An
Imaginery Place
Called Home

Mnzlee Stories

Leena Al-Nasser

Illustrations Haidar Al-Haibie

black dog press

Contents

Foreword

Loring M. Danforth

When Leena Al-Nasser invited me to travel with a group of students to Saudi Arabia, she opened my eyes to a new world. With her first book, *An Imaginary Place Called Home: Mnzlee Stories*, Al-Nasser will open the eyes of her readers to many new worlds—worlds of the imagination, insight, and invention; worlds of childhood, dreams, and our innermost selves. The ideas explored in these stories of home—all too often the rarified domains of philosophers—are presented here through simple but eloquent prose and glorious watercolor paintings.

This book invites us to appreciate more fully the relationships between childhood imagination, scientific discoveries, and technological innovations. More specifically, *An Imaginary Place Called Home* honors the miracles of life and growth, the wonder of color and sight; and the joy of words, the magic of language, and the miracle of translation. Among the visions from the inspired world conjured by Al-Nasser that will stay with me and enrich my life are the images of remembering as sewing, translating as alchemy, and reading as hugging. Perhaps the most moving of all—at least for someone who has spent much of his scholarly life in dictionaries as I have—is from the story "Kalimat" (Words), which features images of a Word Caravan with a Word Menu from which we can order words to share with others.

The art of Haidar Al-Haibie is equally inspiring. His graceful and tender watercolors beautifully complement Al-Nassar's text. I was delighted by the redness and roundness of his tomatoes, the sensuous purple of his eggplants, and the all-encompassing whorl of his snail shell. I found the story "Imagine" to be the most powerful visually. This account of mathematical, scientific, and technological discoveries is not presented in what to an English-speaking public is the more usual context of Christian cathedrals and European capitals, but rather in the context of magnificent mosques and Near Eastern cities. In this history of science, the Banū Mūsā Brothers and Ismail Al-Jazari take the place of Leonardo da Vinci and Sir Isaac Newton. Al-Haibie's paintings capture the beauty of the House of Wisdom in the City of Peace (the Grand Library in the city of Baghdad), which was the center of Islamic and Arab learning from the 8th to the 13th centuries.

While enjoying Al-Haibie's paintings of these Muslim men of learning, wearing their fezzes and turbans and pouring over their illuminated manuscripts, I can almost smell the smoky candles, the crumbling paper, and the drying ink. In a totally different style, one that to me evokes the tradition of Persian miniatures, Al-Haibie has redrawn the fantastical inventions depicted in *The Book of Ingenious Devices* and *The Book of Knowledge of Ingenious Mechanisms*. We delight in detailed drawings of gears, pulleys, and levers; elephant clocks, peacock fountains, and self-playing musical instruments. Finally, in what to me is the most powerful image in the book, we see the results of the 1258 Mongol sack of Baghdad: the Tigris River running "black from the ink in the books and red from the blood of slaughter".

Two other stories moved me profoundly. "Bang Bang" and "Tomato" powerfully illustrate the destructive nature of violence. "Bang Bang" demonstrates the way in which violence directed by one actor against another inevitably turns back on itself—like the echo of a shout or the ricochet of a bullet—to harm the perpetrator of the violence as much as the victim. The hunter becomes the hunted; the desire to harm another harms the self. "Tomato" shifts the portrait of violence from the individual level to the collective. It illuminates the ultimate futility, the utter meaninglessness, of violence that is carried out at the state level as a product of colonialism, nationalism, sectarianism, or racism. Minor cultural, religious, or linguistic differences from the distant past all too often continue to inspire violence between groups into the immediate present. With these two stories, *An Imaginary Place Called Home* encourages people who see themselves as enemies to reimagine their relationship as brothers. This is a lesson that needs to be learned in many countries around the world—perhaps nowhere more in the context of this book than Syria, Yemen, and Palestine.

With *An Imaginary Place Called Home* Leena Al-Nasser and Haidar Al-Haibie have created a treasure—a beautiful book that raises thought provoking questions in a manner accessible to all. Their book encourages us to explore more deeply "the real eternal House of Wisdom, the creator of the future ... the imagination", which exists inside us all.

Introduction

Leena Al-Nasser

Mnzlee, an Arabic word meaning "my home", is derived from the word mnzl, which translates literally as "the place to go down". But what is the significance of going down? Why not go up? Or go nowhere?

The word's context is a nomadic culture of pre-Islamic Arabia, where people traveled on camels to find home. Traveling by camel is a regal experience; the camel—itself a majestic animal—must kneel to let you down. In this way, finding home was not separate from the animal, and it was not just a place, but a process, an action, a rooting in the earth, a kneeling, a claiming, a making, a verb. Home changes, it moves. It doesn't just happen. You make home.

The world was on lockdown, collectively enduring an internal pilgrimage. Pilgrimages are marked by specific things—confinement, repetition, monotony being a few. They necessarily require a shutting out of noise and the experience of boredom.

During lockdown, I did not have my camel—but I did have my majestic being Milou and his best friend Luna with me during this time.

I woke up there one morning, looking ahead at another day of that same boredom. It was like every other morning—except one thing. A voice. I don't know if this voice had always been there or if I finally reached some sort of threshold that day, but as soon as I heard her, I acted.

As a child my mom had given me the nickname "garbage collector", referring to my habit of collecting treasures that others deemed garbage. And the spoils of my collecting had a home in the second drawer of my bedroom dresser, which on the morning in question, I rushed to open. Inside, there lay a mountain of scraps and pages from magazines and old books, cutouts capturing all manner of shapes, sizes, countries, and histories.

I took them out to the sunlit living room where I sat on the silky carpet next to my companions Milou and Luna and spread them across the coffee table, and there, I invited her, my imagination, to play a game—or maybe she invited me.

"What can you make with these images?" I said. Very quickly, my hands began moving pieces together. Story after story spilled from my mind, and I recorded my voice speaking them aloud.

It became obvious to me that my imagination was the one talking, and that there was a common thread in all the stories she told—*her*! Her power, her ability, her vitality, all but discarded by the adults in the world. Some of her stories were fantastical, others romantic and whimsical, and others still historical and factual. But to me, the message was clear: fact or fiction, science or art, it was all imagined—created from nothing, as if out of thin air, like magic. Everything. Everything came from her.

This was my pilgrimage. My place to kneel, to pause. To find home. To find her.

> "Home isn't Mom and Dad and Sis and Bud. Home isn't where they have to let you in. It's not a place at all. Home is imaginary. Home imagined comes to be. It is real, realer than any other place, but you can't get to it, unless your people show you how to imagine it – whoever your people are. They may not be your relatives. They may never have spoken your language. They may have been dead for a thousand years. They may be nothing but words printed on paper, ghosts of voices, shadows of minds. But they can guide you home. They are your human community. All of us have to learn how to invent our lives, make them up, imagine them. We need to be taught these skills; we need guides to show us how. If we don't, our lives get made up for us by other people." — Ursula K Le Guin, "The Operating Instructions" (2002)

BECOME

Some things feel so still, like they've always been there.

A body of water.

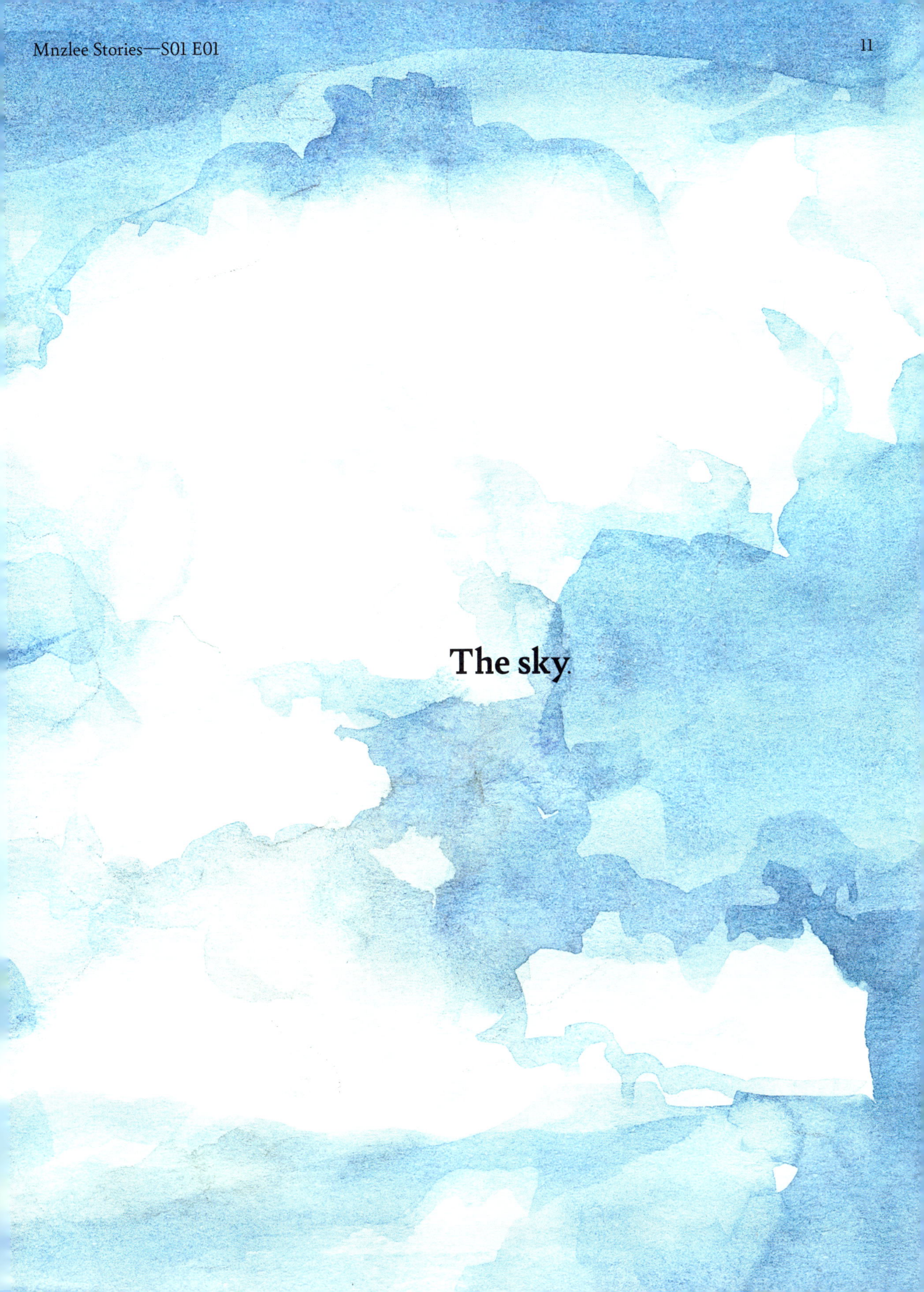

The sky.

Some things have been there for a very, very long time.

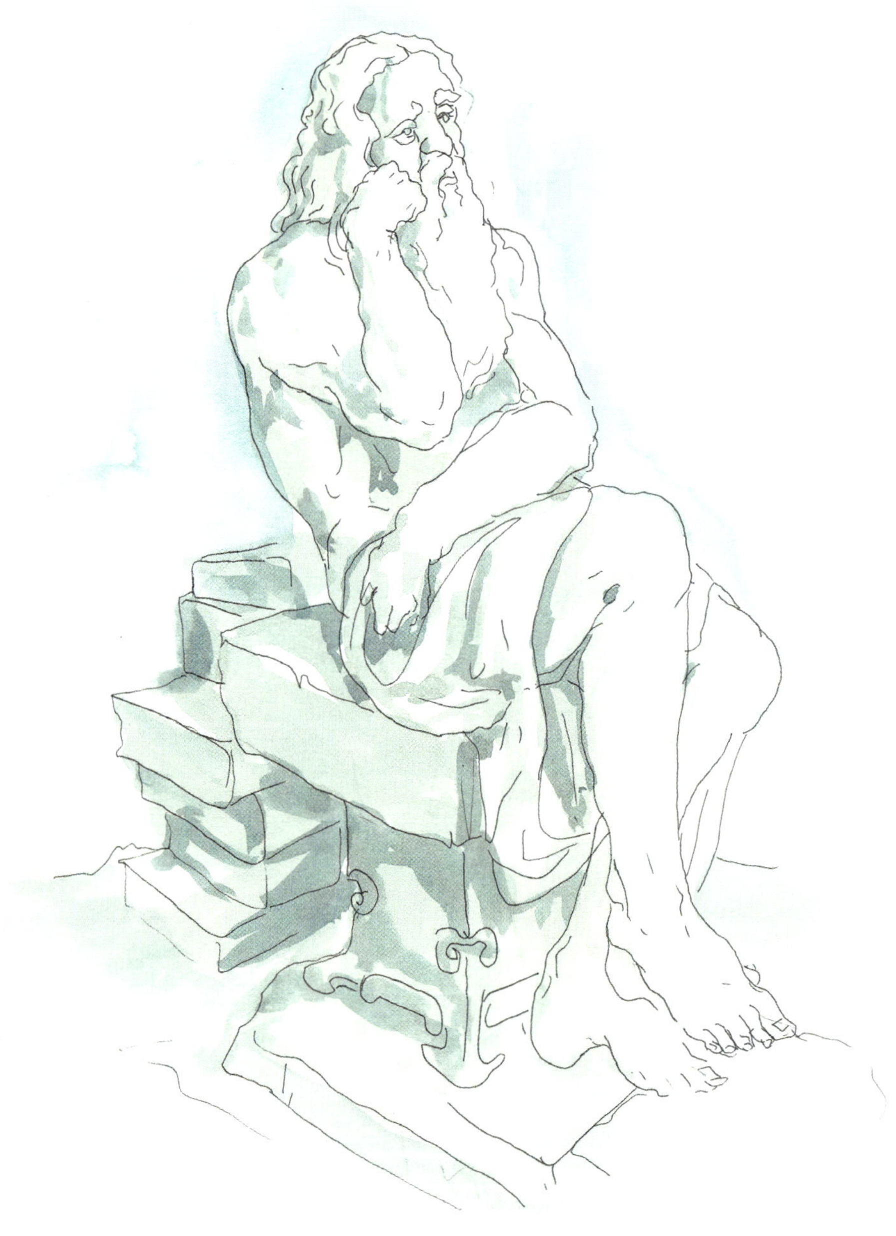

Maybe all your life.

They also feel still.

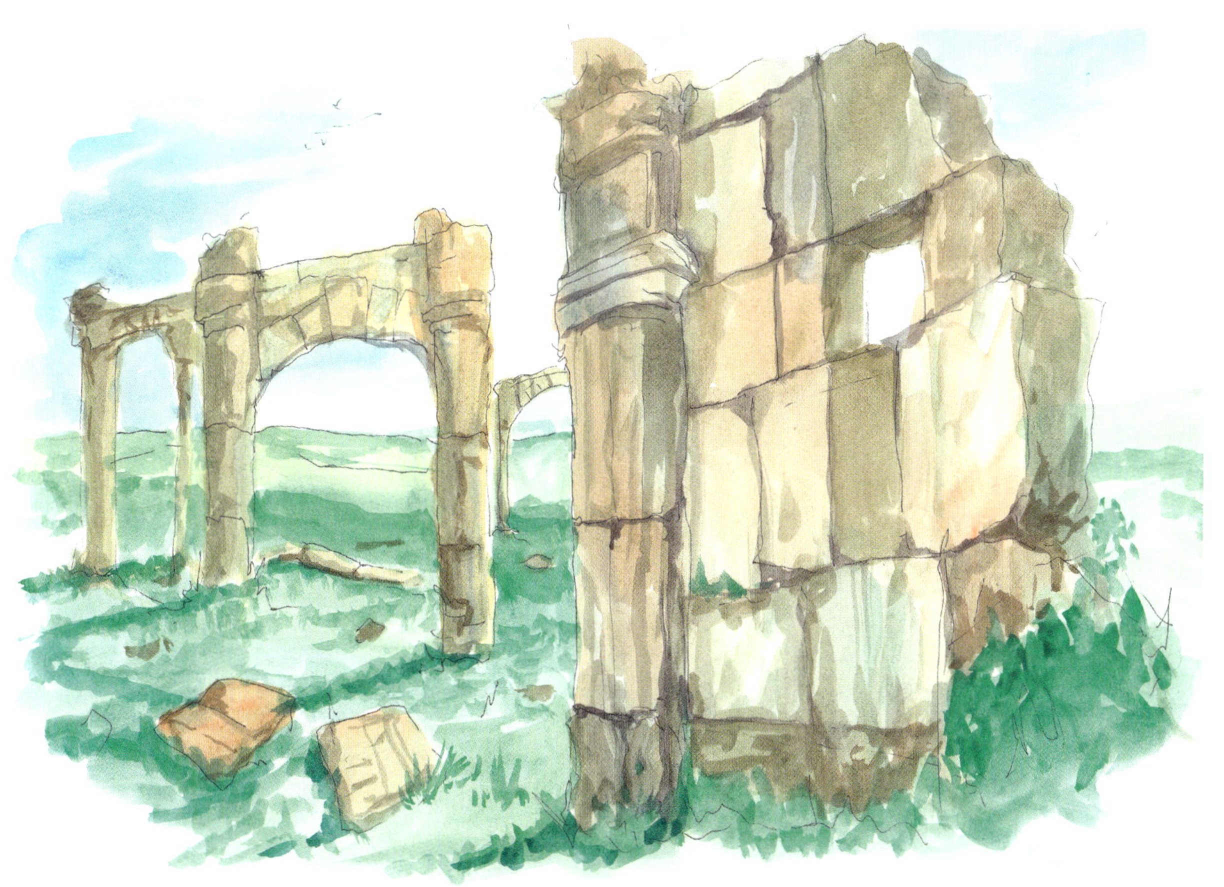

Are they still?
Have they always been there?

Who made them?

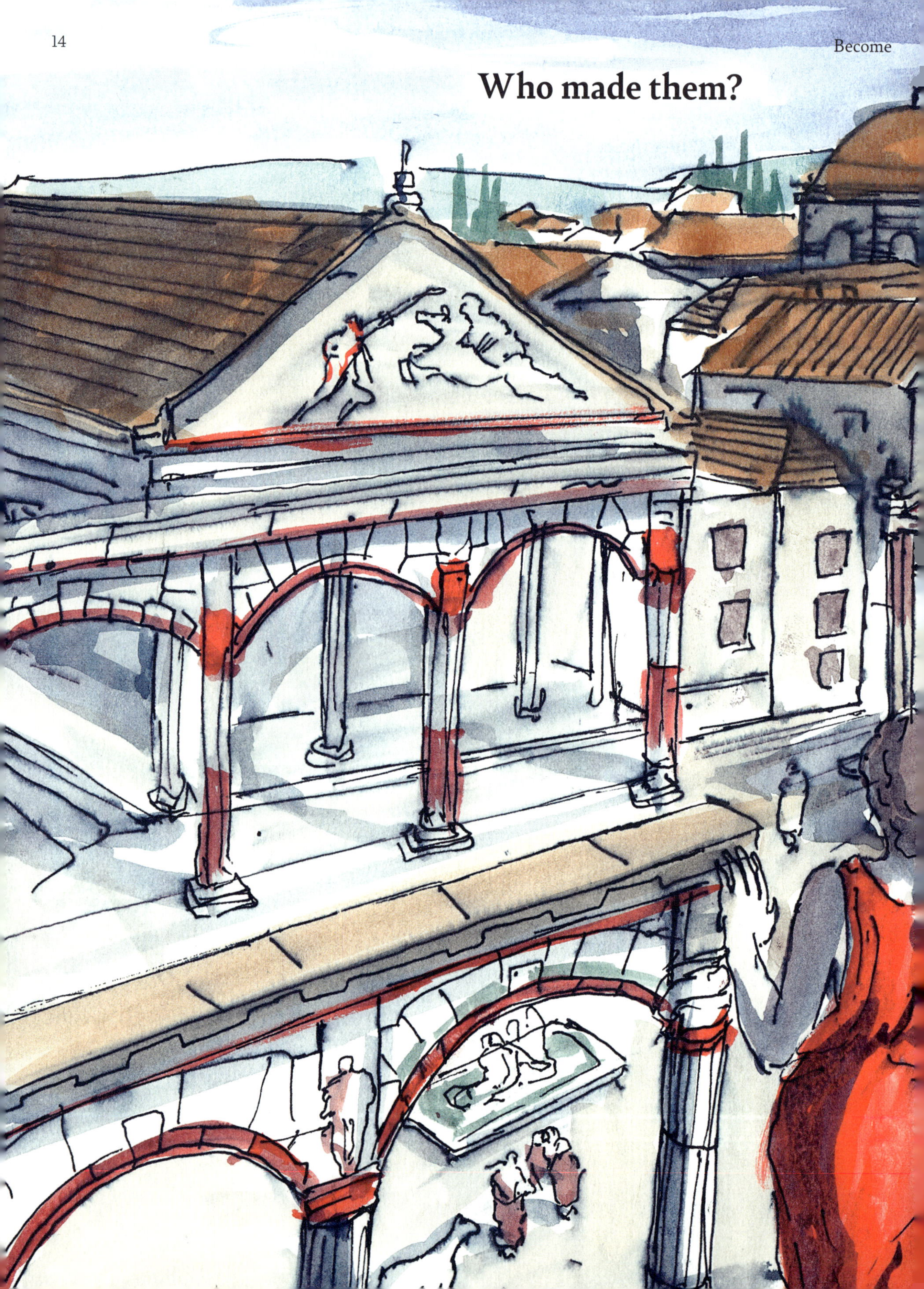

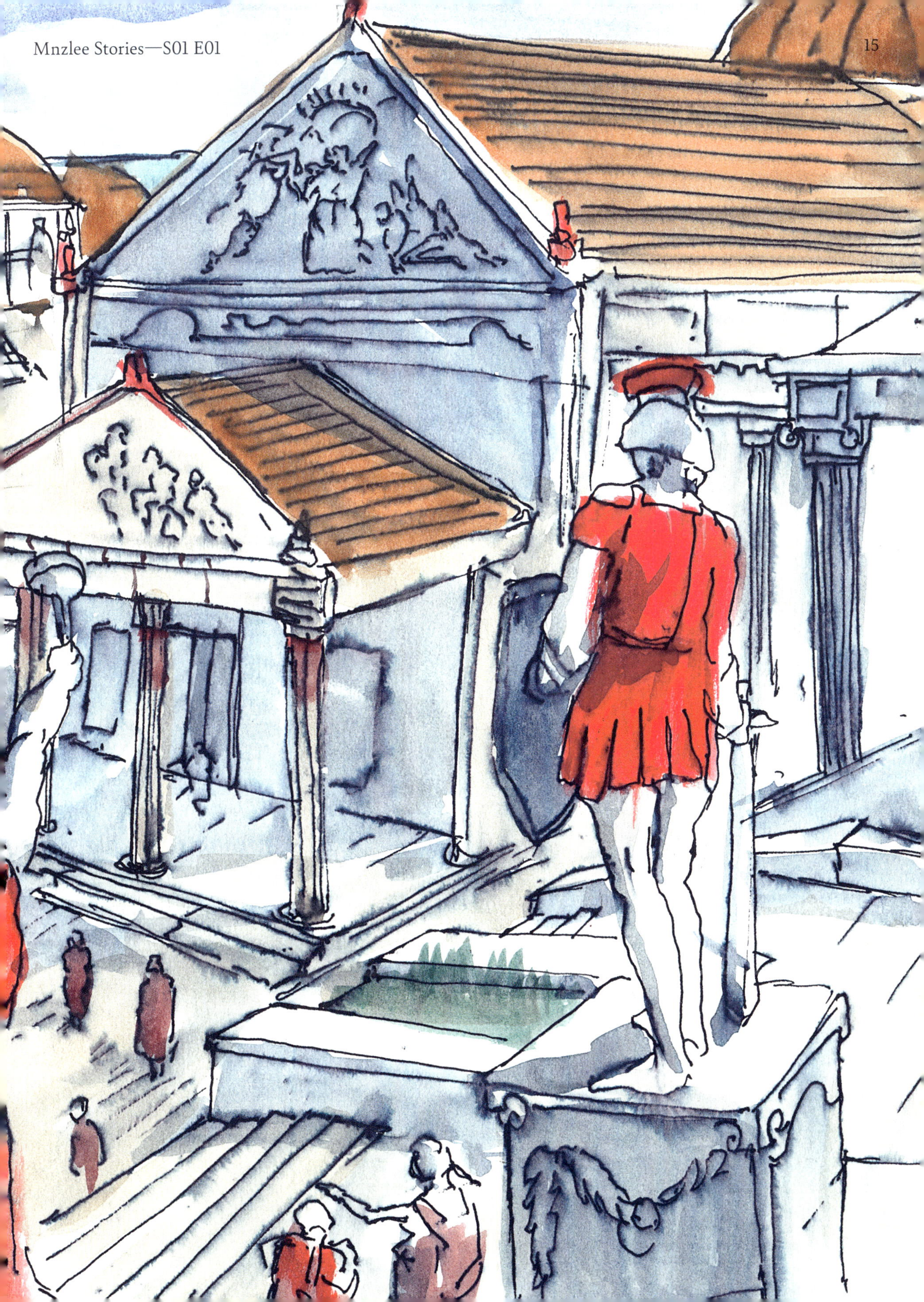

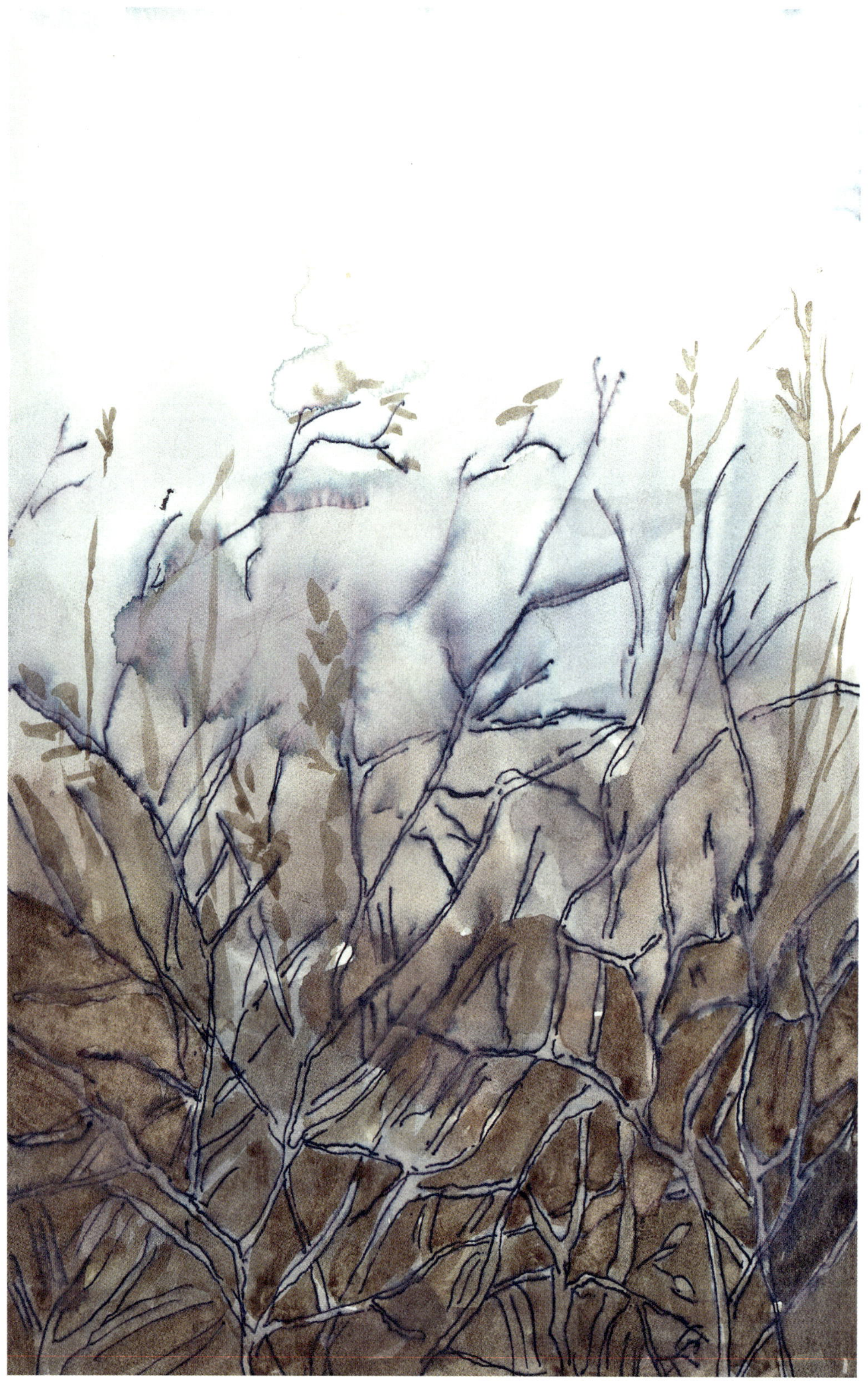

How did this

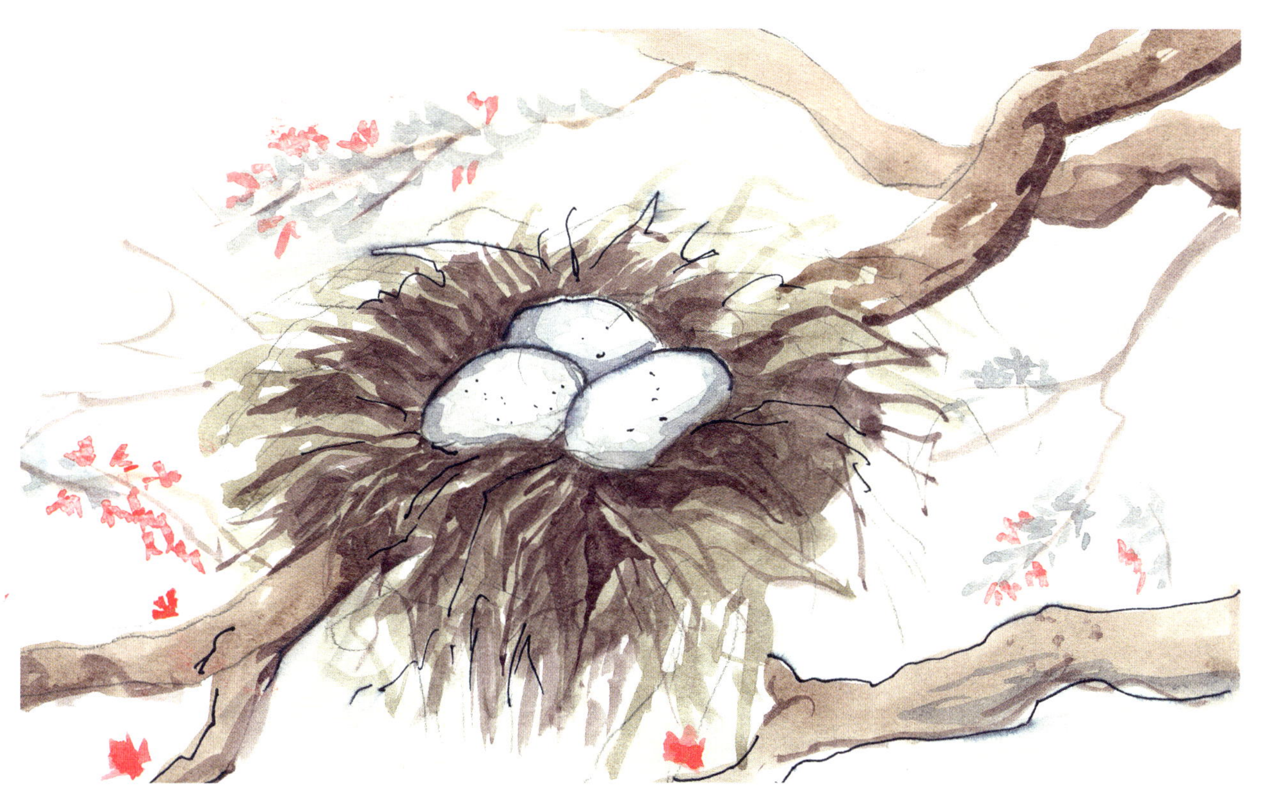

become that?

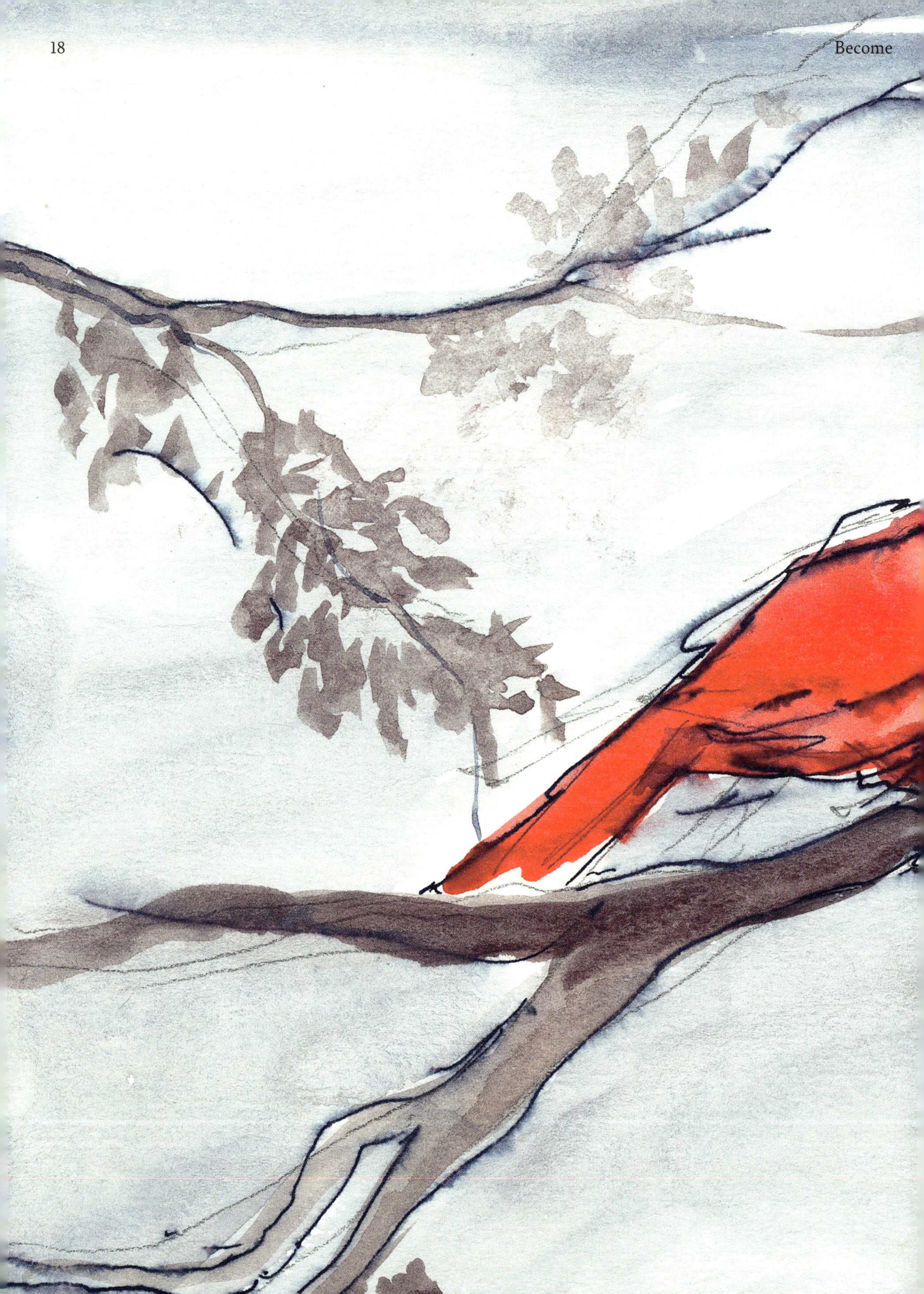

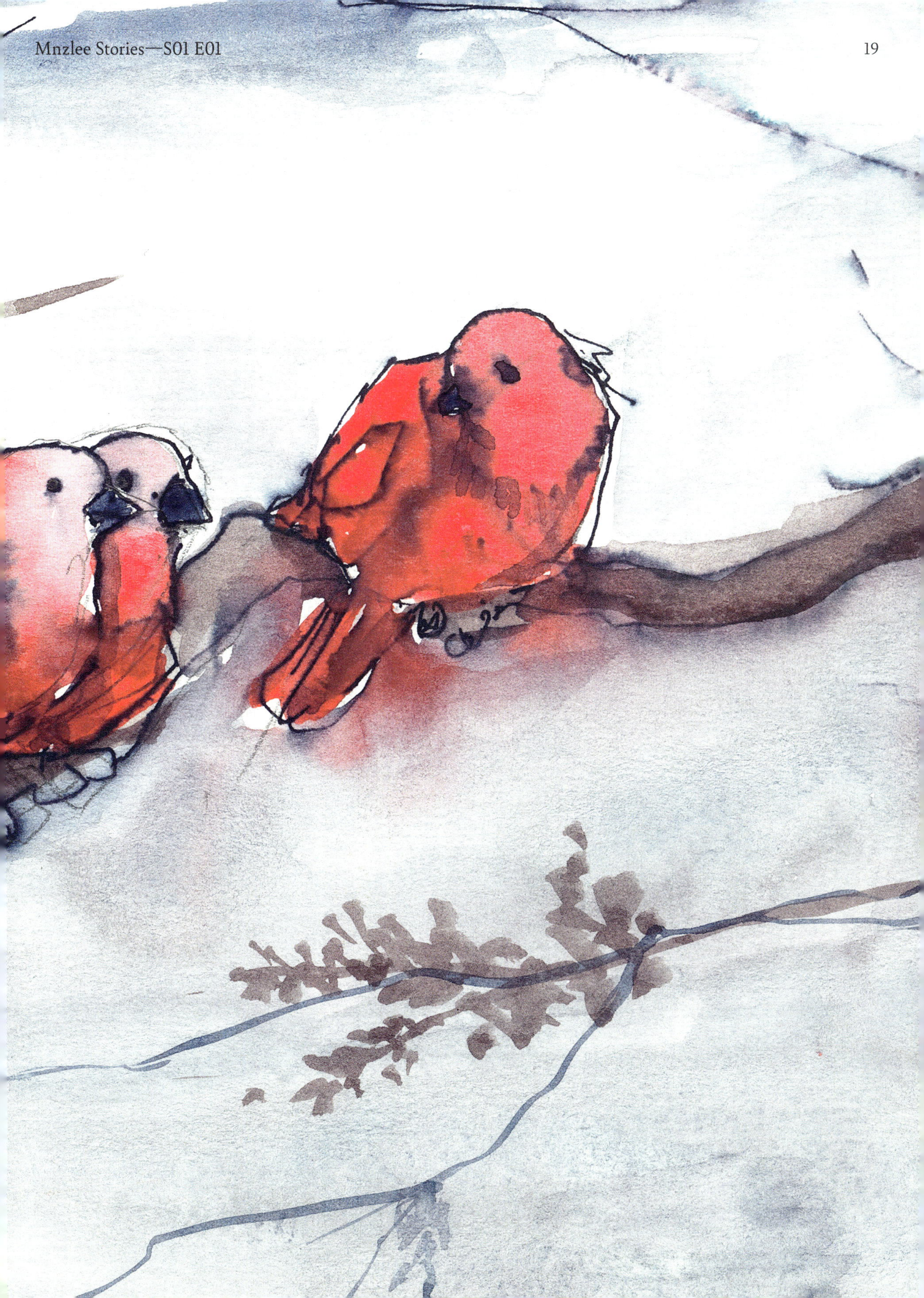

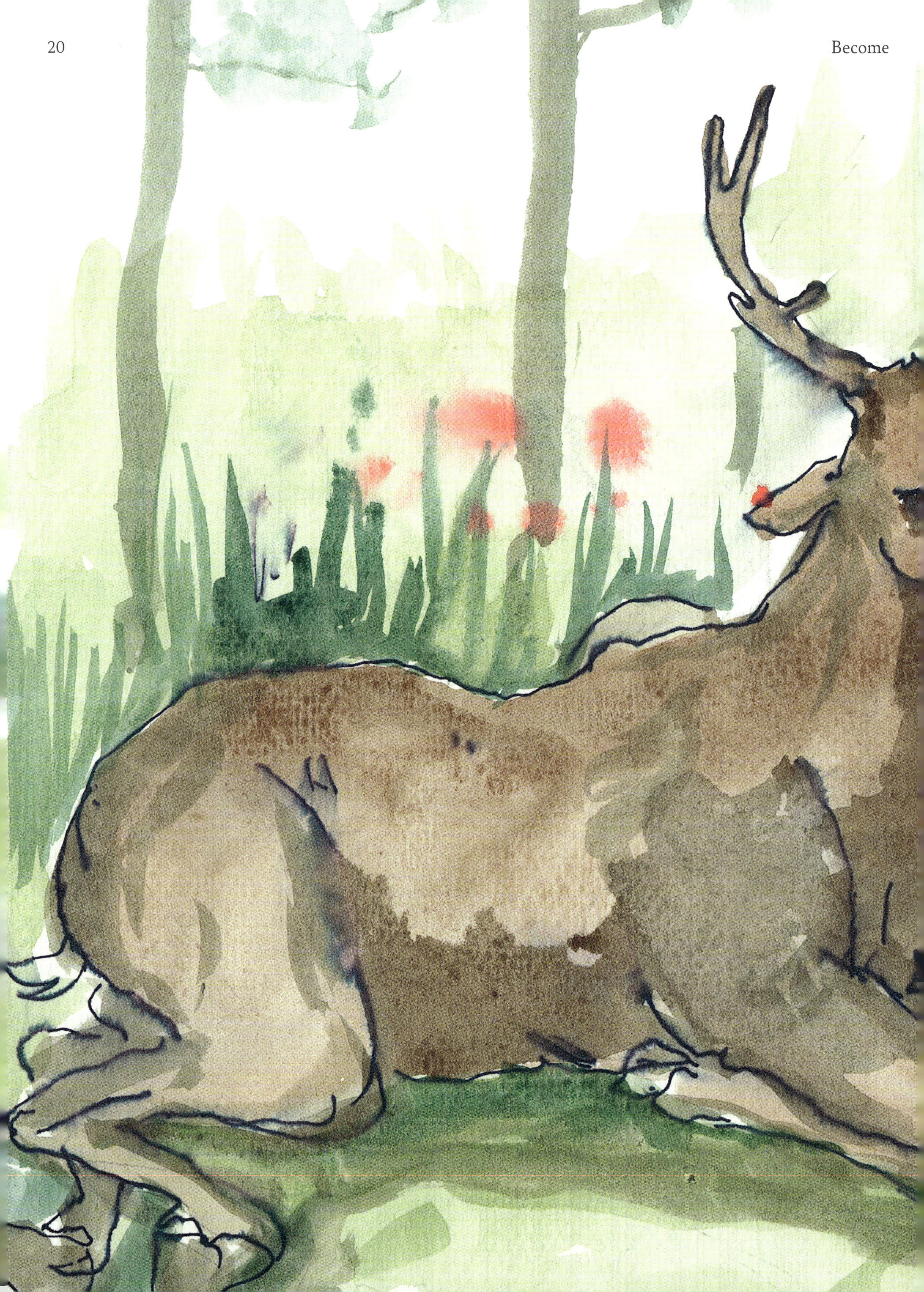

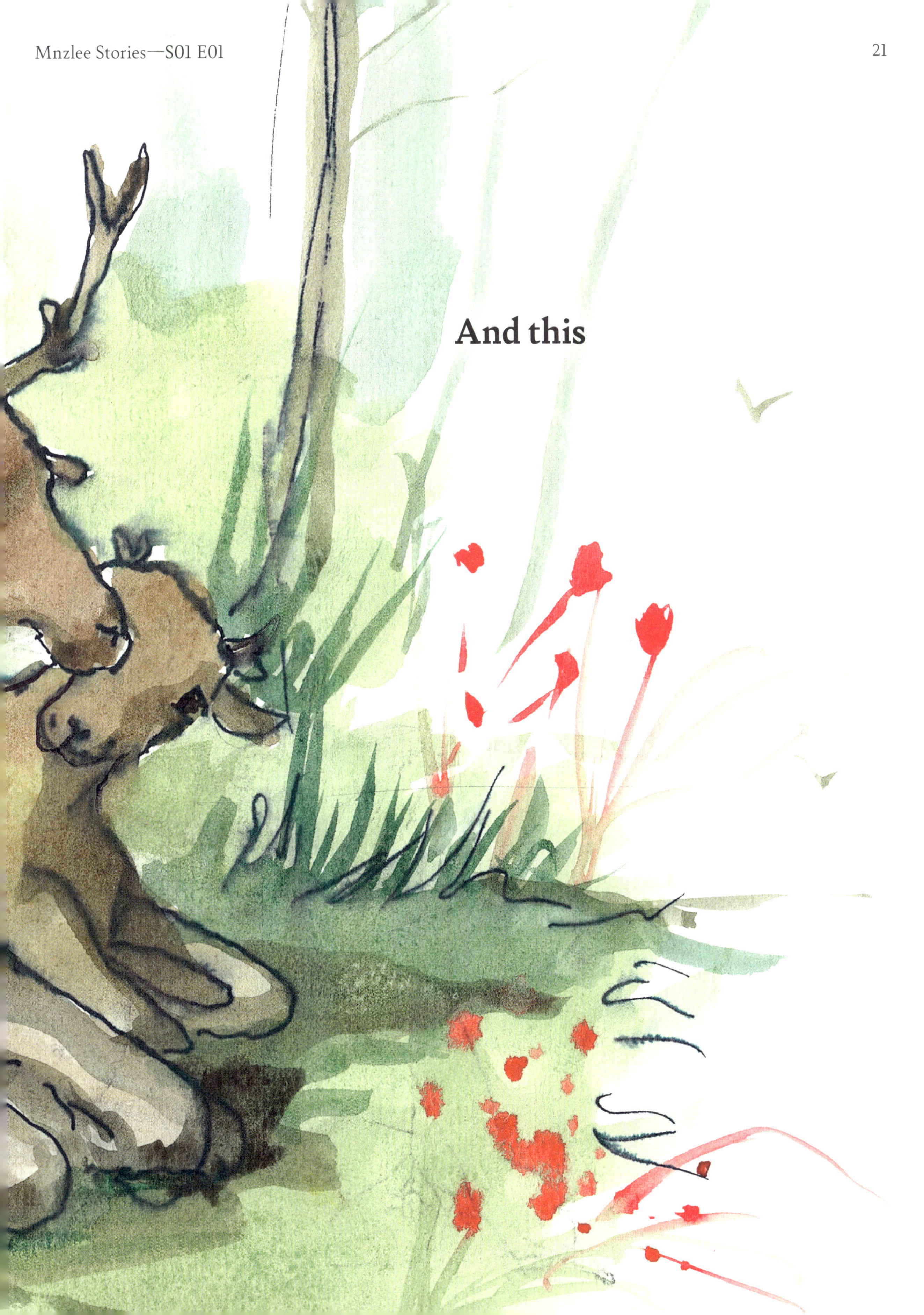
And this

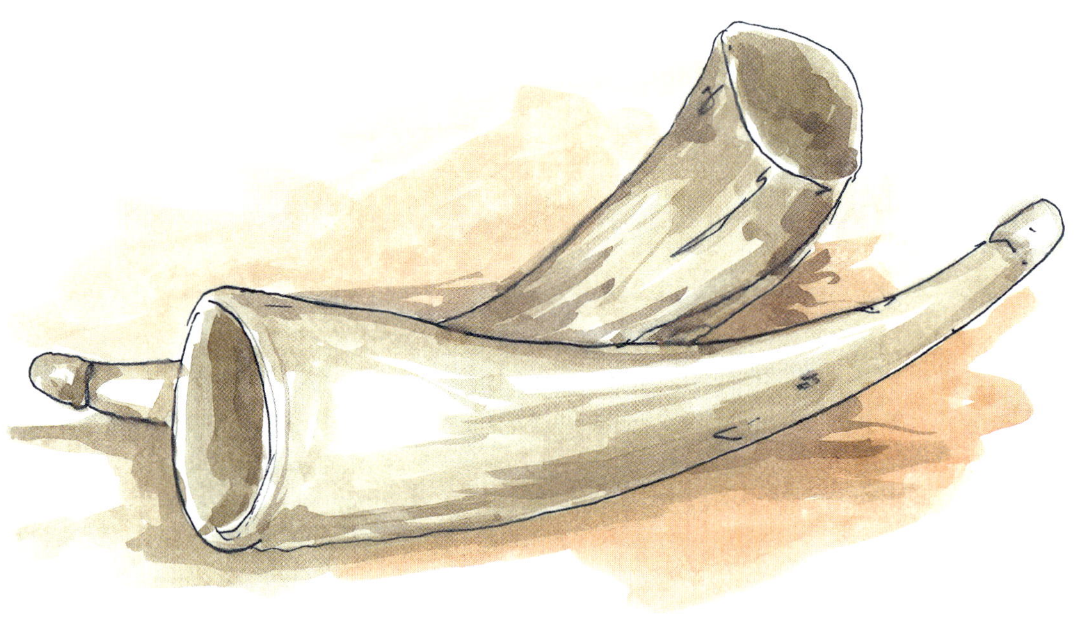

become that?

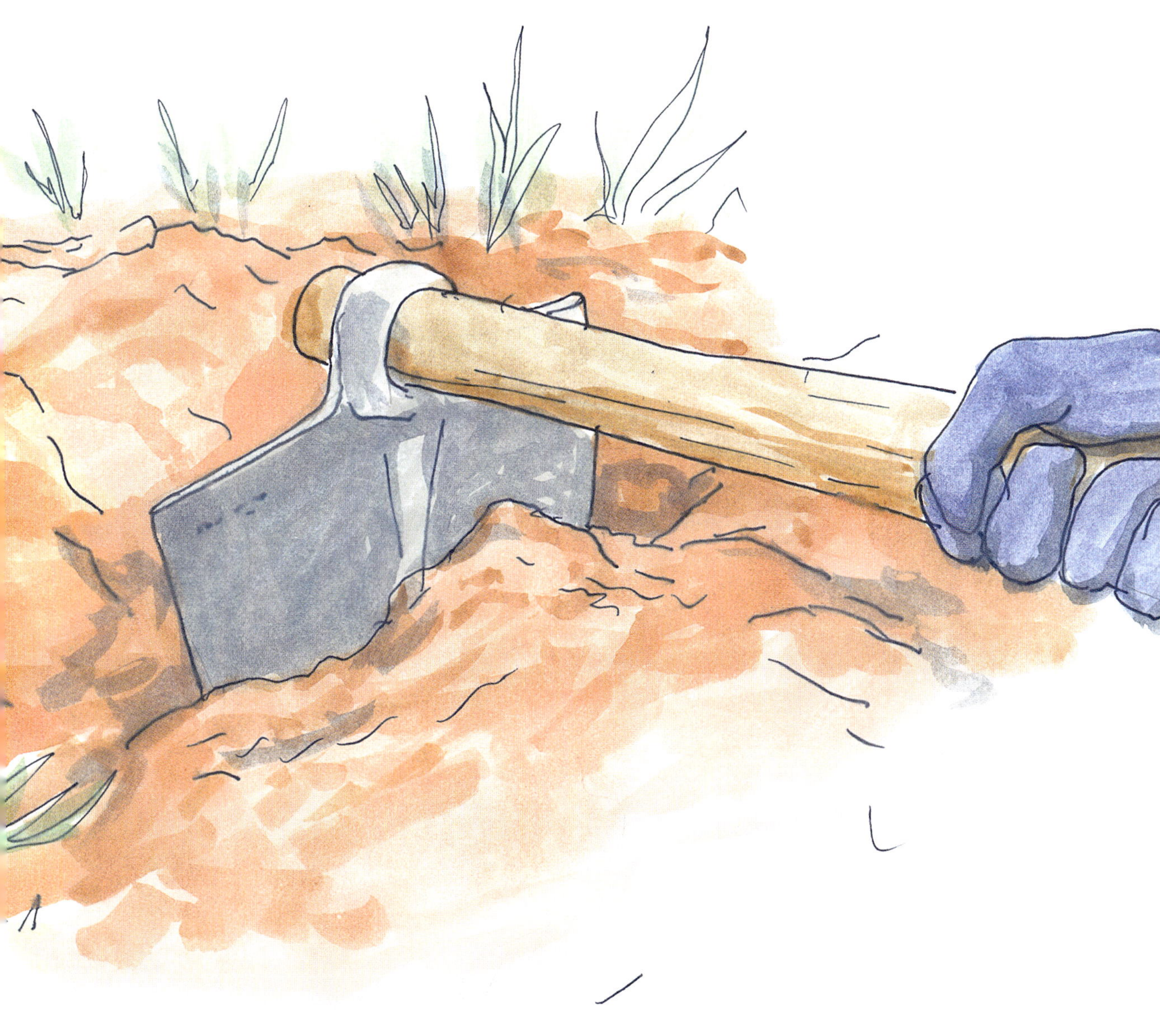

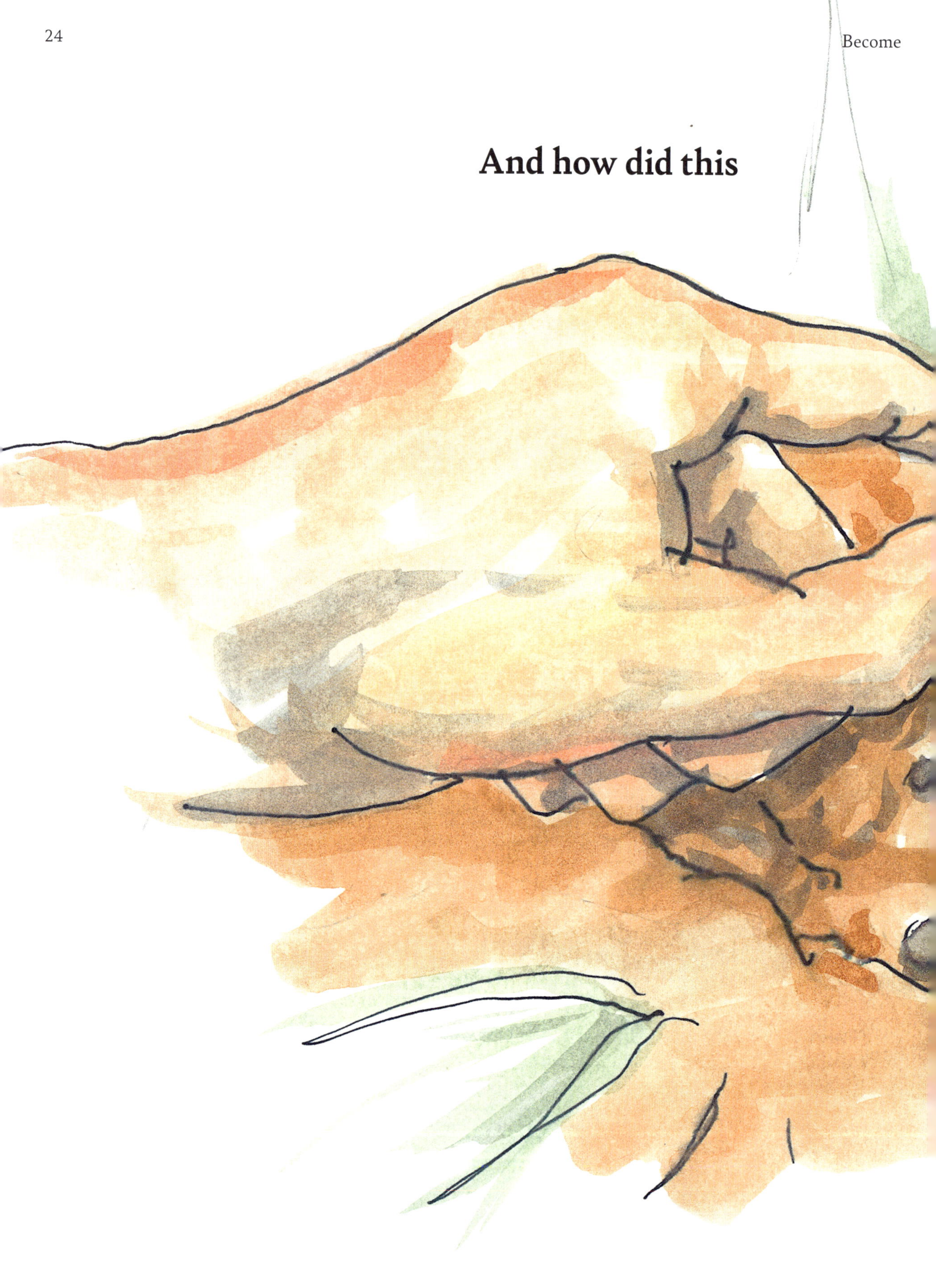

Become
And how did this

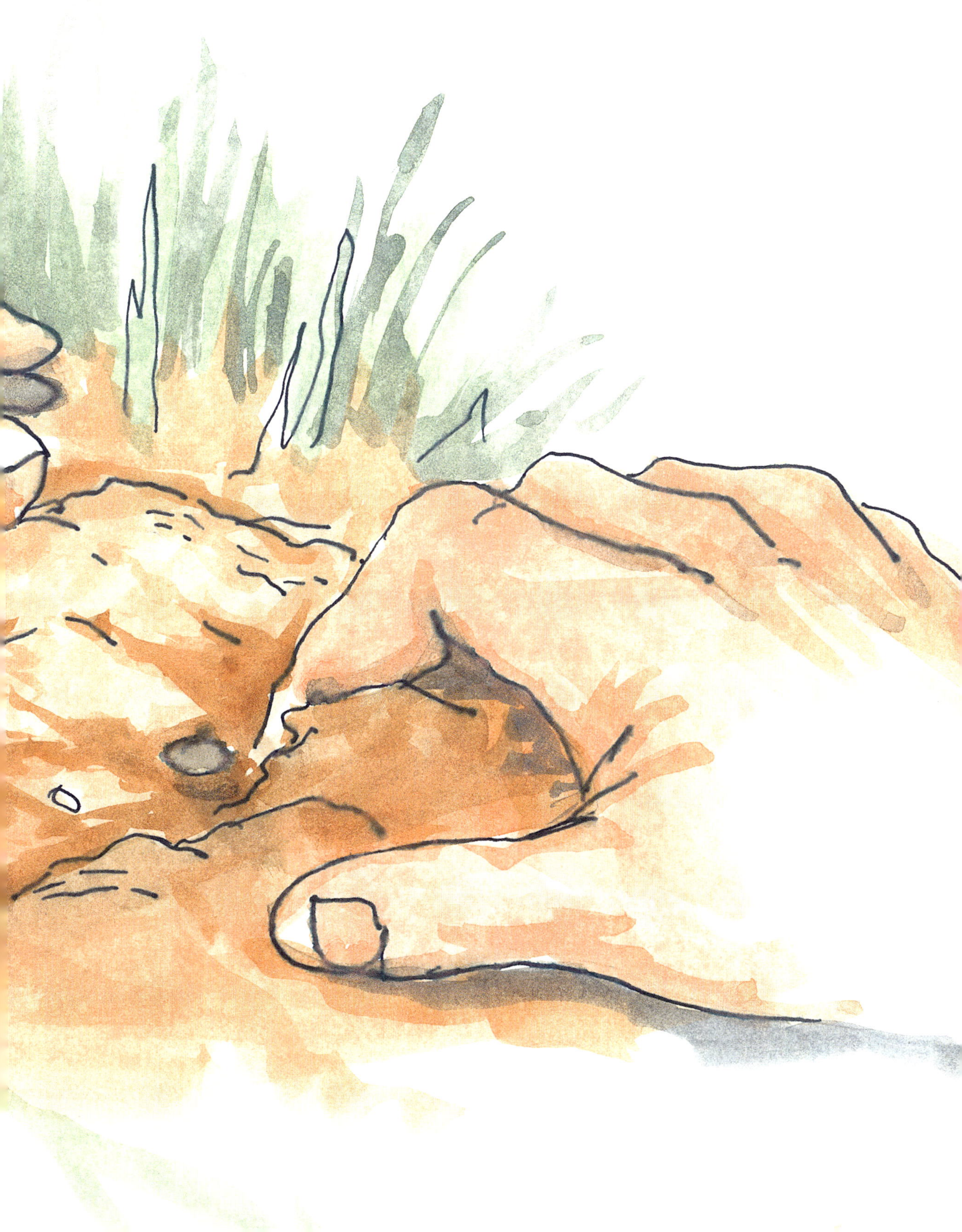

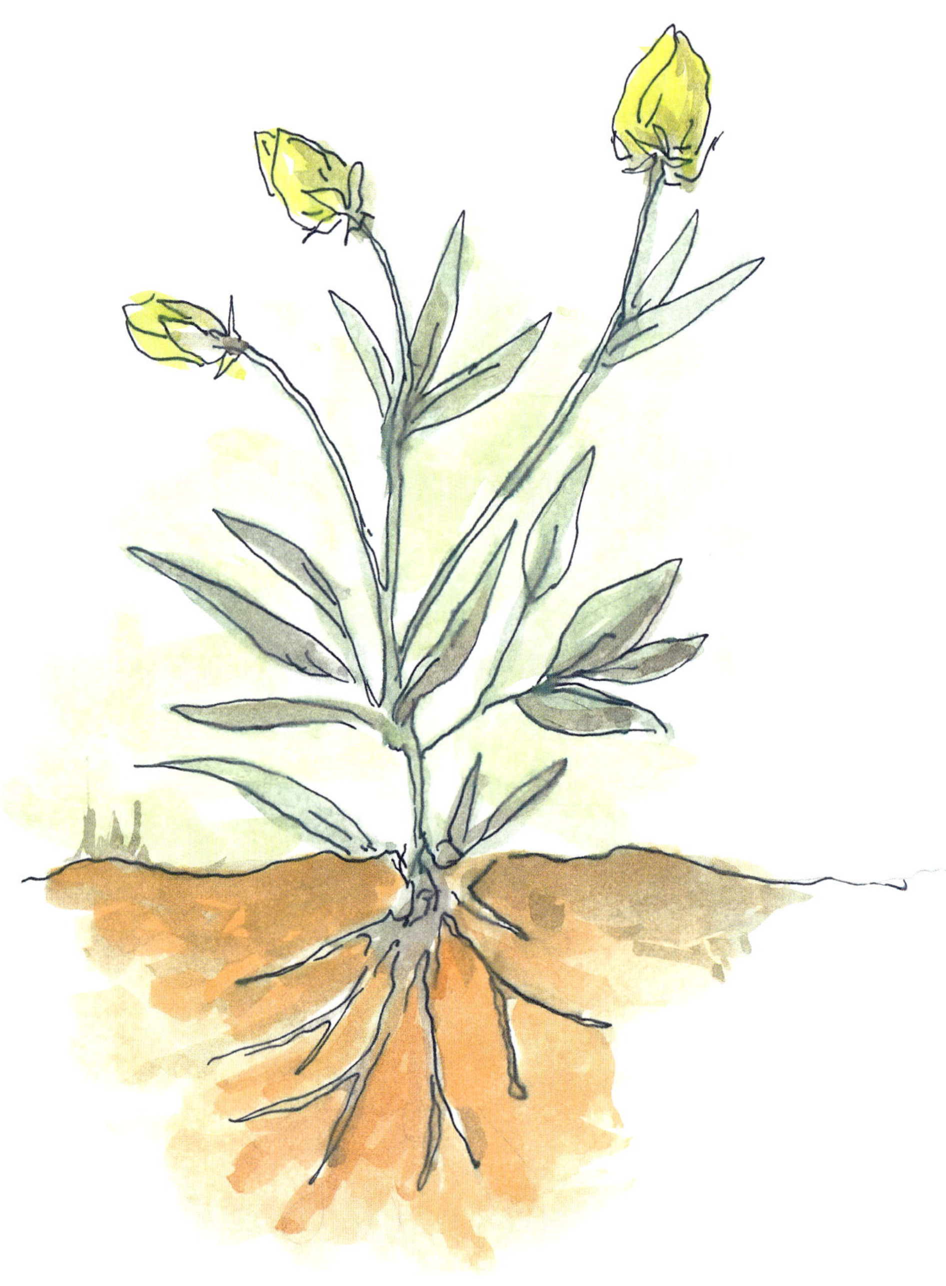

become this?

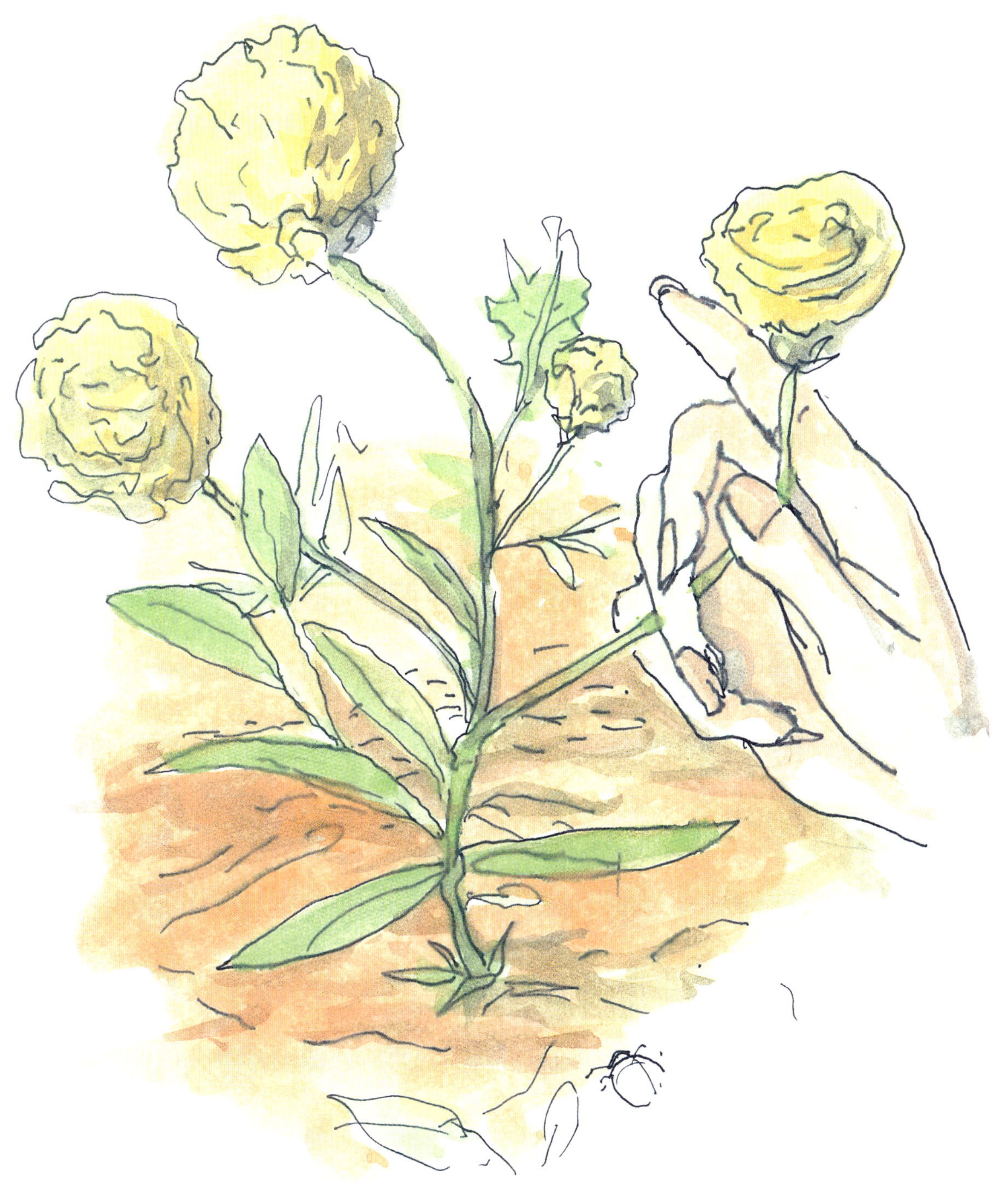

And that.

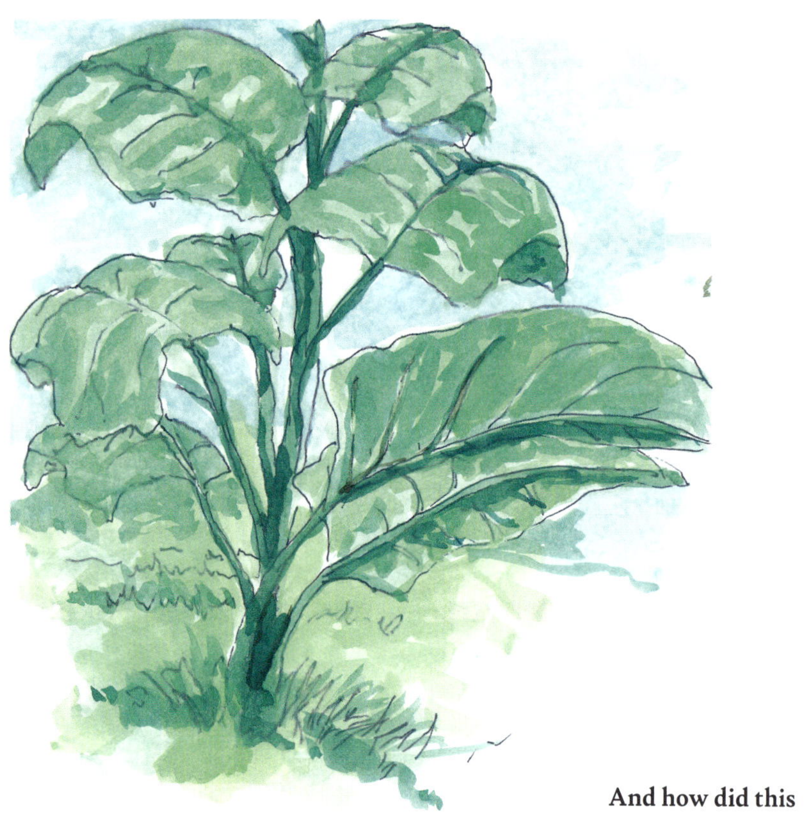

And how did this

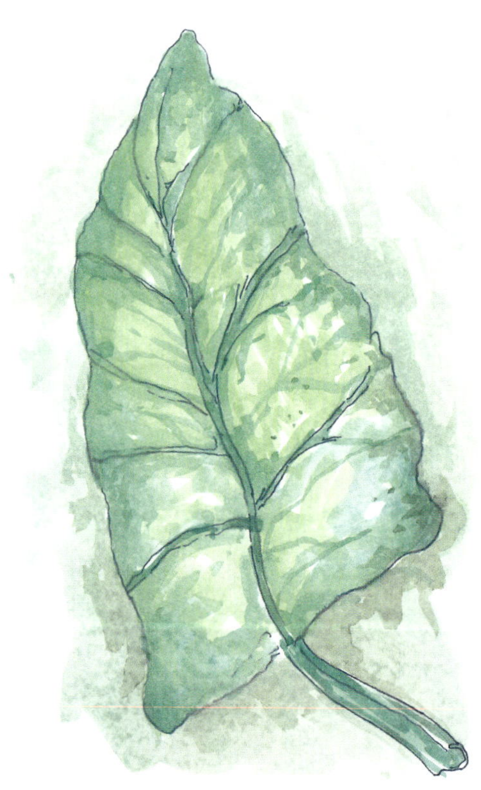

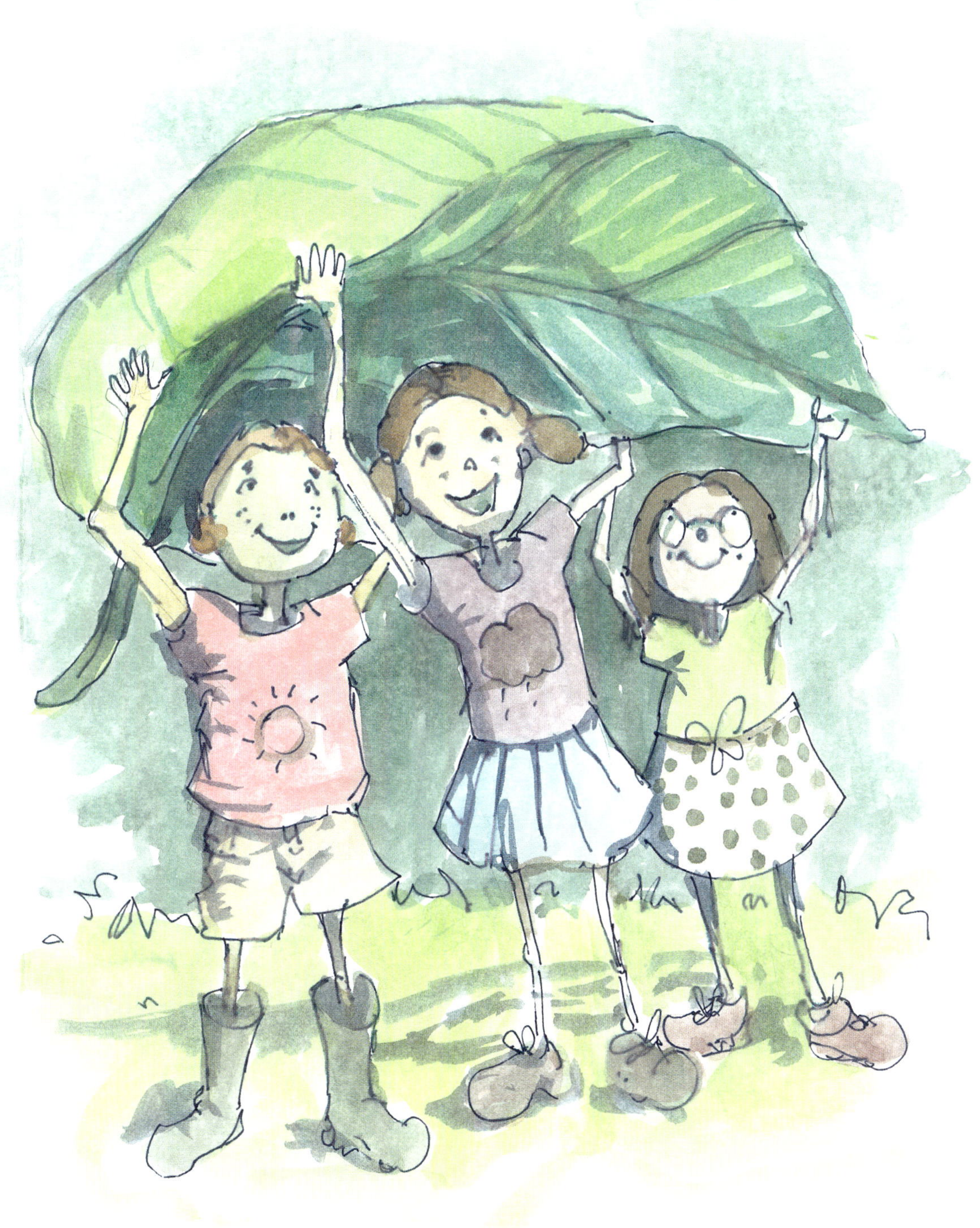

turn into that?

That.

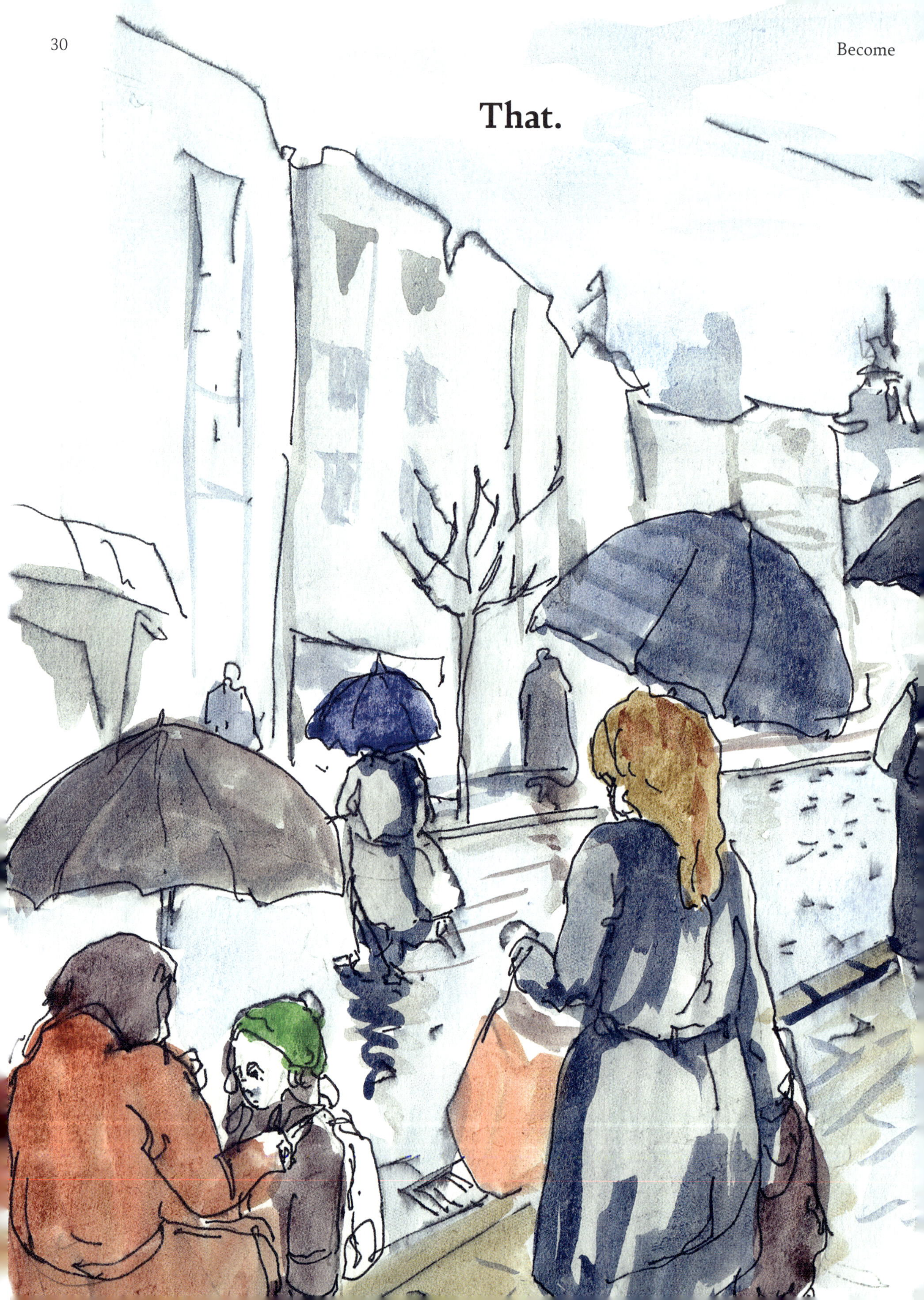

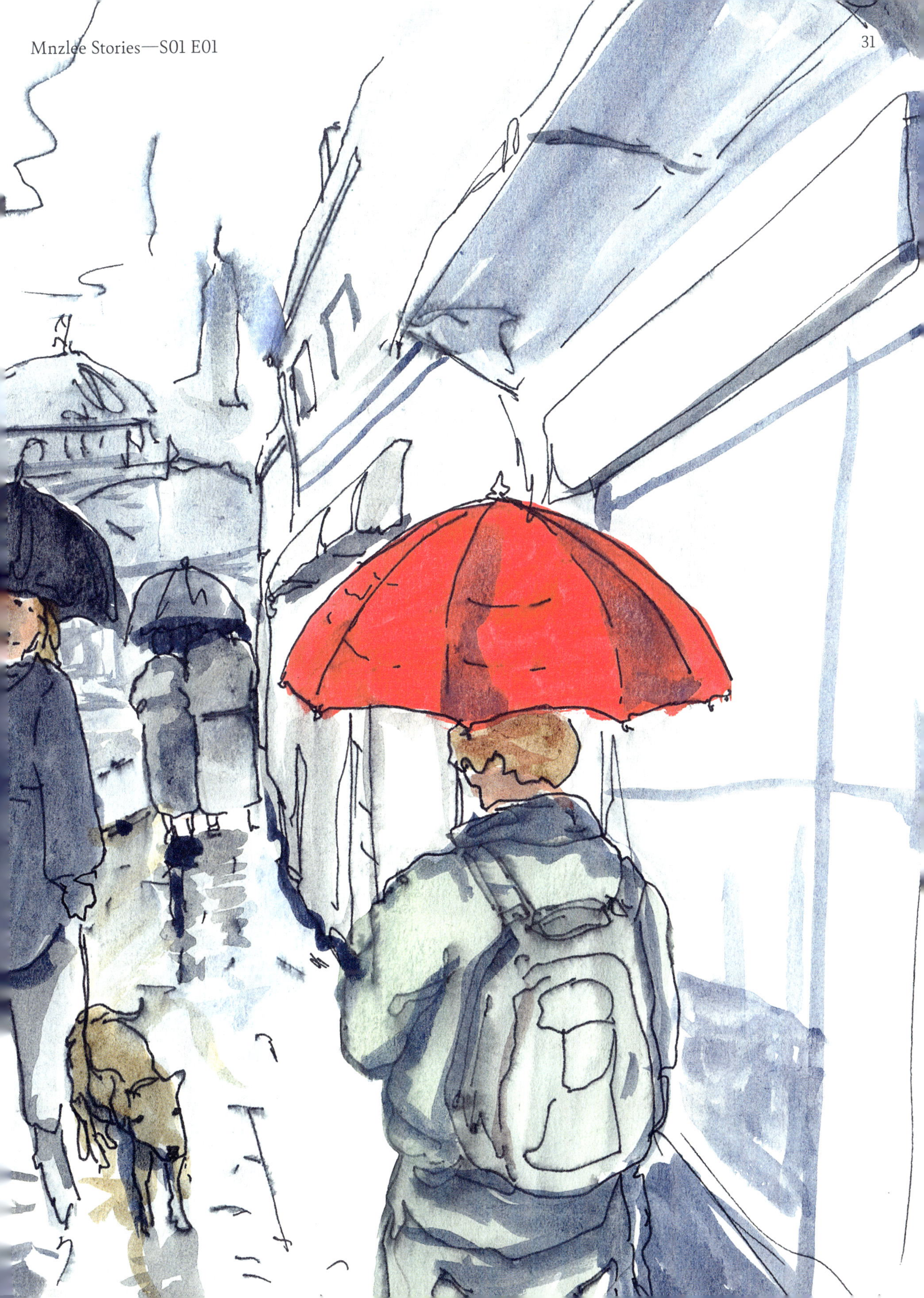

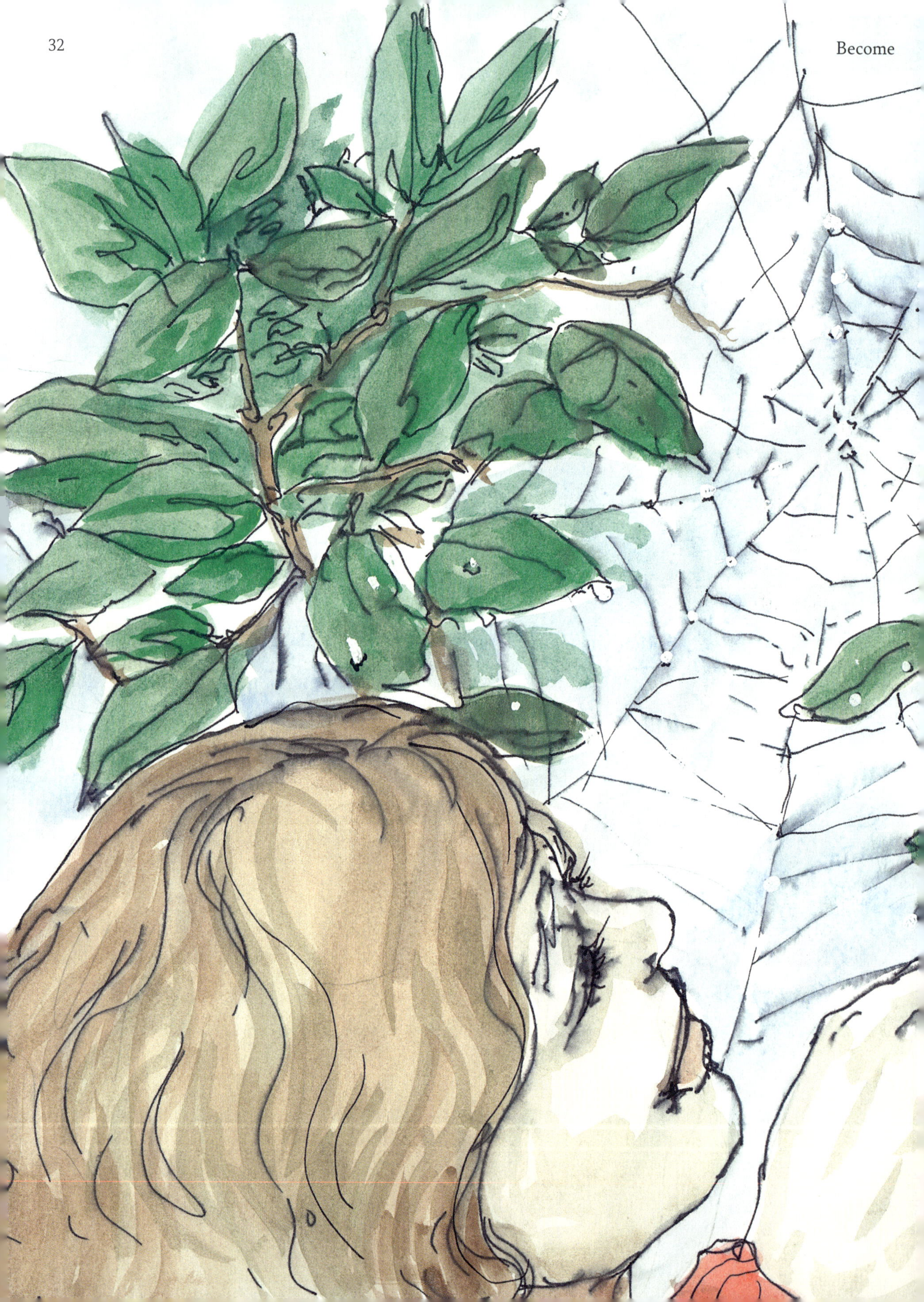

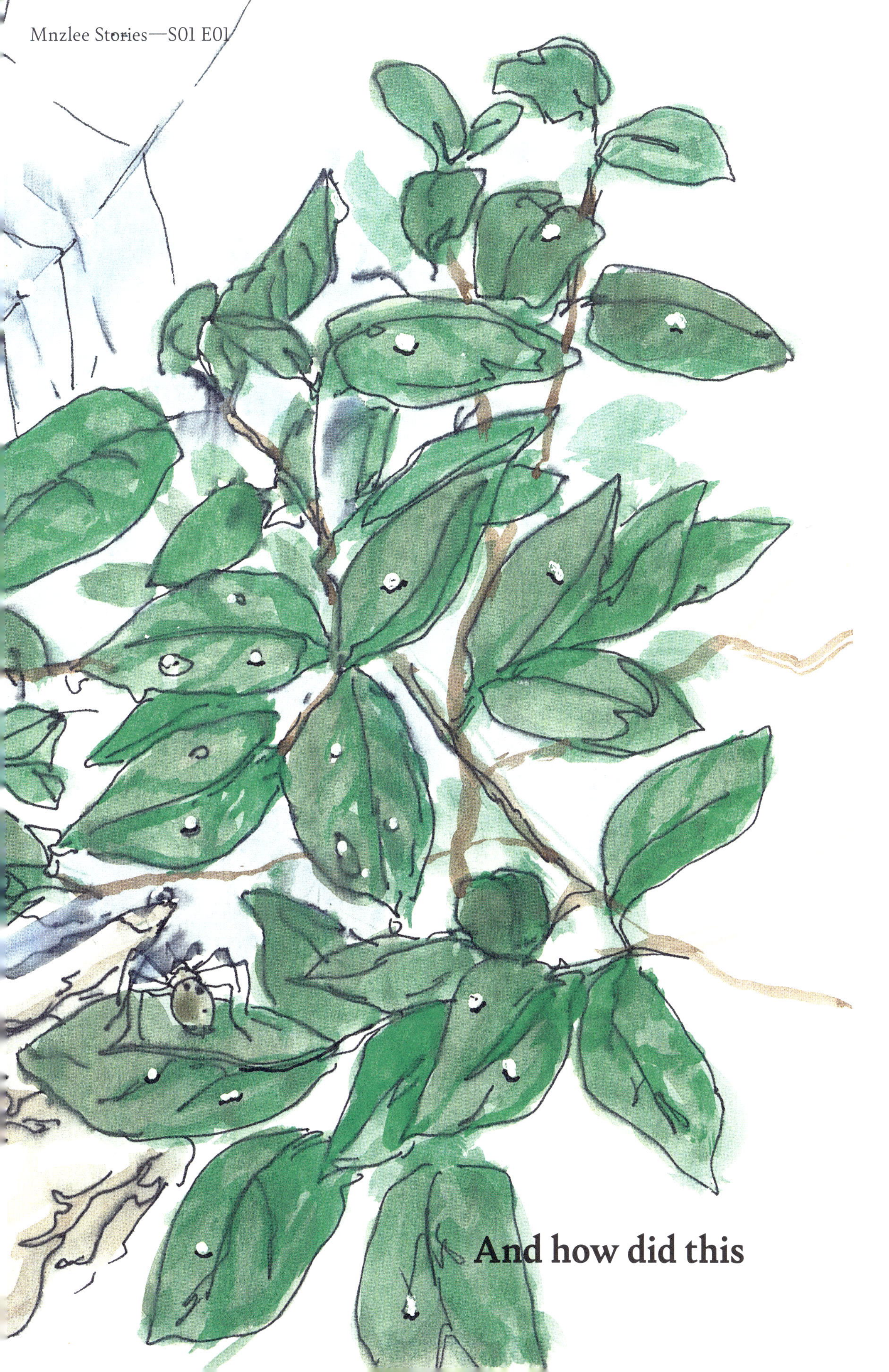

And how did this

become that?

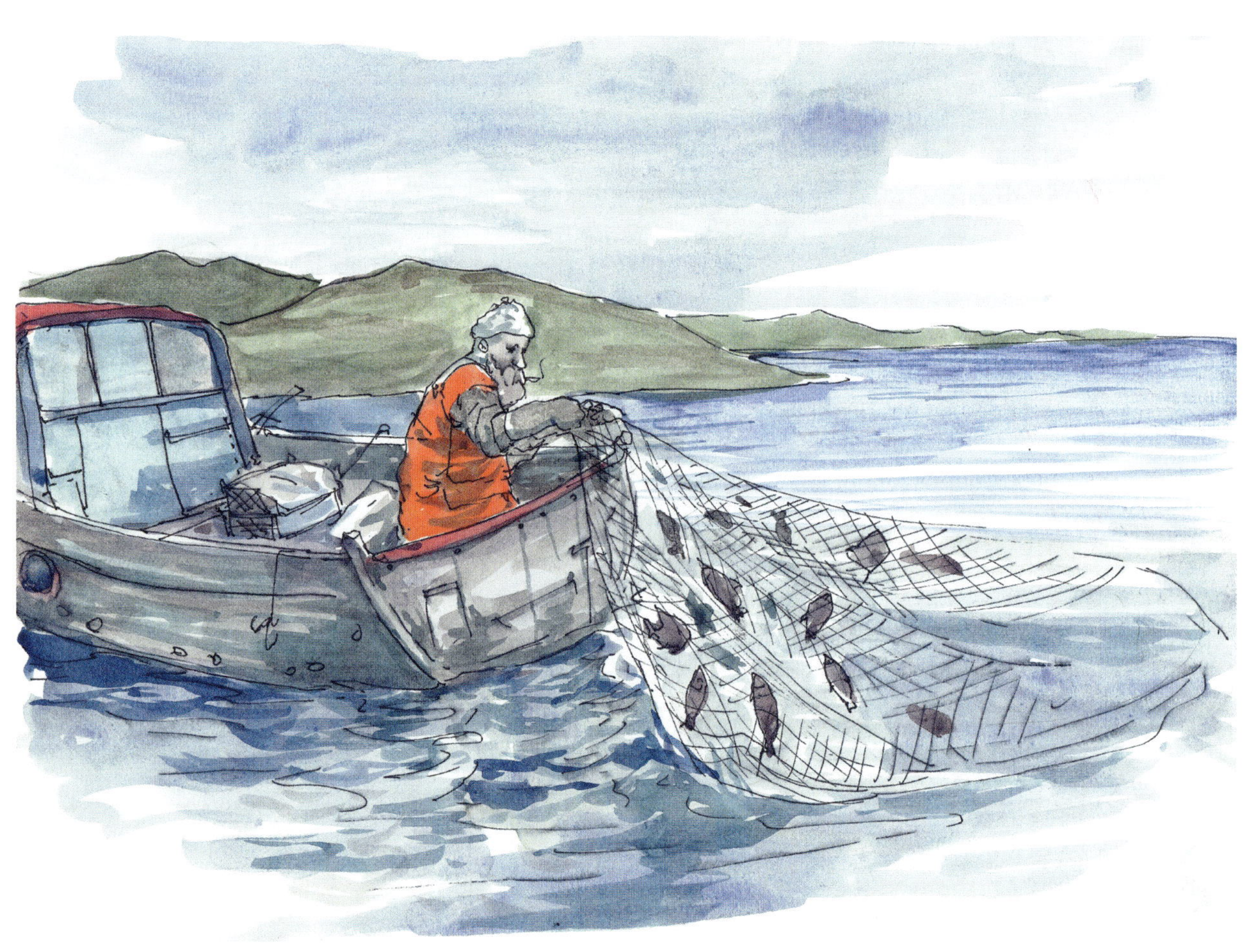

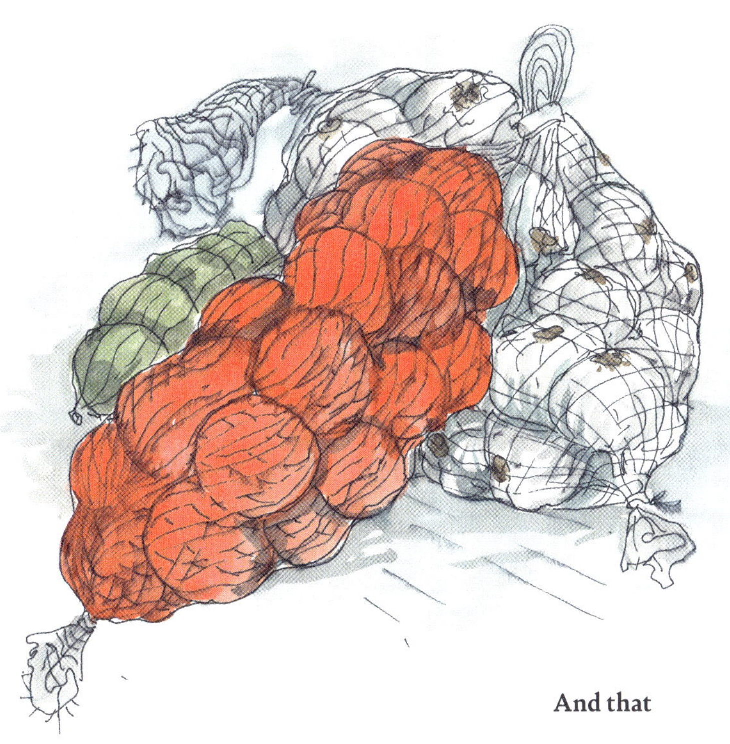

And that

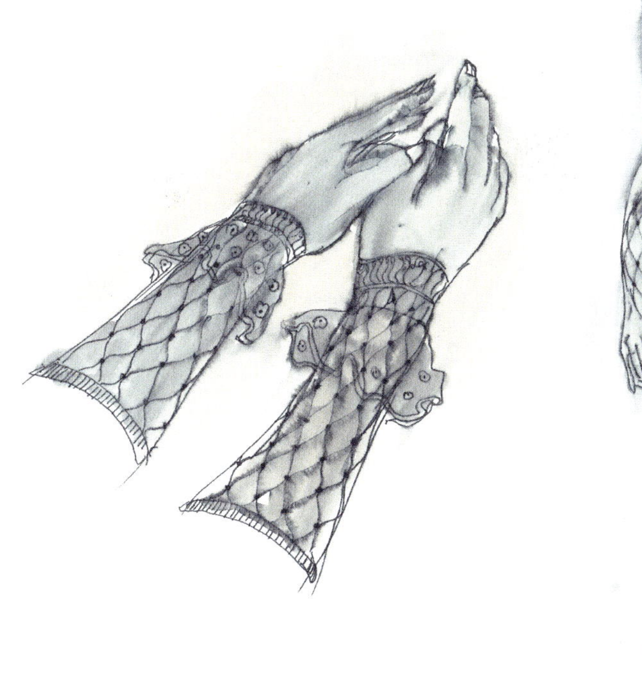

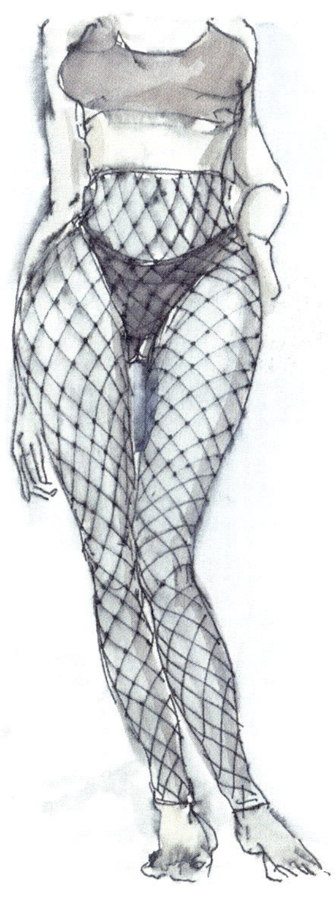

becomes this?

And how did this

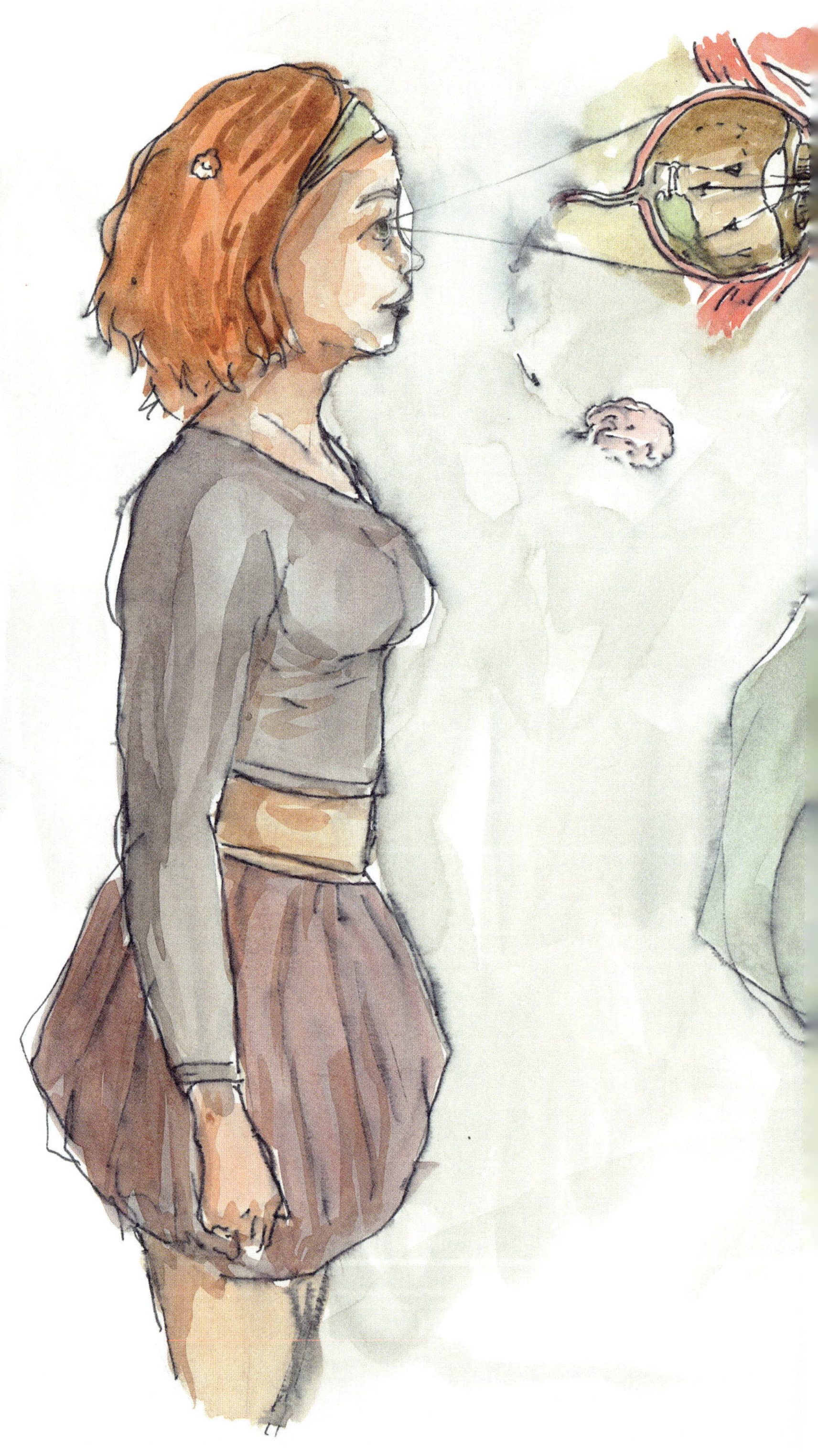

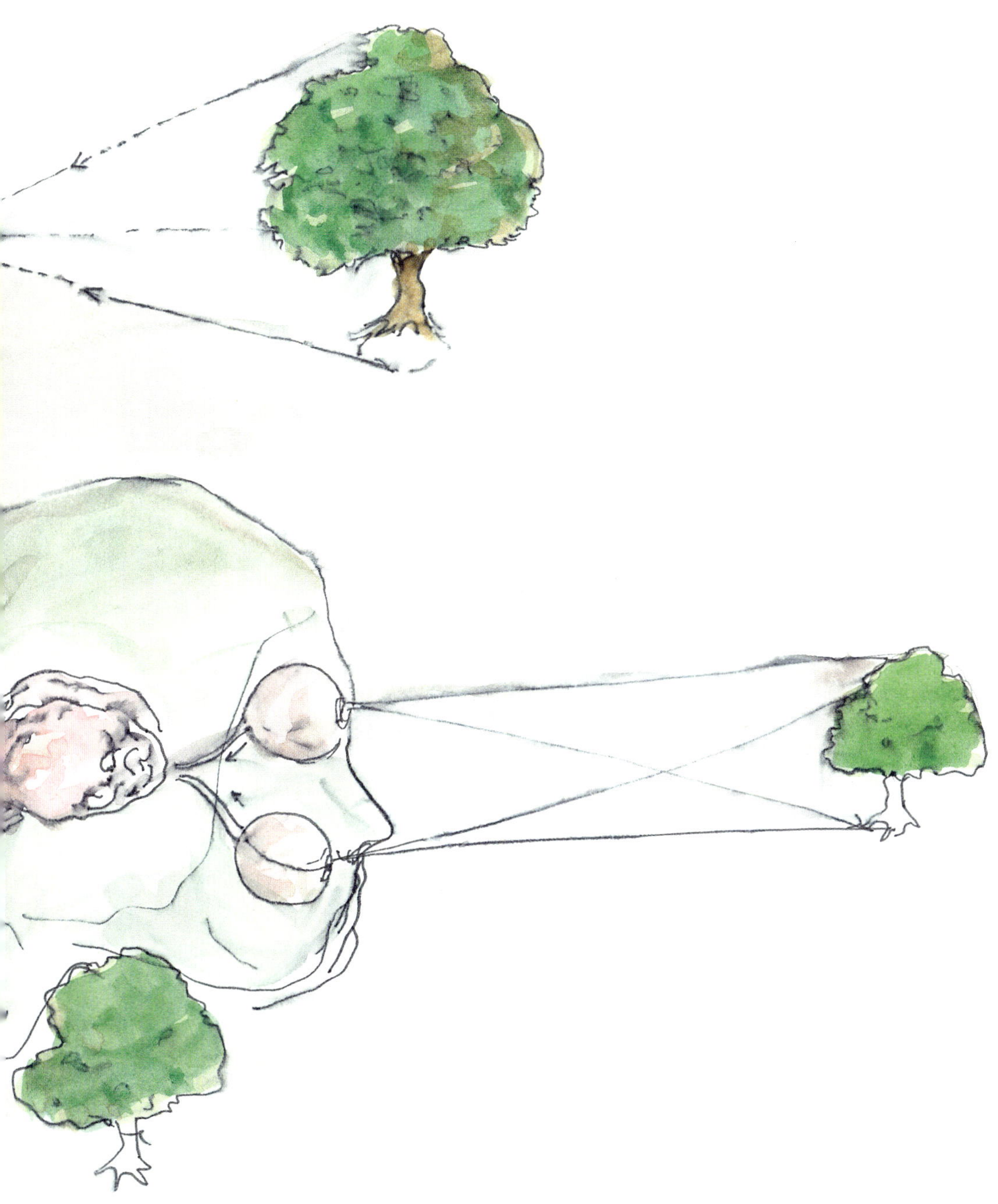

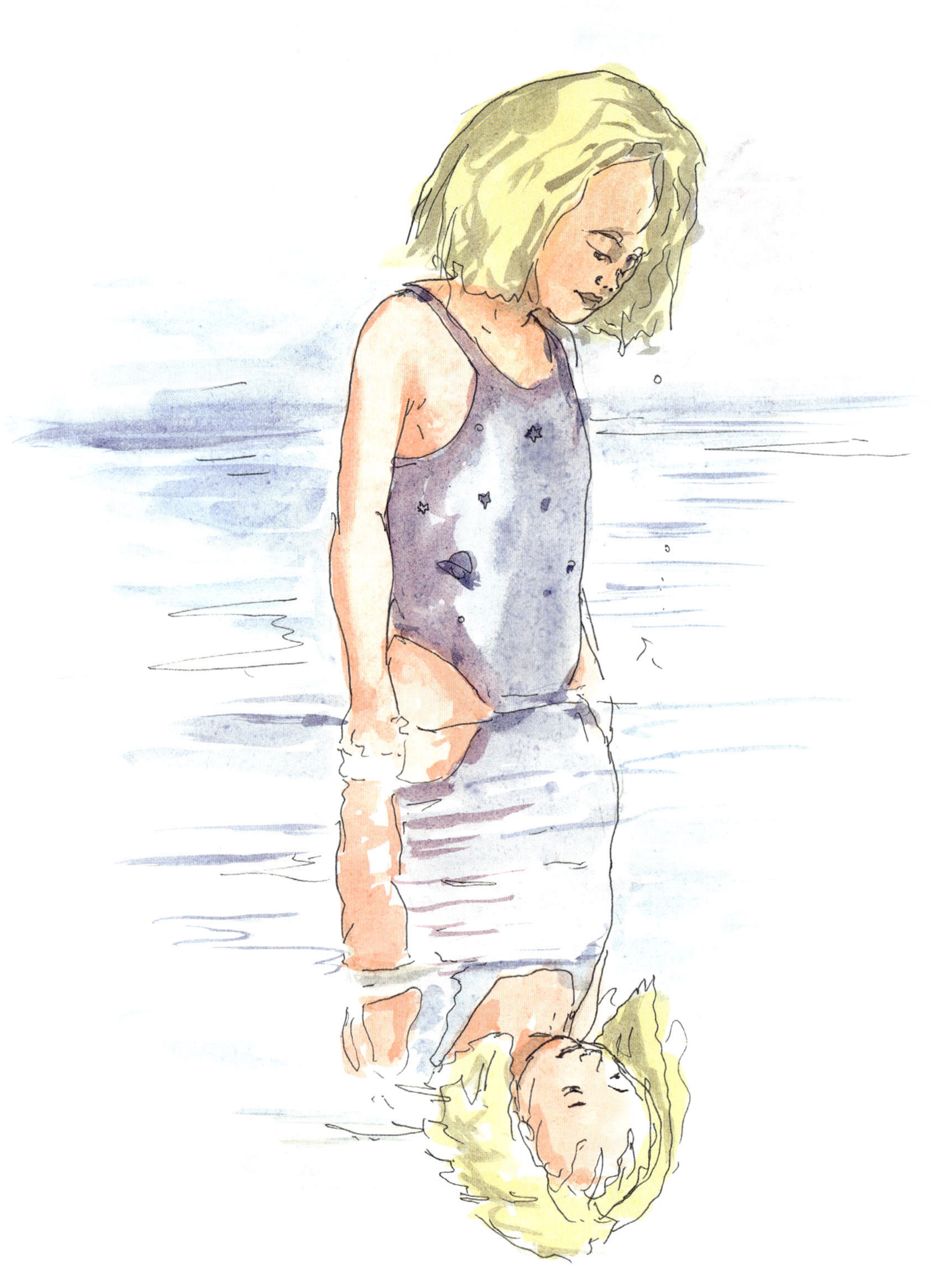

become this?

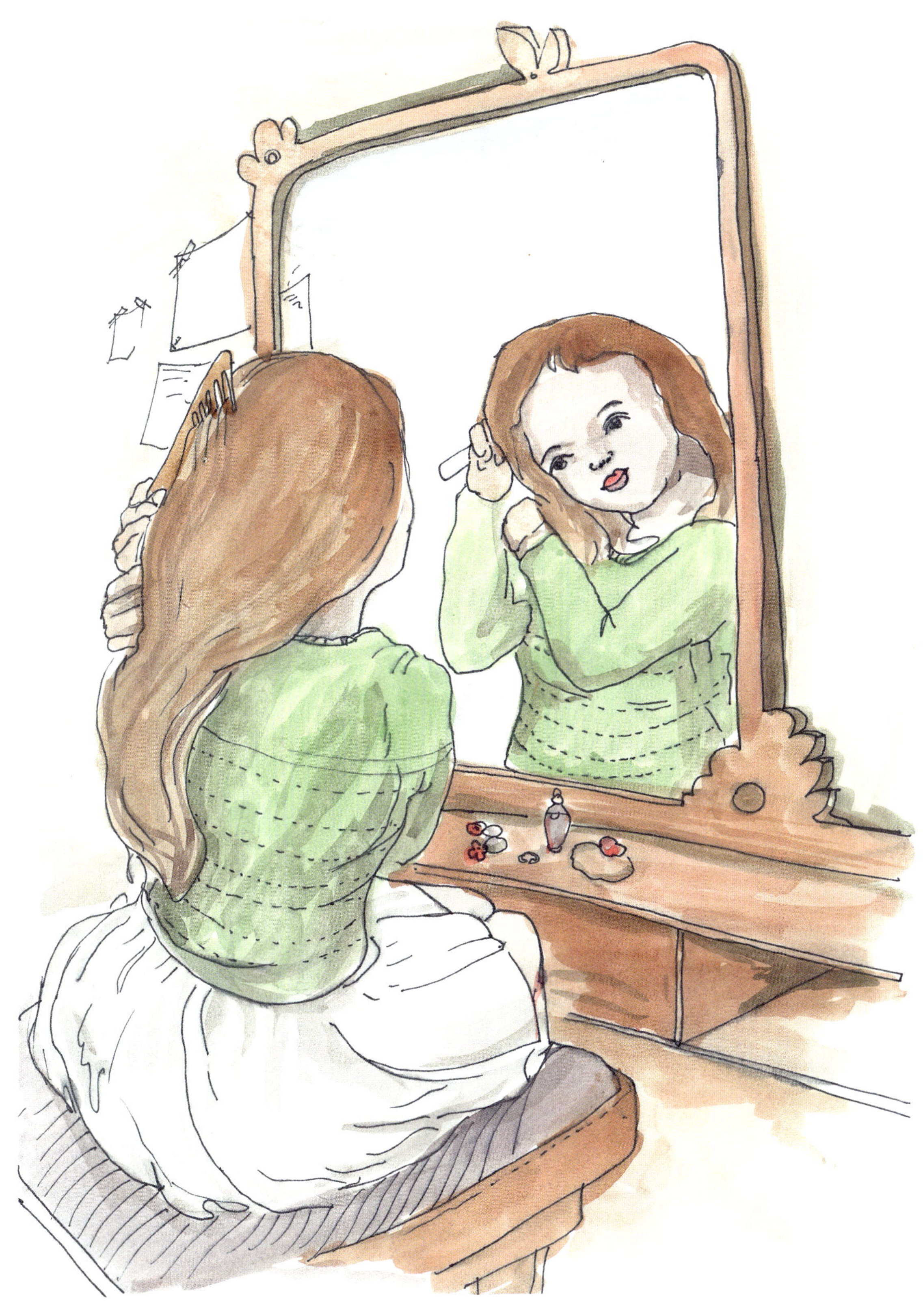

And that.

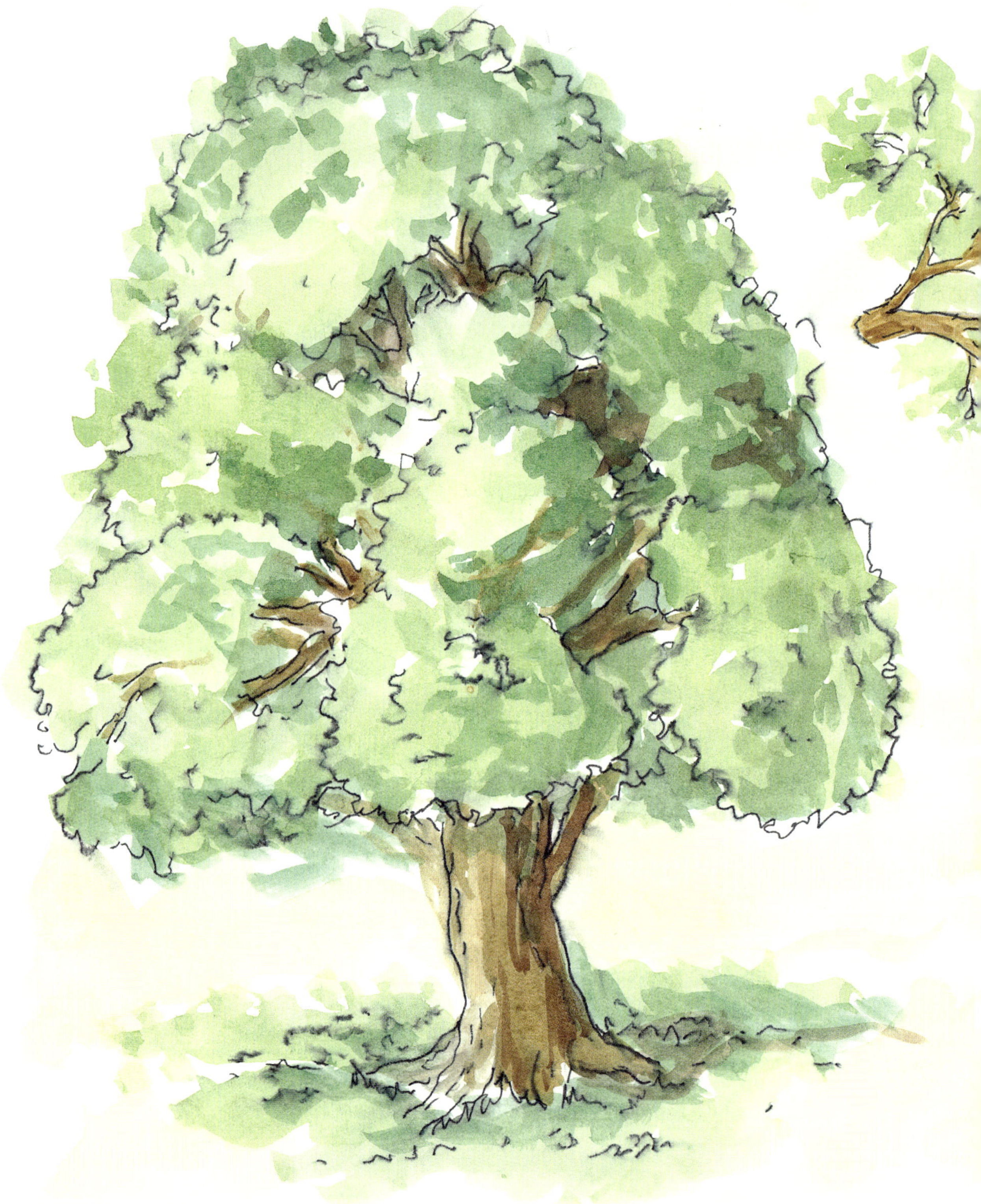

**And how did this

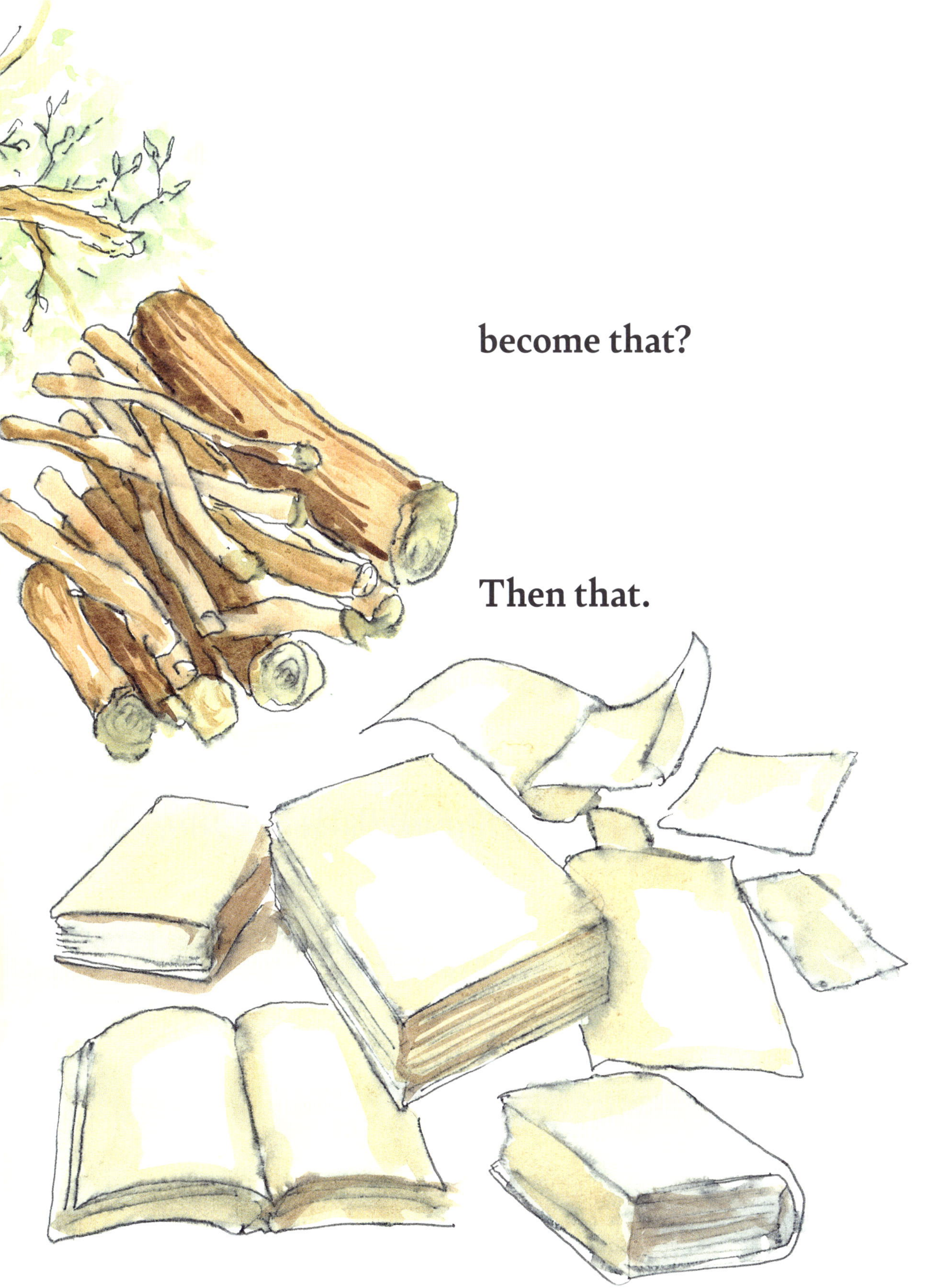

become that?

Then that.

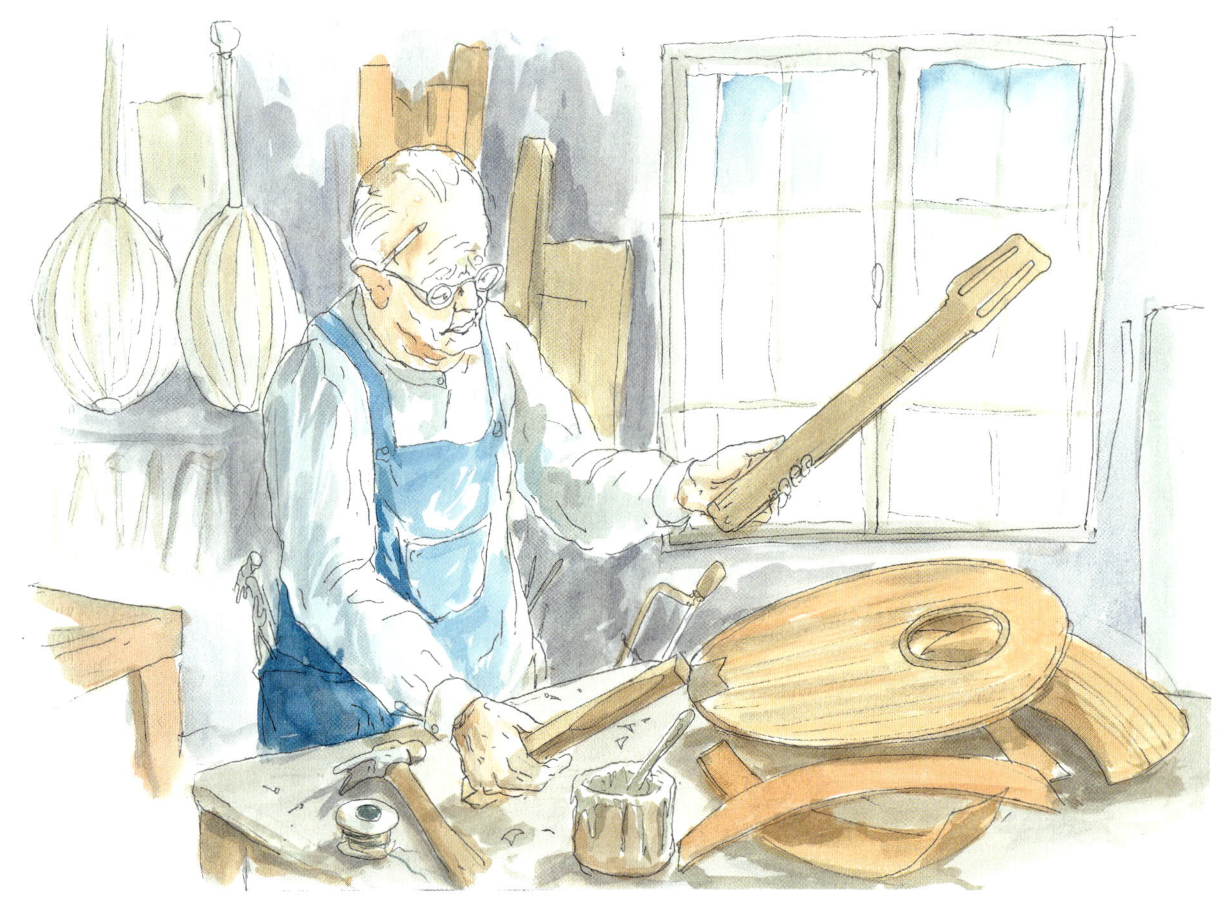

That

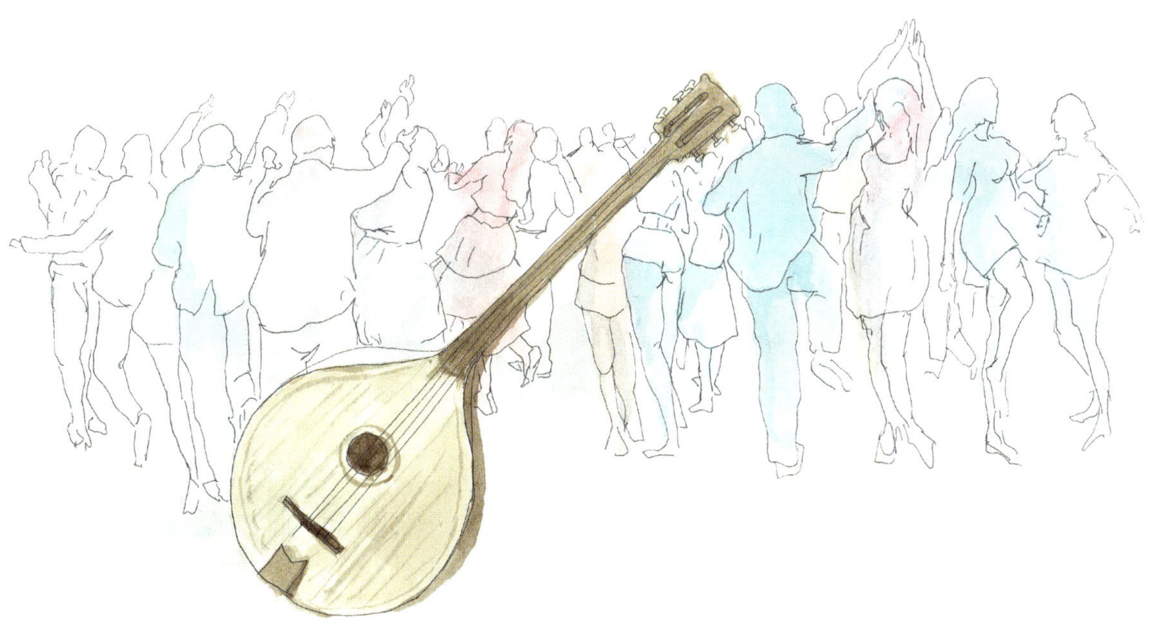

becomes this?

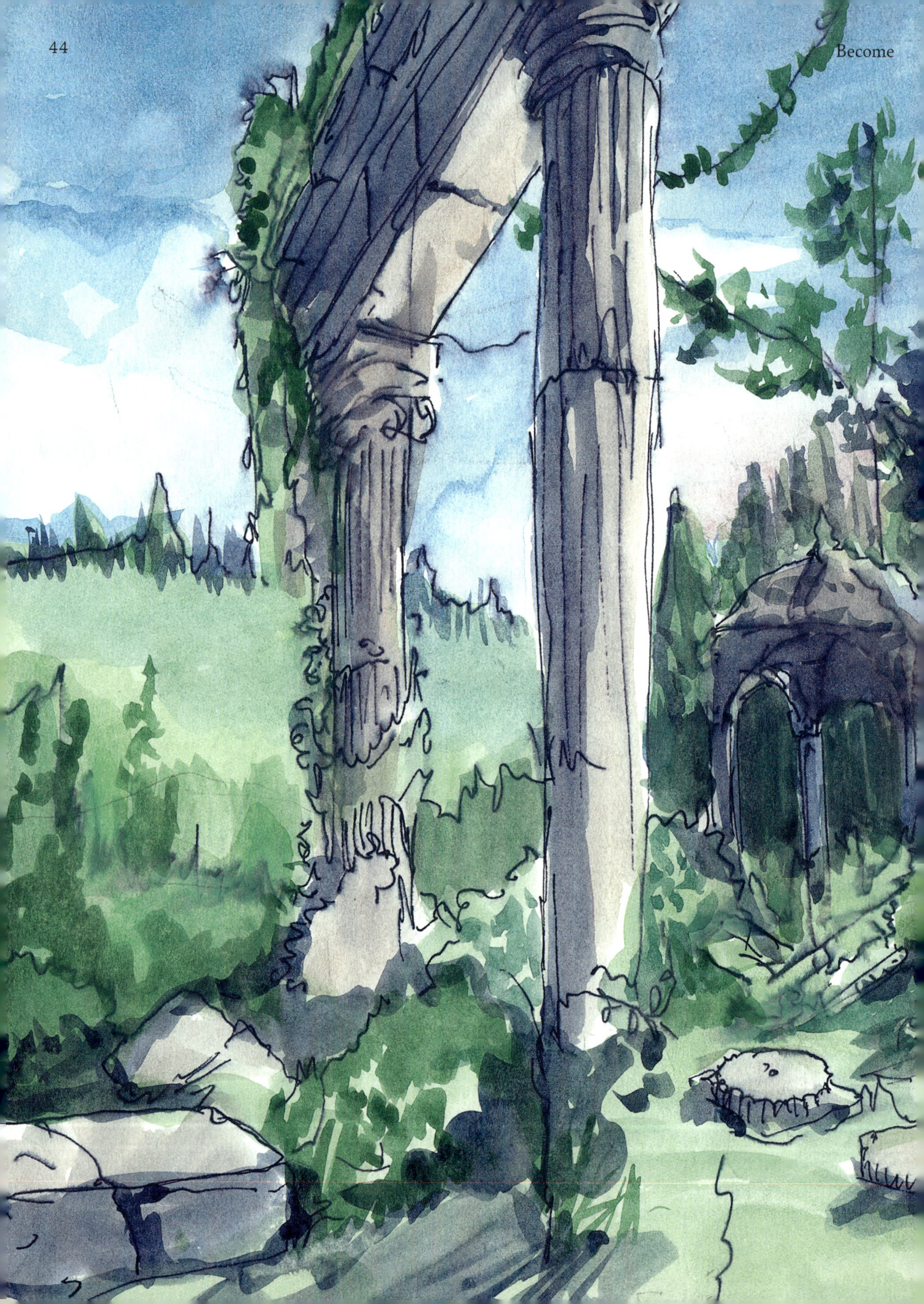

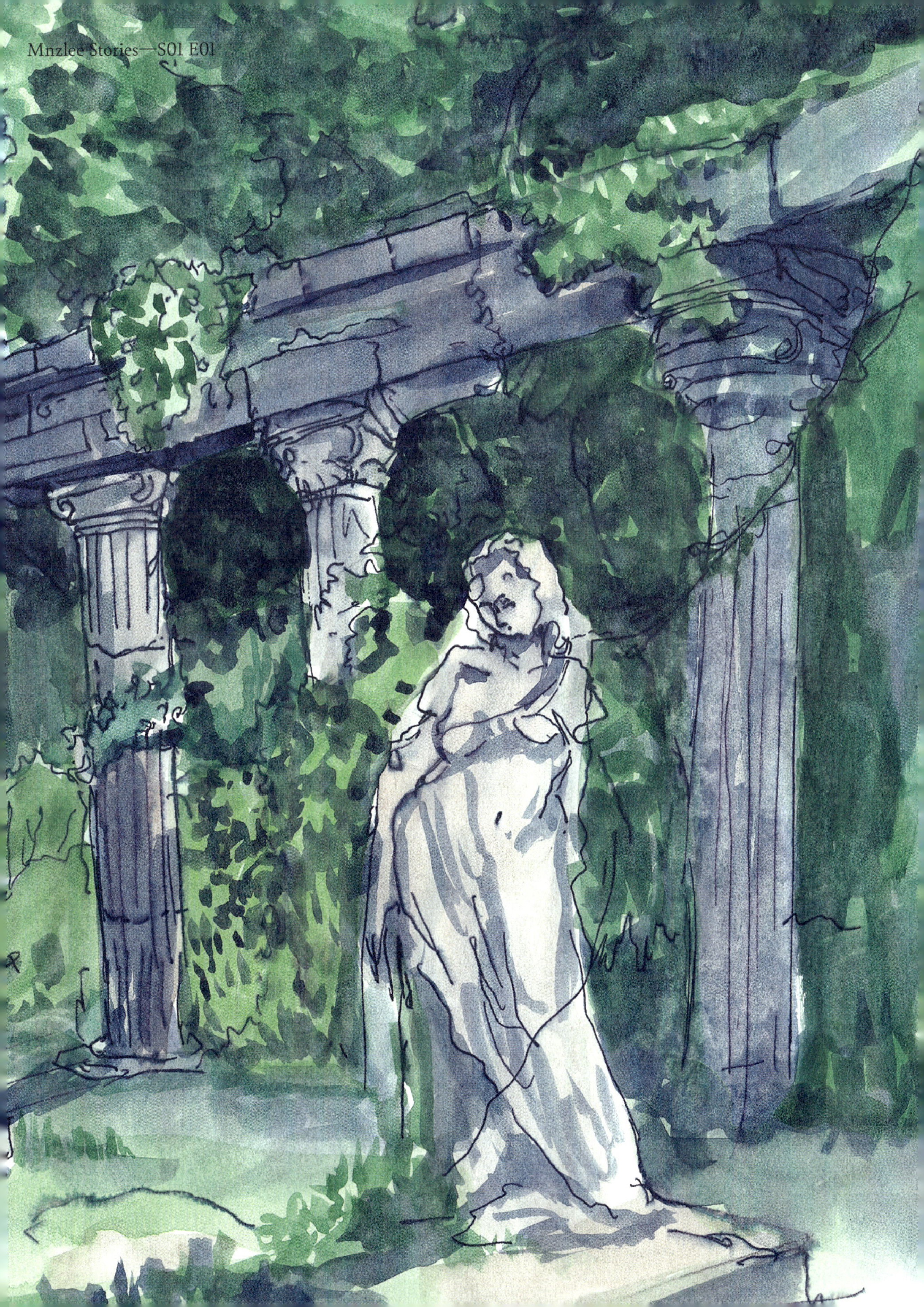

Some things feel so still, like they've always been there.
They're not still, nor have they always been there.

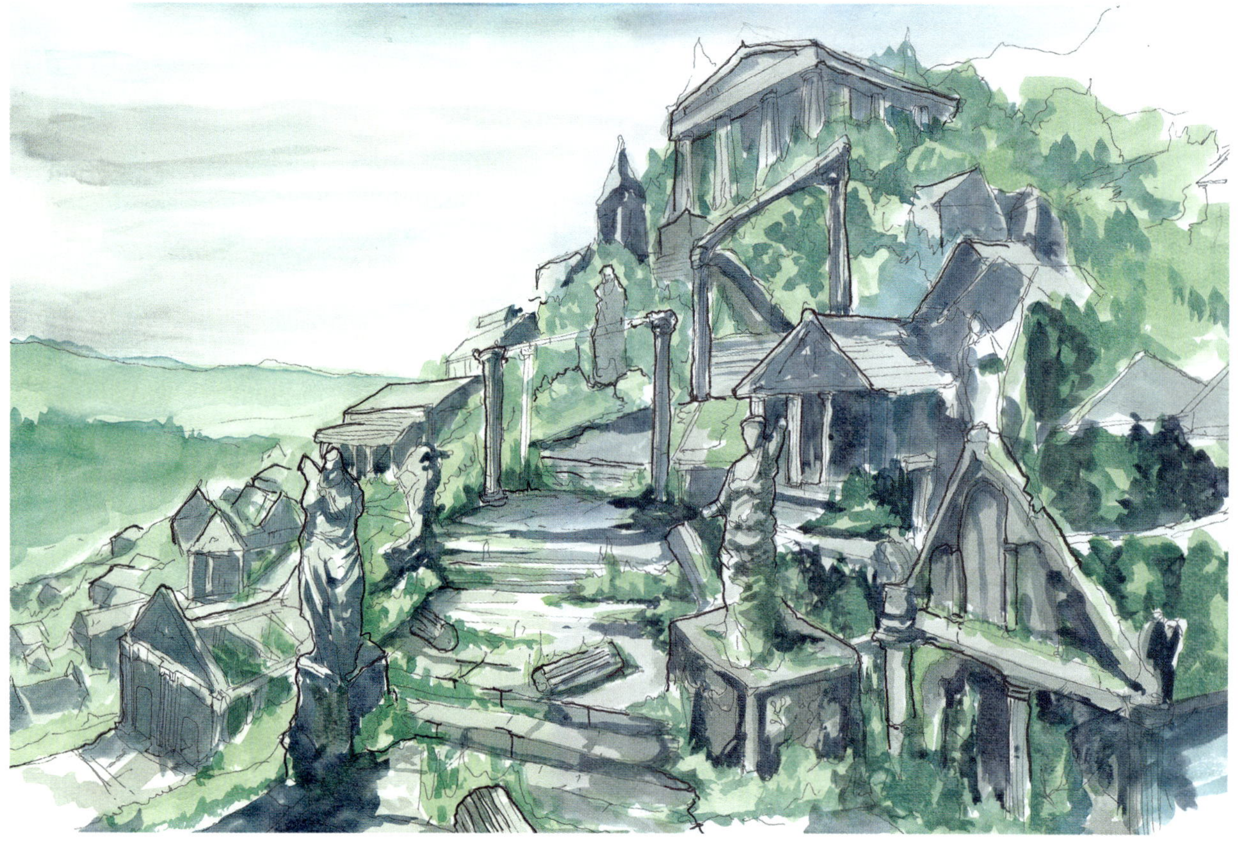

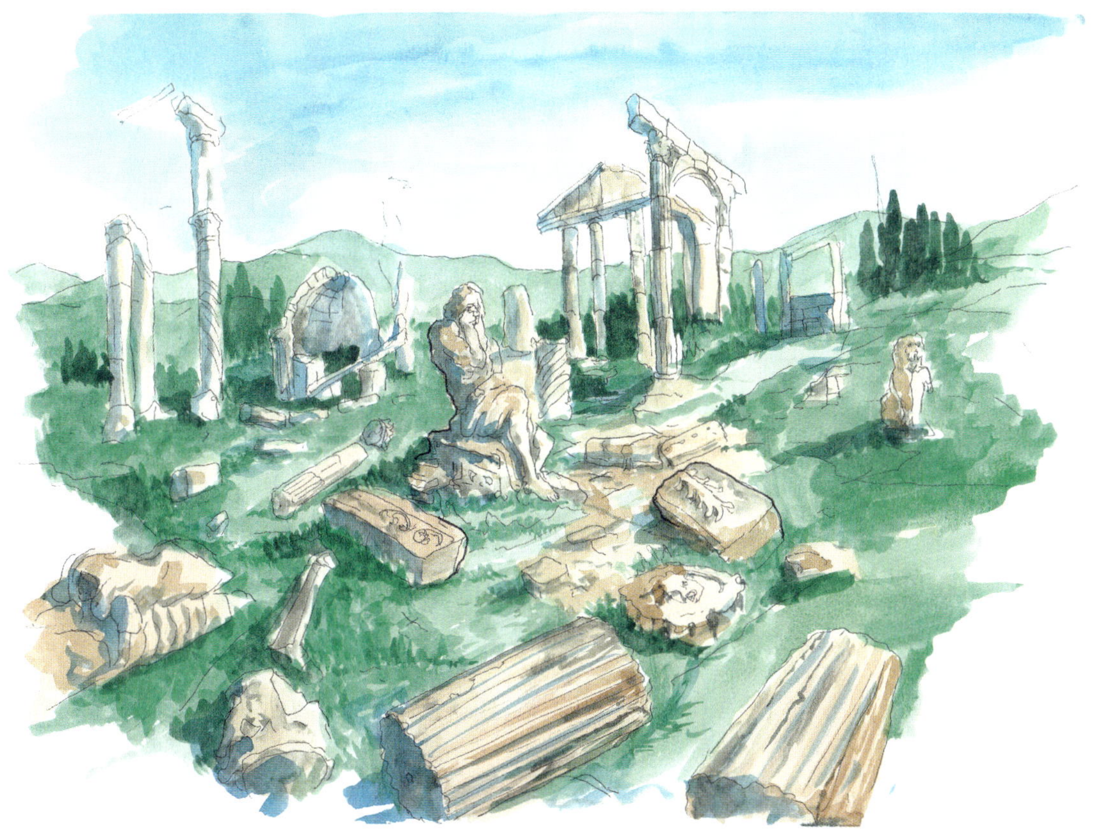

They have been made up.

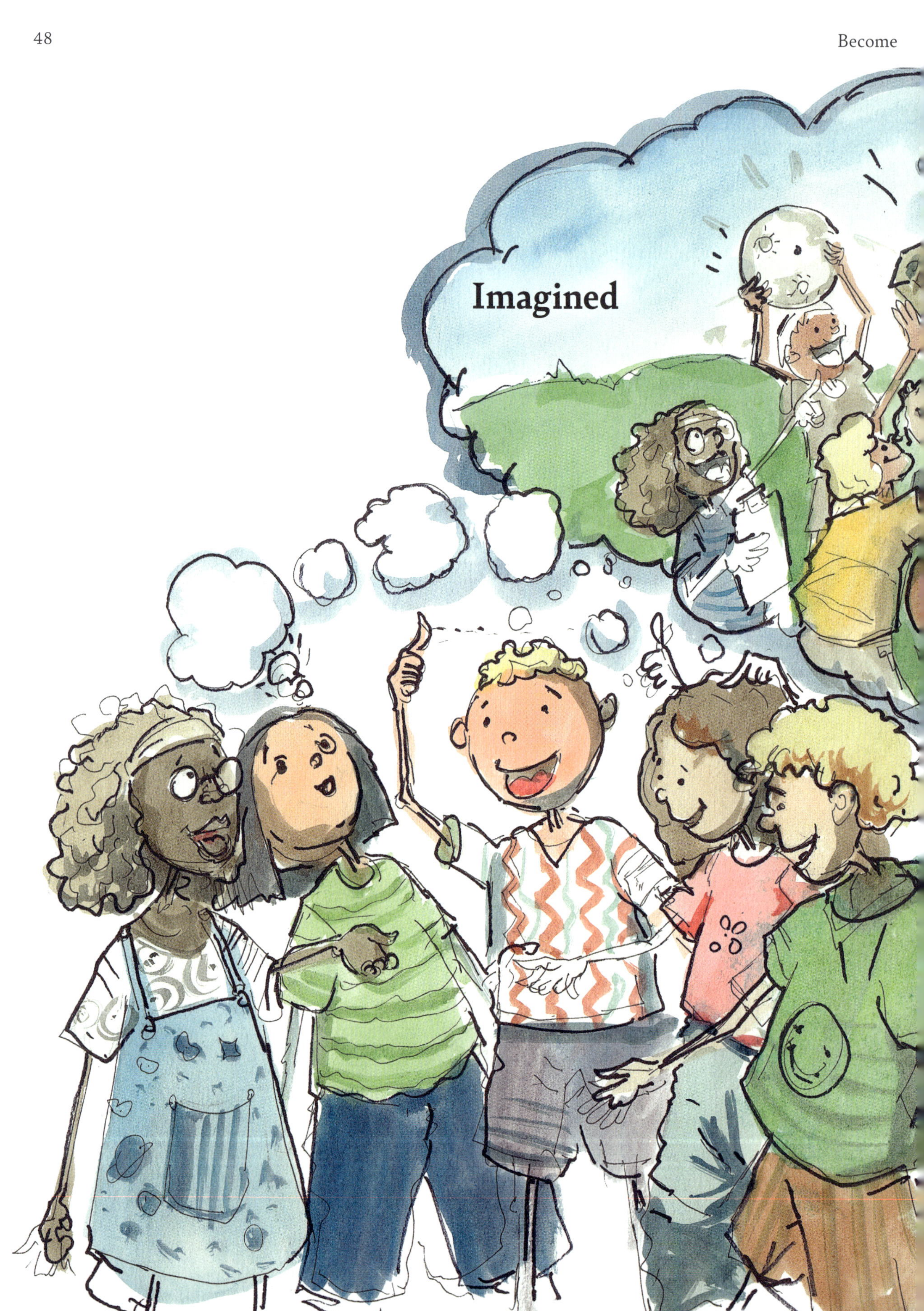
Imagined

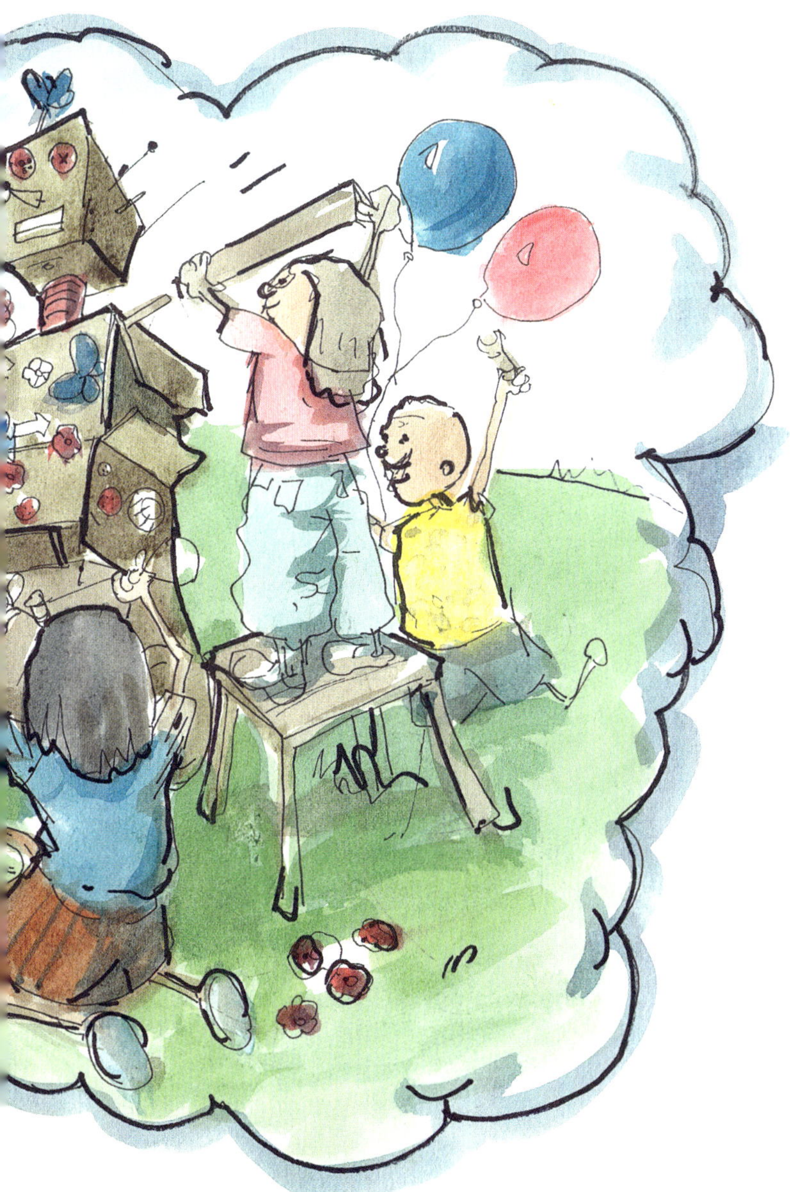

**by those who dare to dream
in what is not yet.**

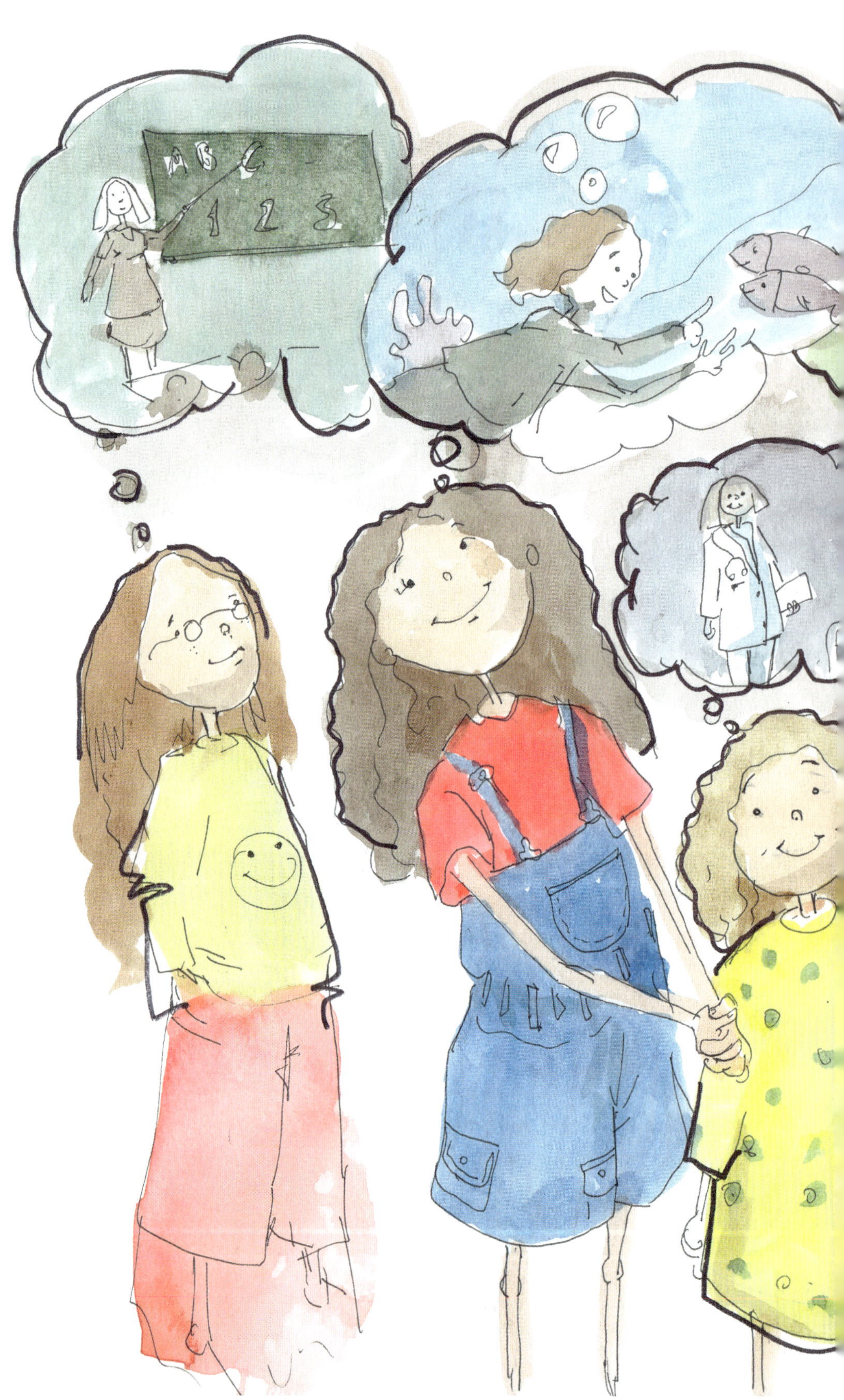
ABC
123

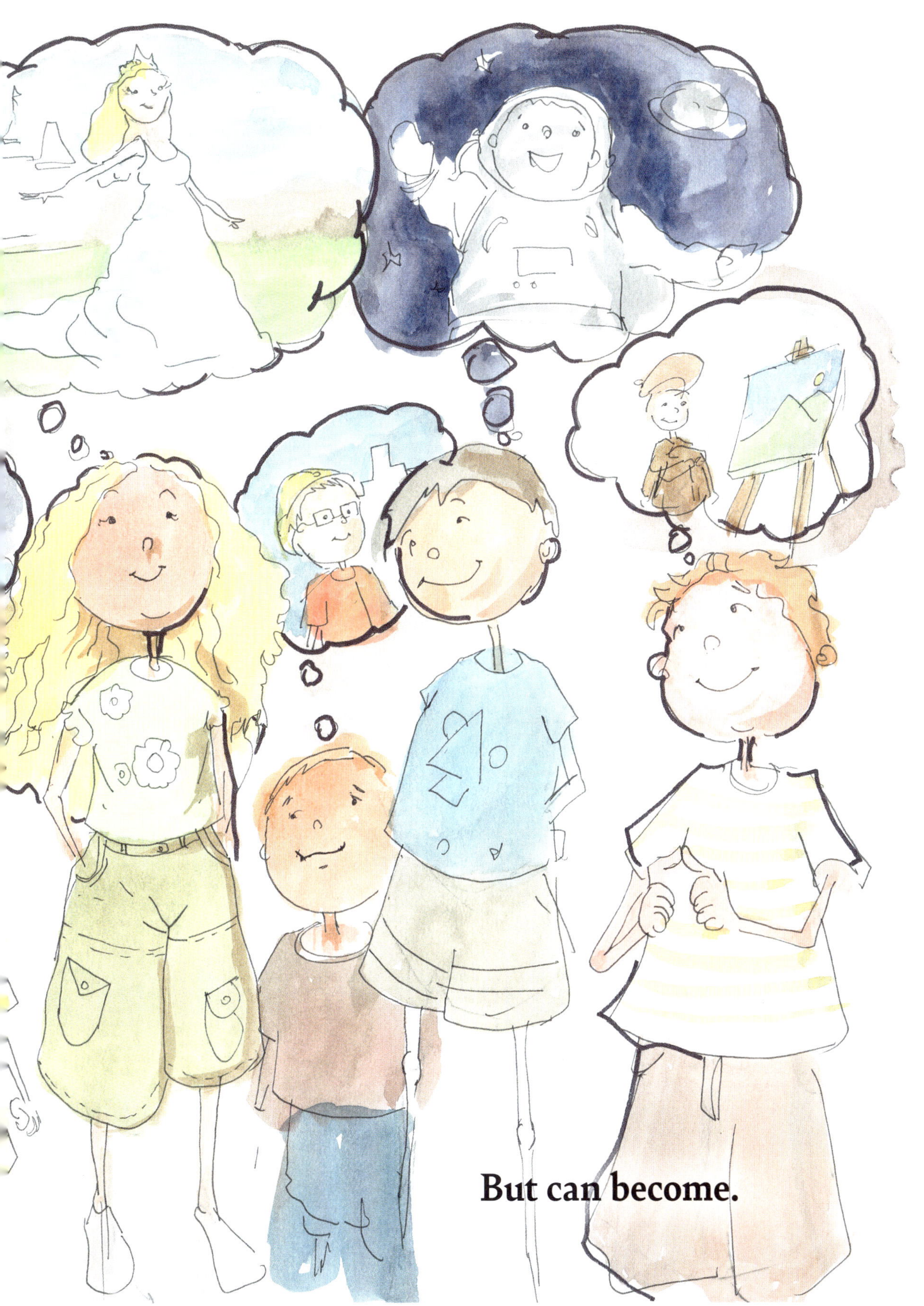

But can become.

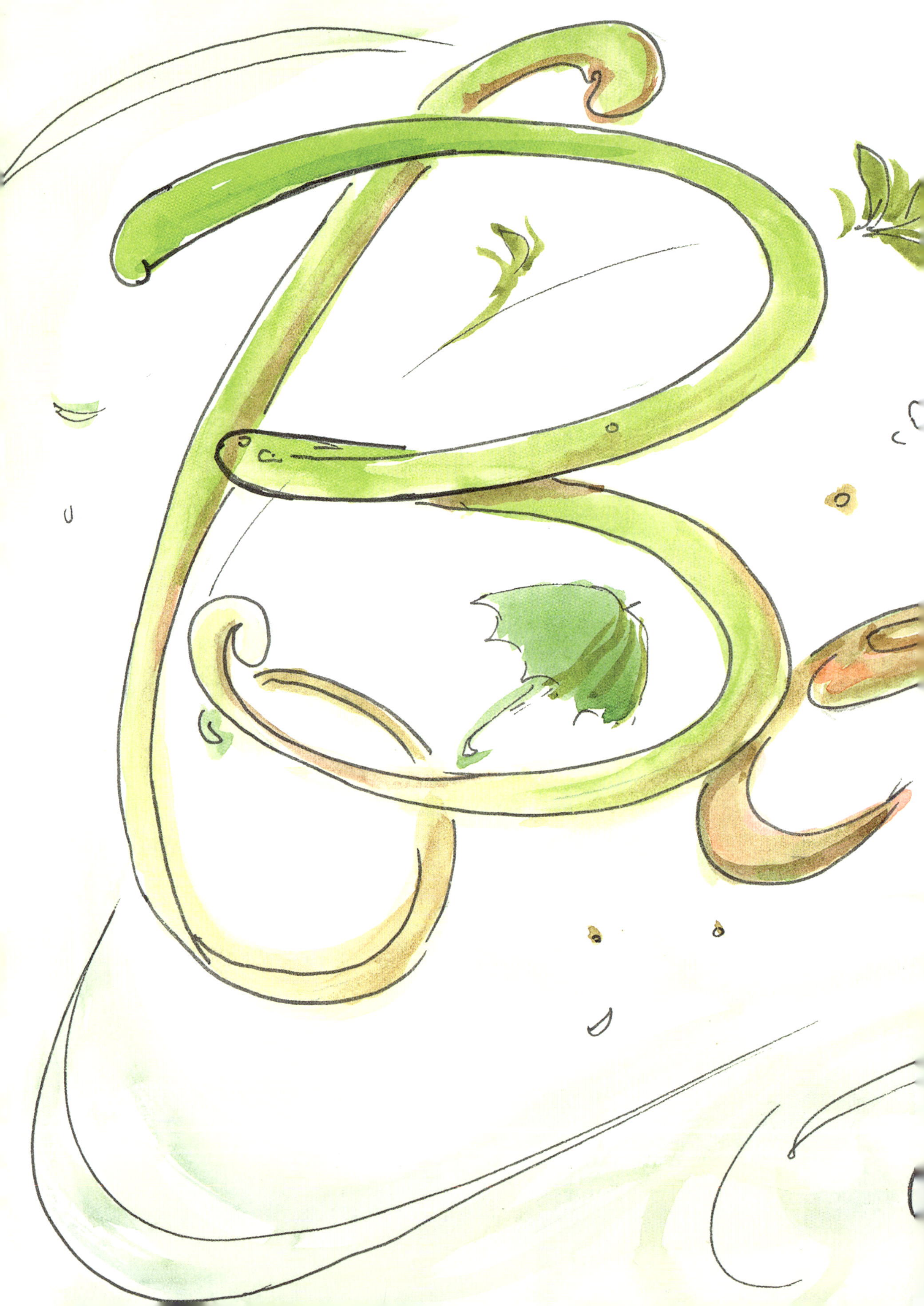

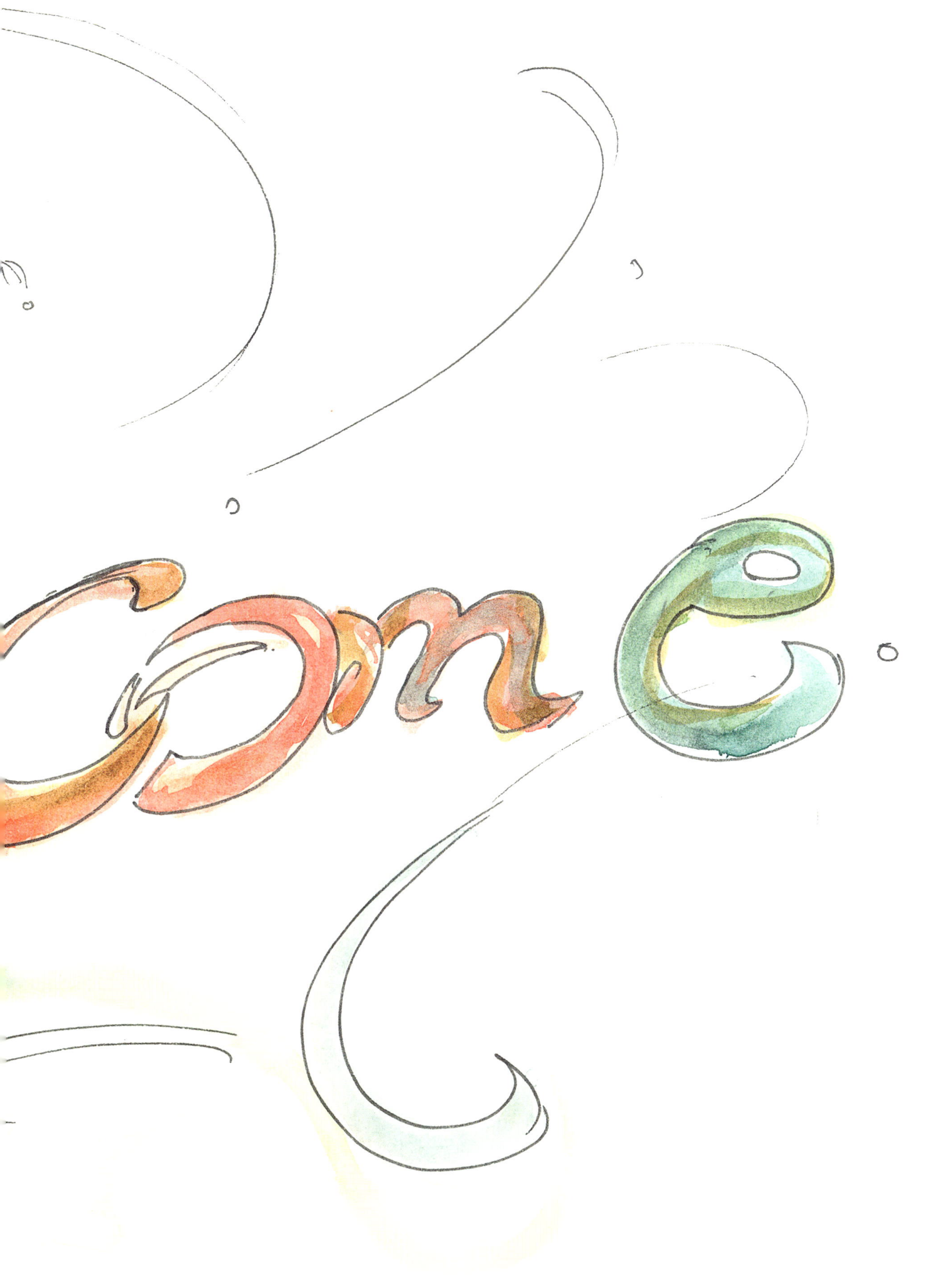

BANG BANG

Mnzlee Stories — S01 E02

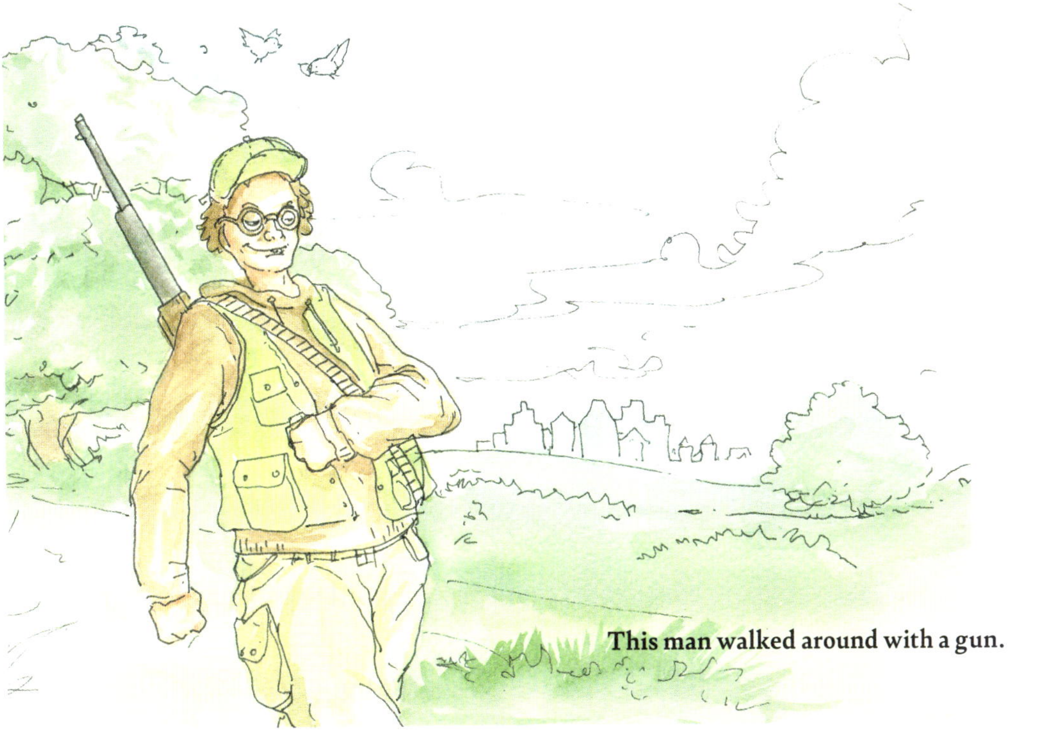

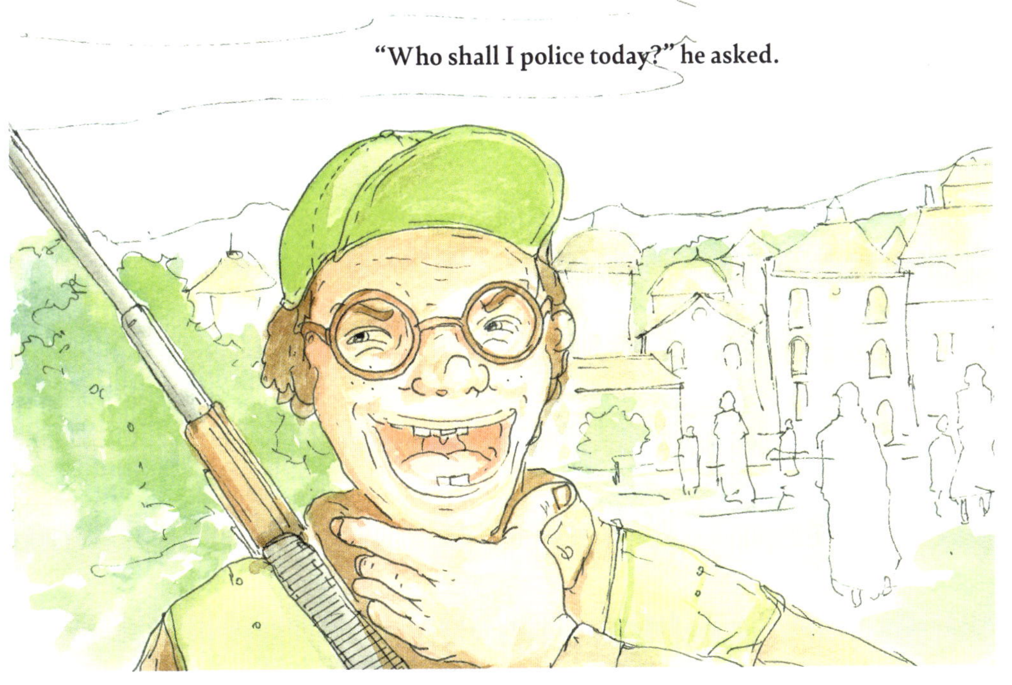

This man walked around with a gun.

"Who shall I police today?" he asked.

"Ah, no one to police, what a boring, boring day."

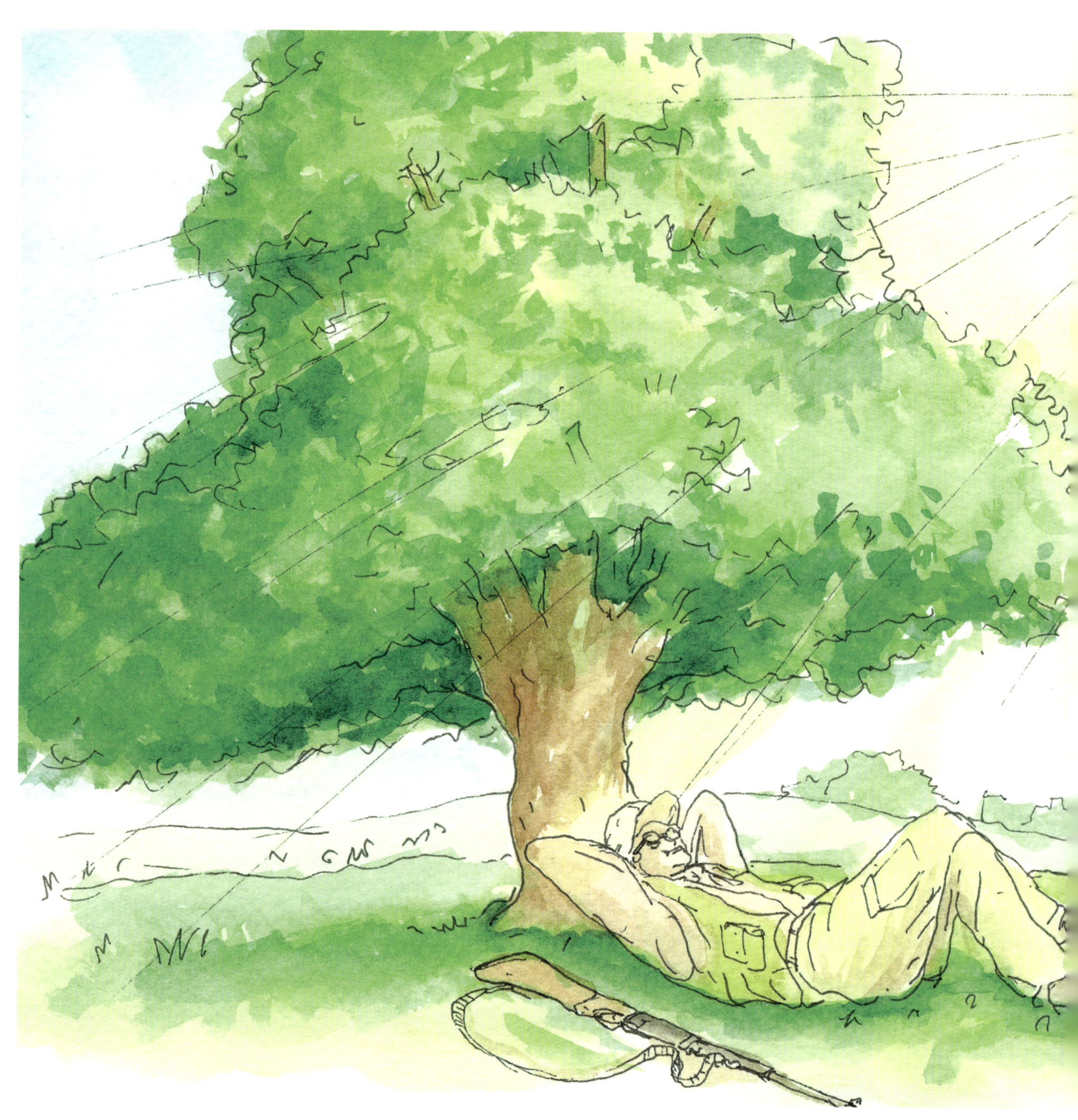

And so under the shaded tree, he slept.

And the sun, who does not discriminate, cast her light on him.

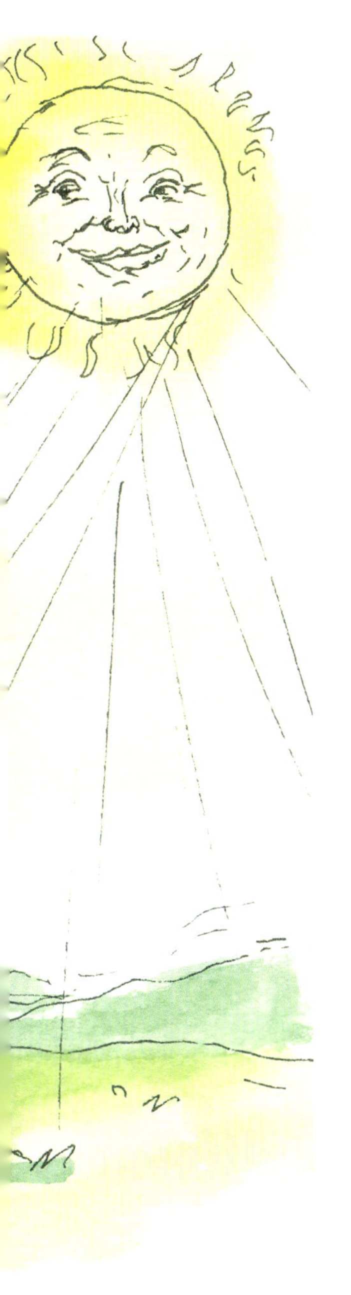

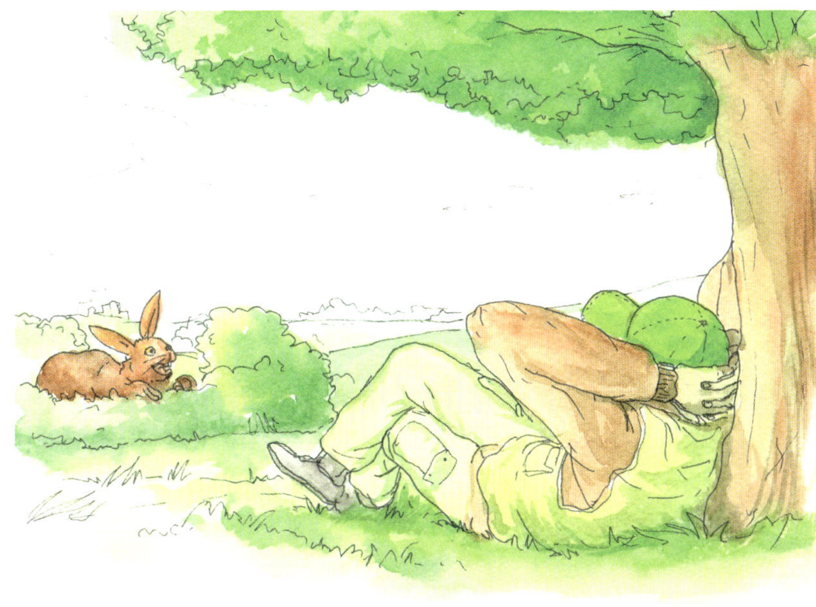

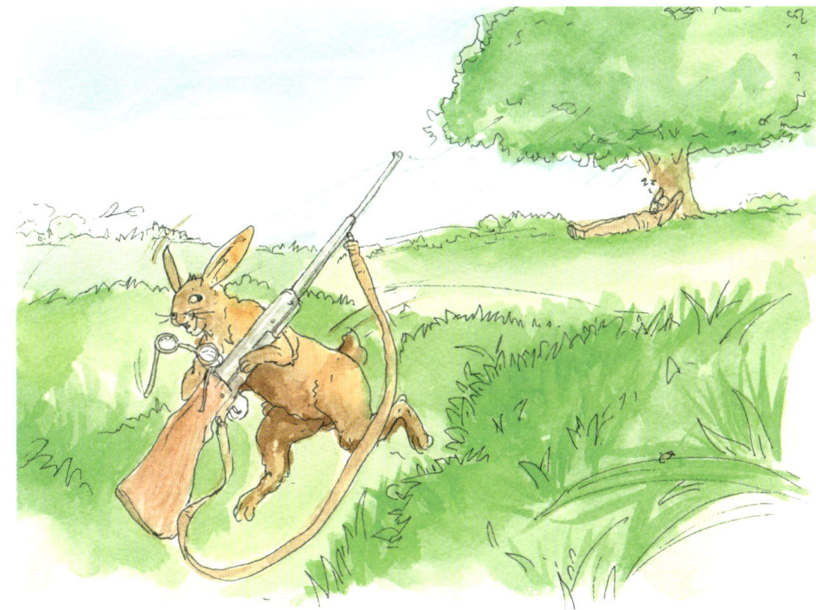

And out of the bushes, a sweet fuzzy bunny appeared and stole his gun and glasses.

Bang bang.
Fuzzy bunny shot the man.

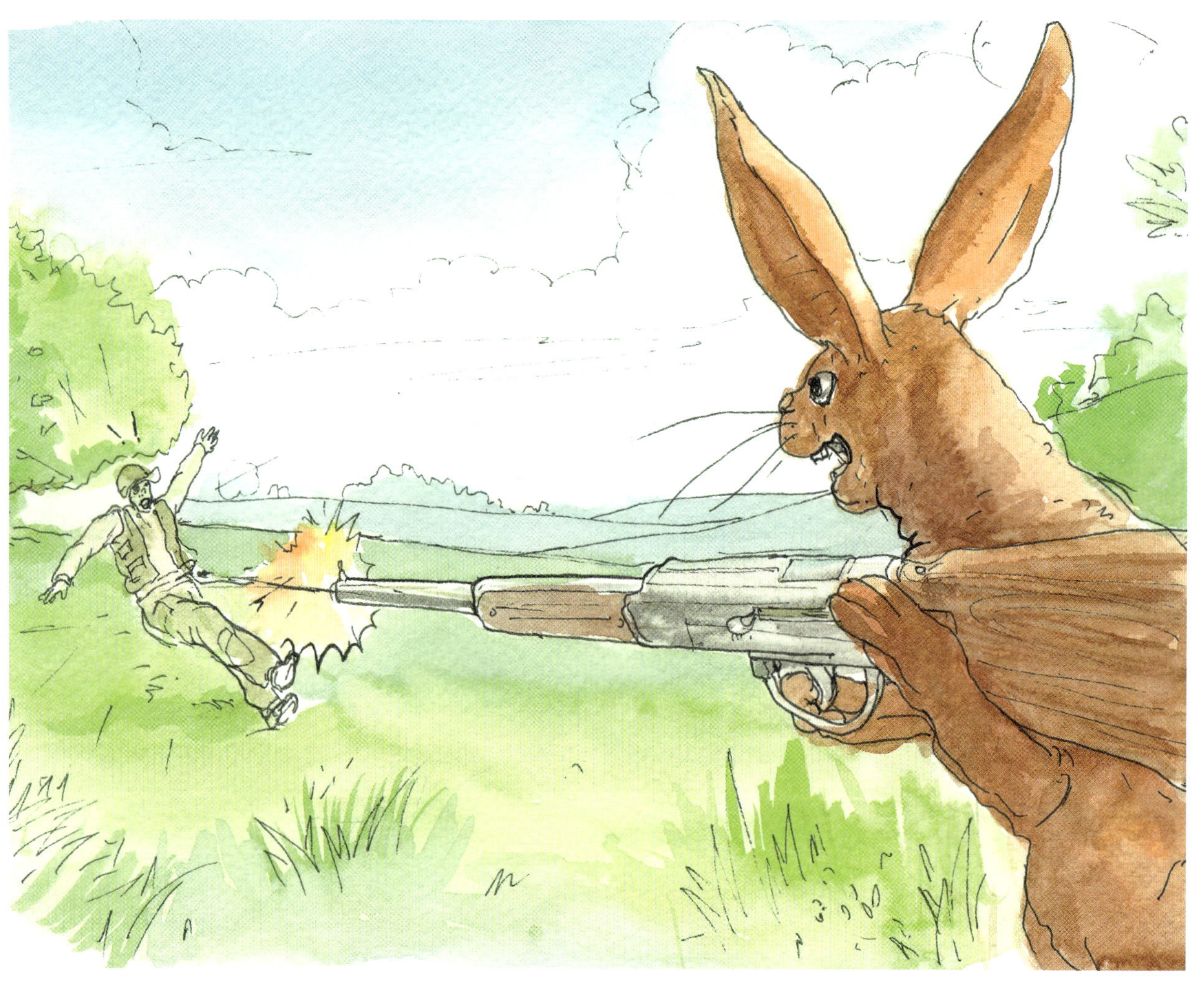

He felt so happy and victorious.

But little did the sweet fuzzy bunny know that he was a figment of the man's imagination.

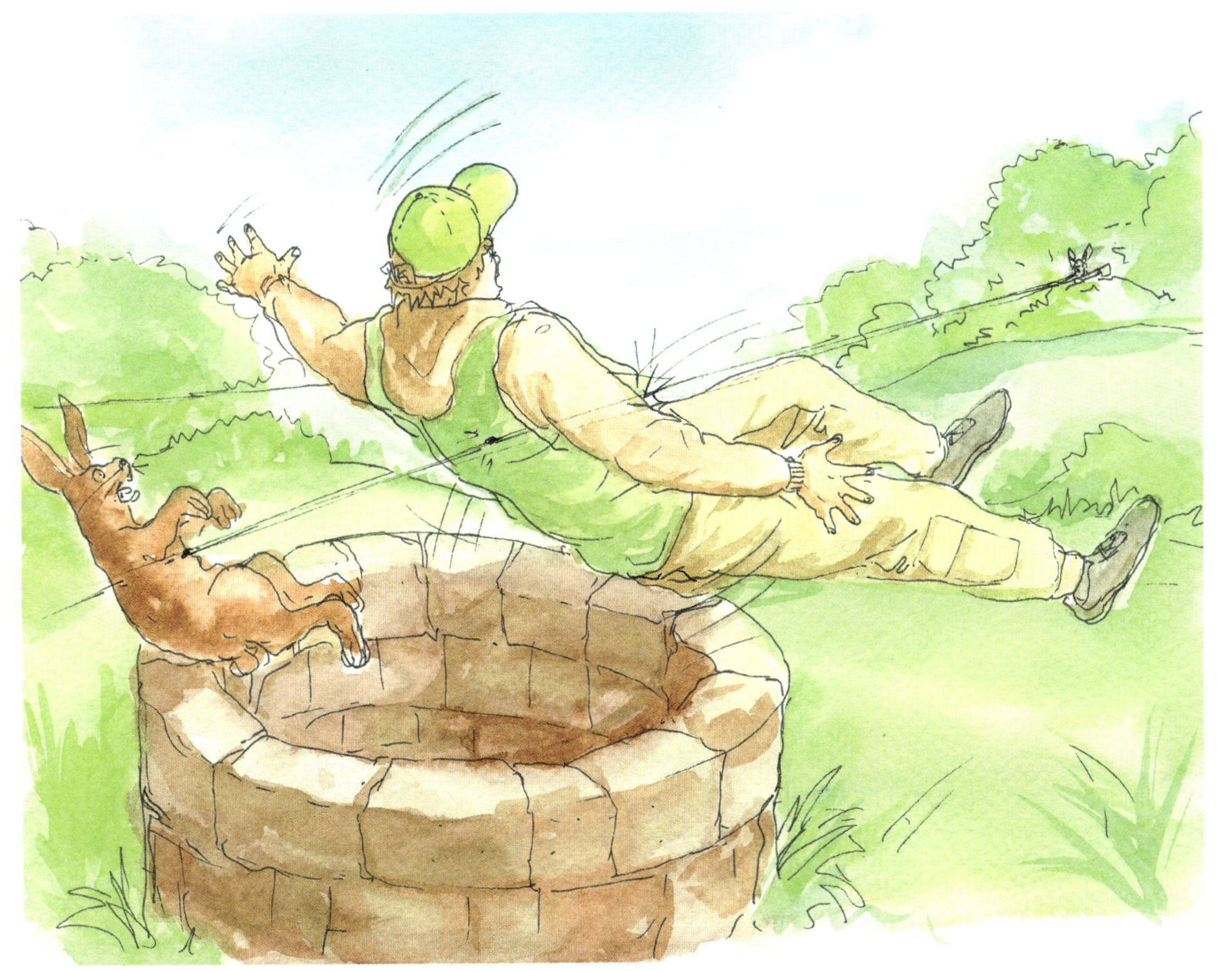

In fact, he was the man.

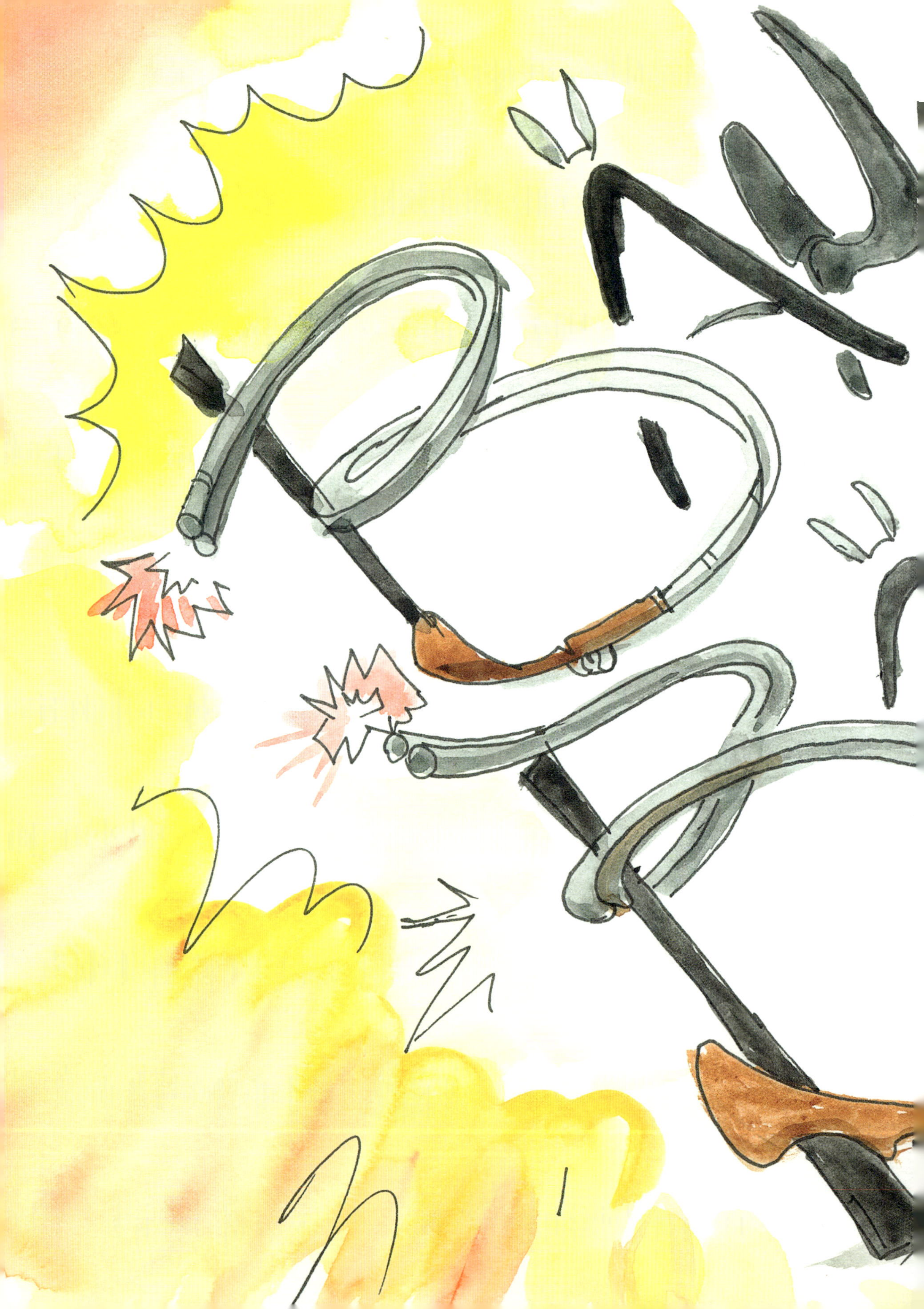

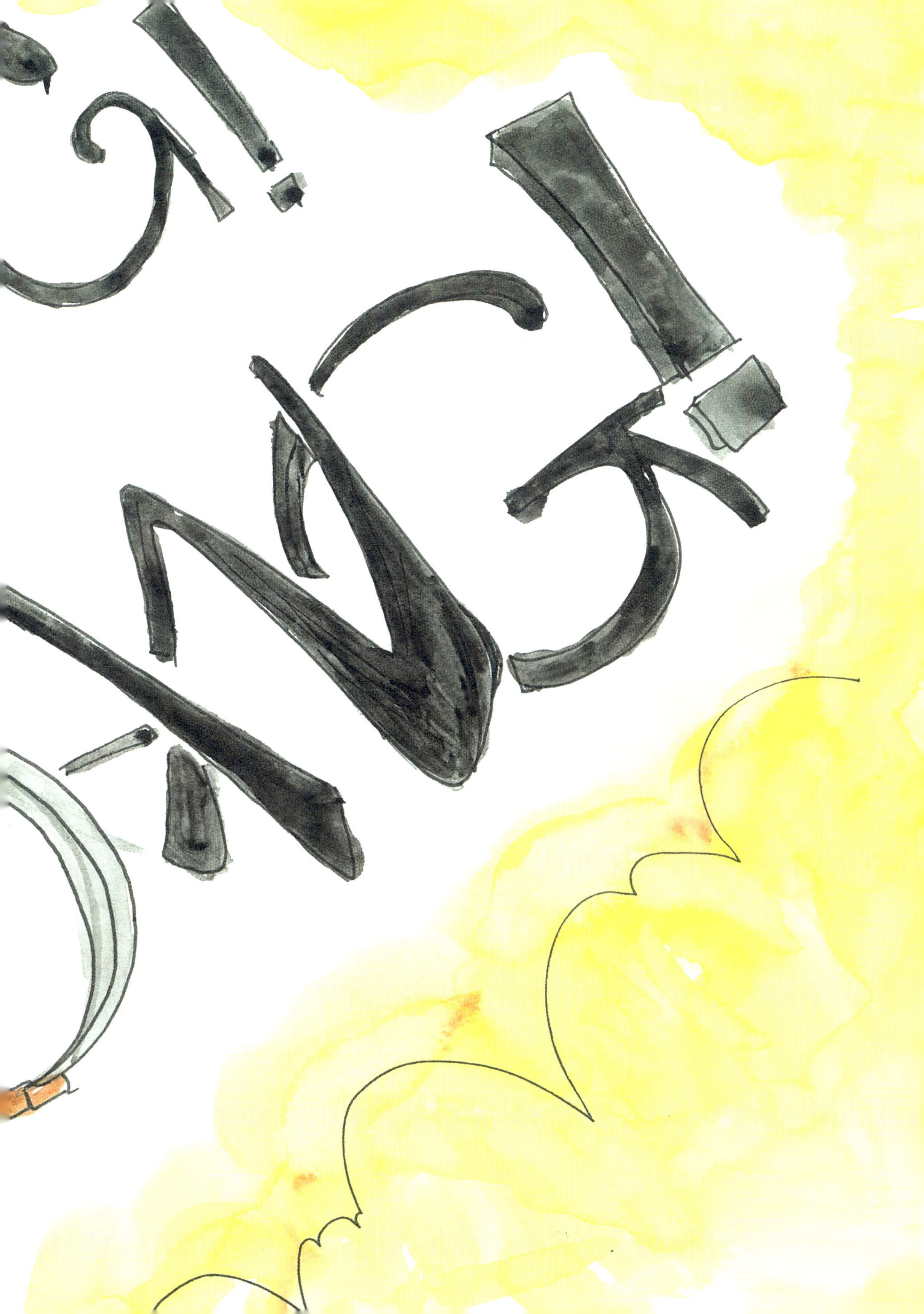
OMG!

TOMATO

Mnzlee Stories — S01 E03

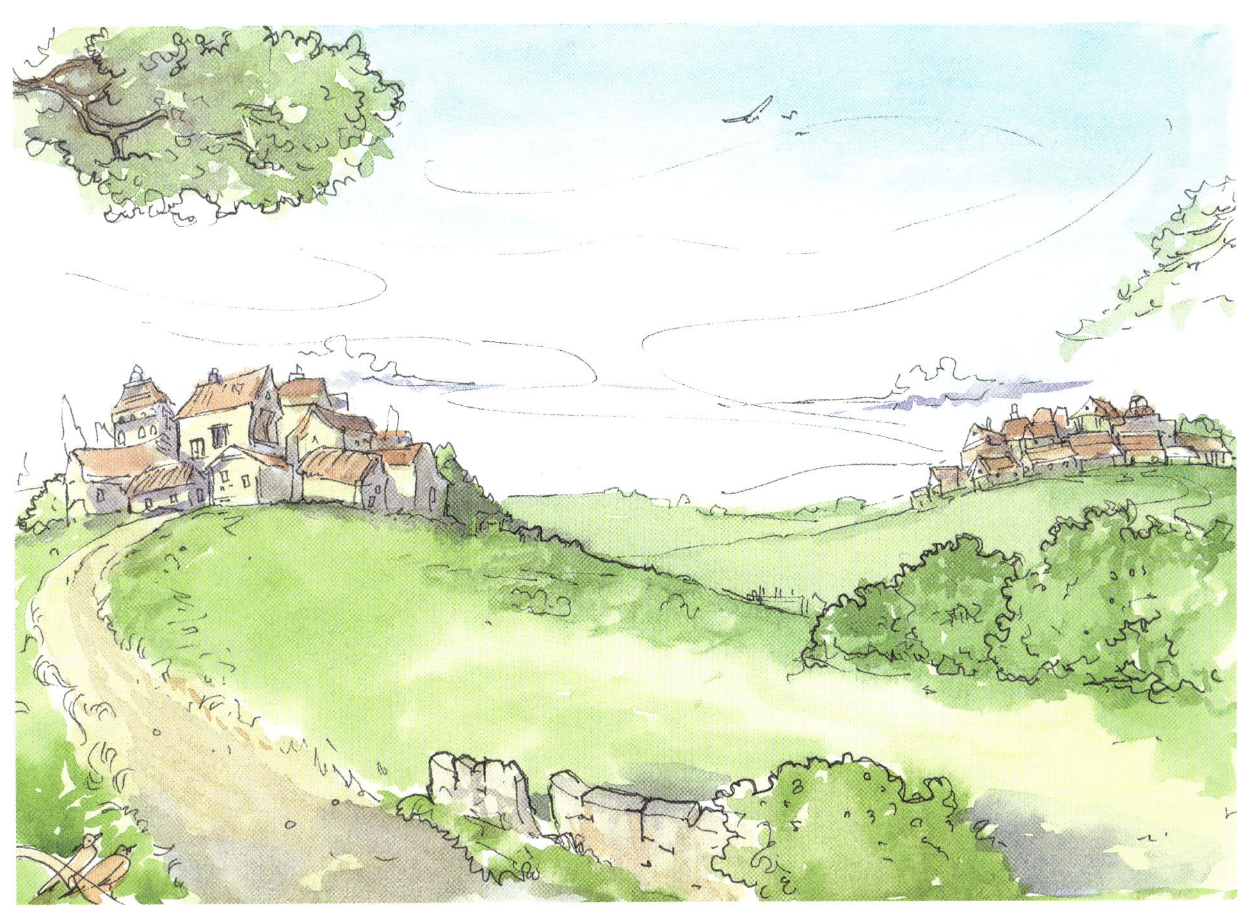

Two boys were chosen at birth by the world to settle one matter once and for all.

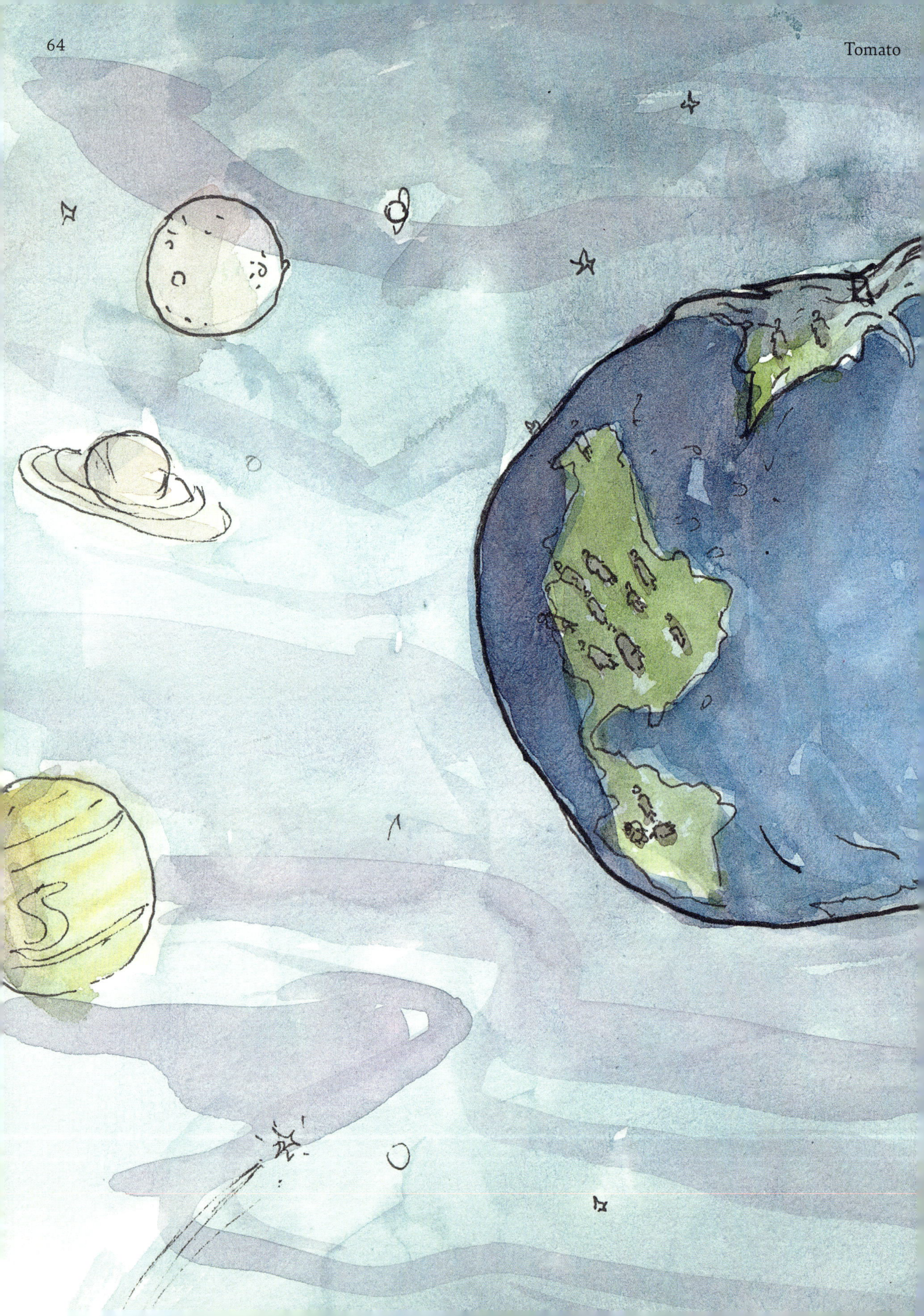

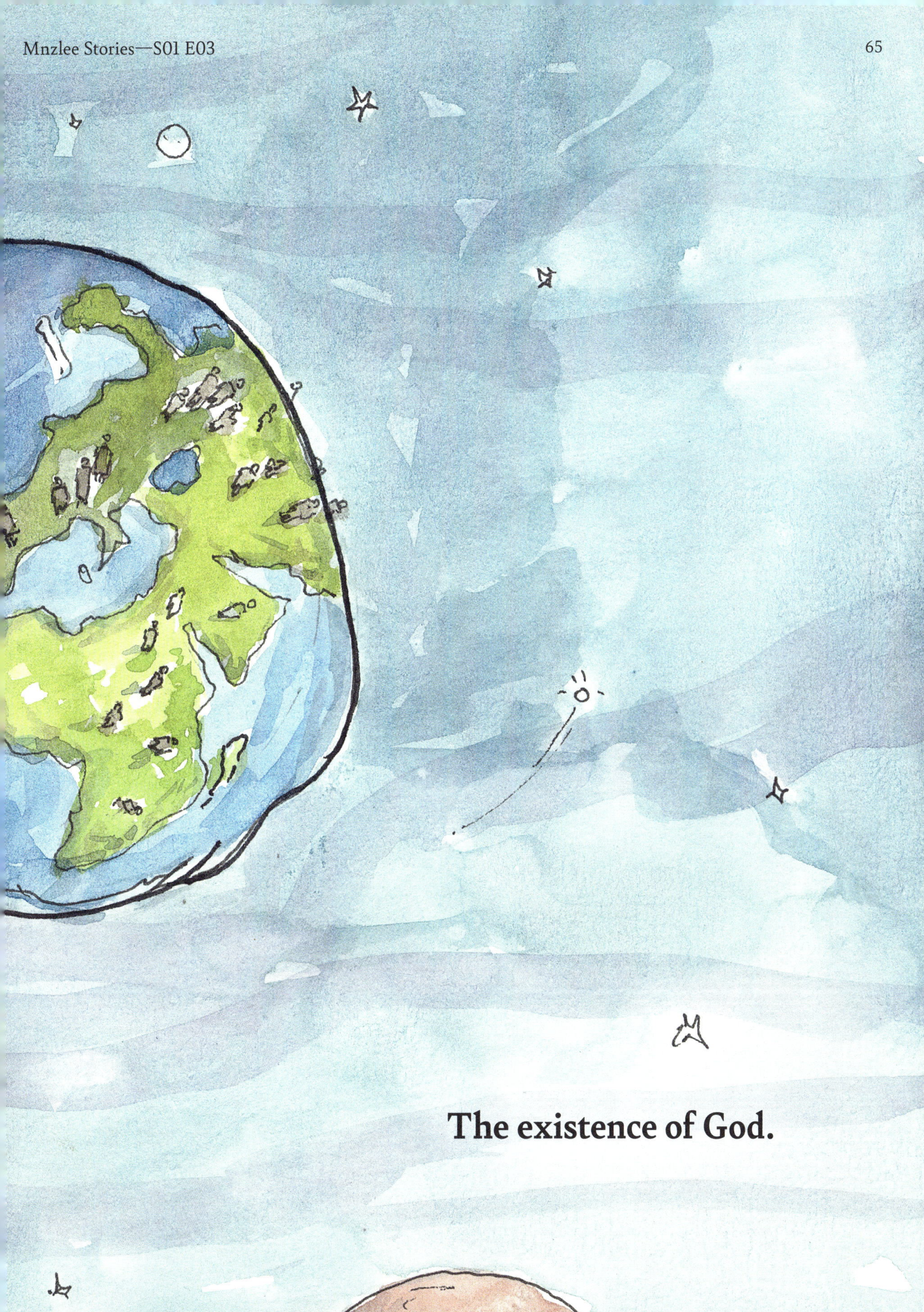

The existence of God.

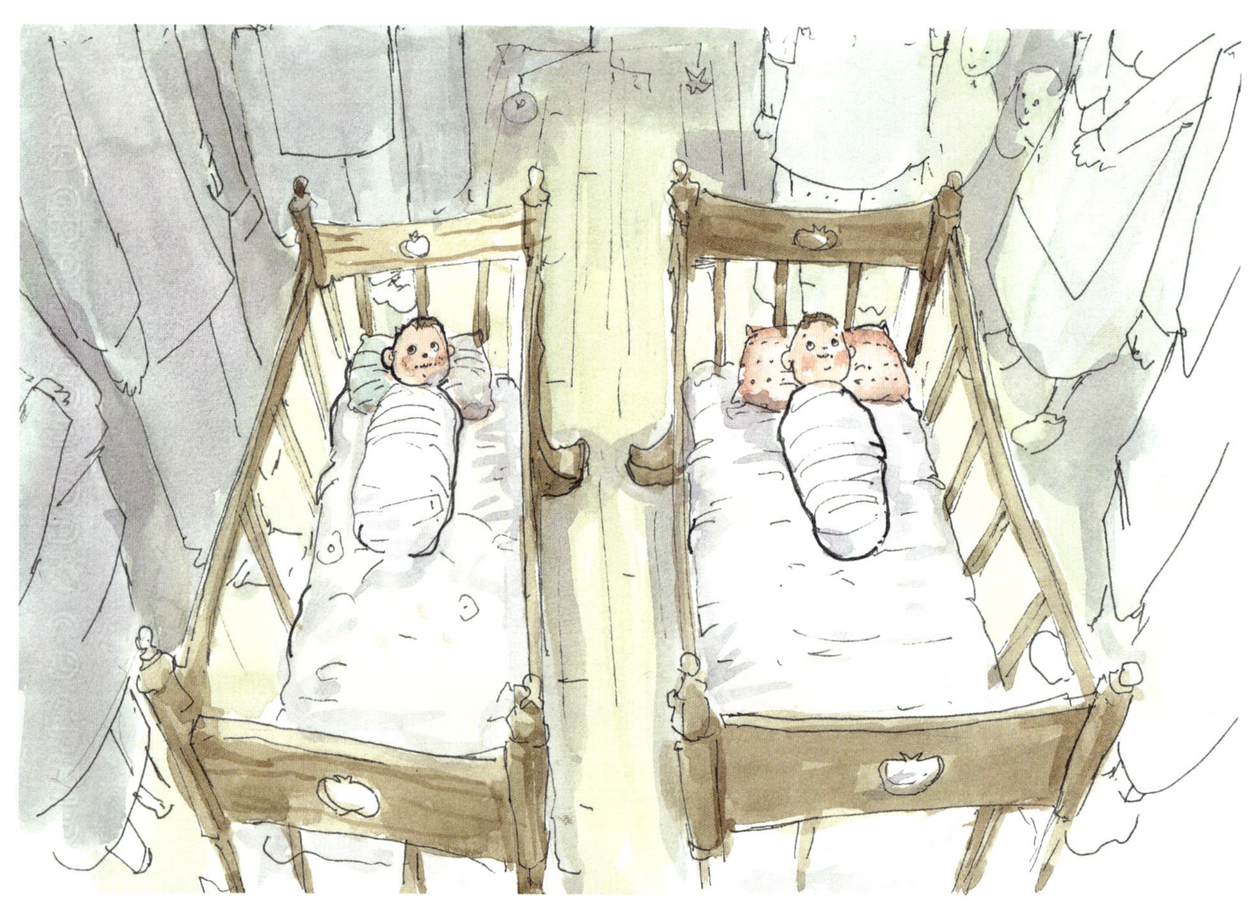

They were bred and prepared for
their important meeting.

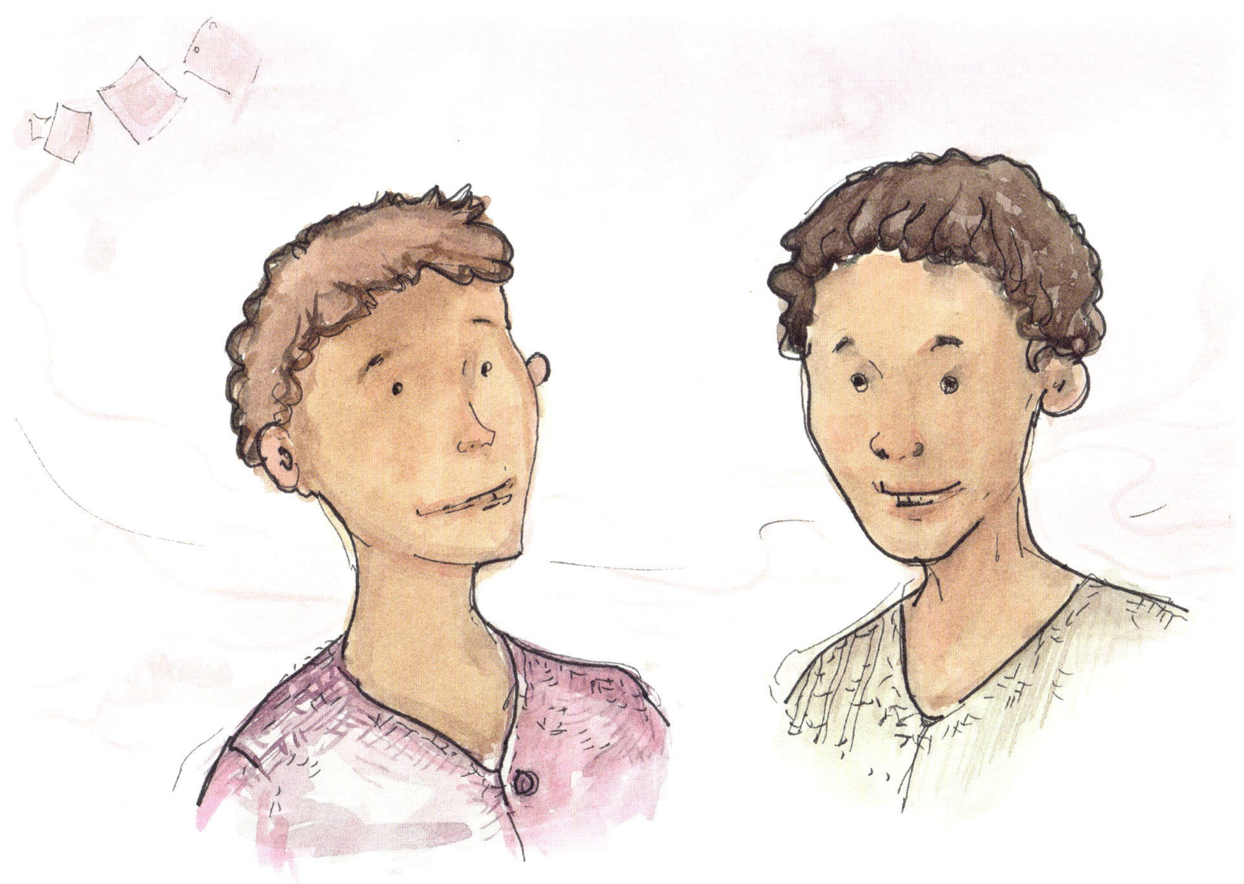

And when they turned of age, they were placed into a house together for their discussion to begin.

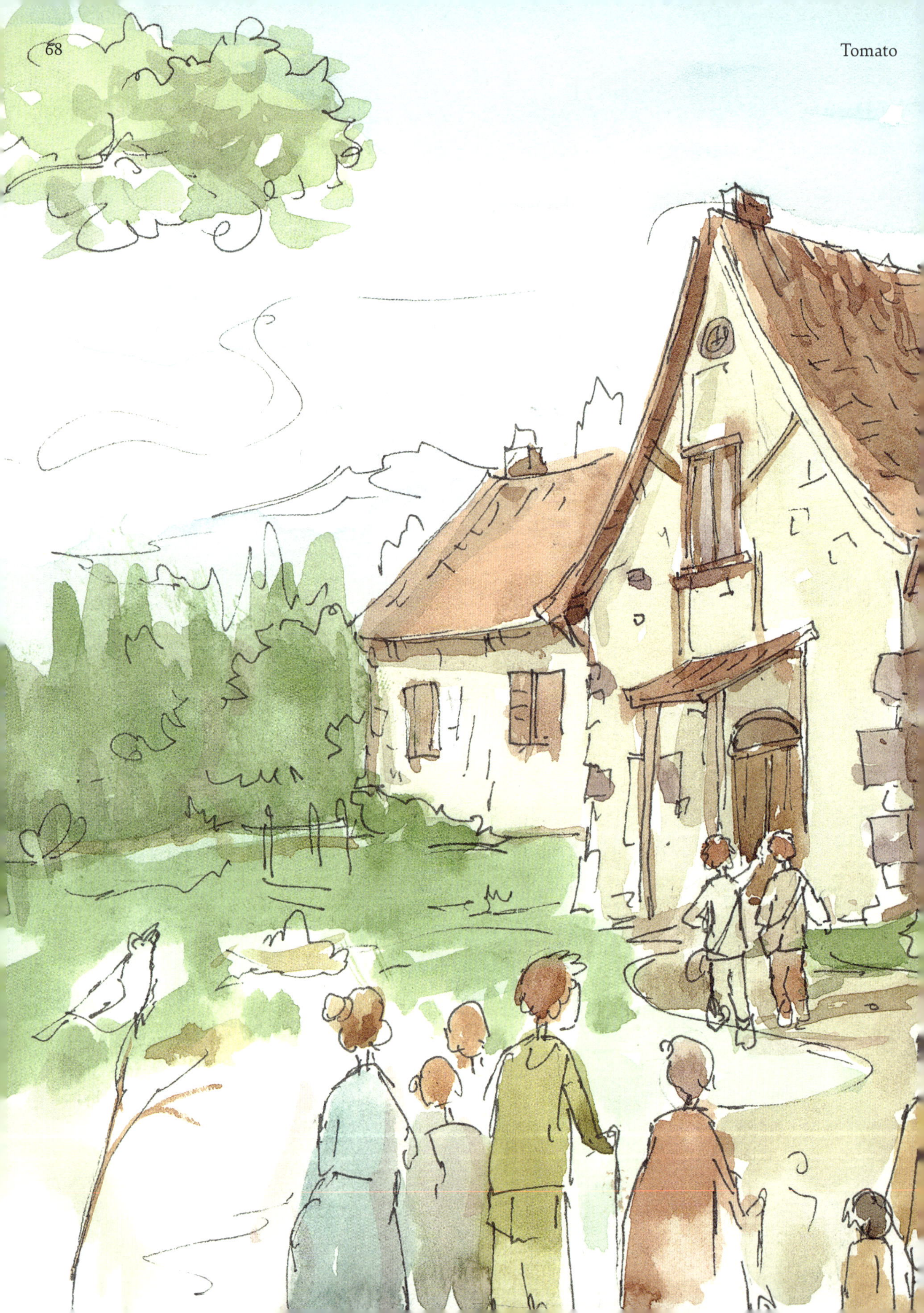

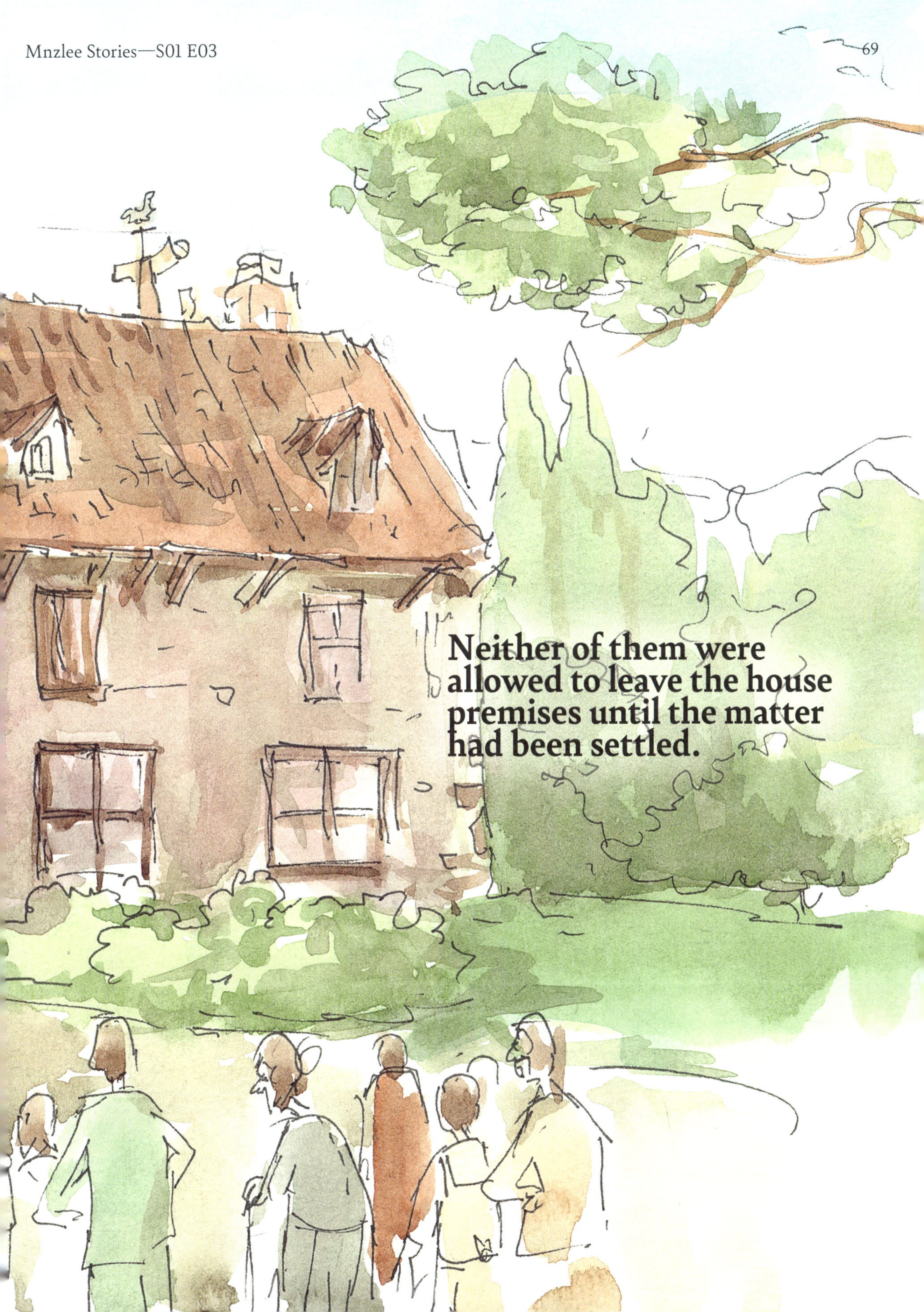
Neither of them were
allowed to leave the house
premises until the matter
had been settled.

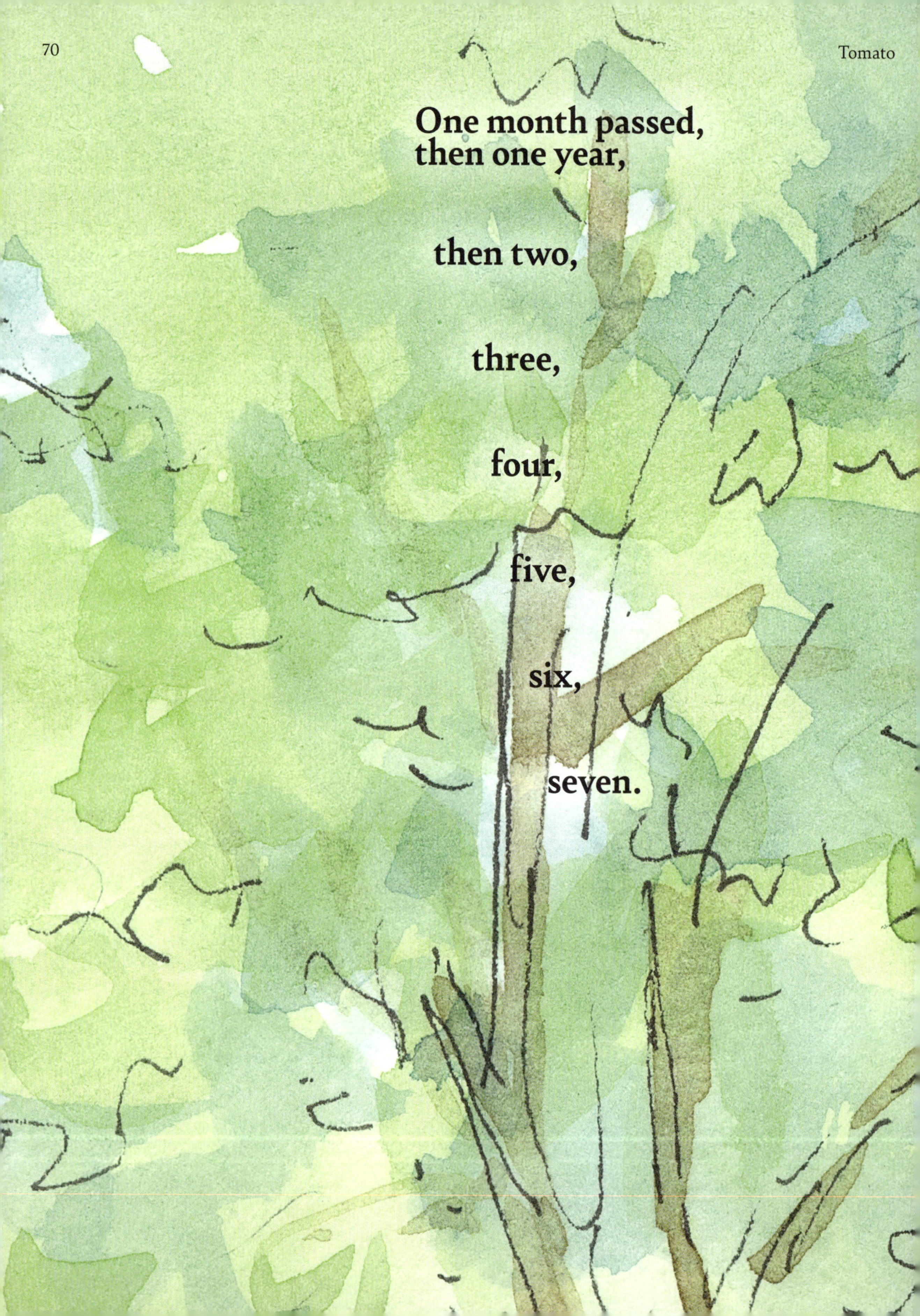
One month passed,
then one year,

then two,

three,

four,

five,

six,

seven.

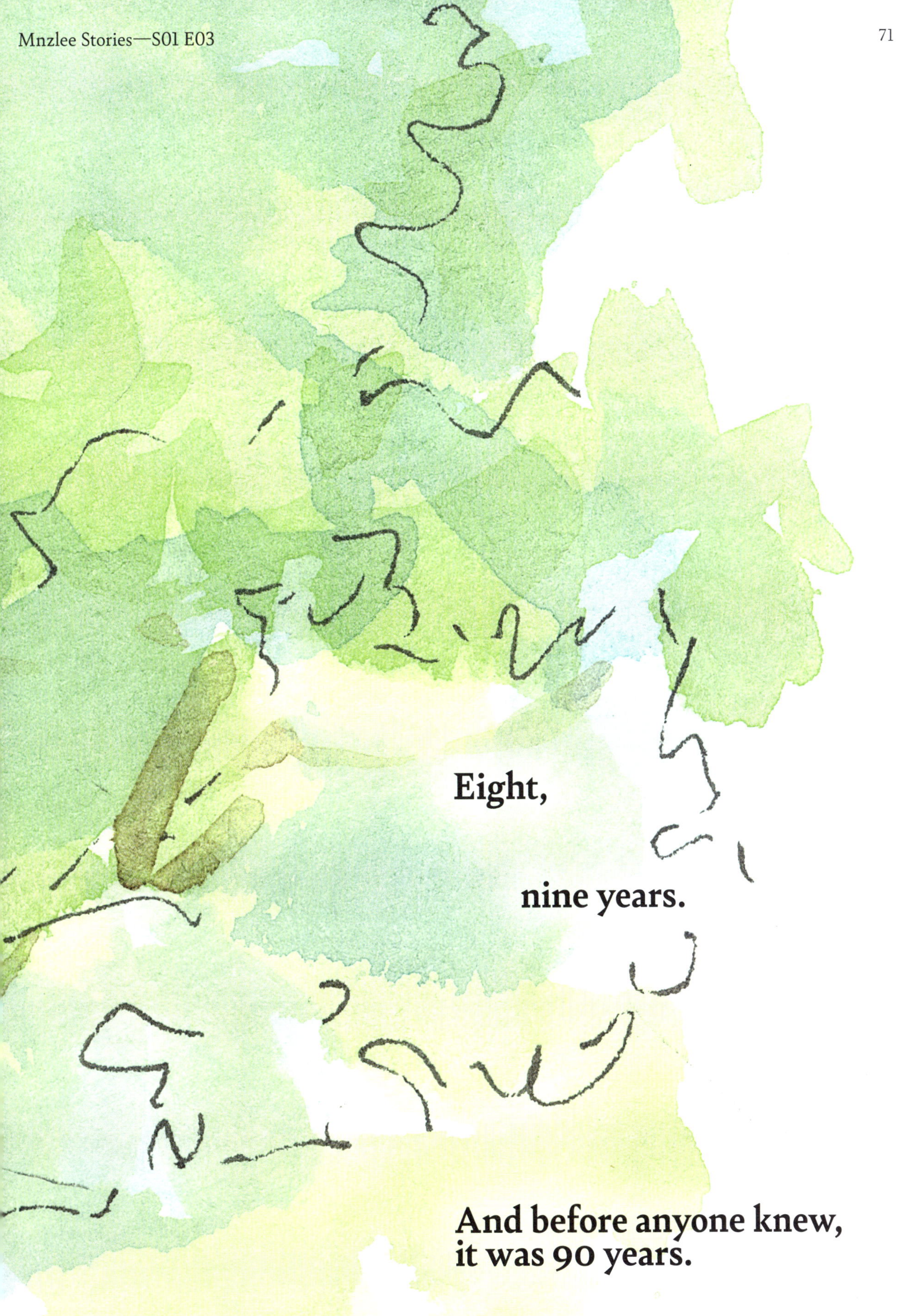
Eight,
nine years.
And before anyone knew,
it was 90 years.

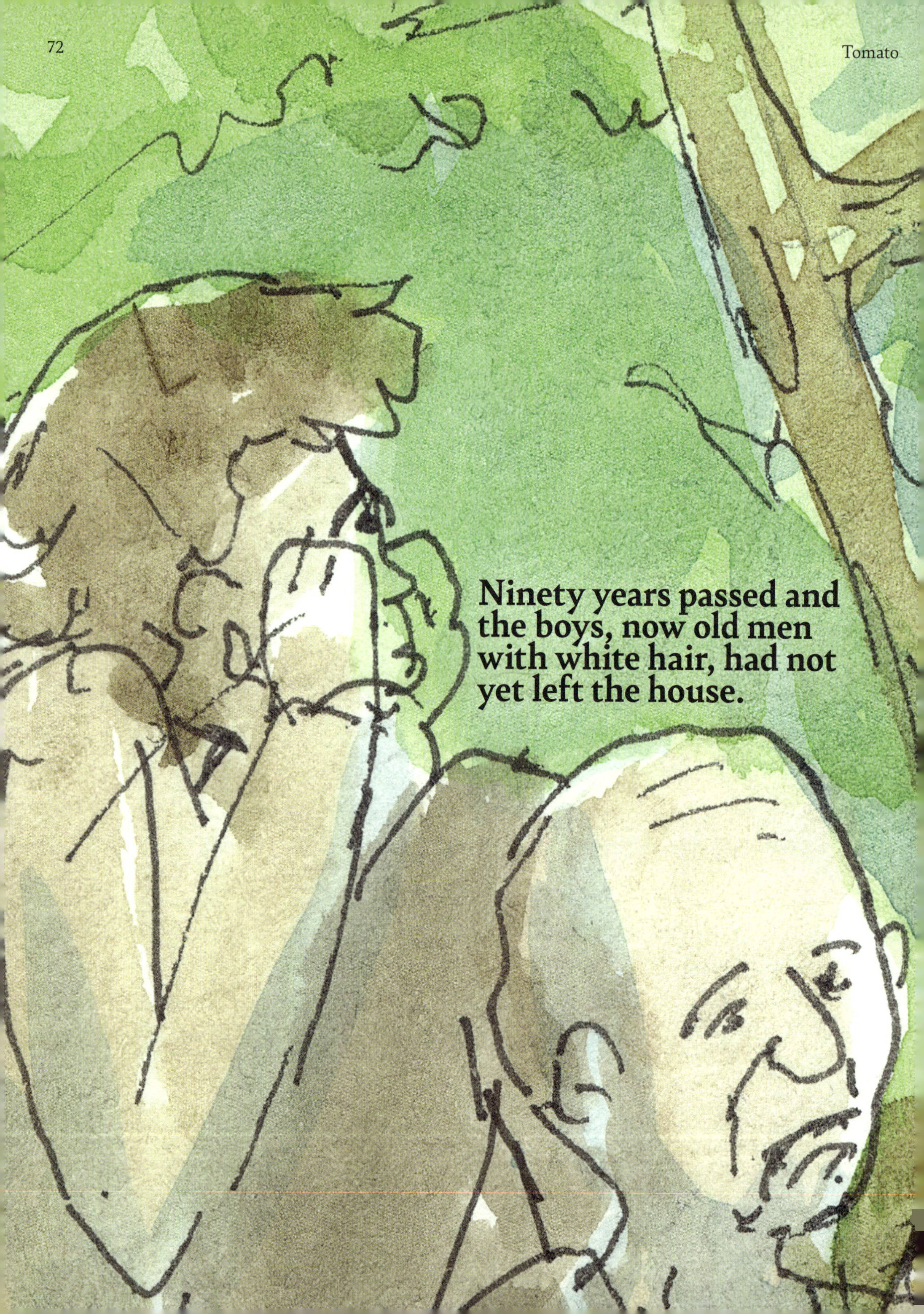
Ninety years passed and the boys, now old men with white hair, had not yet left the house.

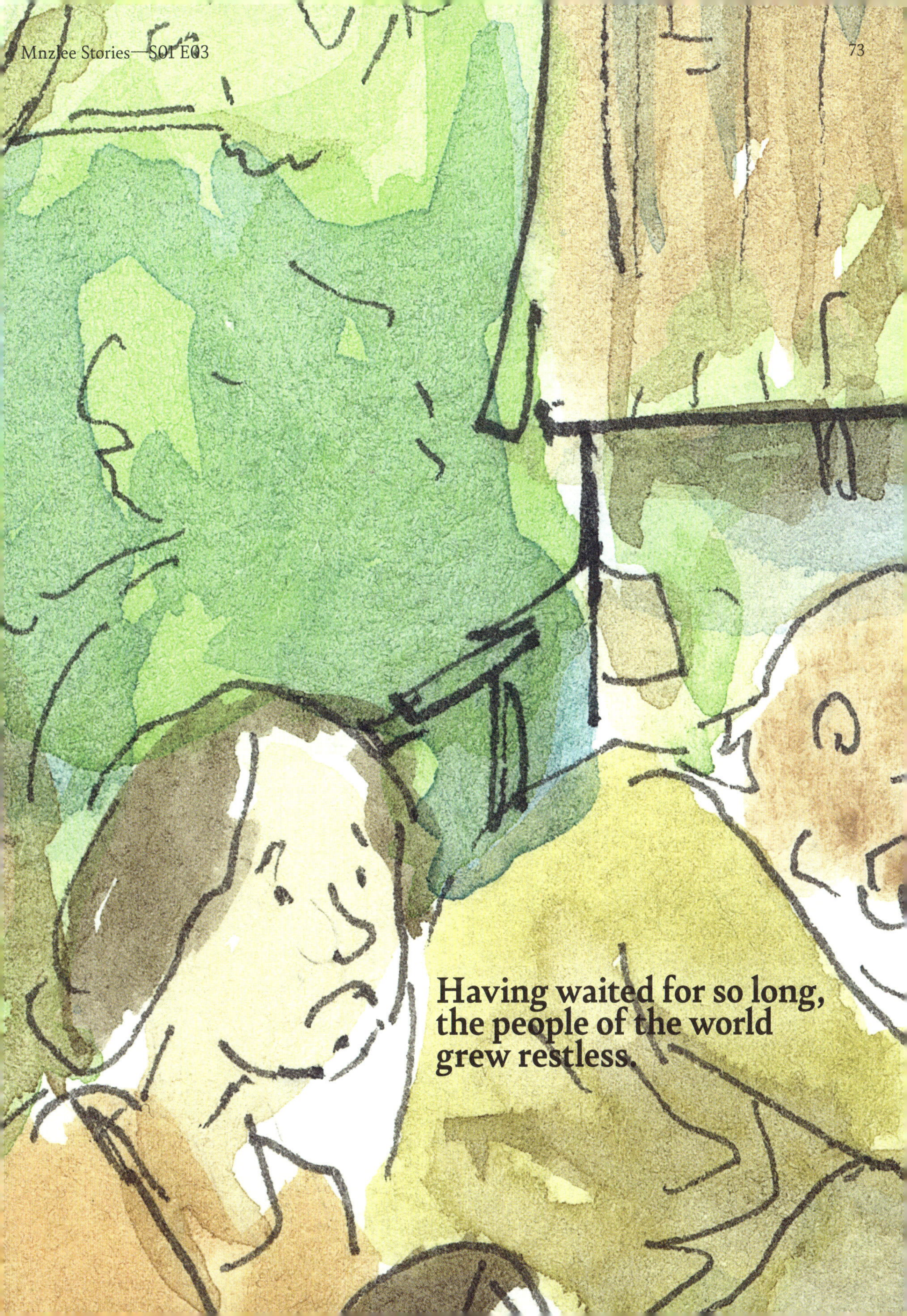
Having waited for so long,
the people of the world
grew restless.

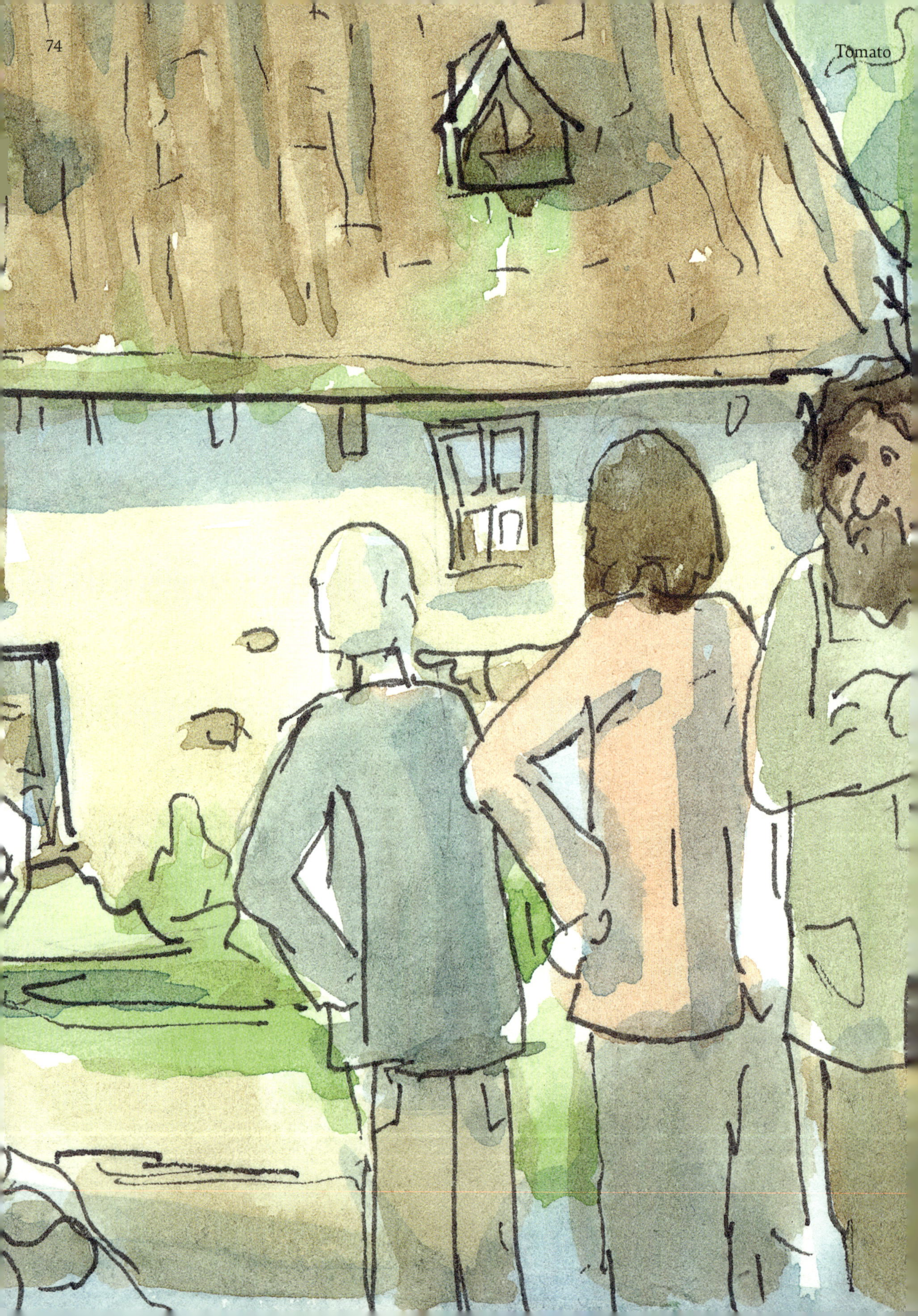

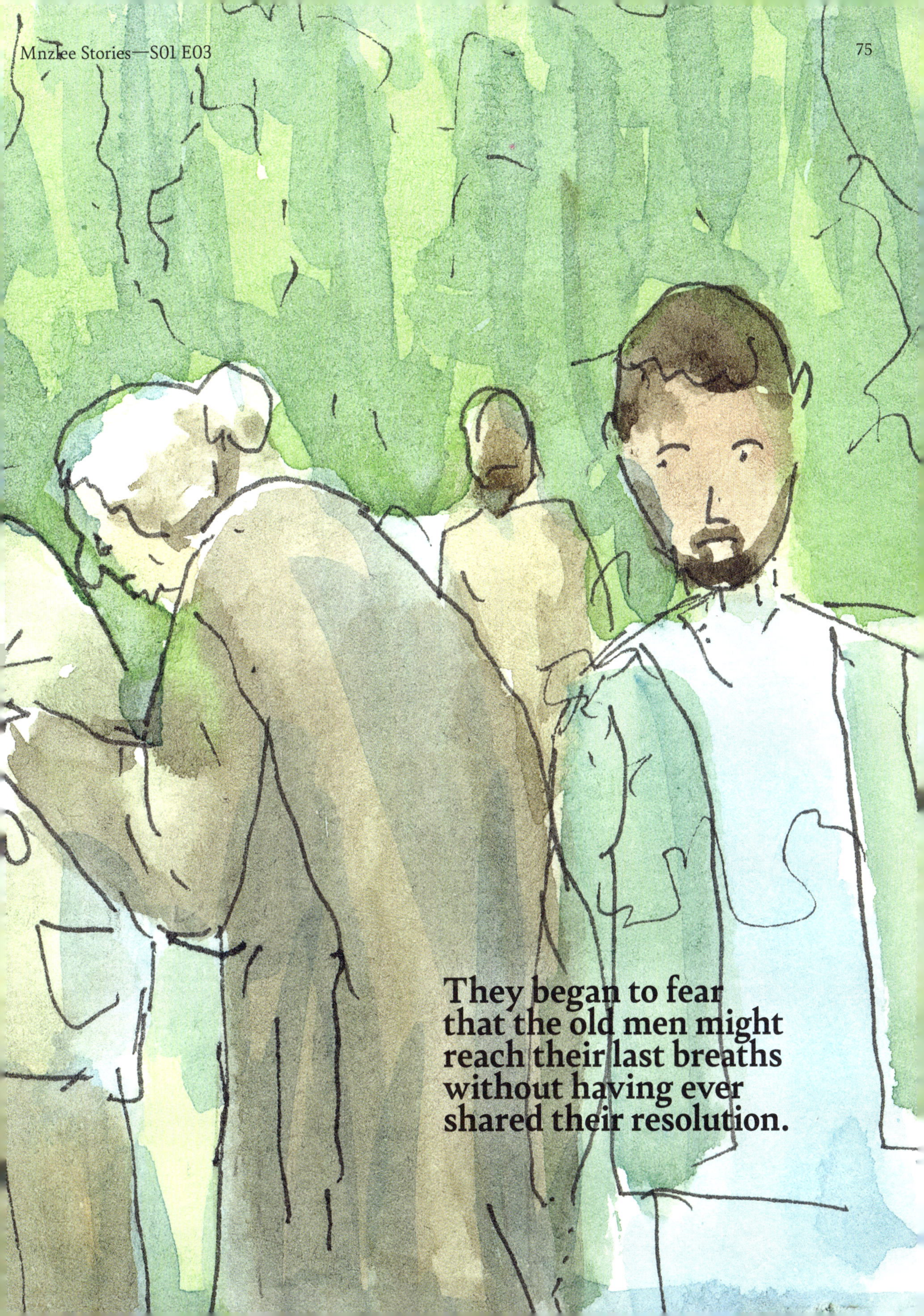

They began to fear
that the old men might
reach their last breaths
without having ever
shared their resolution.

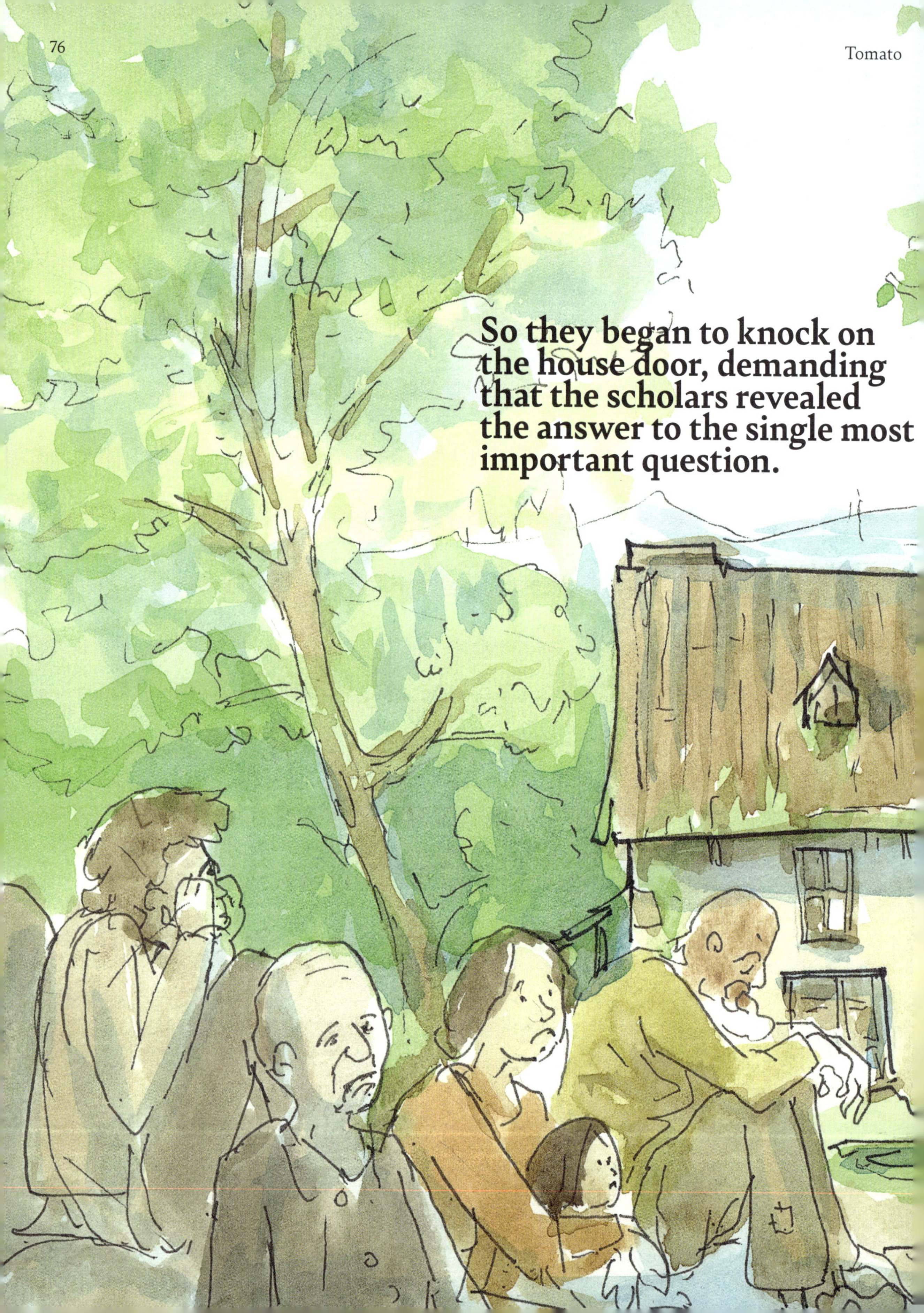
So they began to knock on the house door, demanding that the scholars revealed the answer to the single most important question.

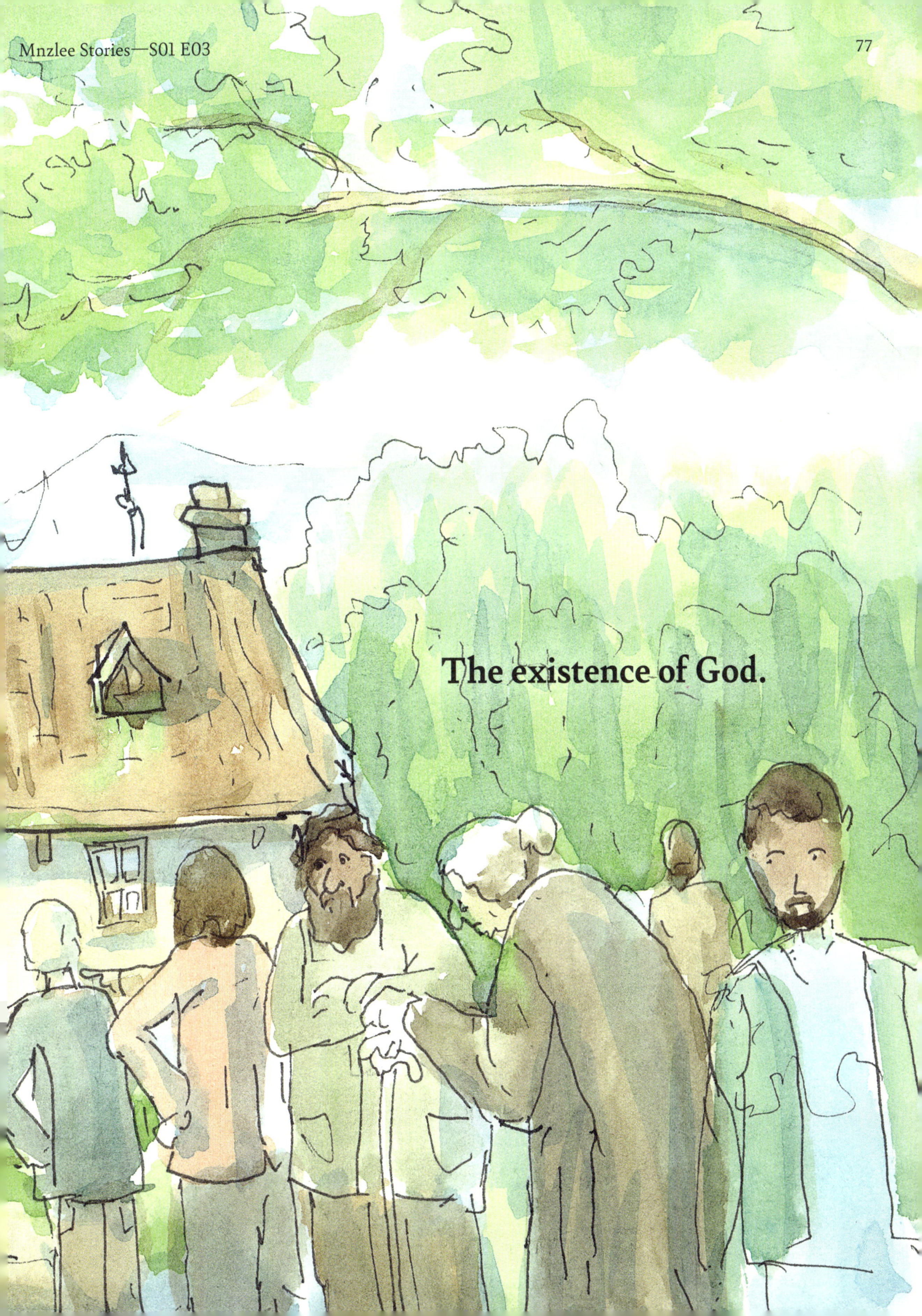
The existence of God.

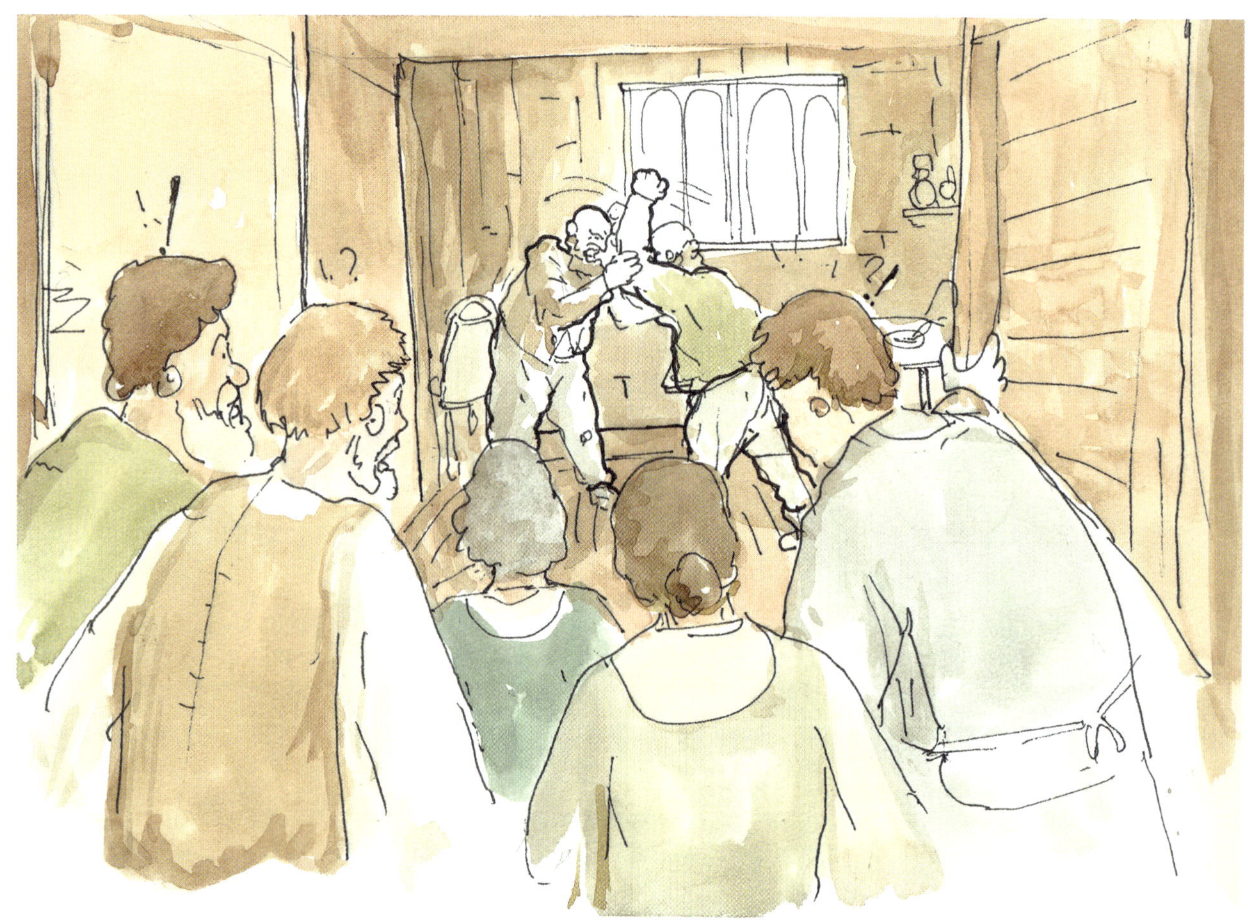

After a series of failed knocks the people broke down the front door, only to find the two men at each other's throats, loudly screaming.

The people stopped them and demanded to hear their resolution of their prolonged quest.

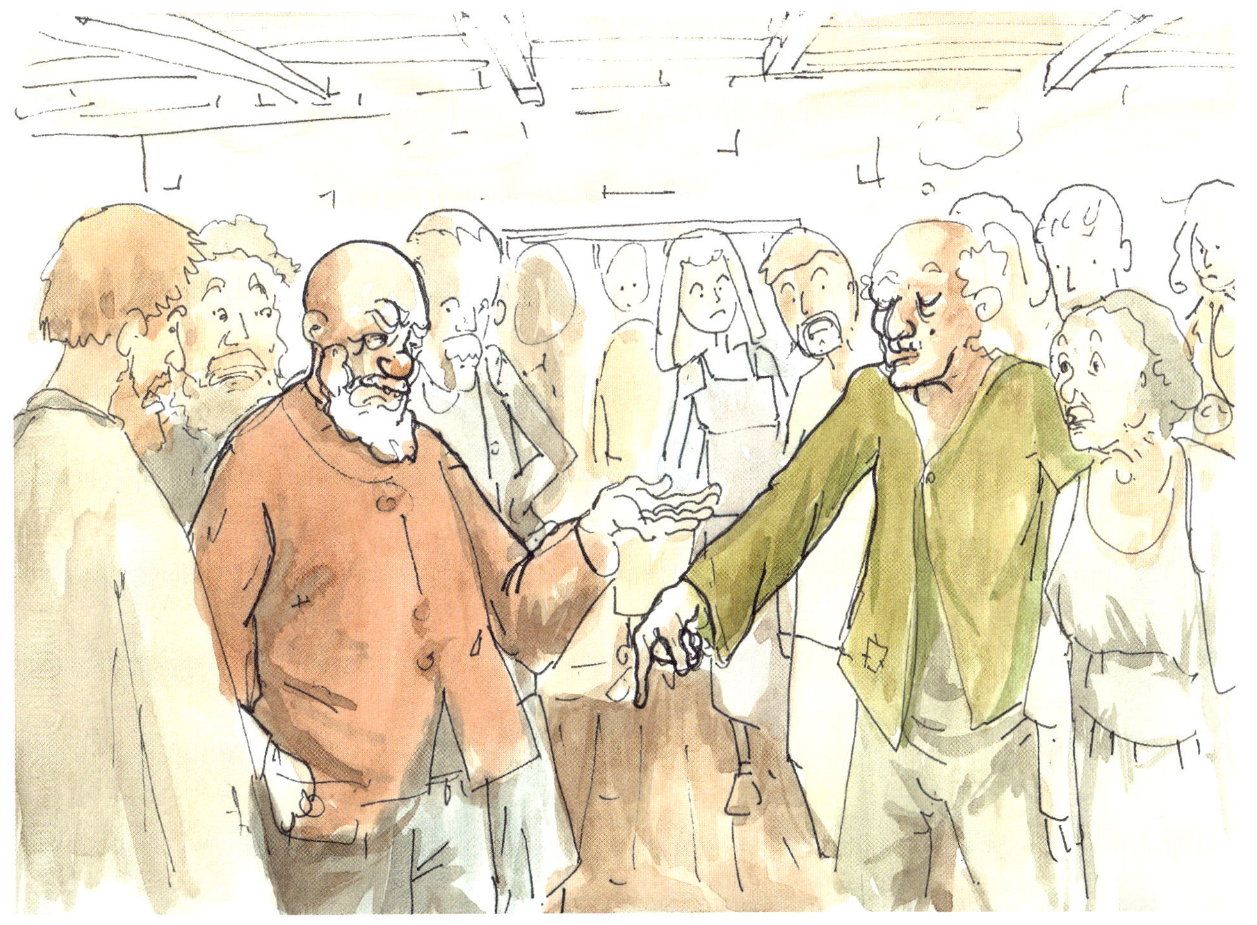

"Ah, thank you for bringing us back on track," said the first scholar. "To tell you the truth, what we have decided to focus on is something that urgently came up after our first meal together ninety years ago."

"What is that?" the people anxiously asked. "Maybe that holds the answer to the quest."

And the second scholar continued,

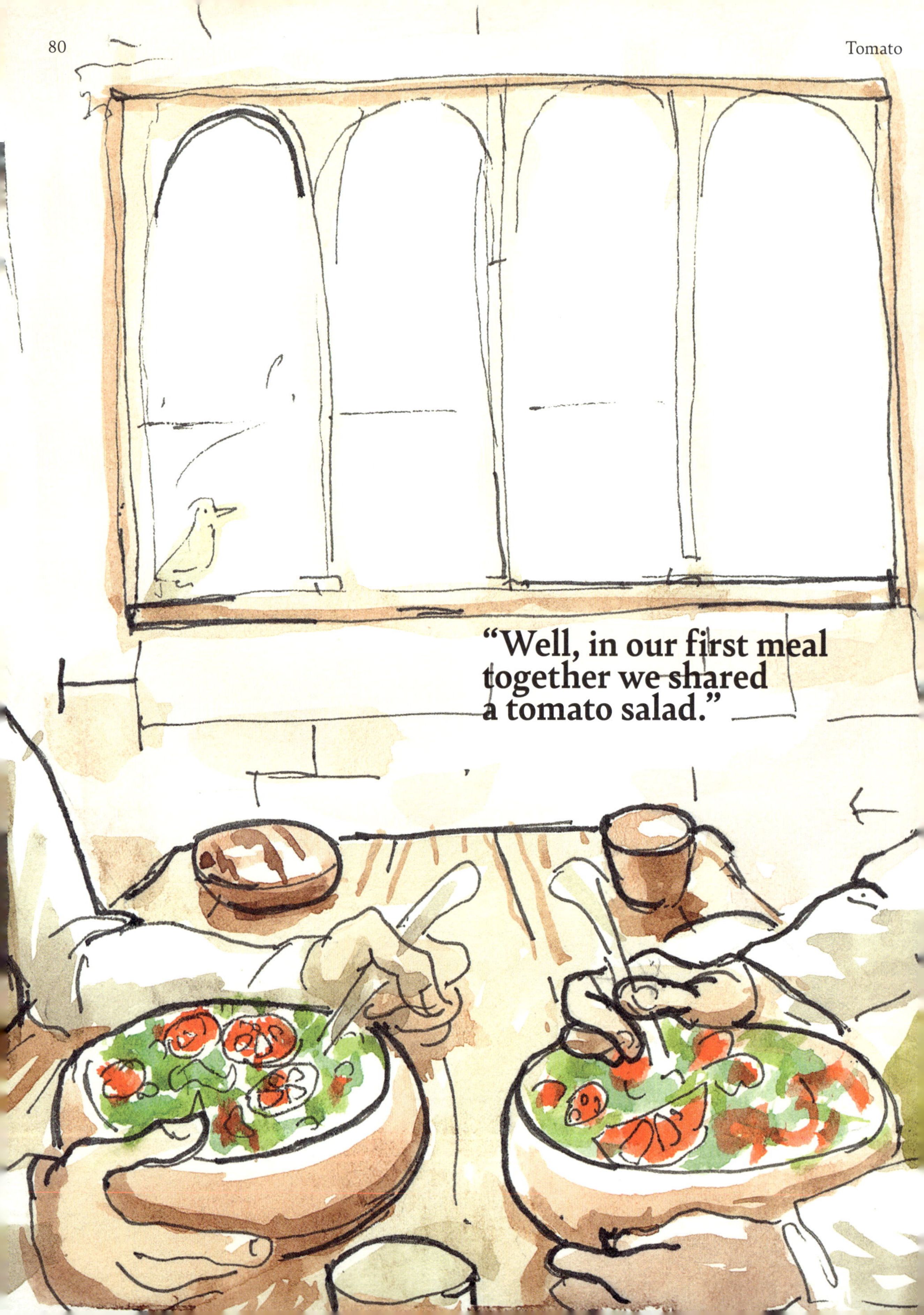
"Well, in our first meal
together we shared
a tomato salad."

"And after agreeing on how delicious the tomatoes were, I proudly said that those tomatoes came from my farm."

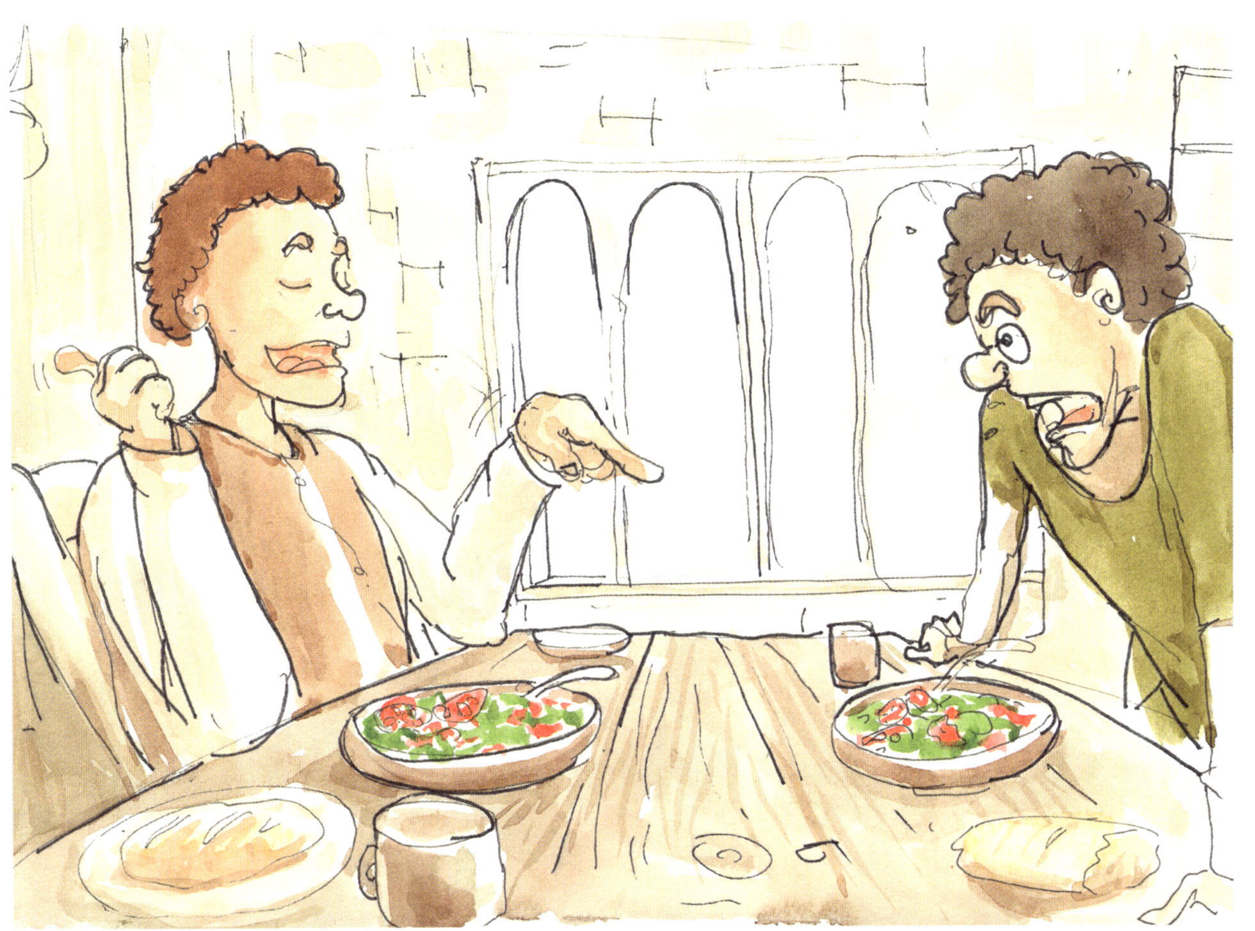

"And he said, 'No they came from my farm.'"

"And that of course is not true, so we began this argument and have not been able to settle it yet."

The people gasped—how could they have spent all this valuable time discussing something so silly?

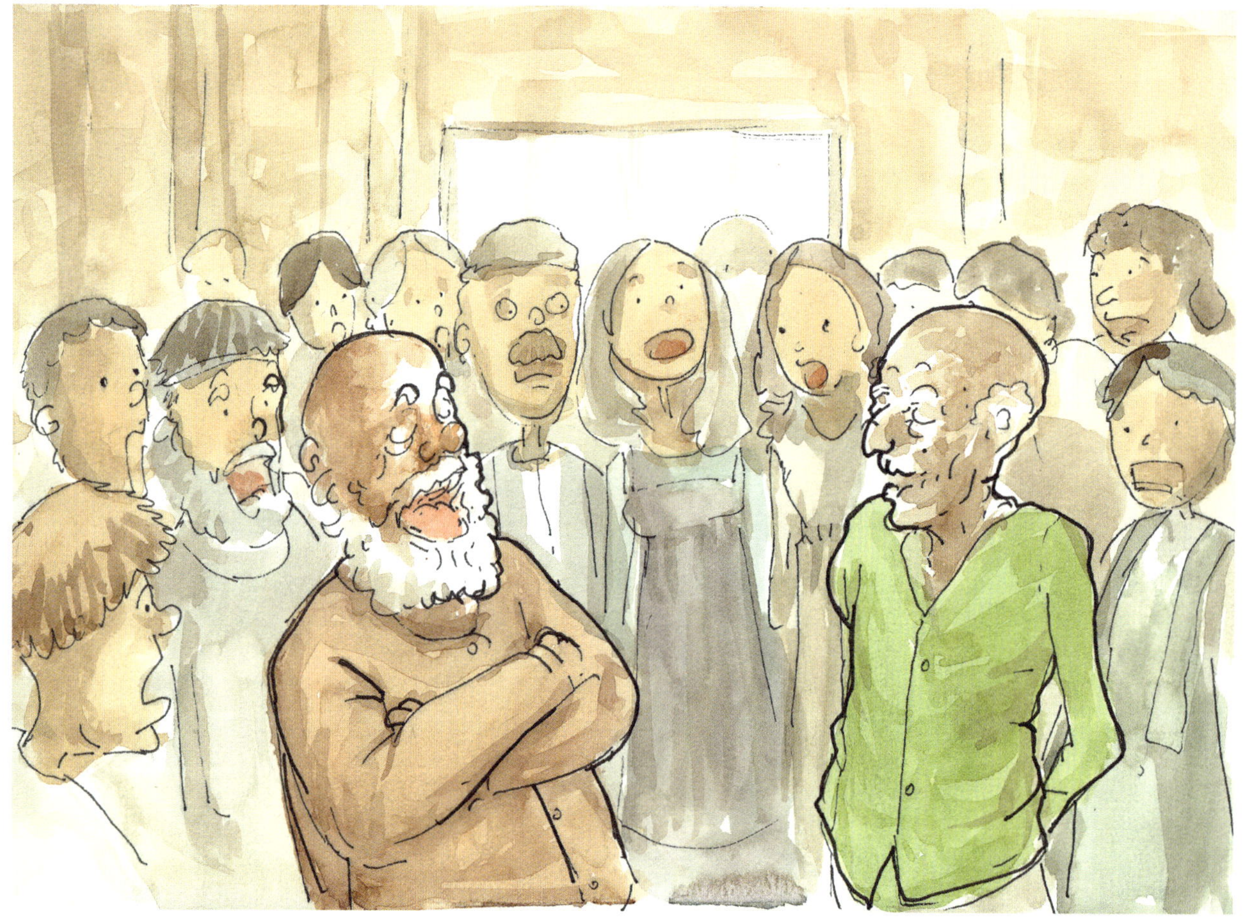

The two scholars looked around at the people. "Perhaps you all can help us resolve this once and for all."

"Which farm did the tomatoes come from?"

People began murmuring at first.

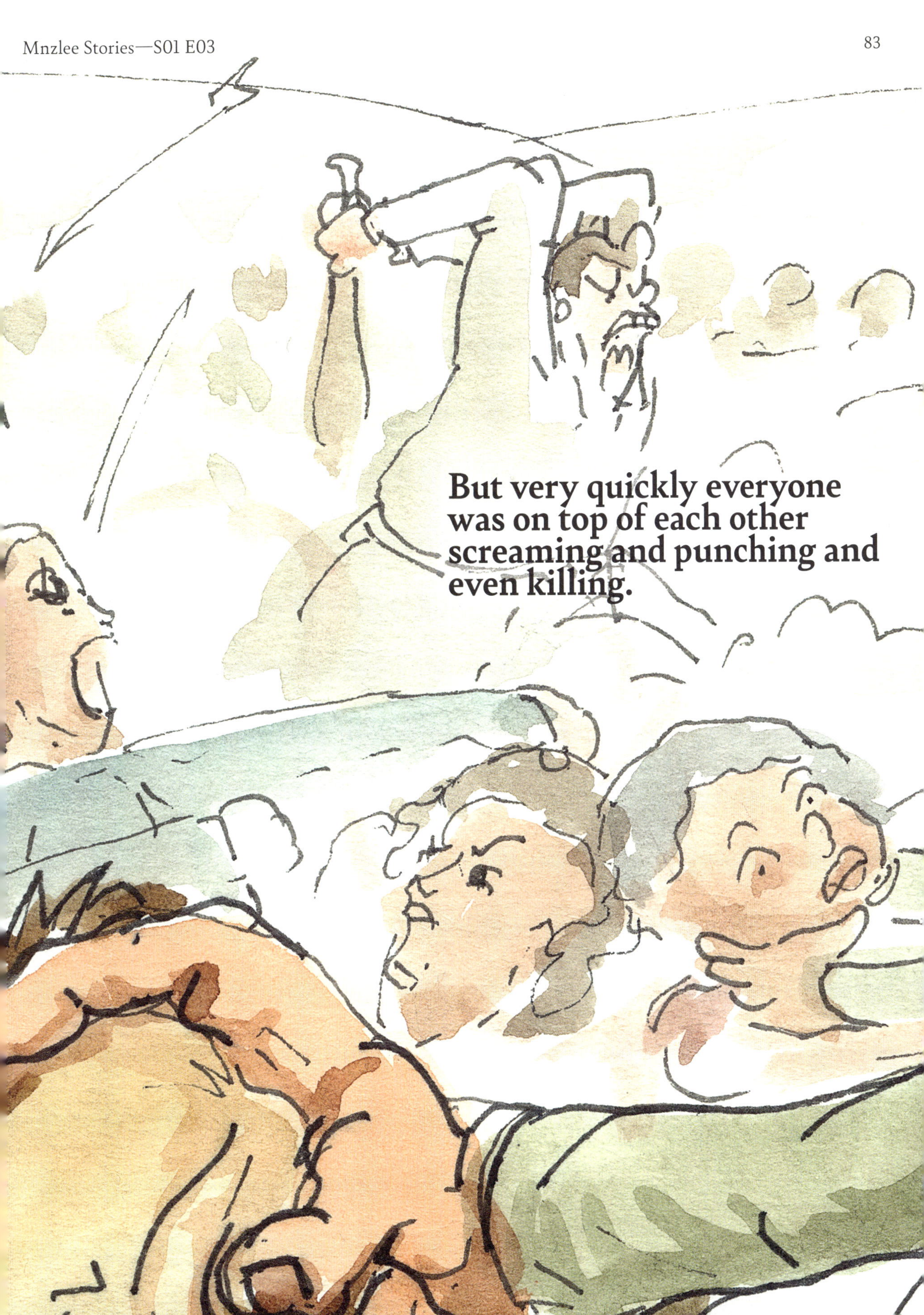

But very quickly everyone was on top of each other screaming and punching and even killing.

The two men unfortunately died before they were ever able to resolve the quest on the existence of God.

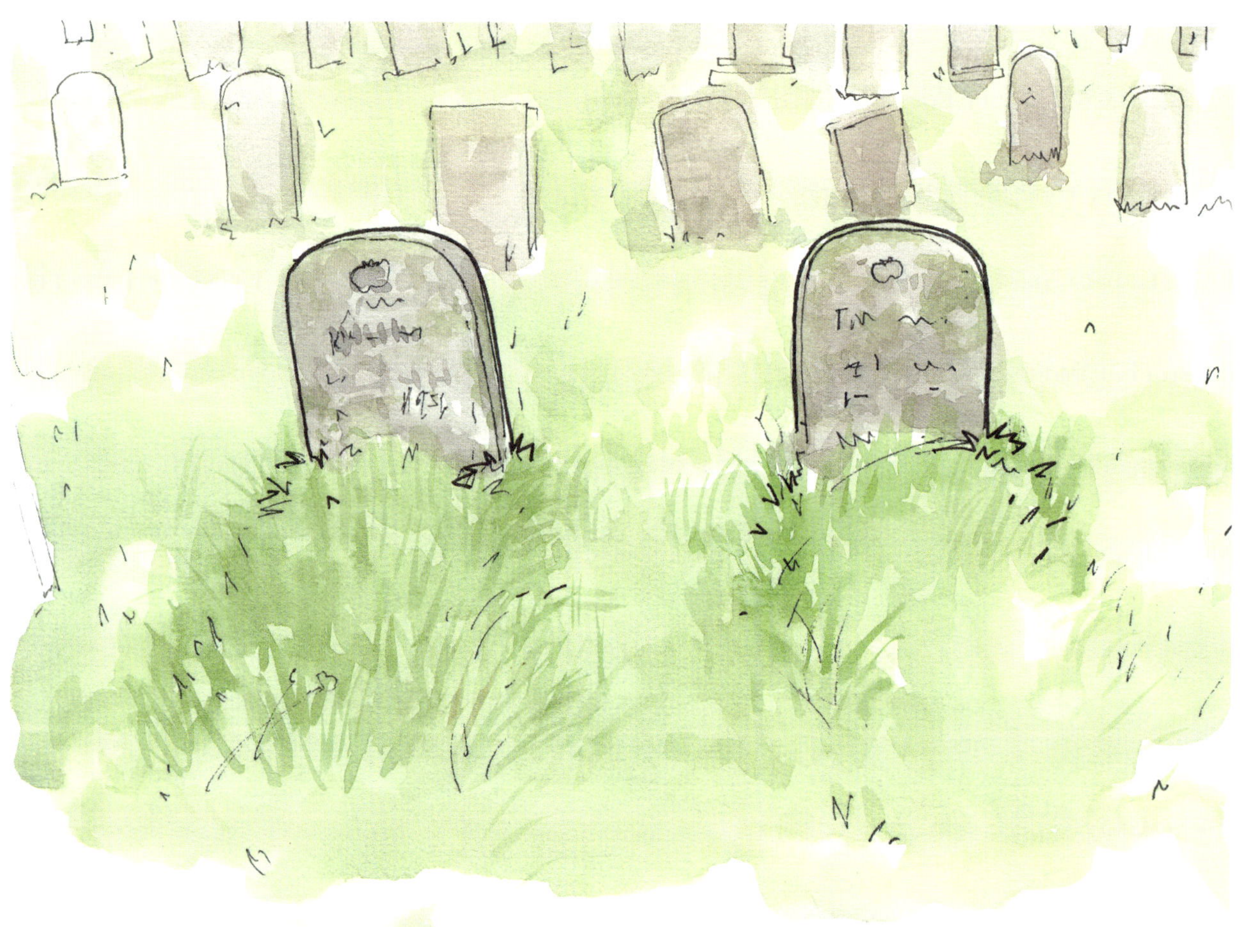

But their legacy continues.

It is said that the war over the tomato has been going on for hundreds of years and that no-one can agree on who those tomatoes really belonged to.

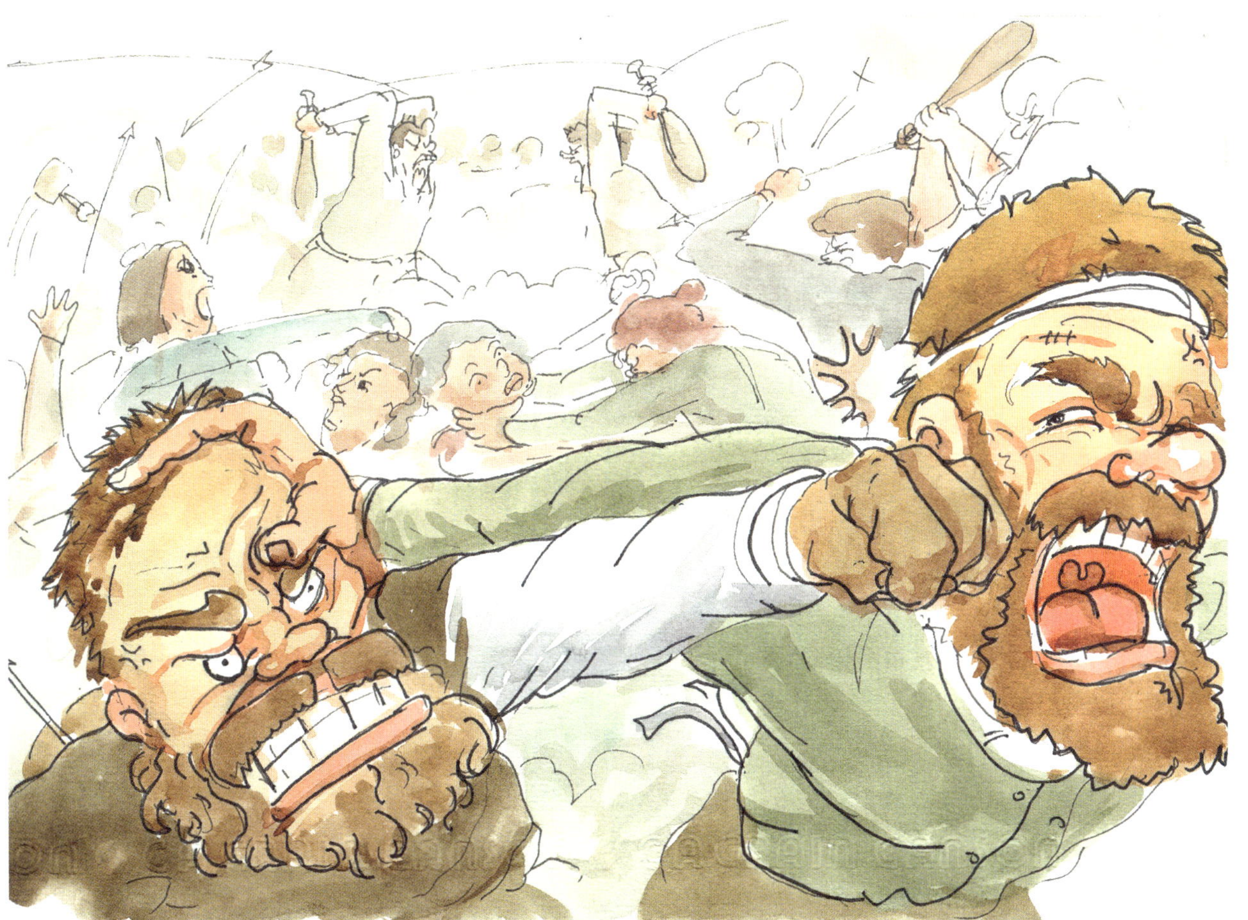

No-one really knows why they are fighting about tomatoes anymore. But it seems important enough that their ancestors fought for it.

To continue the effort.

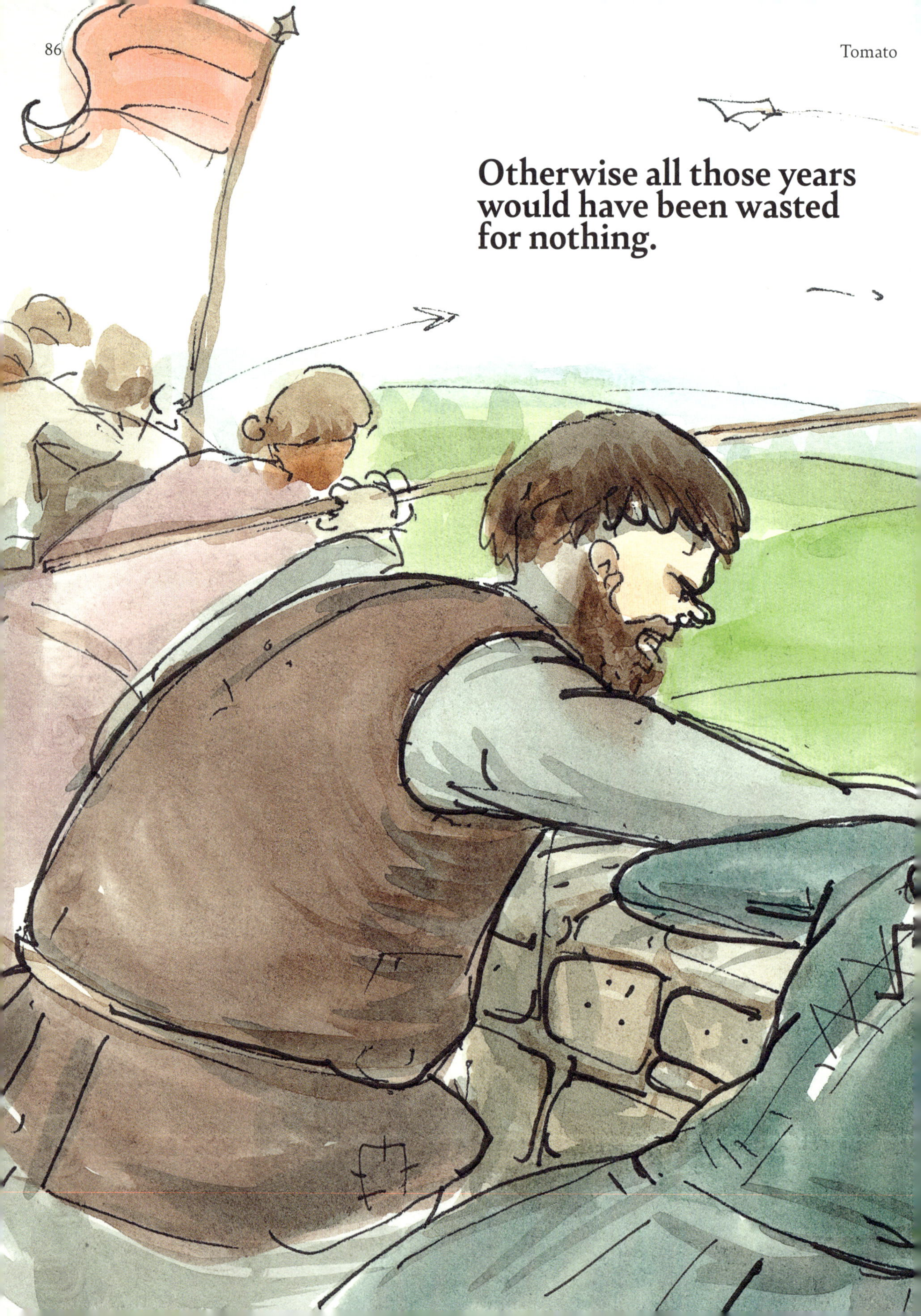
Otherwise all those years
would have been wasted
for nothing.

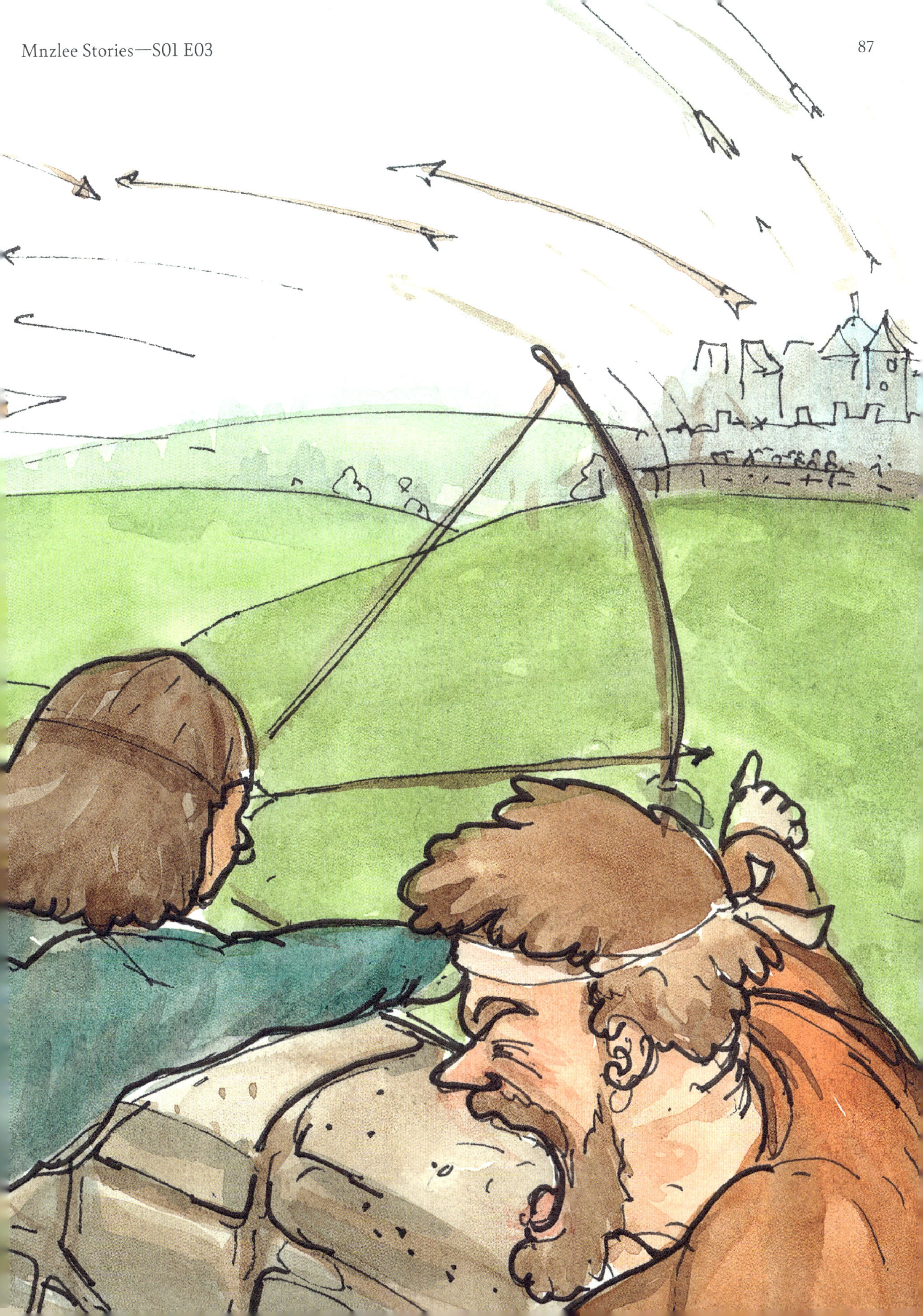

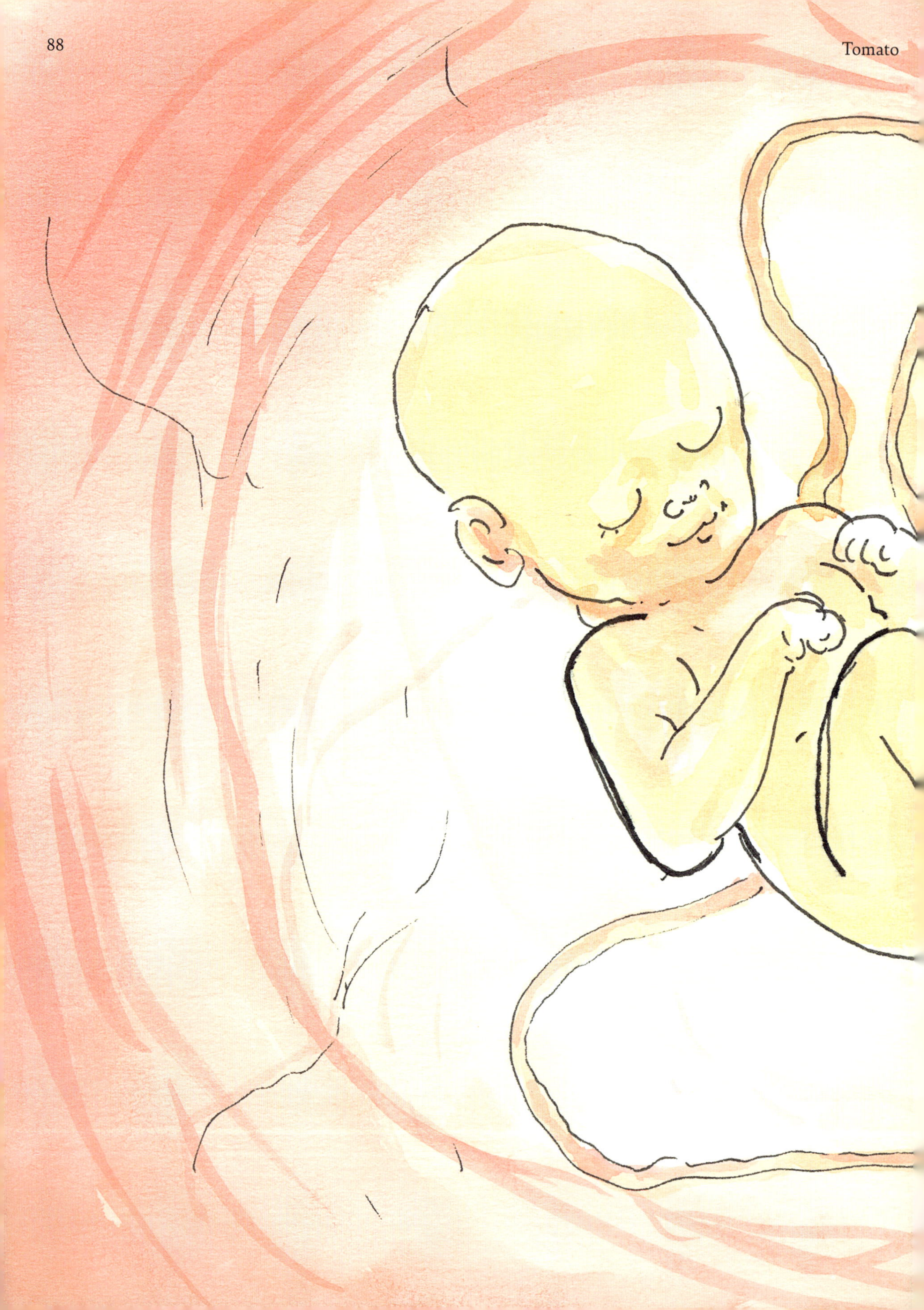

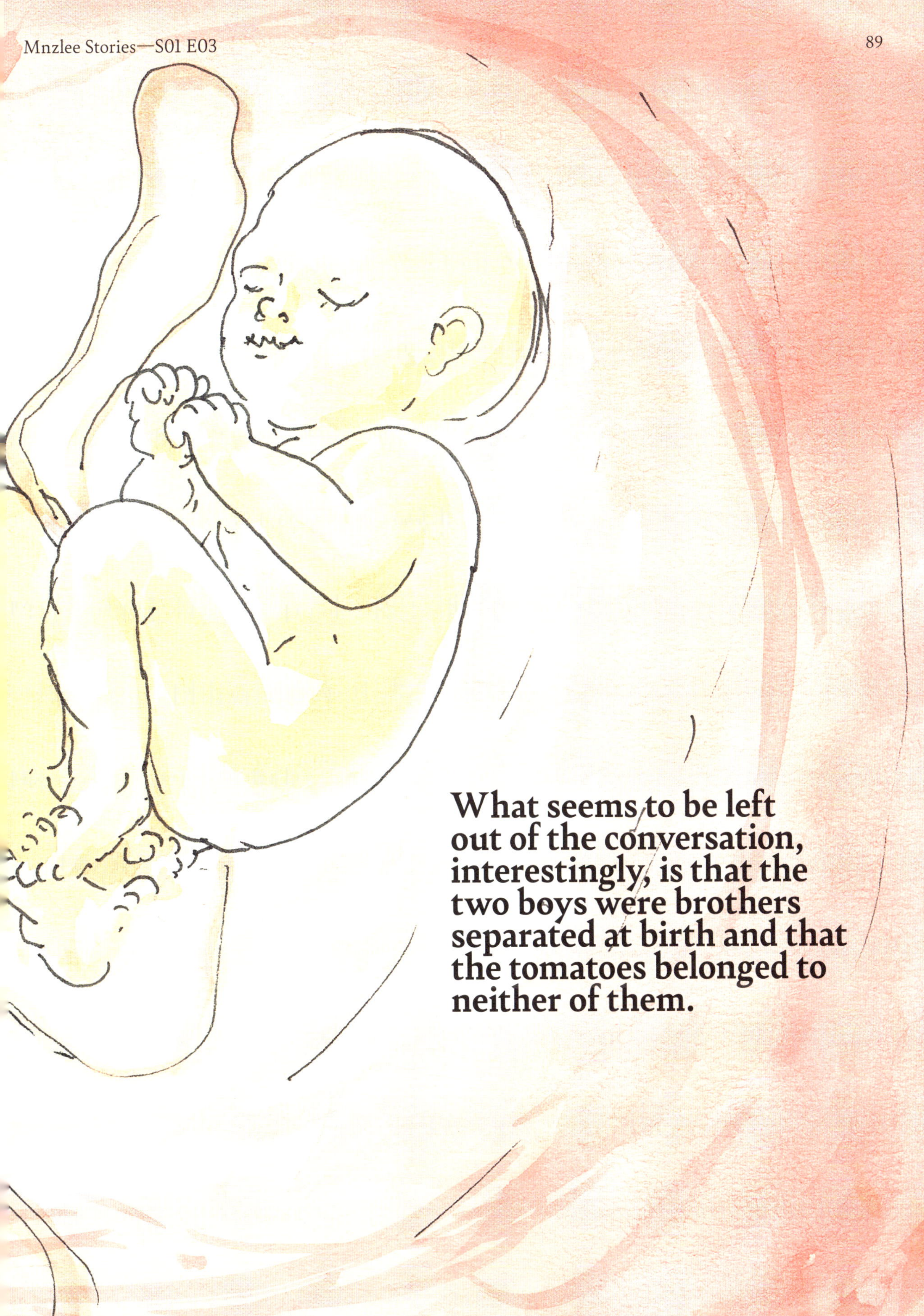

What seems to be left out of the conversation, interestingly, is that the two boys were brothers separated at birth and that the tomatoes belonged to neither of them.

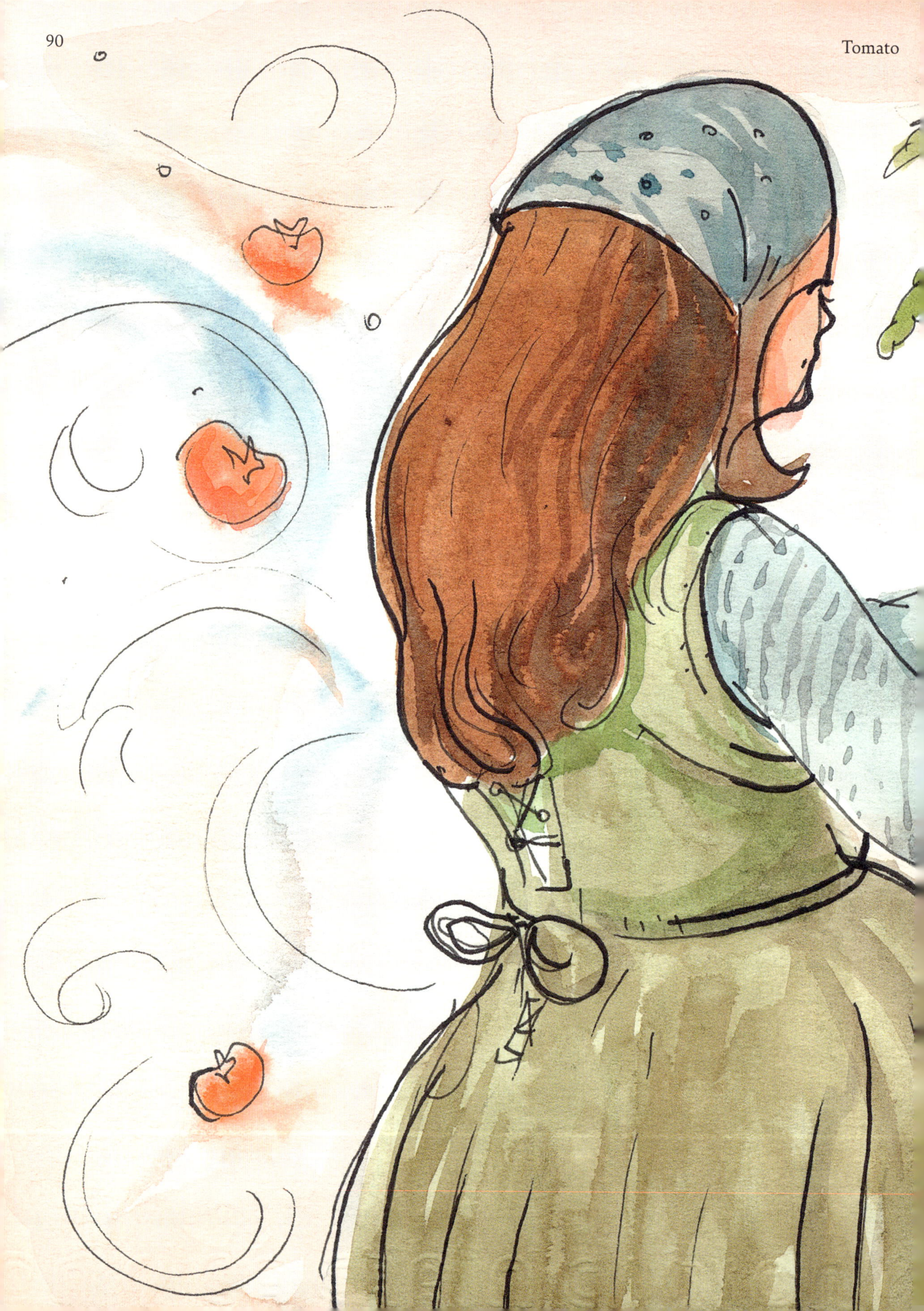

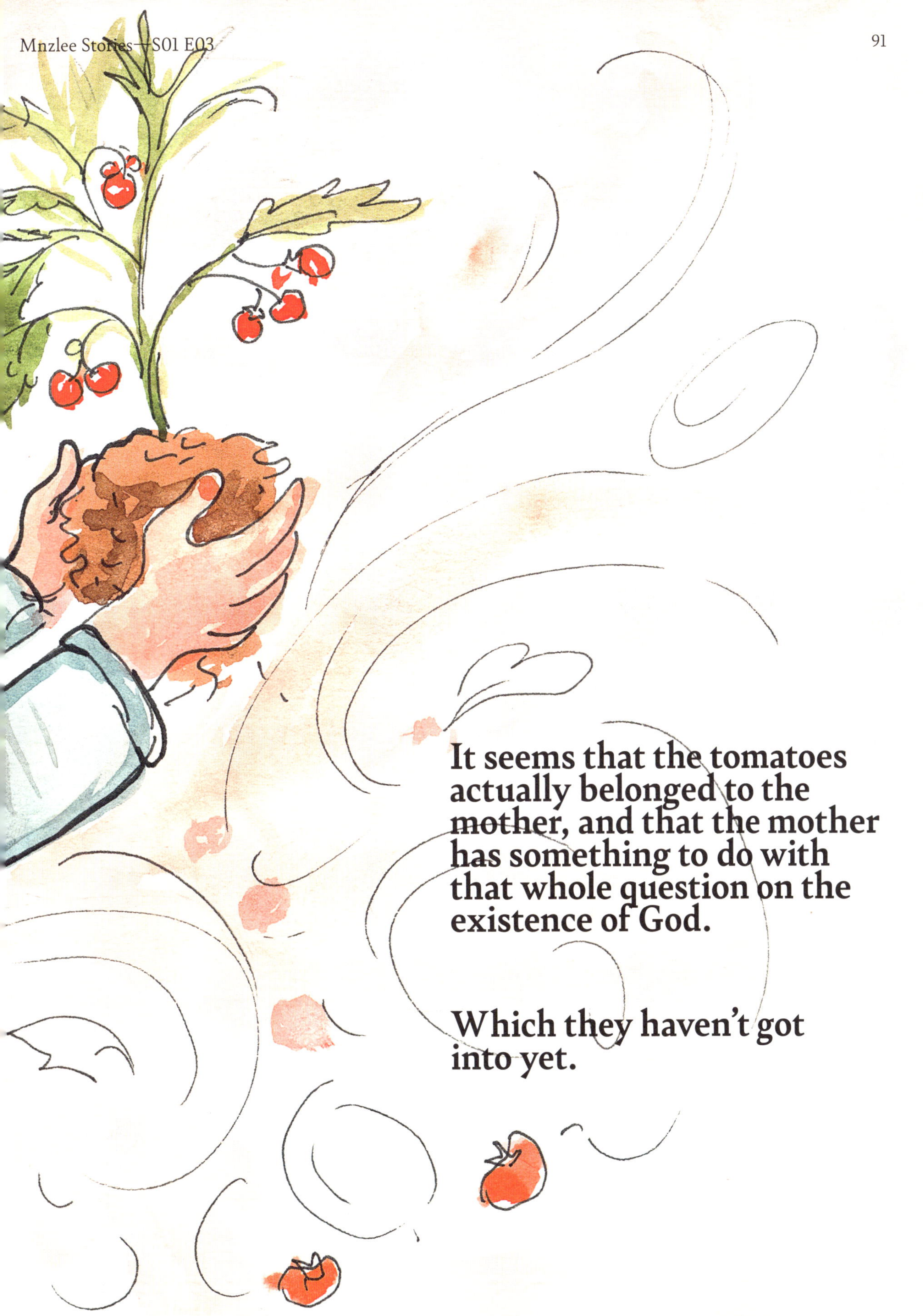

It seems that the tomatoes actually belonged to the mother, and that the mother has something to do with that whole question on the existence of God.

Which they haven't got into yet.

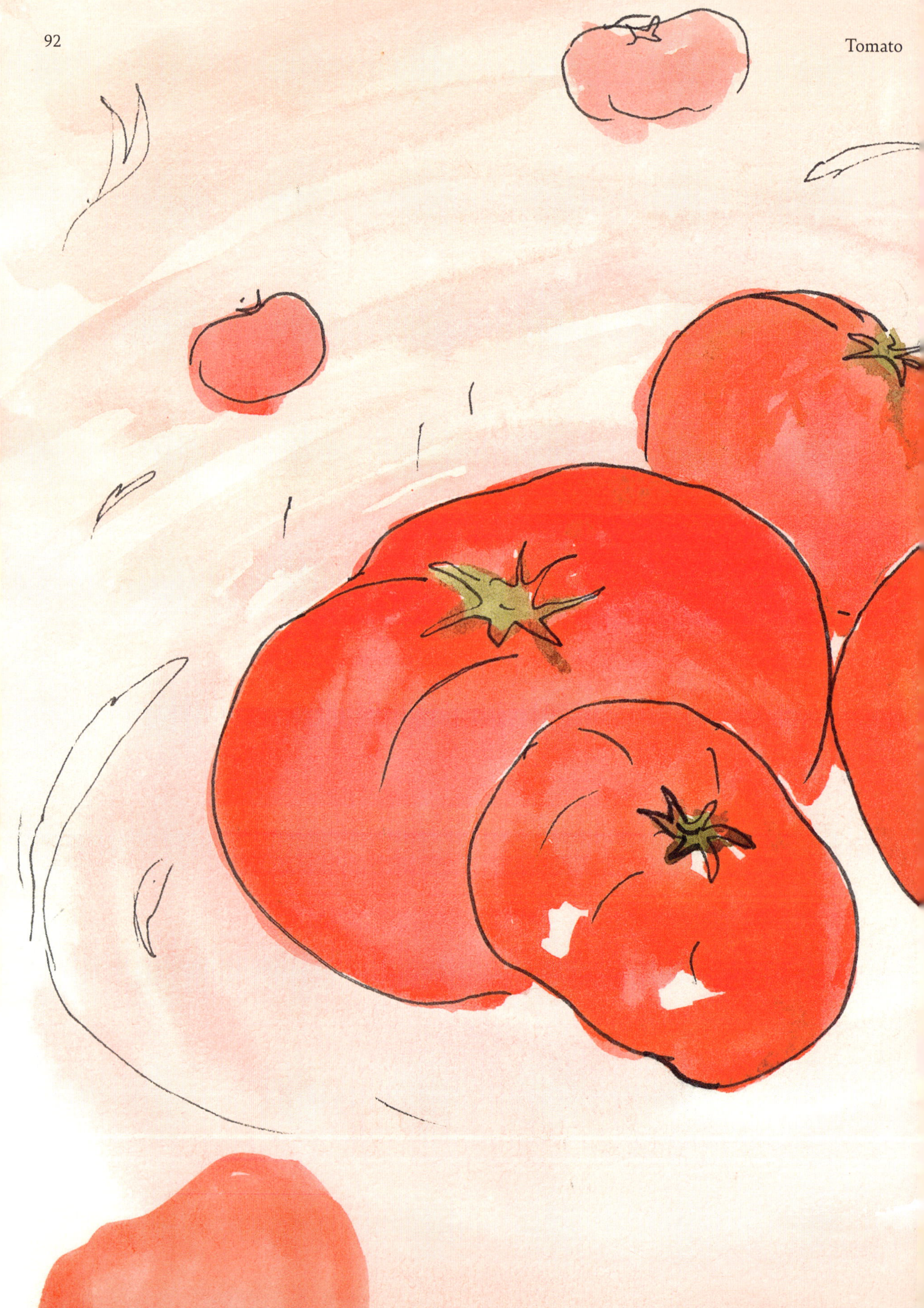

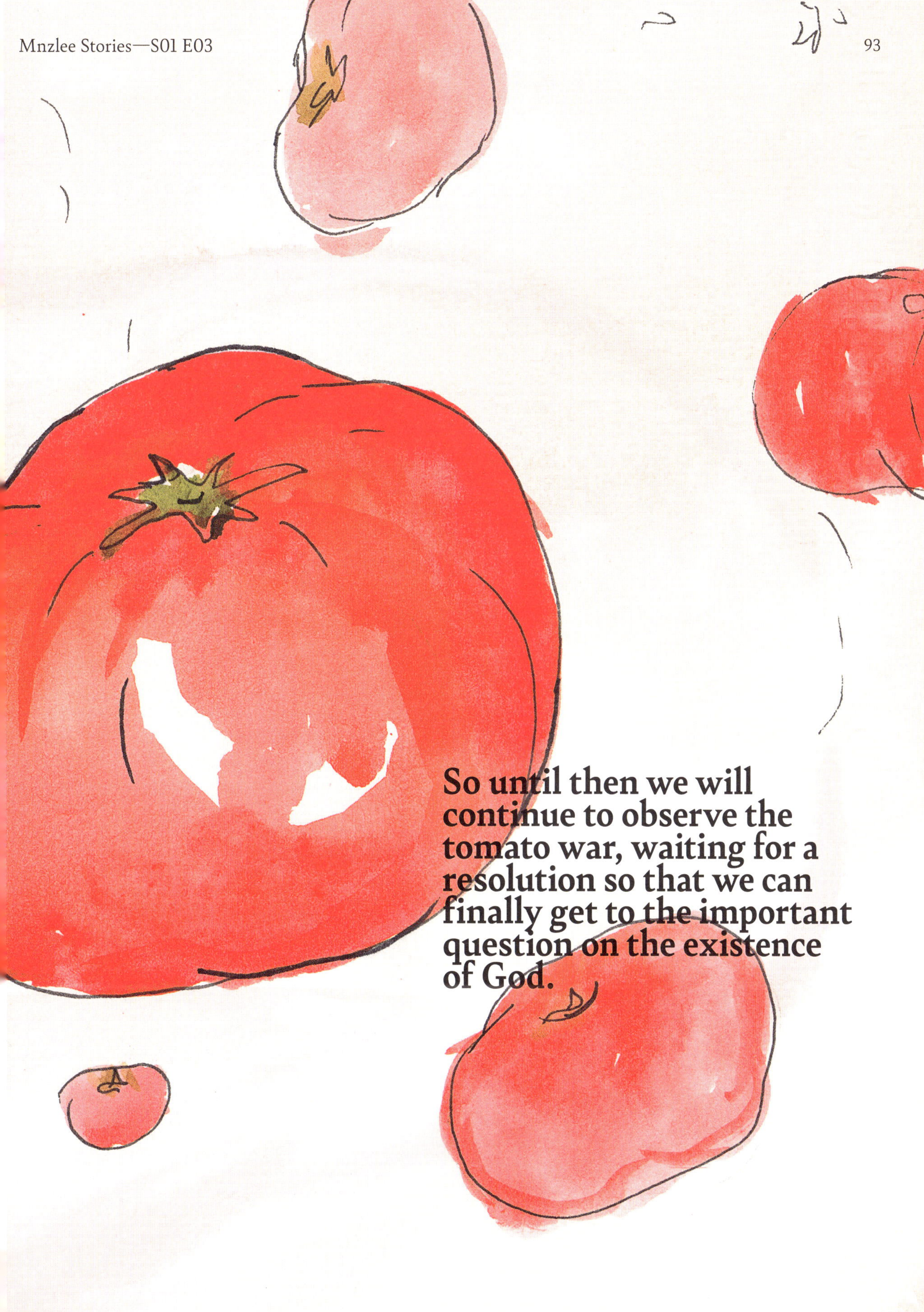
So until then we will
continue to observe the
tomato war, waiting for a
resolution so that we can
finally get to the important
question on the existence
of God.

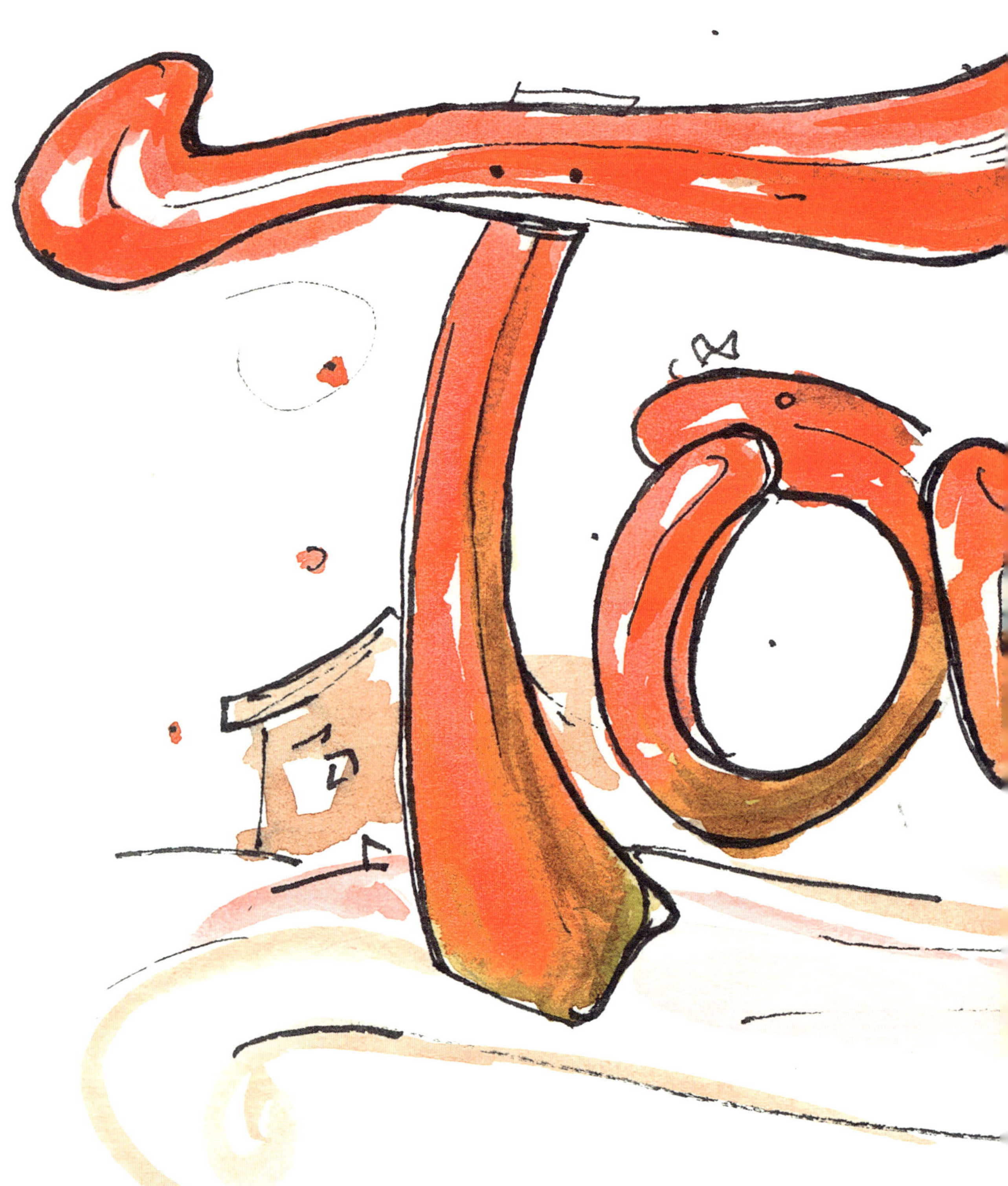

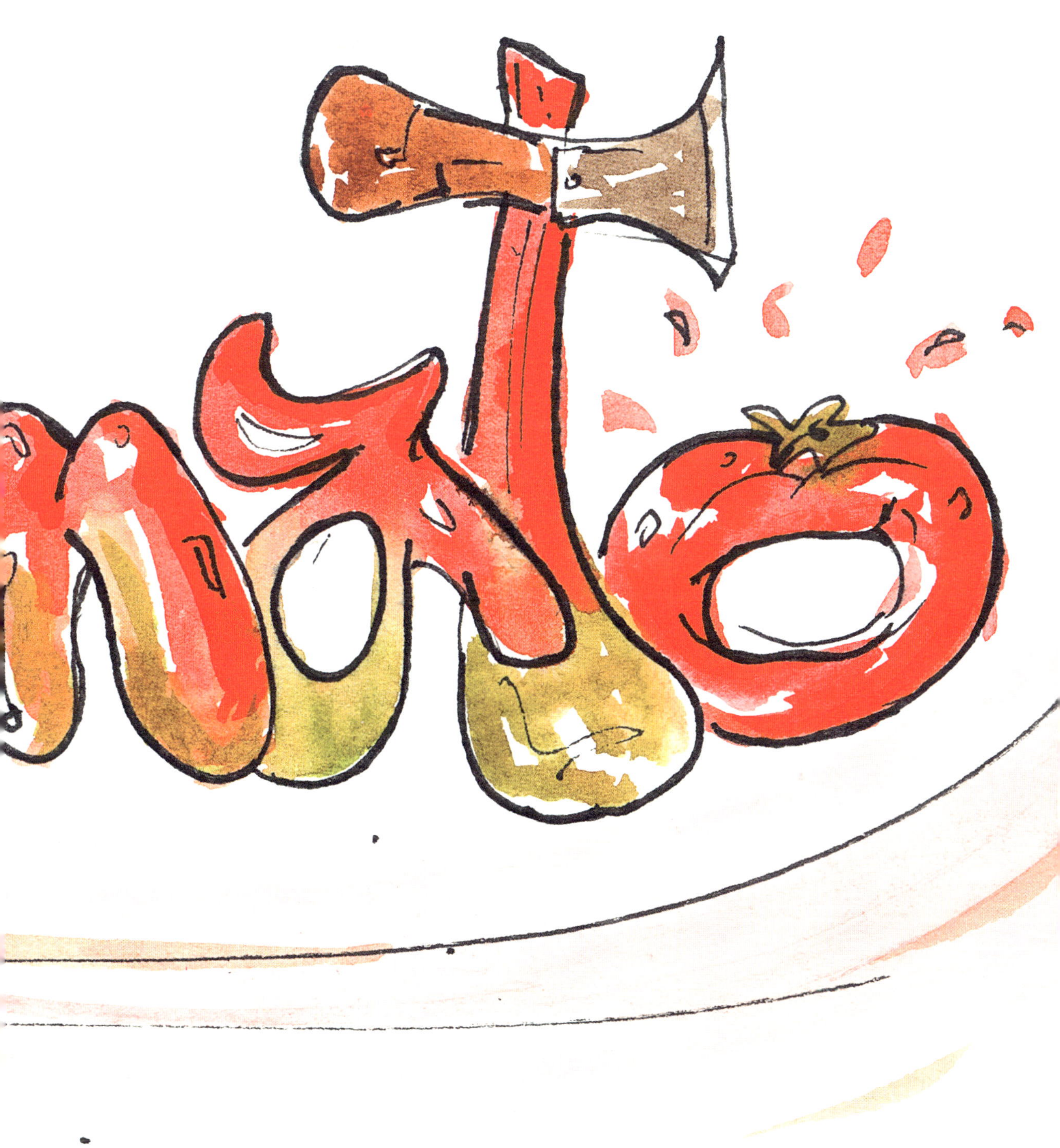

MEMORY

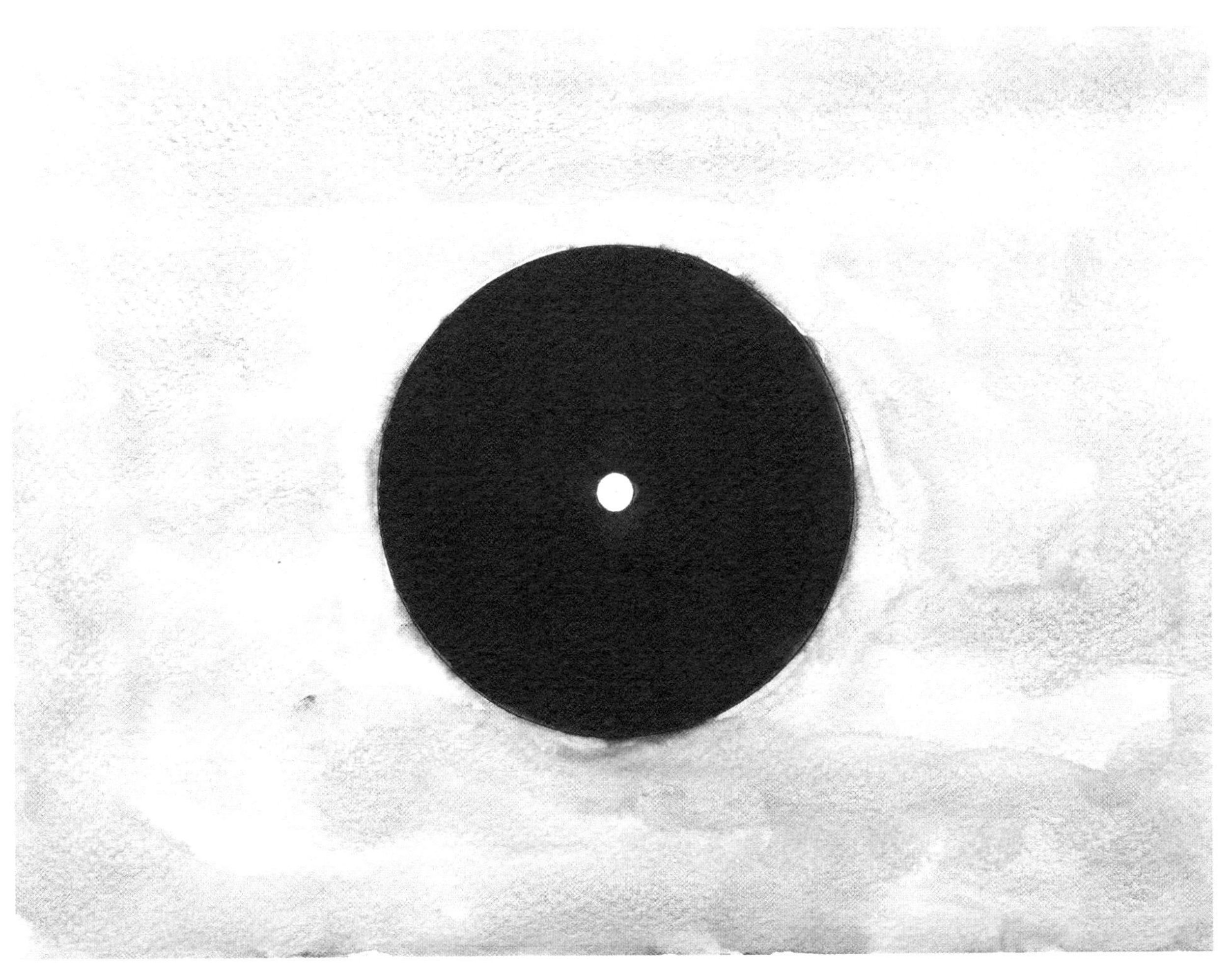

(فَاذْكُرُونِي أَذْكُرْكُمْ) [البقرة: ١٥٢]
(فَاذْكُرُوا اللَّهَ كَذِكْرِكُمْ آبَاءَكُمْ) [البقرة:٢٠٠]
(أَو يَذَّكَّرُ فَتَنْفَعَهُ الذِّكْرَى)[عبس: ٣]

Where does life come from

and where does death come from?

Once upon a time there was
a girl who came from India
as early as 200 BCE,

she was a dot,

people drew her everywhere,

the point from which all things emerged,

the creation of something

from nothing.

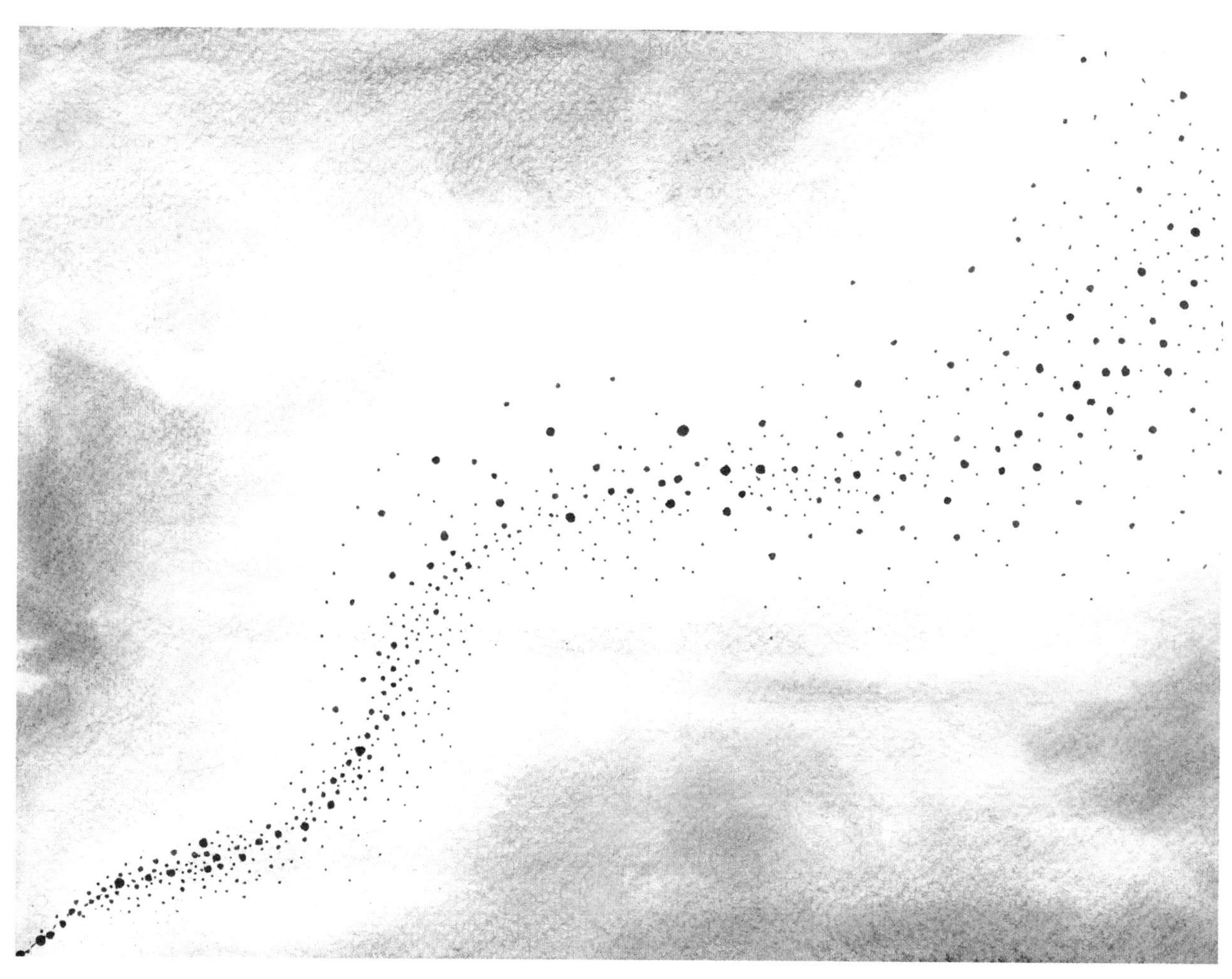

People drew her again and again

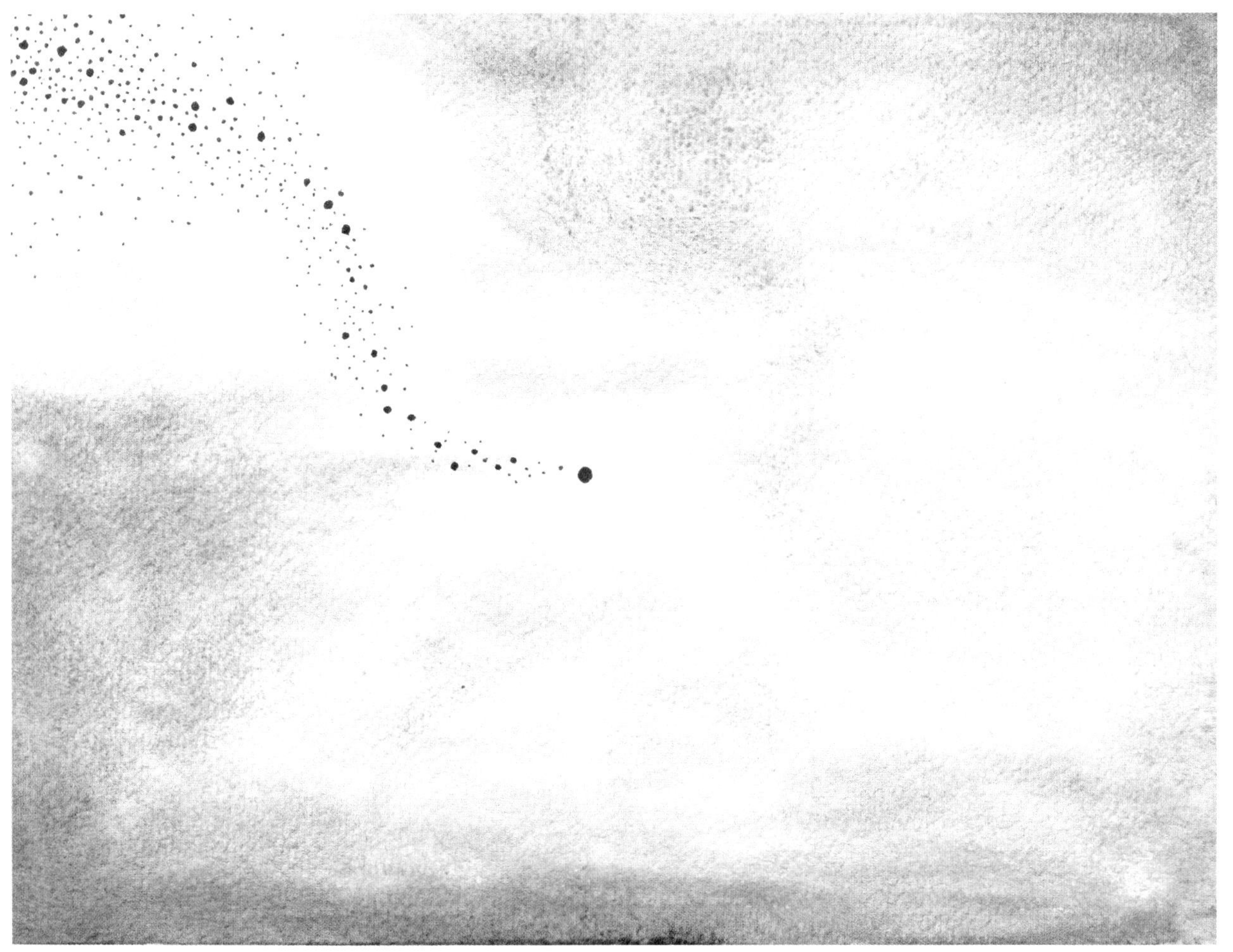

until the drawing of her made it to the Muslim world.

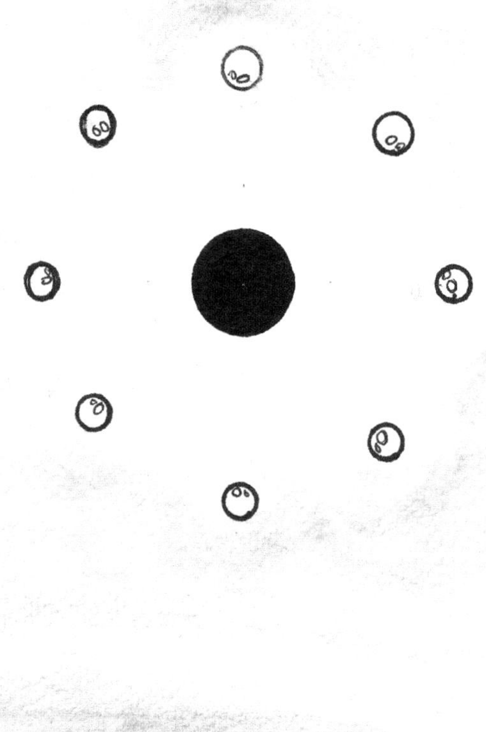

In the middle ages Muslim scholars understood the great value

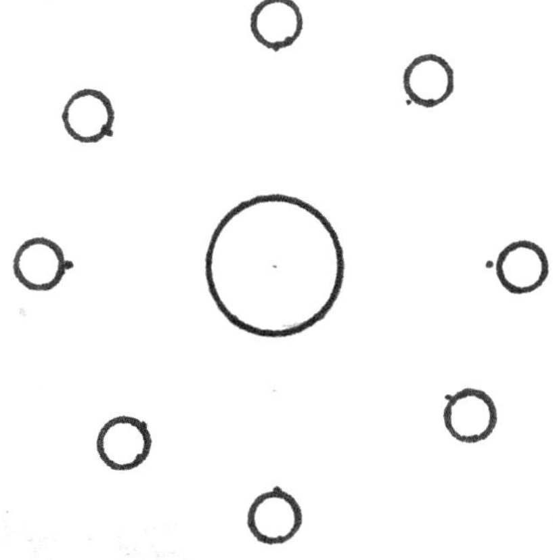

in her non-value.

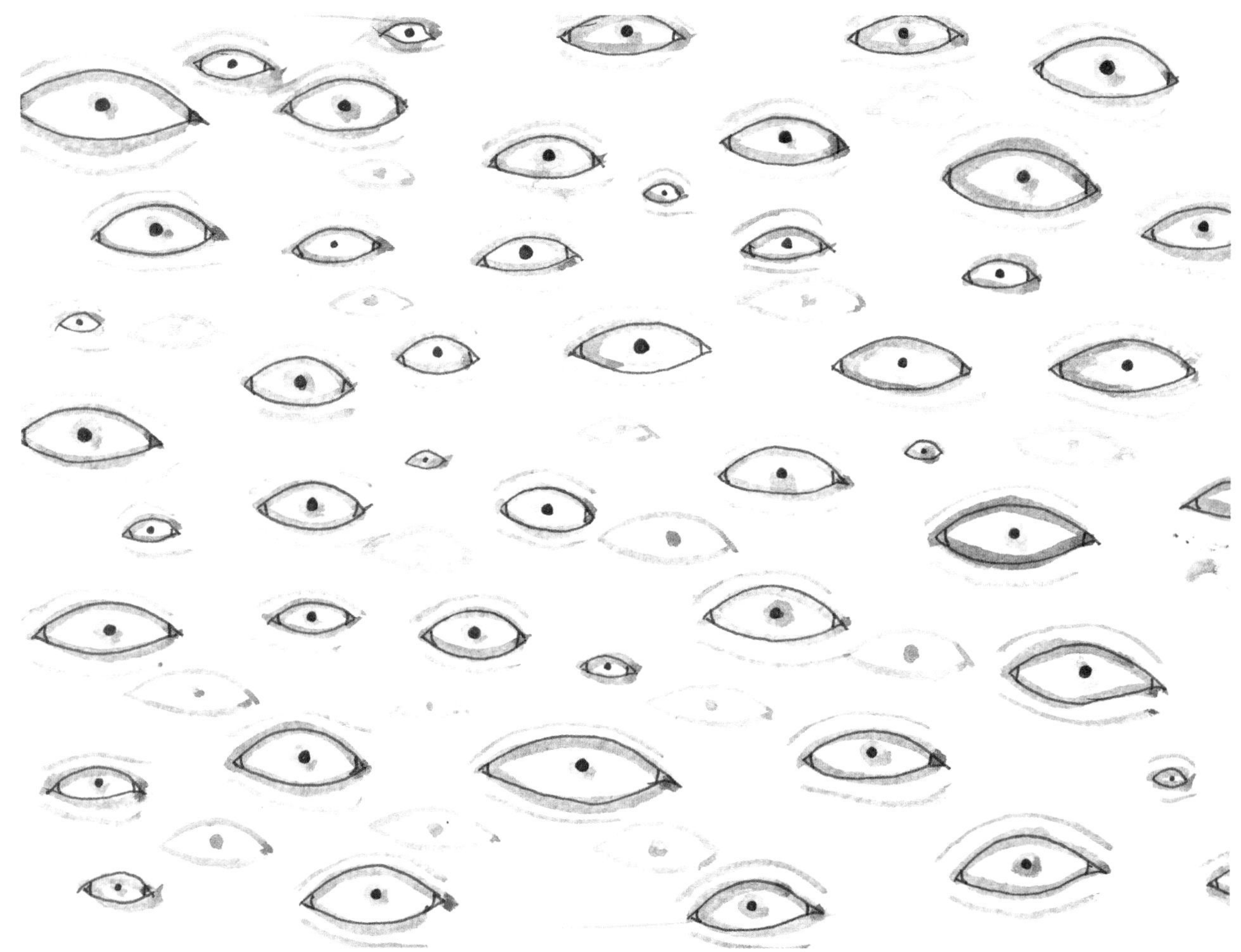

The existence

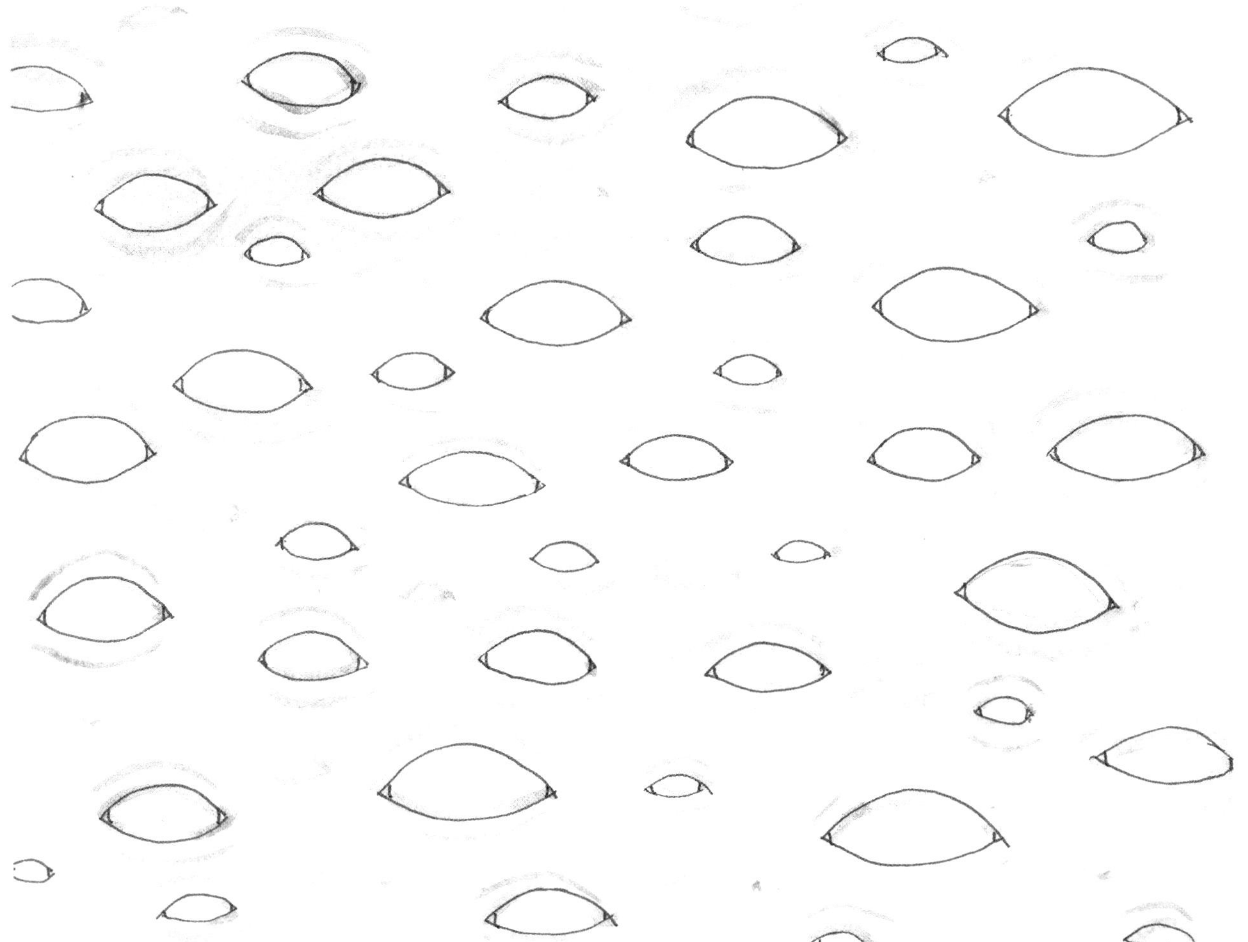

of her non-existence.

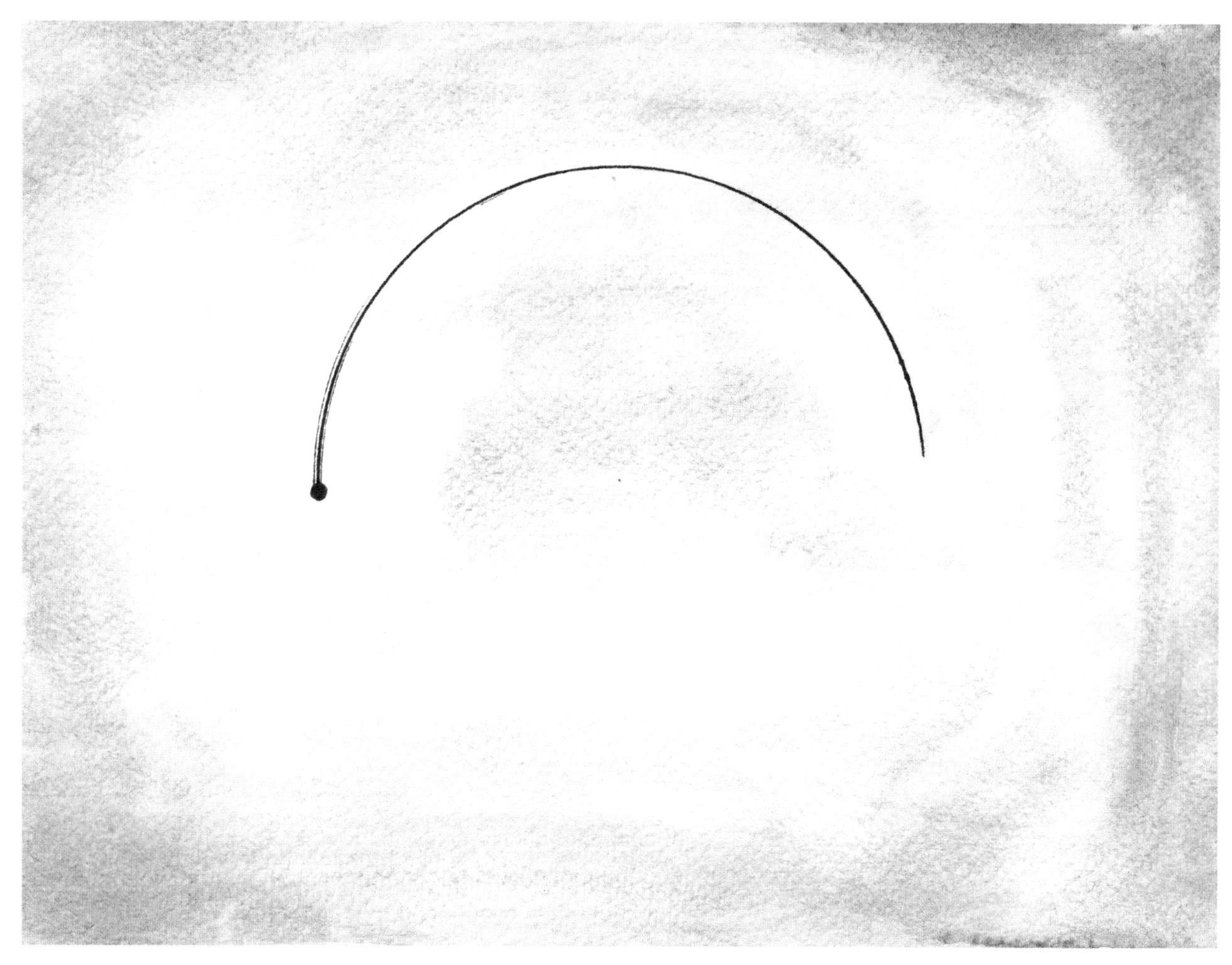

and in looking more closely at her, they began to draw

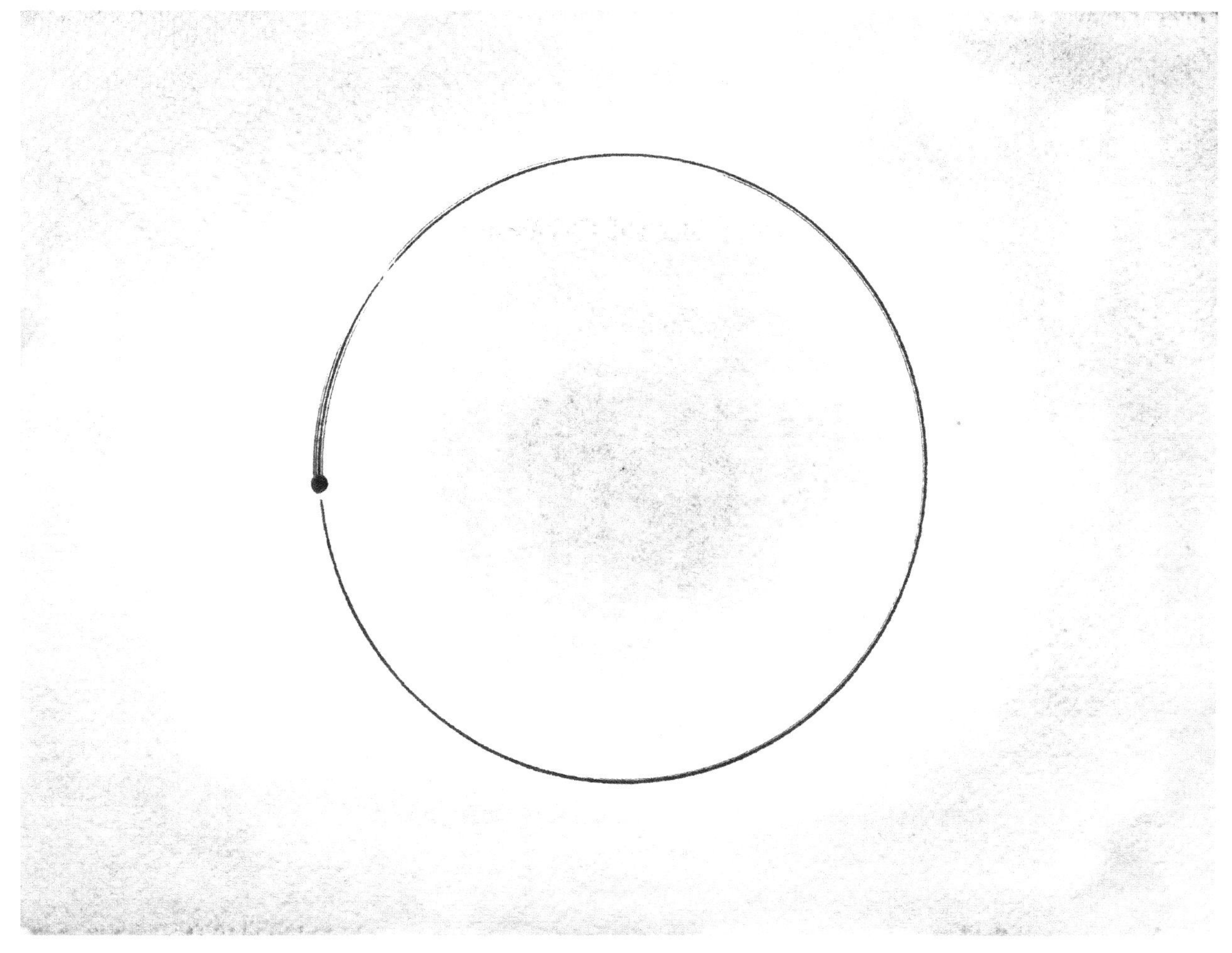

her as a circle.
And they gave her the name Sifr, Zero.

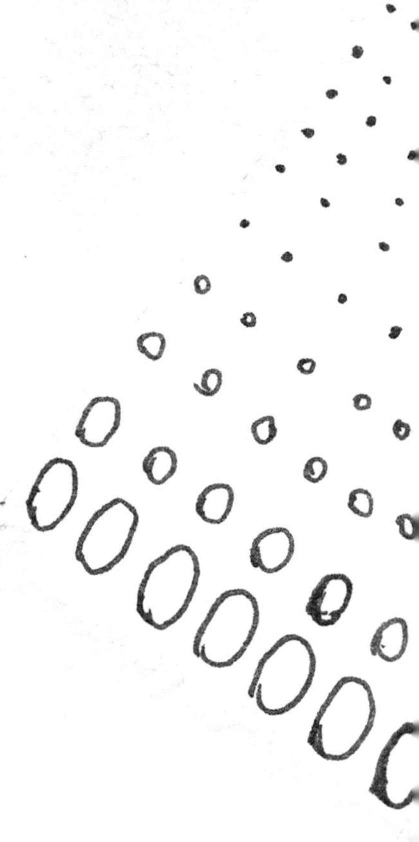

**They drew her at the
beginning of numerology**

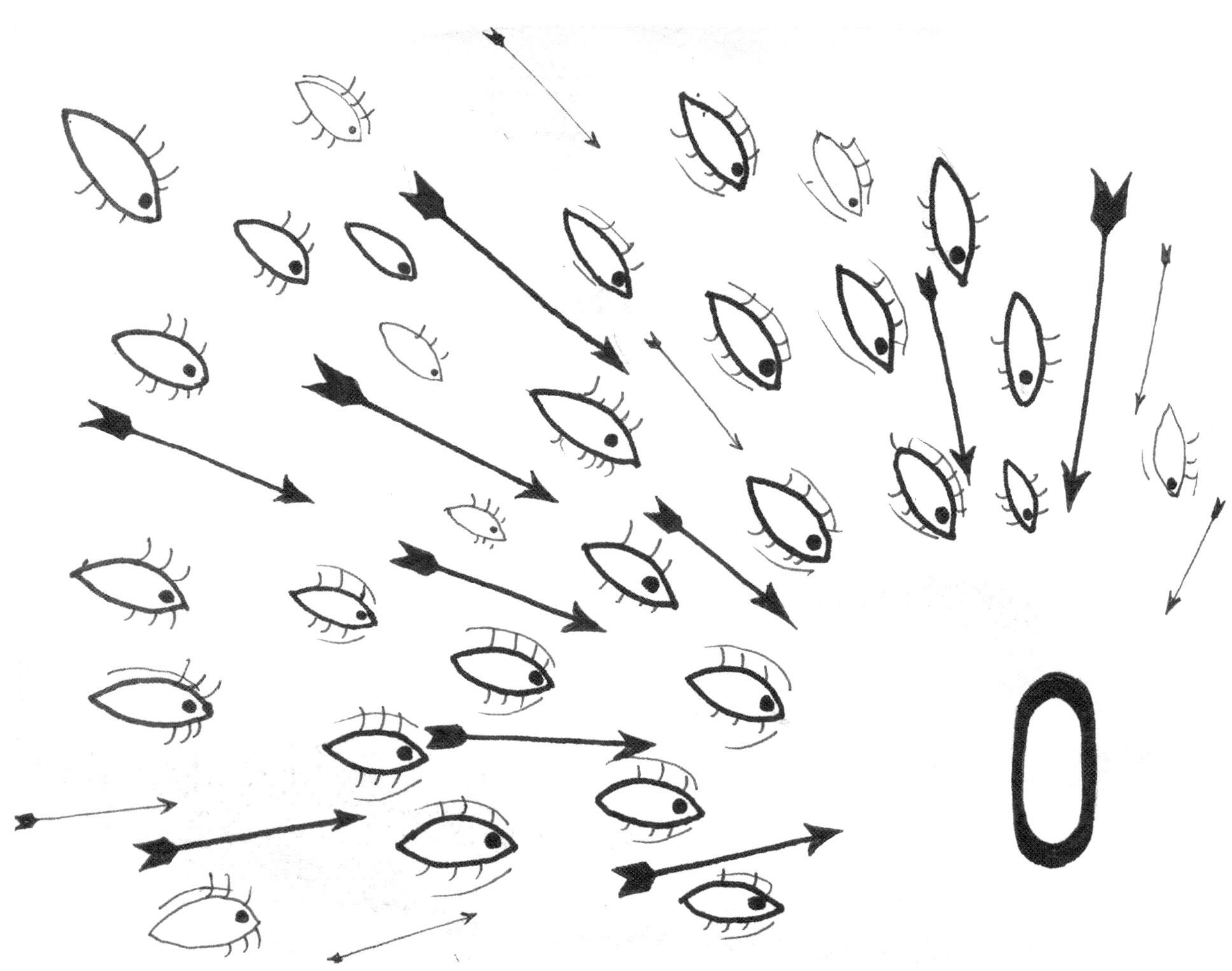

and brought her to Europe, where she was not received well,

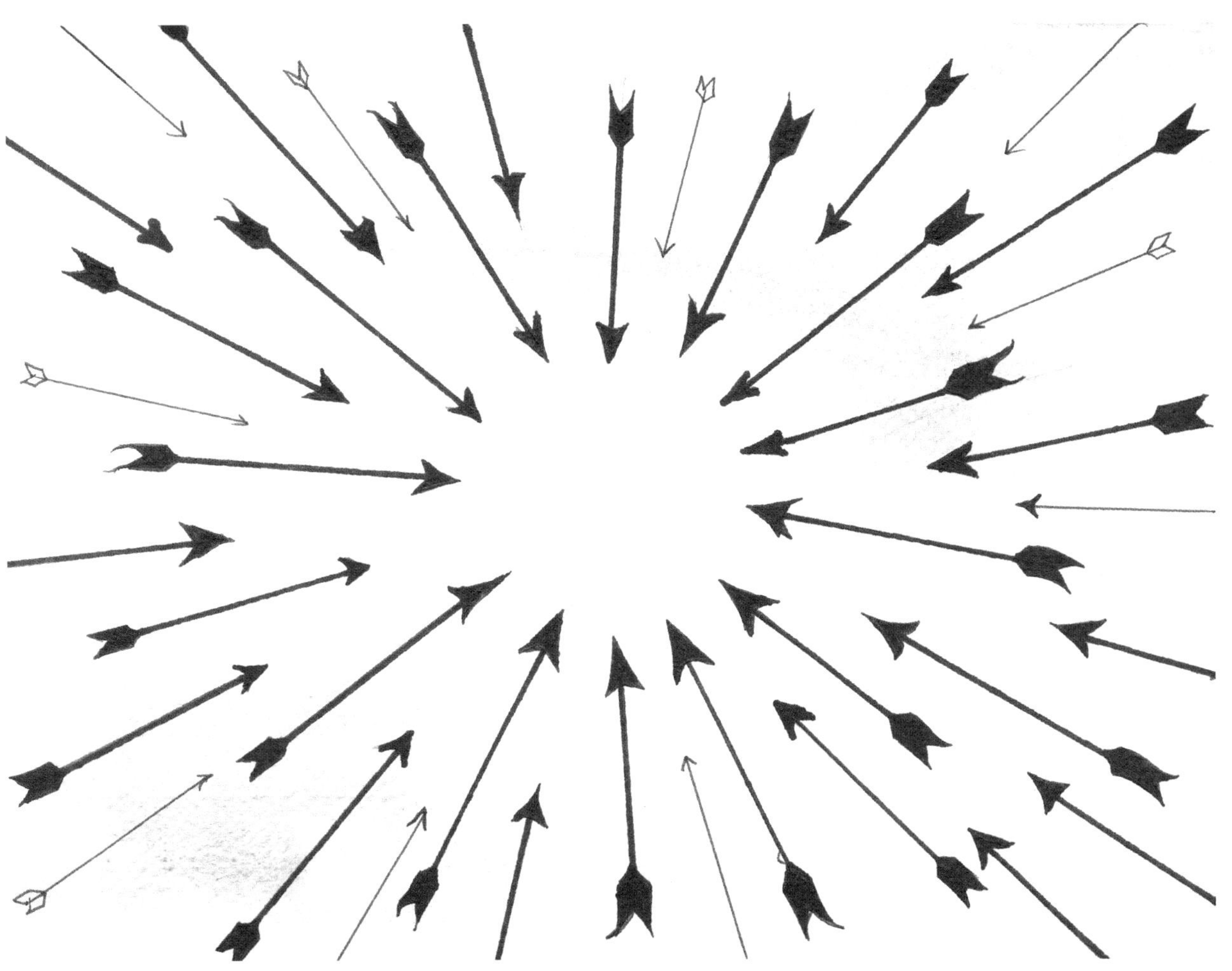

for the Romans and the Greeks were frightened of her power.

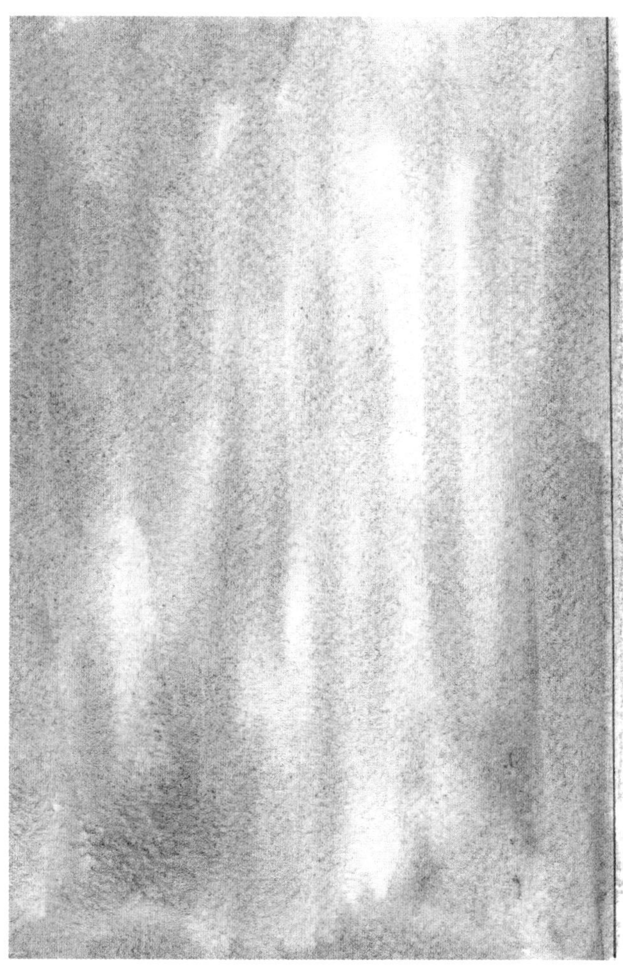

How can nothing be something?

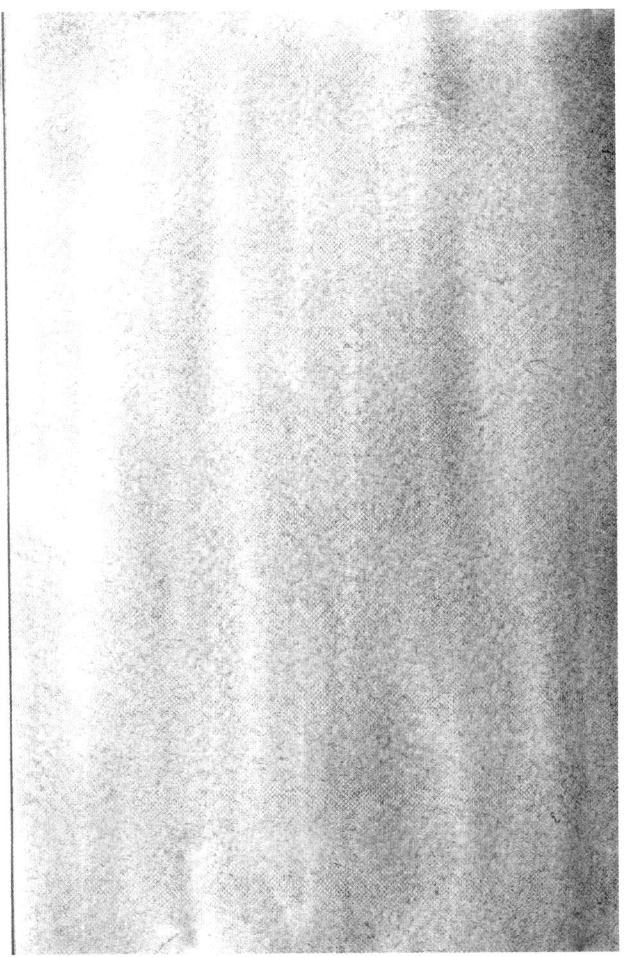

How can something be nothing?

Something,

nothing,

something,

nothing,

something,

nothing,

something,

nothing,

nothing,

something,

nothing,

something,

nothing,

something,

nothing,

something.

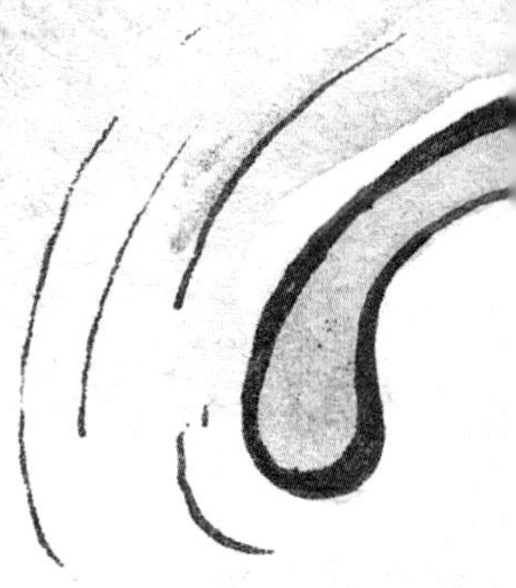

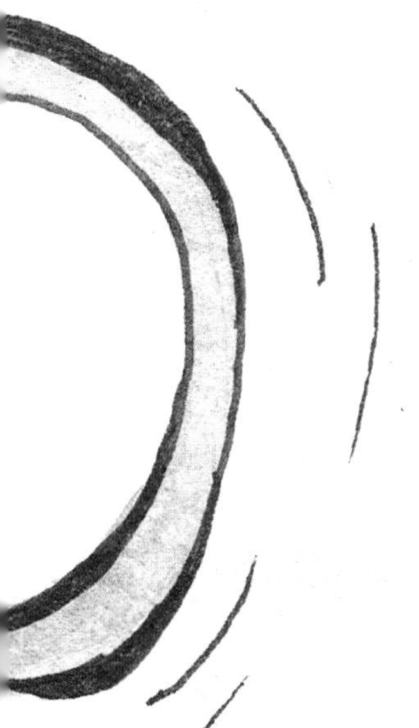

How?

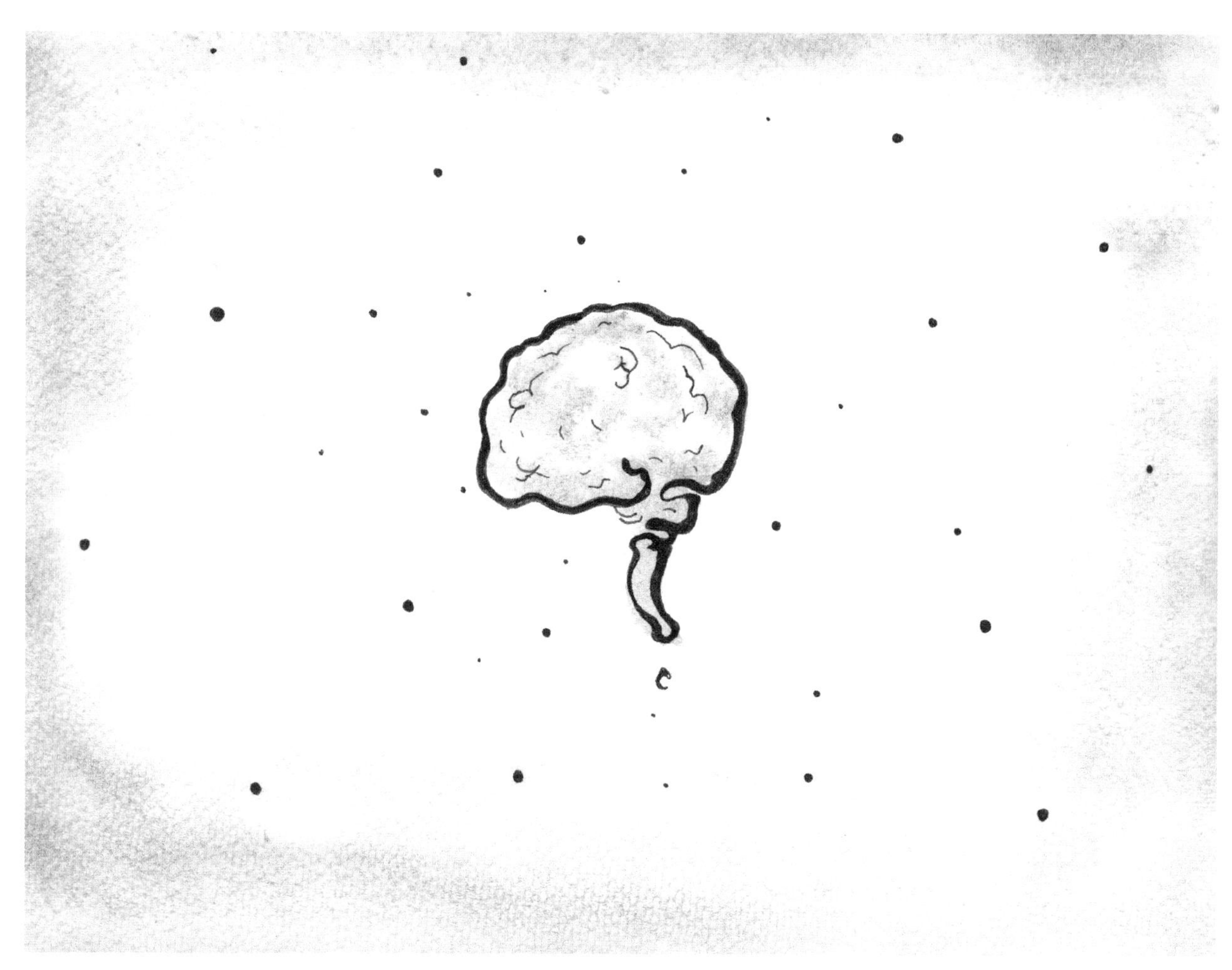

Forgetting is like nothing, like Zero, Sifr.

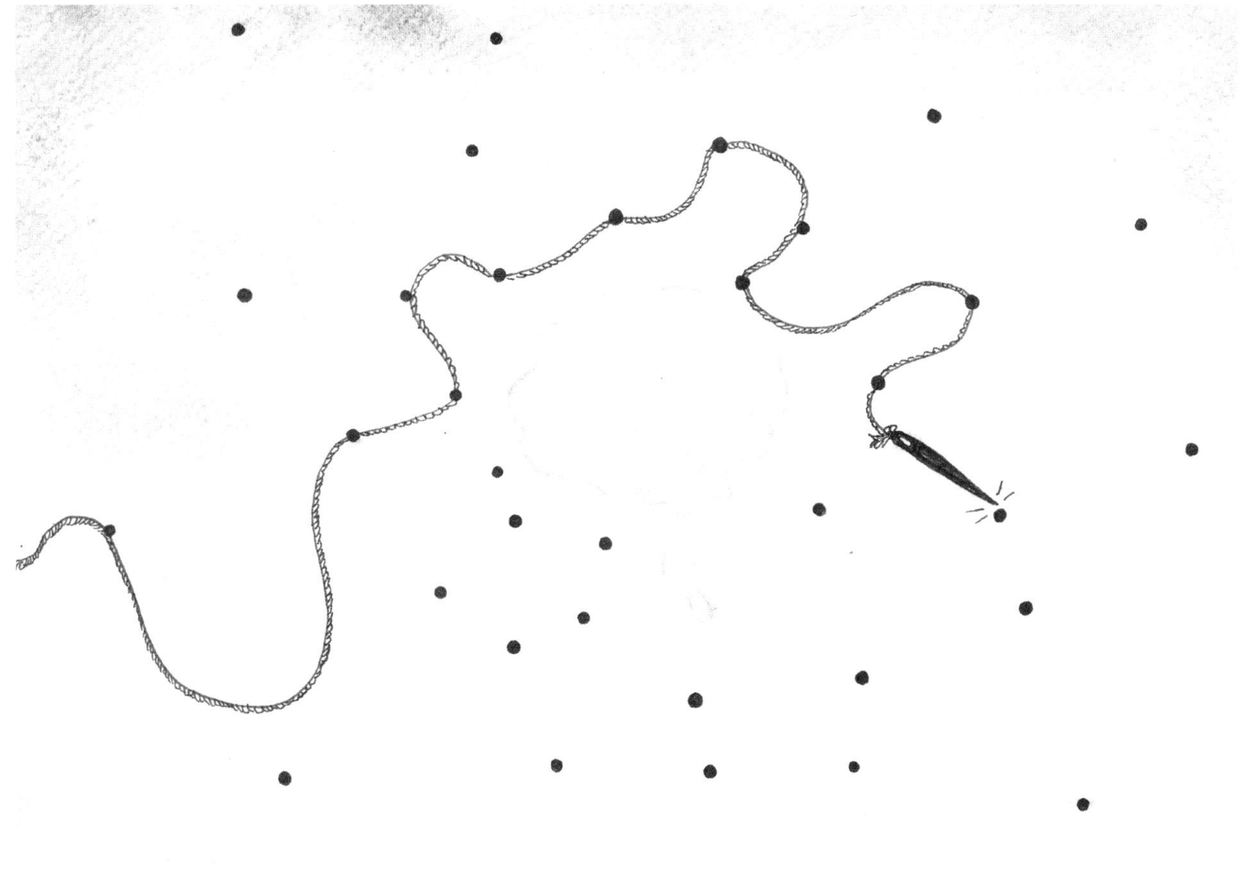

And remembering is like sewing,

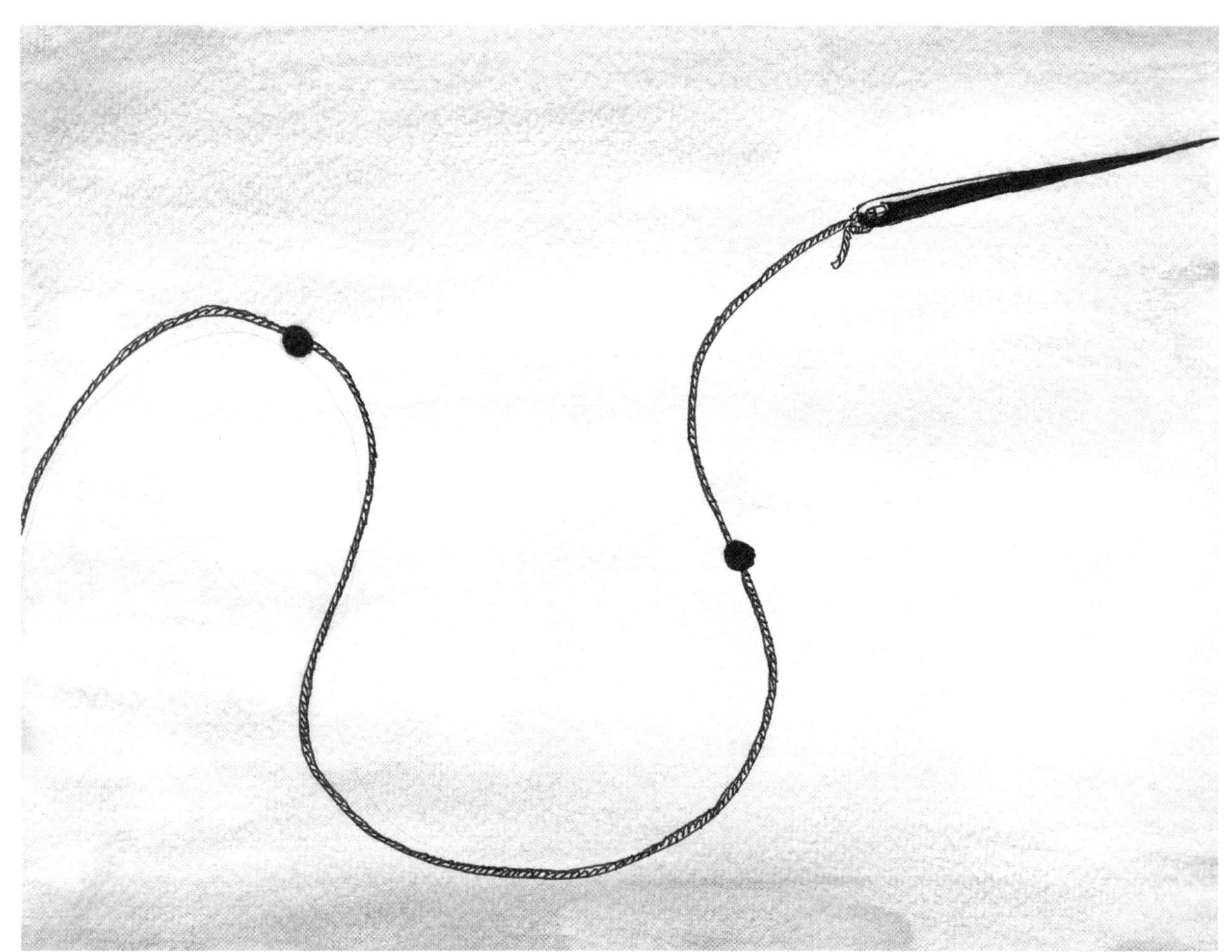

like stringing the zeros,

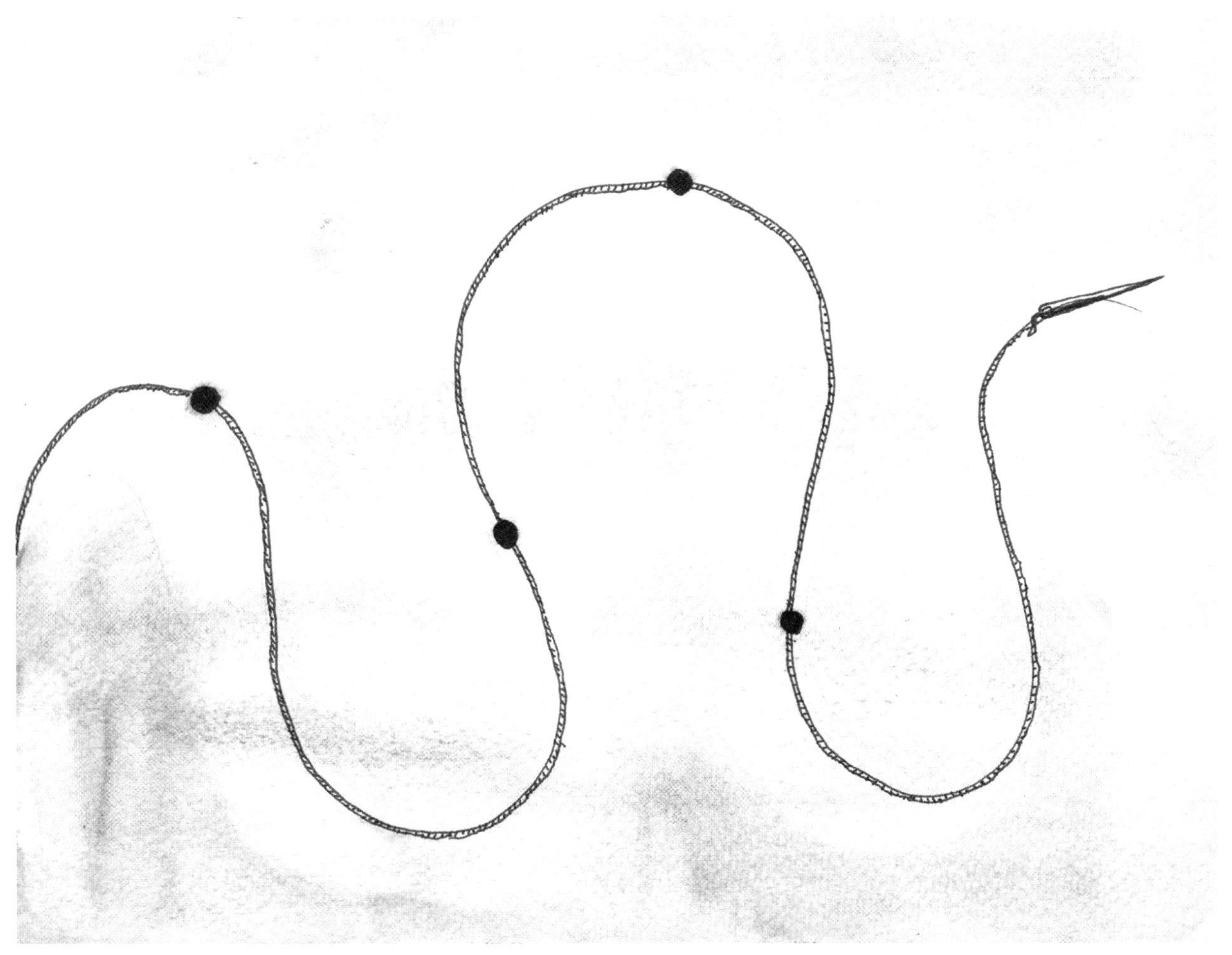

again and again and again.

Like ritual,

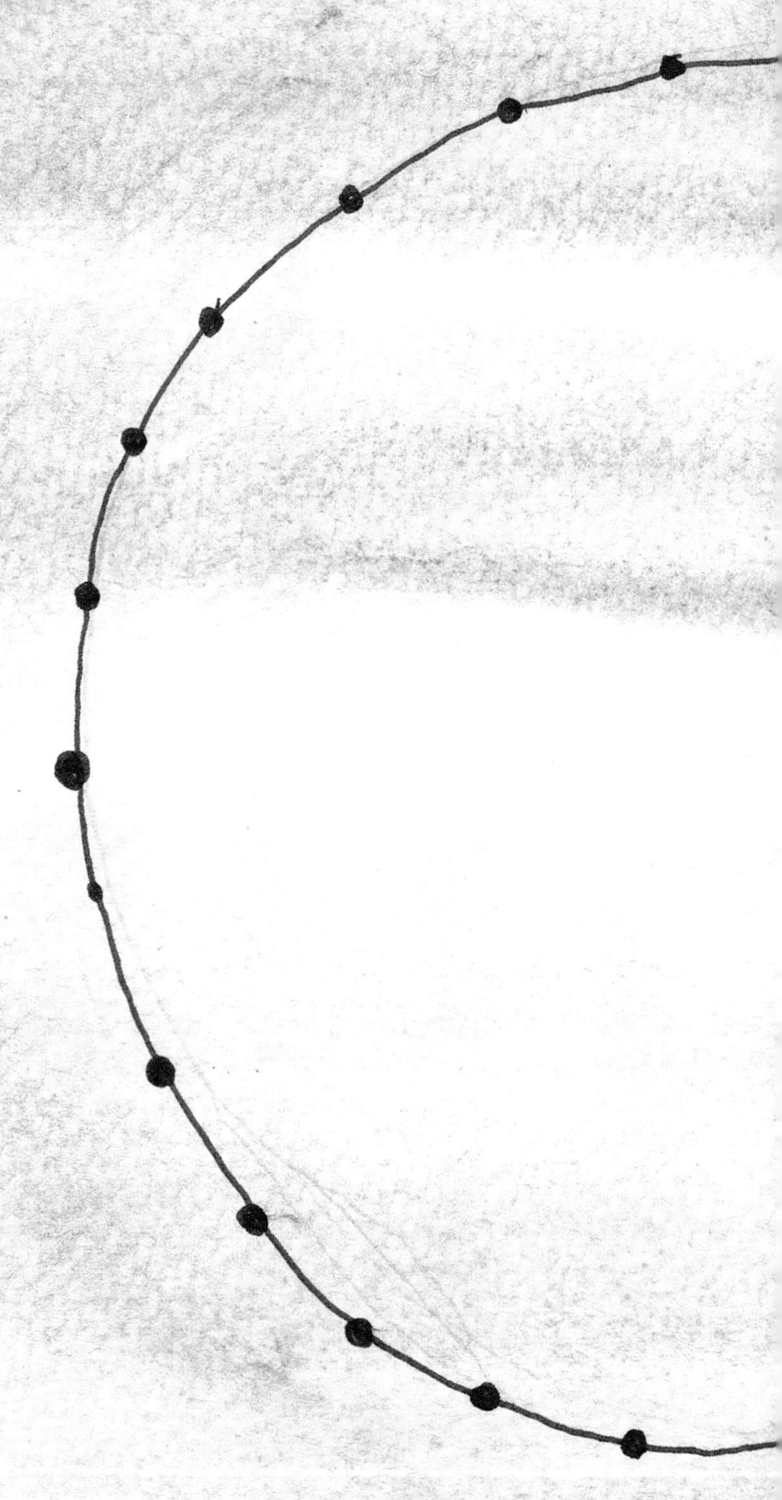

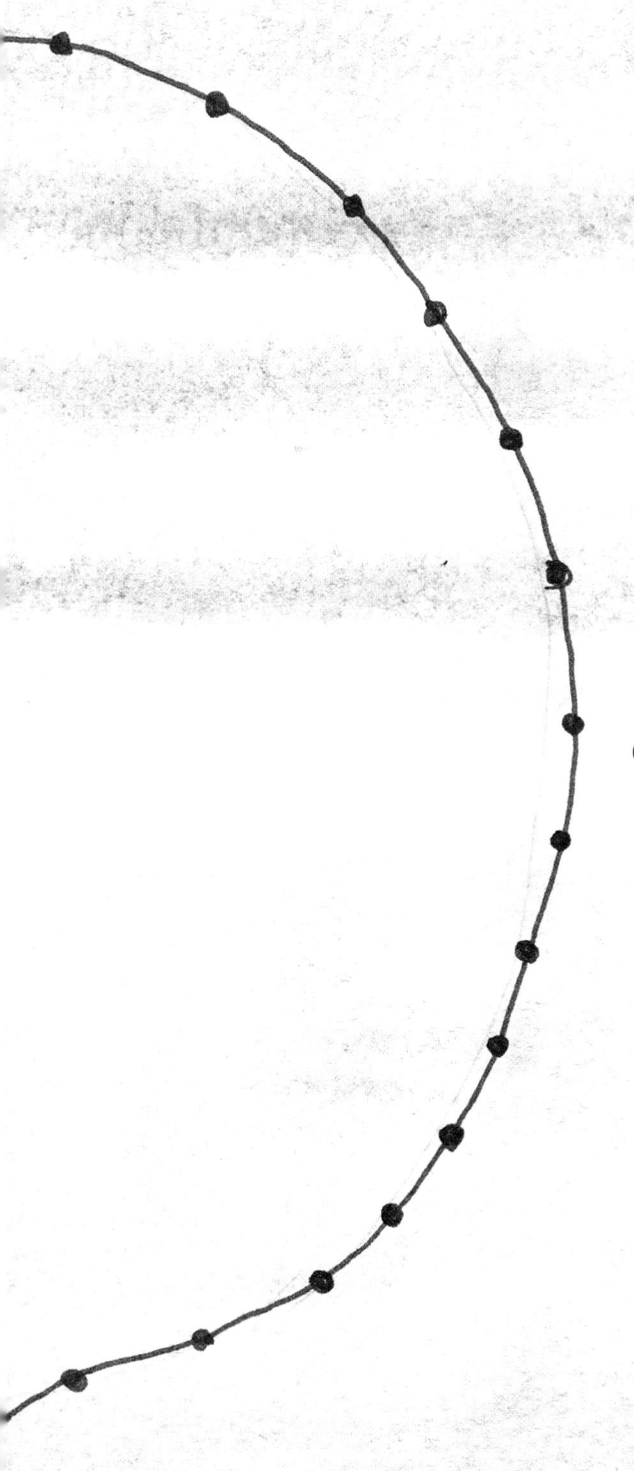

connecting back to zero.

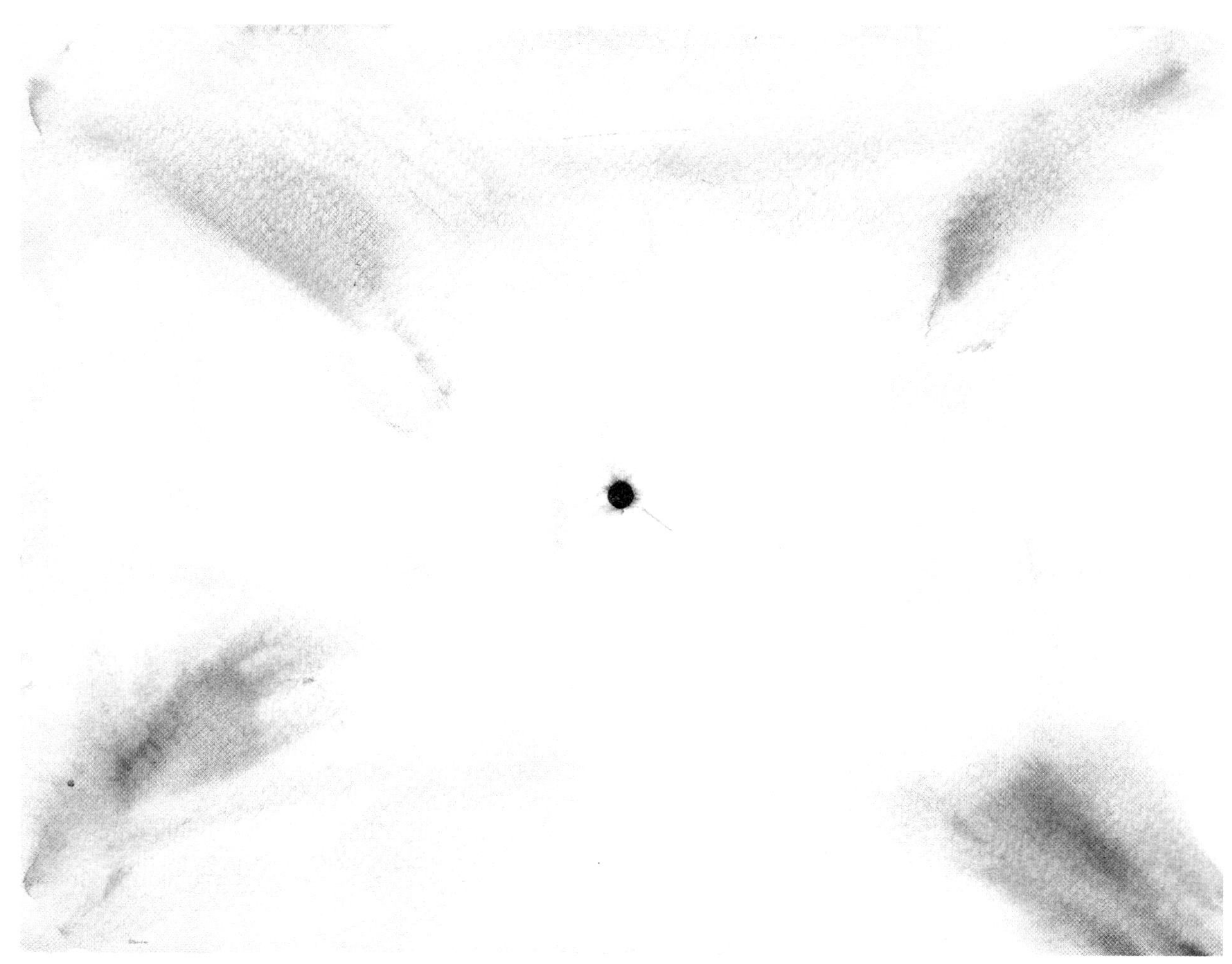

Back to nothing,

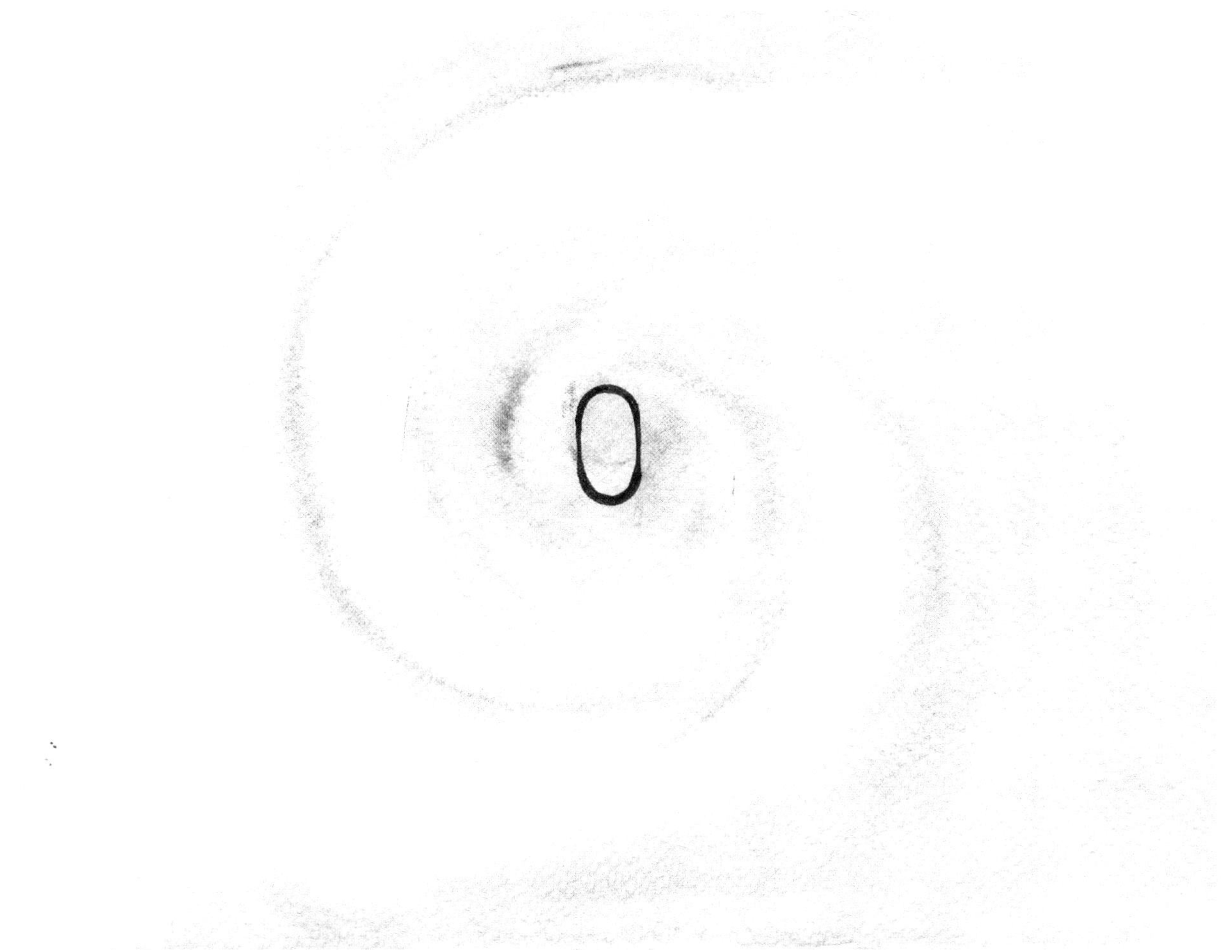

back to her.

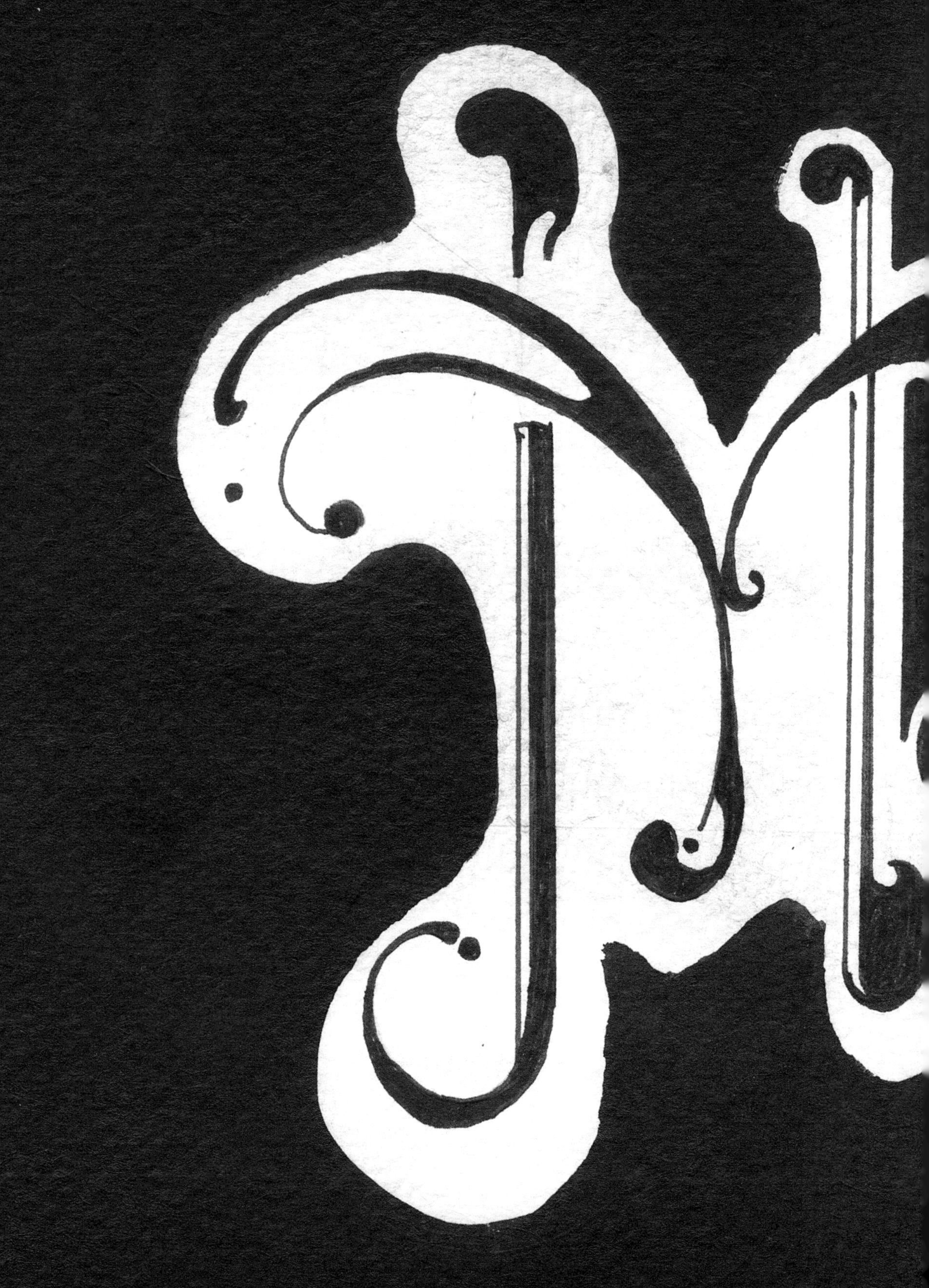

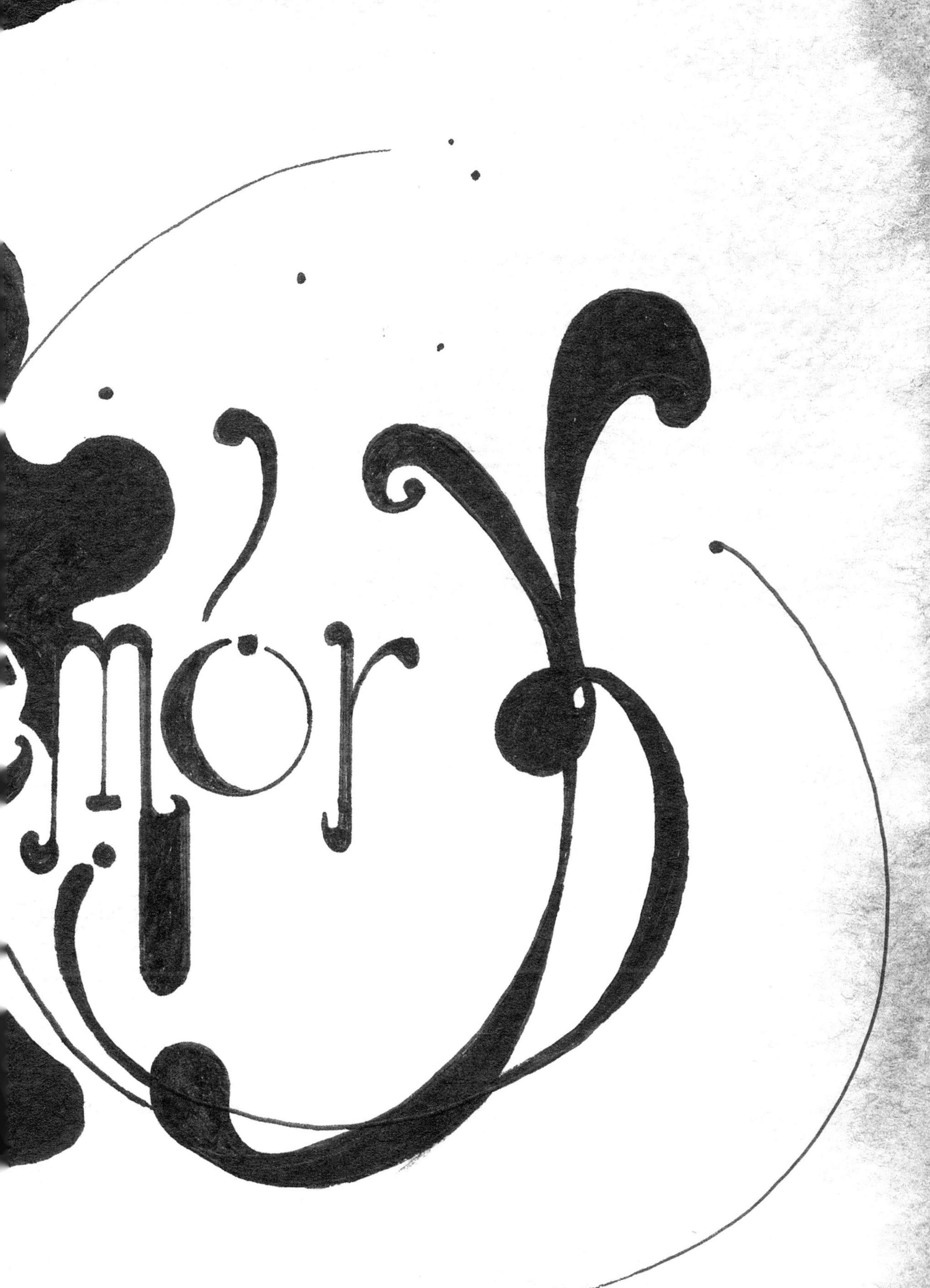

COLOR

Mnzlee Stories — S01 E05

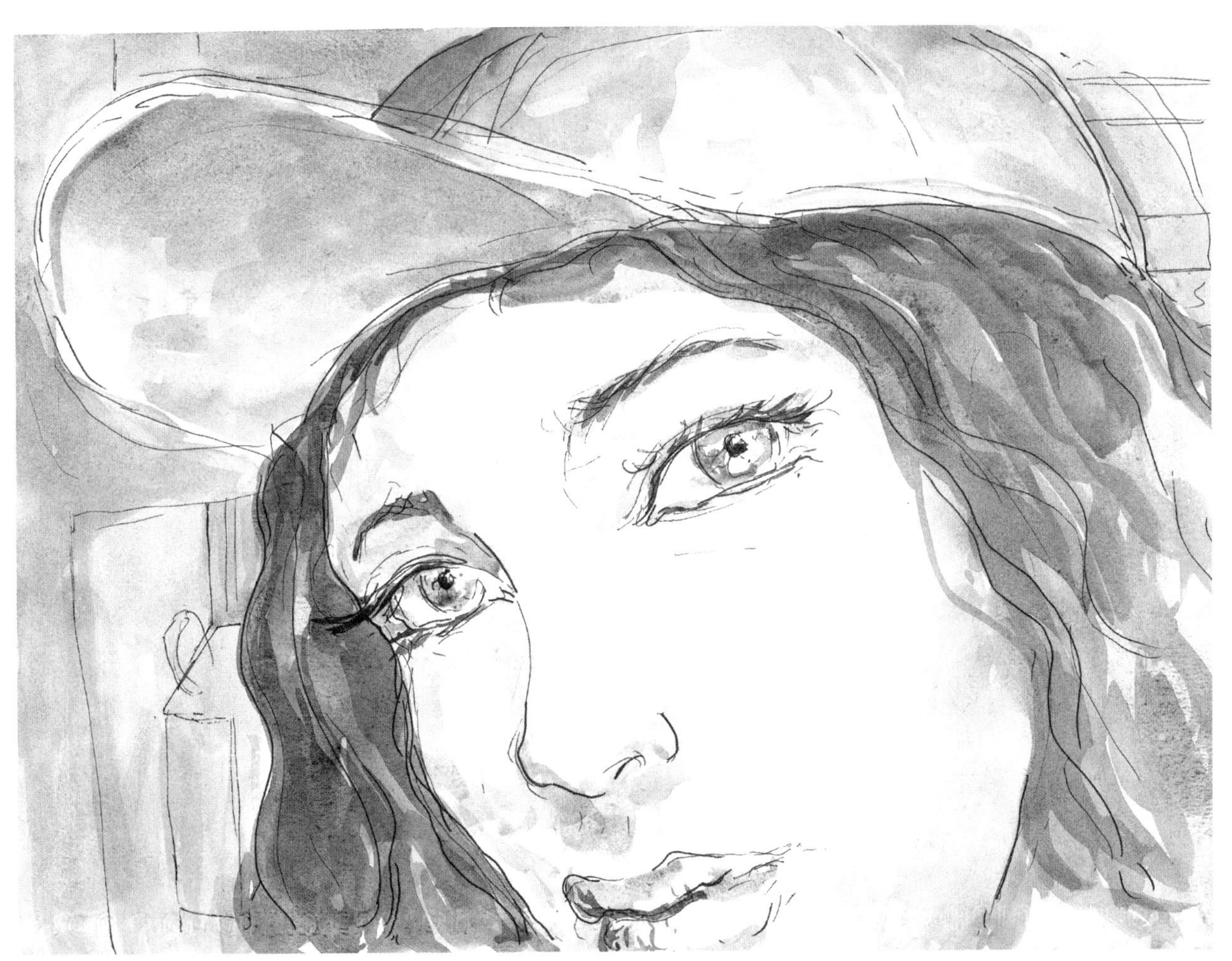

There was a girl who wanted to hide.

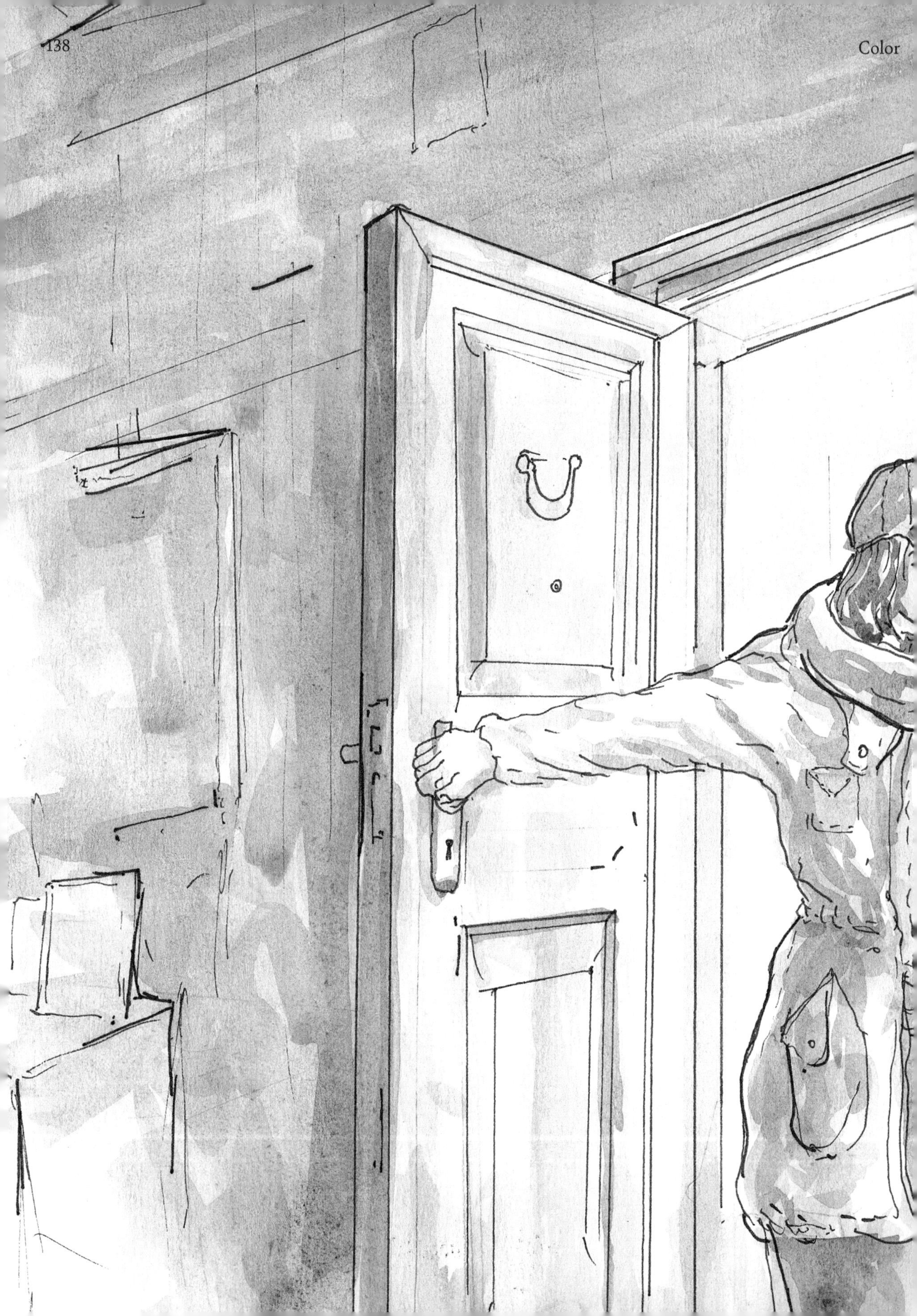

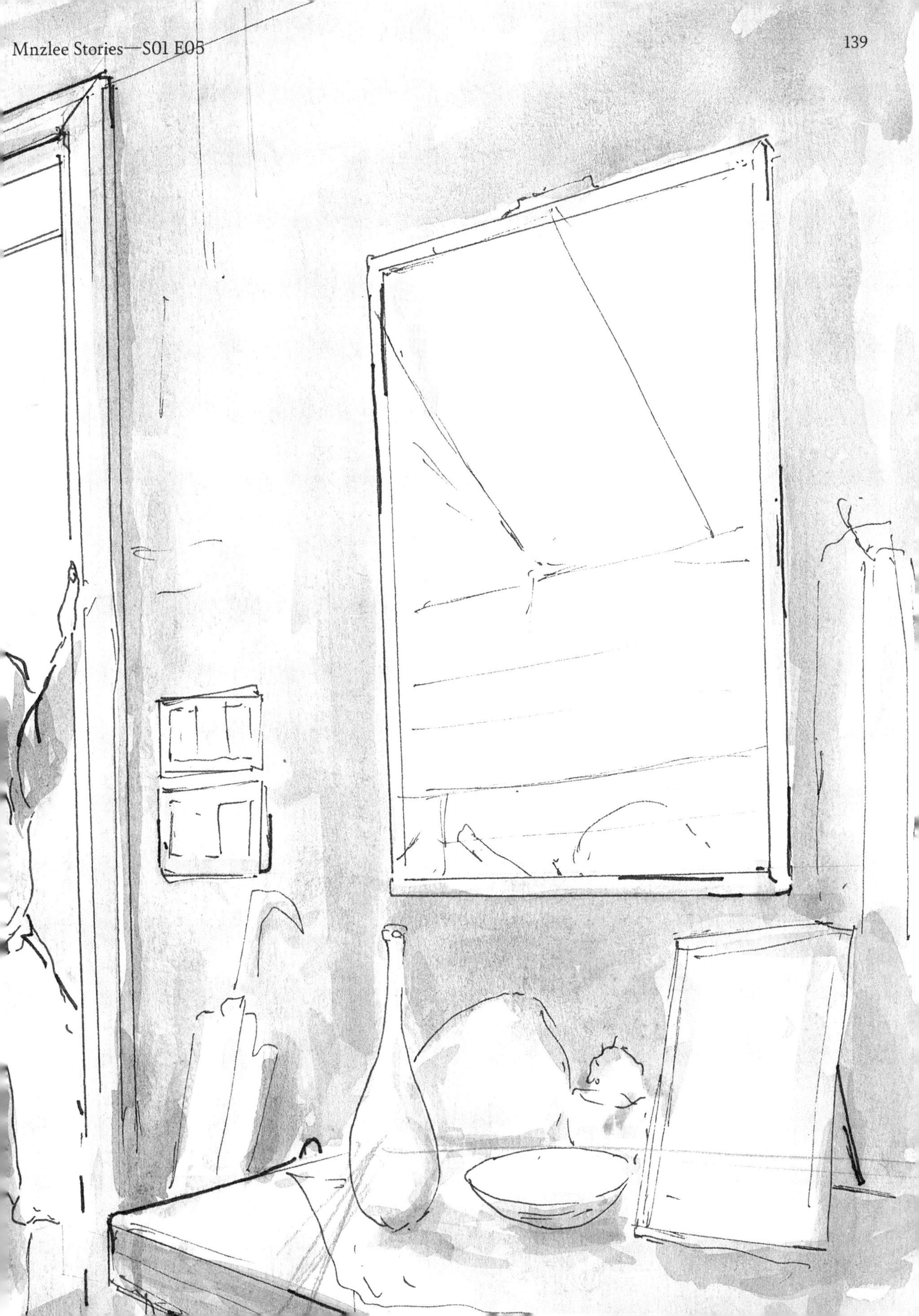

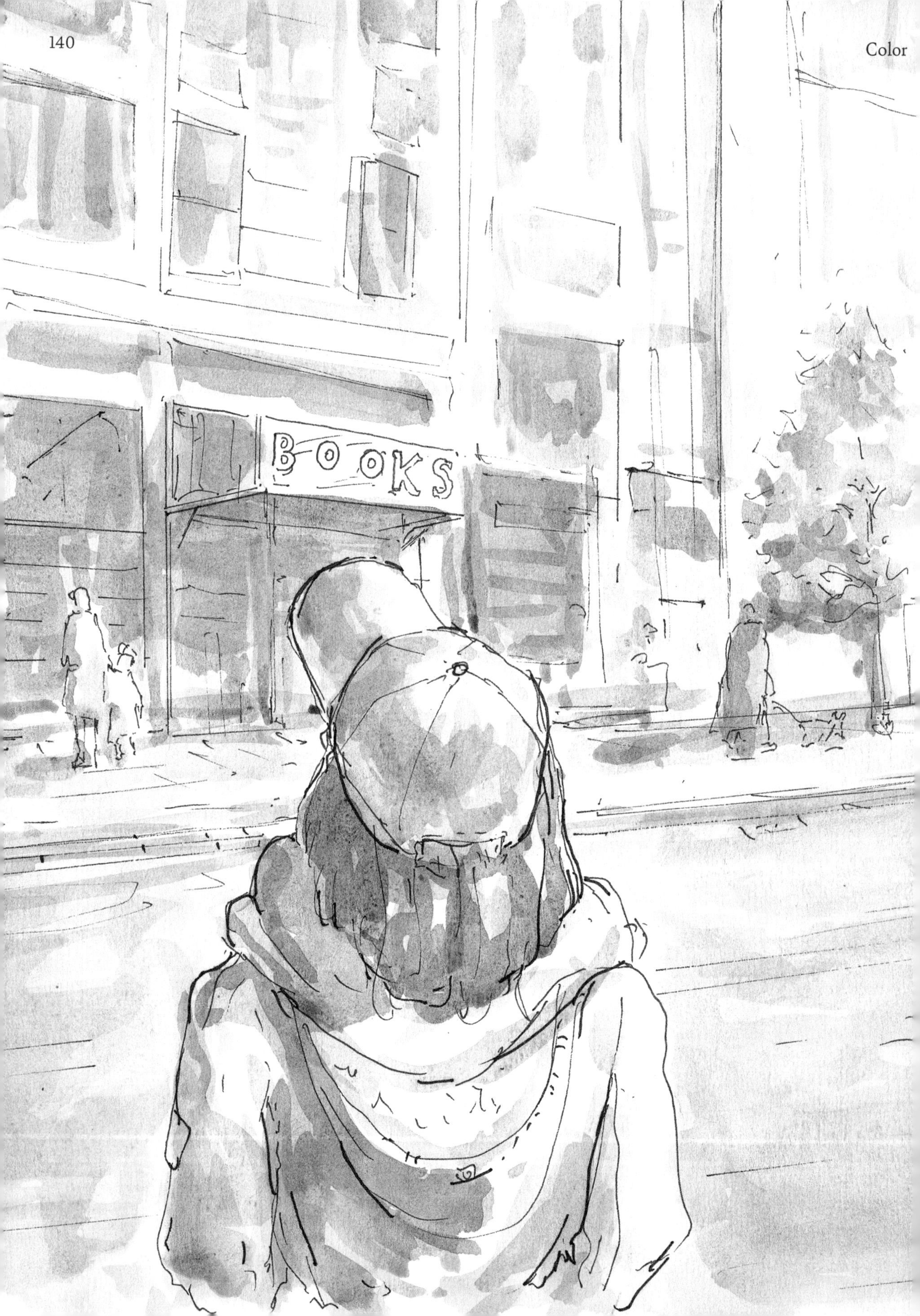
BOOKS

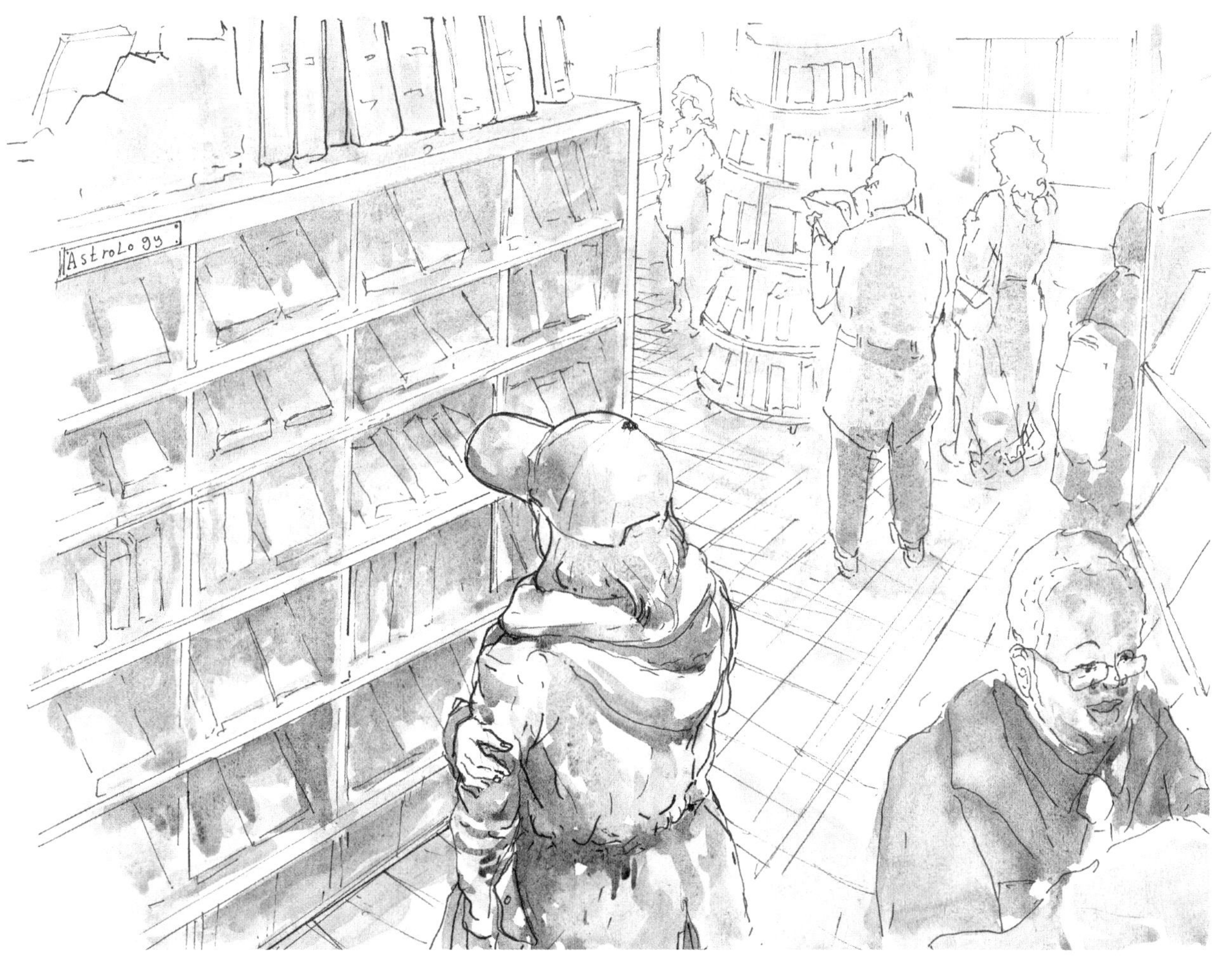

She walked into the local book store.

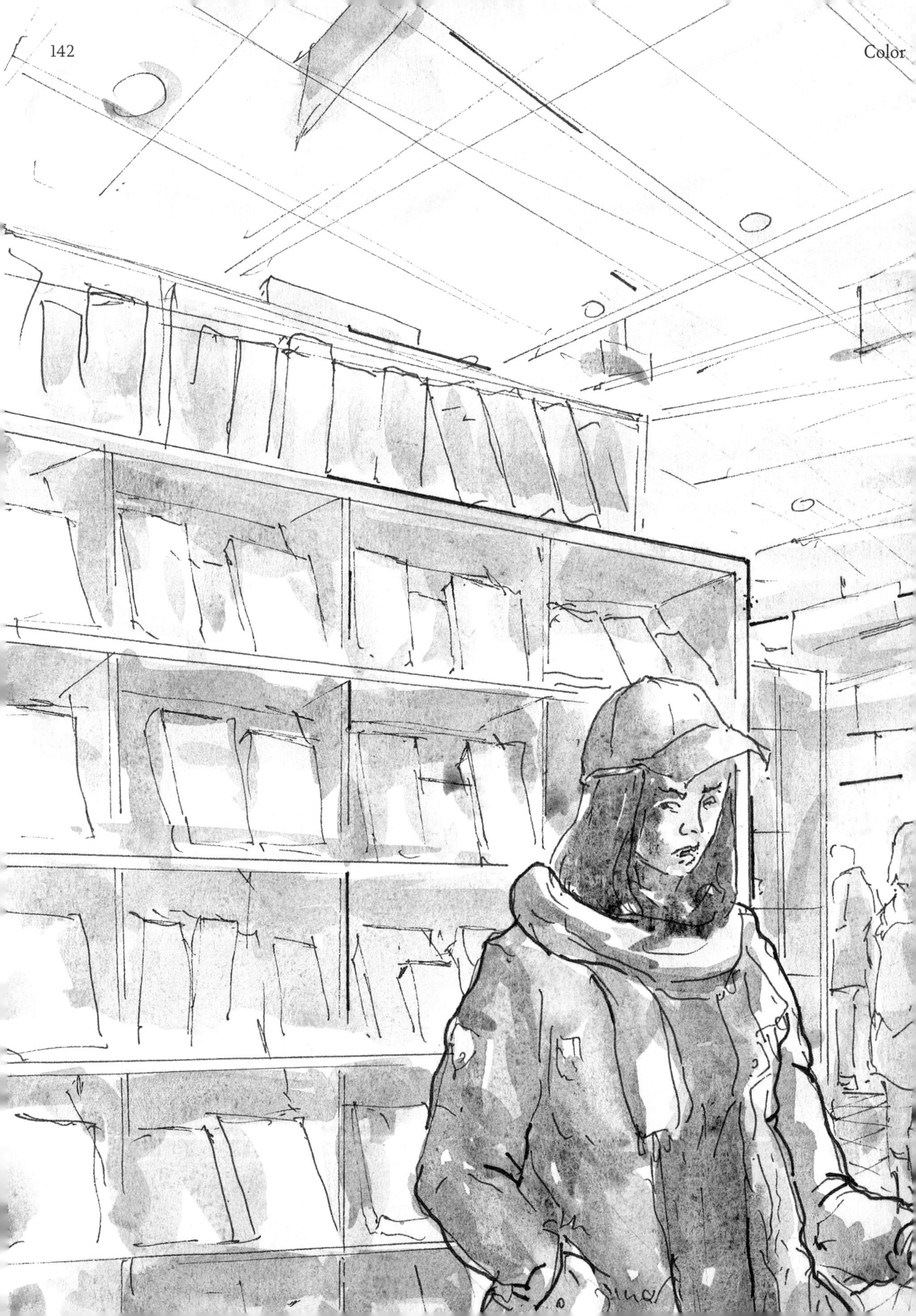

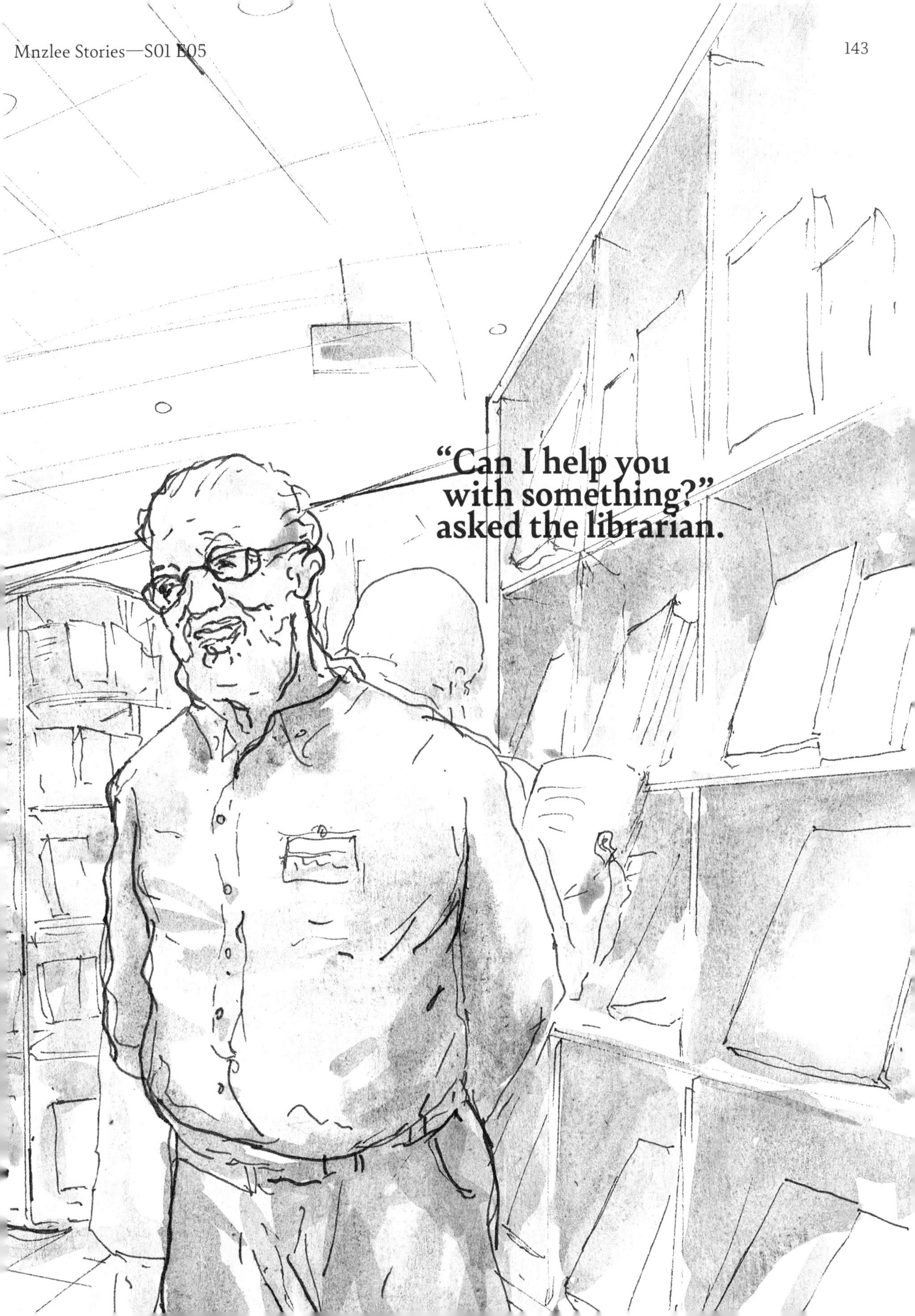
"Can I help you
with something?"
asked the librarian.

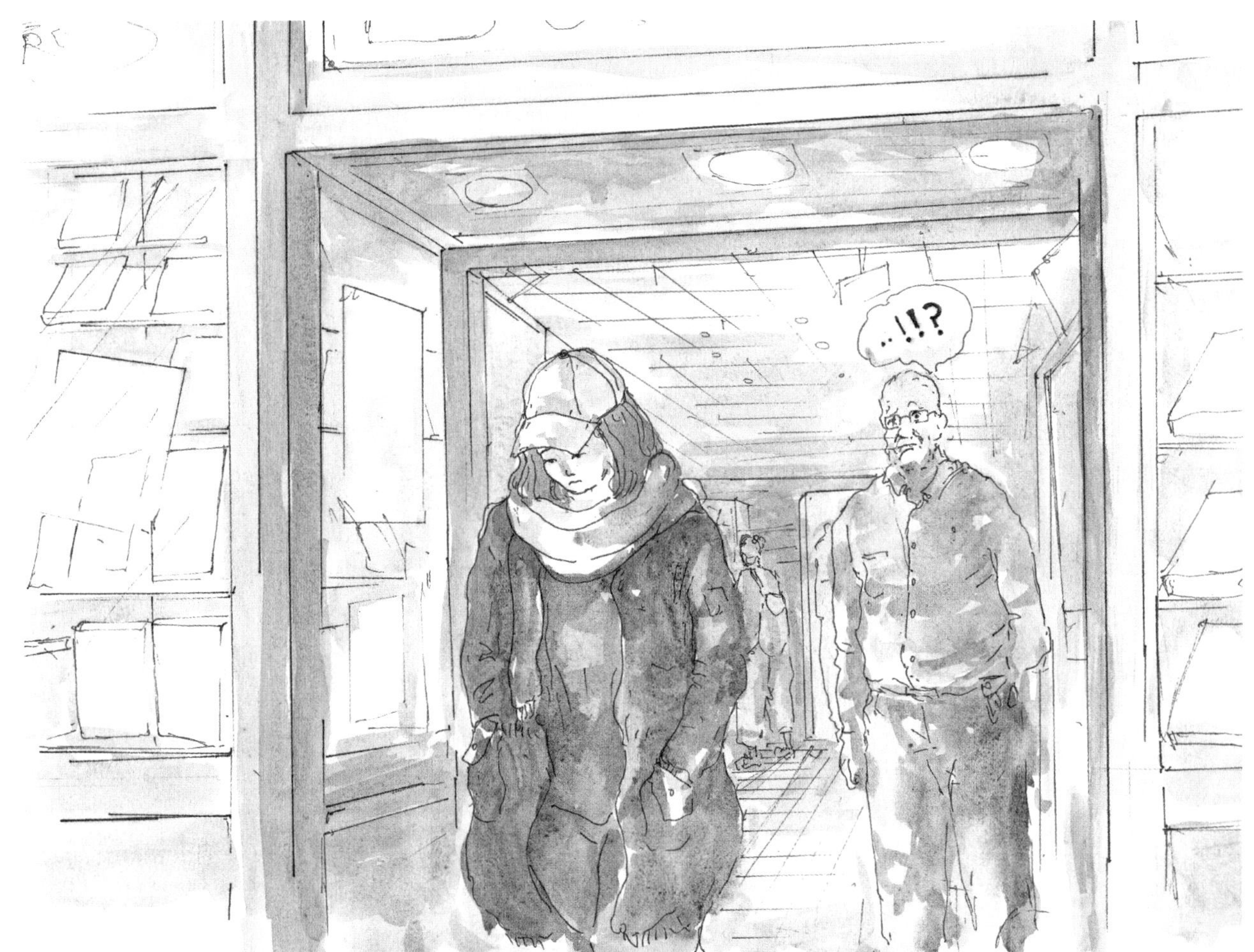

"No!" she yelled and left quickly.

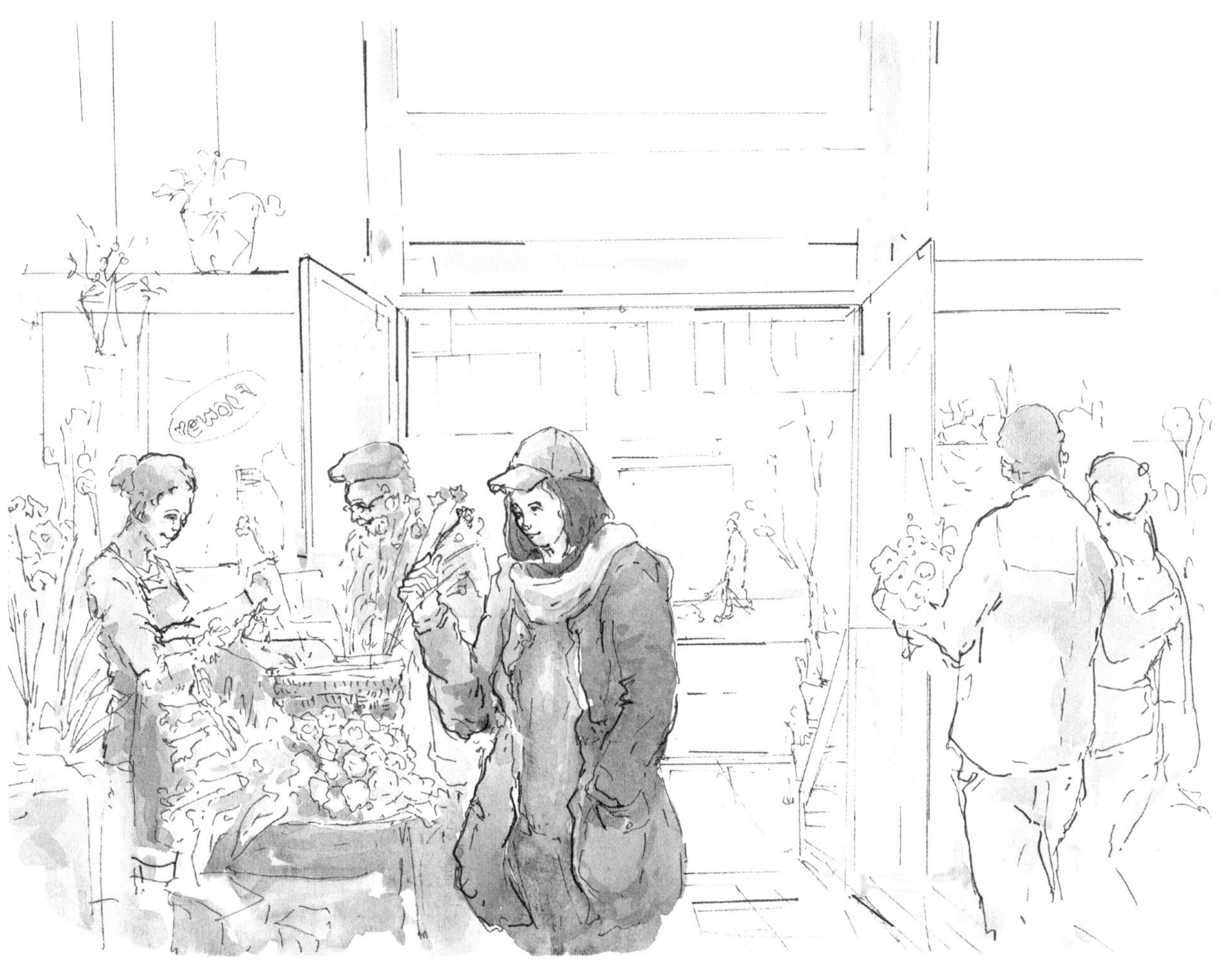

She stepped into a flower shop.

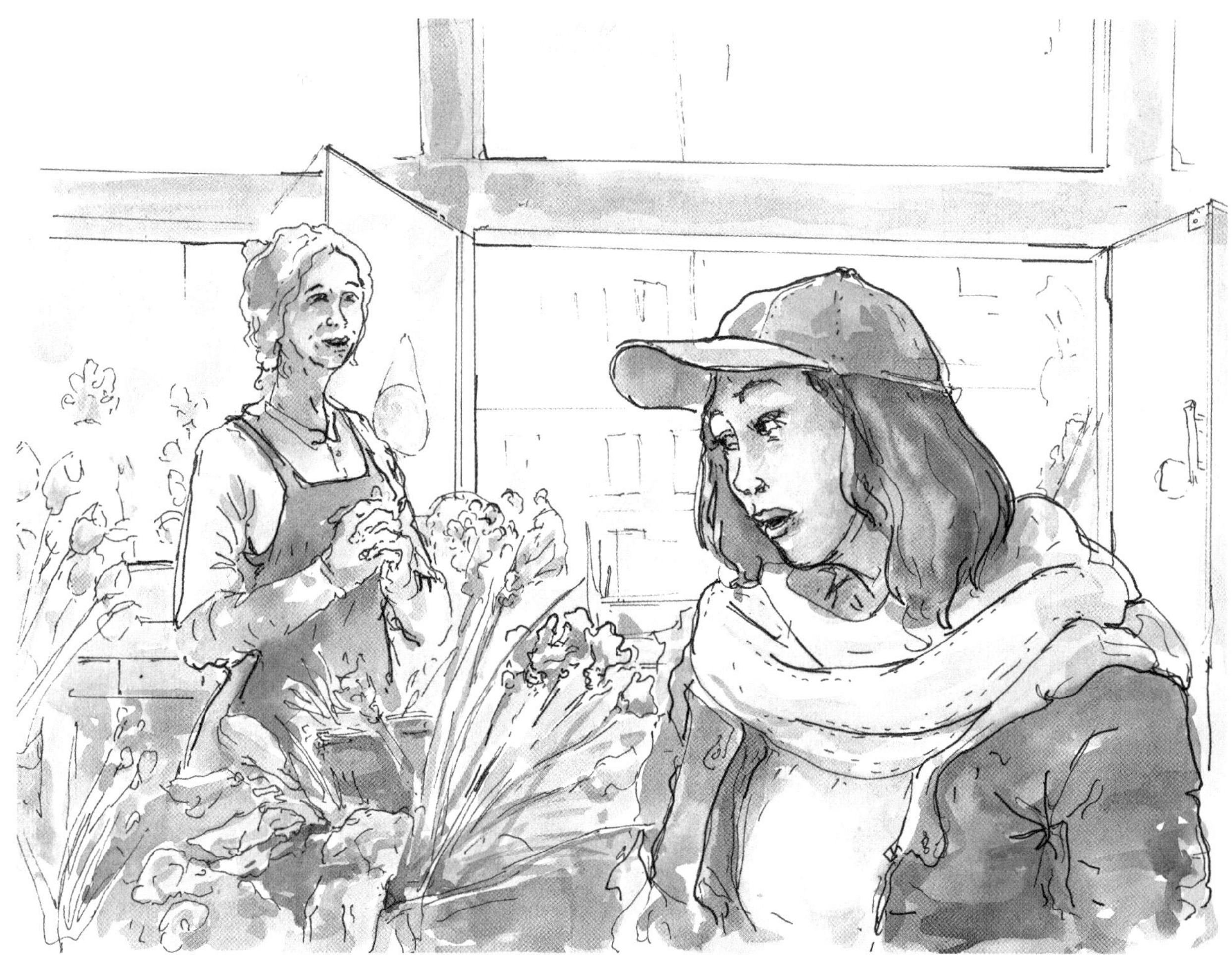

"Oh, good morning, want to smell that flower?"
asked the owner.

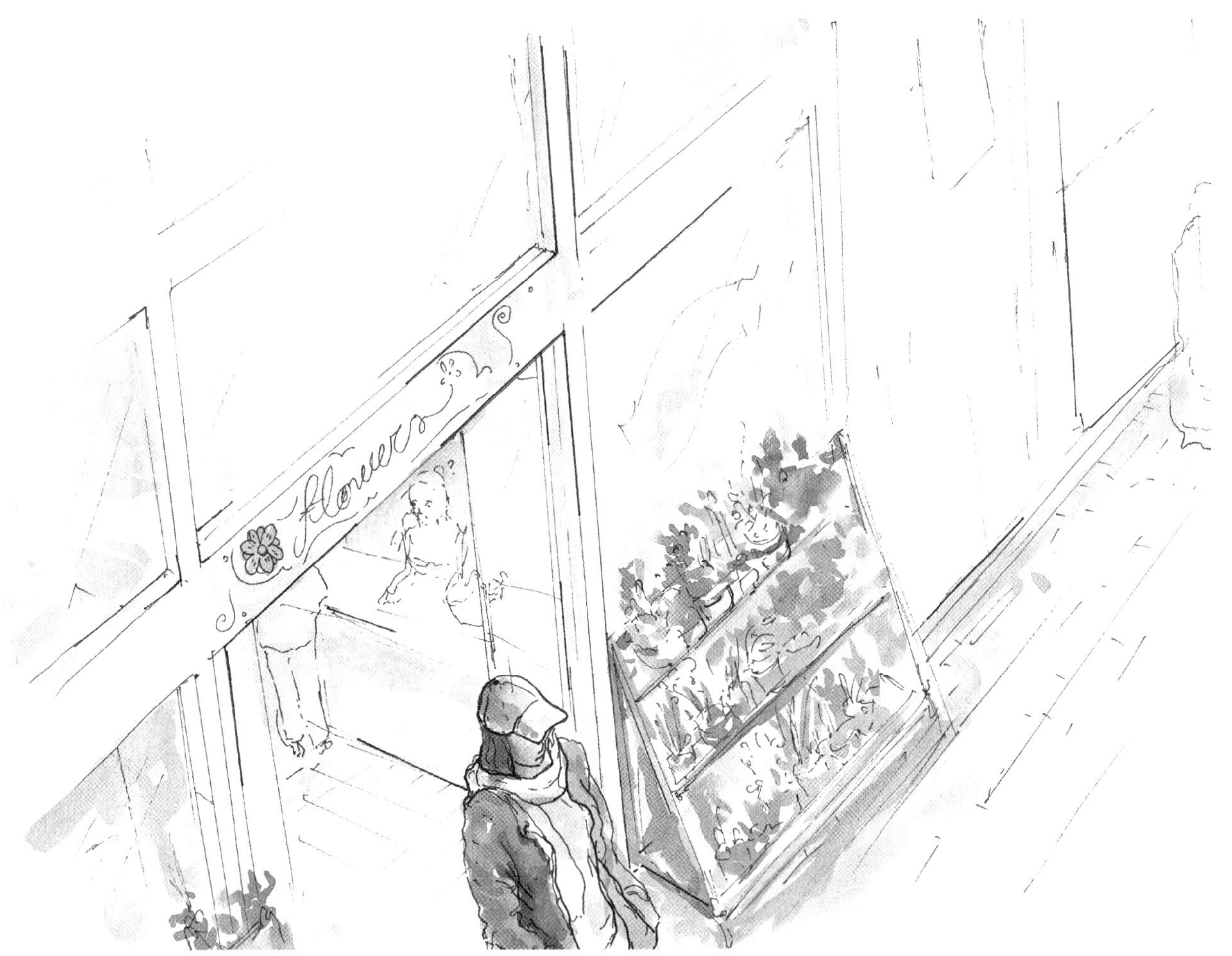

"No!" she yelled and ran off.

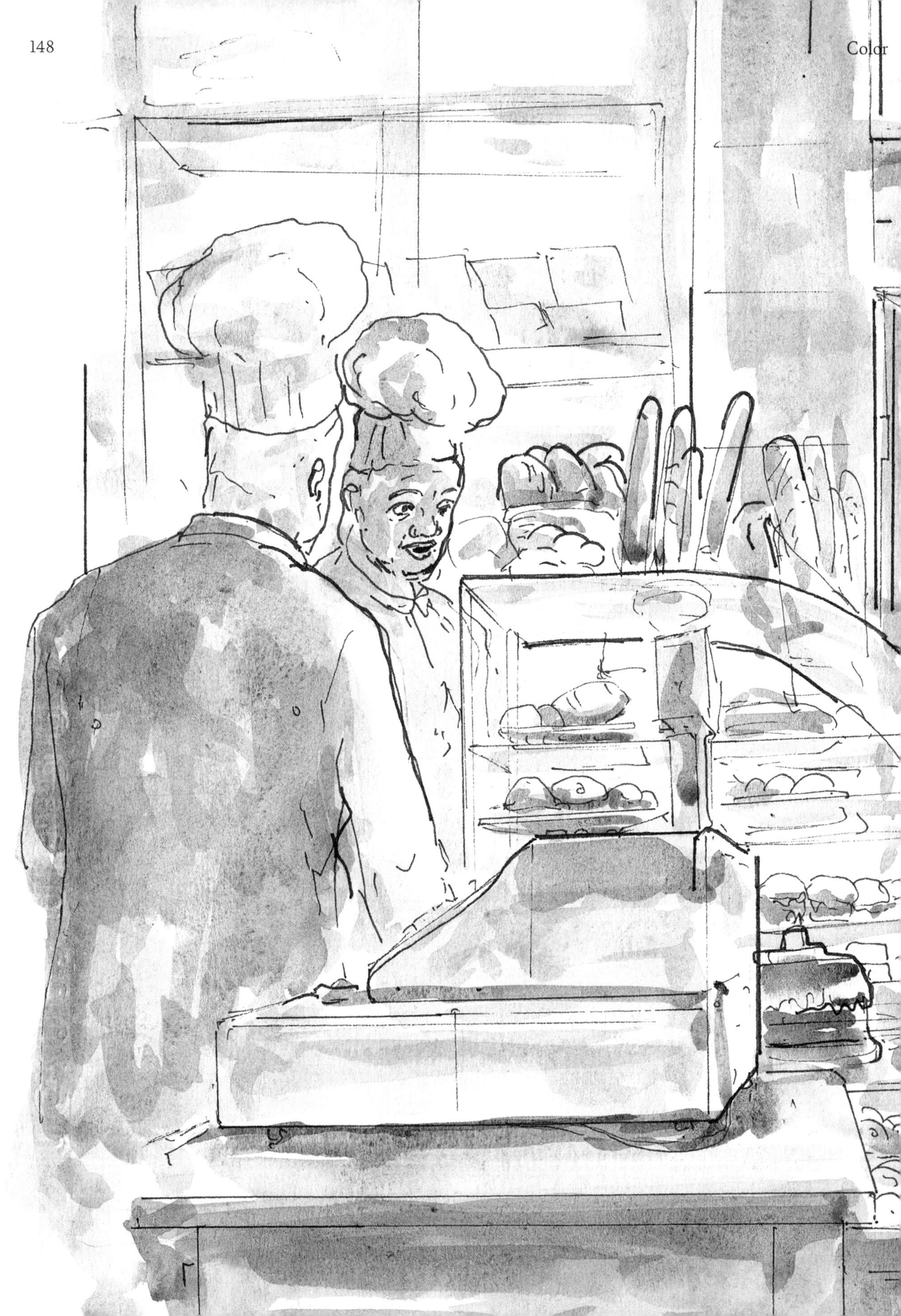

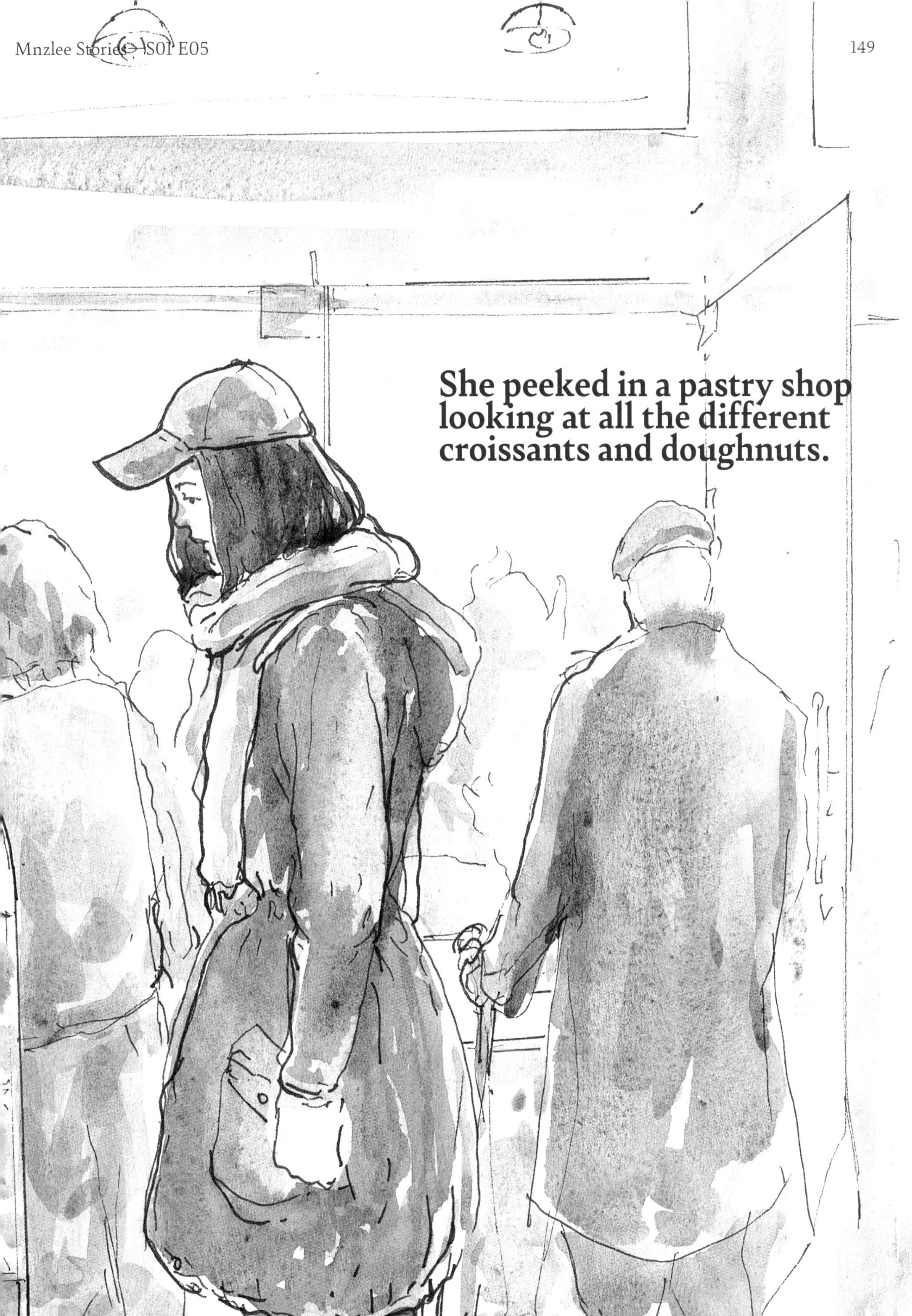

She peeked in a pastry shop looking at all the different croissants and doughnuts.

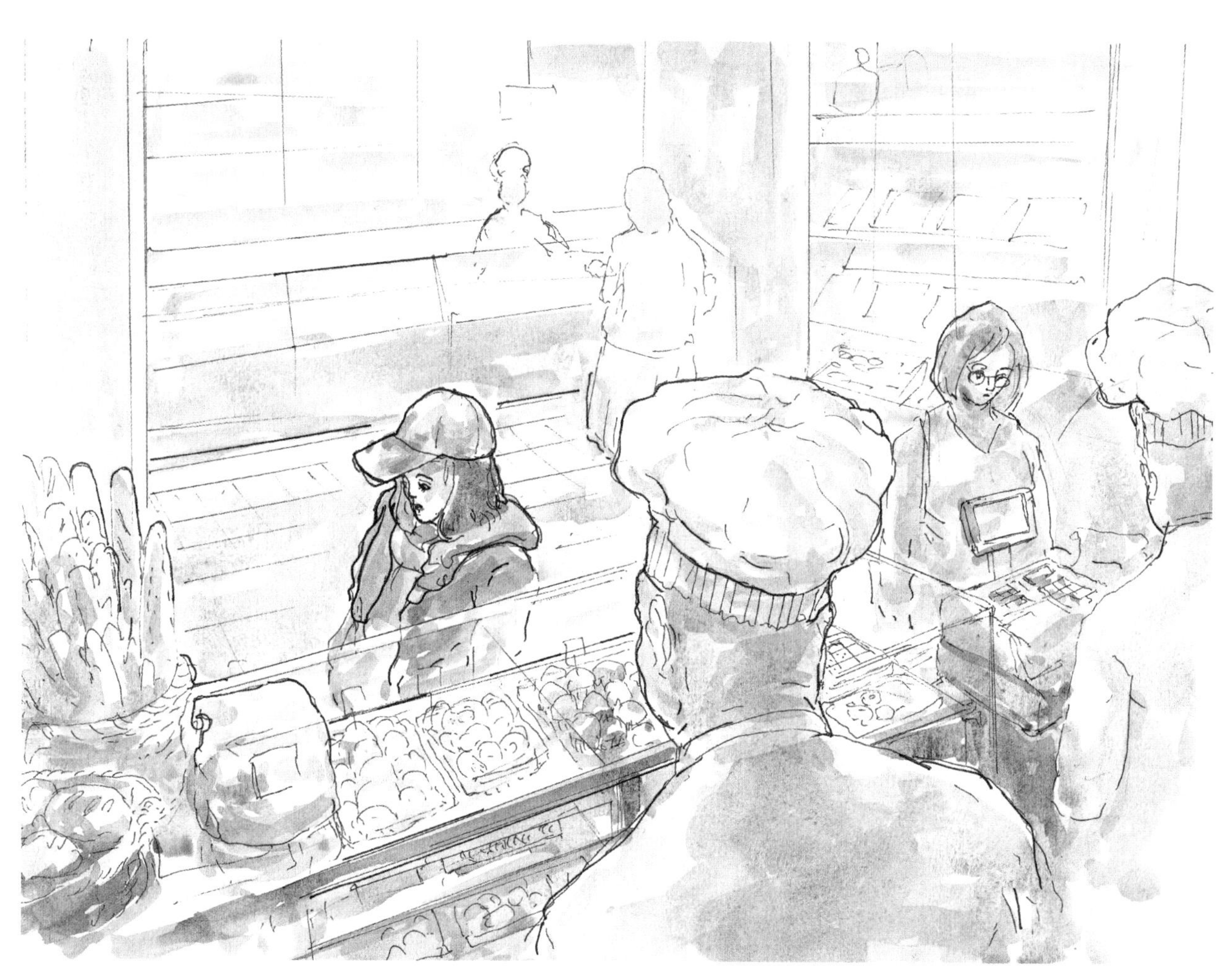

"Can I help you order?"

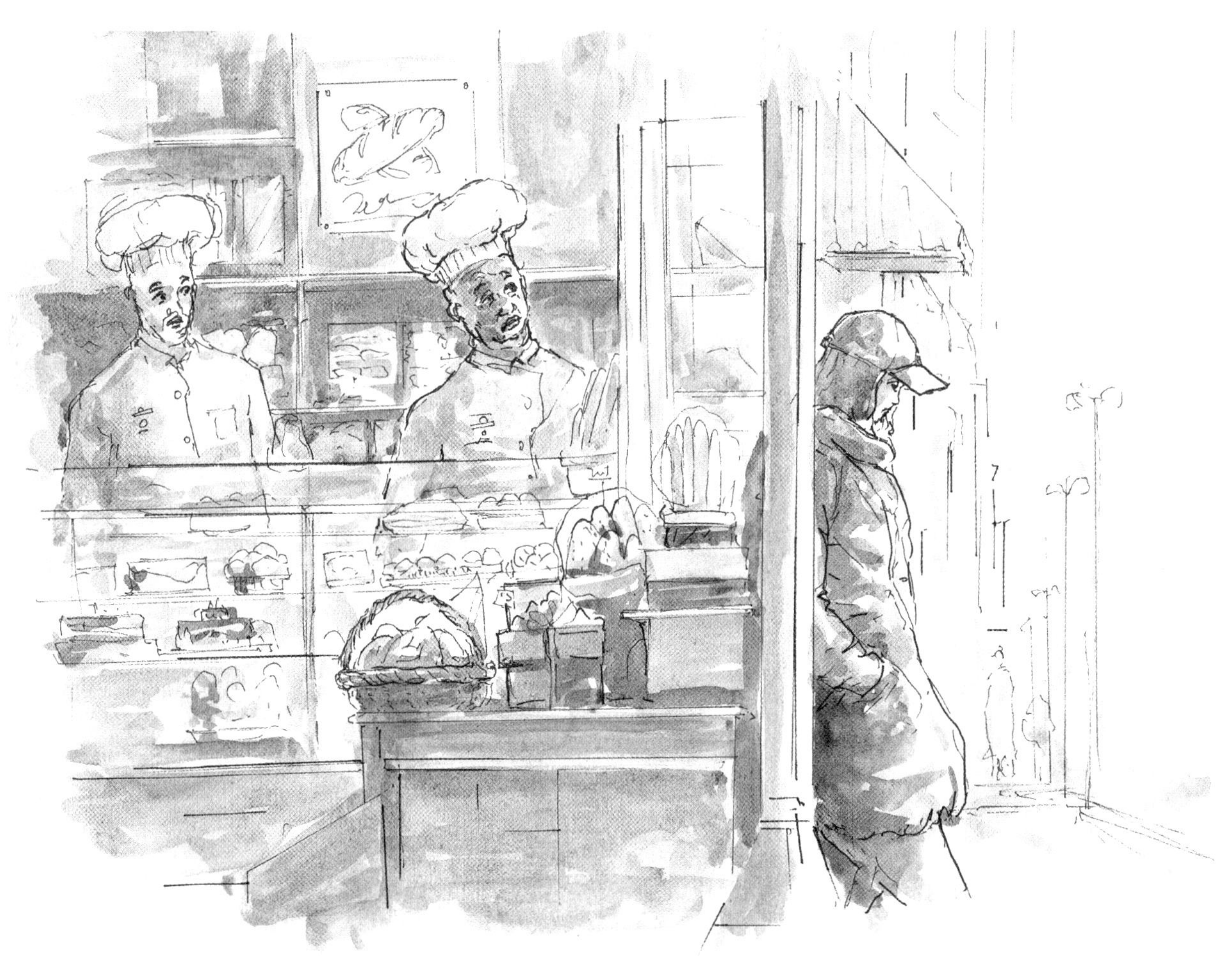

"No!" she yelled. "I am leaving."

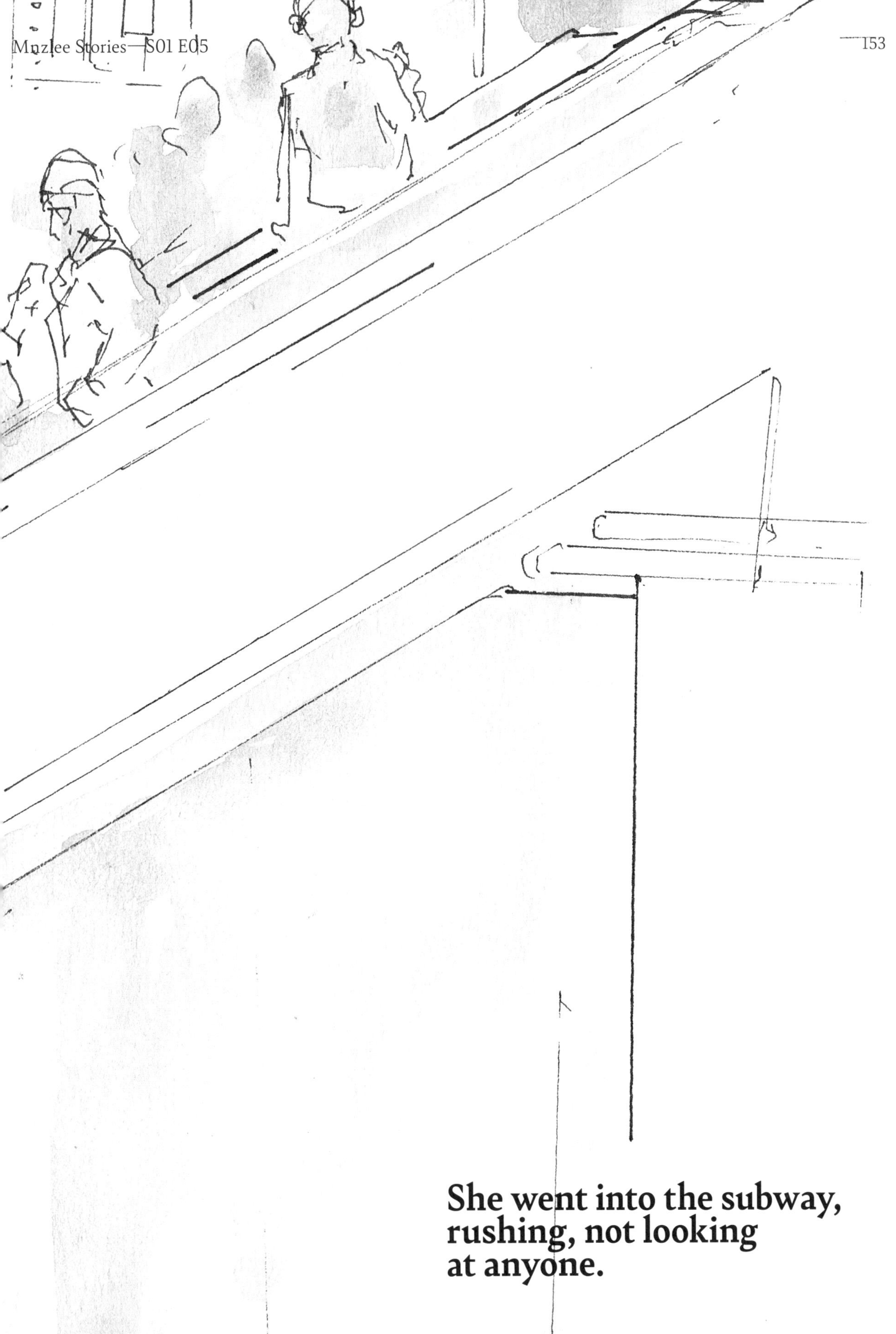

She went into the subway, rushing, not looking at anyone.

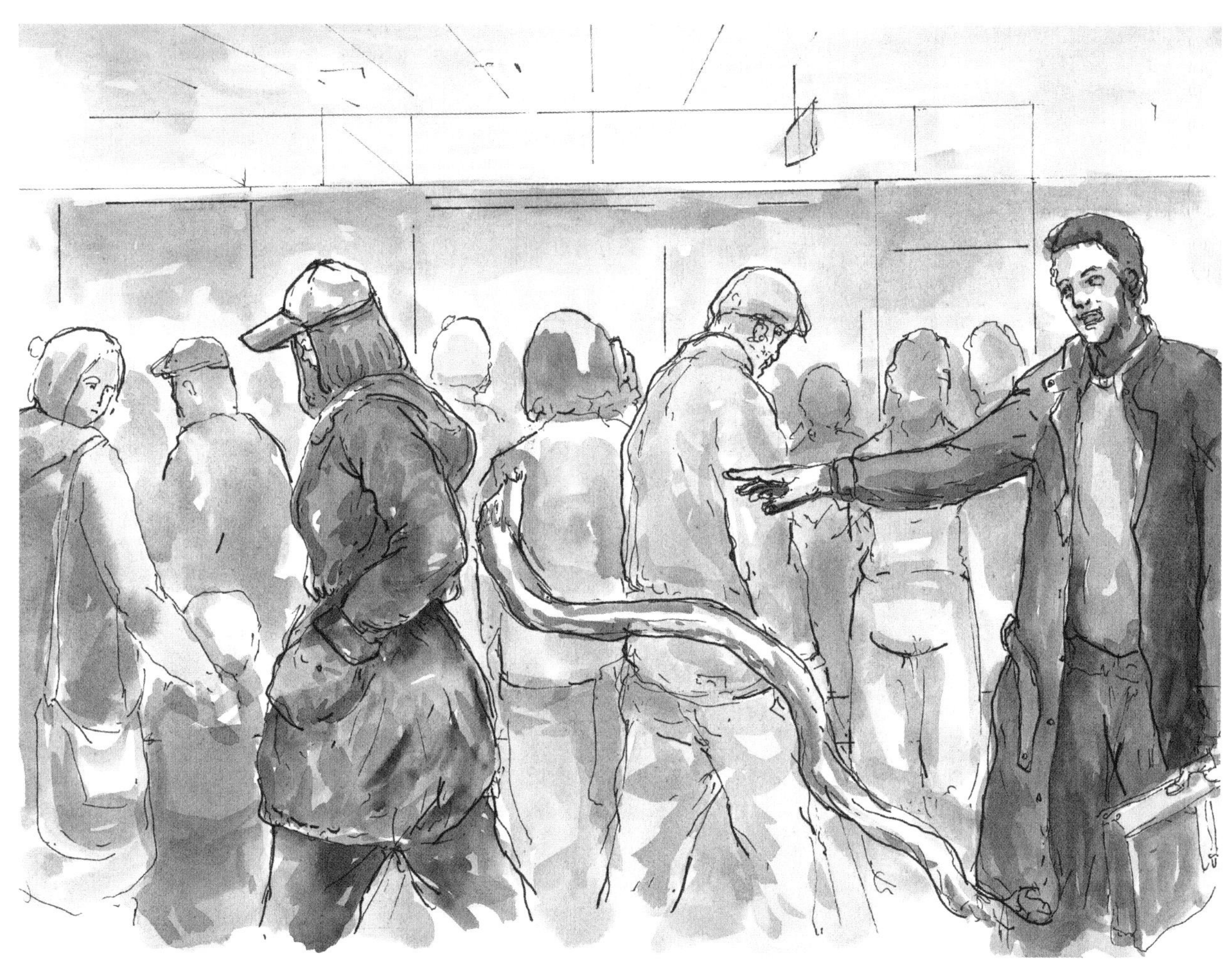

Someone ran after her trying to give her the scarf she dropped.

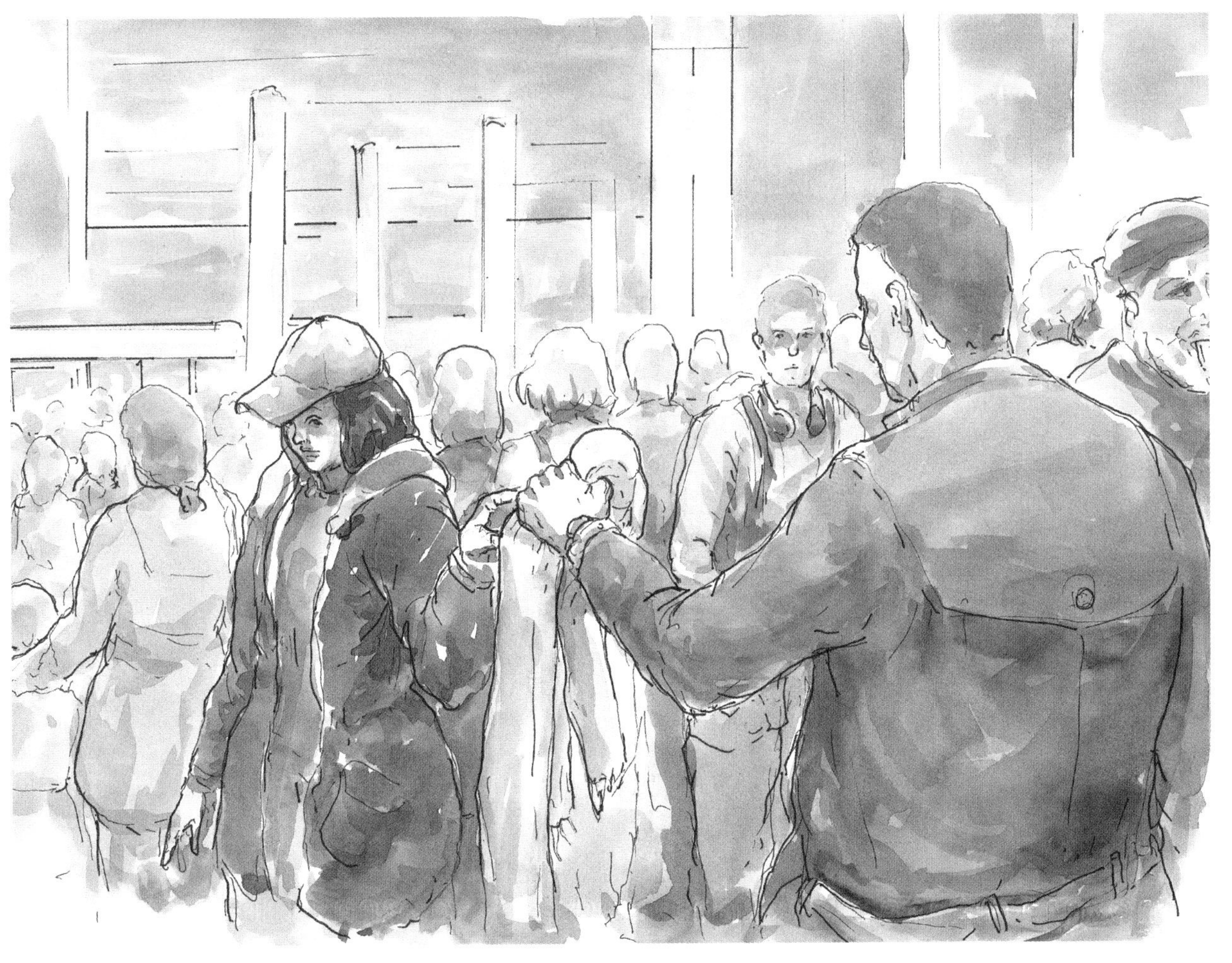

"You dropped this!
You dropped this!"

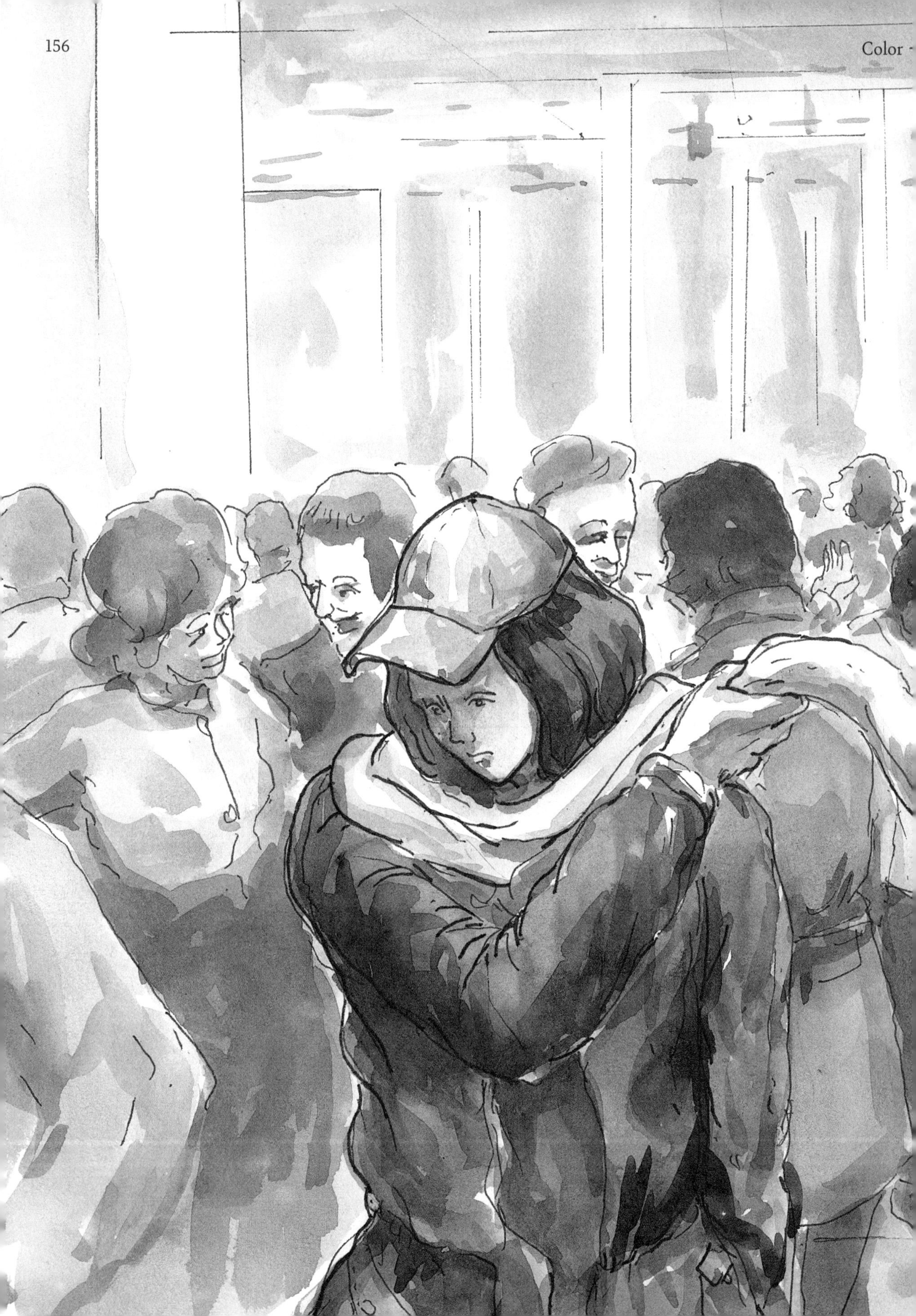

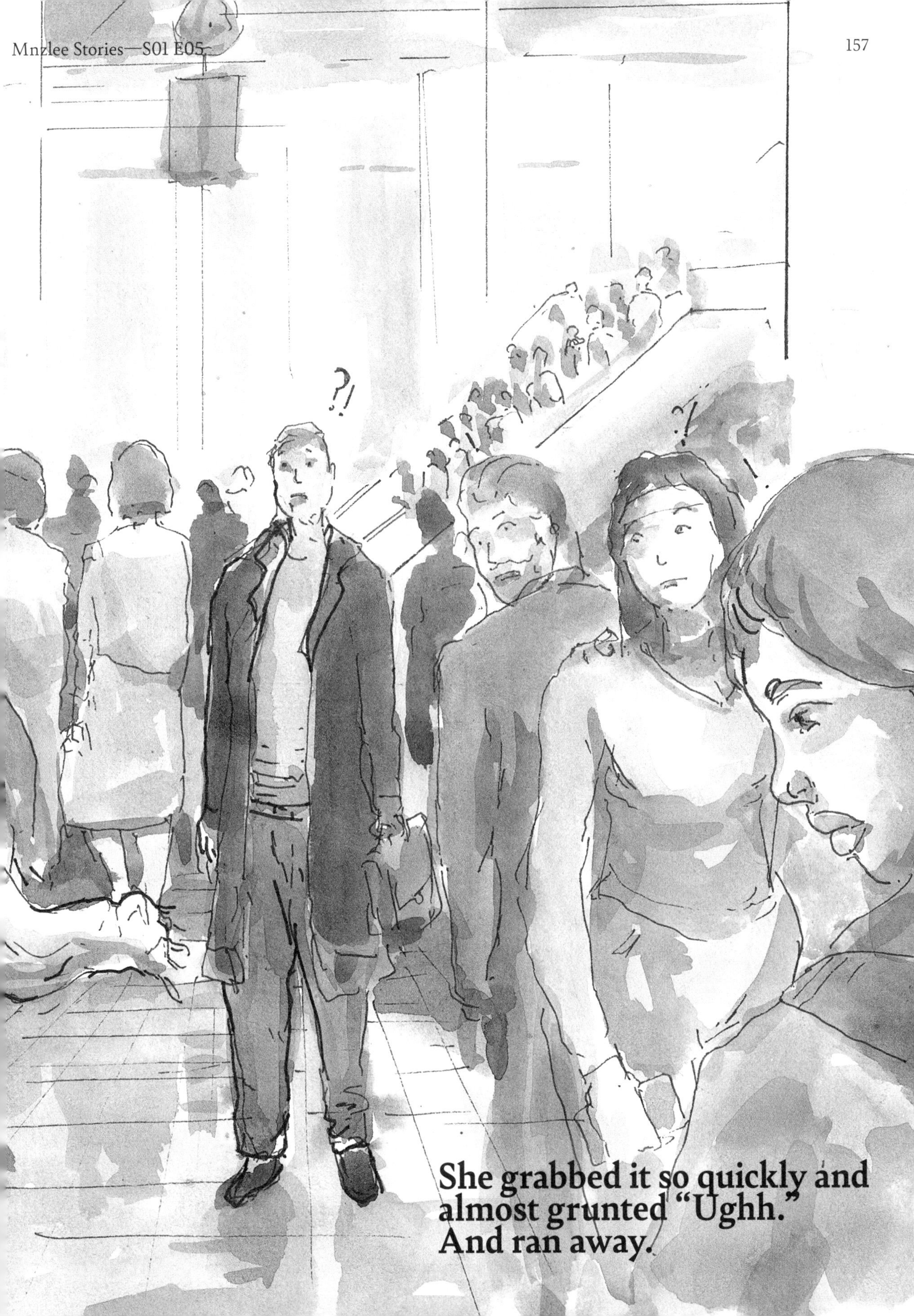

She grabbed it so quickly and
almost grunted "Ughh."
And ran away.

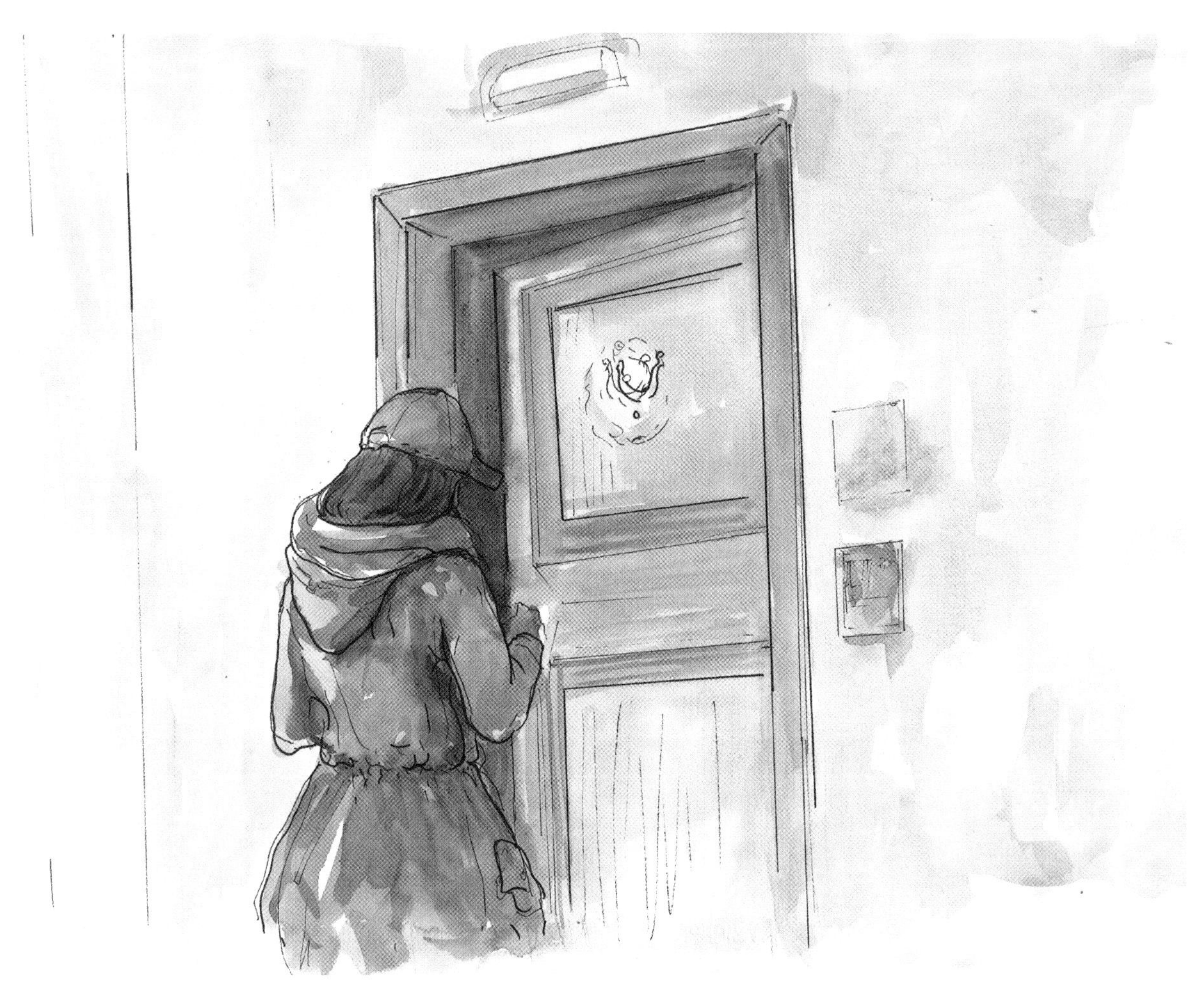

When she finally got home at the end of that long, long day, she unlocked her door.

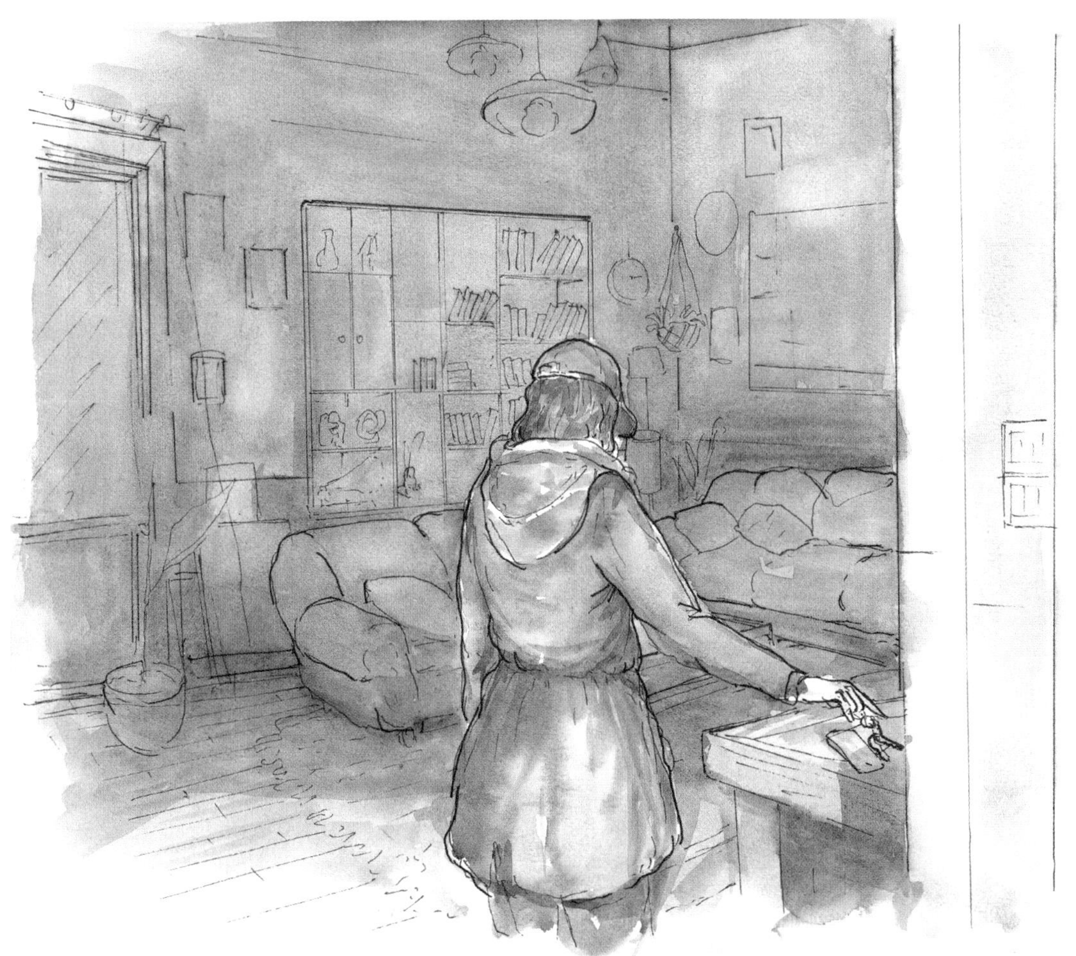

"I hope no-one saw it," she whispered to herself.

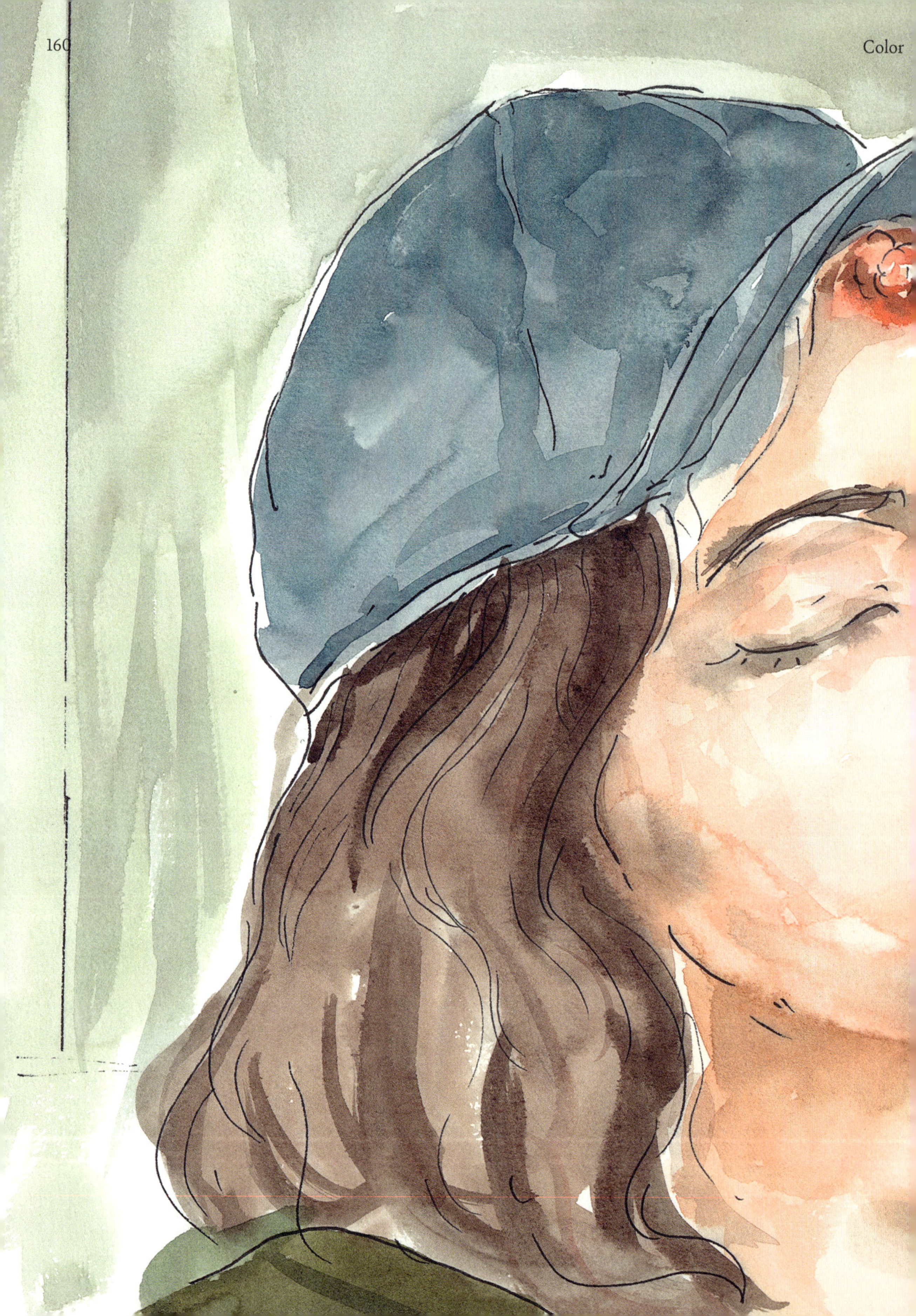

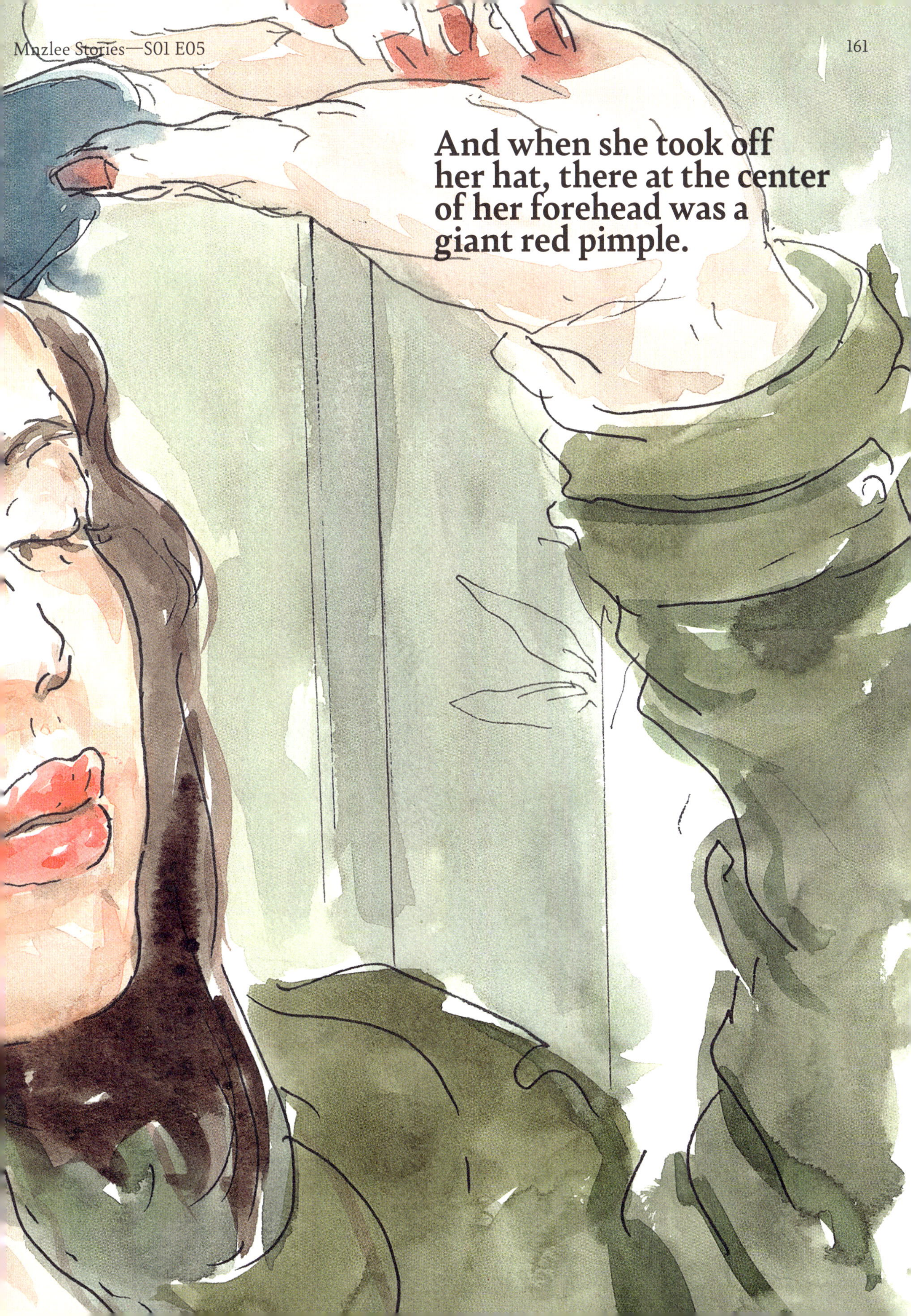
And when she took off her hat, there at the center of her forehead was a giant red pimple.

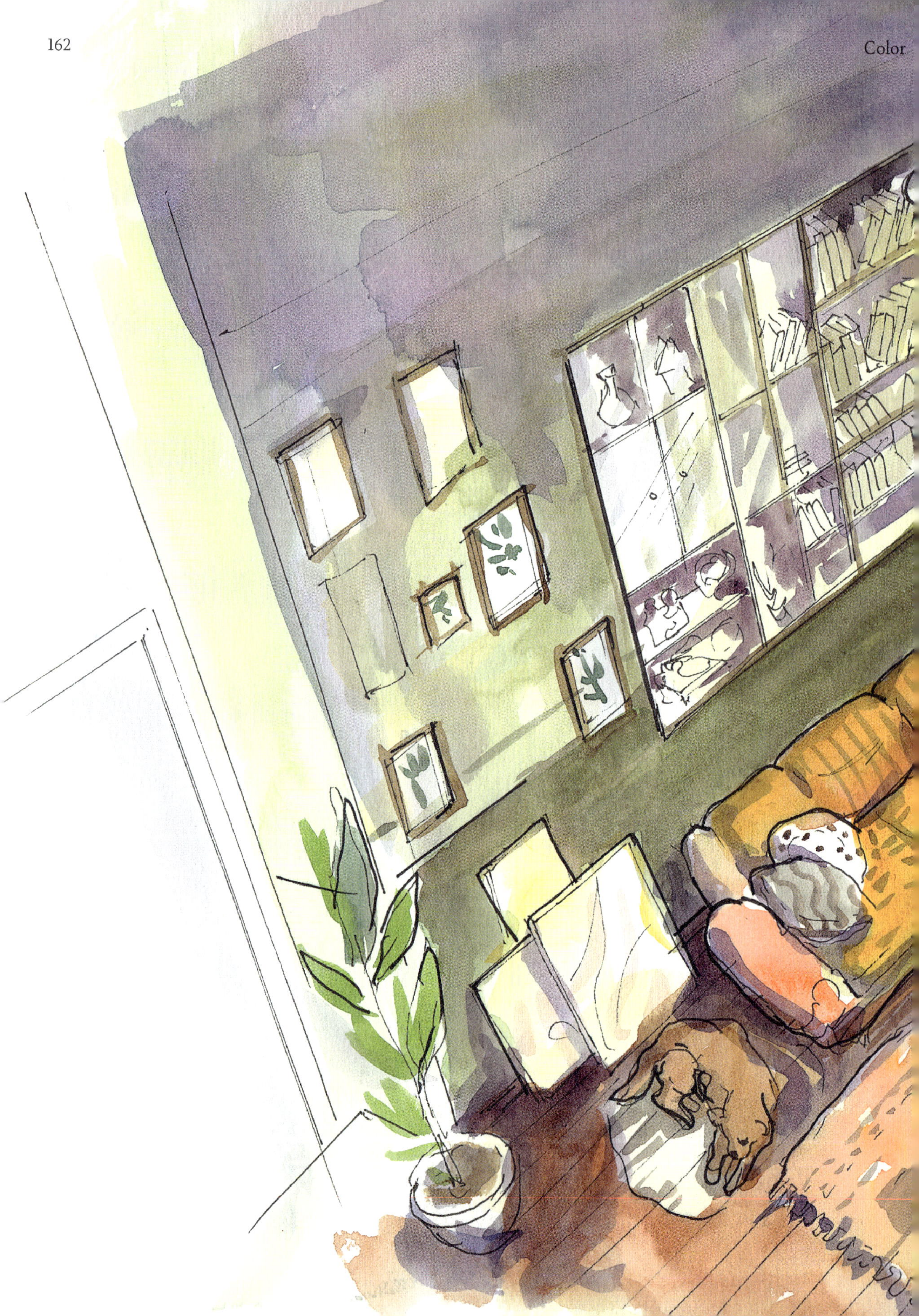

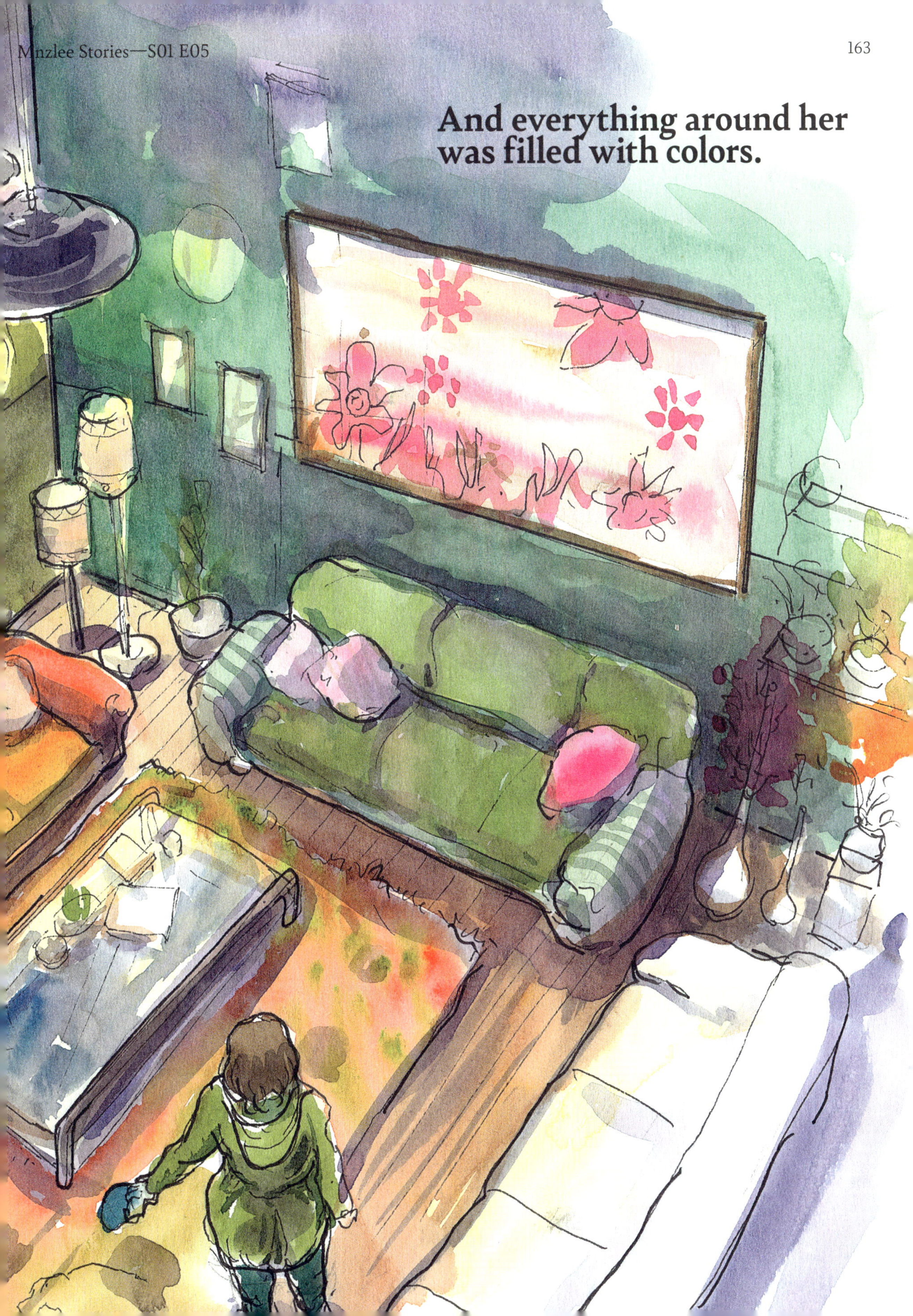
And everything around her
was filled with colors.

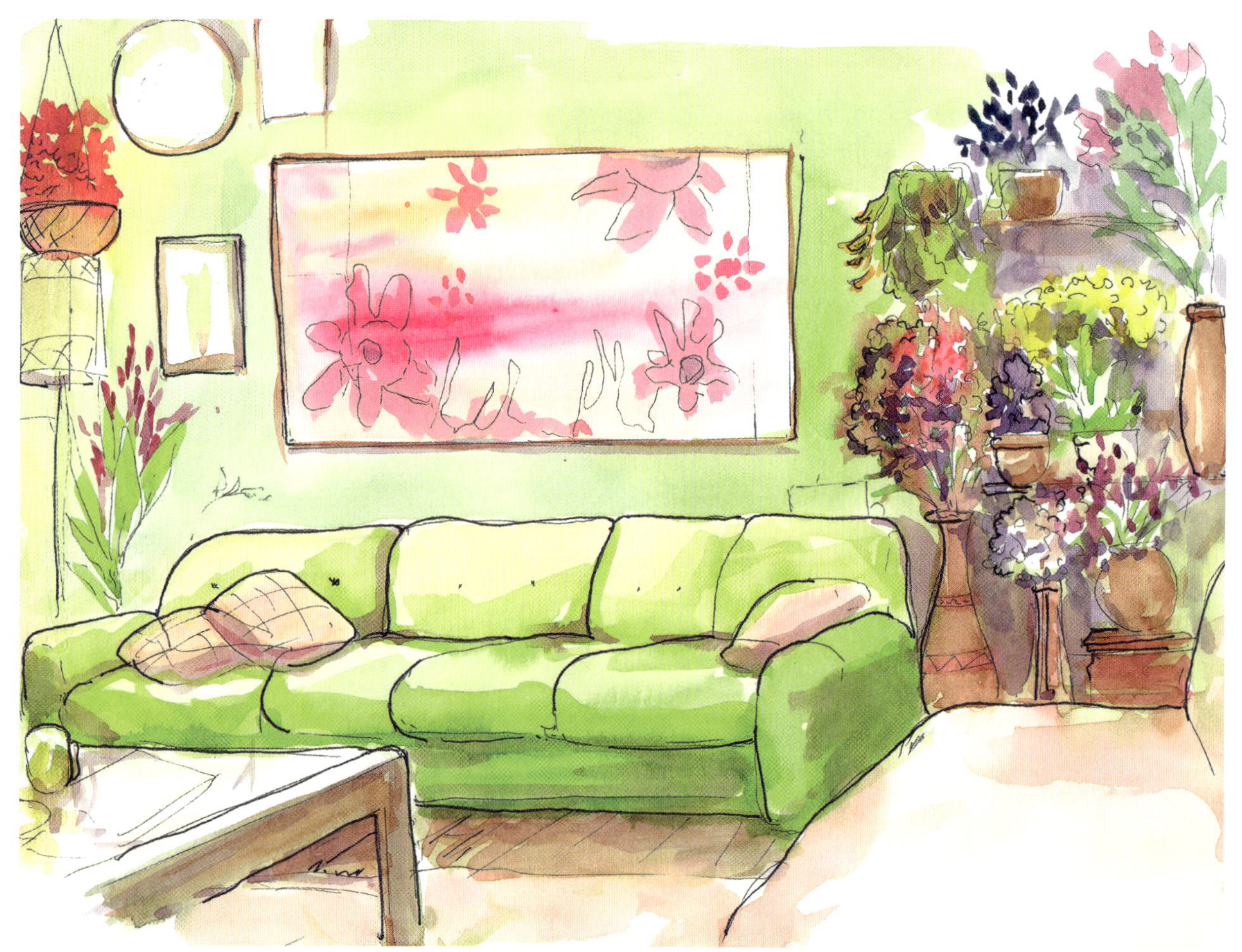

Paintings on the walls, flowers everywhere.

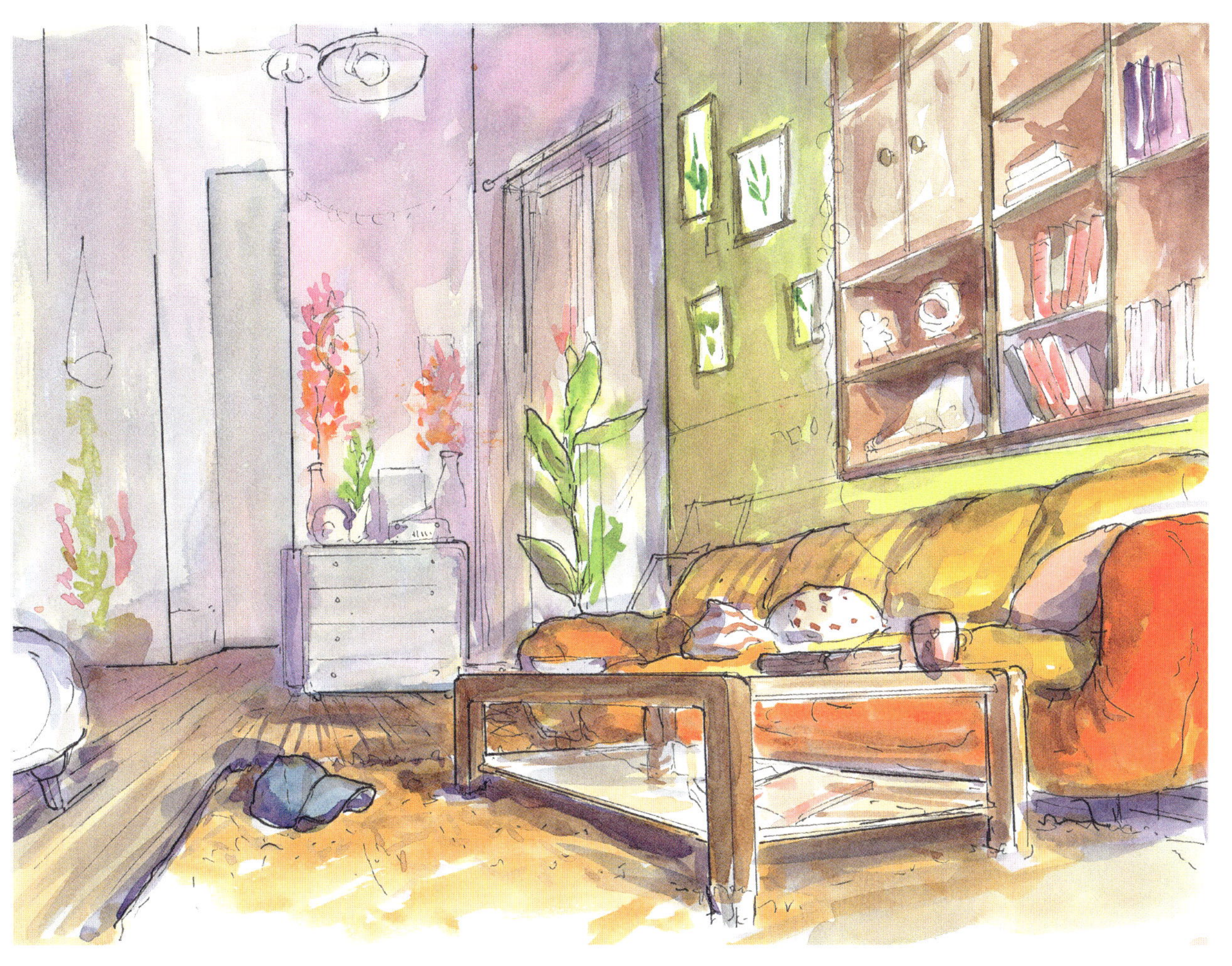

Lots and lots of cards.

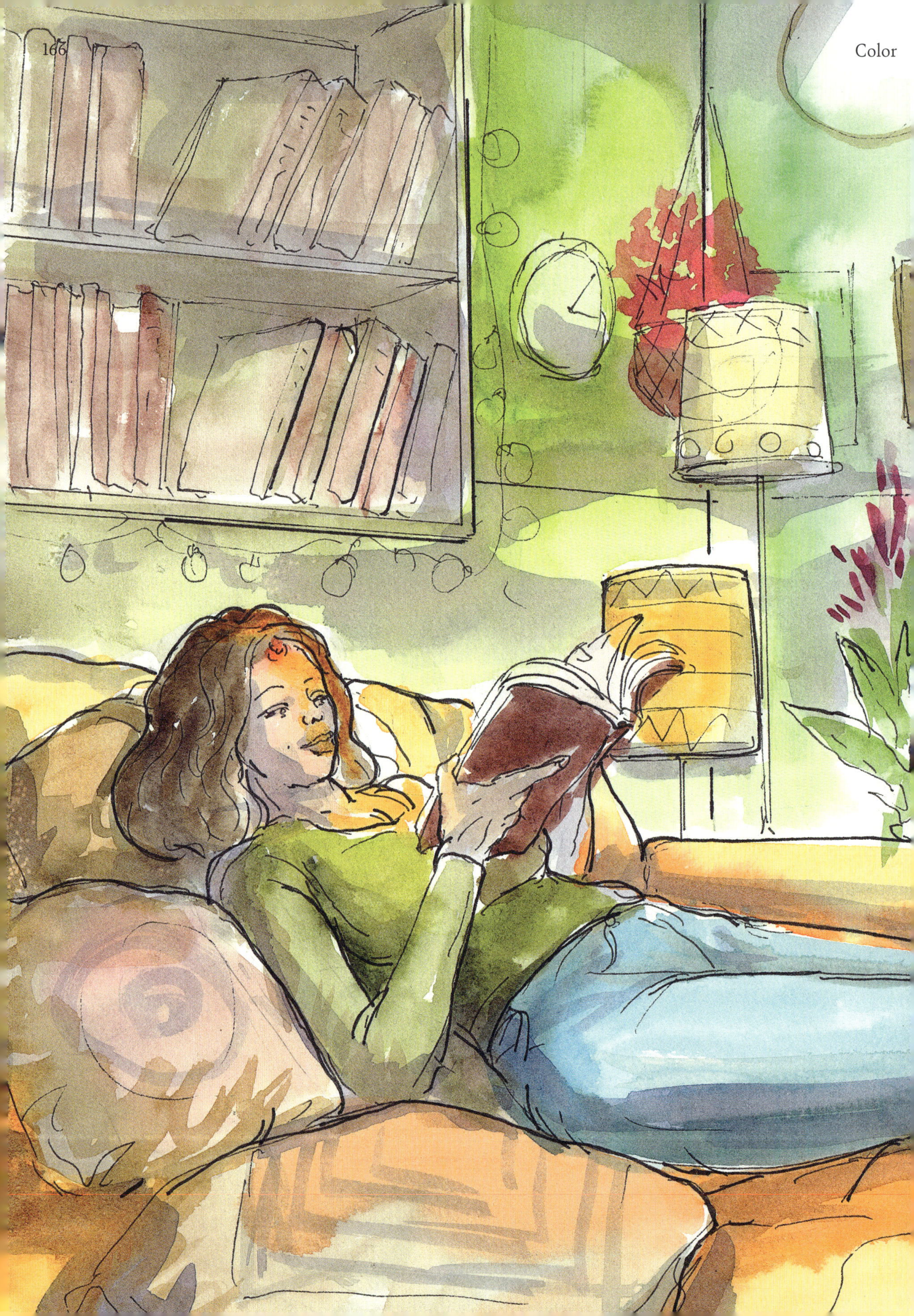

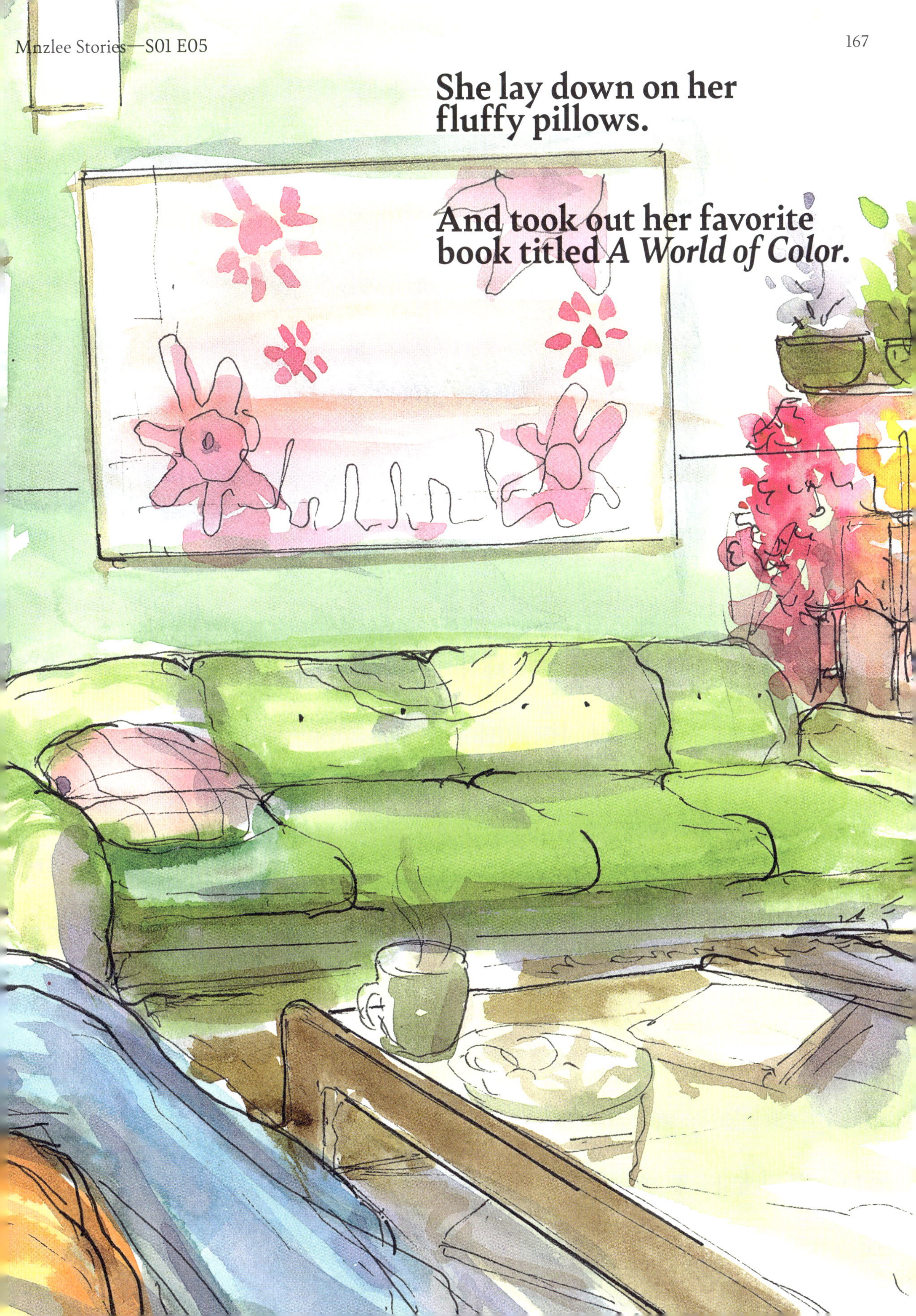
She lay down on her
fluffy pillows.

And took out her favorite
book titled A World of Color.

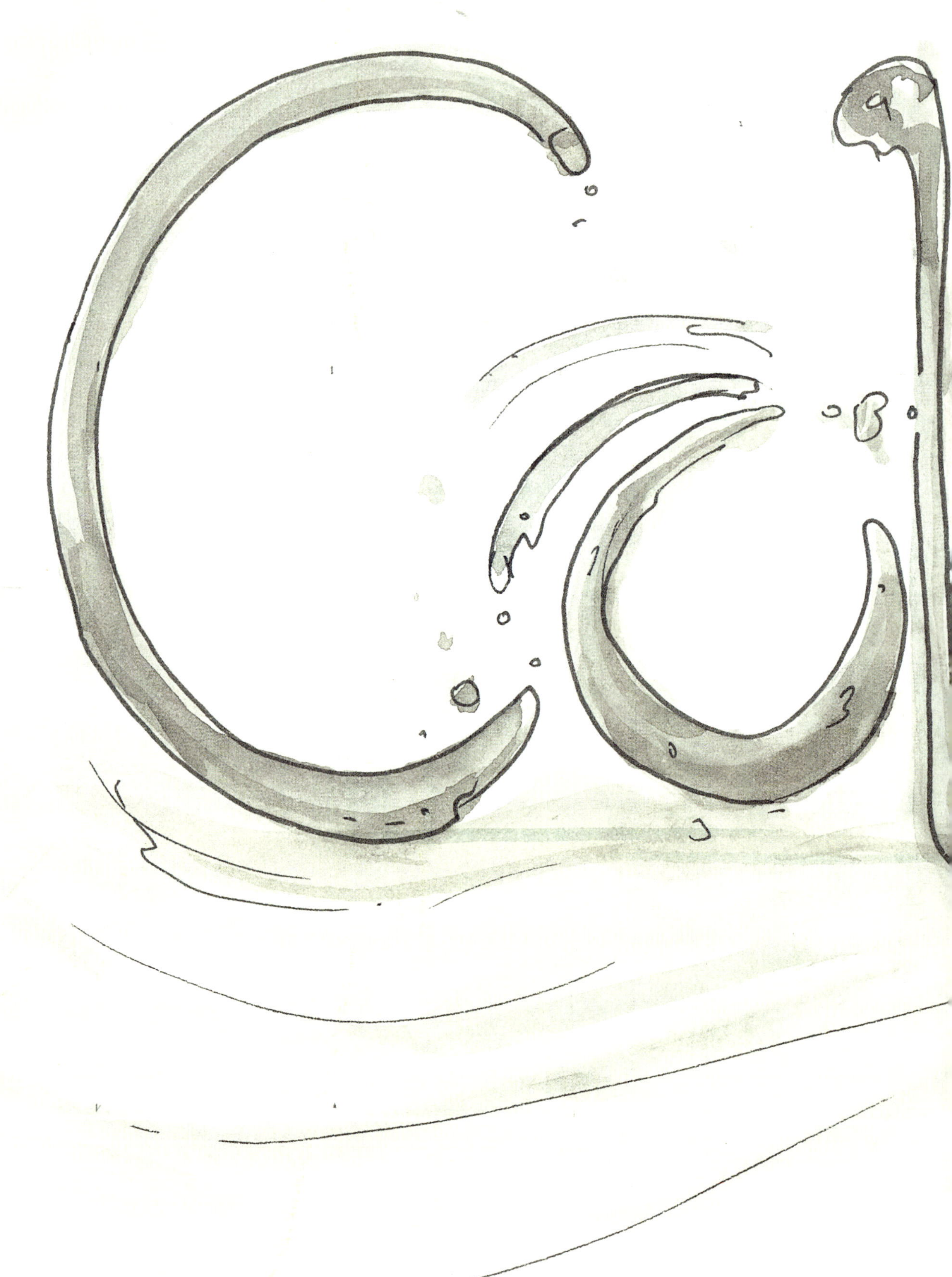

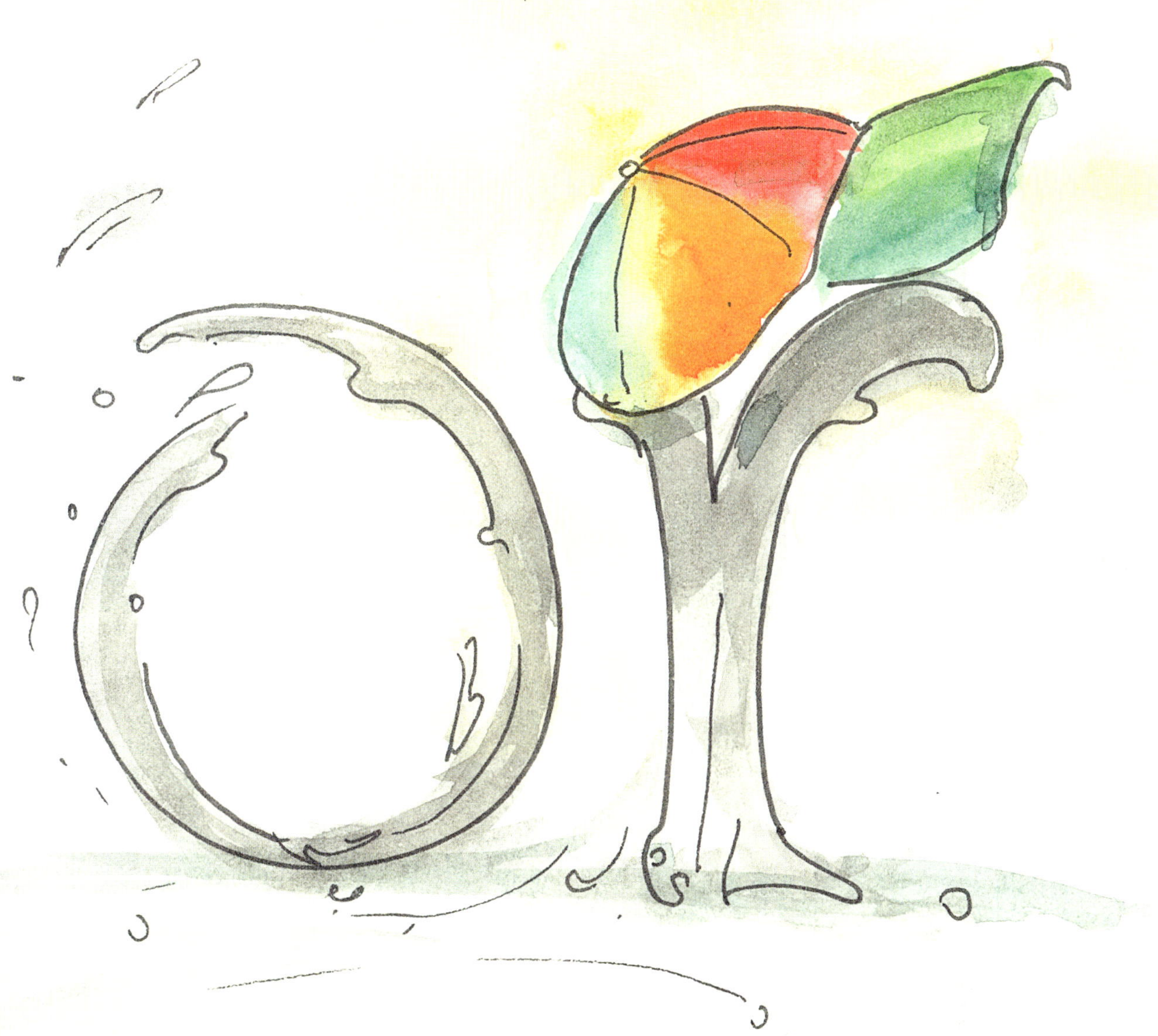

IMAGINE

Mnzlee Stories — S01 E06

In 760 CE, 8th century, a very special city existed named Madīnat al-Salām, City of Peace.

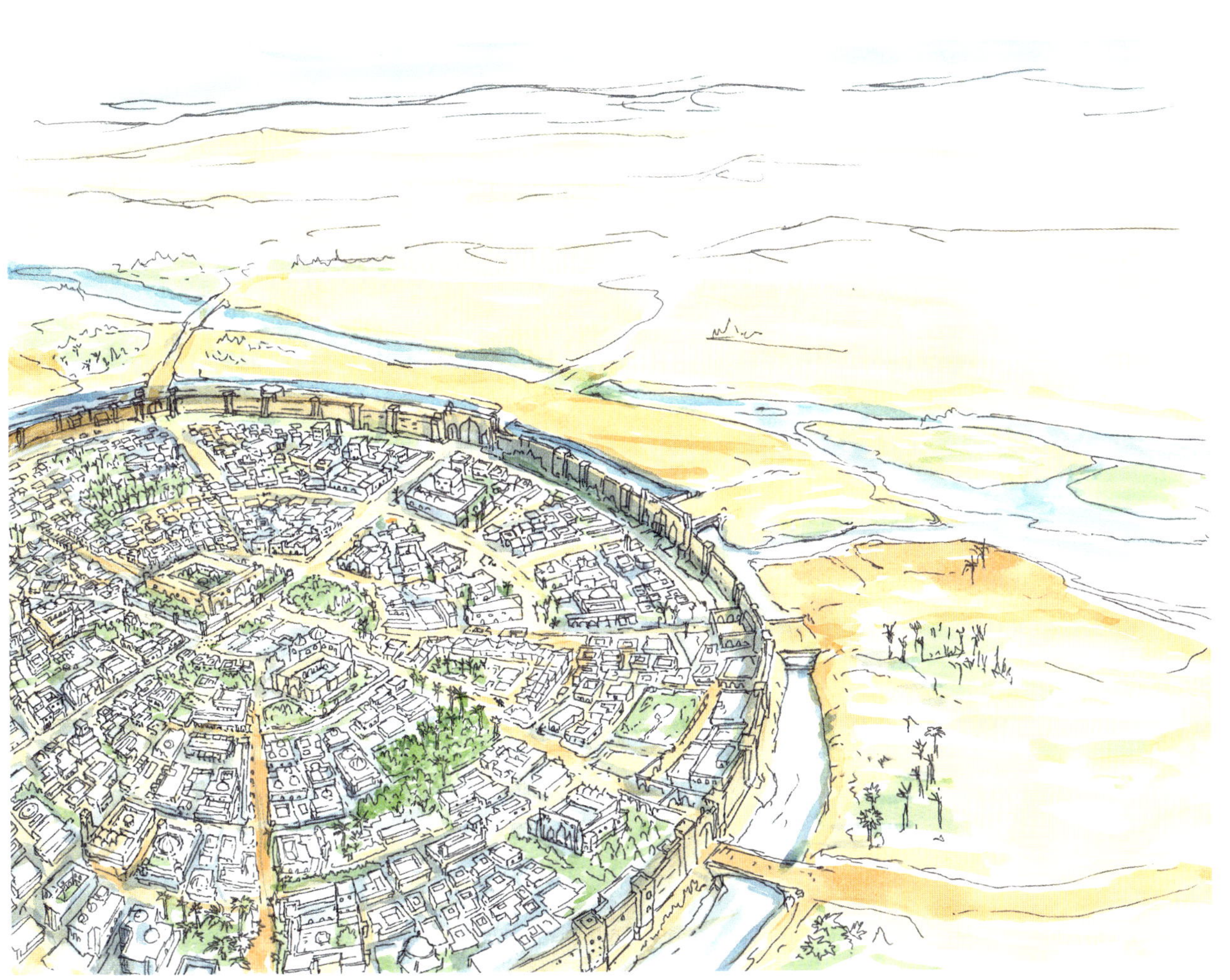

This city had a population of around 1 million.

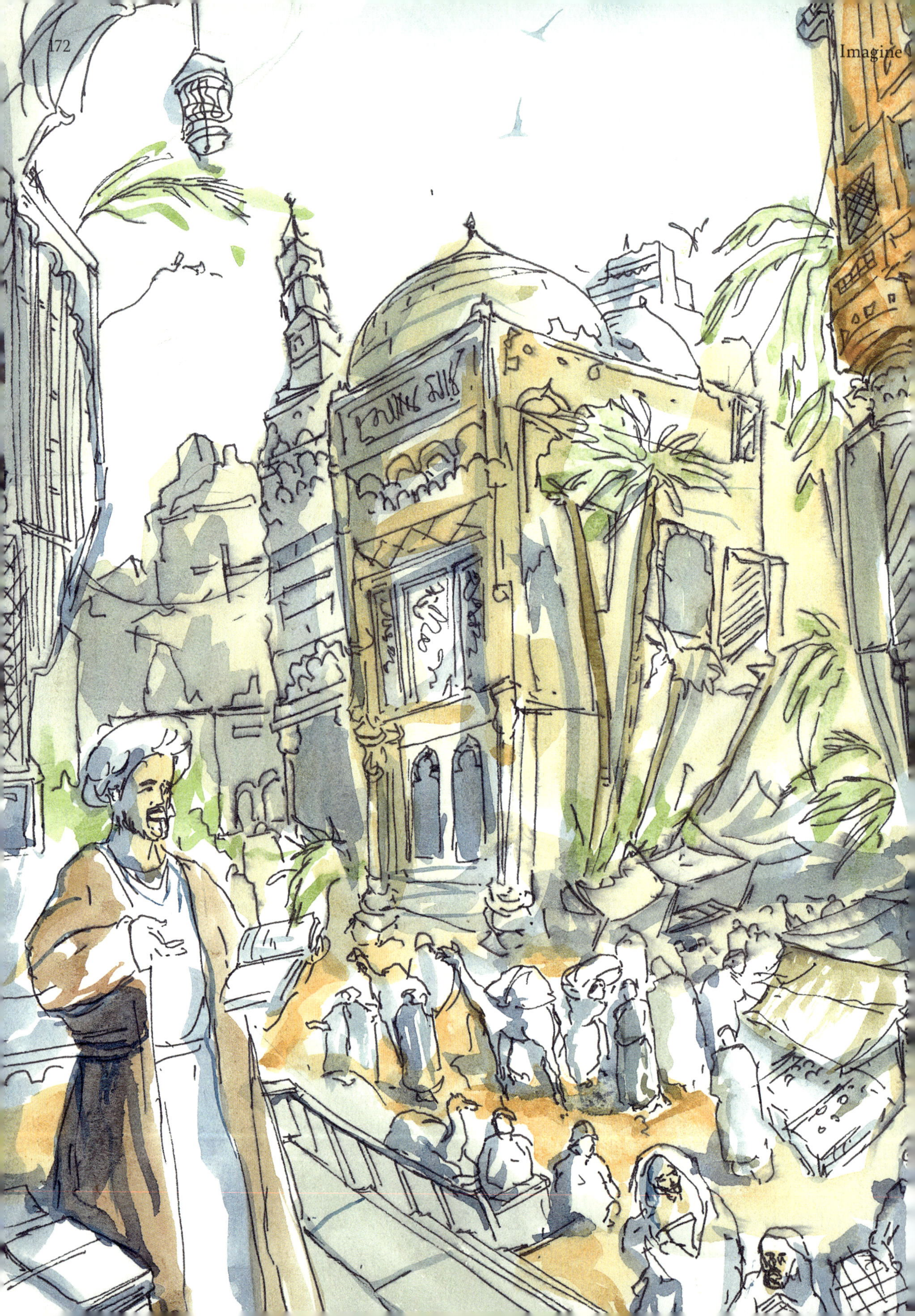

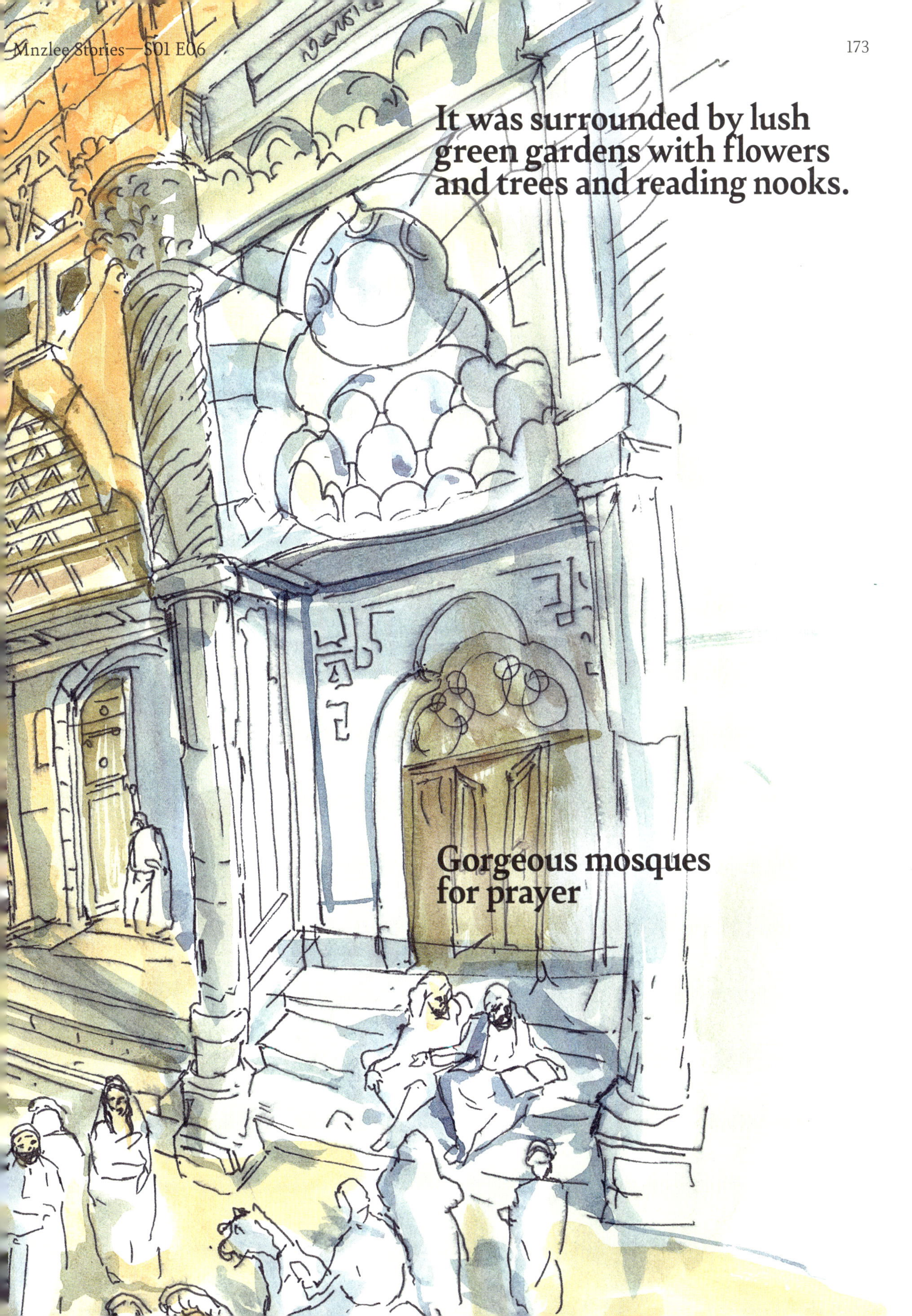
It was surrounded by lush green gardens with flowers and trees and reading nooks.

Gorgeous mosques for prayer

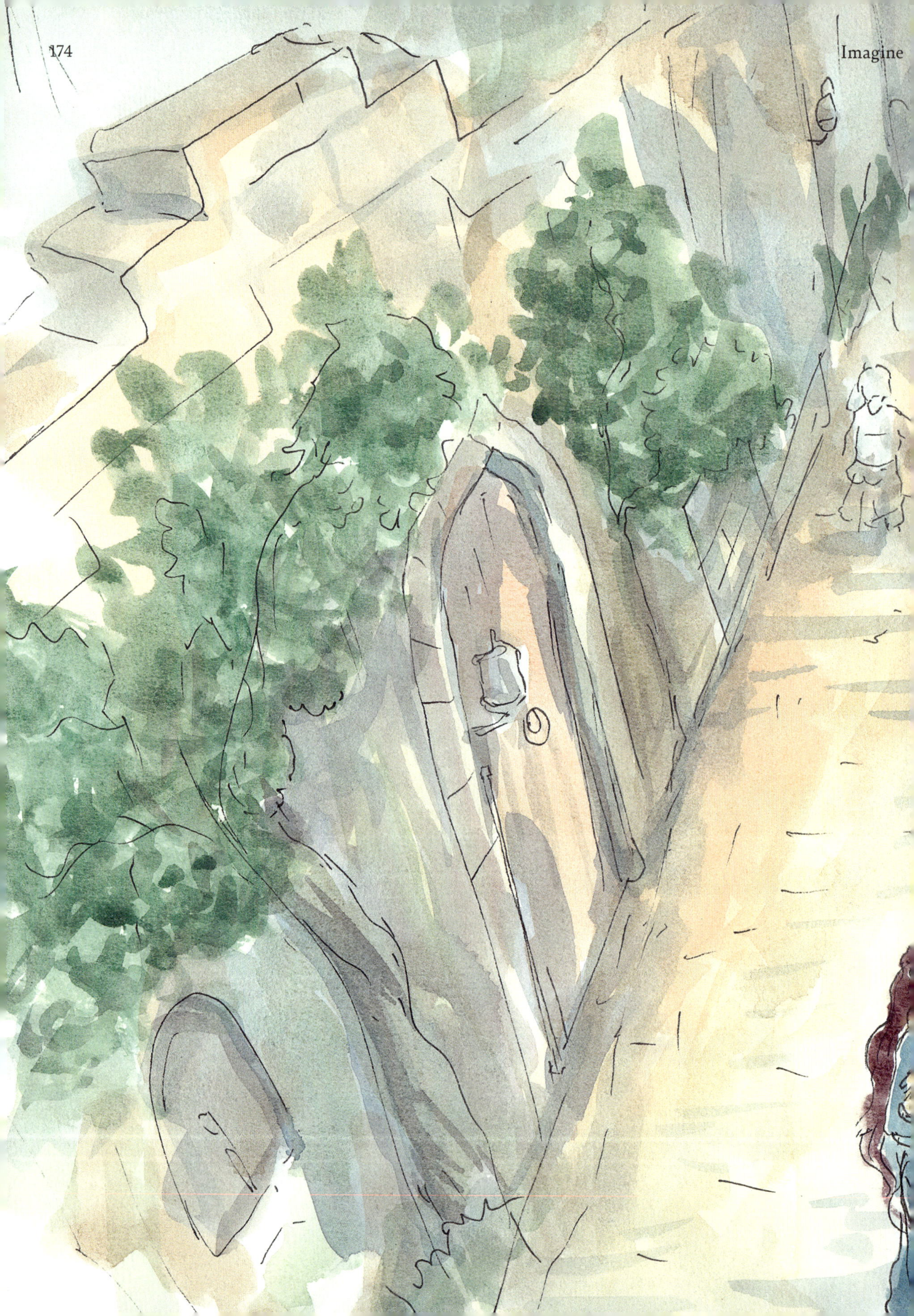

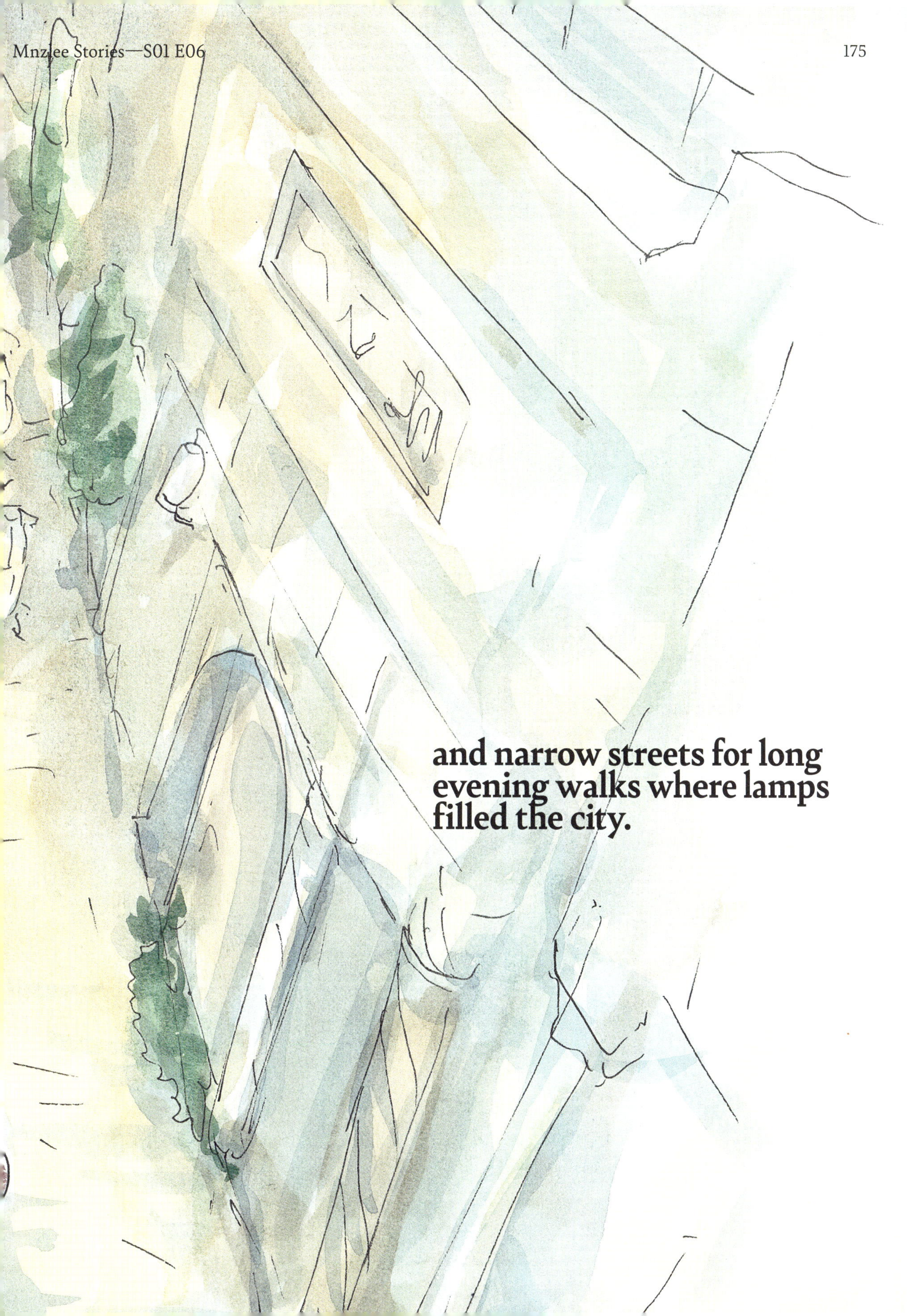
and narrow streets for long
evening walks where lamps
filled the city.

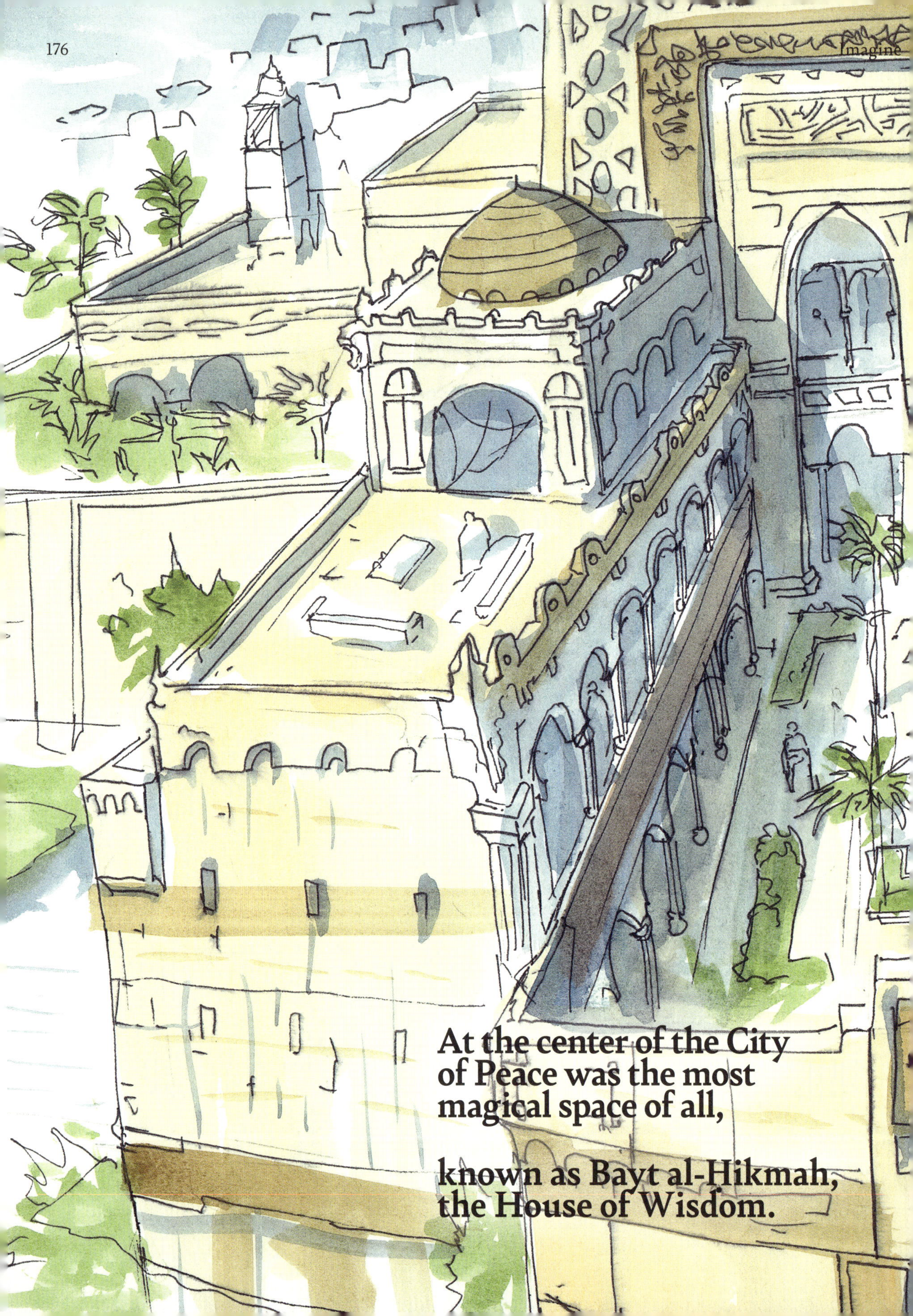
At the center of the City
of Peace was the most
magical space of all,

known as Bayt al-Hikmah,
the House of Wisdom.

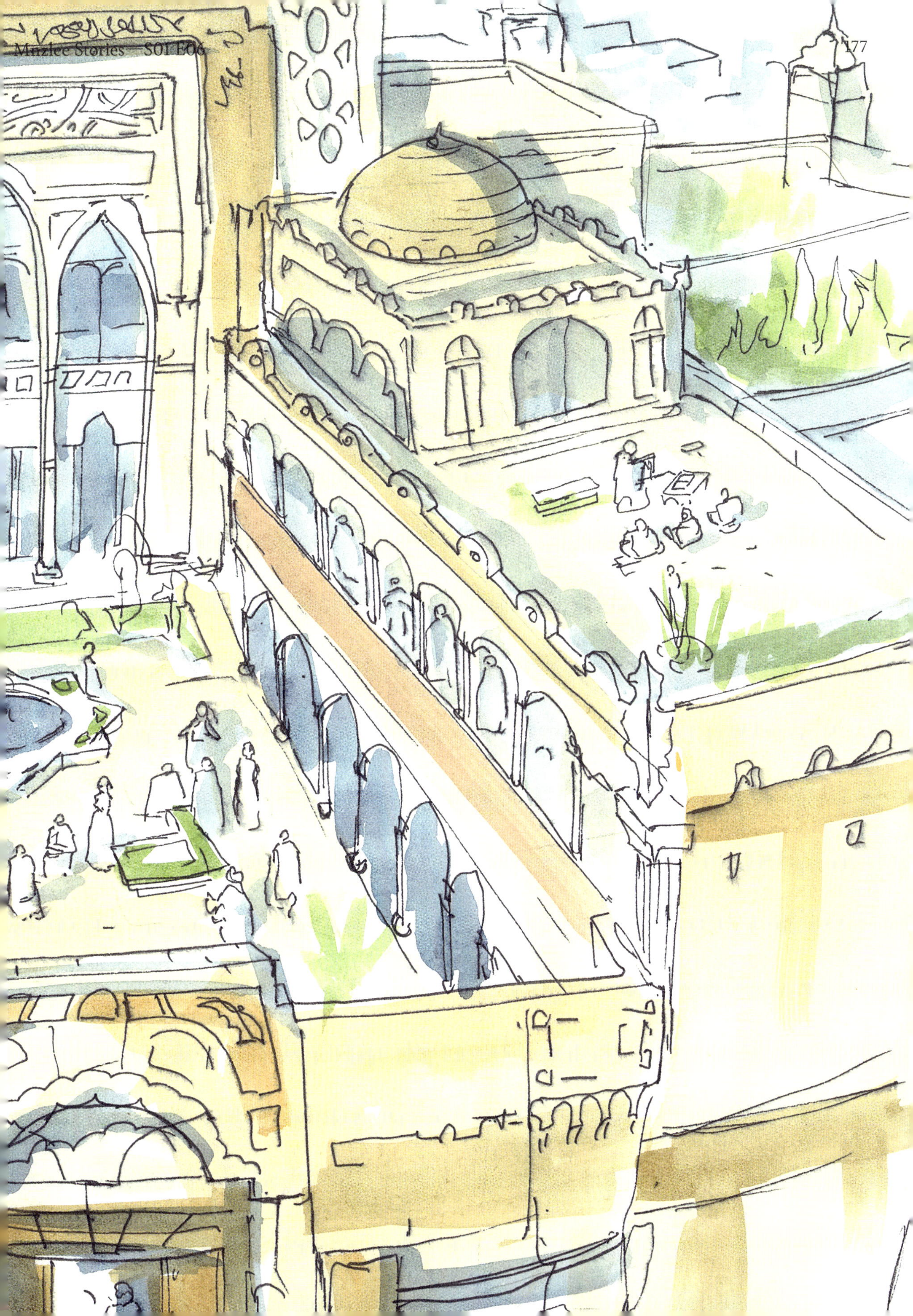

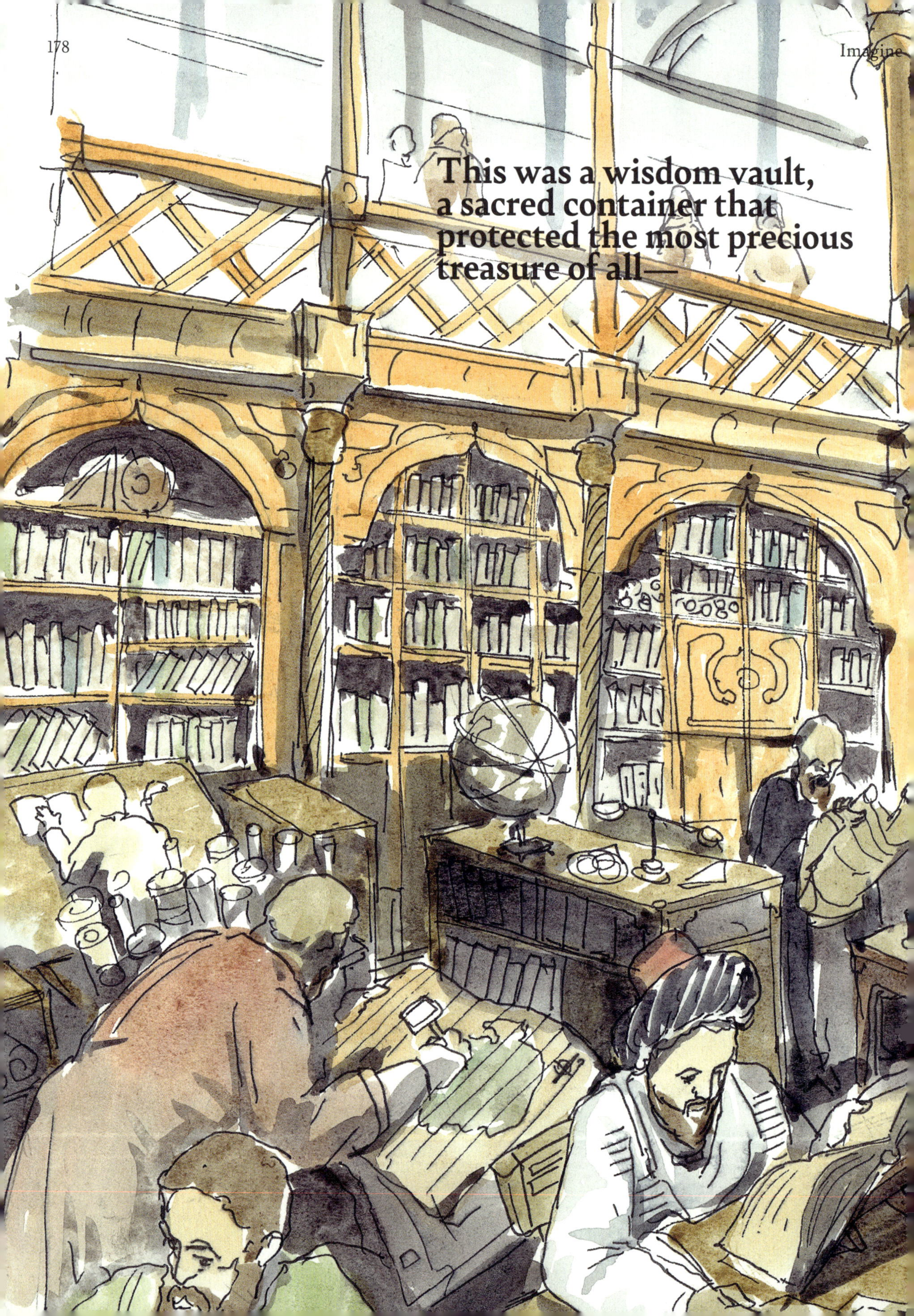
This was a wisdom vault,
a sacred container that
protected the most precious
treasure of all—

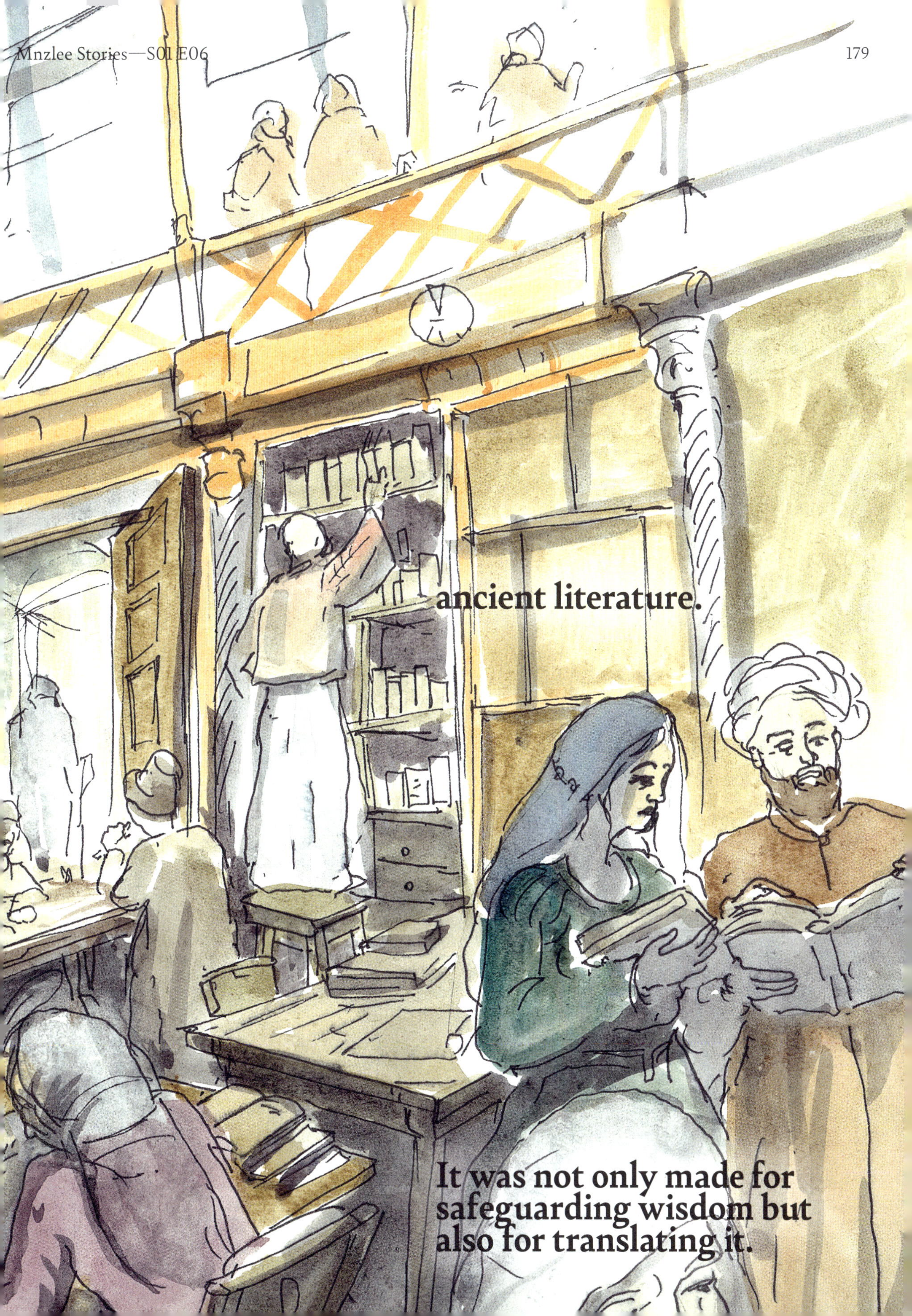
ancient literature.
It was not only made for safeguarding wisdom but also for translating it.

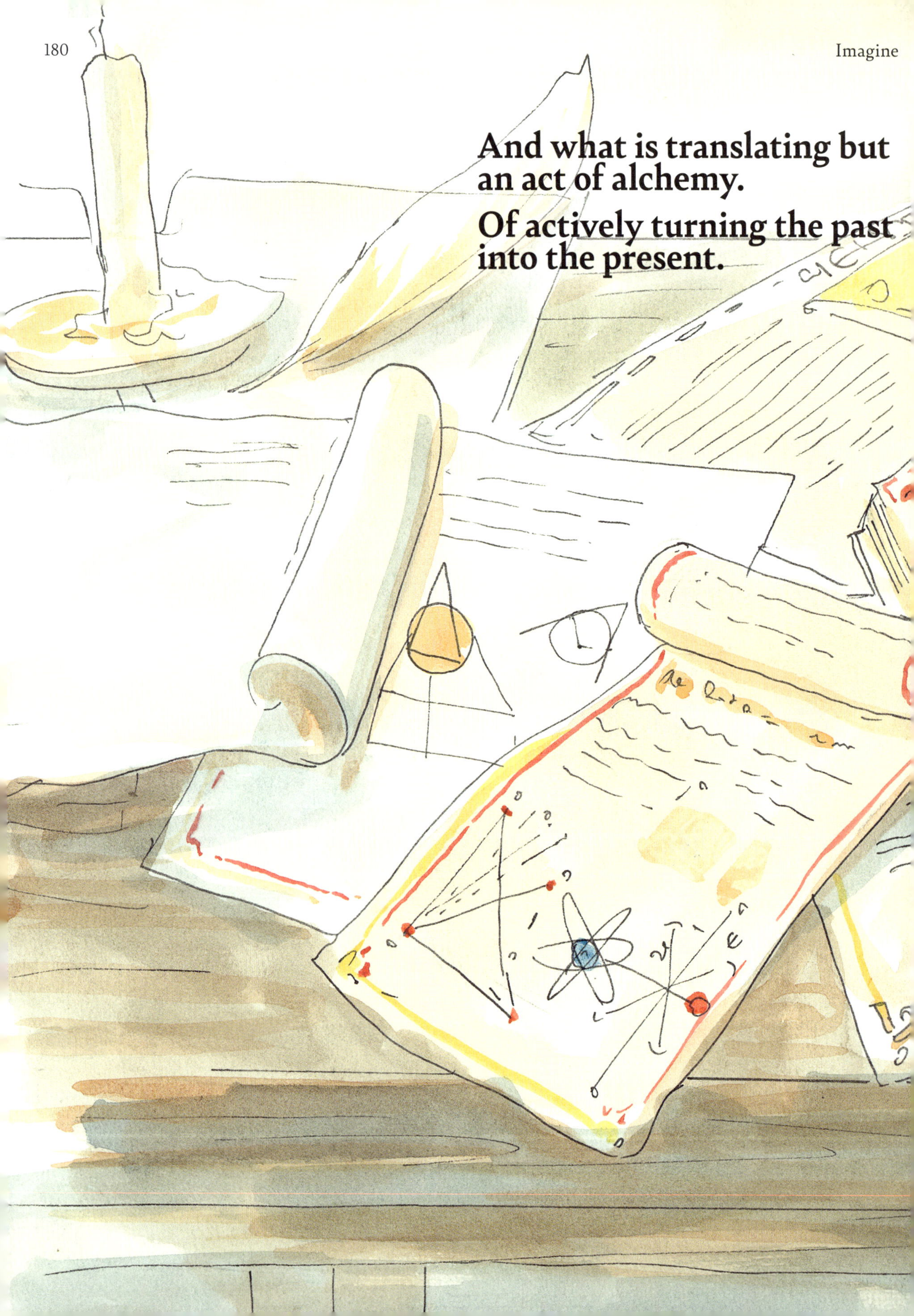

And what is translating but an act of alchemy.

Of actively turning the past into the present.

And so important ancient texts, in math, science, astronomy, engineering, philosophy, were all actively brought back to life, into the Arabic language, and into the City of Peace.

These texts contained works by Plato, Aristotle, Ptolemy, Hippocrates, Euclid, many important Hindu texts from India and more.

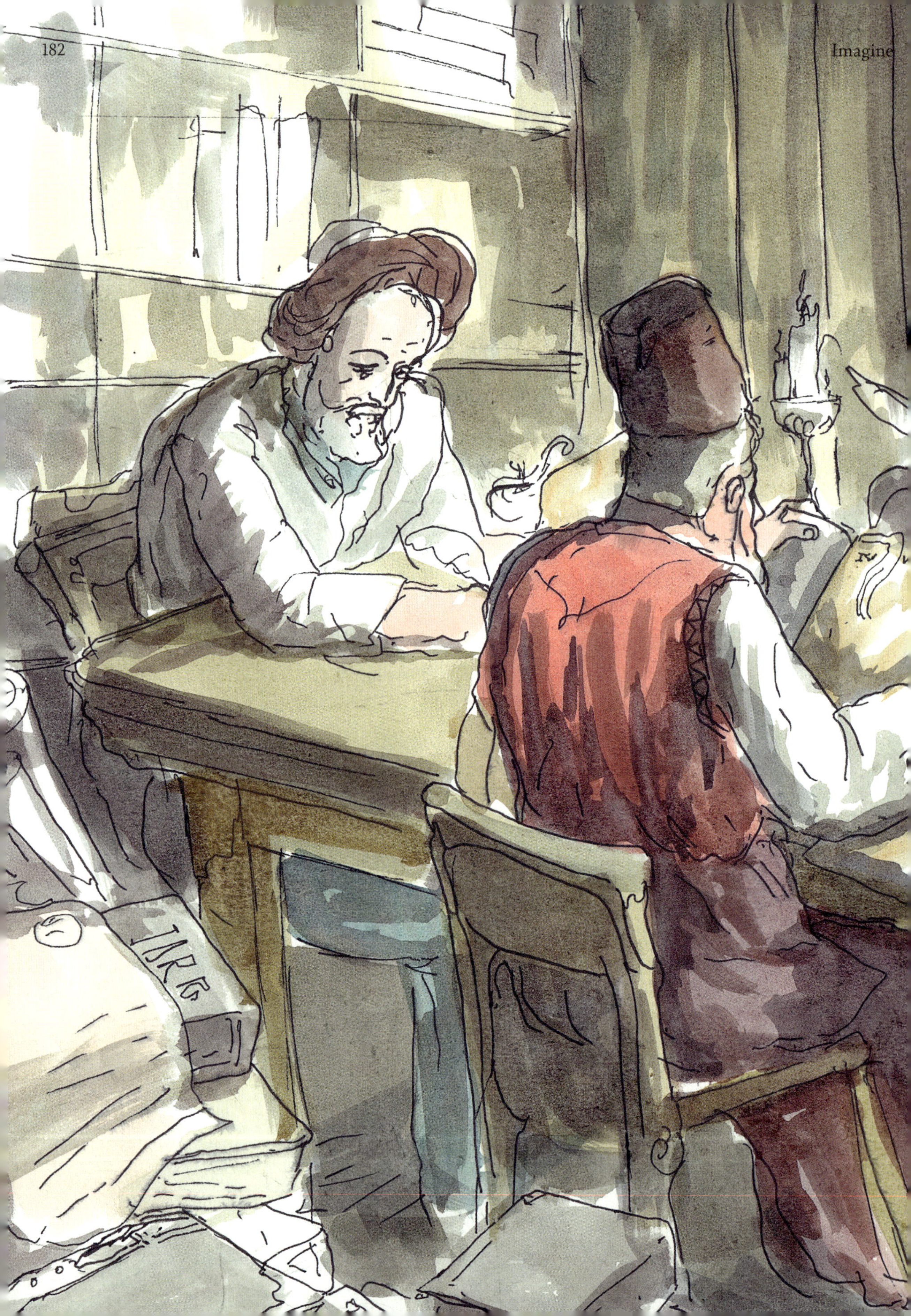

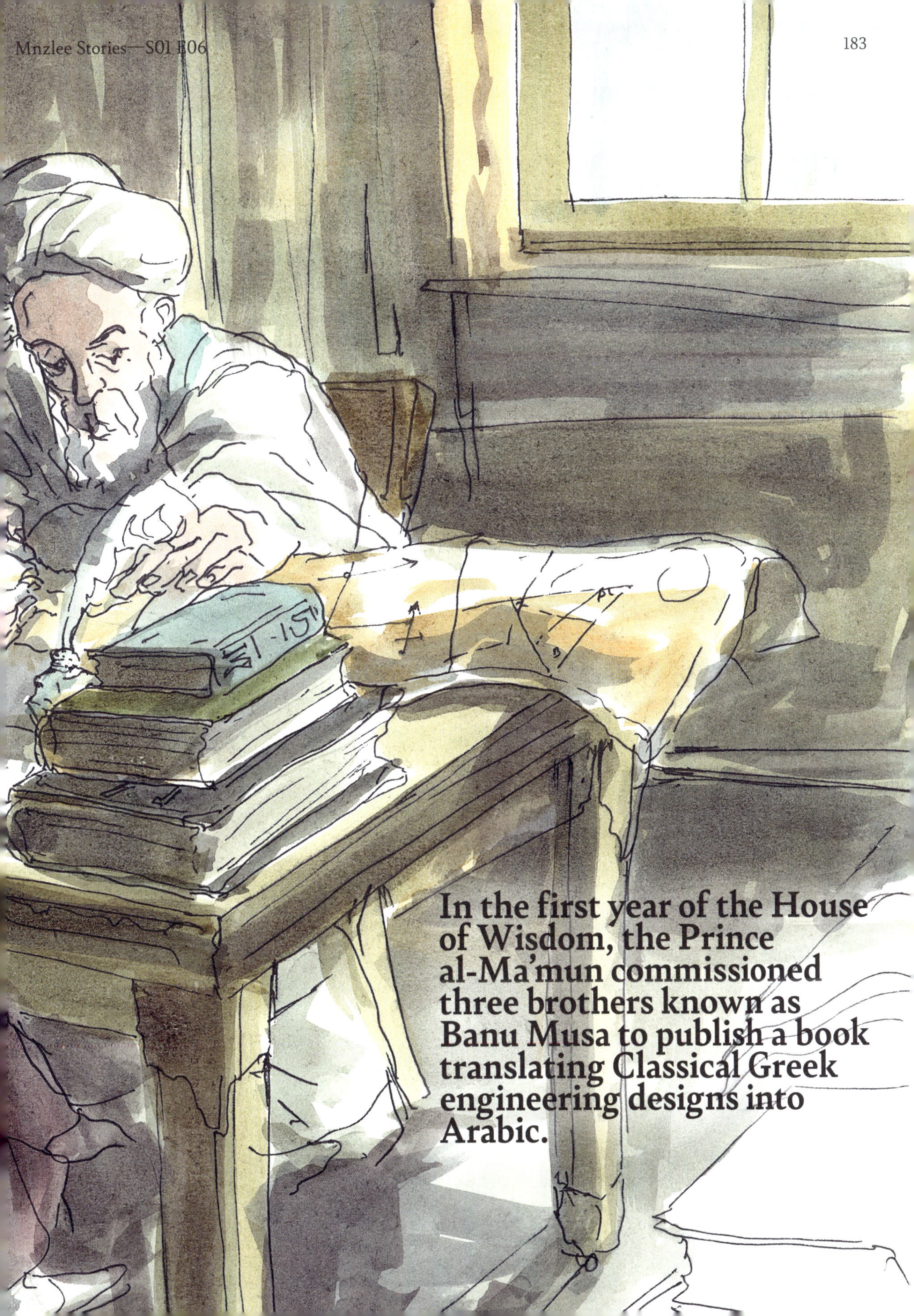
In the first year of the House
of Wisdom, the Prince
al-Ma'mun commissioned
three brothers known as
Banu Musa to publish a book
translating Classical Greek
engineering designs into
Arabic.

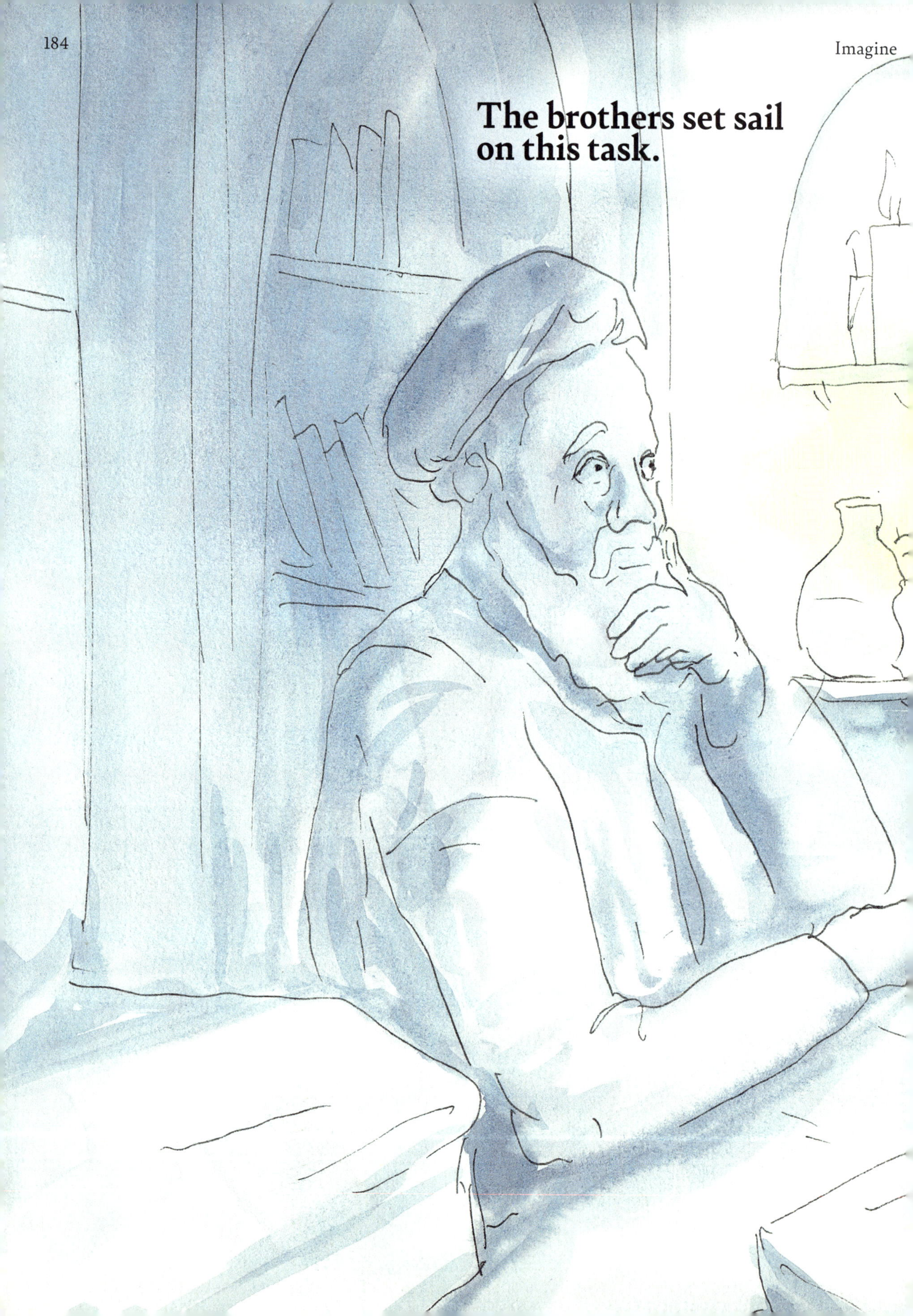

The brothers set sail on this task.

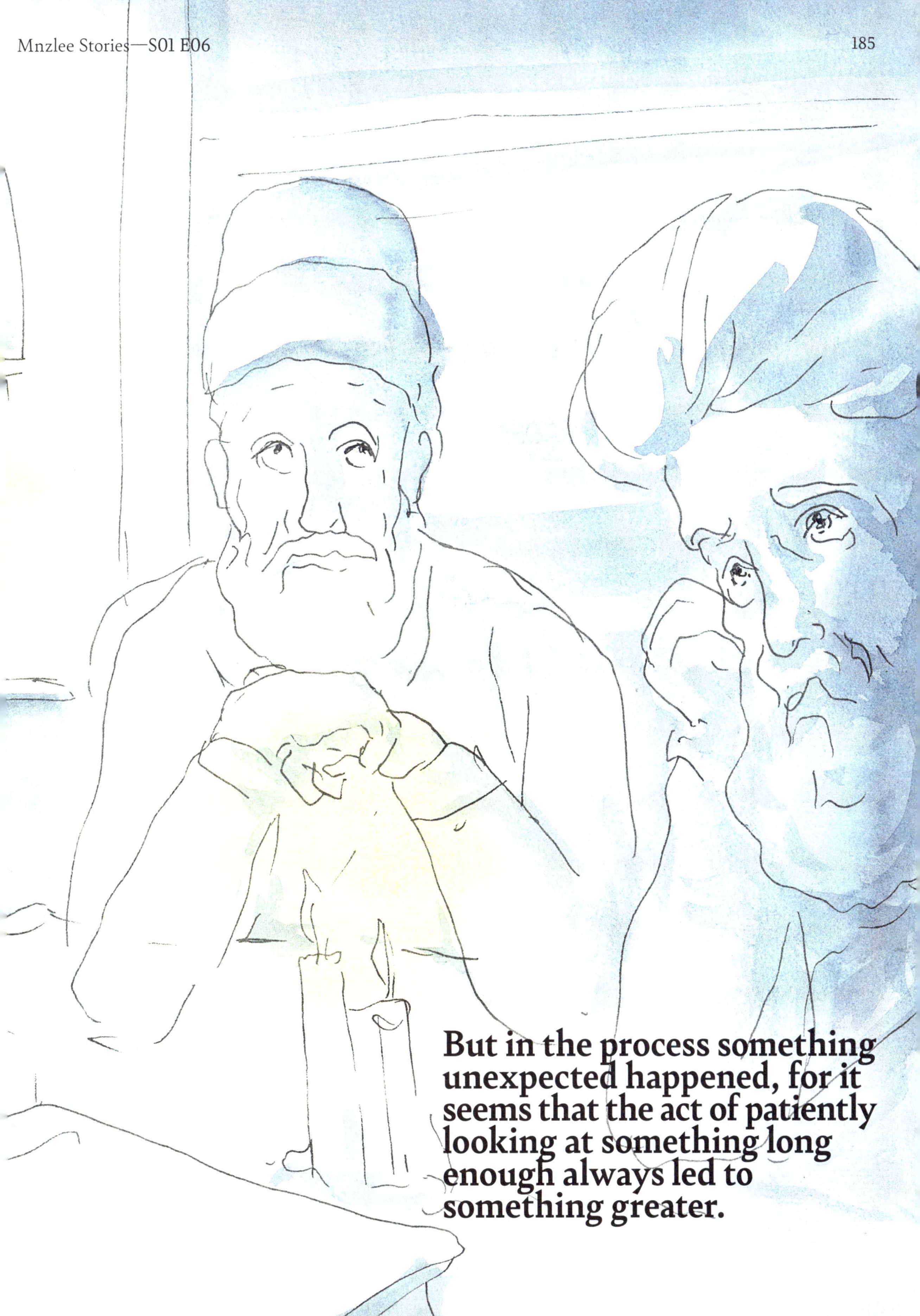

But in the process something unexpected happened, for it seems that the act of patiently looking at something long enough always led to something greater.

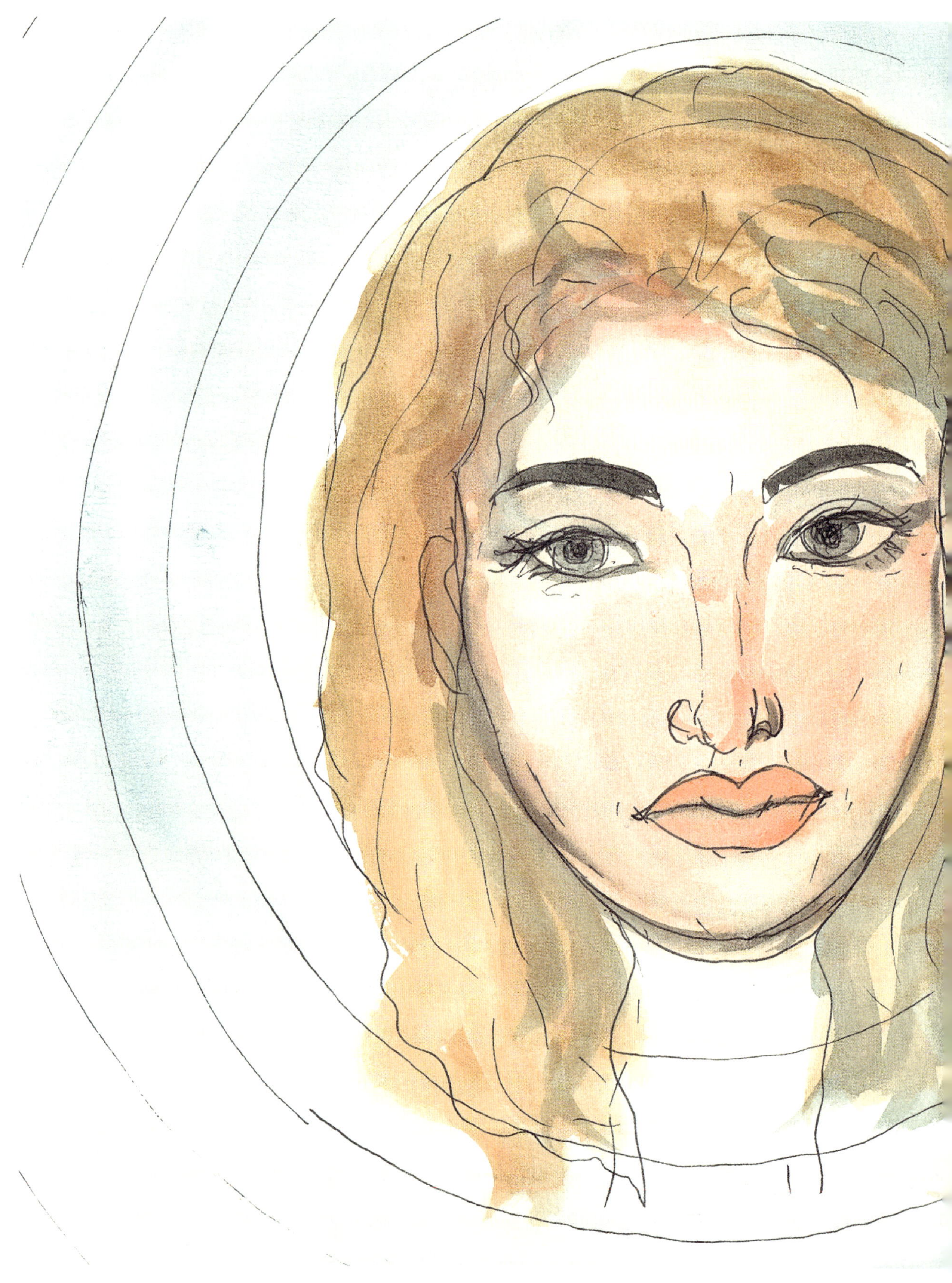

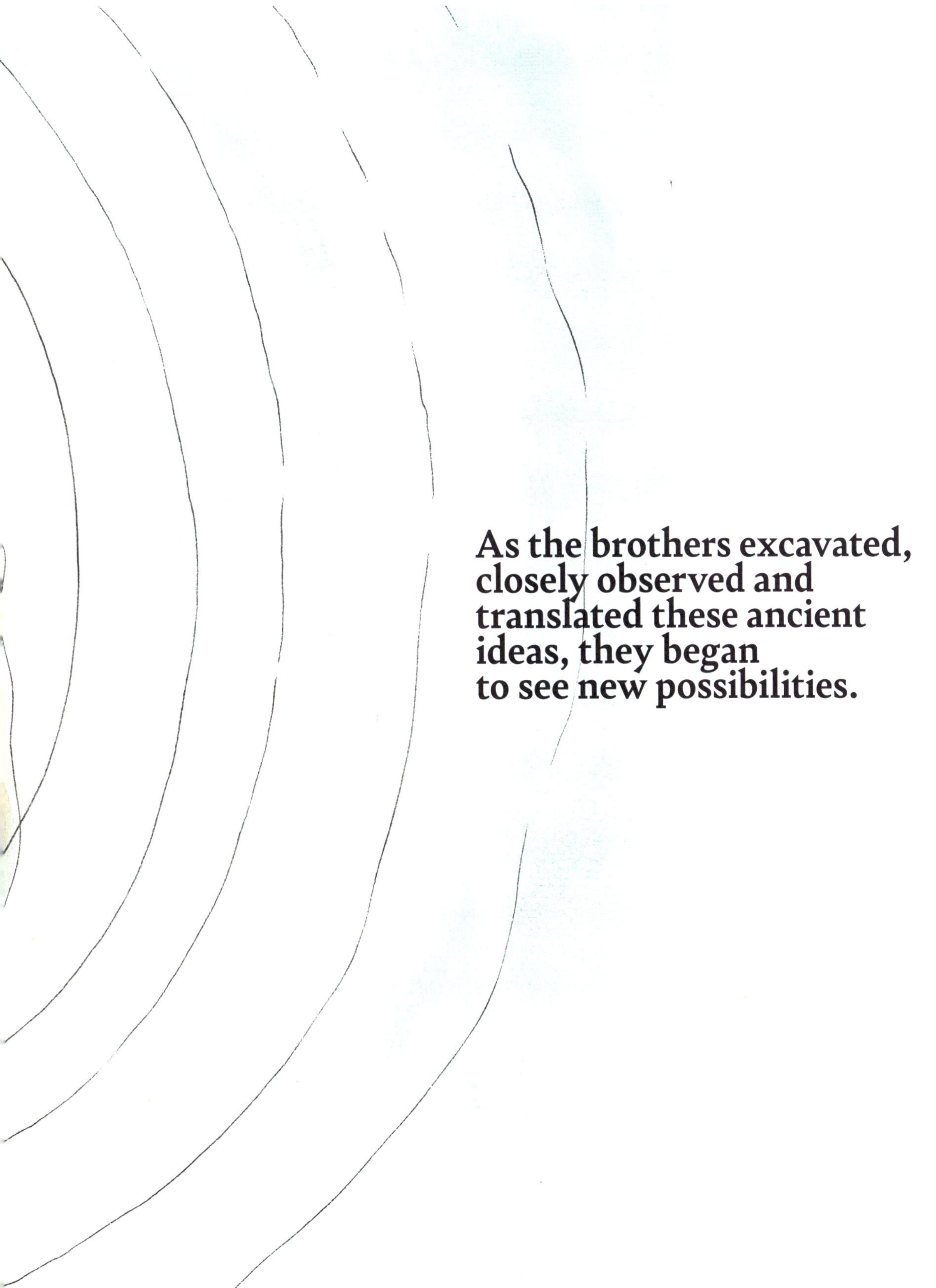

As the brothers excavated,
closely observed and
translated these ancient
ideas, they began
to see new possibilities.

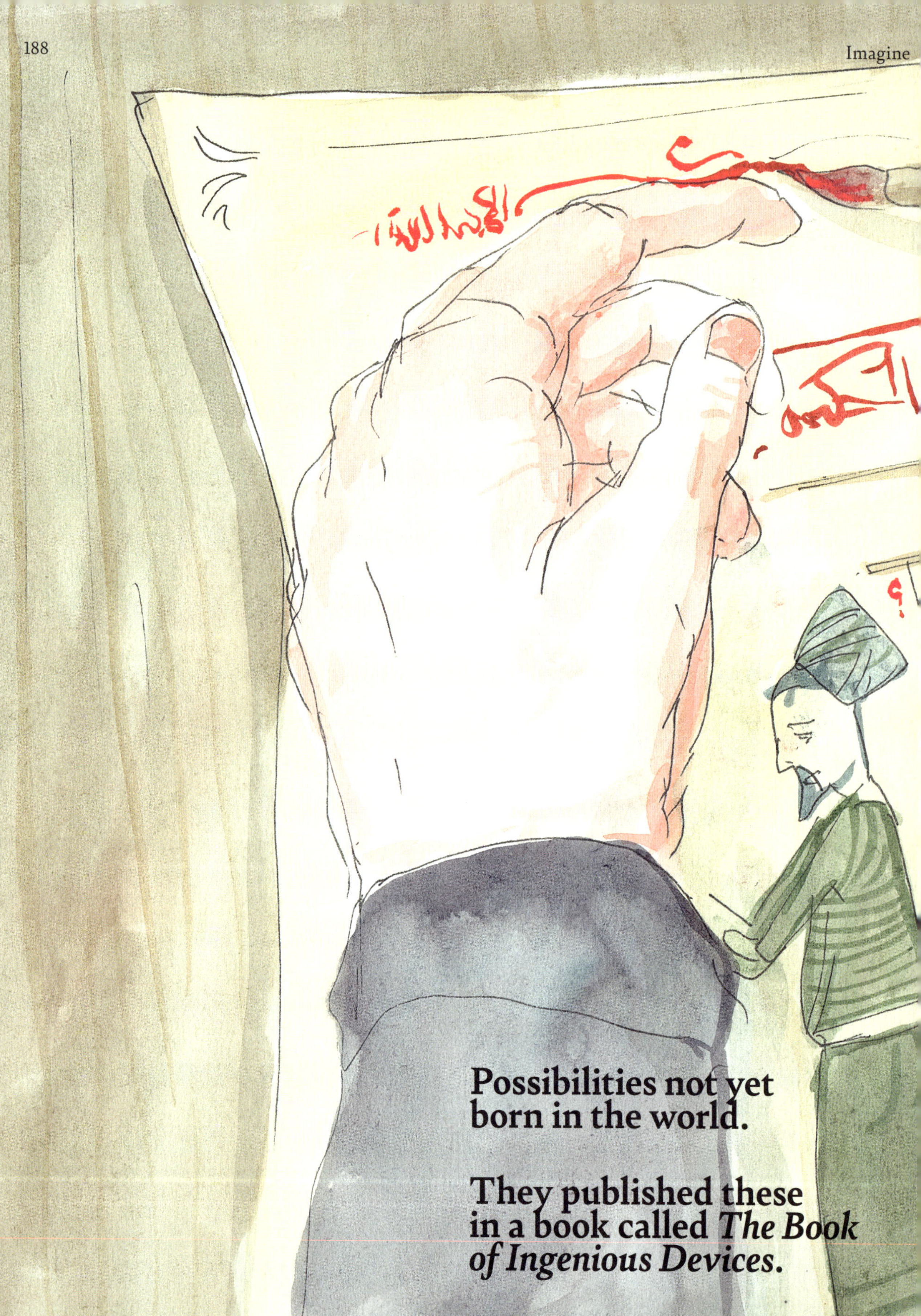

Possibilities not yet born in the world.

They published these in a book called *The Book of Ingenious Devices*.

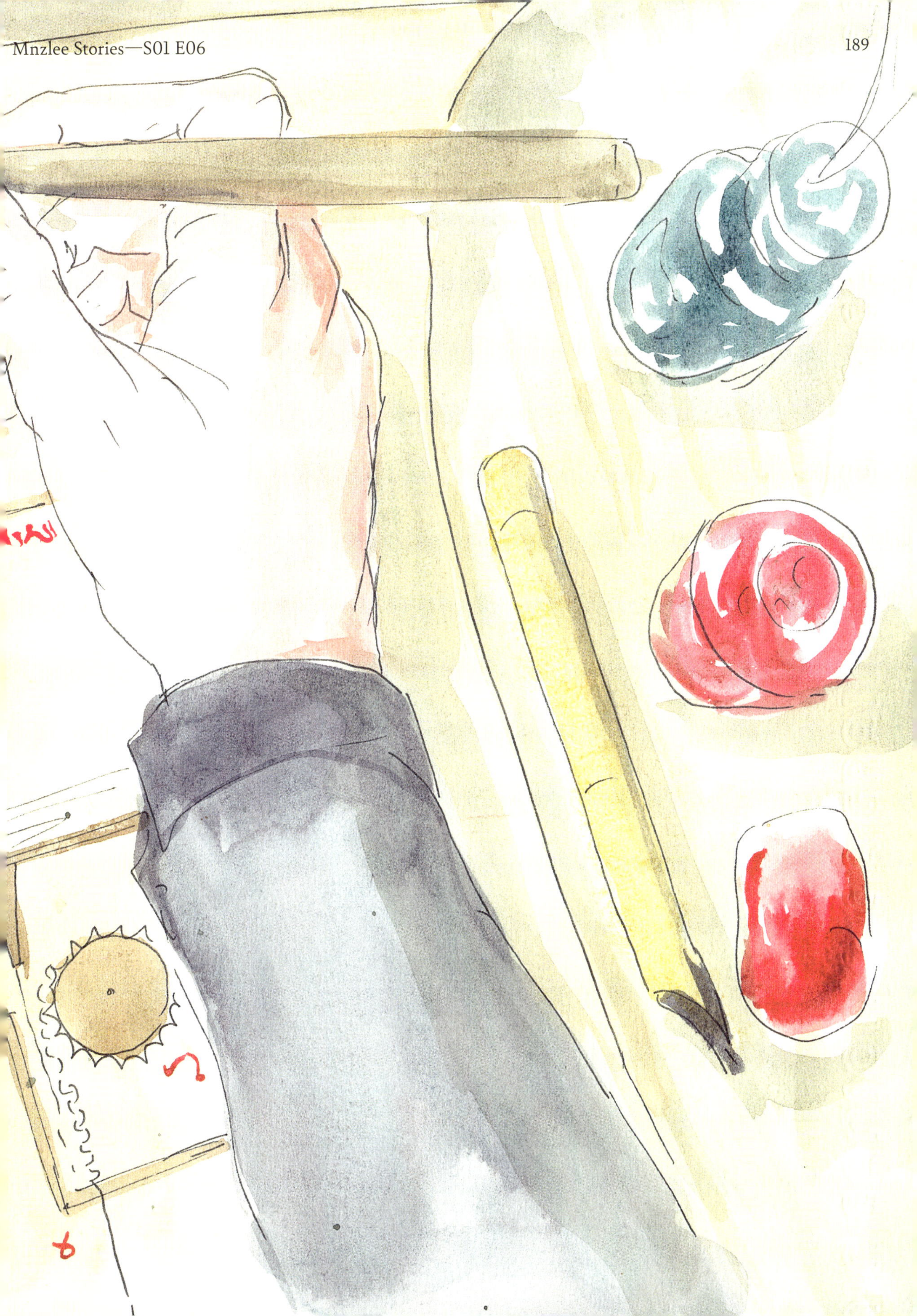

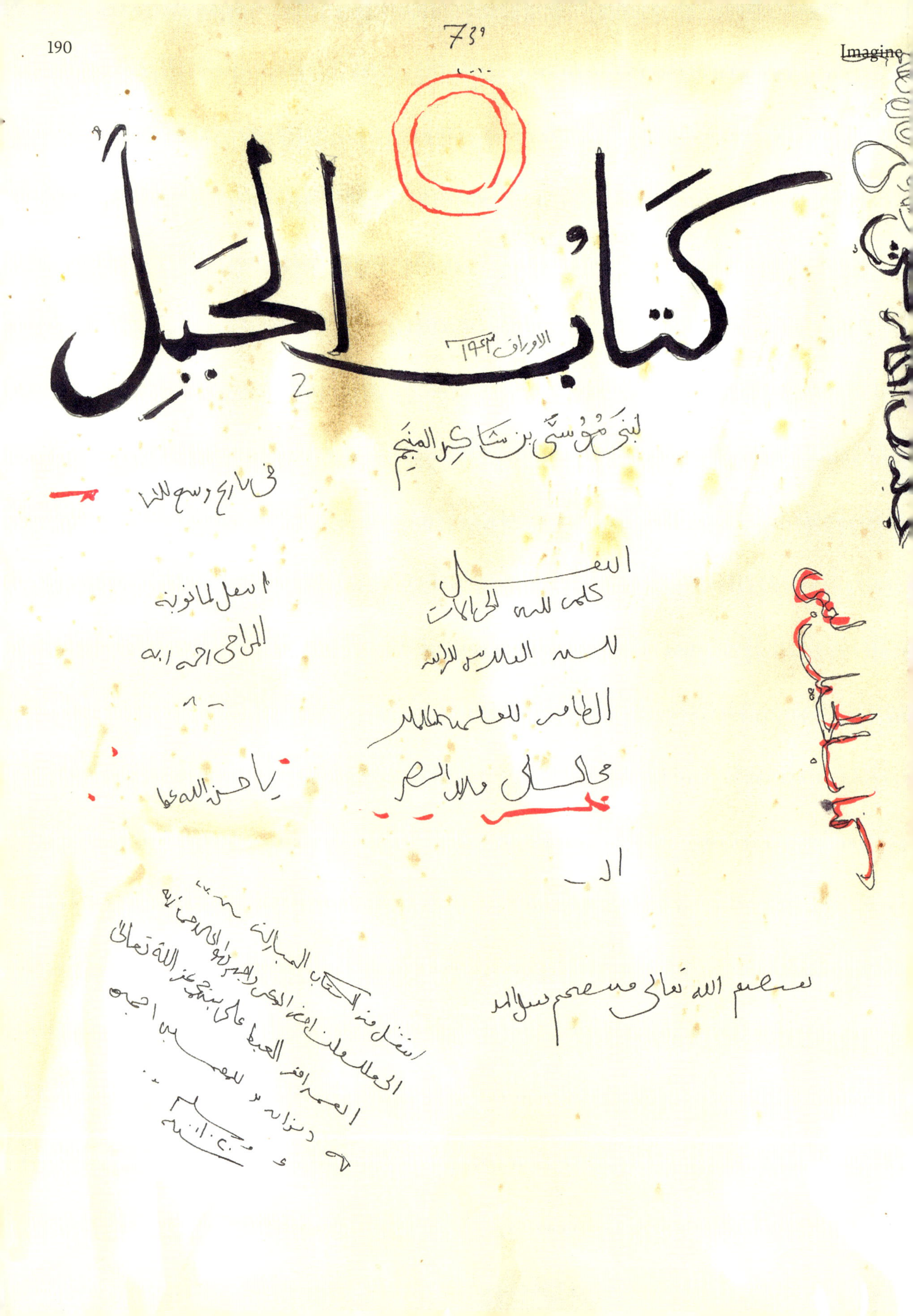

كتاب الحيل

لبني مُوسَّى بن شاكر المنجّم

الاوراق ۱۹۴

في تاريخ وسم الله

وبسم الله تعالى وبه نستعين

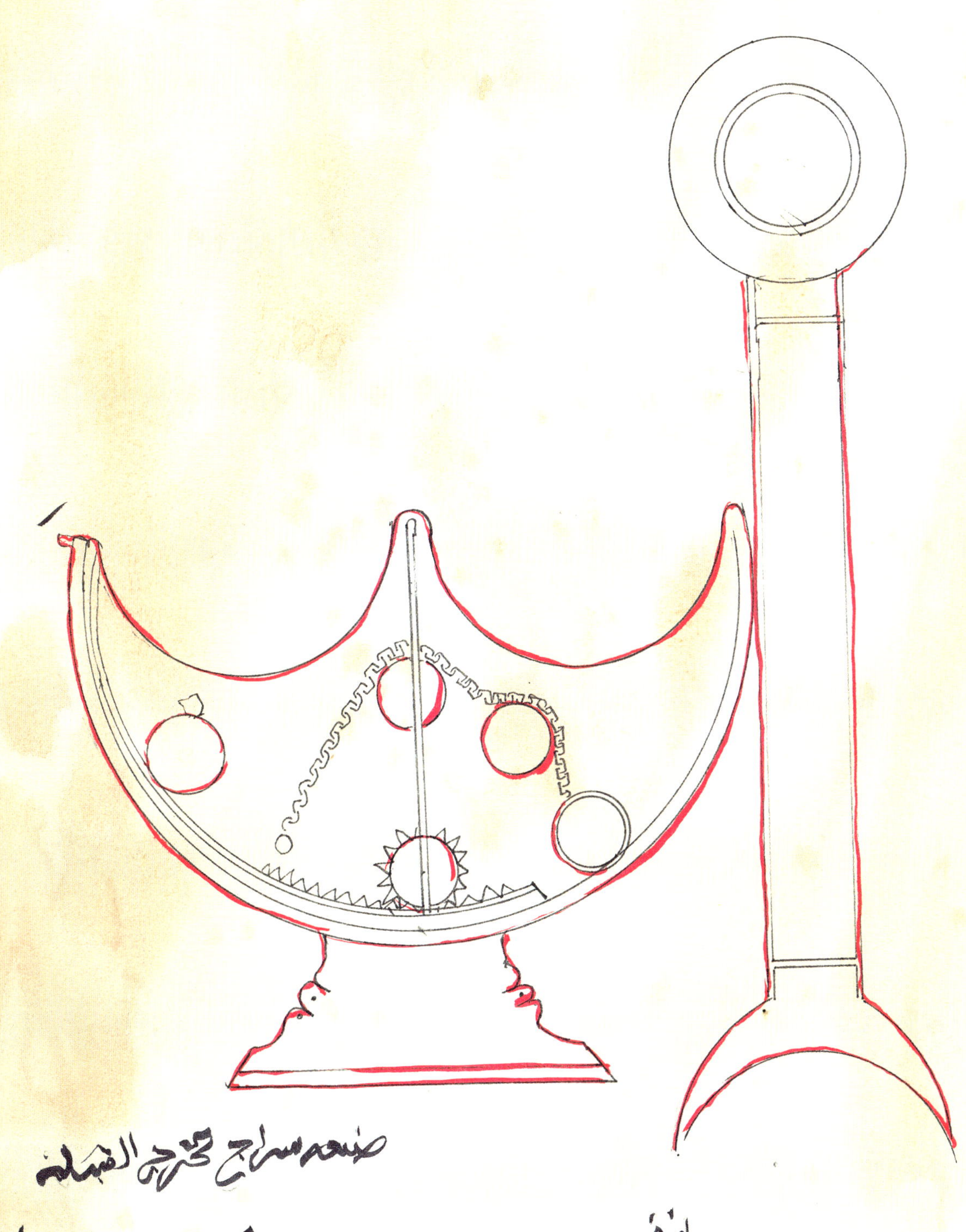
صنعة سراج مخرج القمله

This book included detailed drawings, painted with gorgeous color and detail of what would become.

The industrial revolution.

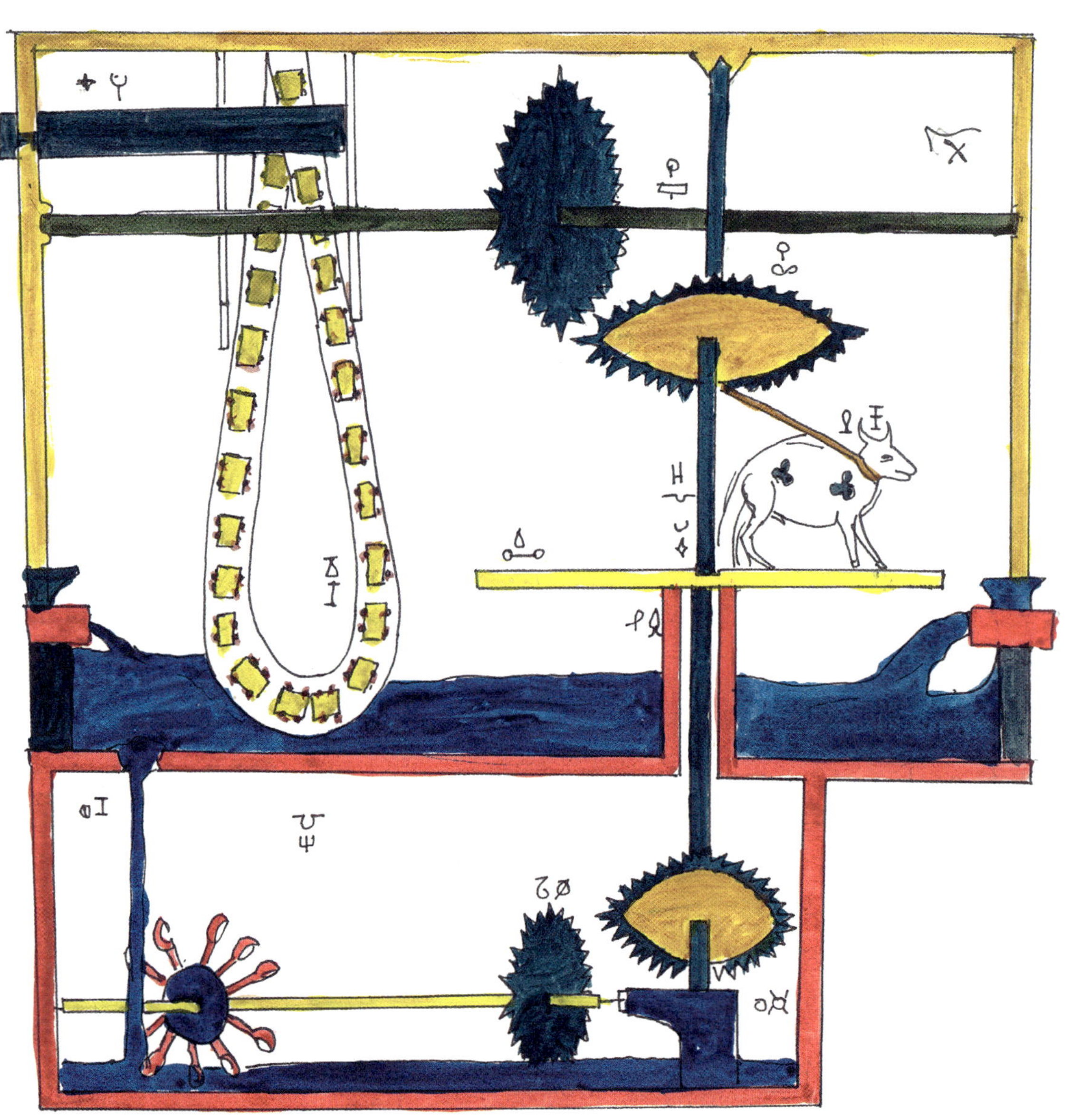

They included twin cylinder pumps with suction.

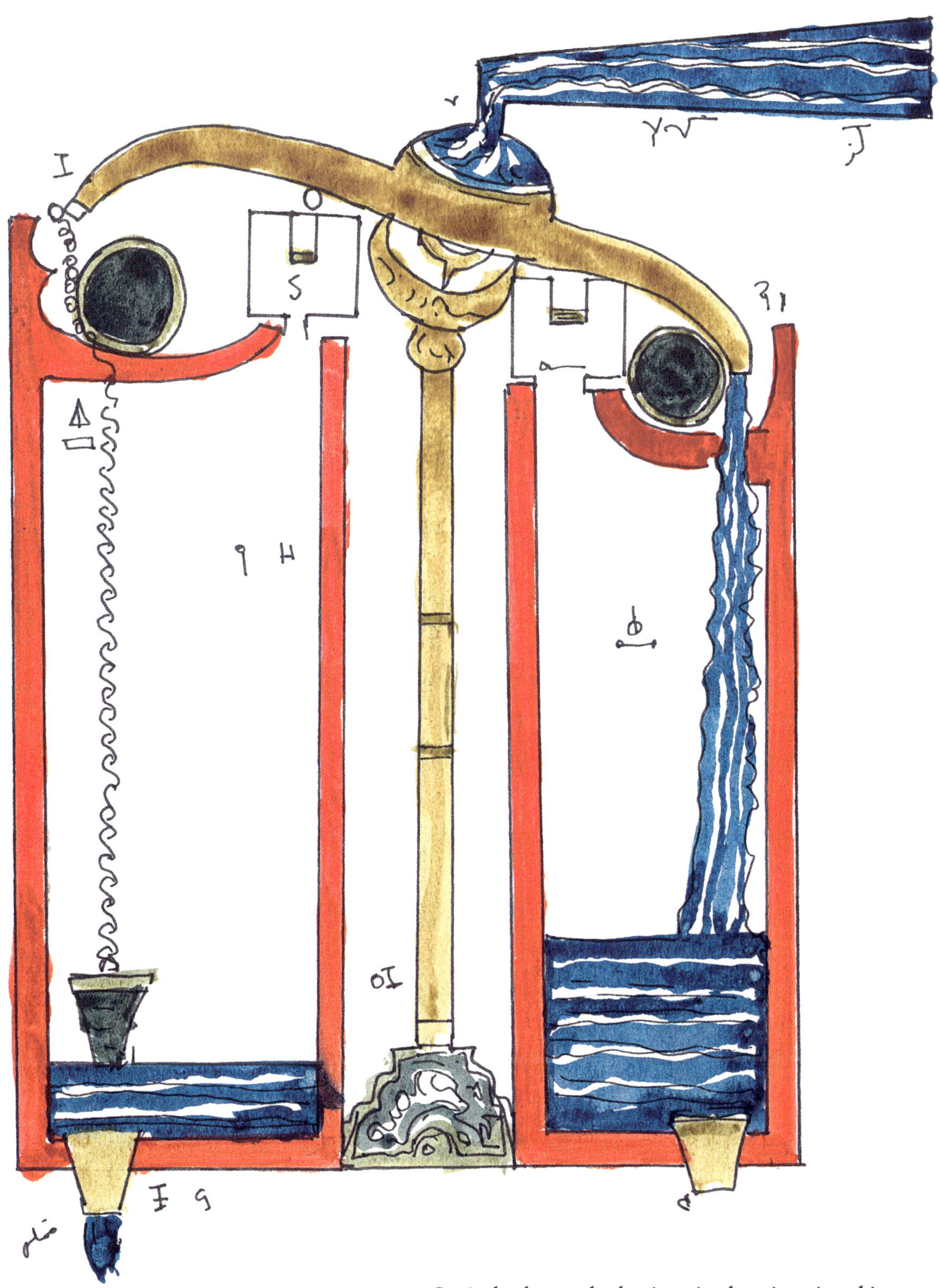

Conical valves and other imagined engineering objects.

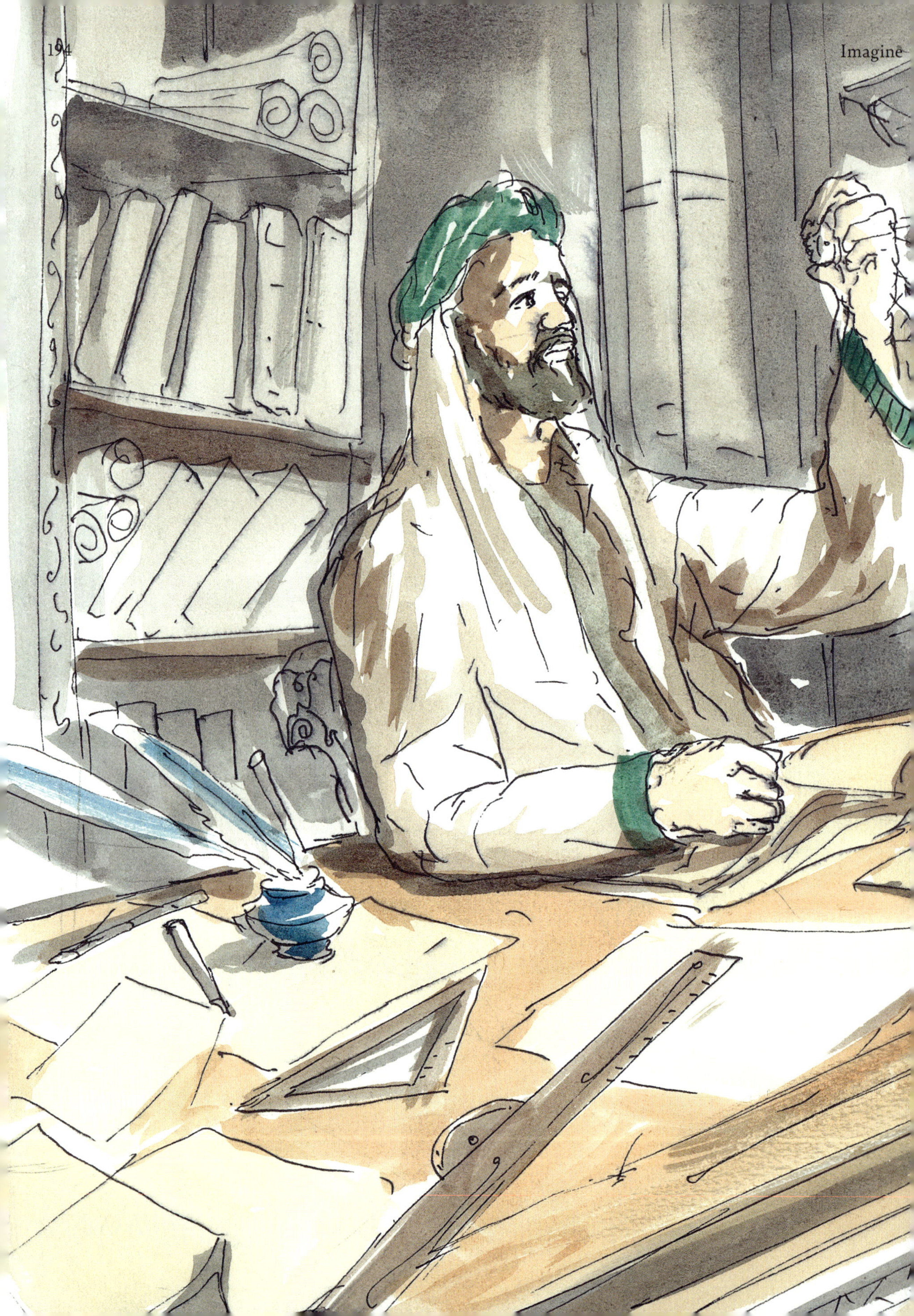

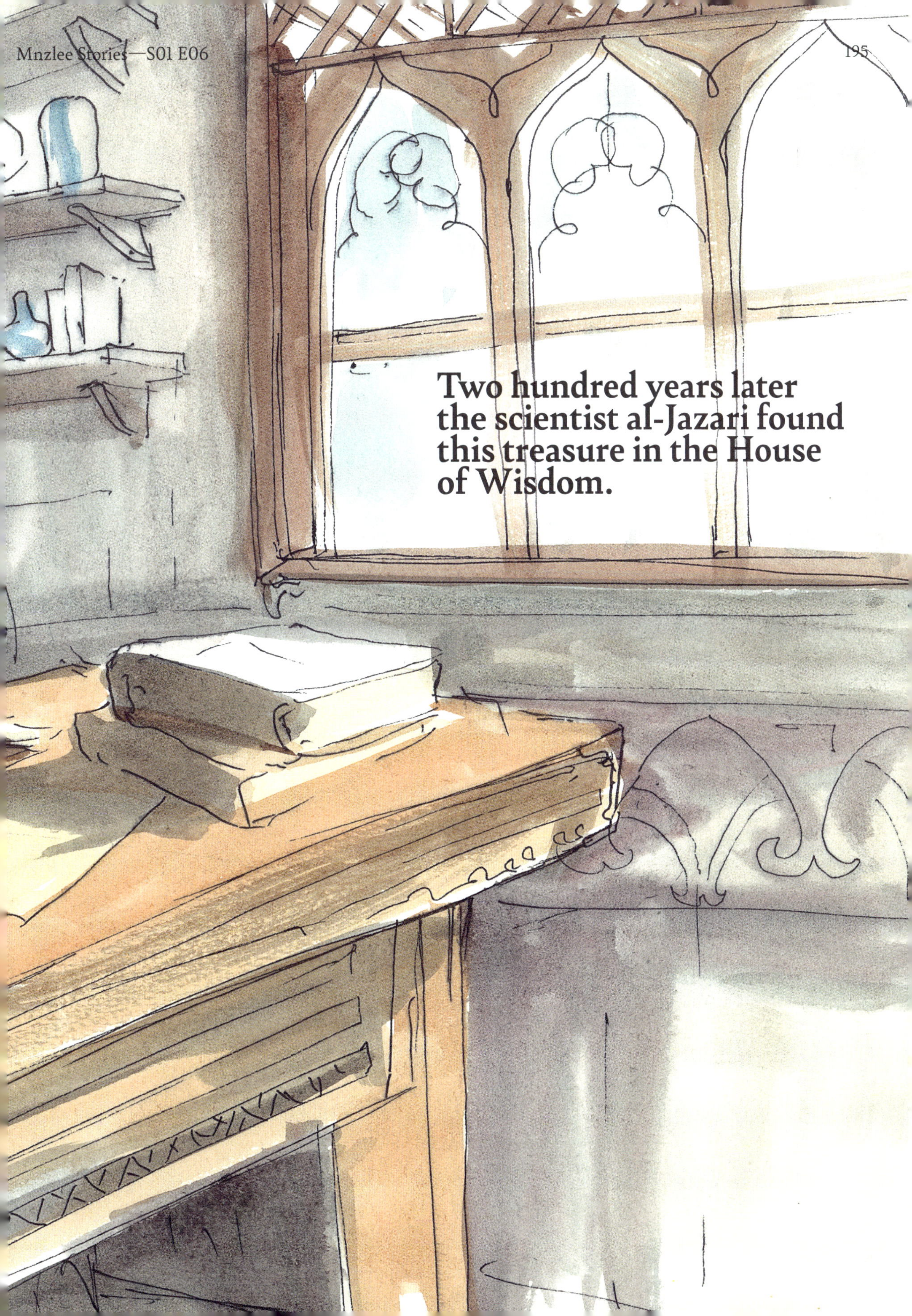
Two hundred years later
the scientist al-Jazari found
this treasure in the House
of Wisdom.

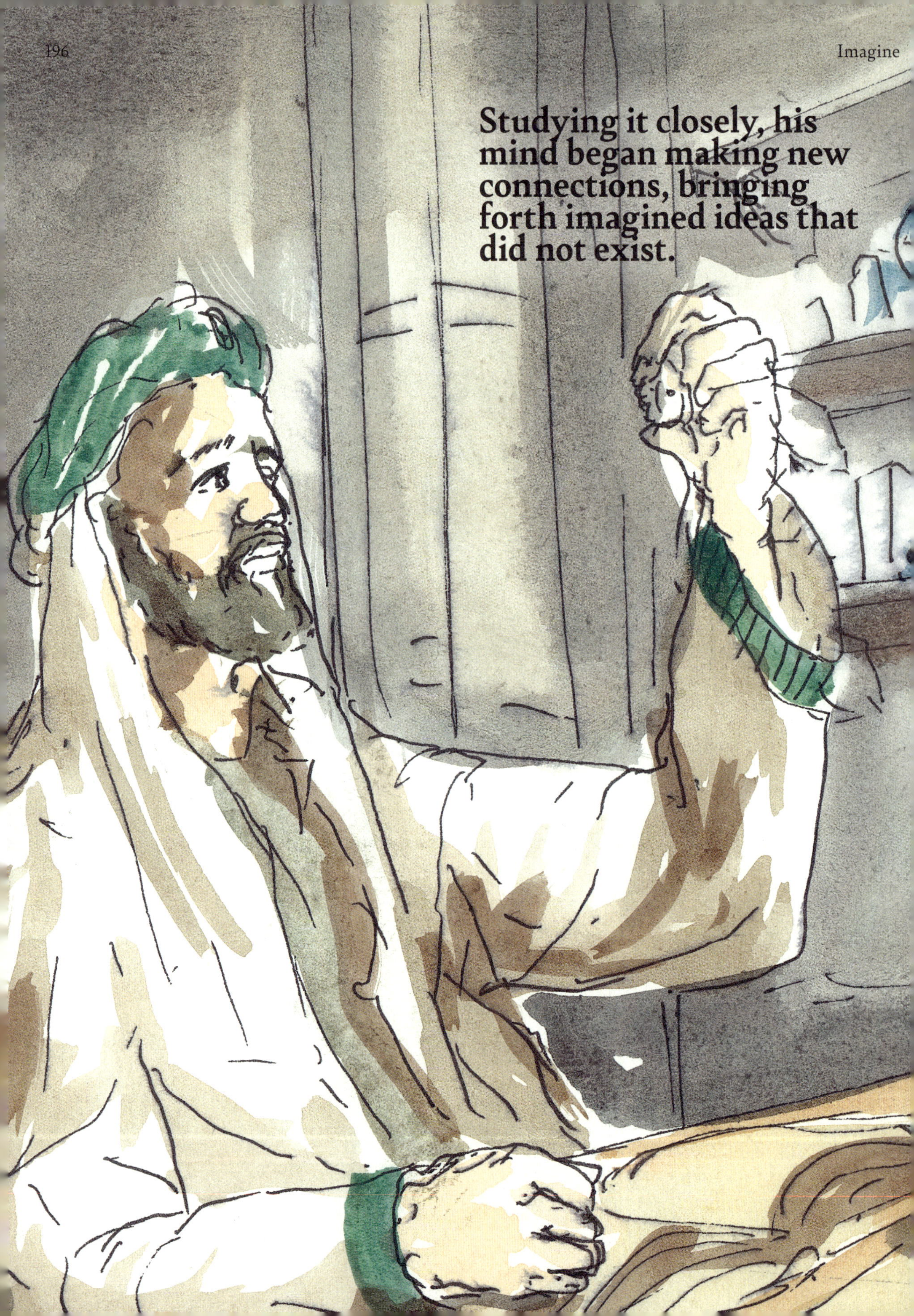
Studying it closely, his
mind began making new
connections, bringing
forth imagined ideas that
did not exist.

إسماعيل بن الرزّاز الجزري

الجامع بين العِلْم والعَمل النَّافع

في صِناعة الحِيَل

He published those in a book known as
The Book of Knowledge of Ingenious Mechanisms.

His book contained incredible drawings of inventions.

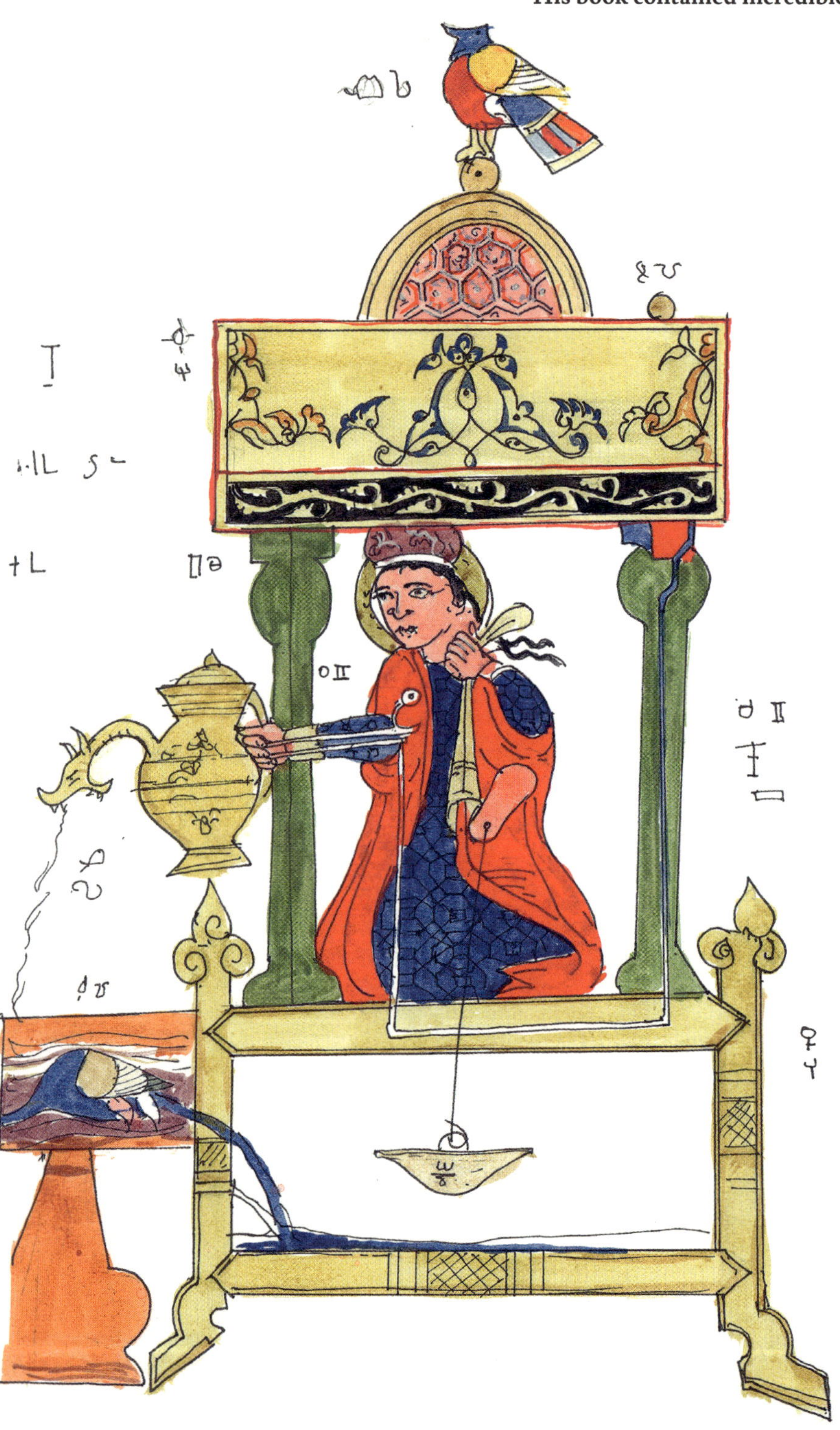

**painted with gorgeous bright colors in gold leaf with
notes on how he imagined each invention might work.**

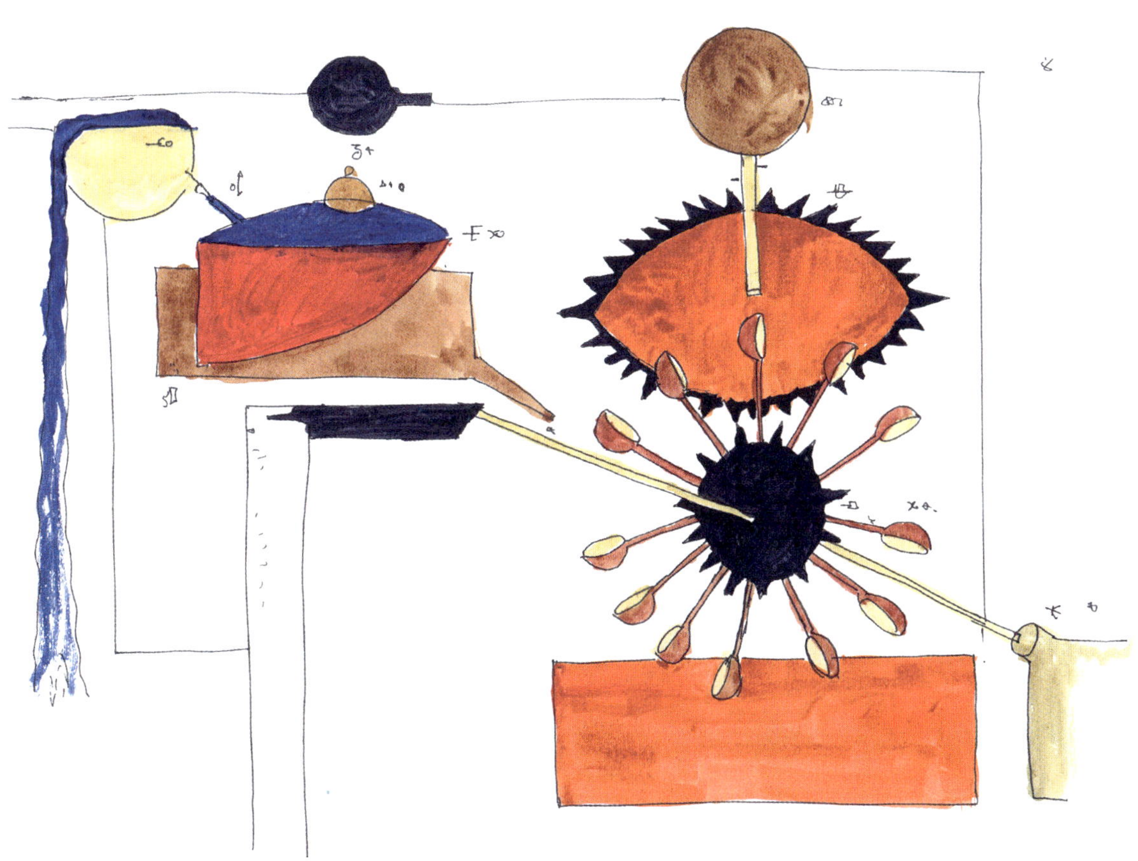

Float valves that illustrated the design of what would become modern toilets.

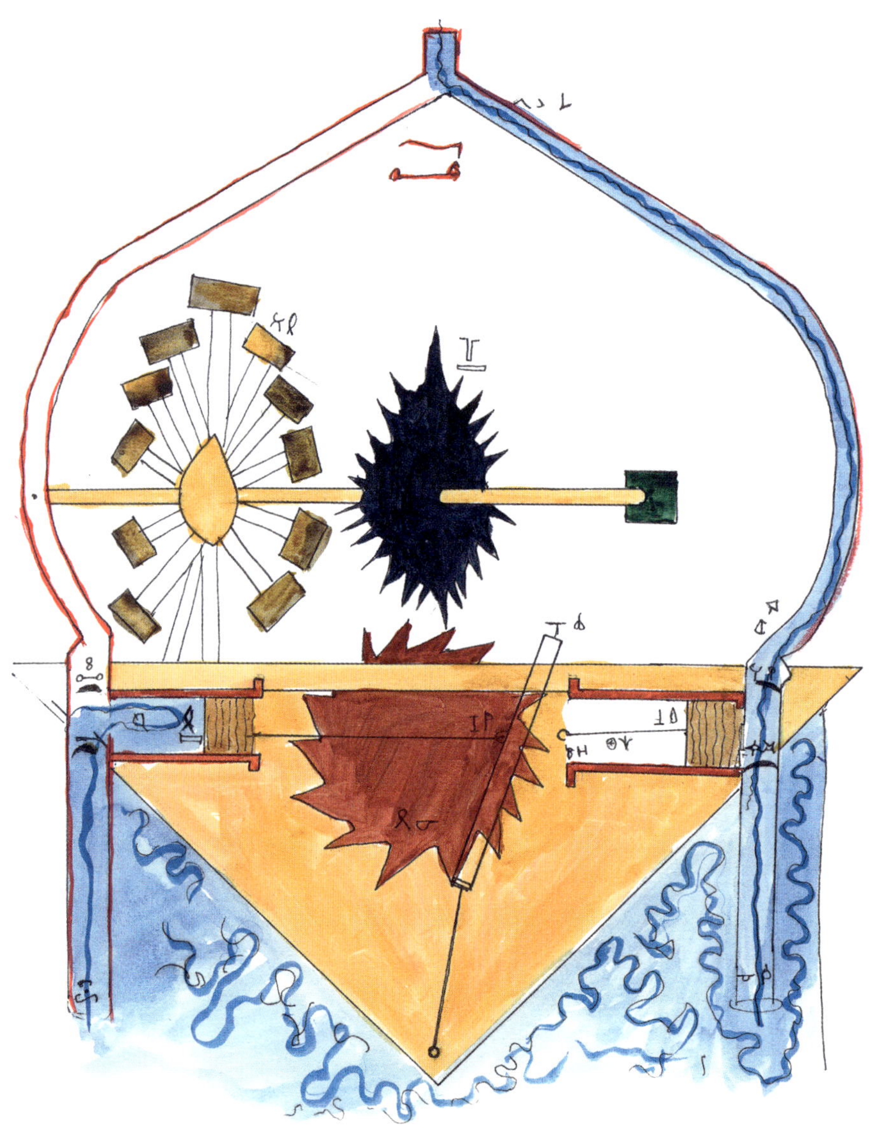

Flow regulators that would be used in the future for hydro-electric dams, internal combustion engines.

Water clocks that could tell time.

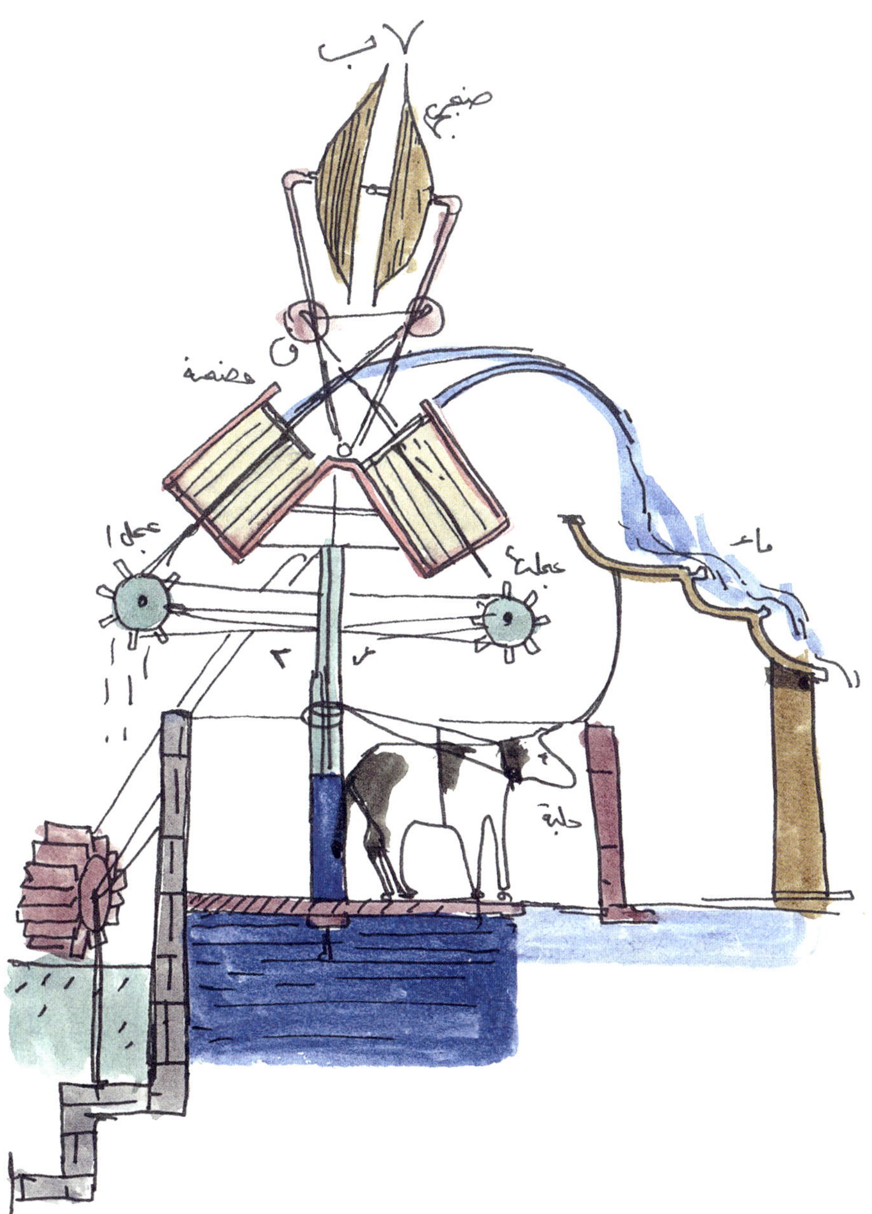

Steven Johnson, author of *Wonderland: How Play Made the Modern World,* makes the acute observation that there is something very strange about these books.

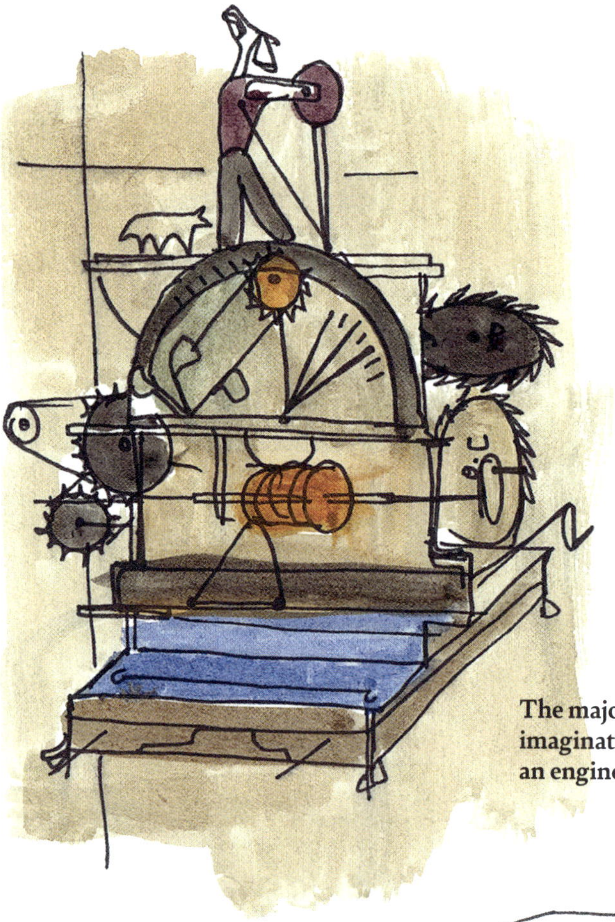

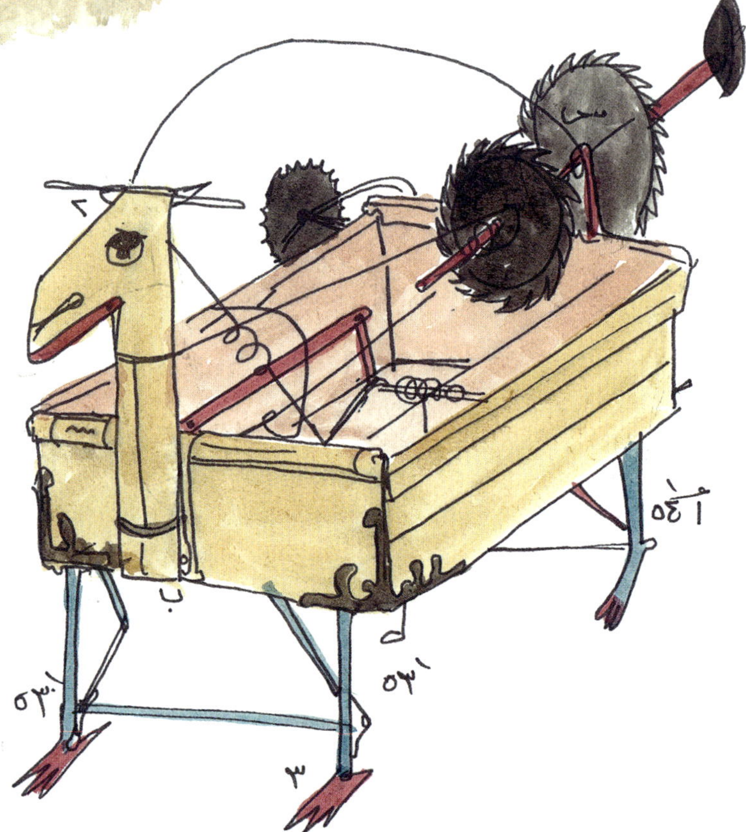

The majority of them include objects of play, imagination and amusement, not what you might think an engineering book would have.

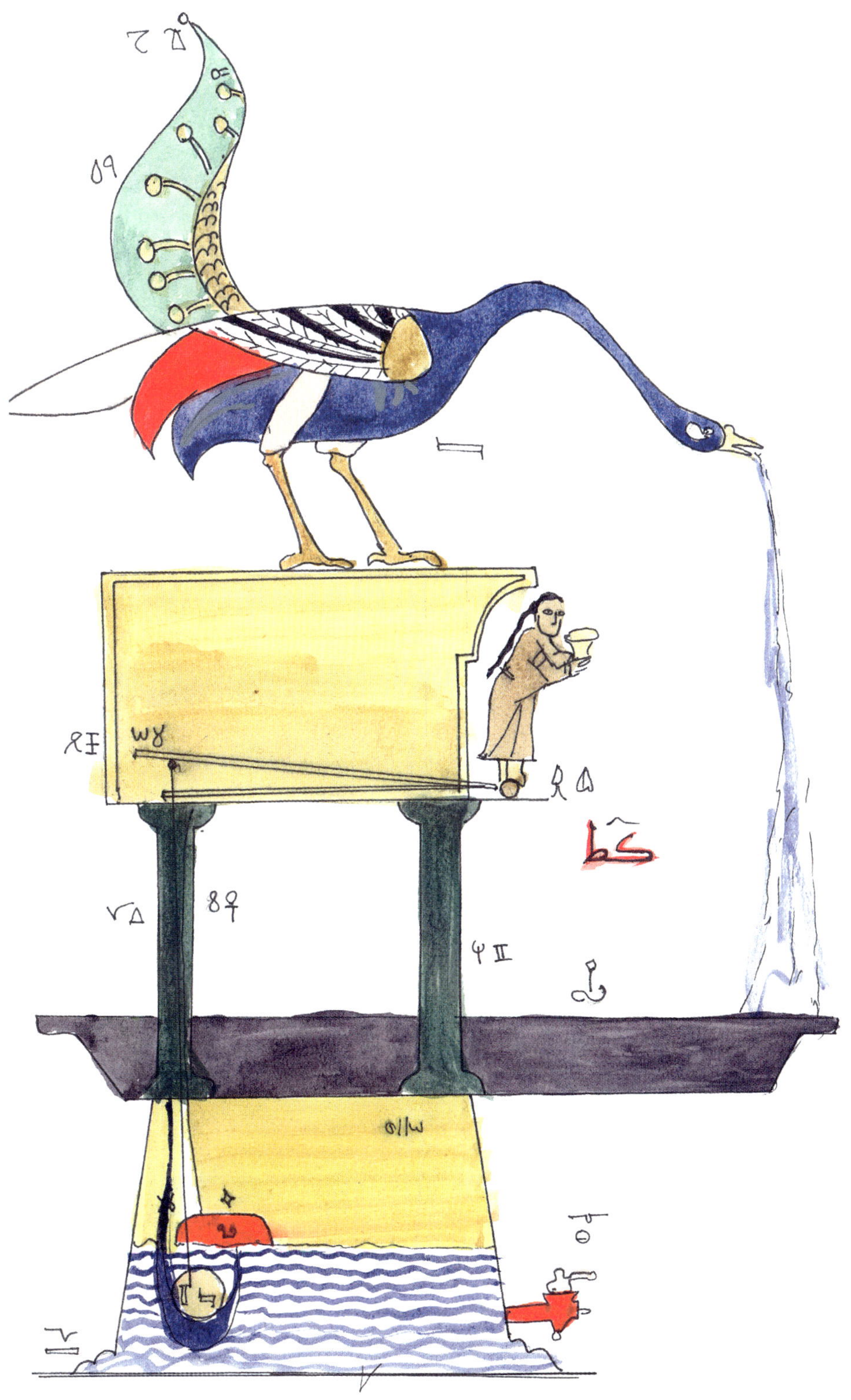

A peacock that releases water when you pull its feathers and offers you a miniature person holding soap to wash your hands with.

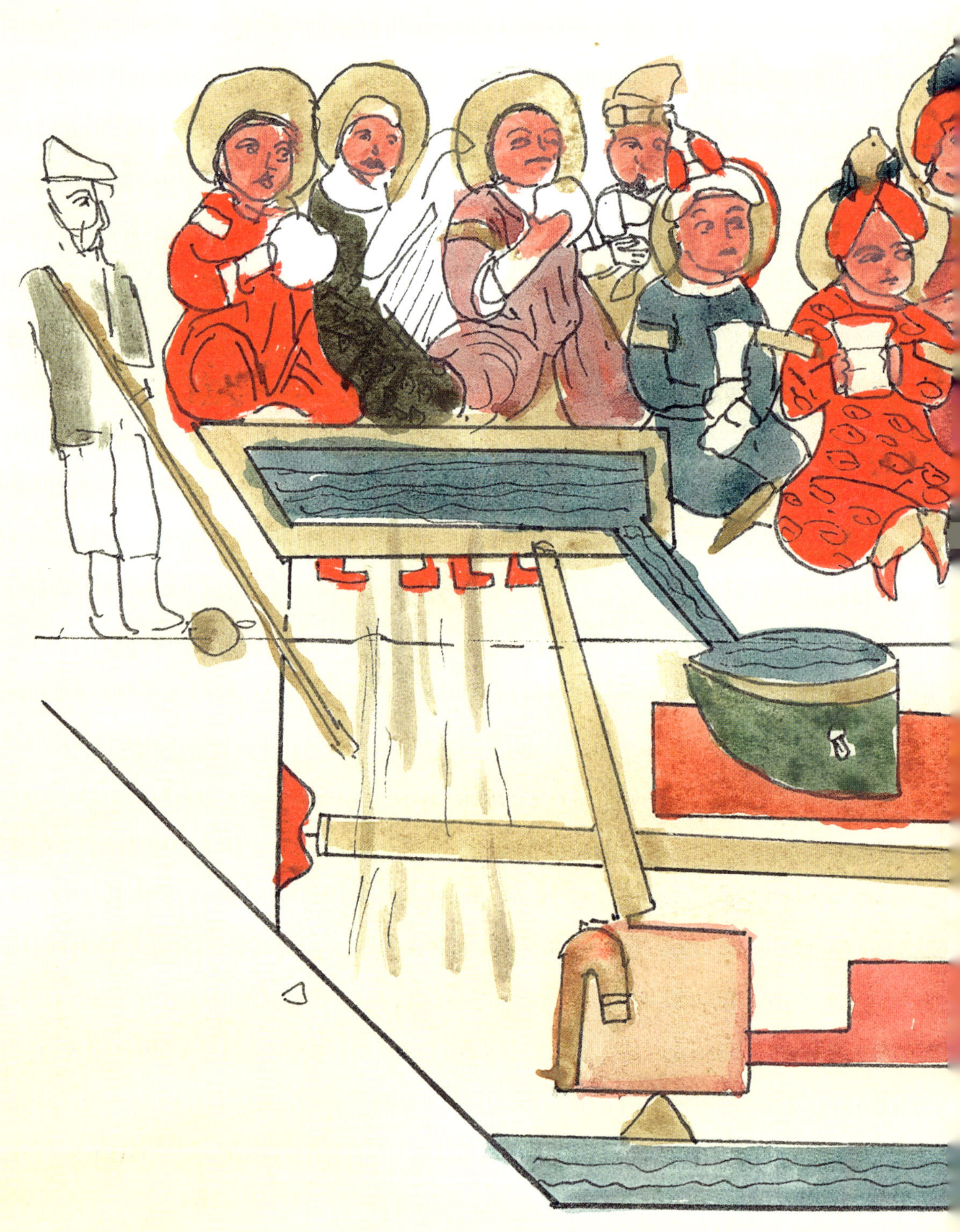

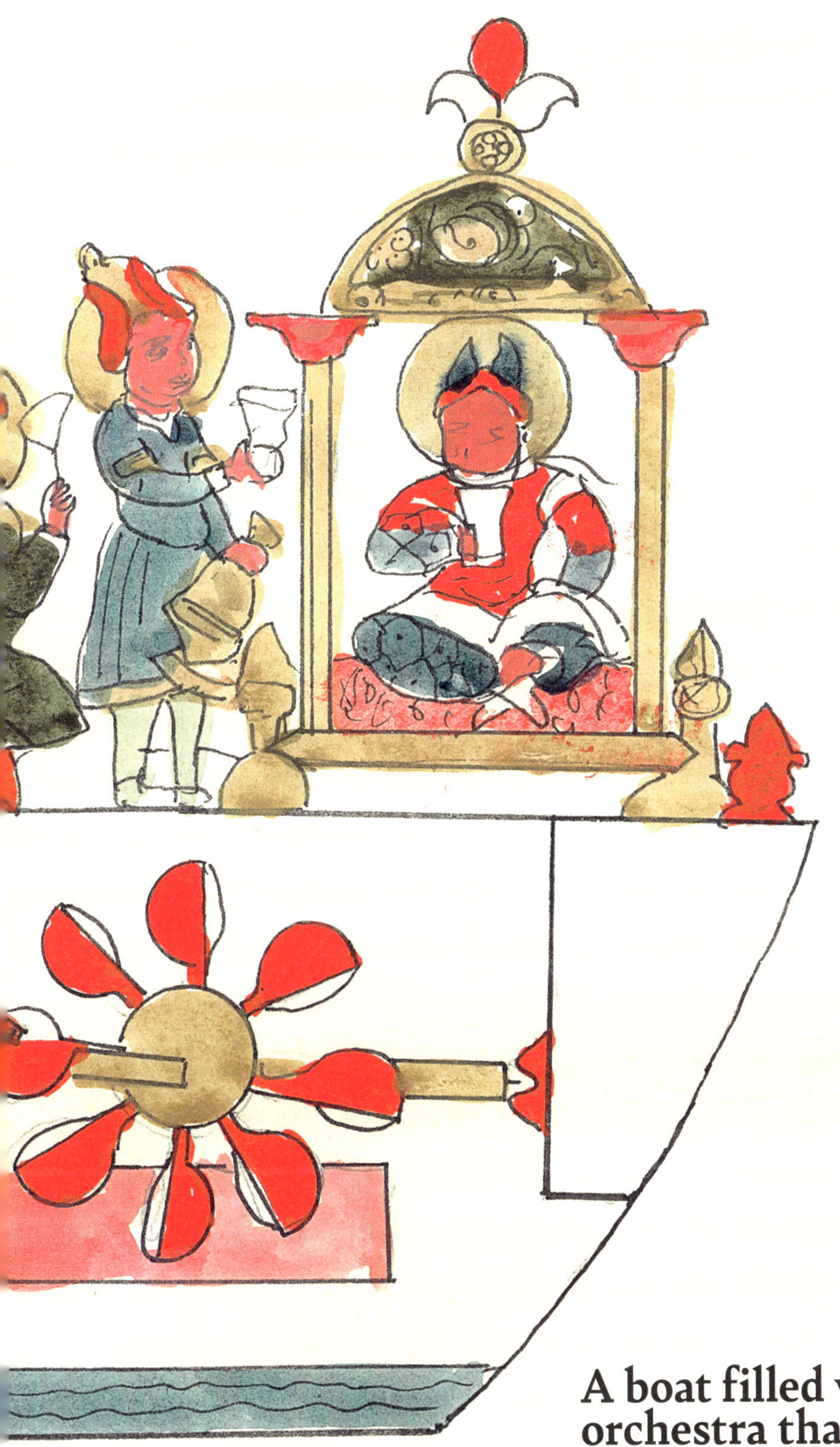

A boat filled with a robotic
orchestra that can play
music while people enjoy
the lake.

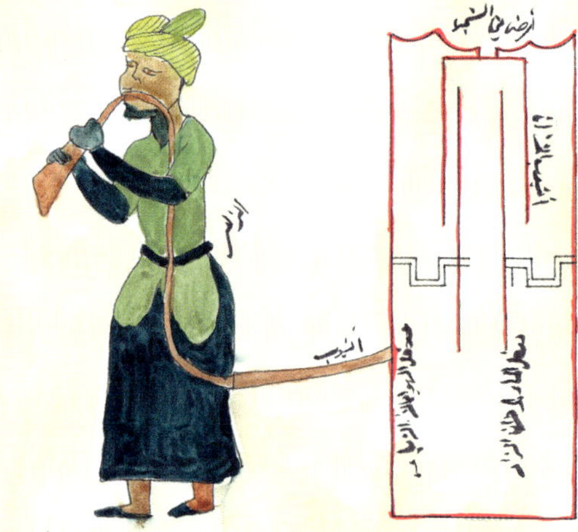

An automated self-playing flute and drums.

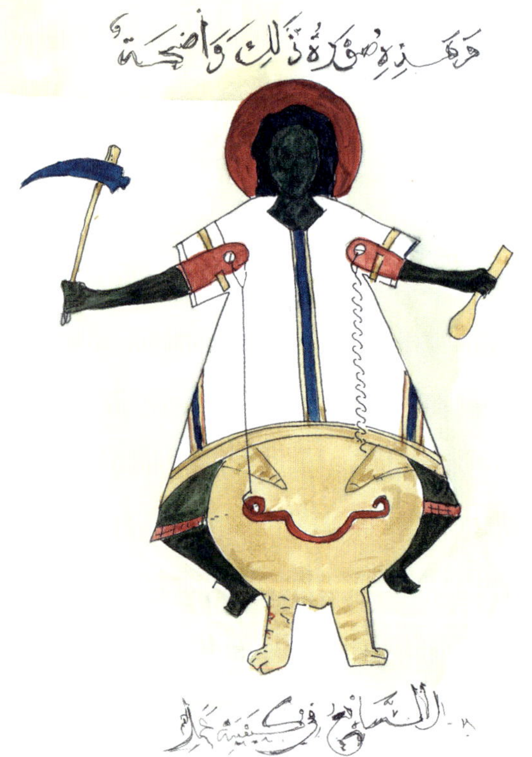

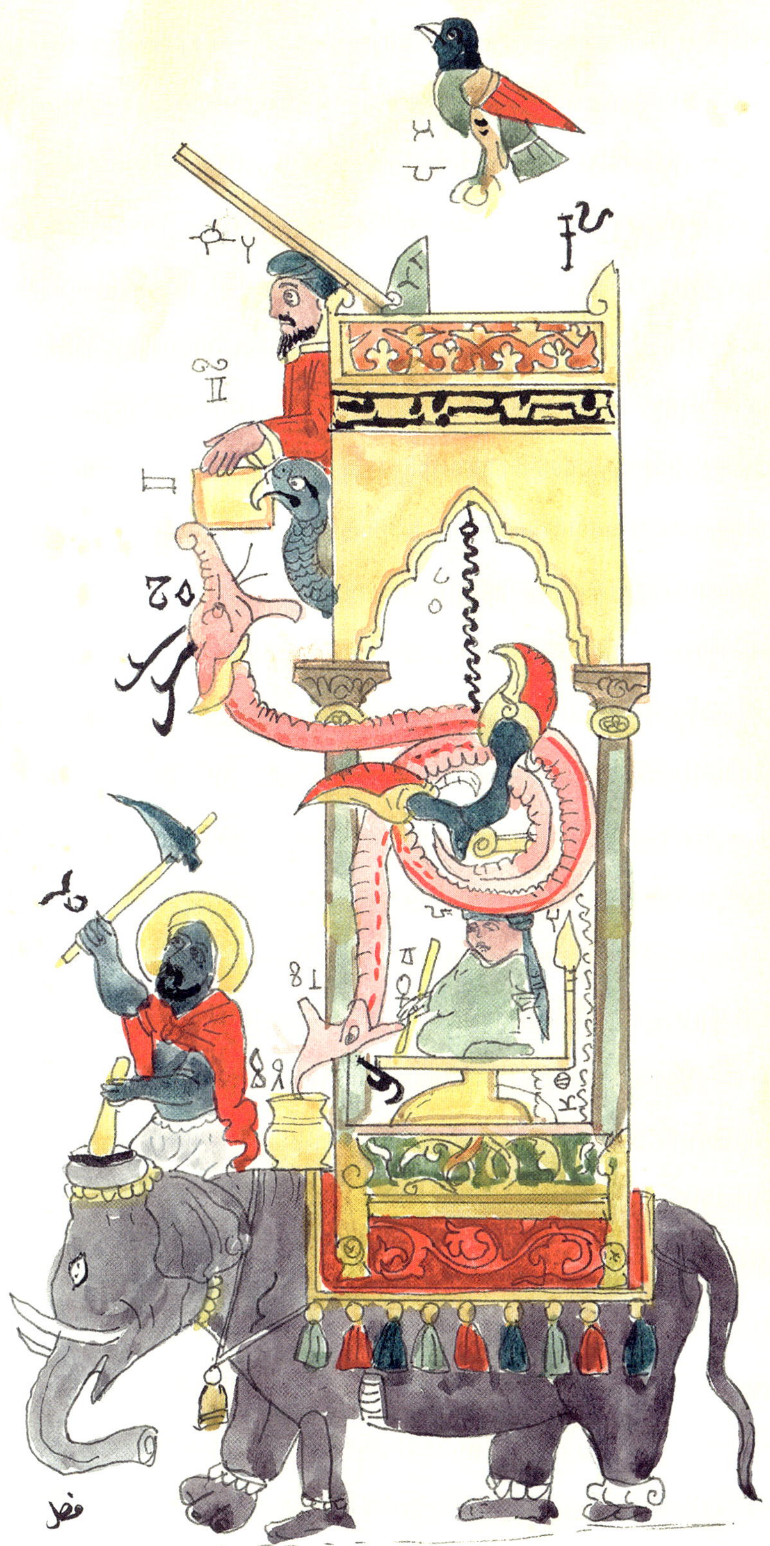

An elephant clock that would automatically sing on the half hour to tell you the time.

The influence these two books have had on the industrial age is completely understated.

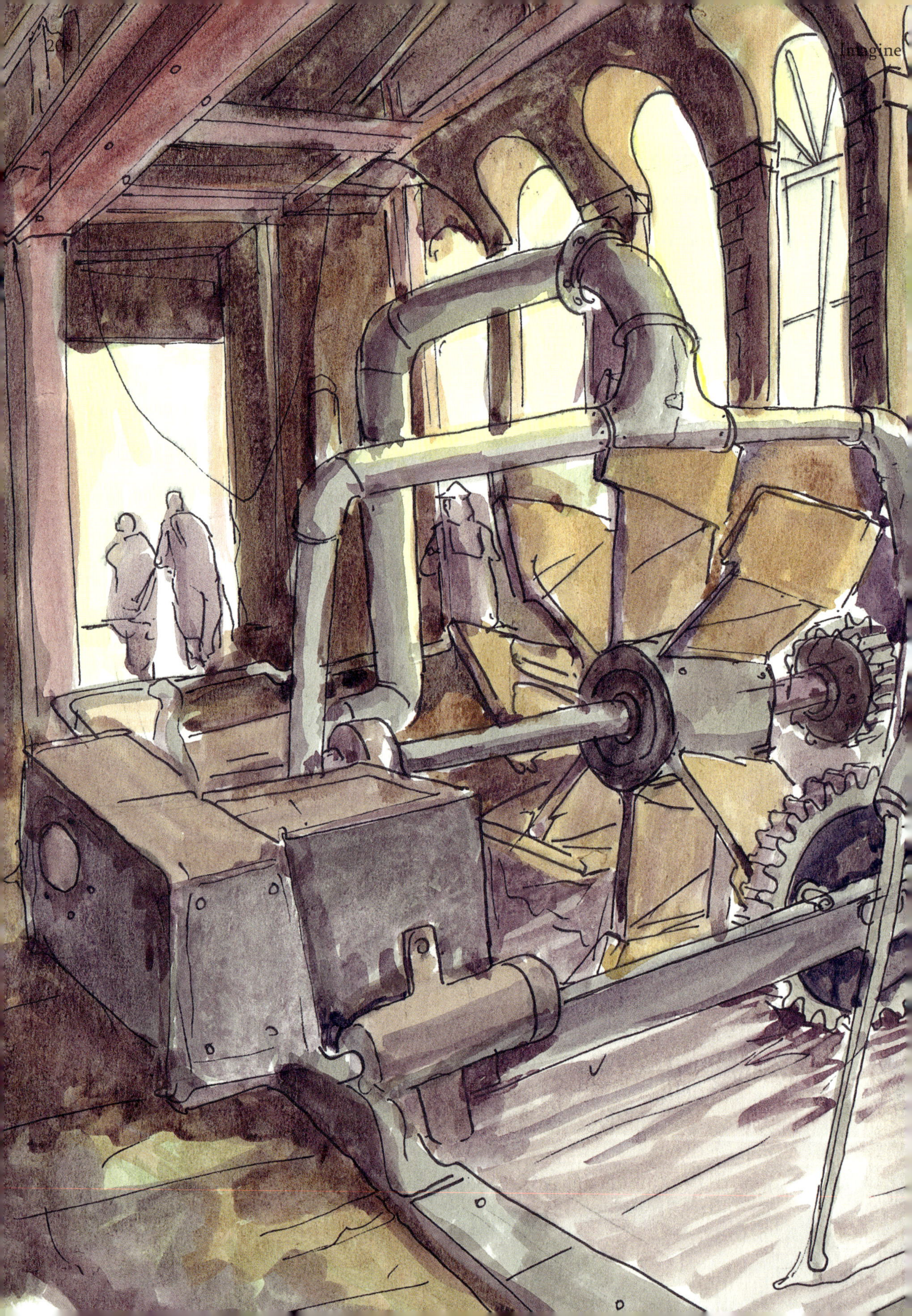

Imagine

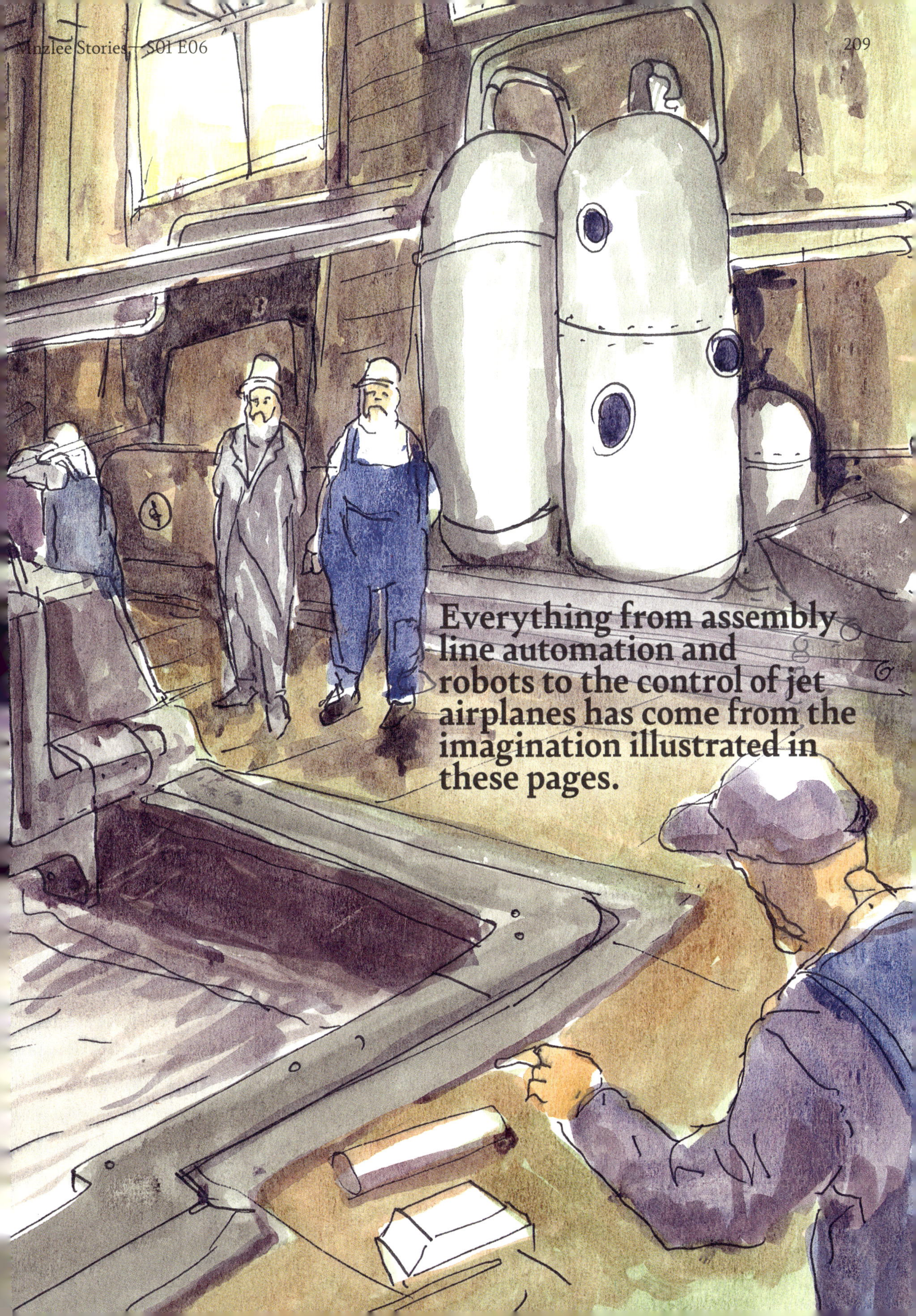
Everything from assembly
line automation and
robots to the control of jet
airplanes has come from the
imagination illustrated in
these pages.

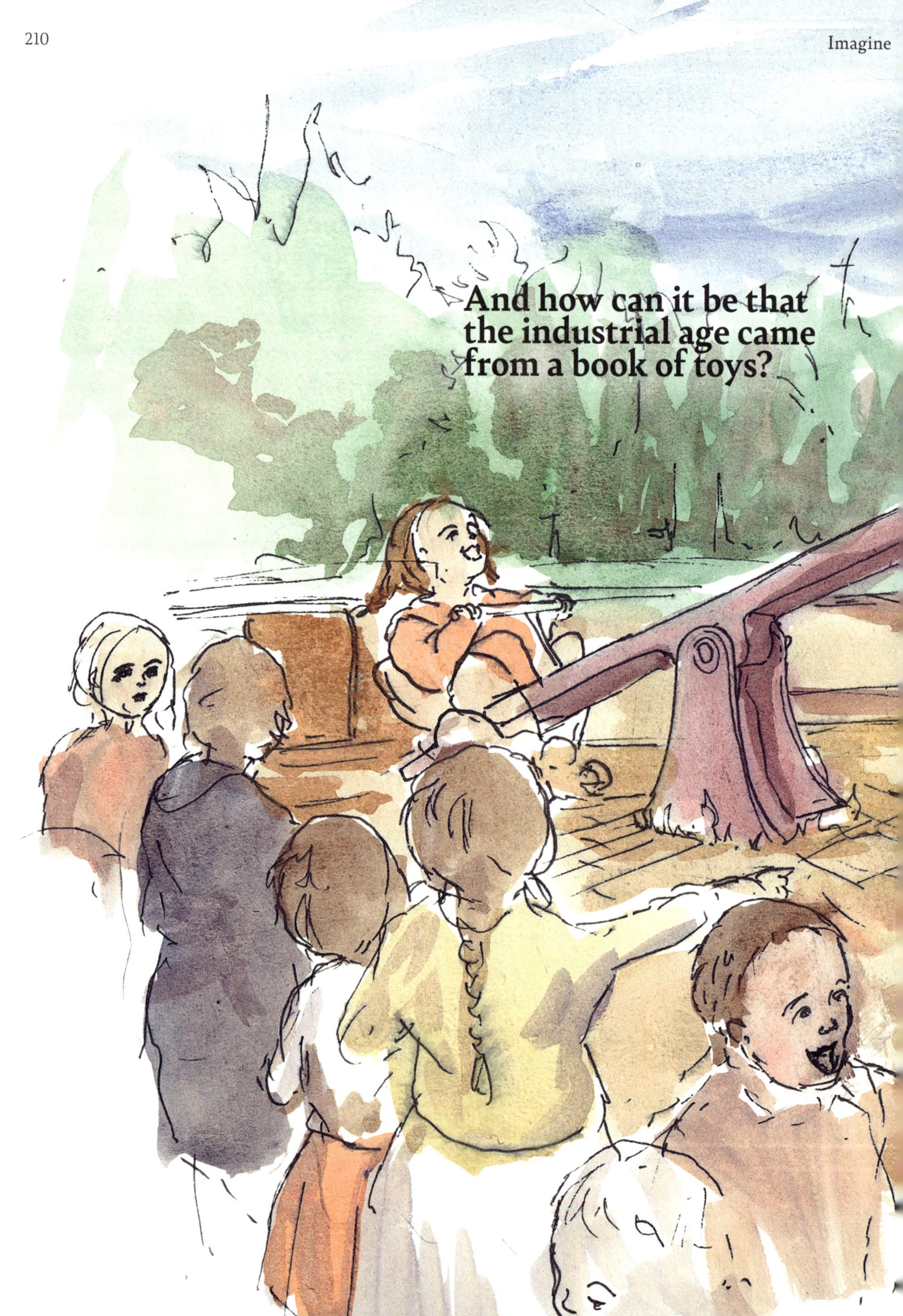
And how can it be that the industrial age came from a book of toys?

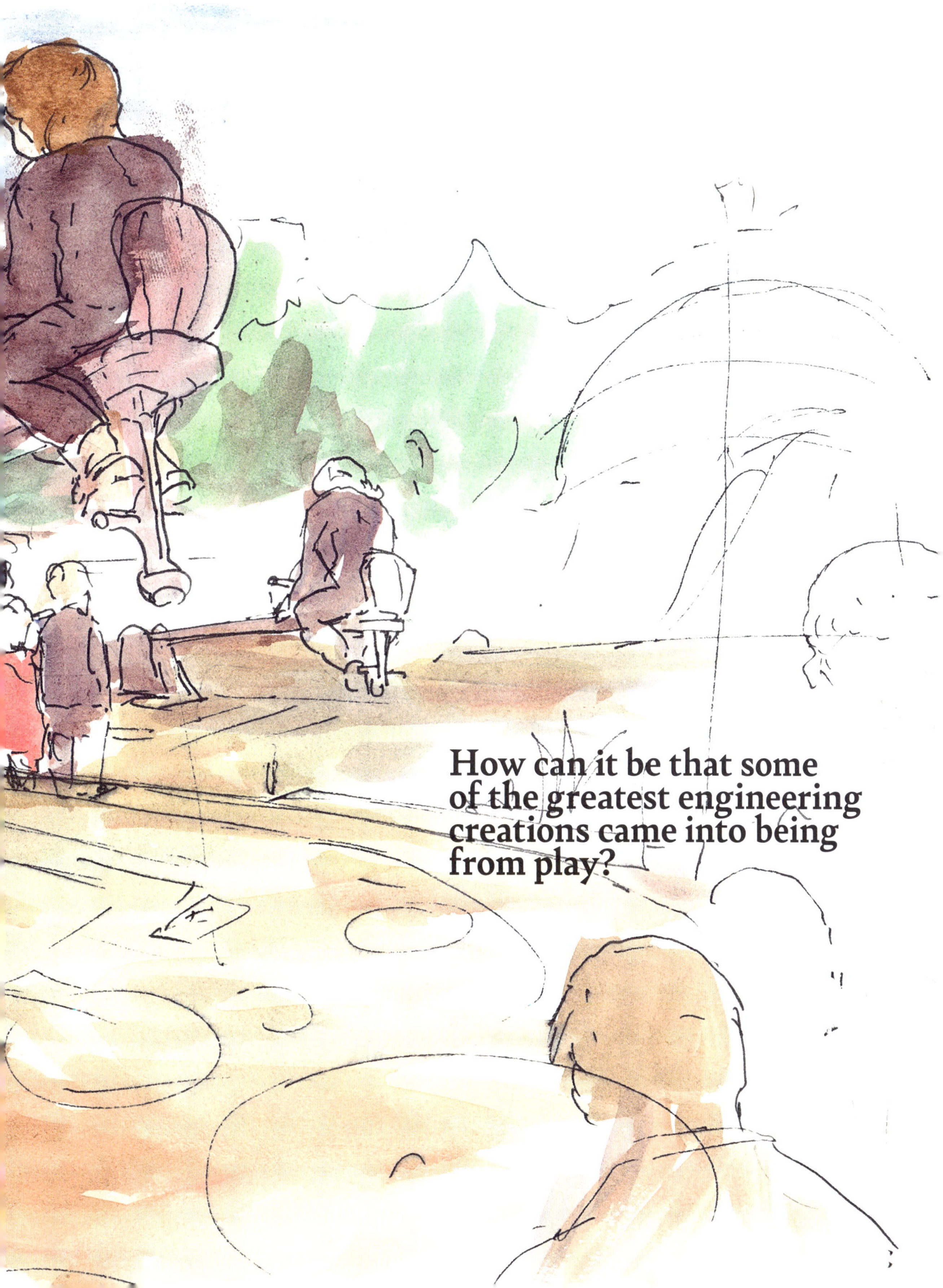

How can it be that some of the greatest engineering creations came into being from play?

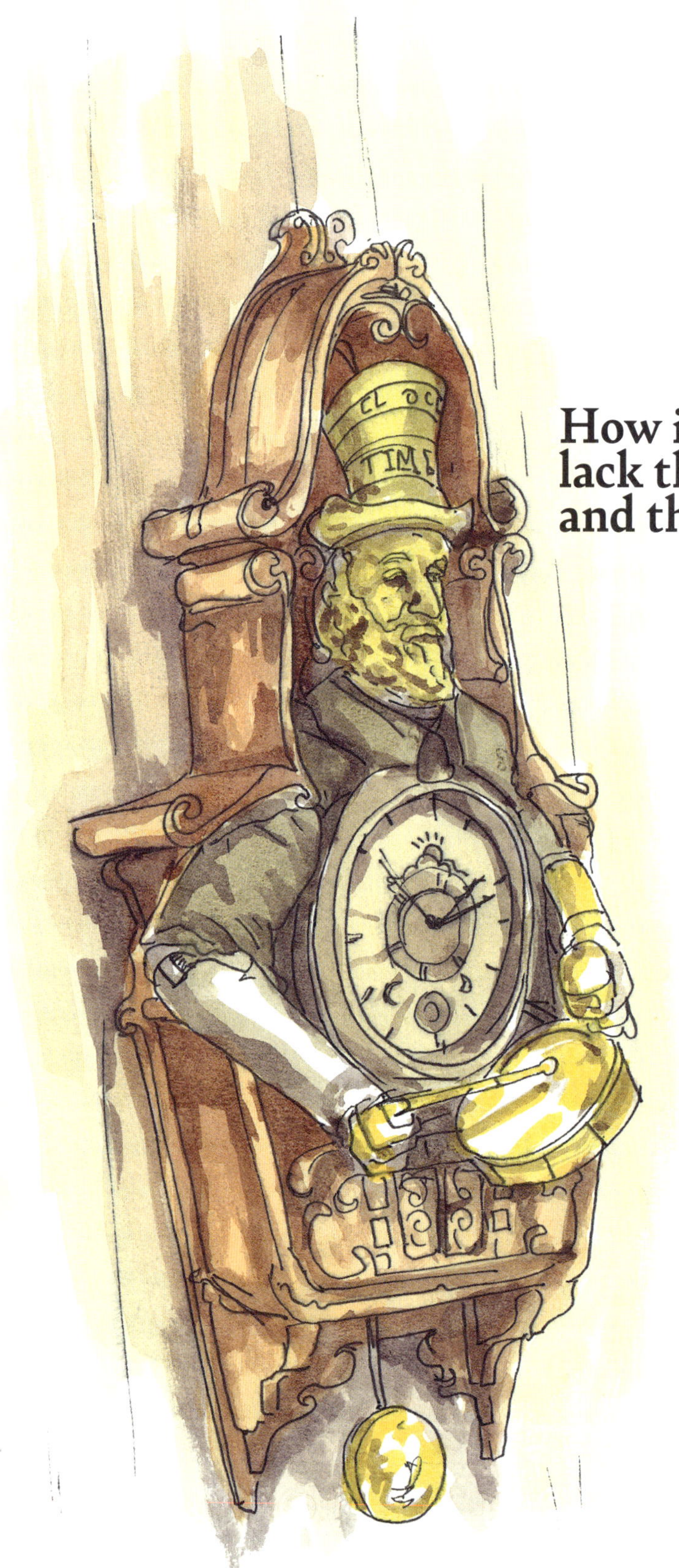

How is our imagination or lack thereof shaping reality and the future?

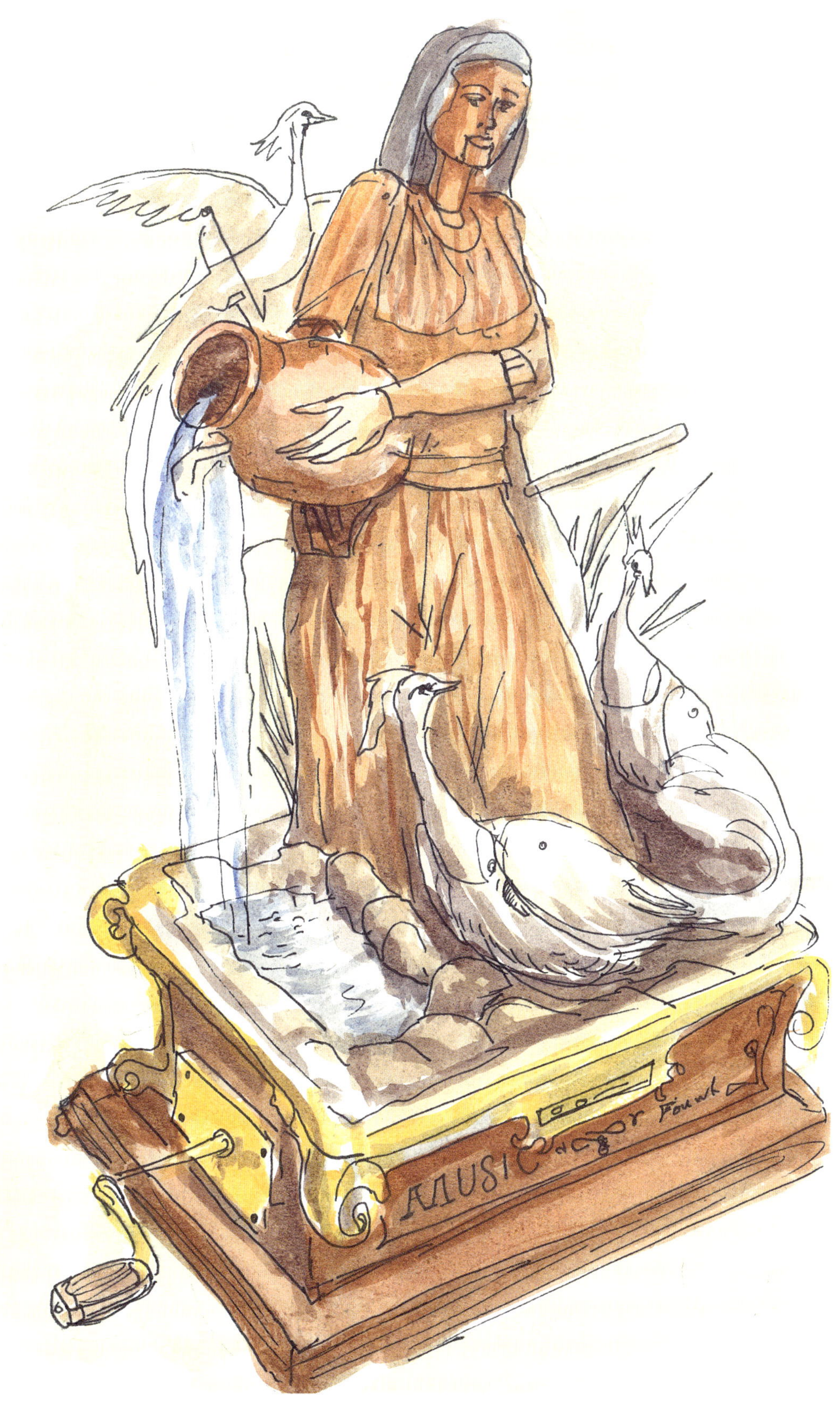
MUSIC

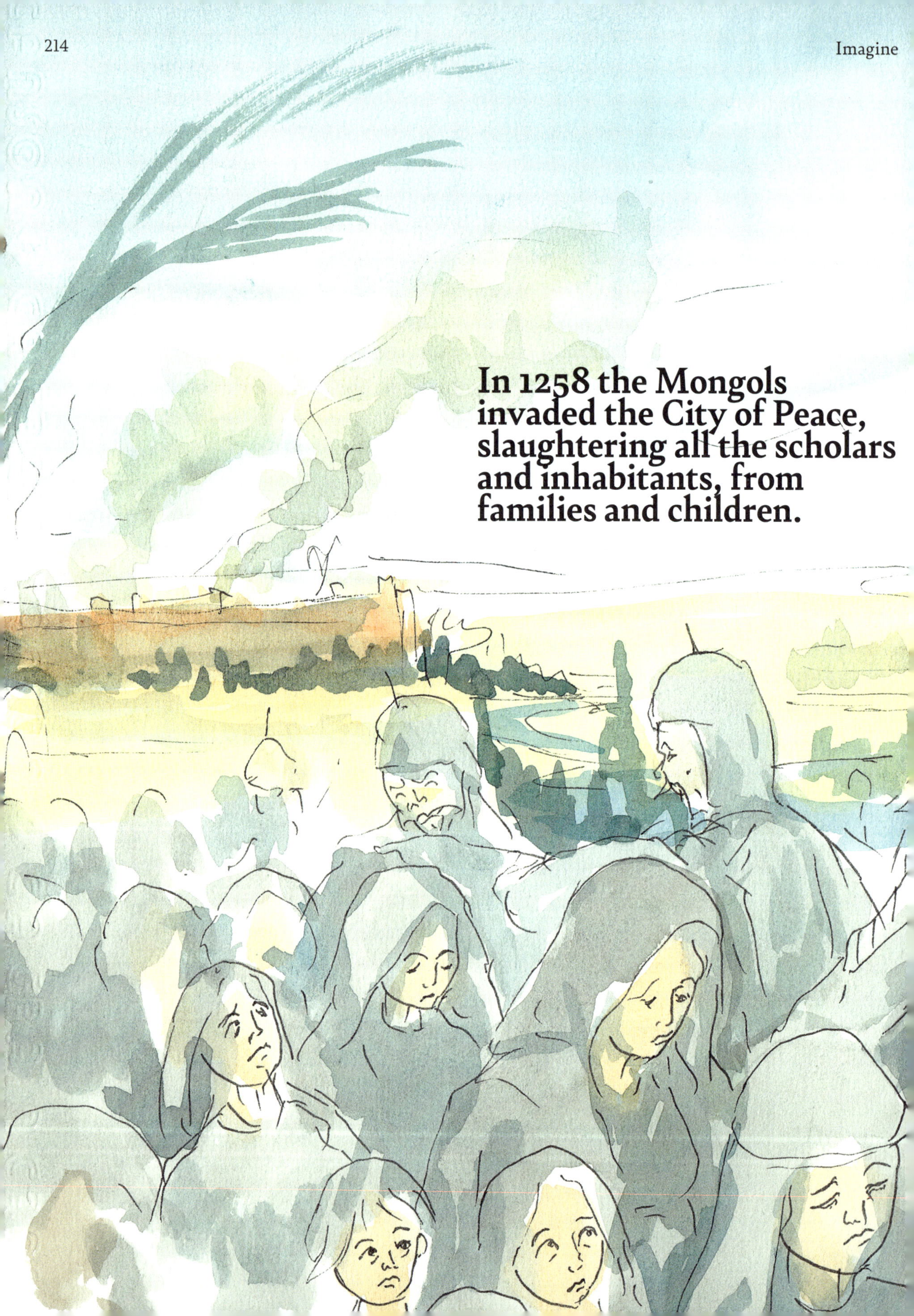
In 1258 the Mongols
invaded the City of Peace,
slaughtering all the scholars
and inhabitants, from
families and children.

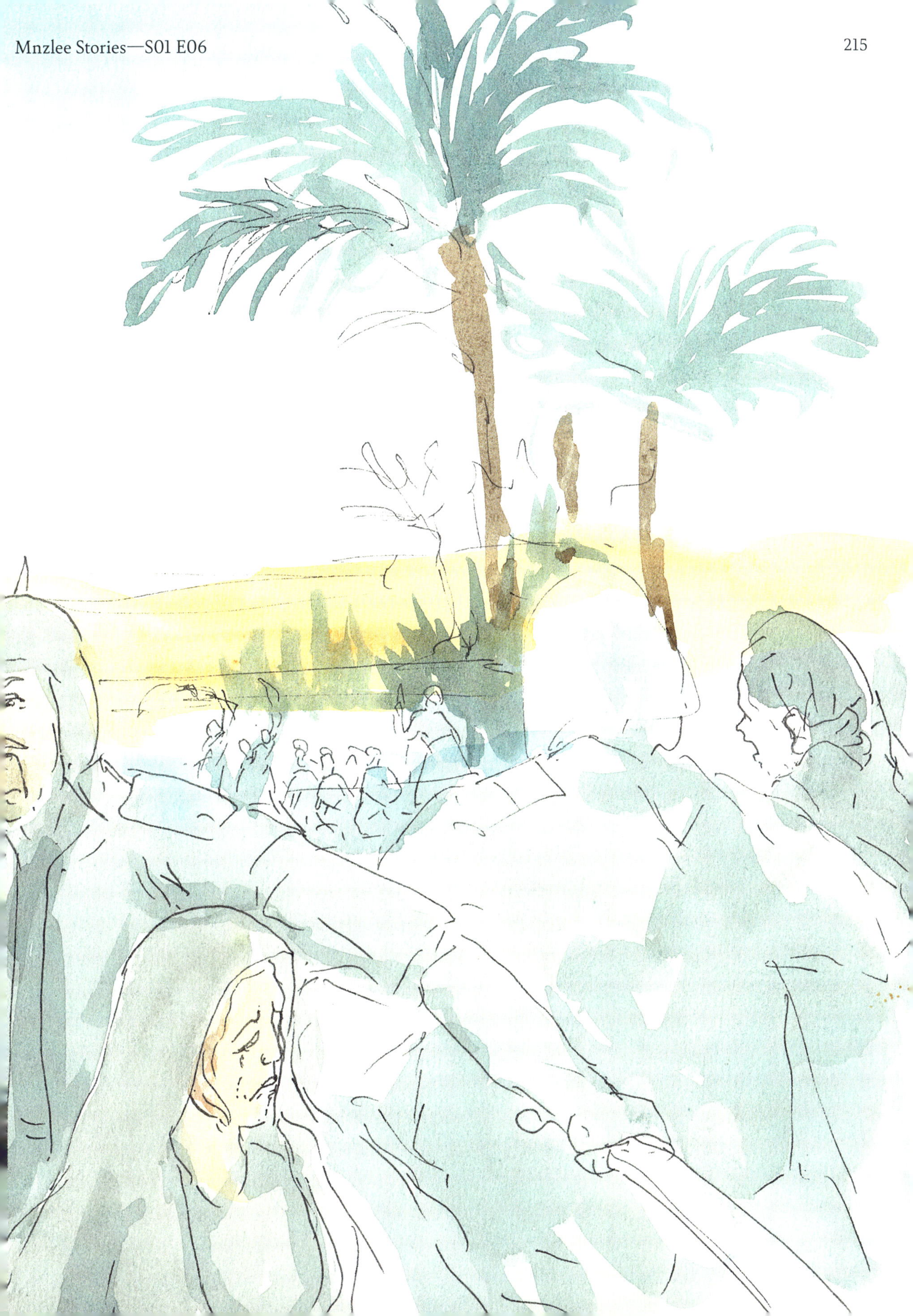

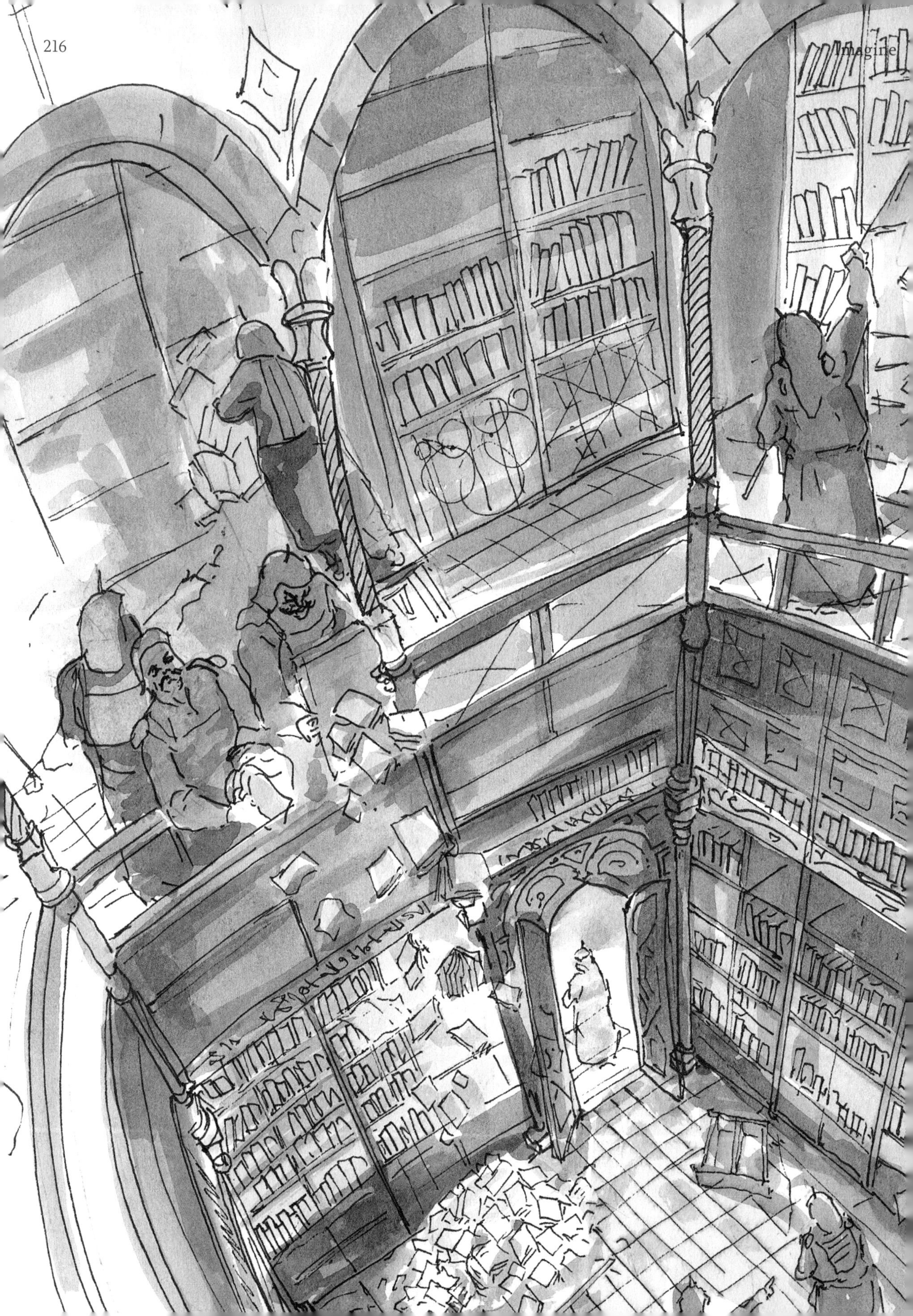

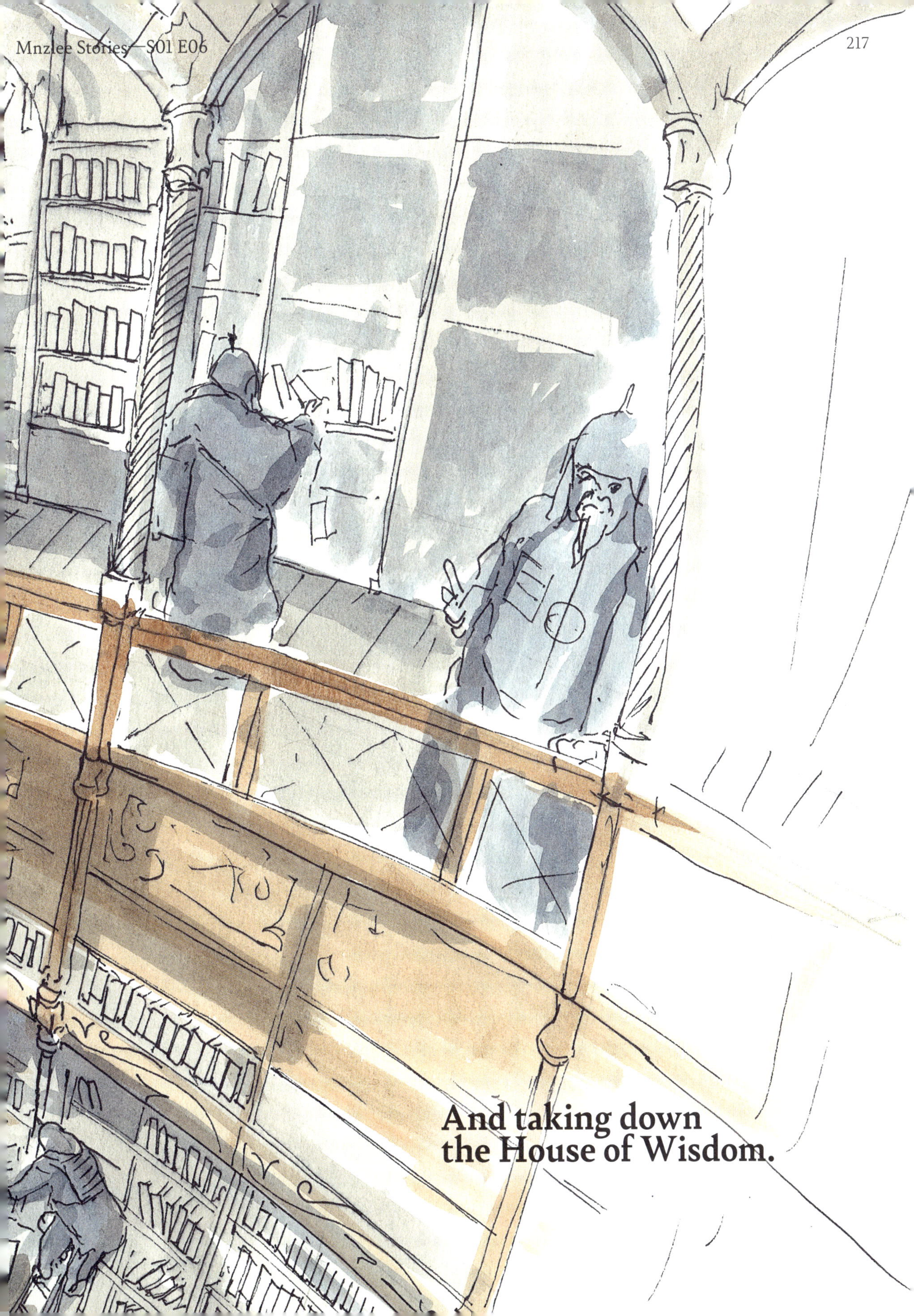

And taking down
the House of Wisdom.

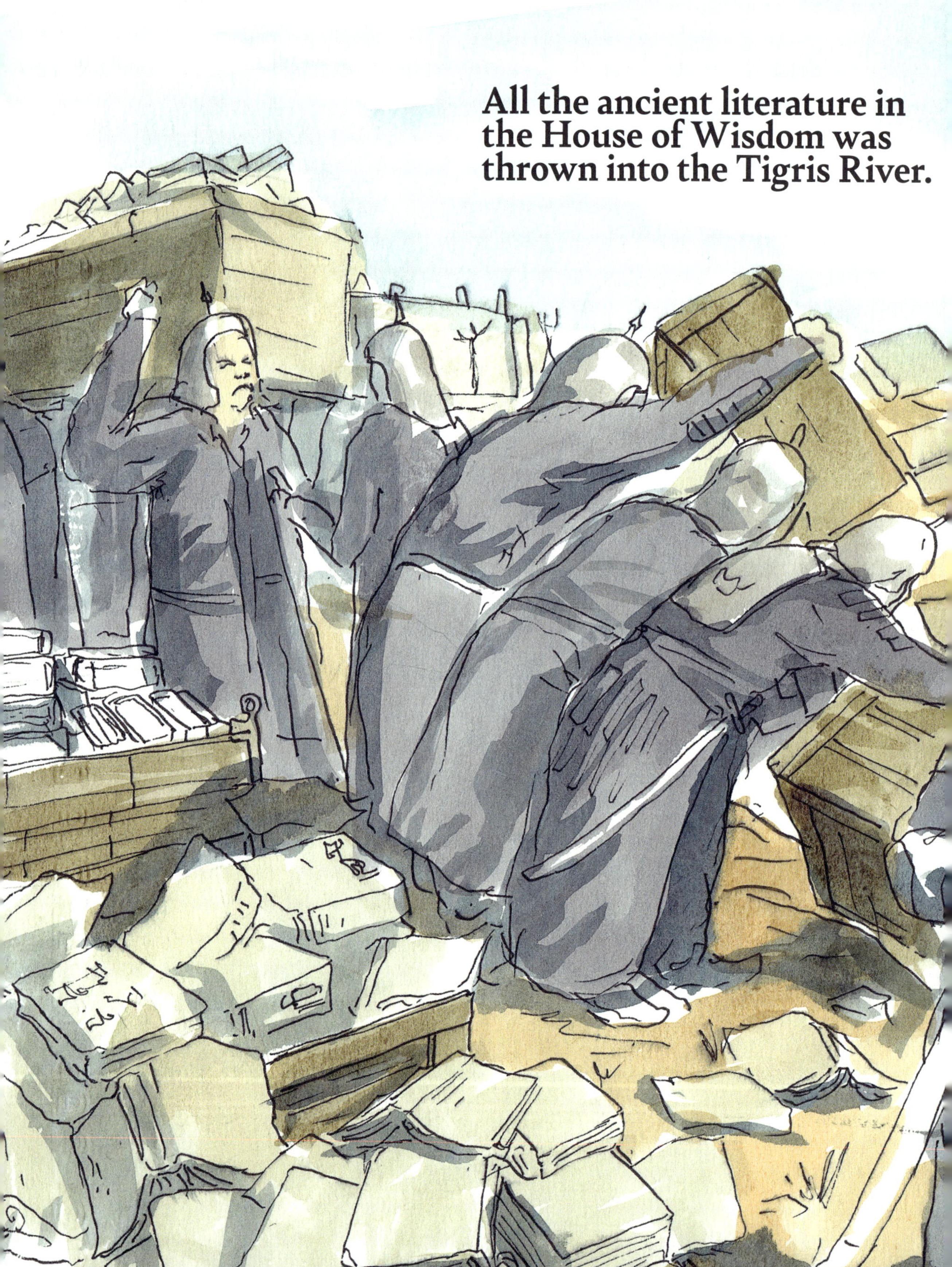

All the ancient literature in the House of Wisdom was thrown into the Tigris River.

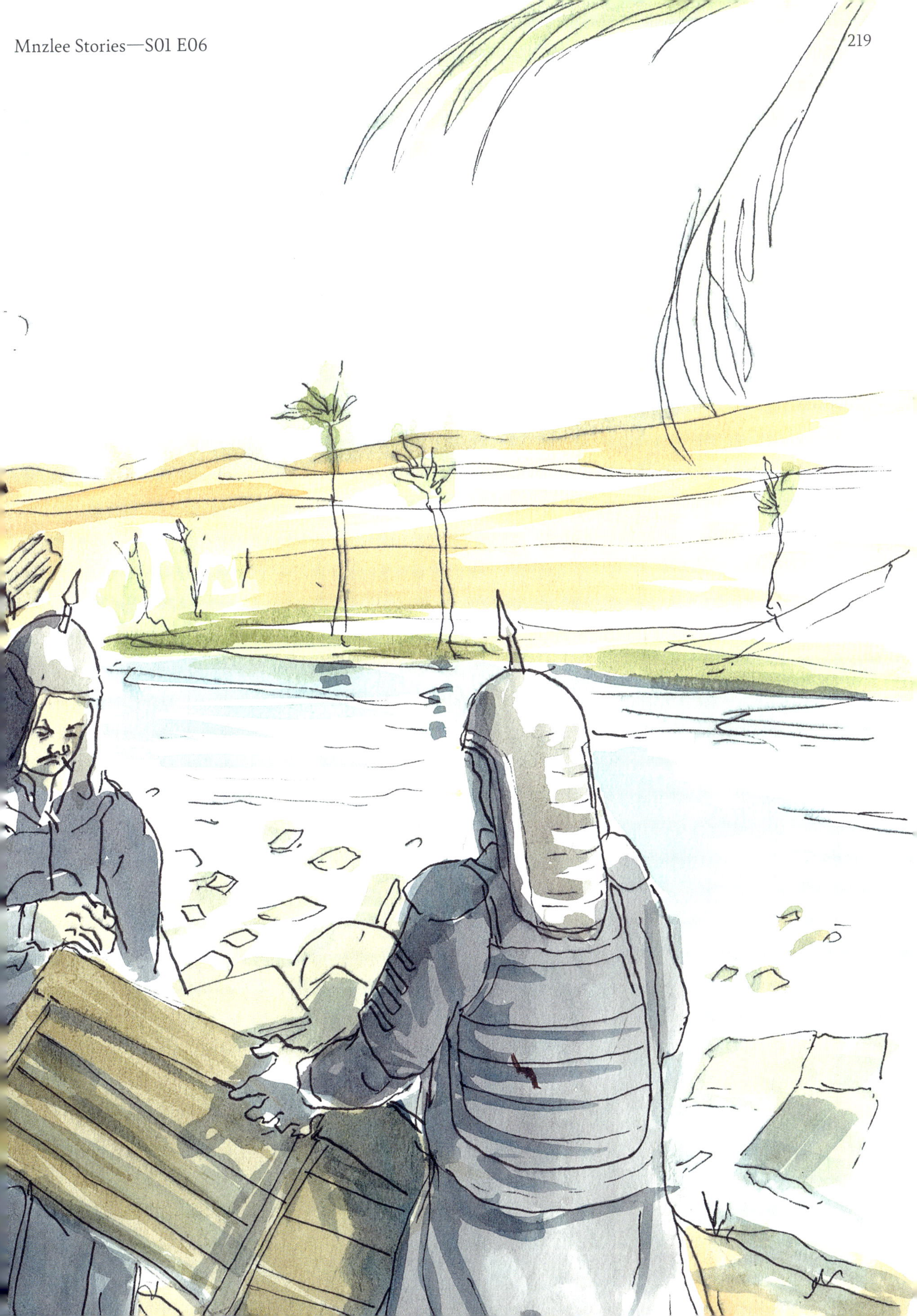

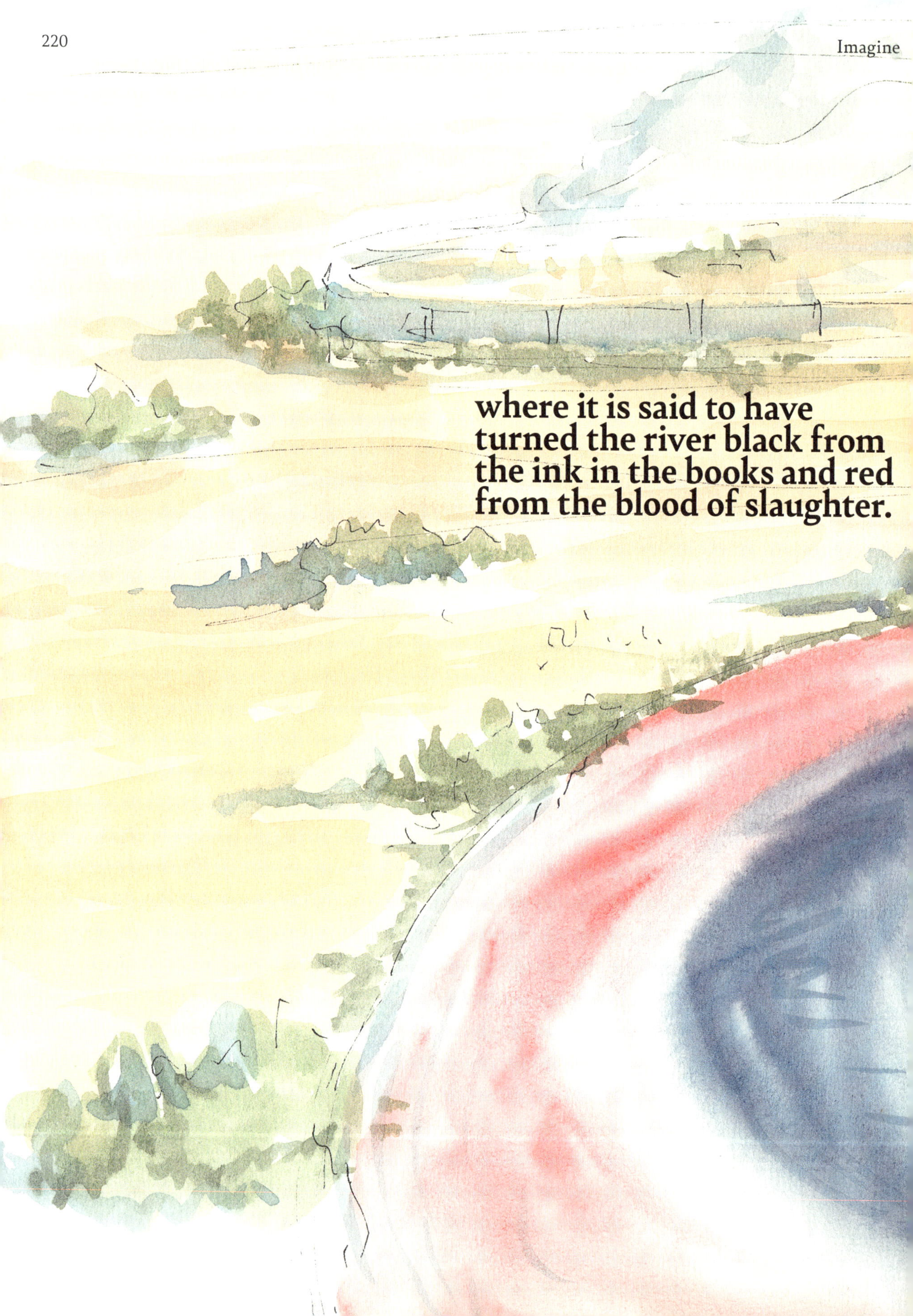
where it is said to have
turned the river black from
the ink in the books and red
from the blood of slaughter.

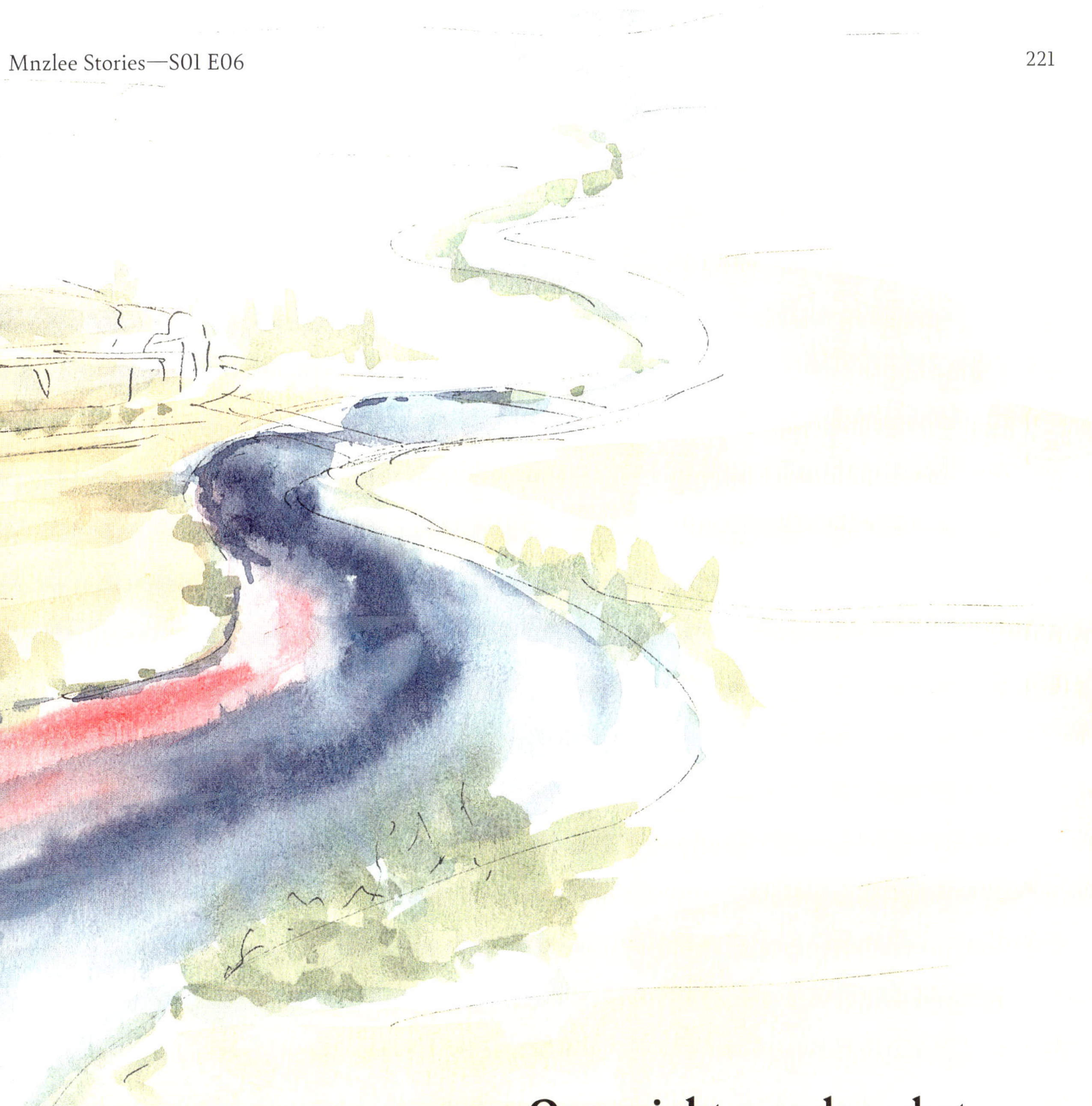

**One might wonder what
other treasures were drowned
in that river that day.**

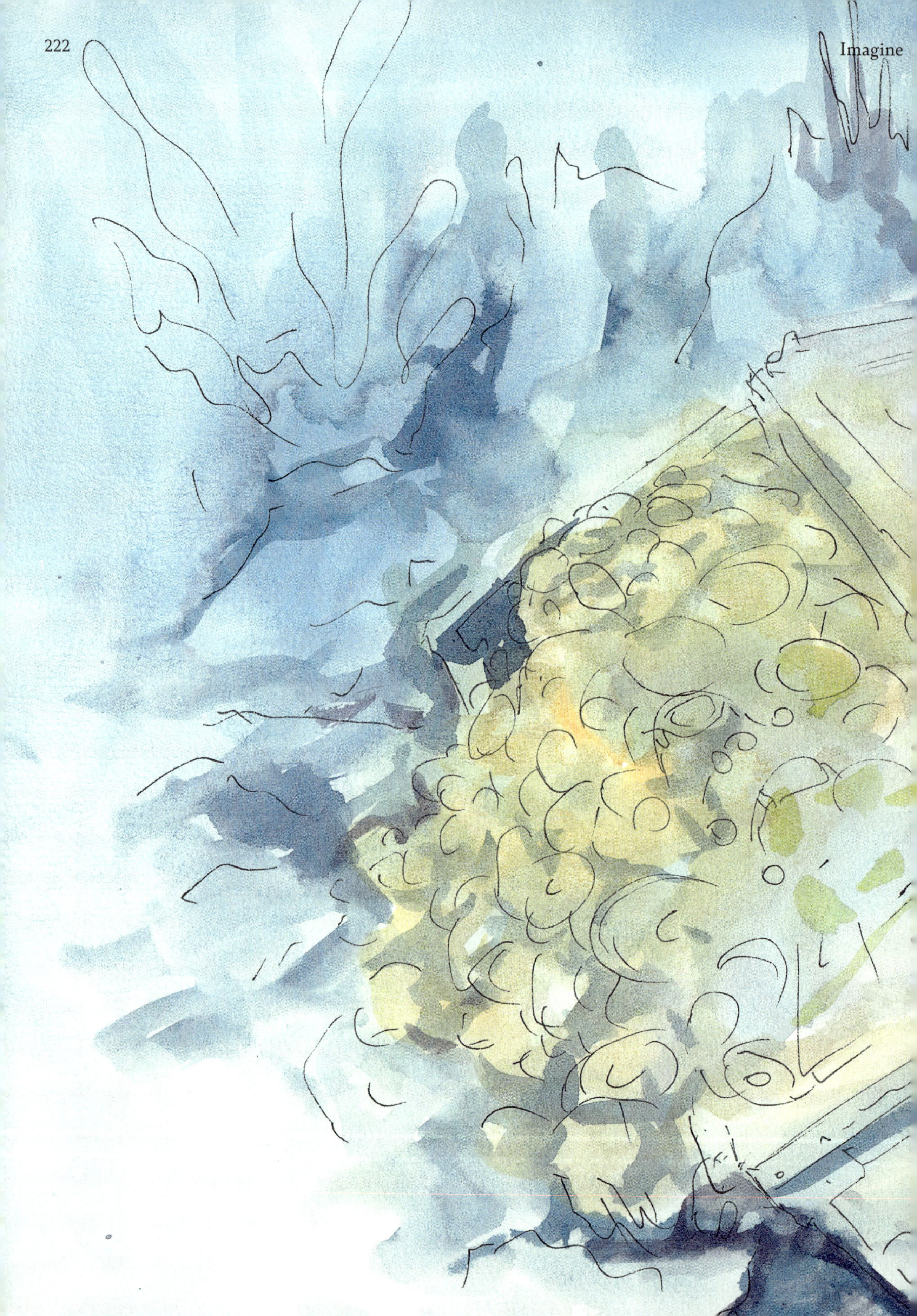

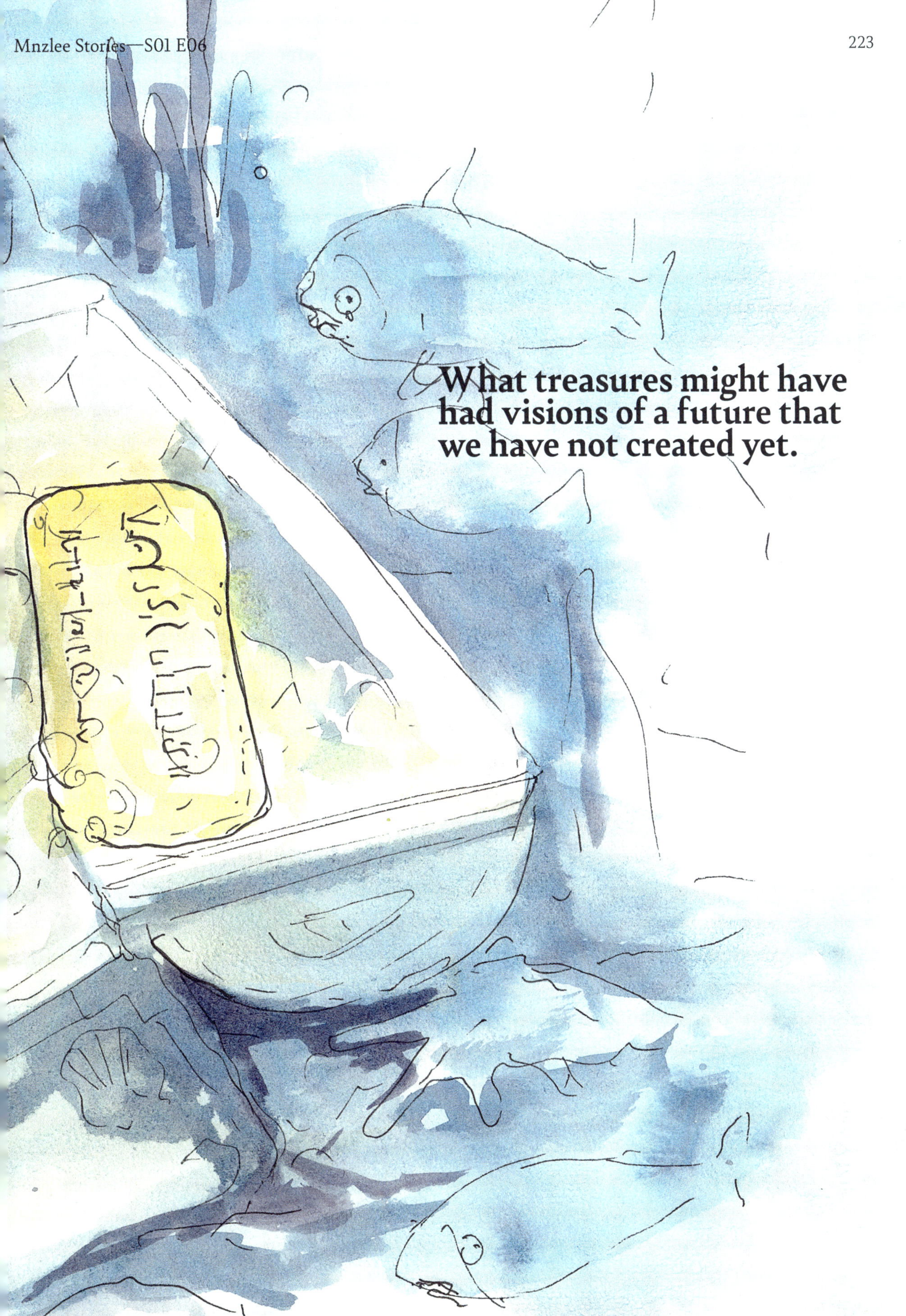
What treasures might have
had visions of a future that
we have not created yet.

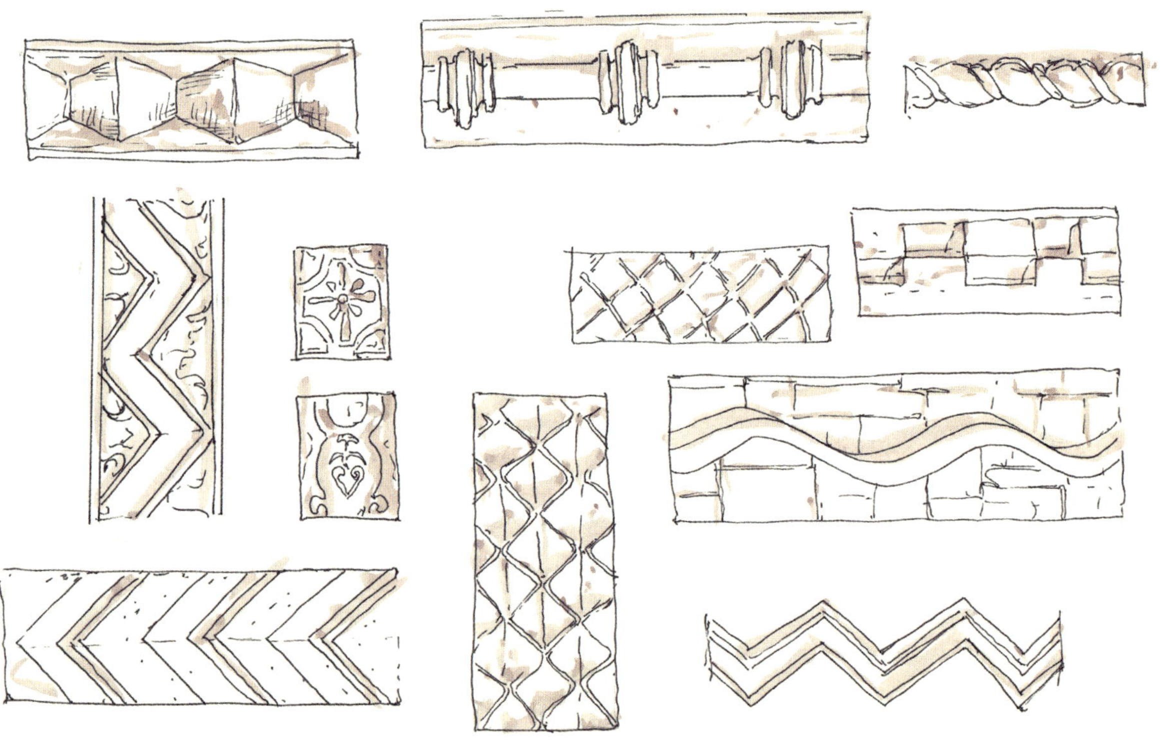

Between what is actually possible...

there is

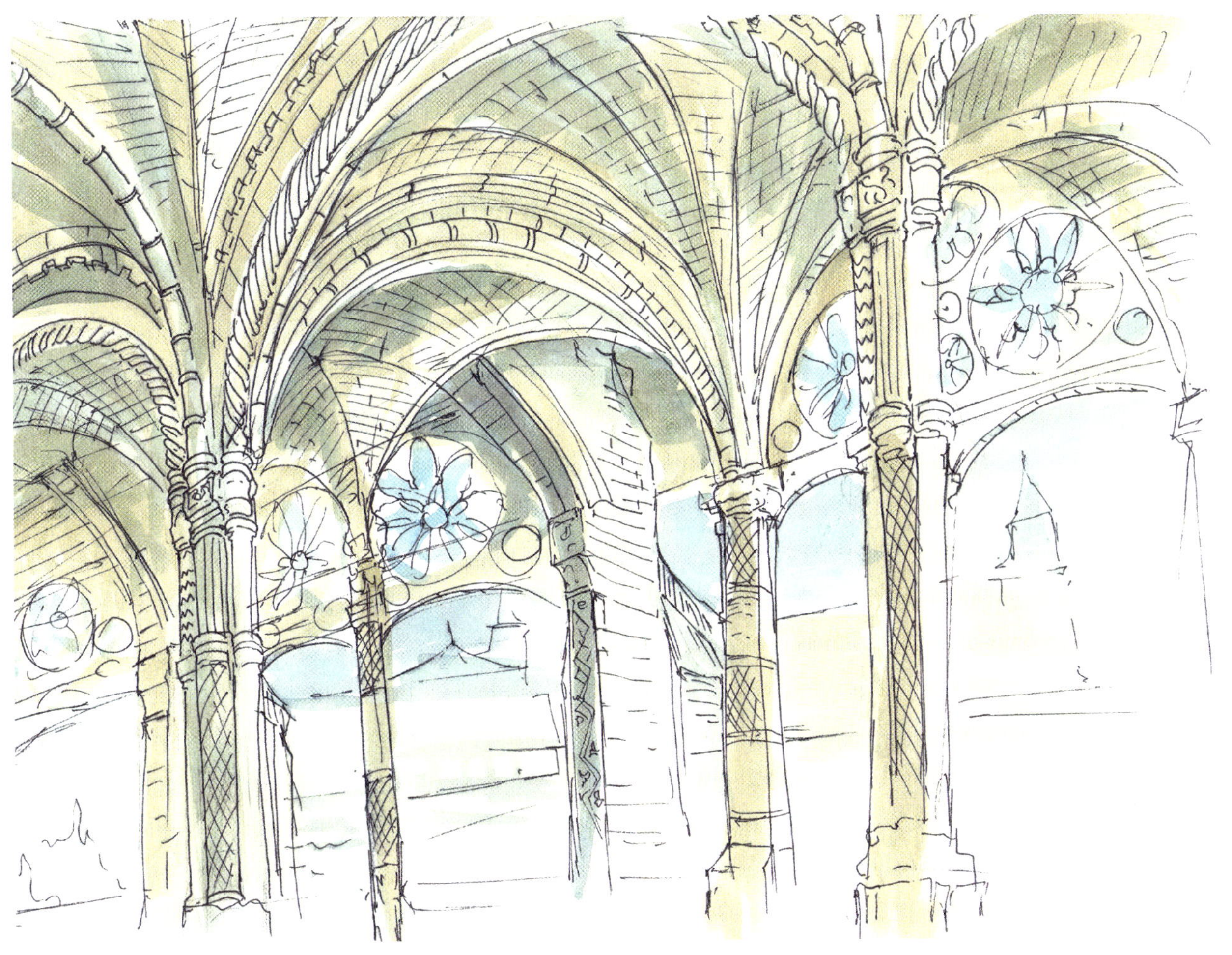

and what we think is possible,

a gap.

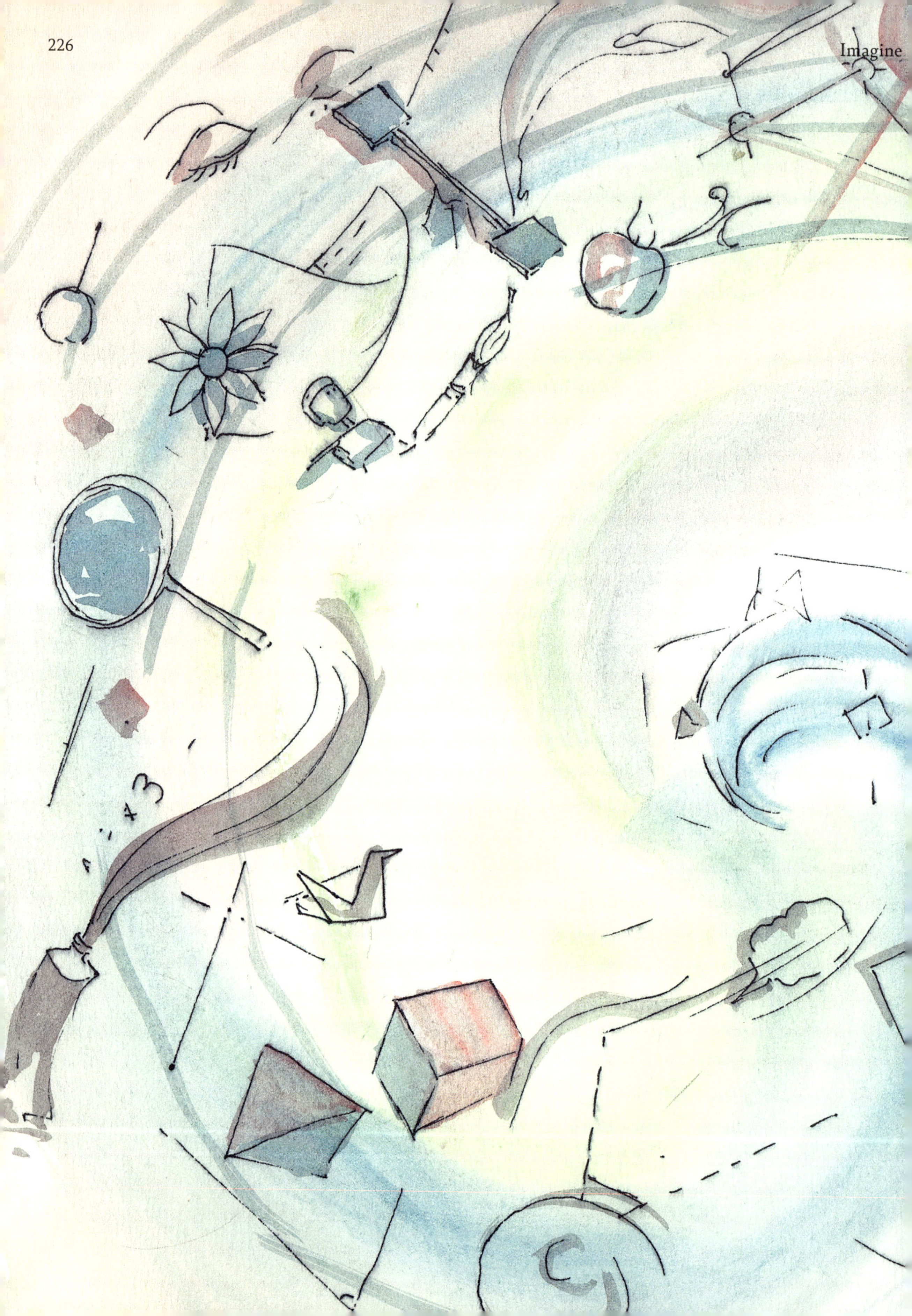

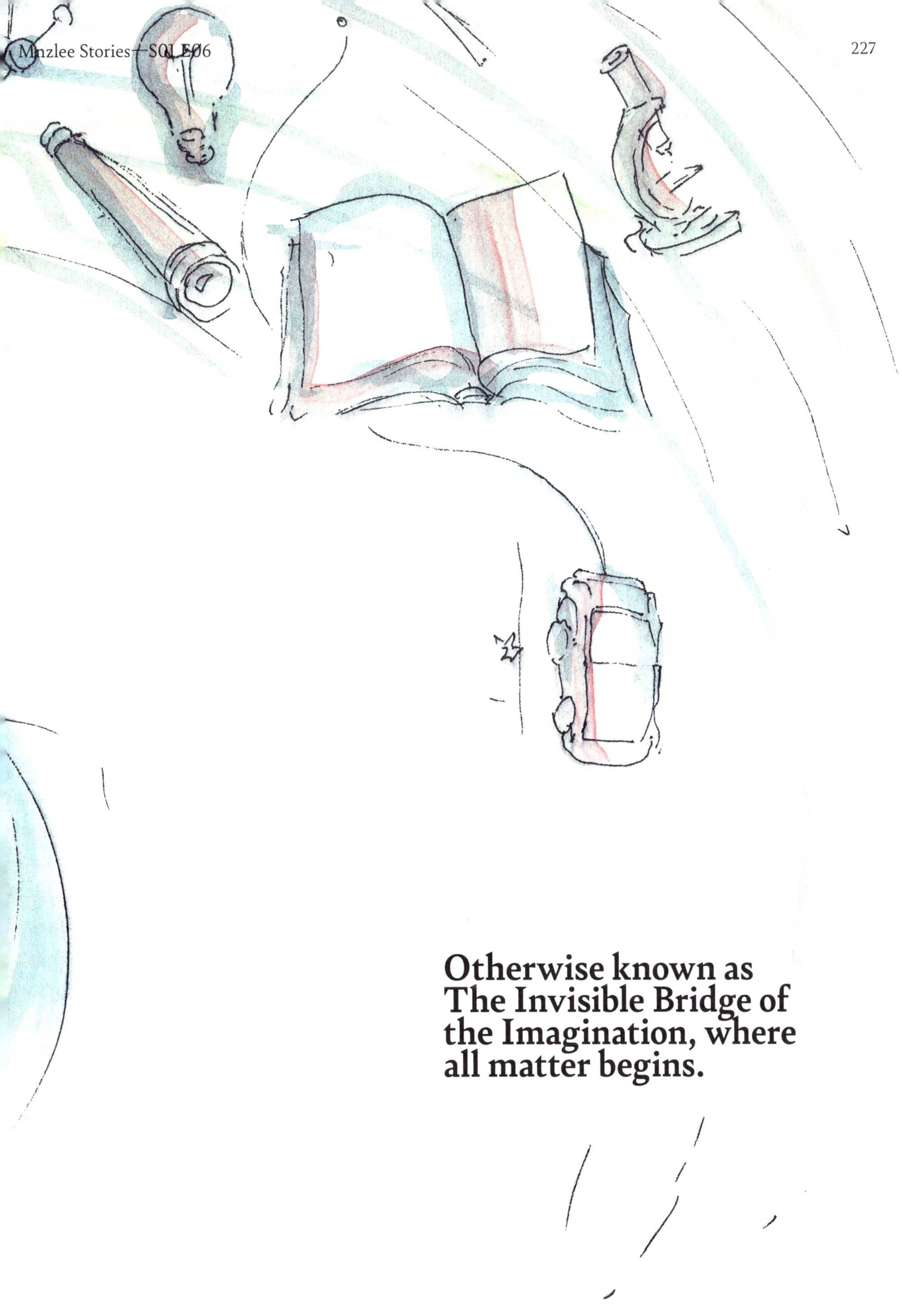

Otherwise known as
The Invisible Bridge of
the Imagination, where
all matter begins.

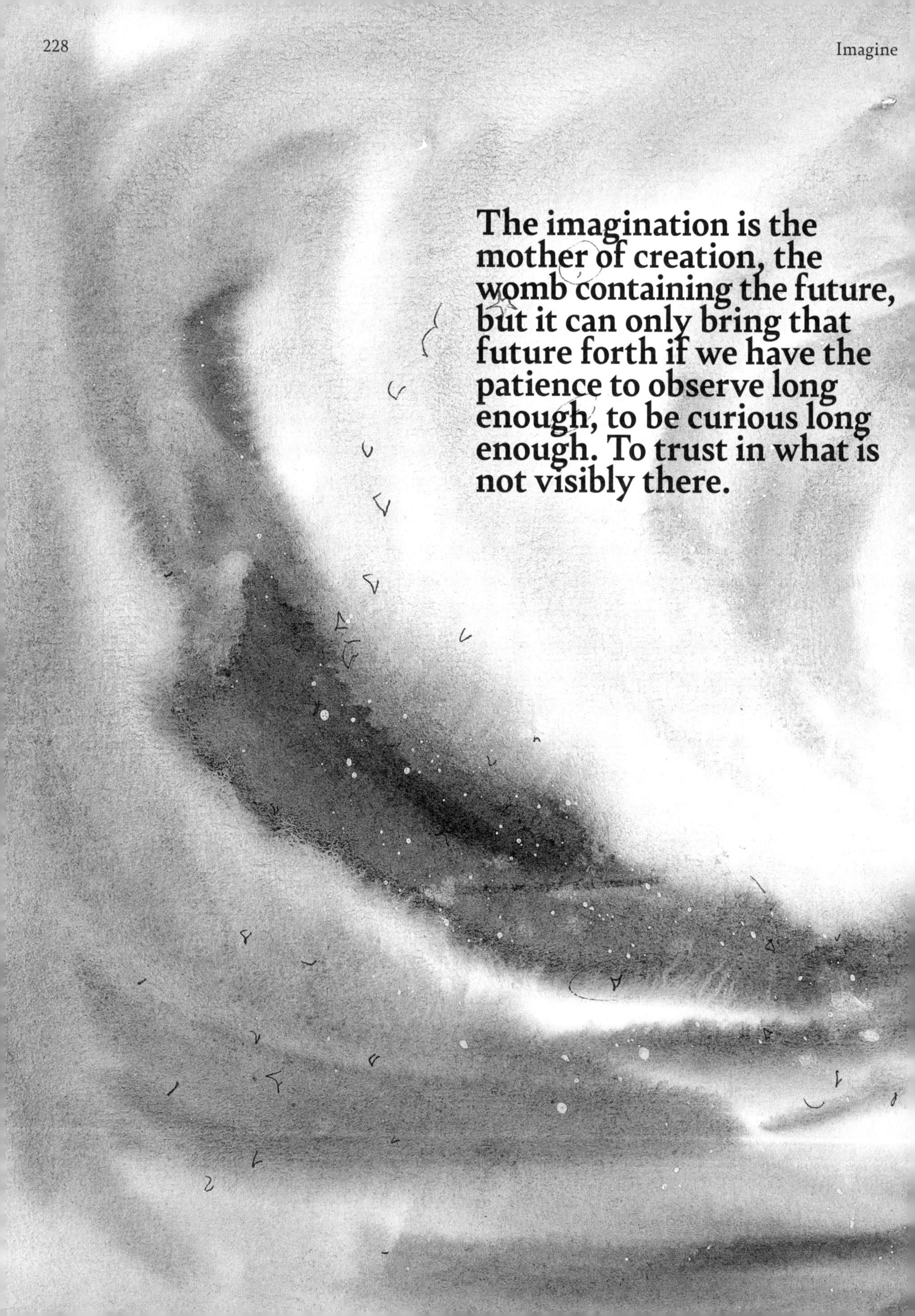

The imagination is the
mother of creation, the
womb containing the future,
but it can only bring that
future forth if we have the
patience to observe long
enough, to be curious long
enough. To trust in what is
not visibly there.

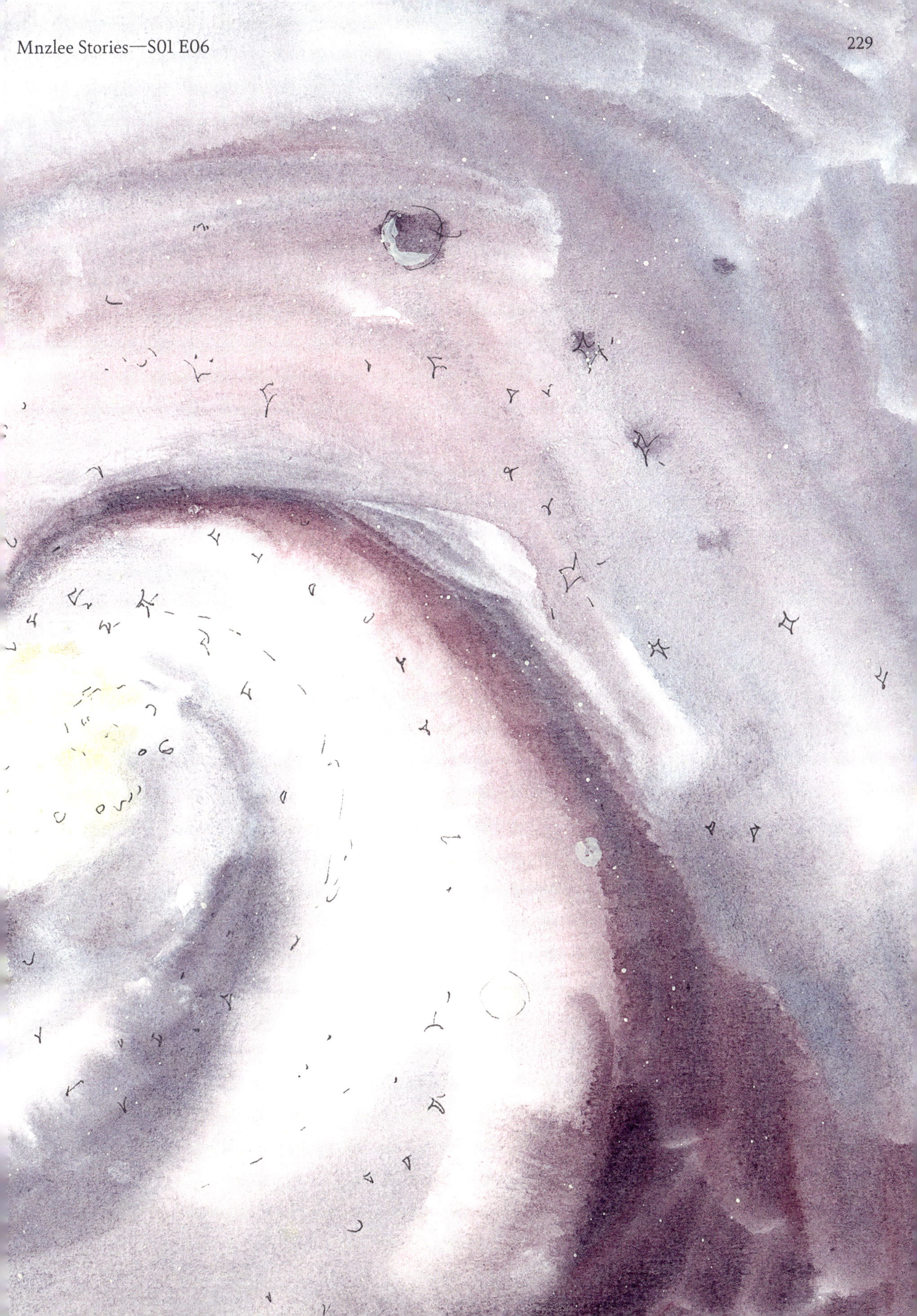

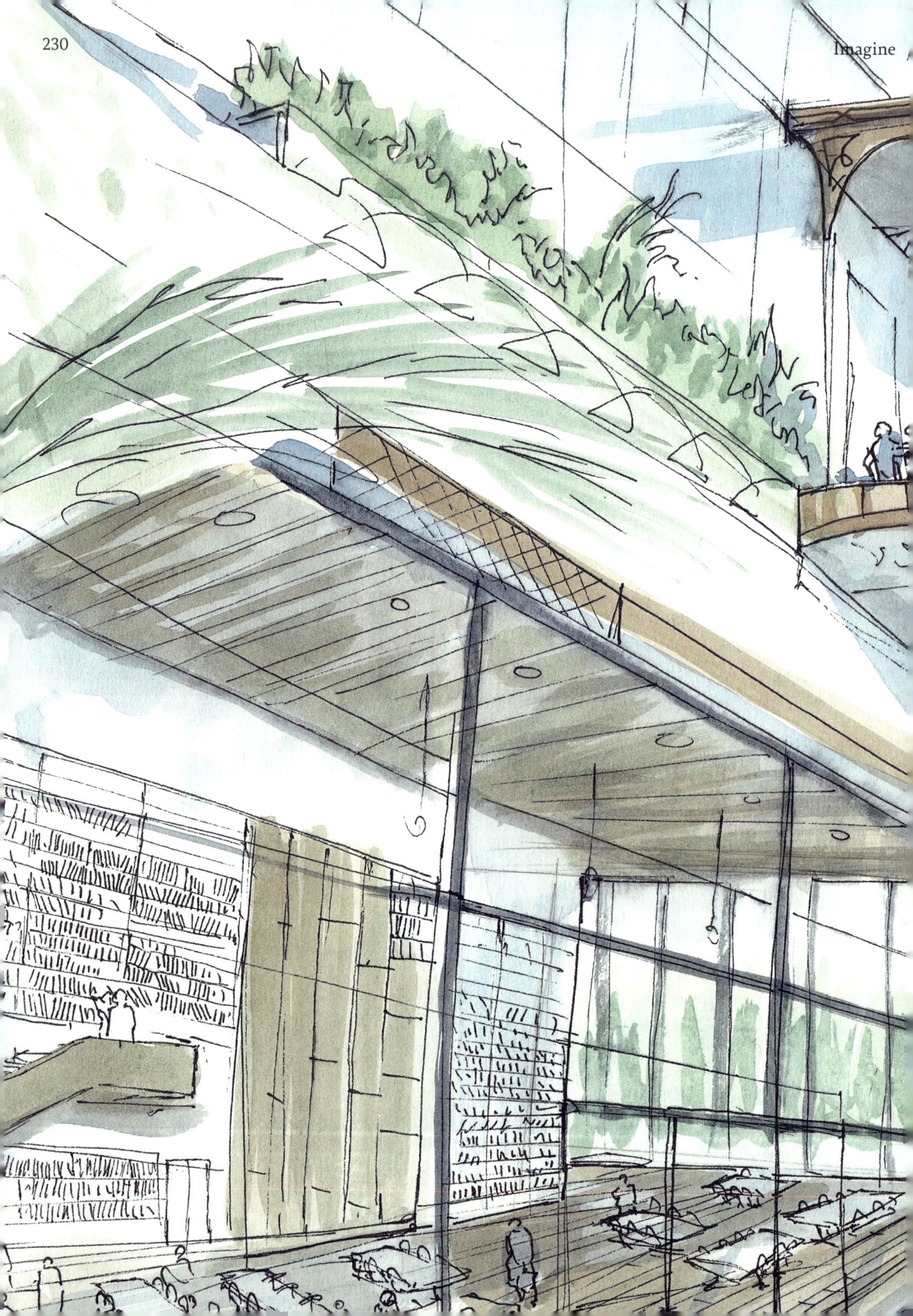

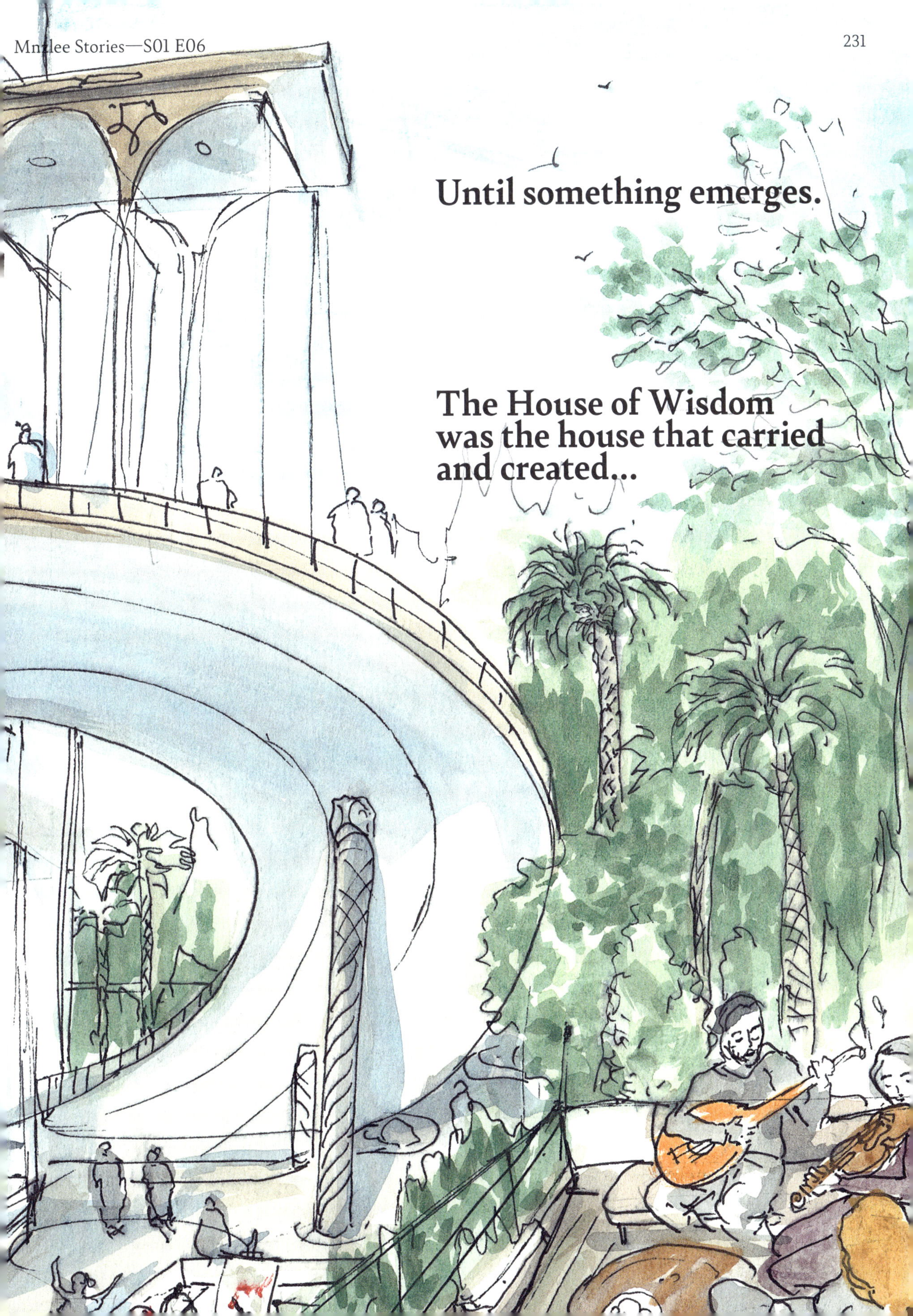
Until something emerges.

The House of Wisdom
was the house that carried
and created...

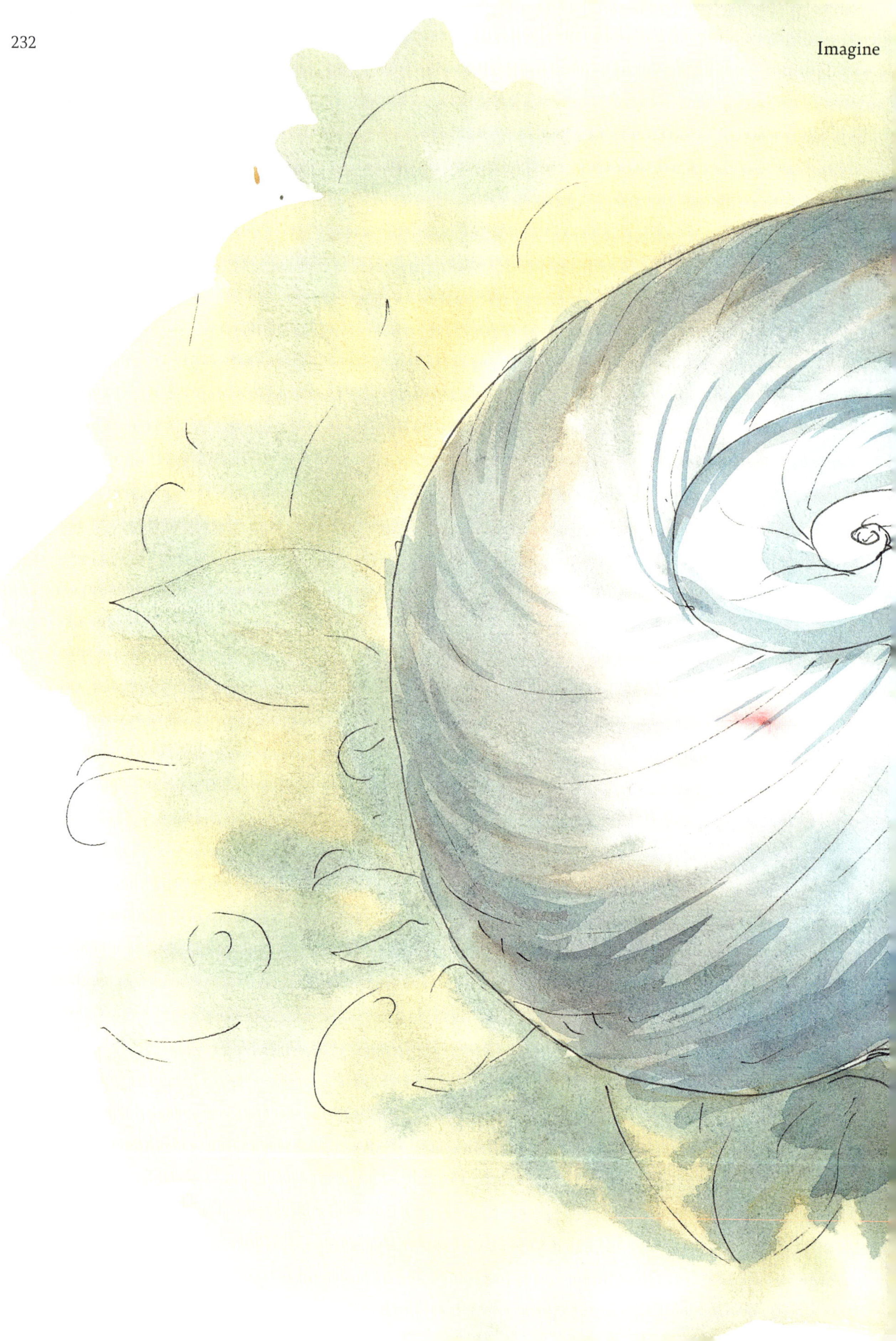

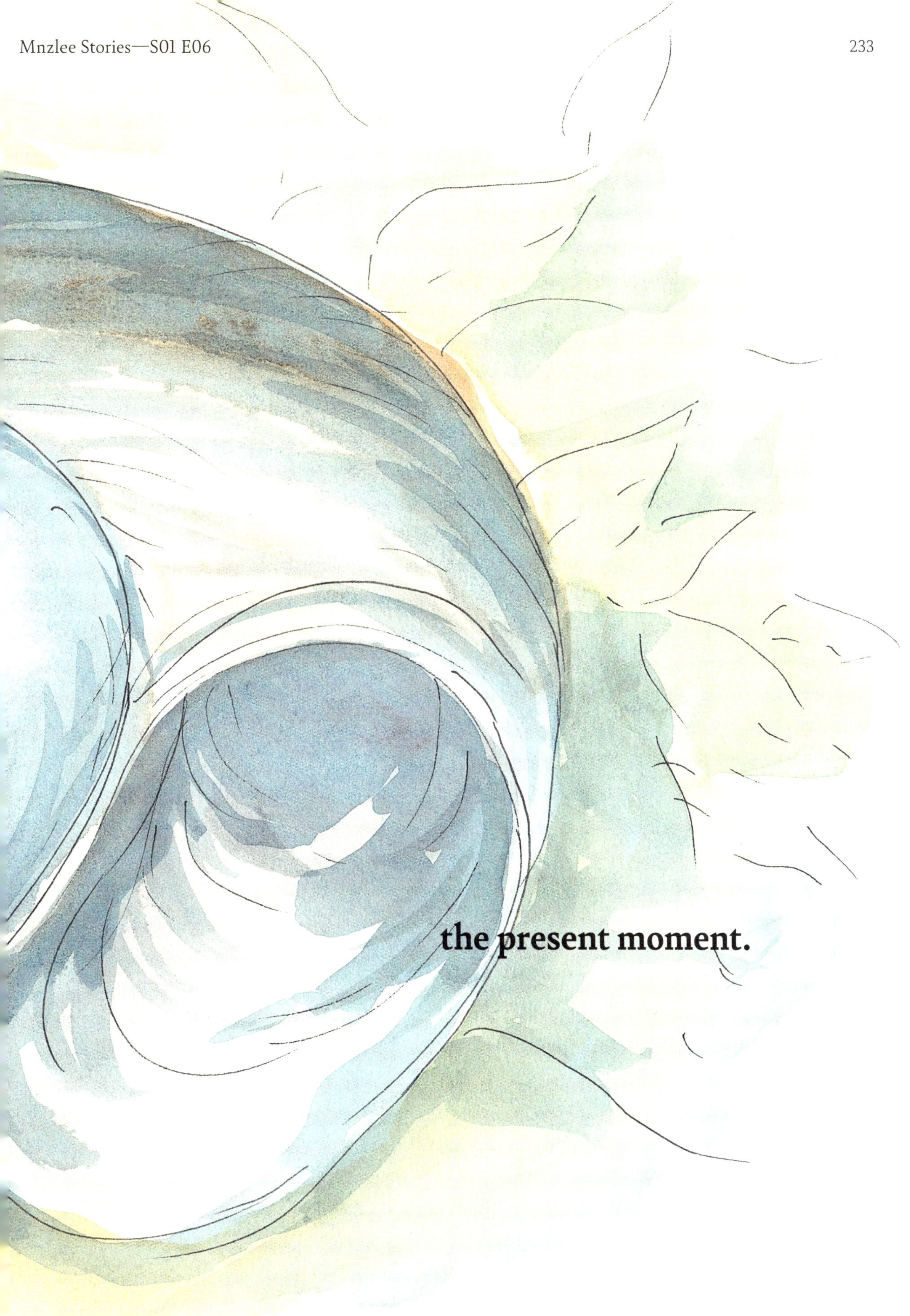

the present moment.

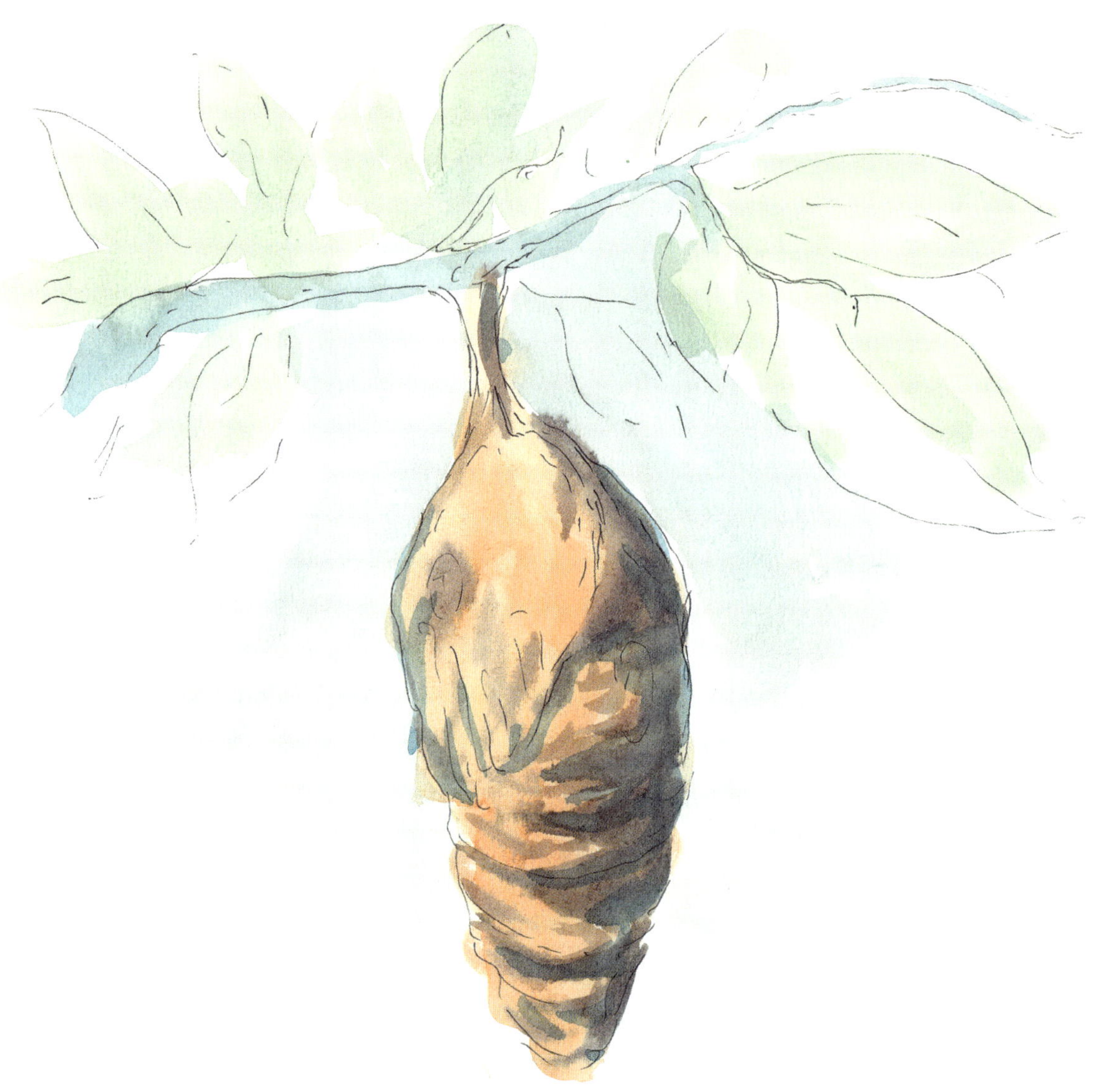

And while it has burnt down,

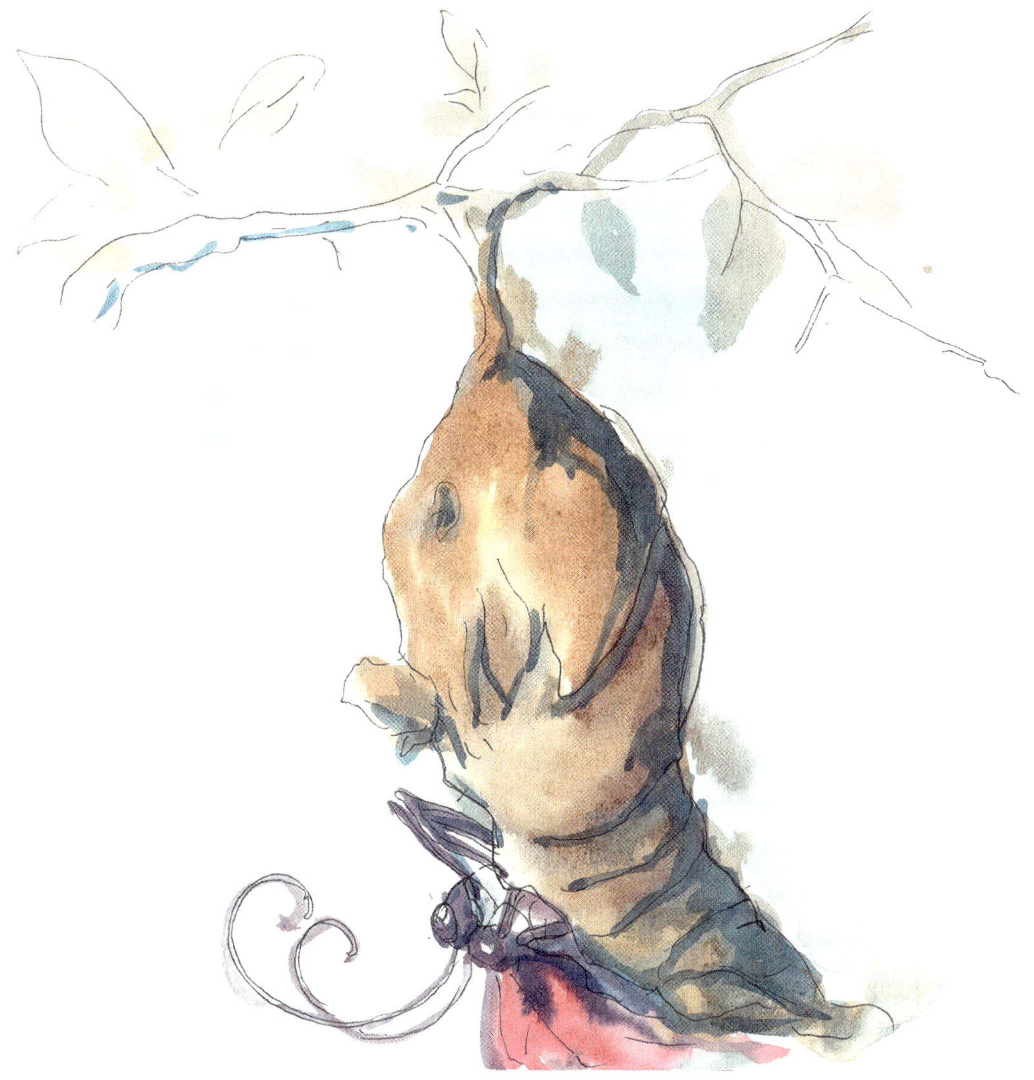

its essence has not.

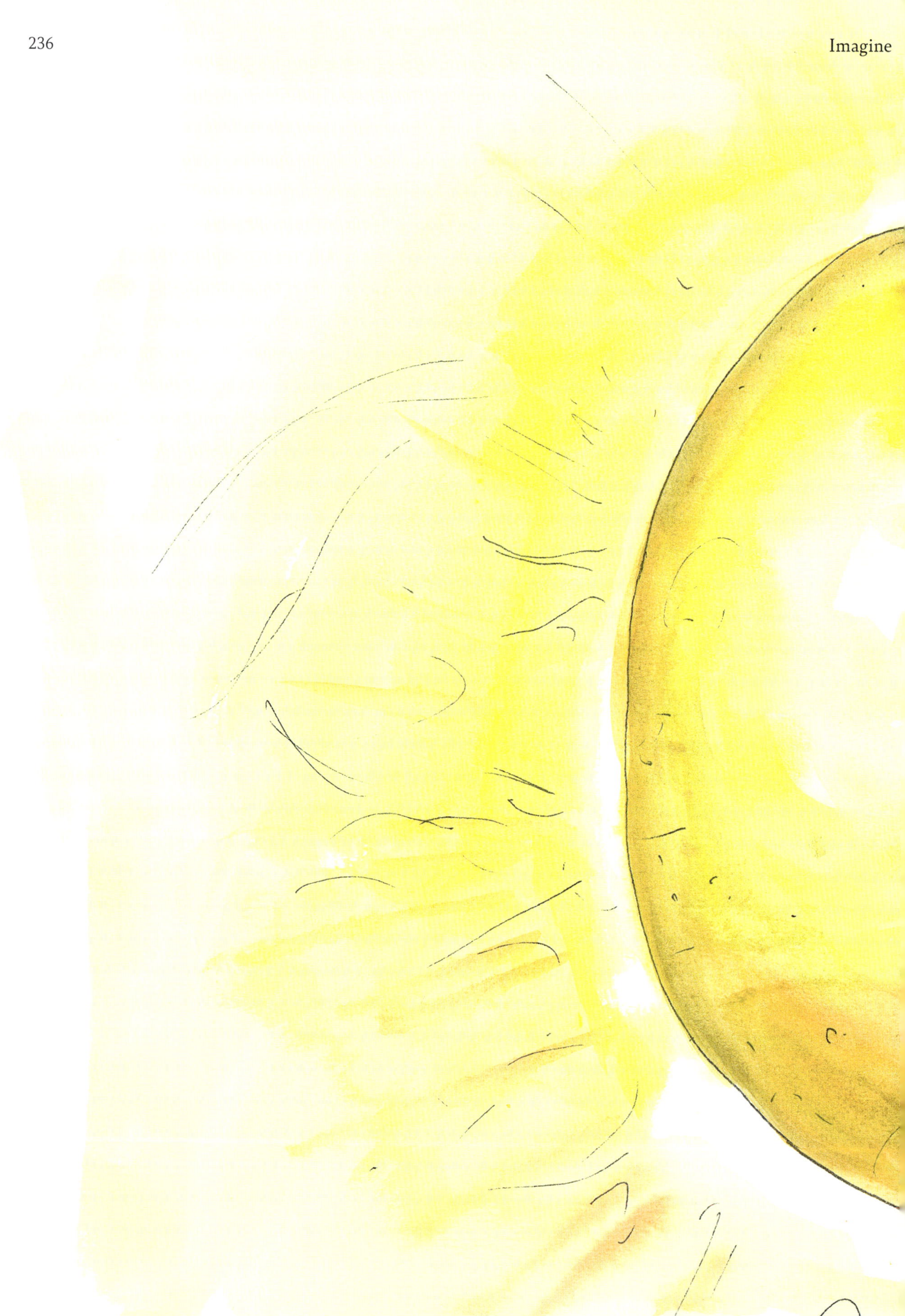

For the real eternal House of Wisdom,

the creator of the future to come, is the imagination,

and it exists inside of you.

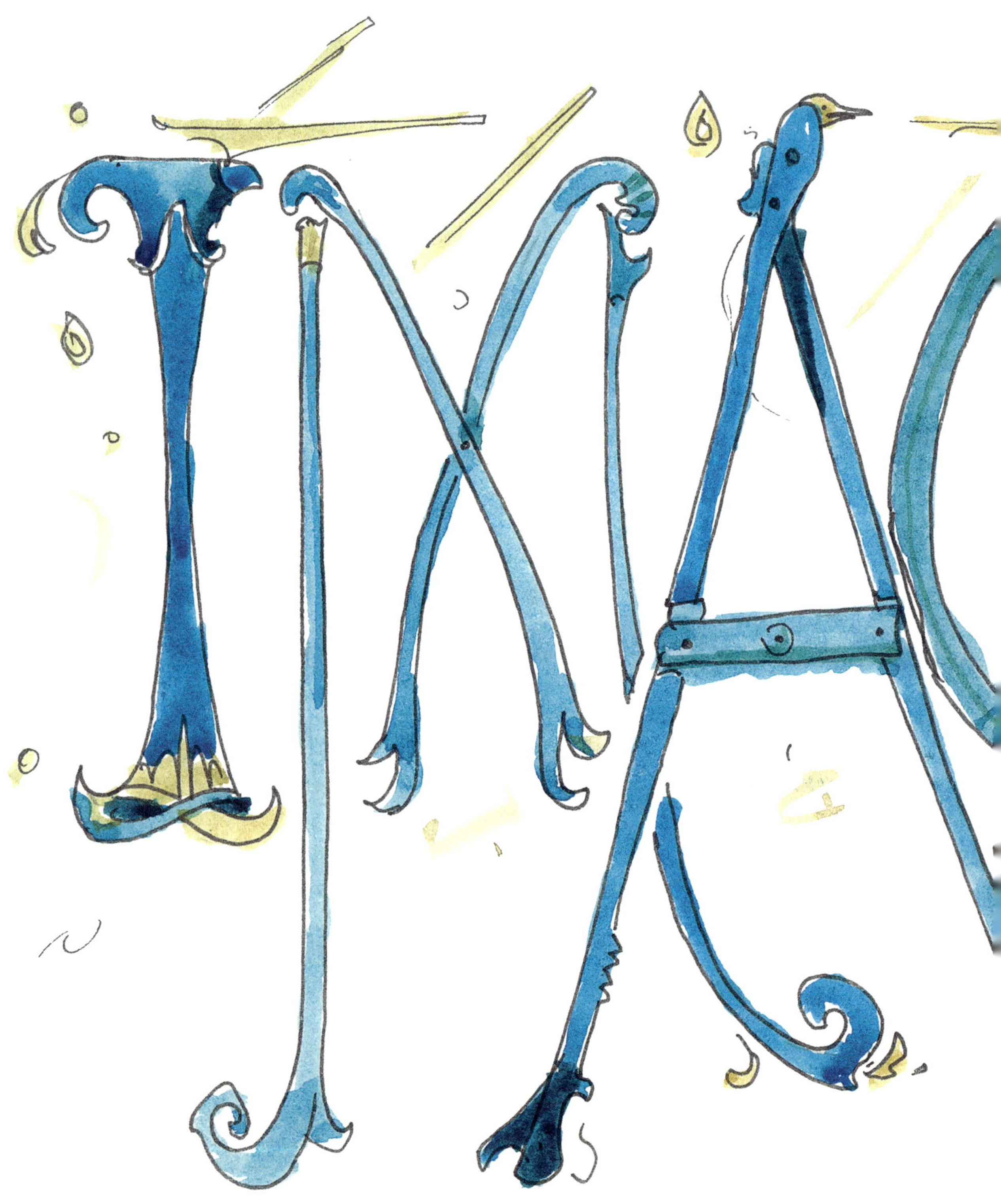

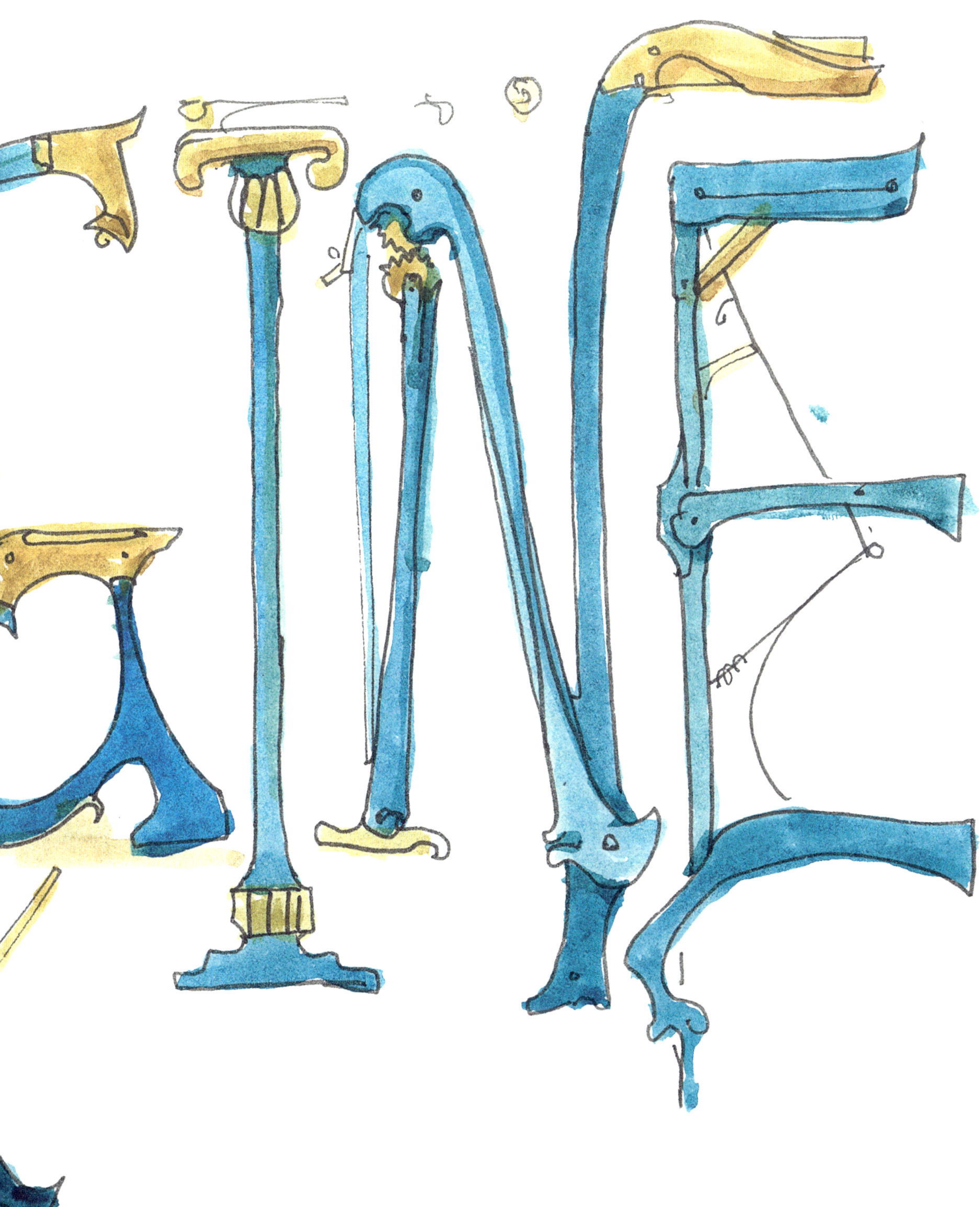

WHOSE

Mnzlee Stories — S01 E07

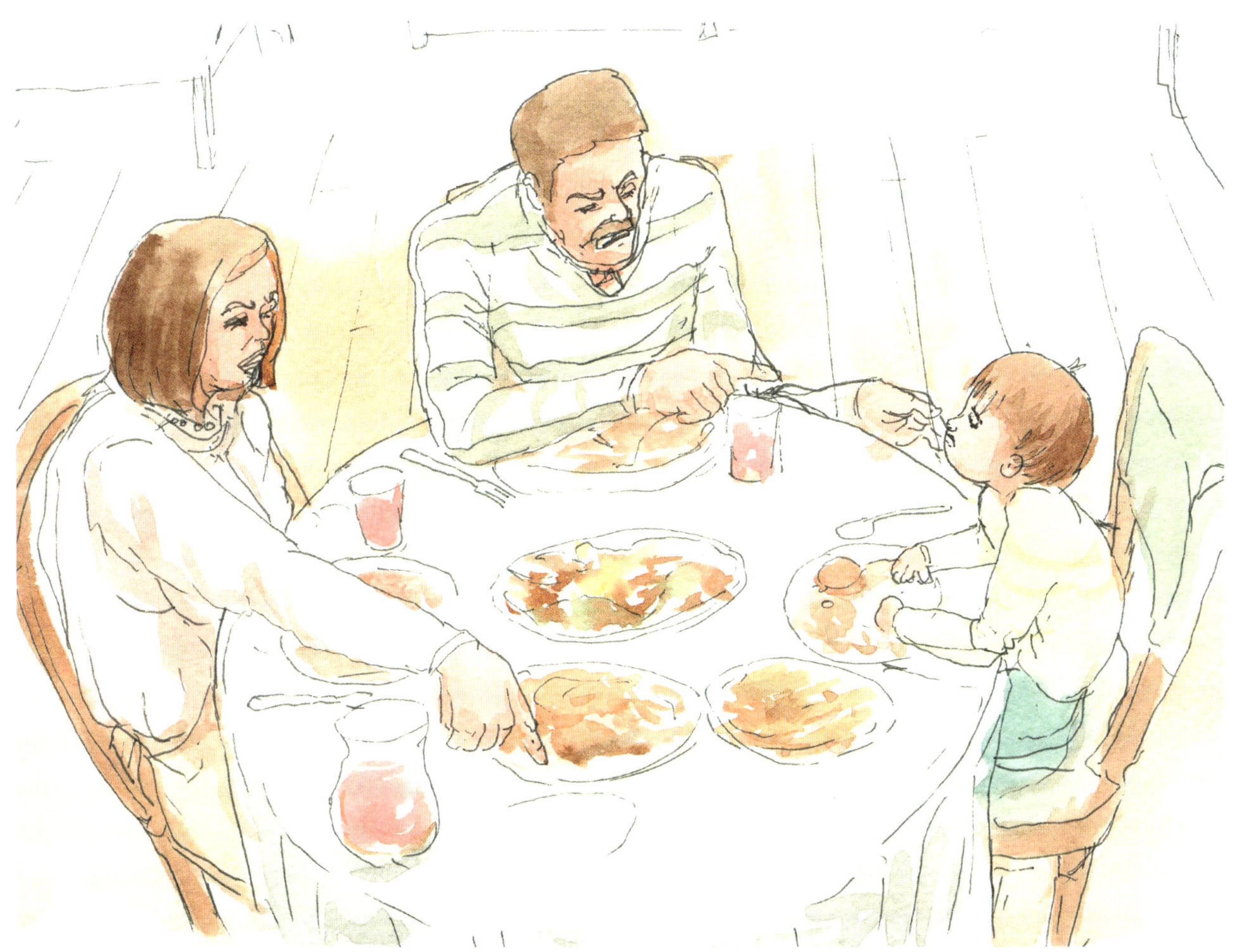

There was a family who was very annoyed with
their child.

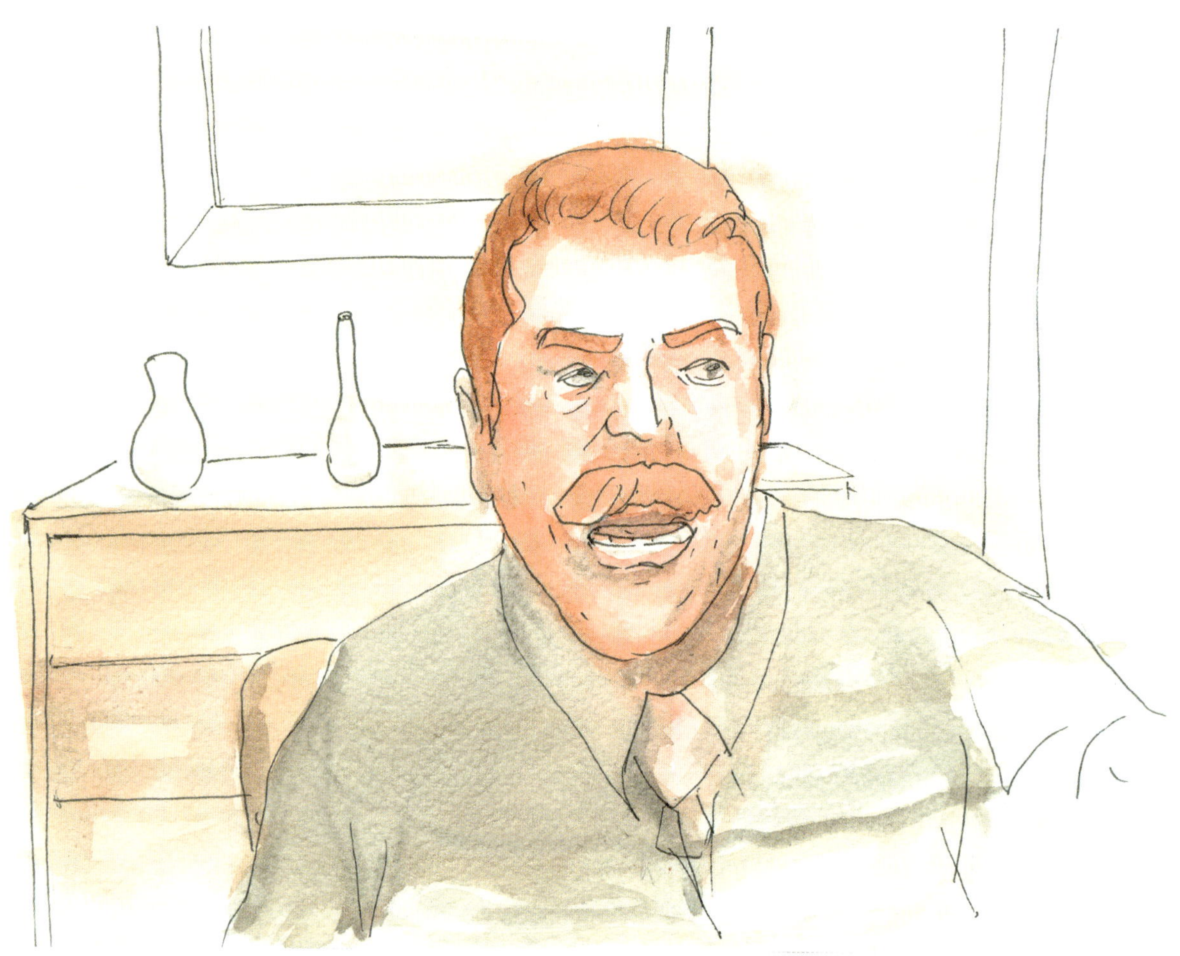

"Stop talking and eat your food," said the father.

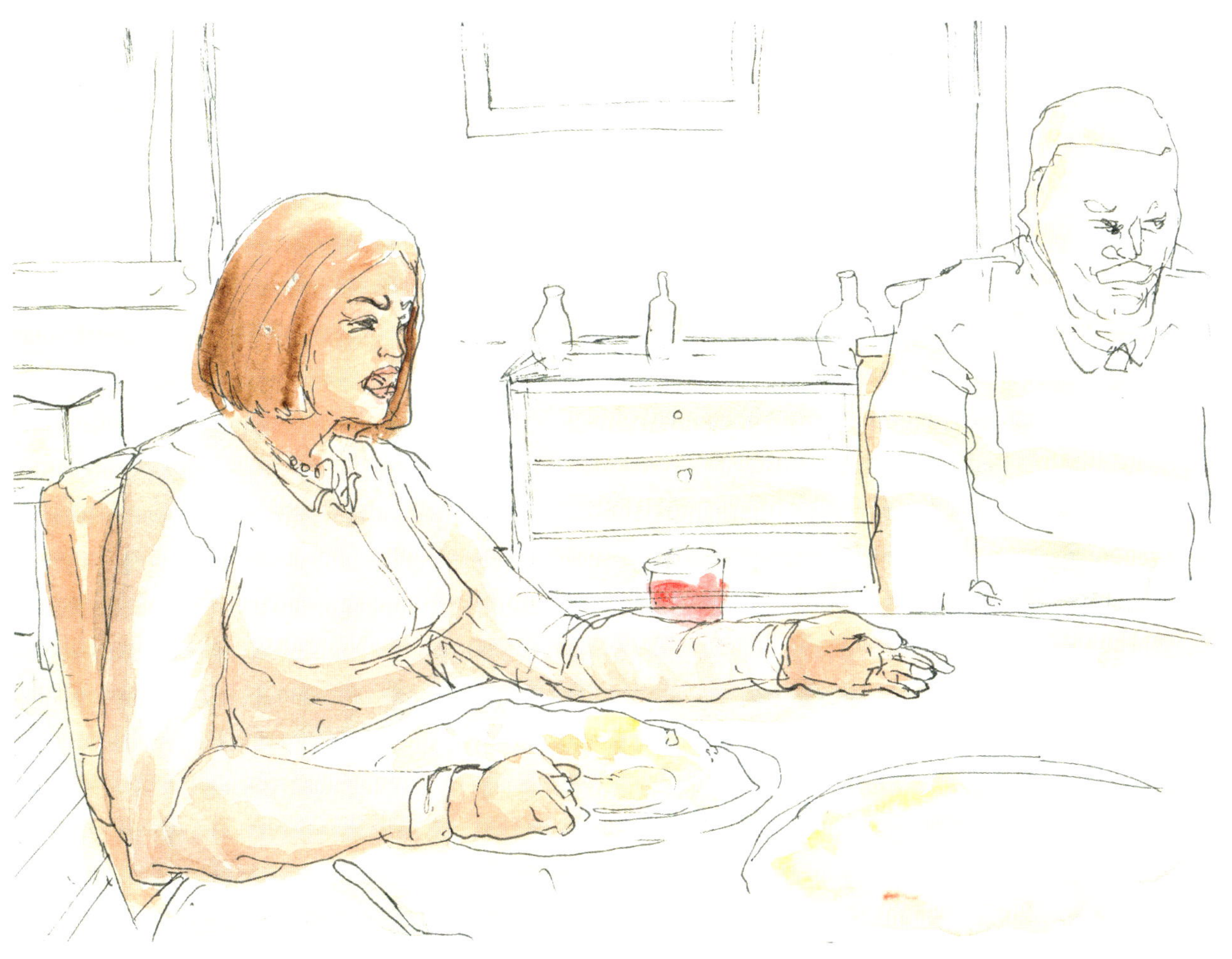

"Sit up straight and quit playing your stupid games." said the mother.

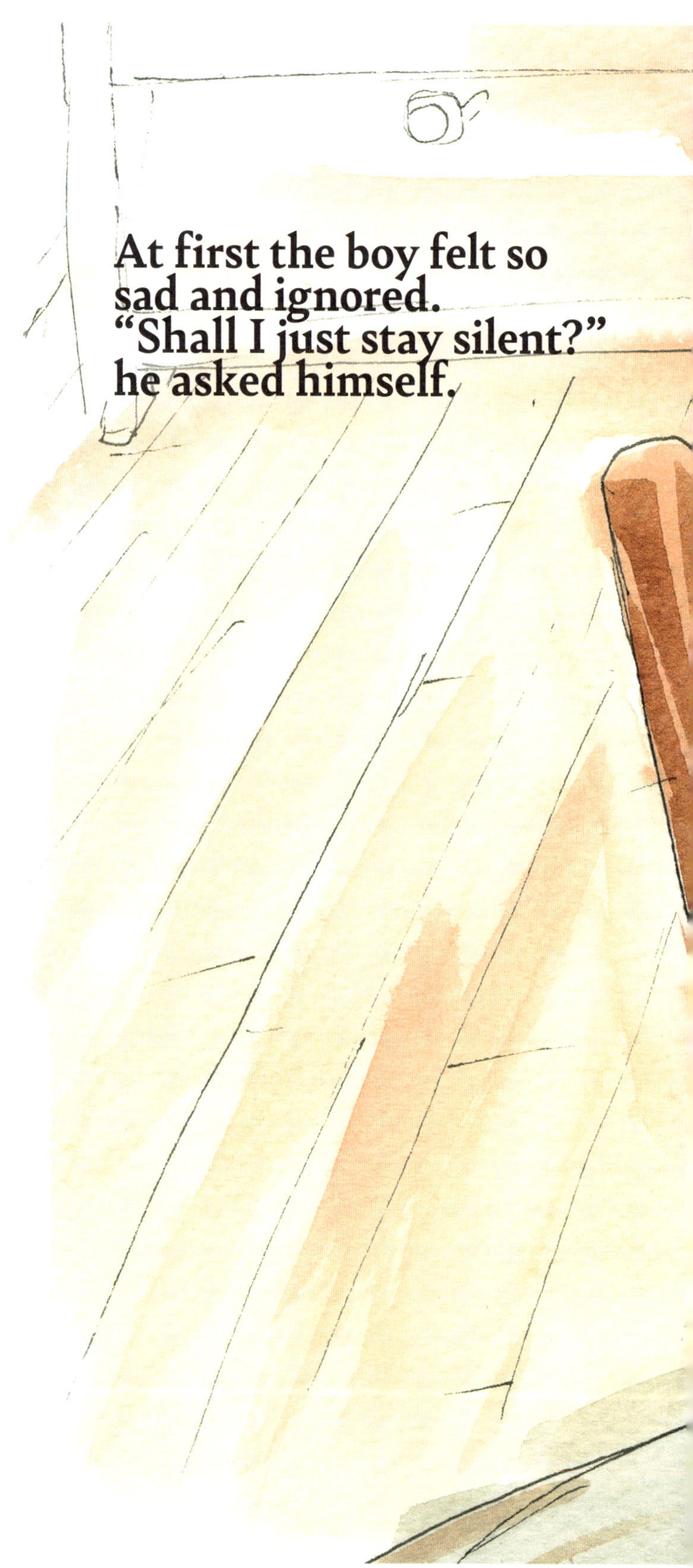

At first the boy felt so
sad and ignored.
"Shall I just stay silent?"
he asked himself.

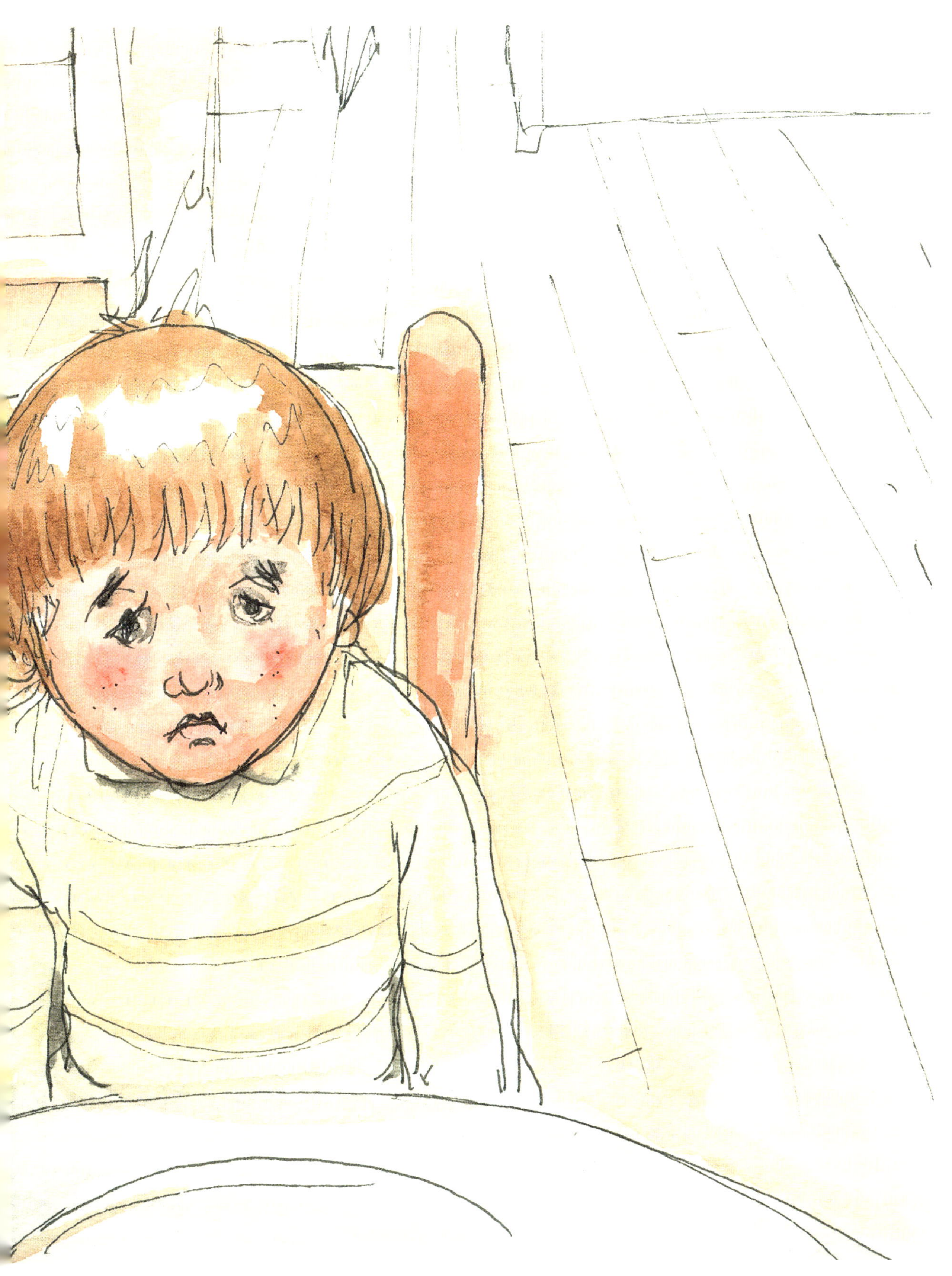

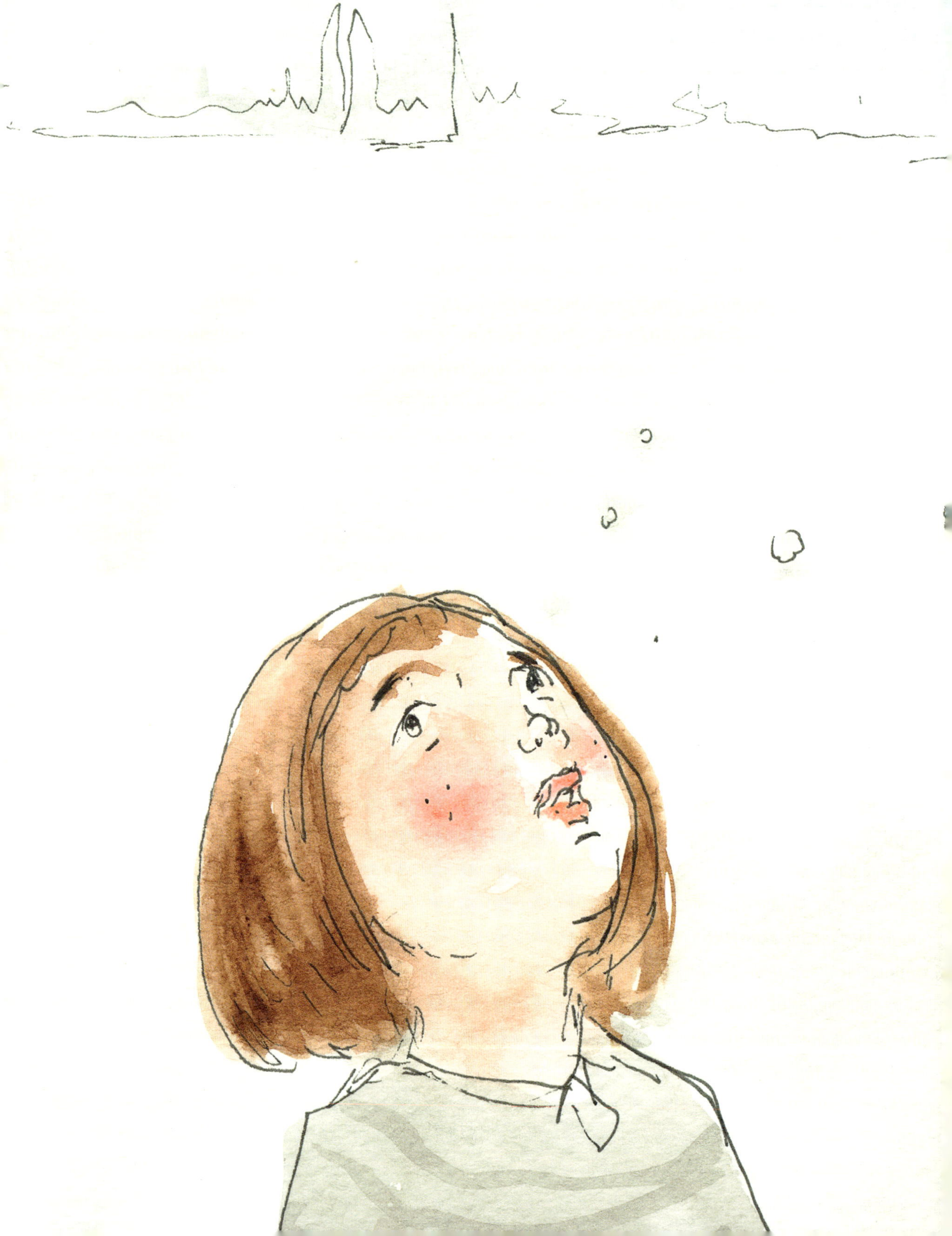

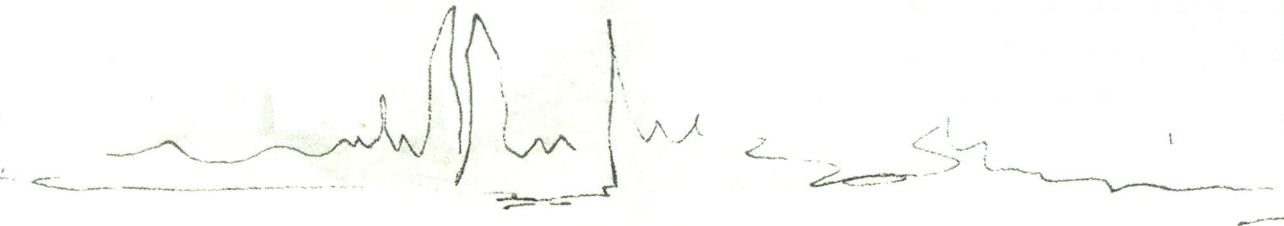

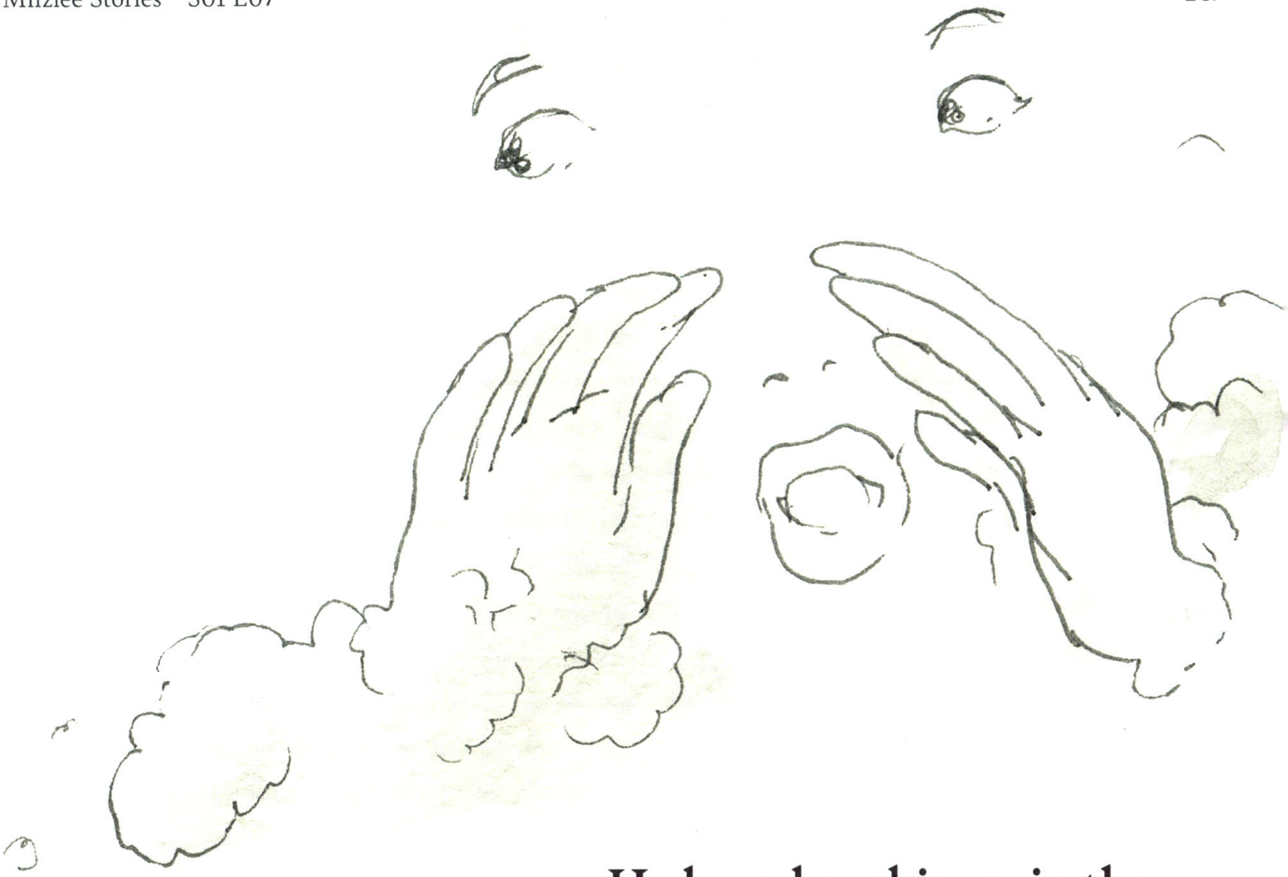

He heard a whisper in the distance saying "Never."

But he didn't see anyone.

"Who is there?" he said.

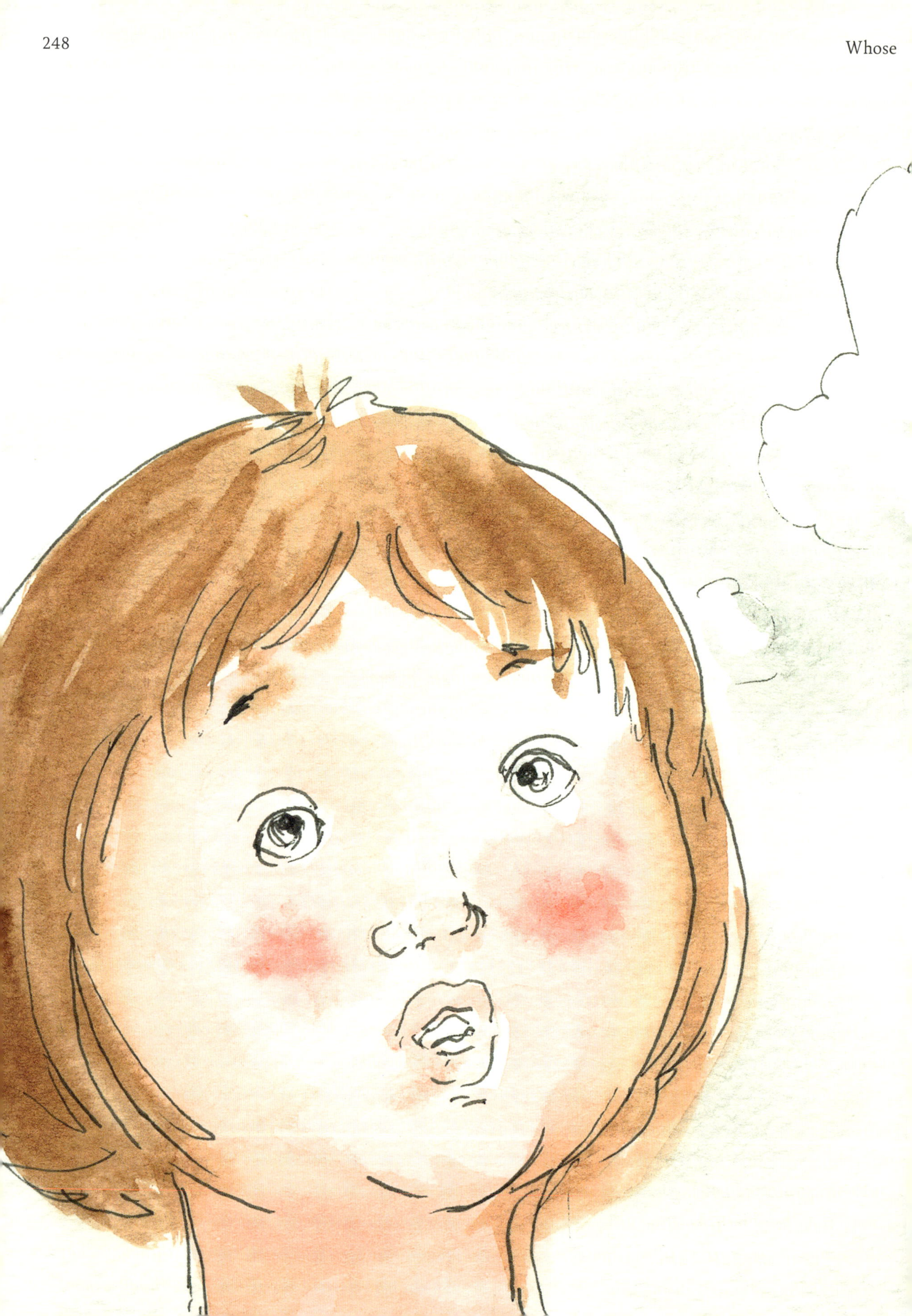

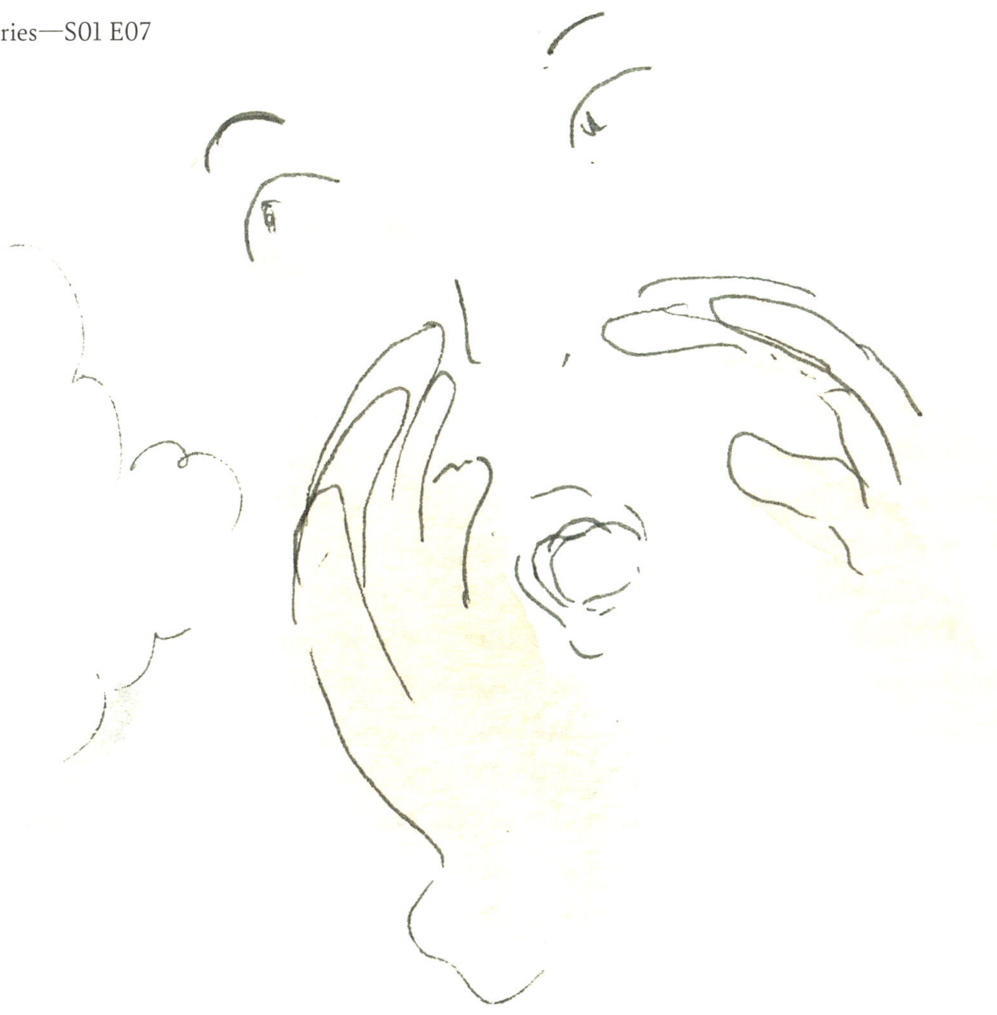

"Whose," the voice whispered back. "My name is Whose."

One day while his mom was putting on his socks, he heard the voice say,

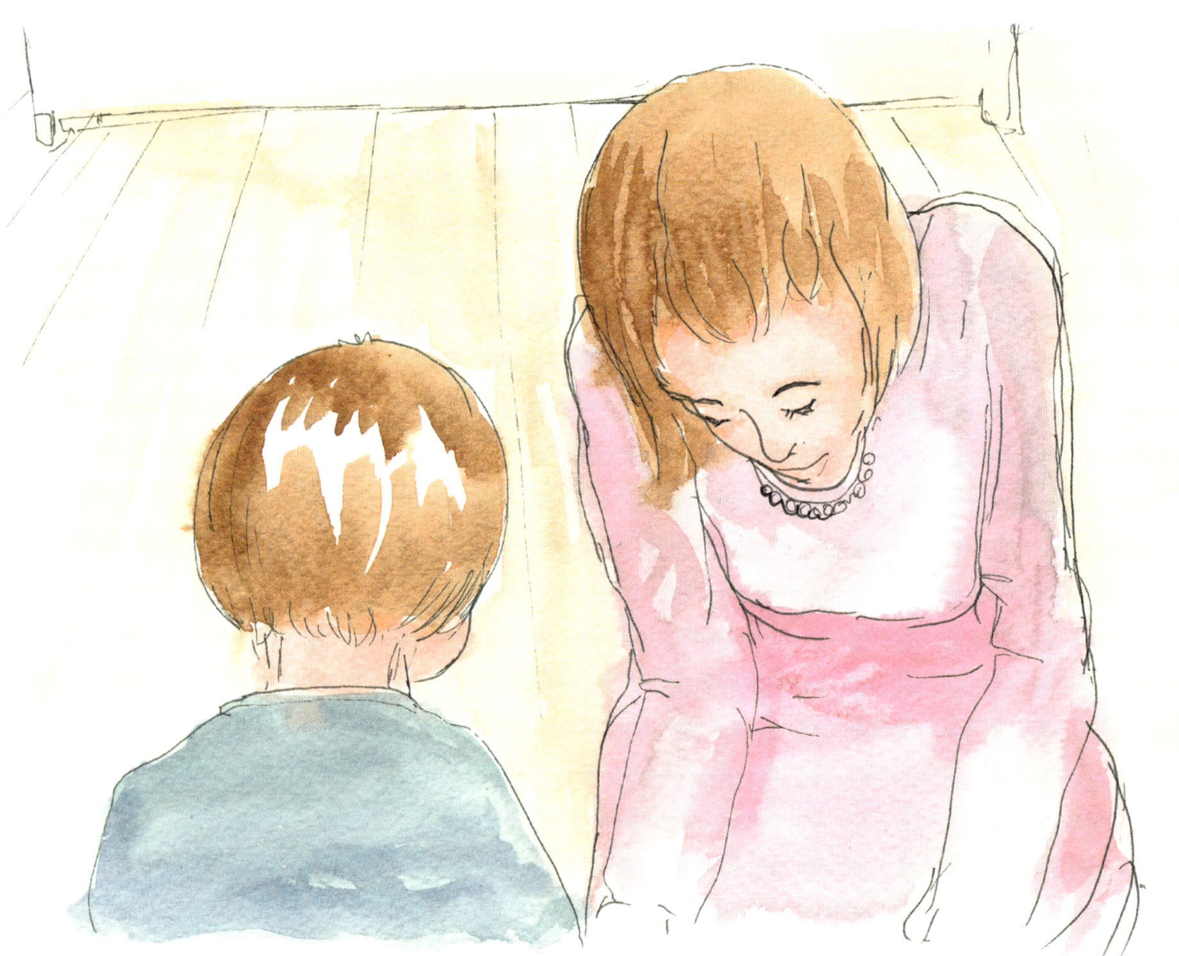

"Tell her about the double magic warm socks idea you had."

And so the boy did.

And the next morning he saw something truly wild.

His parents were making the double magic warm socks.
His idea.

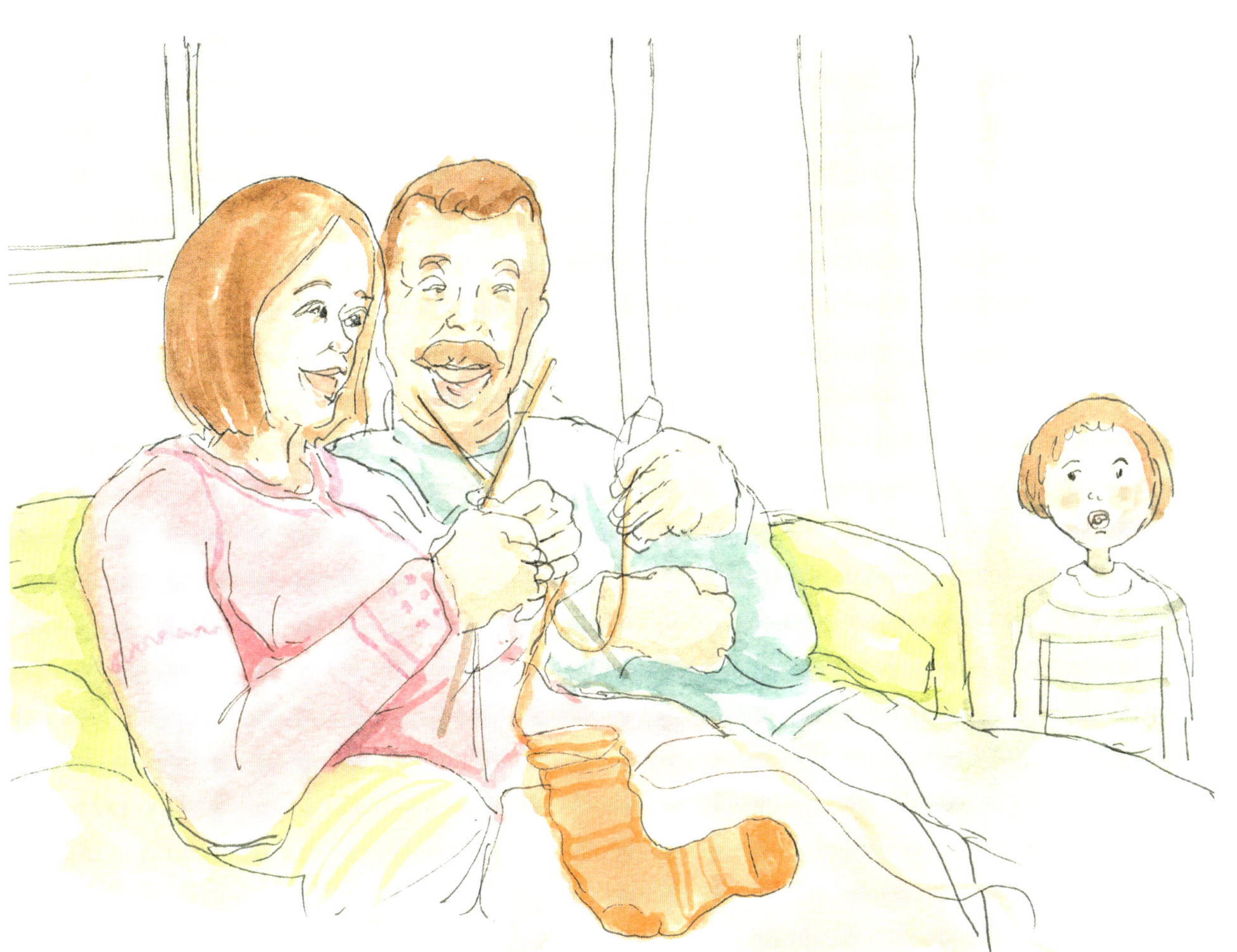

"We are so creative, aren't we, dear."

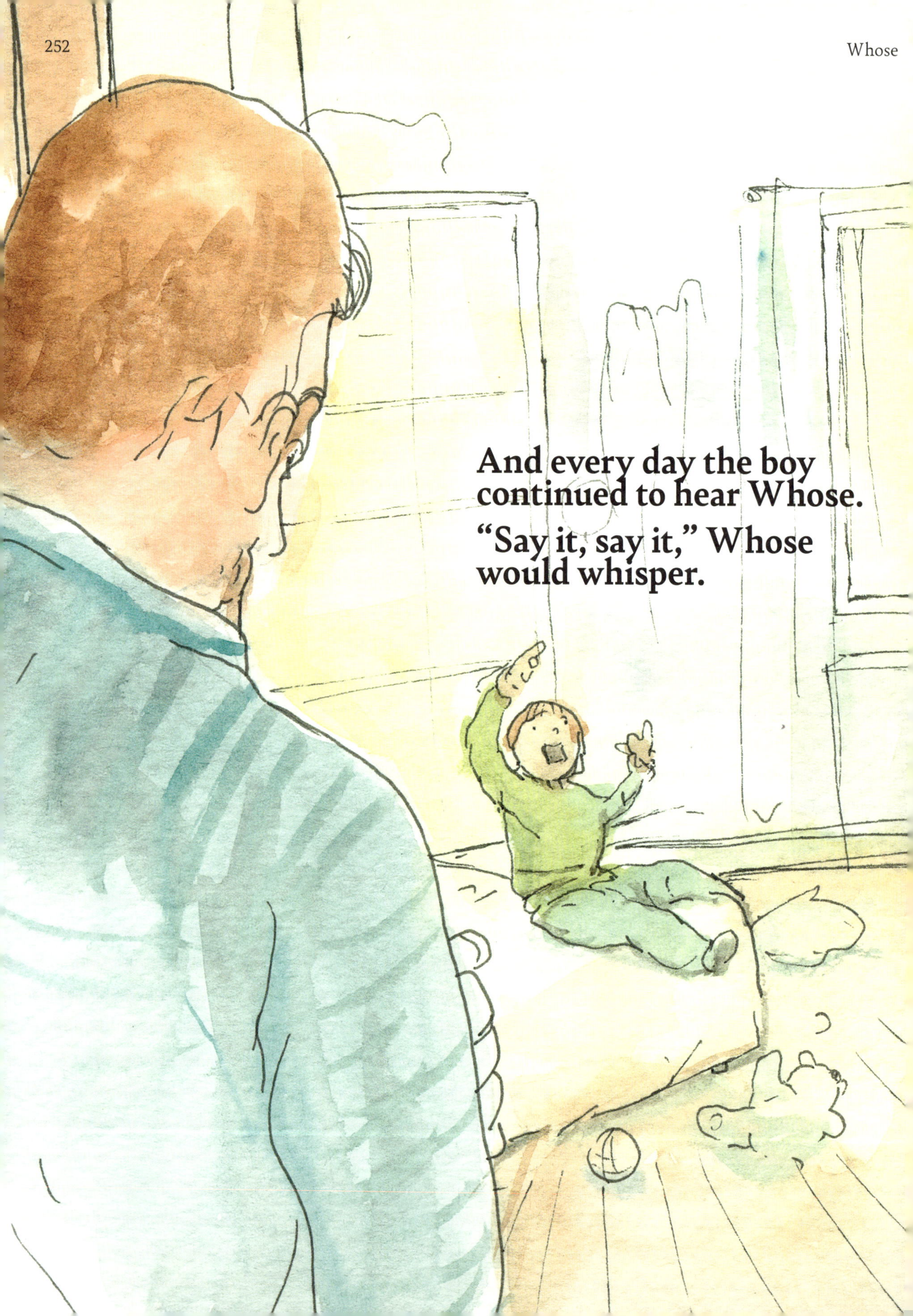

And every day the boy
continued to hear Whose.

"Say it, say it," Whose
would whisper.

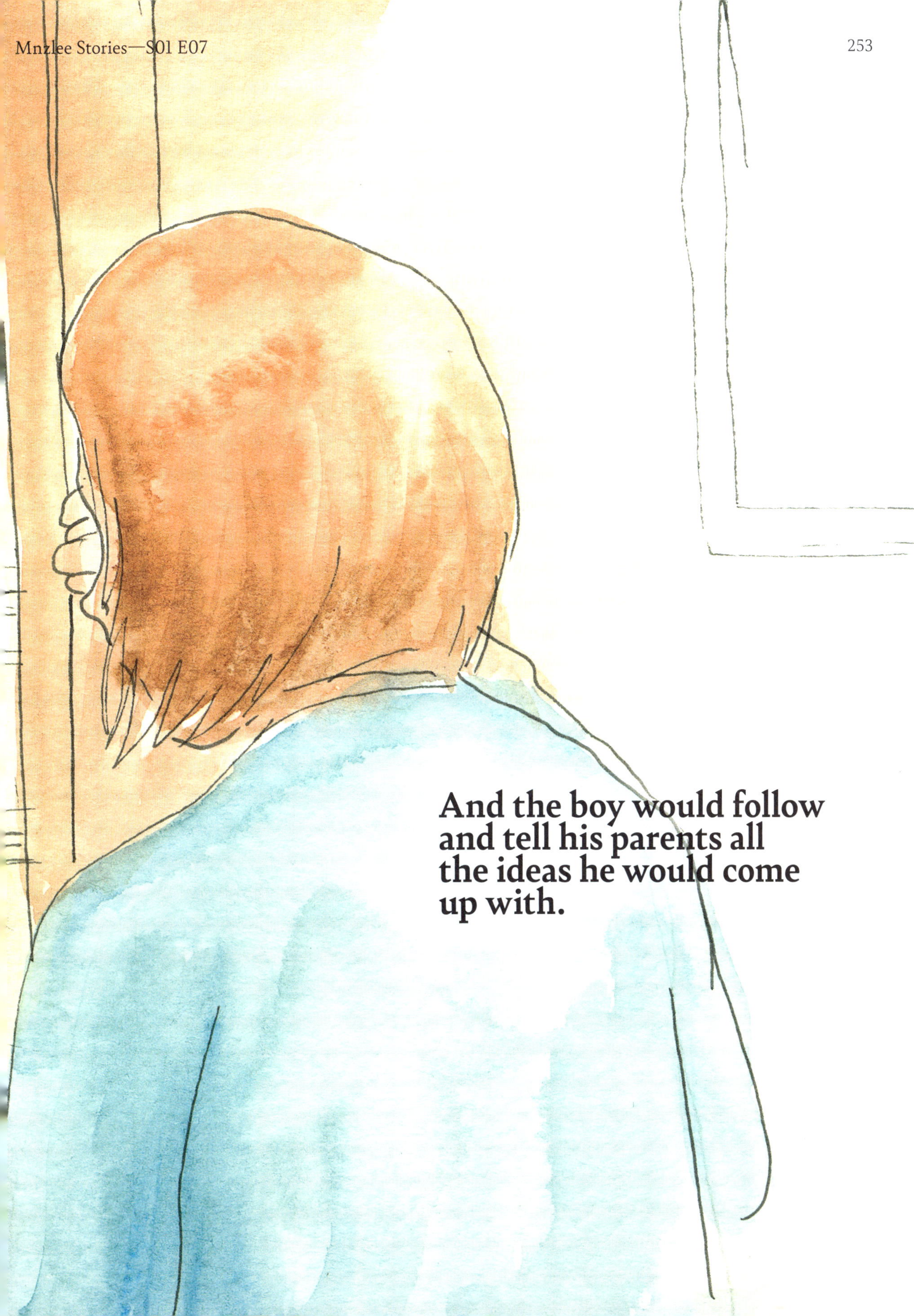

And the boy would follow
and tell his parents all
the ideas he would come
up with.

As he played, ideas would come to him like rain, endless and fun.

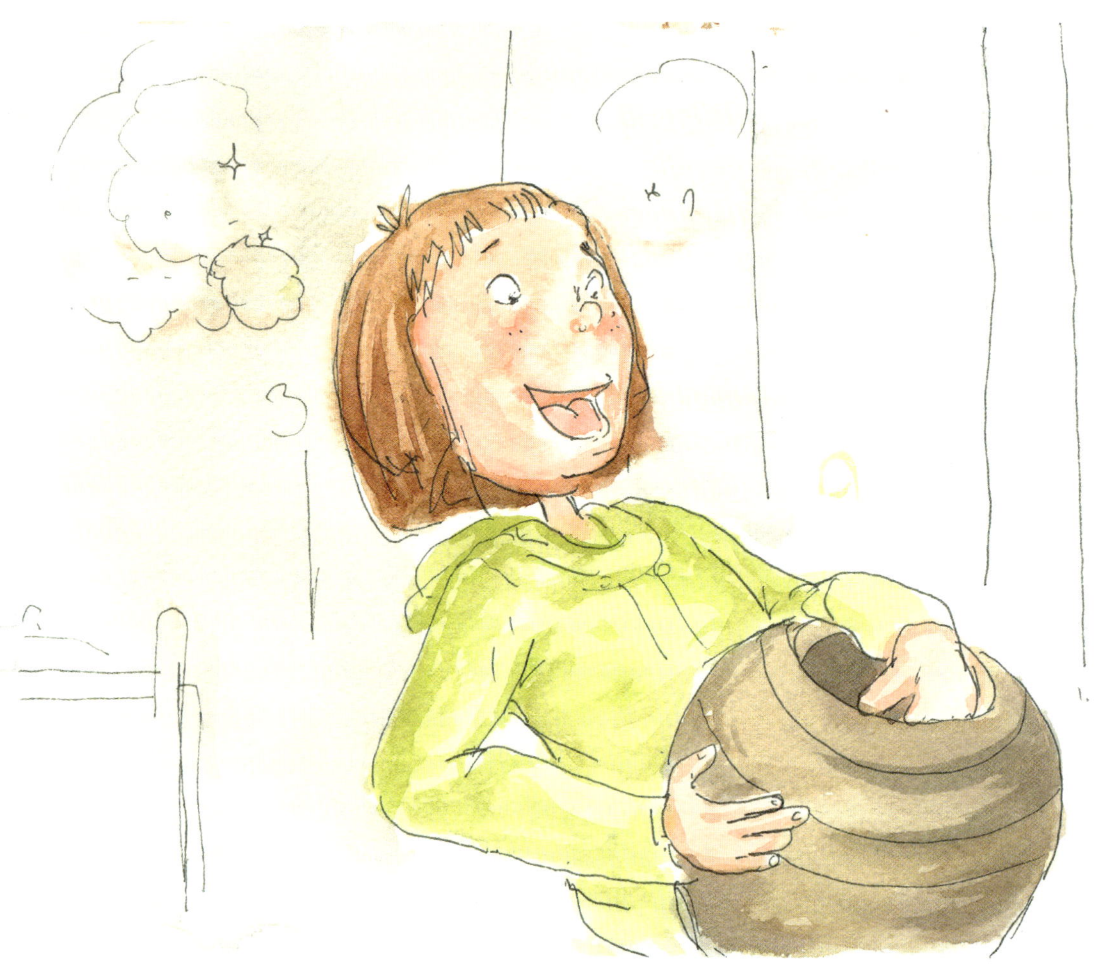

"What if I pulled something magical out of this pot?"

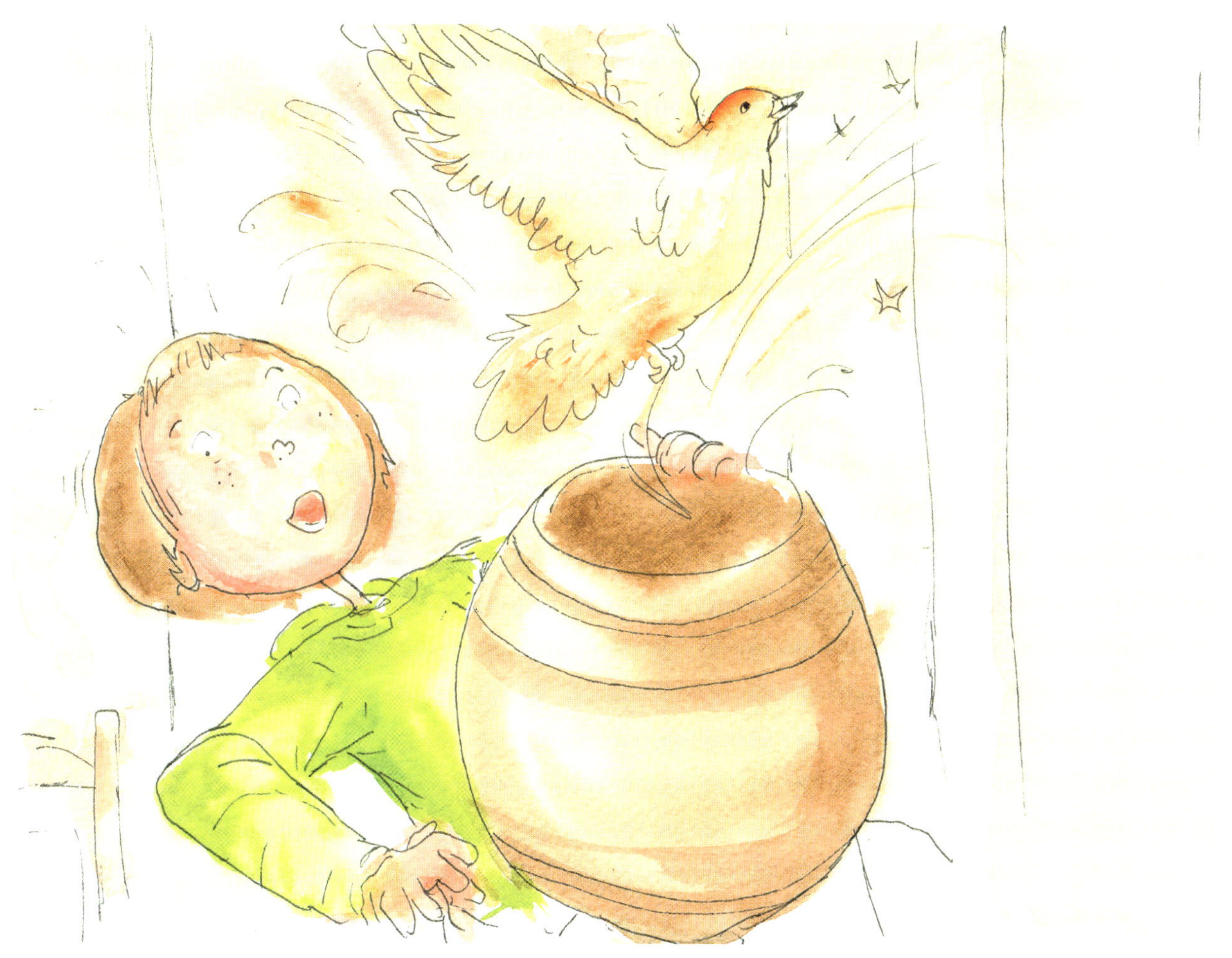

And out of the pot came a magical bird.

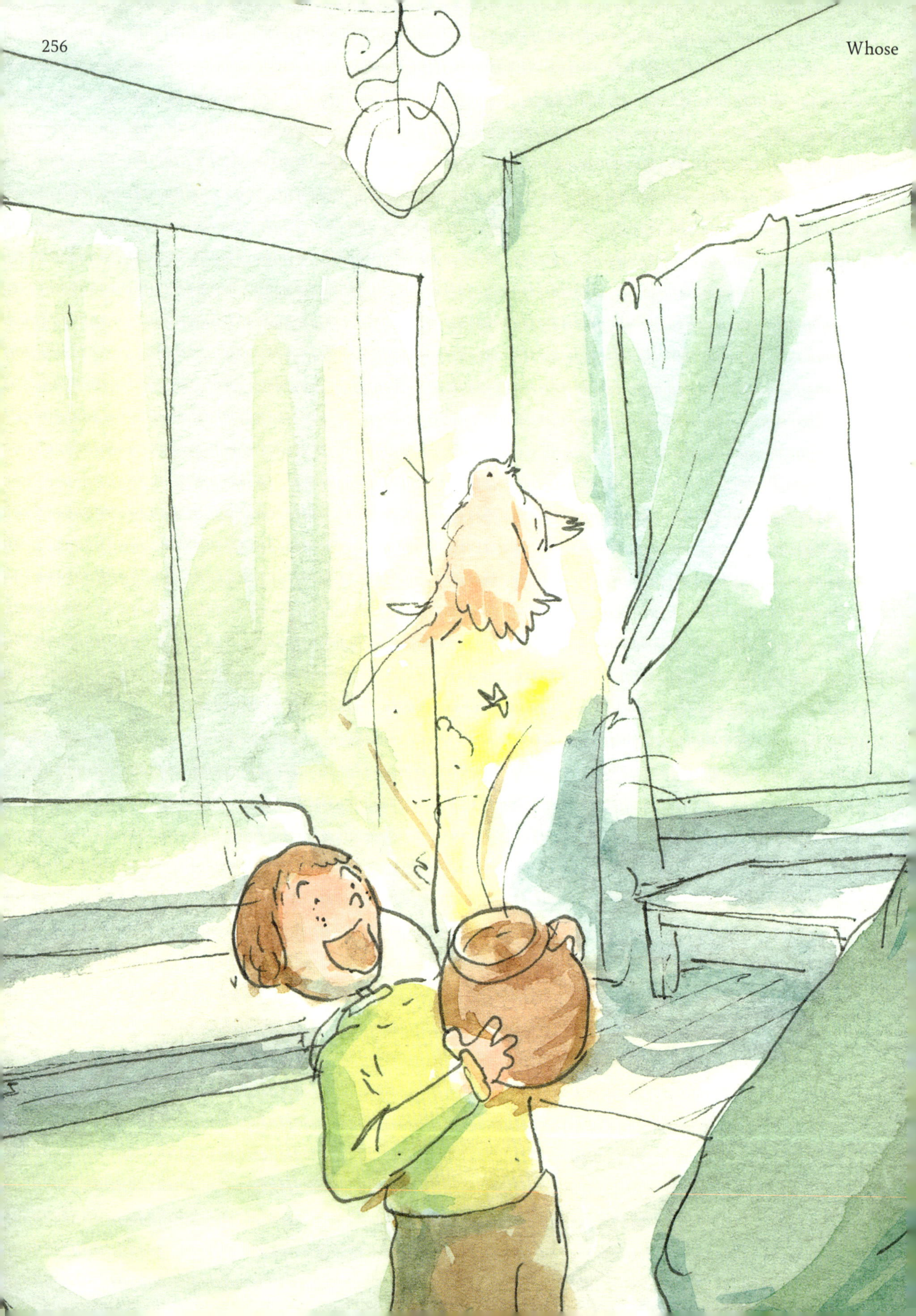

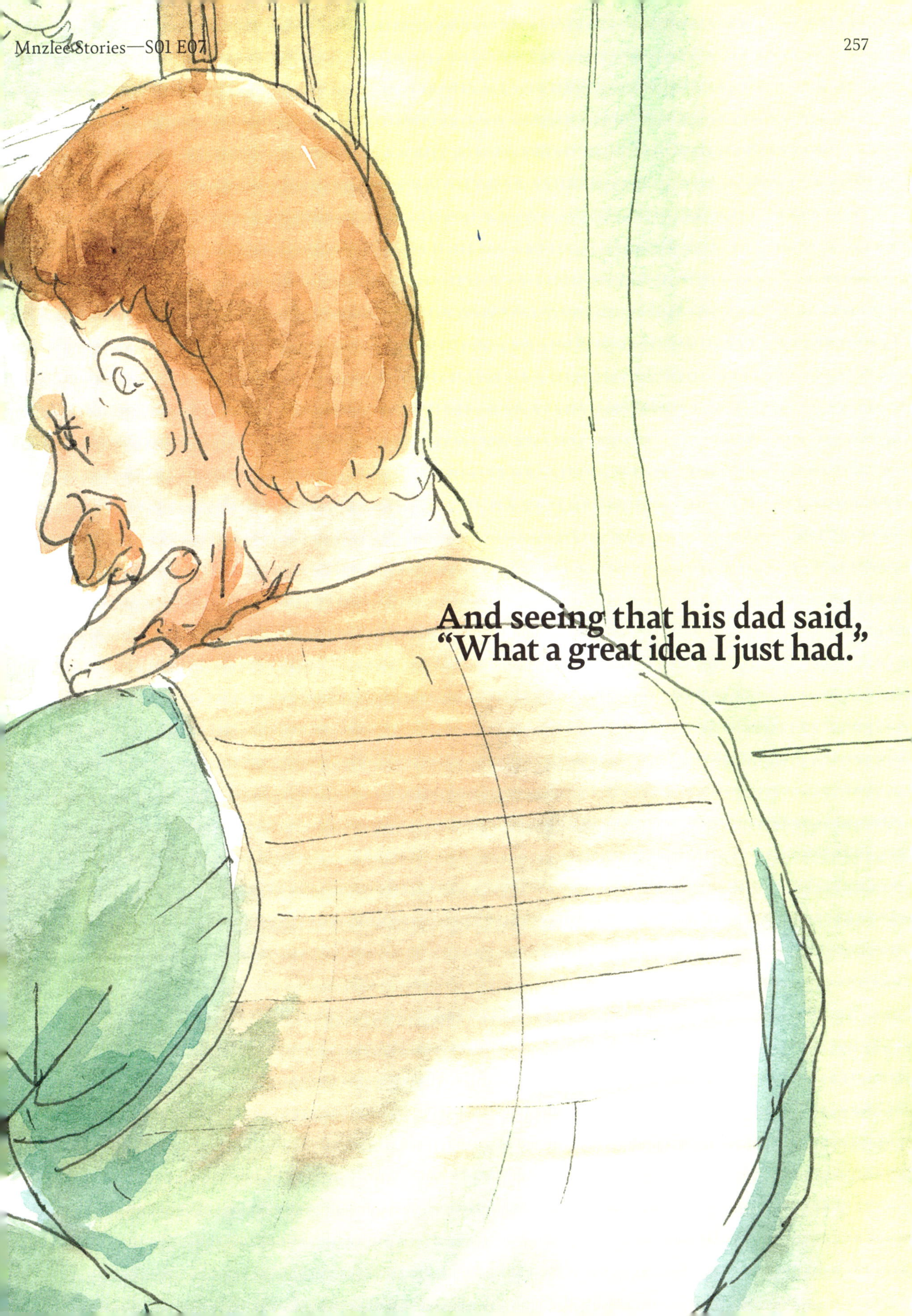

And seeing that his dad said,
"What a great idea I just had."

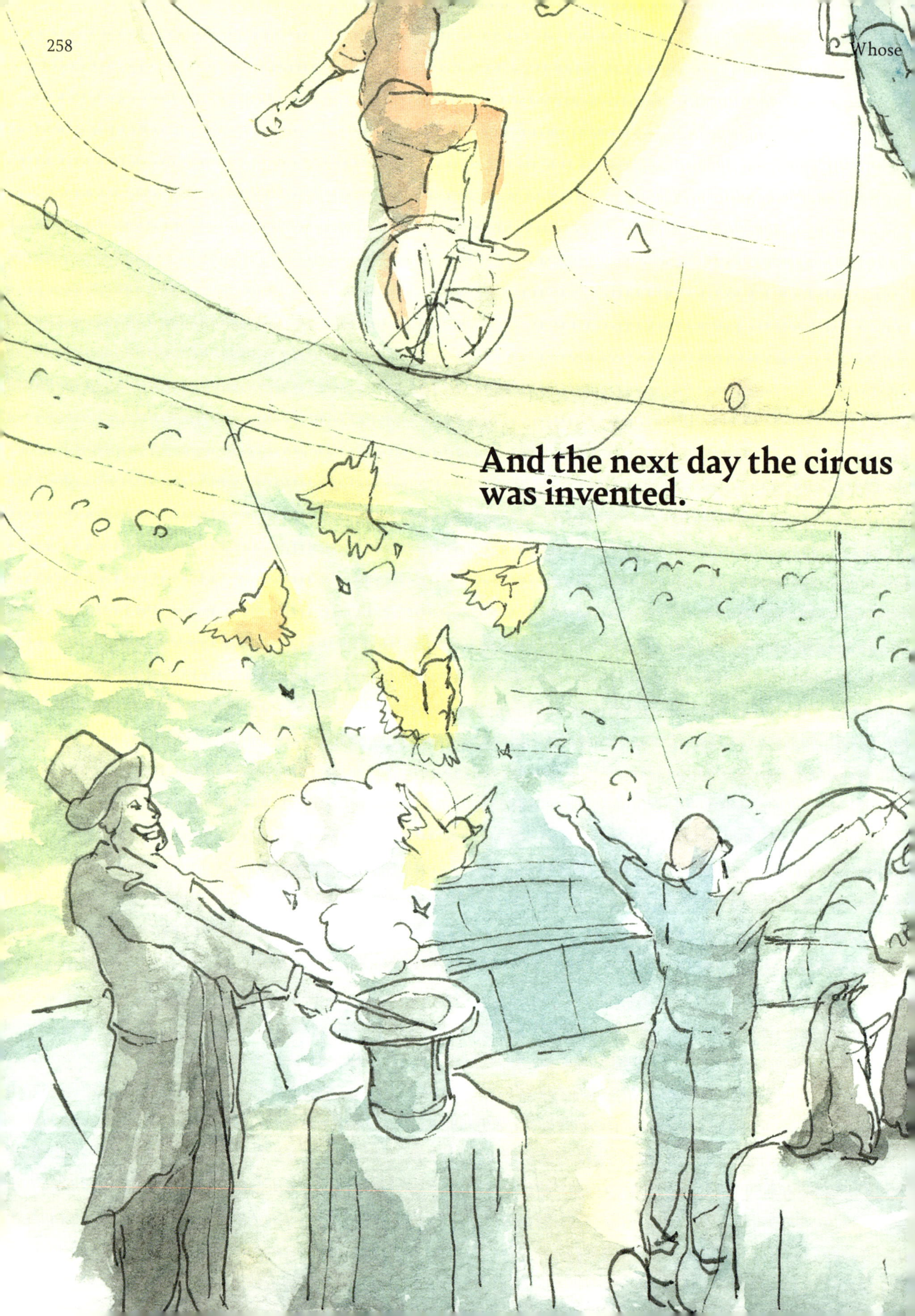

And the next day the circus was invented.

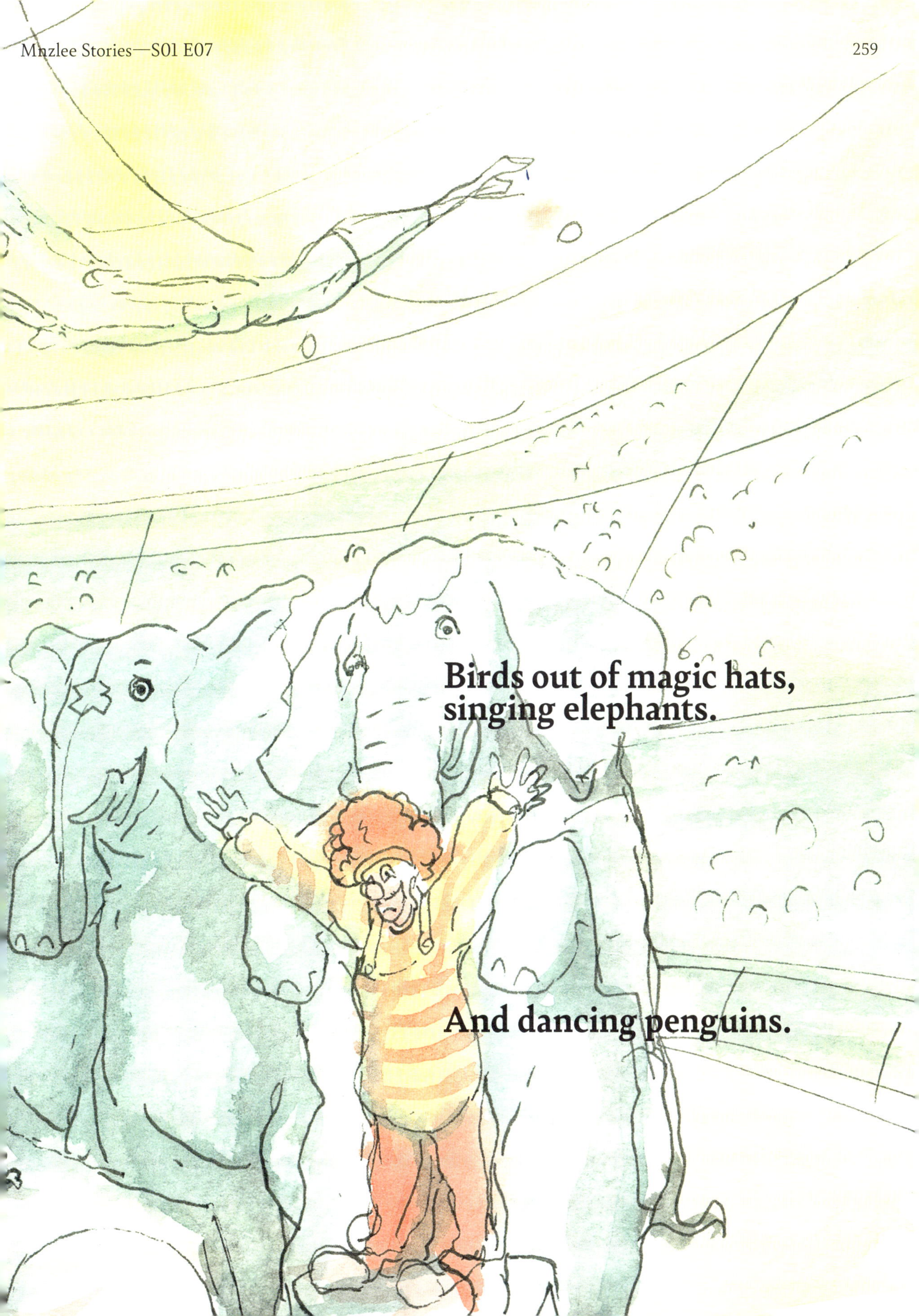
Birds out of magic hats,
singing elephants.

And dancing penguins.

The boy was amazed.
He would just have to whisper something

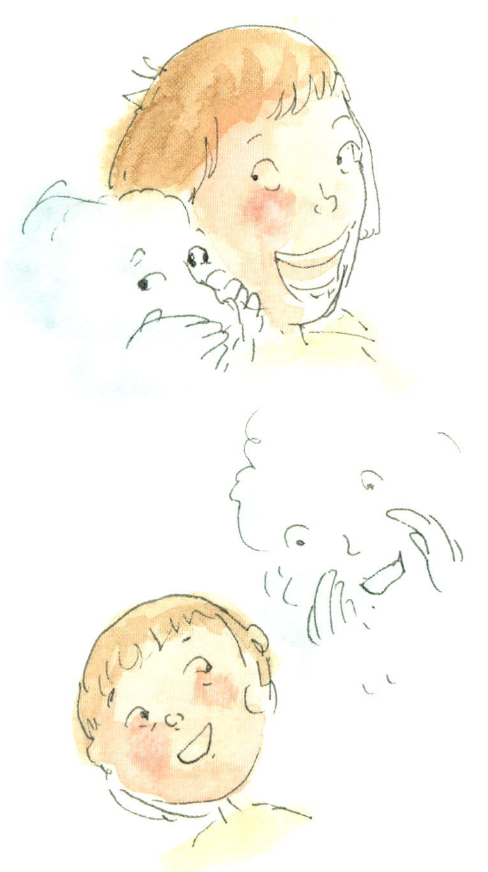

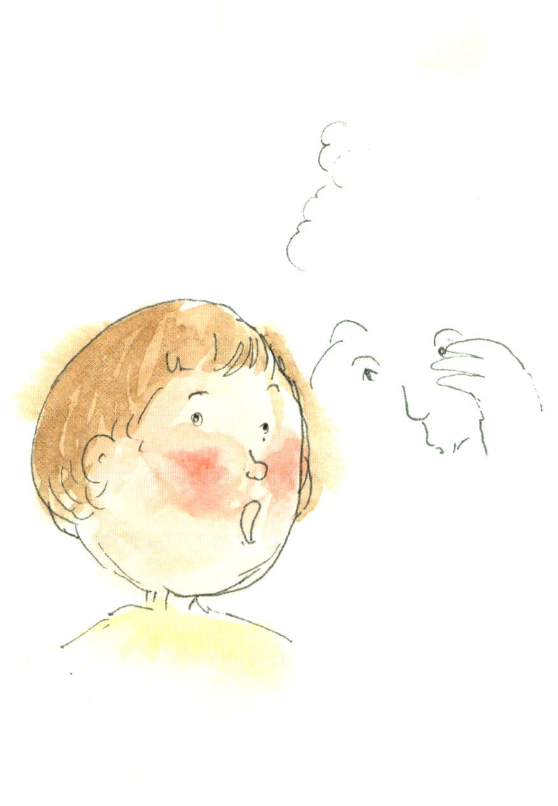

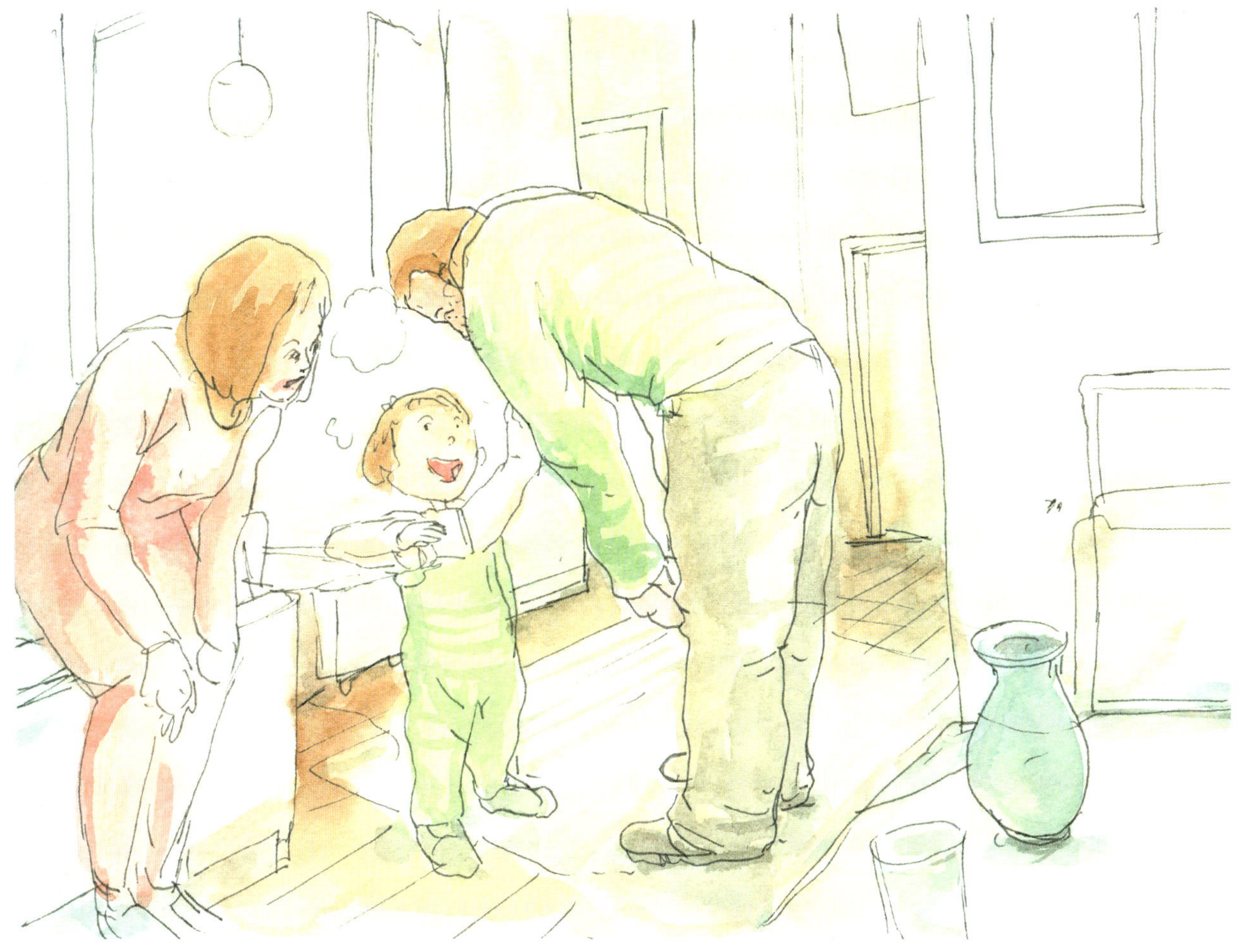

and his parents would jump with enthusiasm and immediately start working on it.

Whisper after whisper led to invention after invention.

"Eureka!" the parents would say.

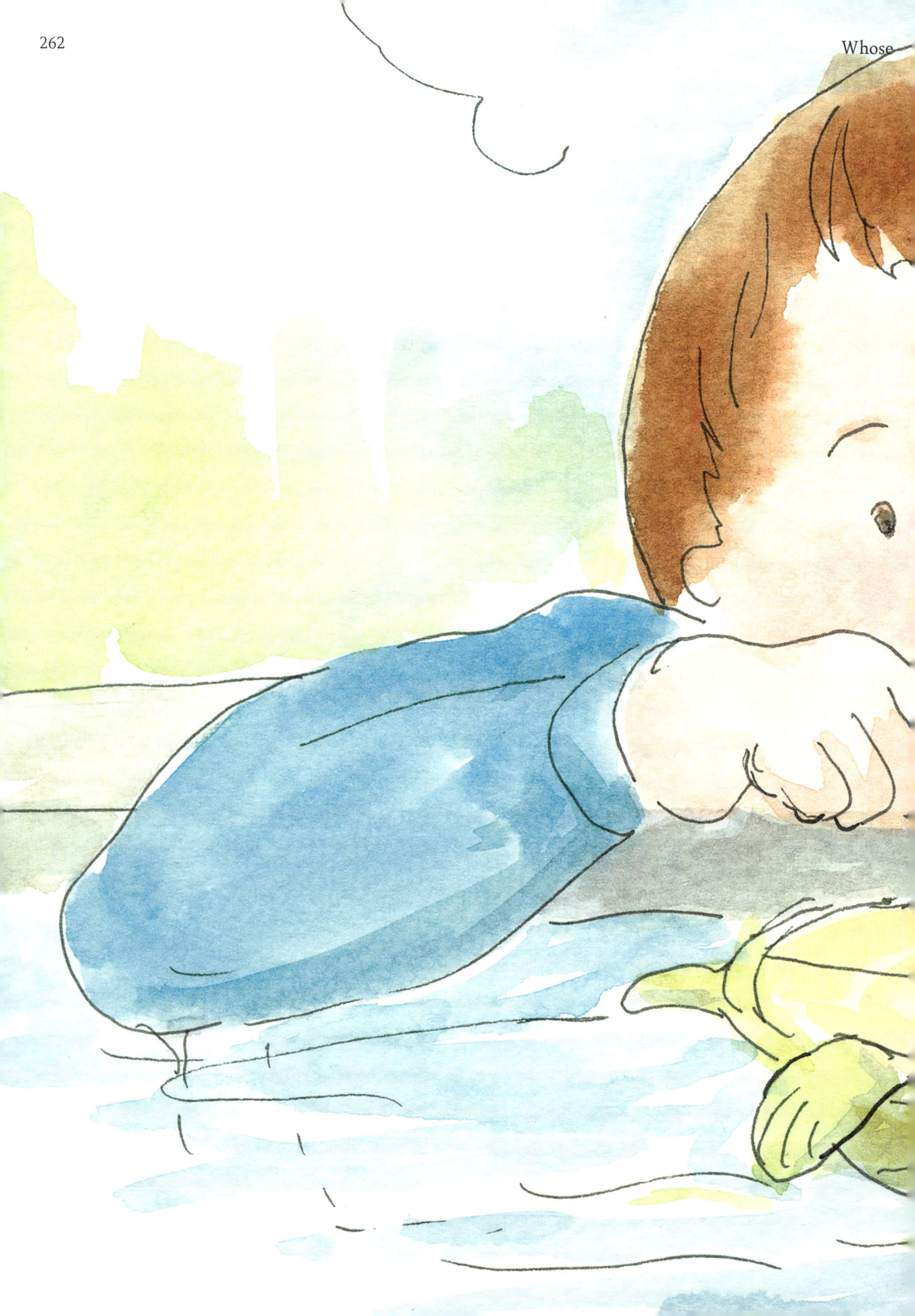

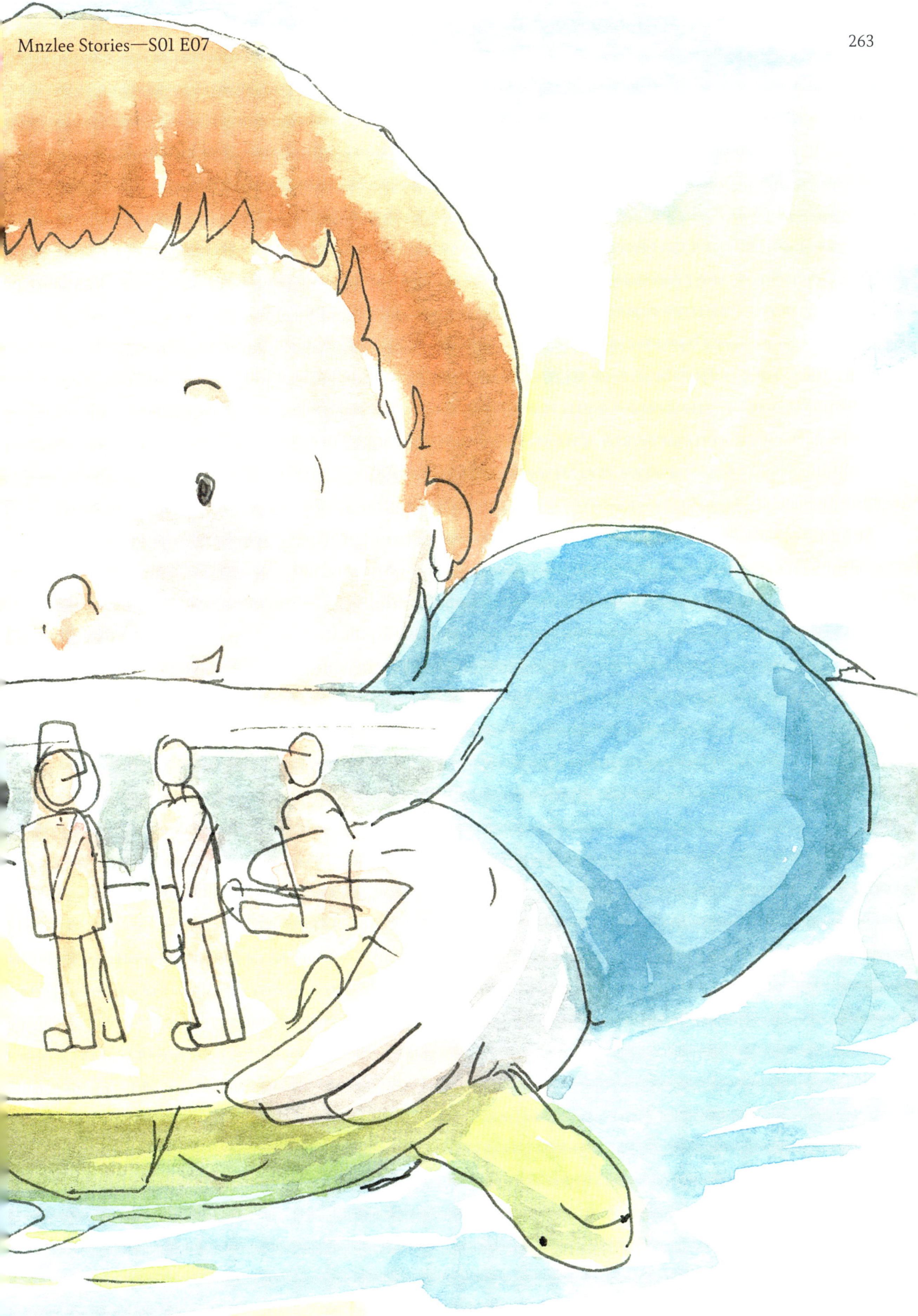

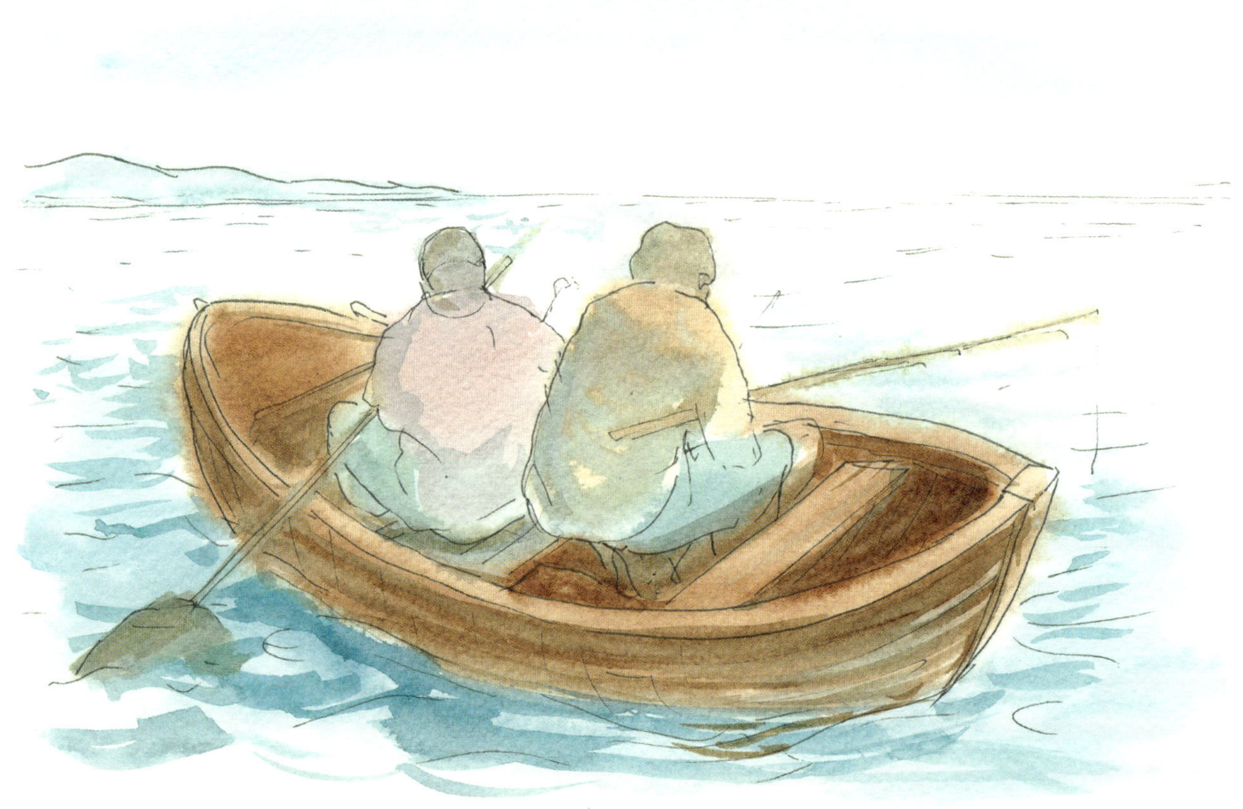

And the boat was invented.

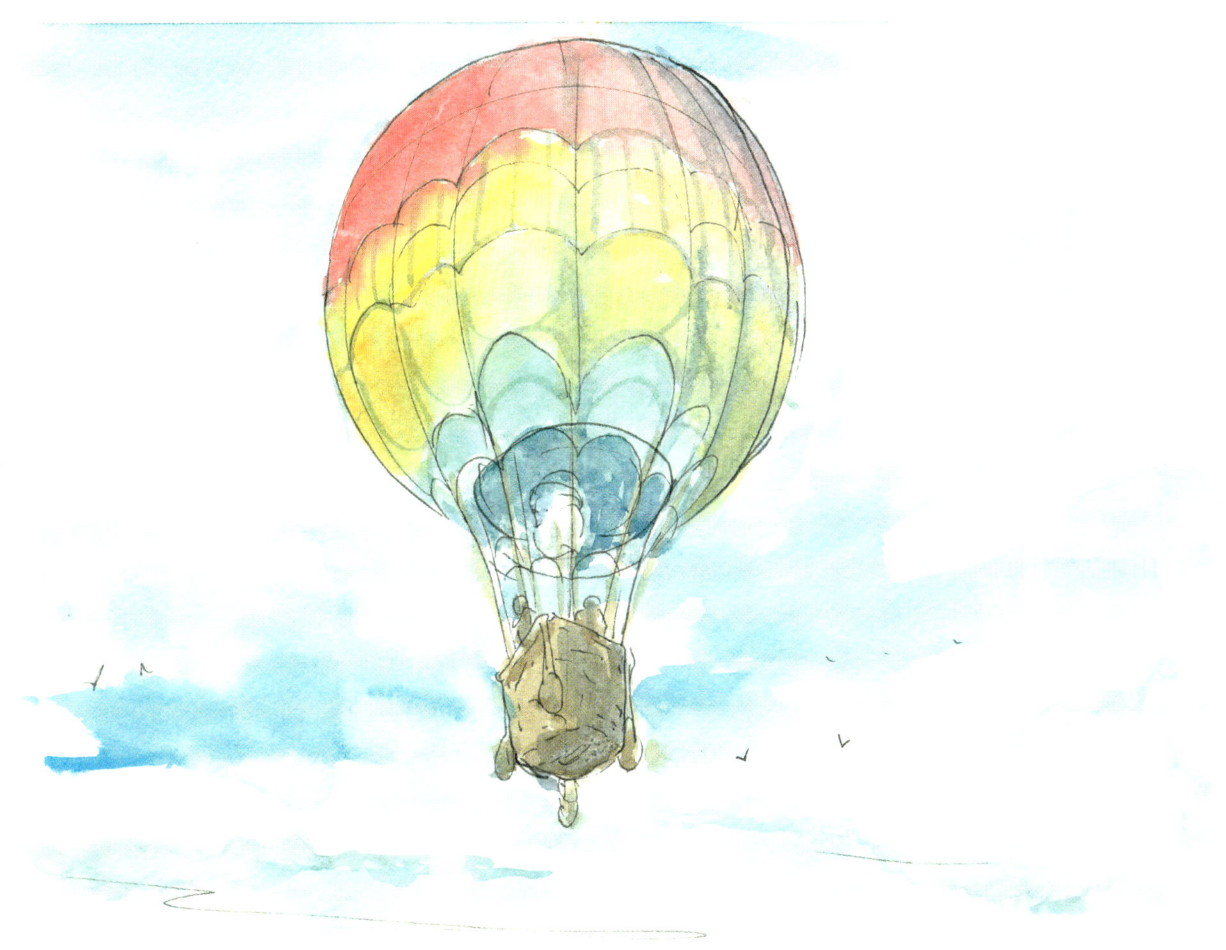

And the air balloon.

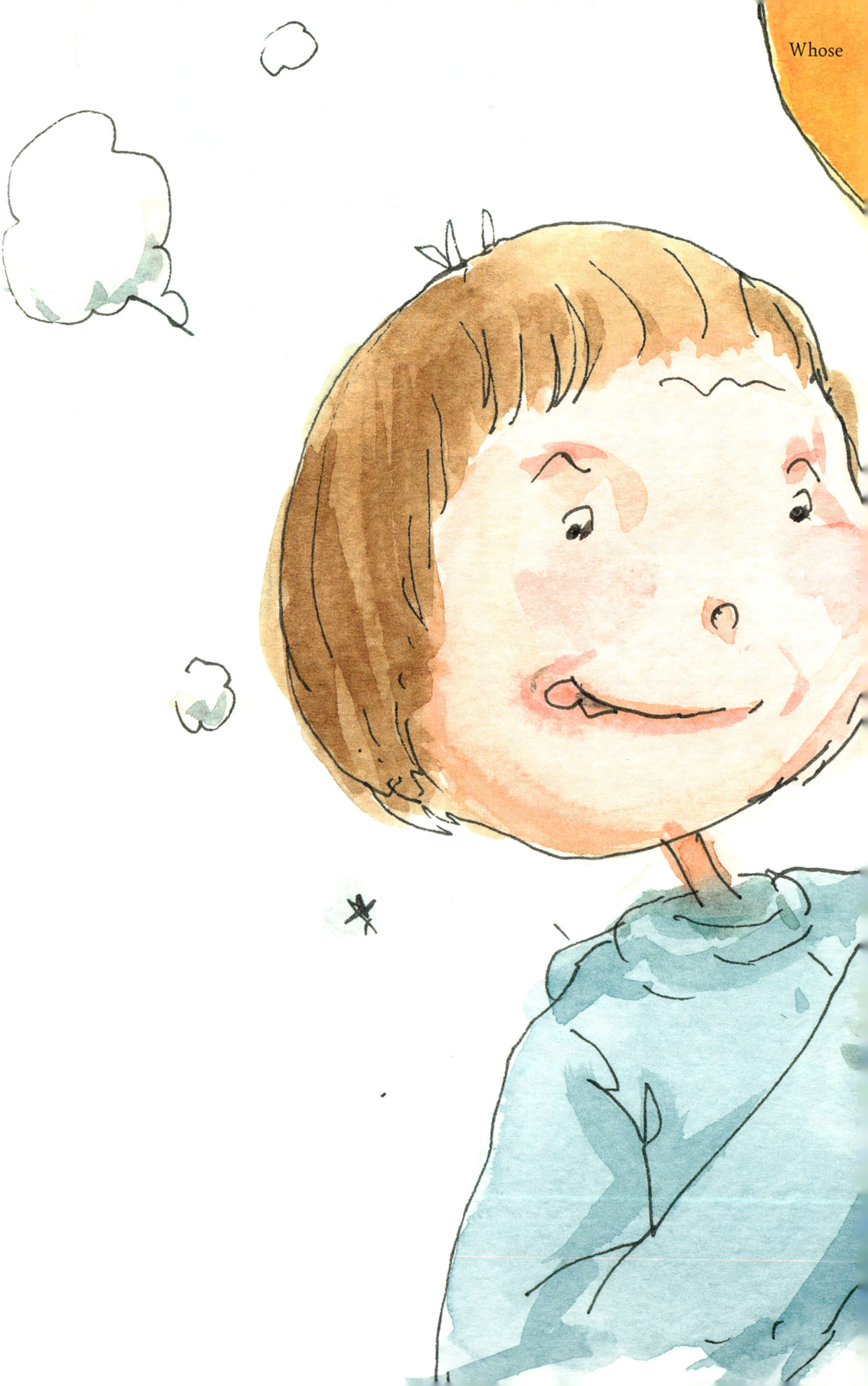

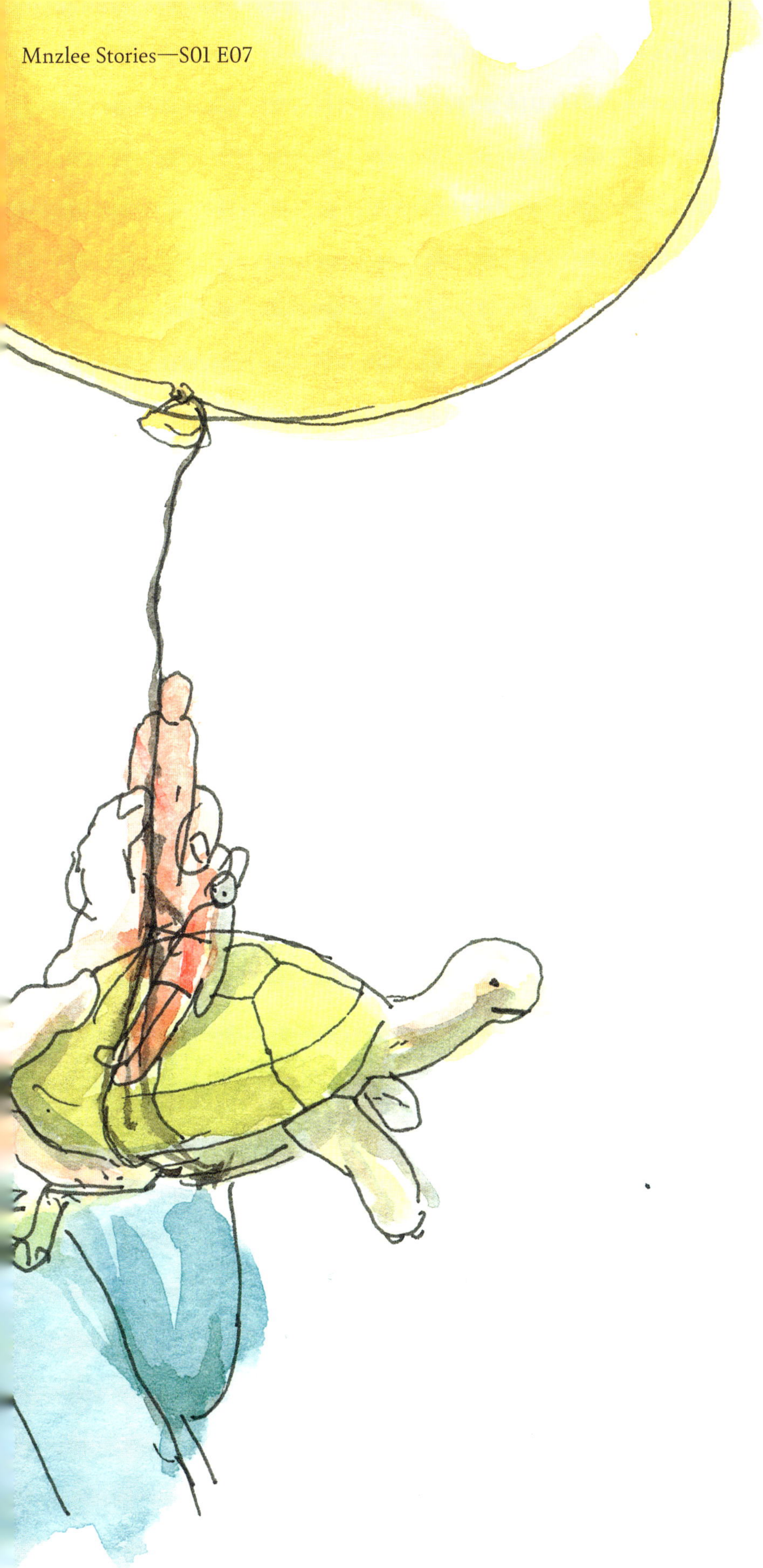

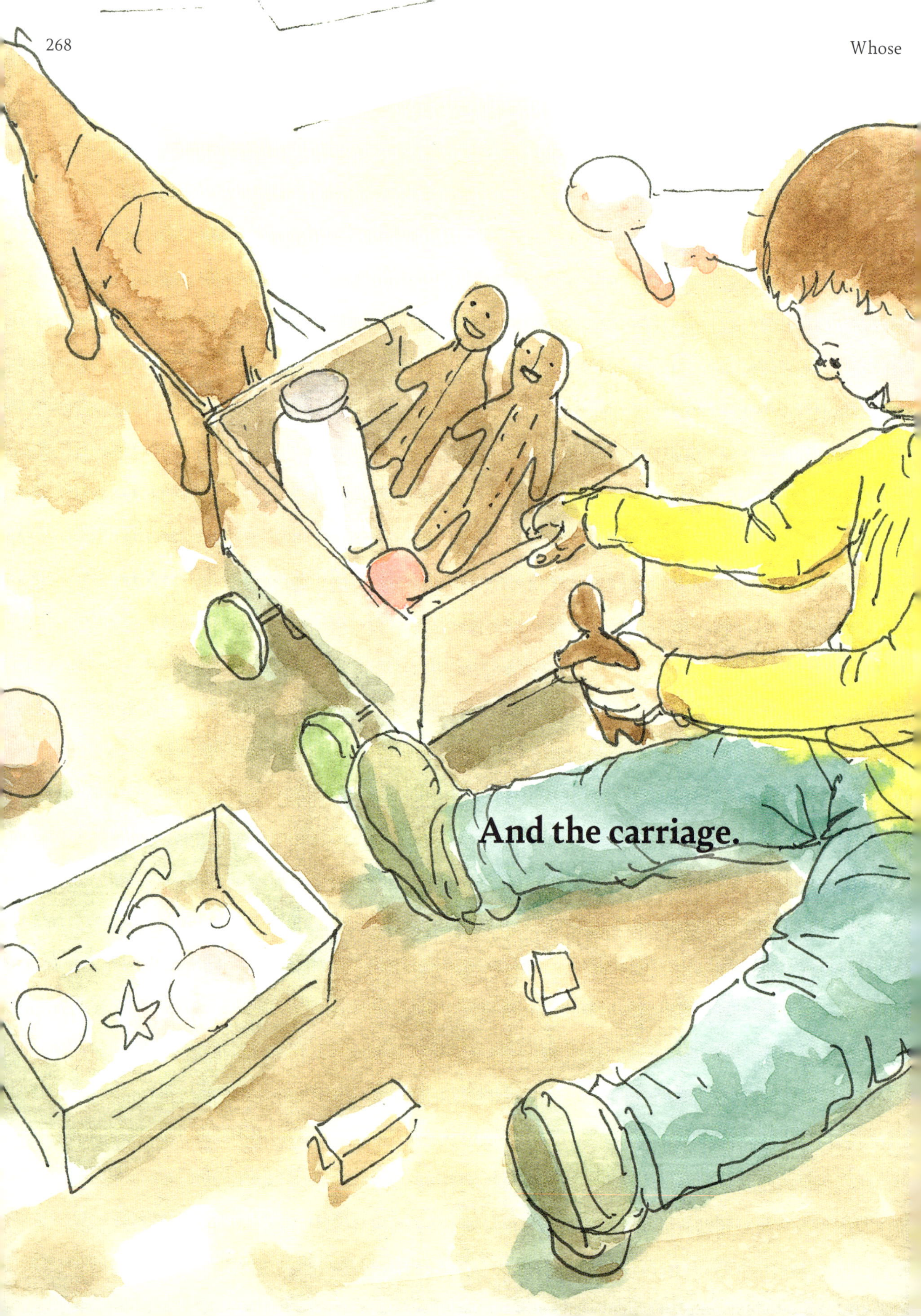
And the carriage.

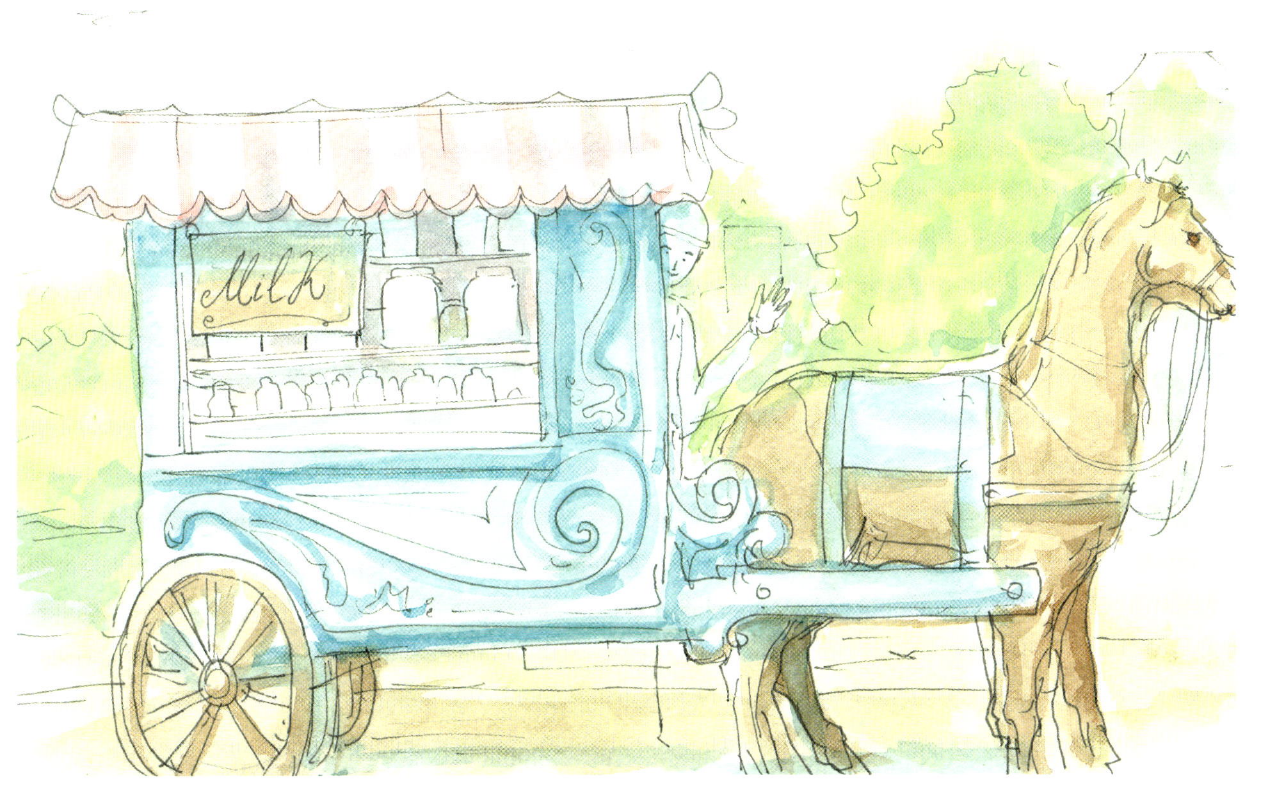

And the milk business on the carriage.

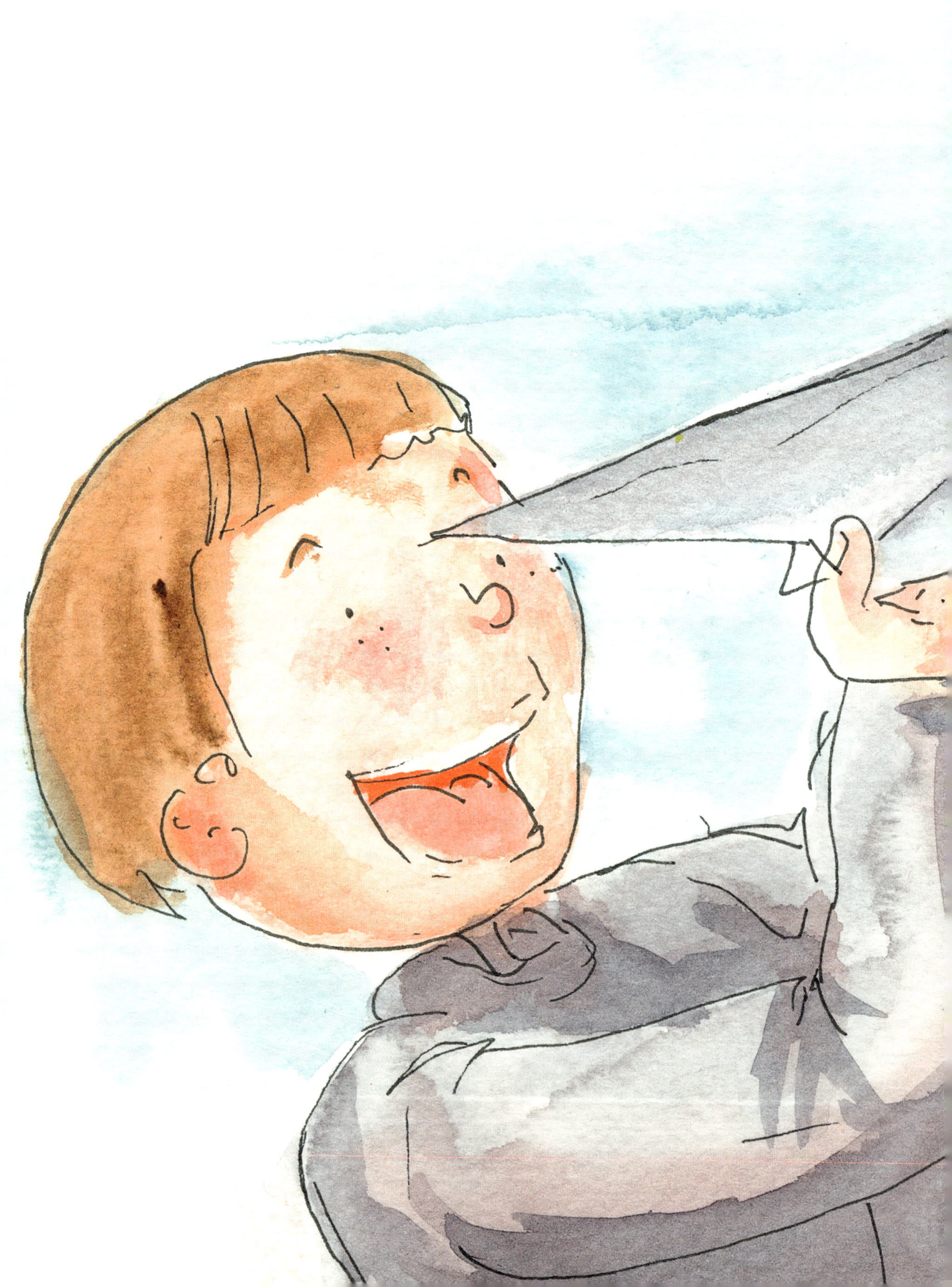

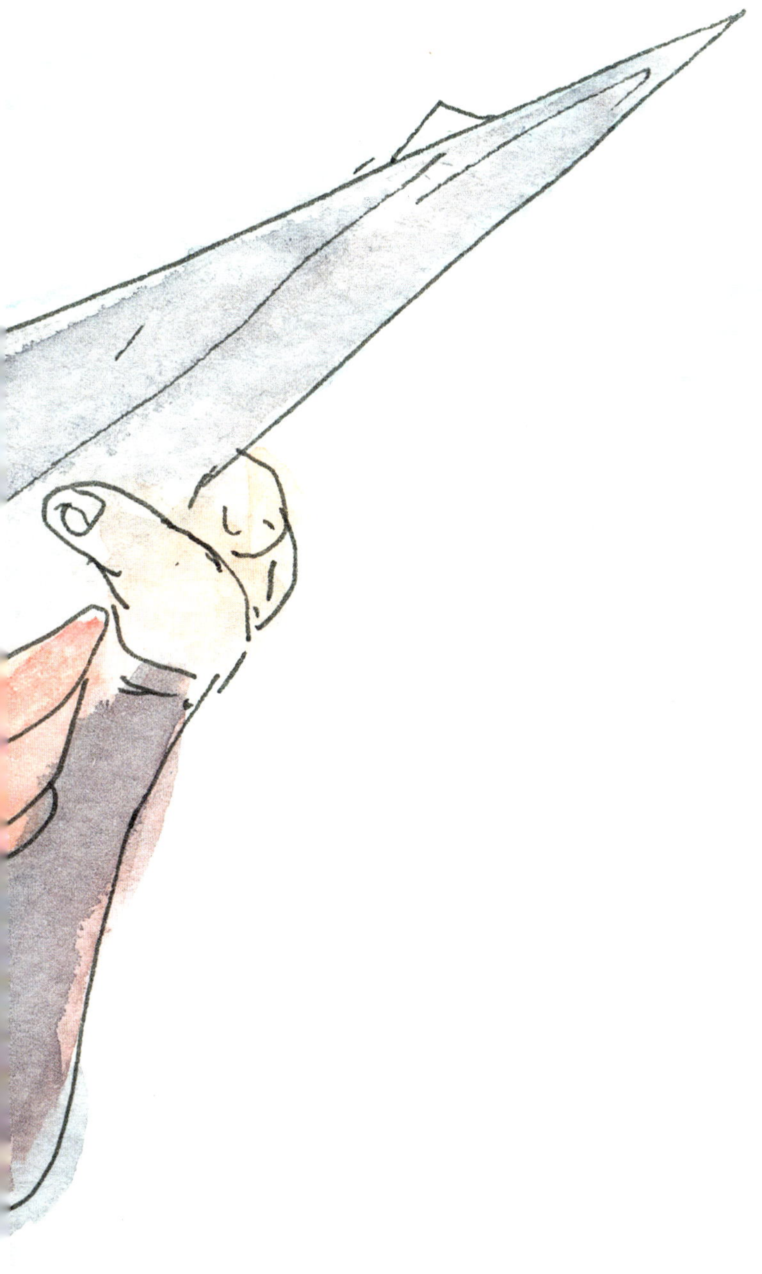

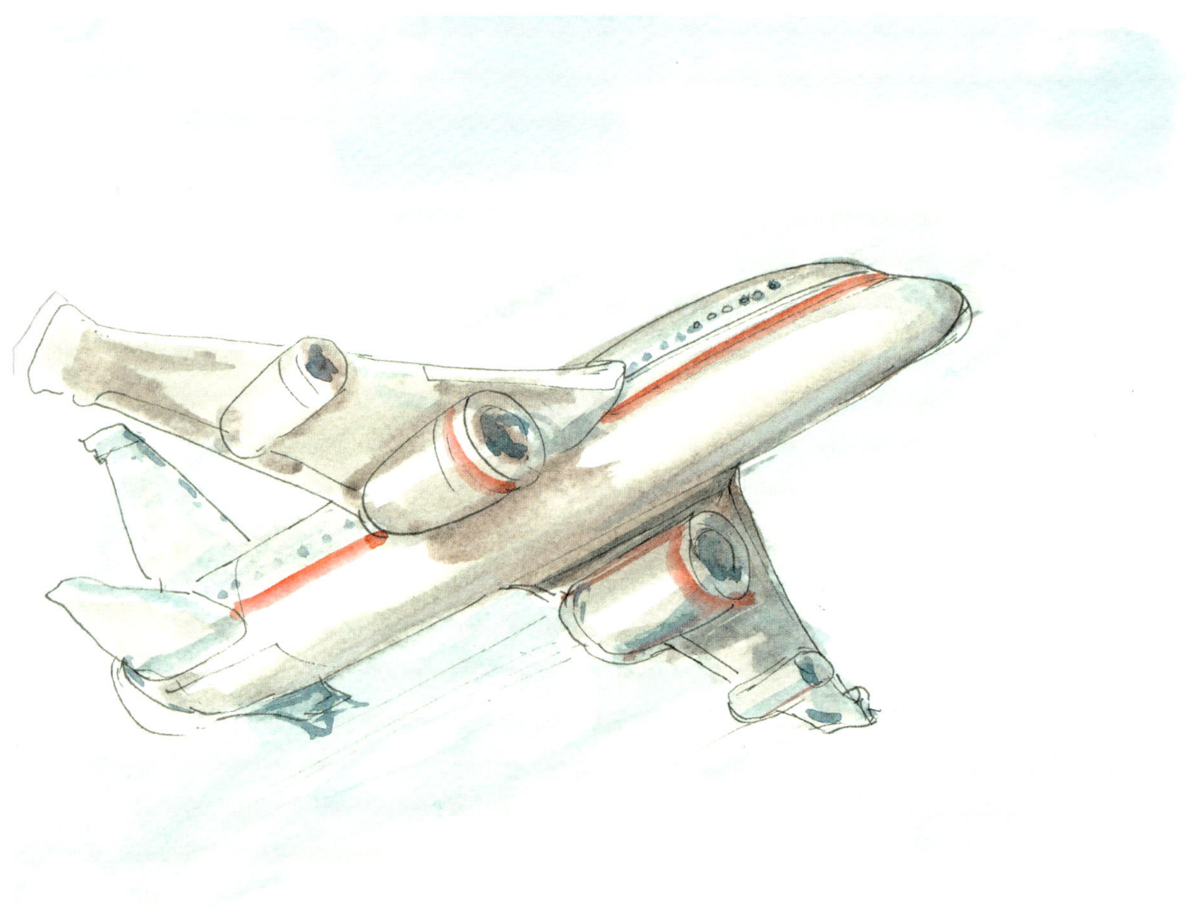

And the airplane.

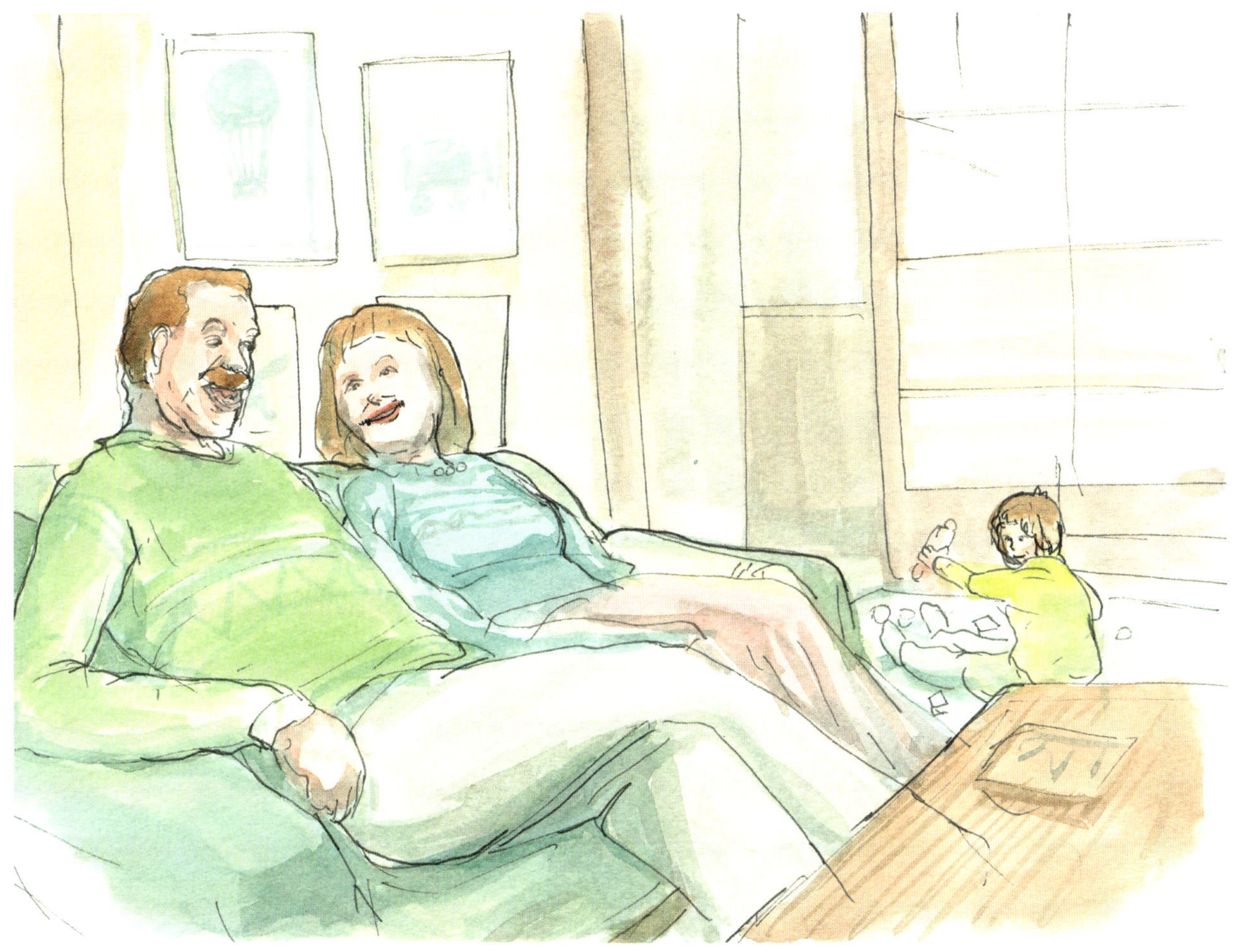

And his parents were so proud of all of their inventions.

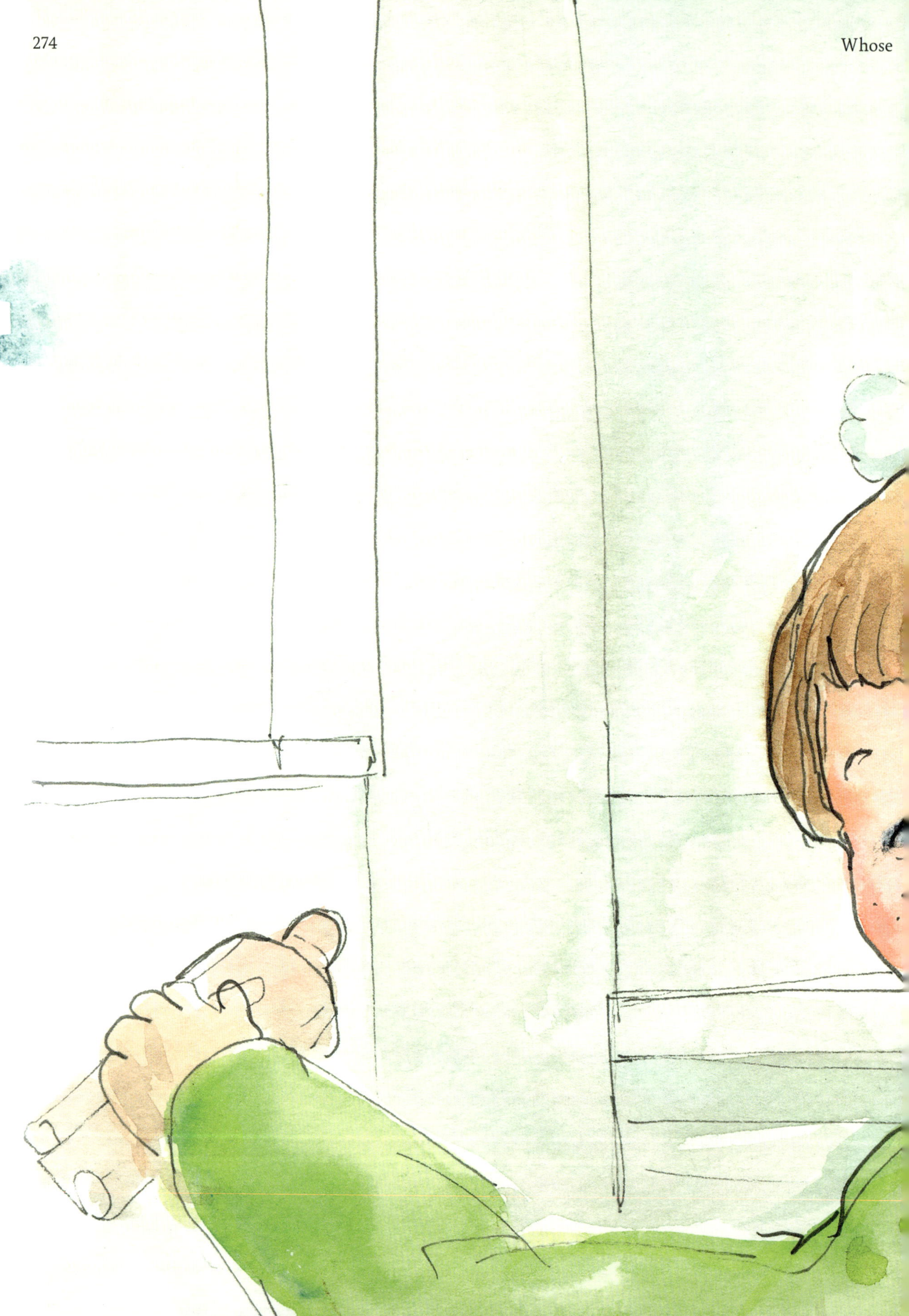

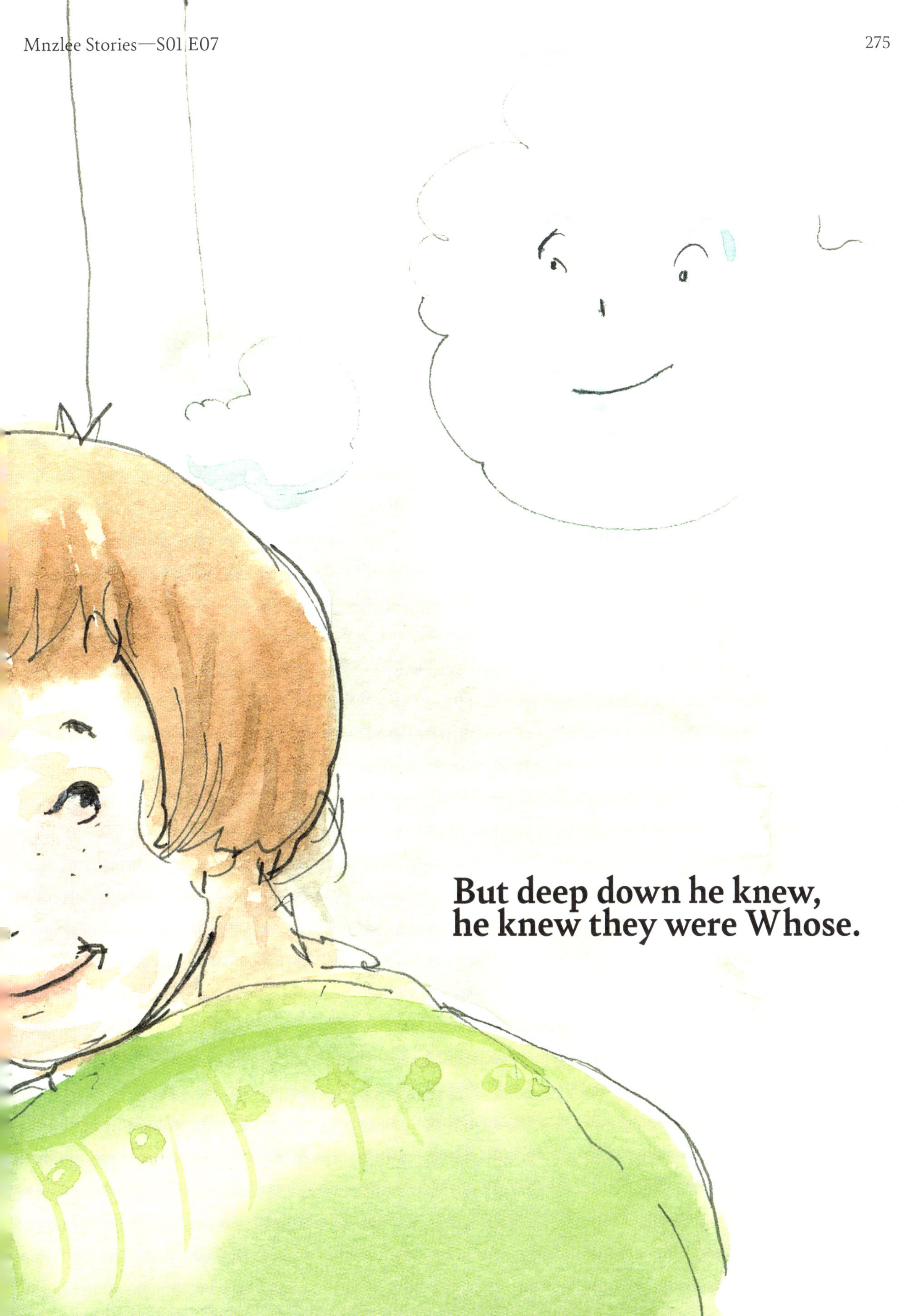

**But deep down he knew,
he knew they were Whose.**

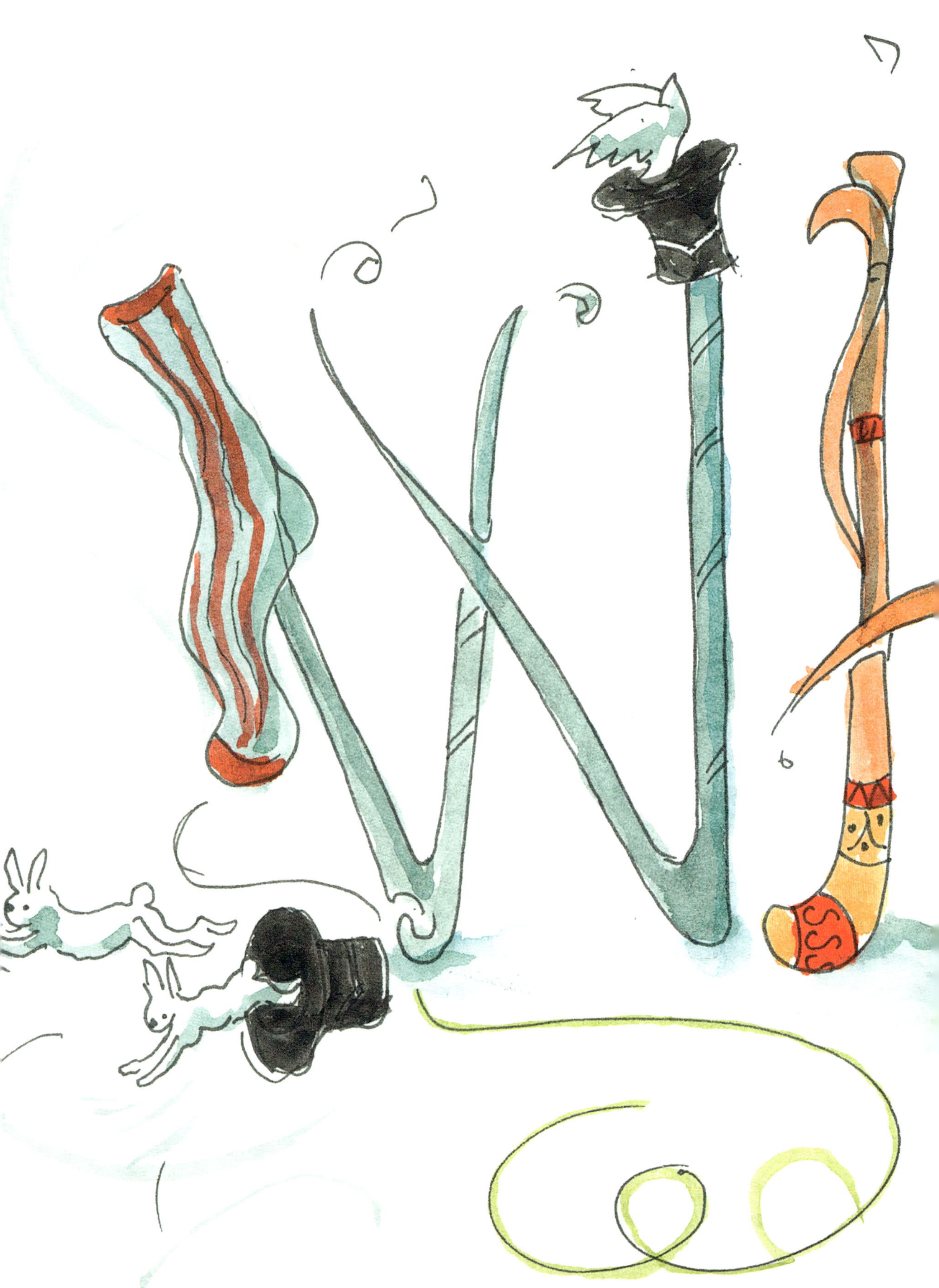

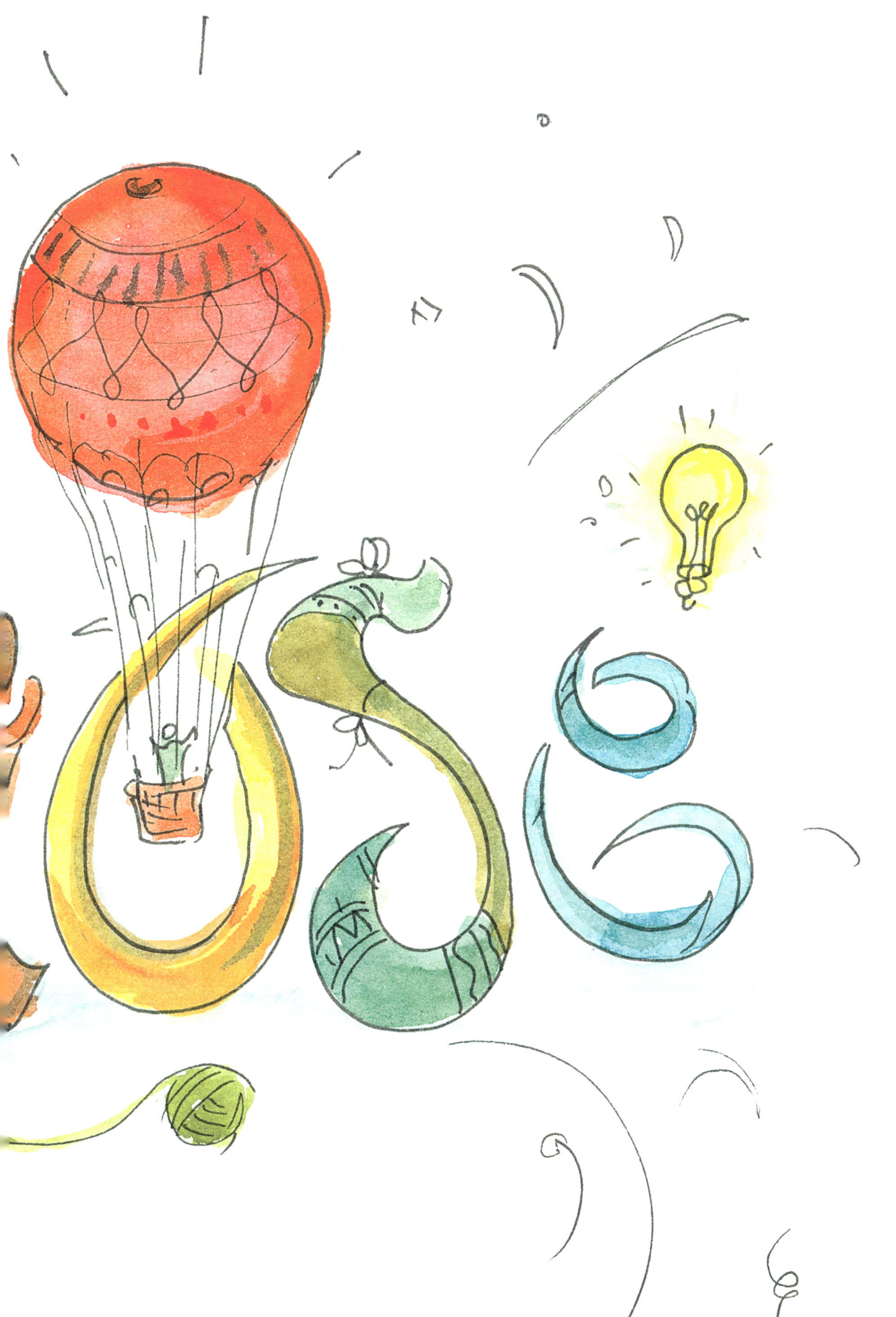

SELVES

Mnzlee Stories — S01 E08

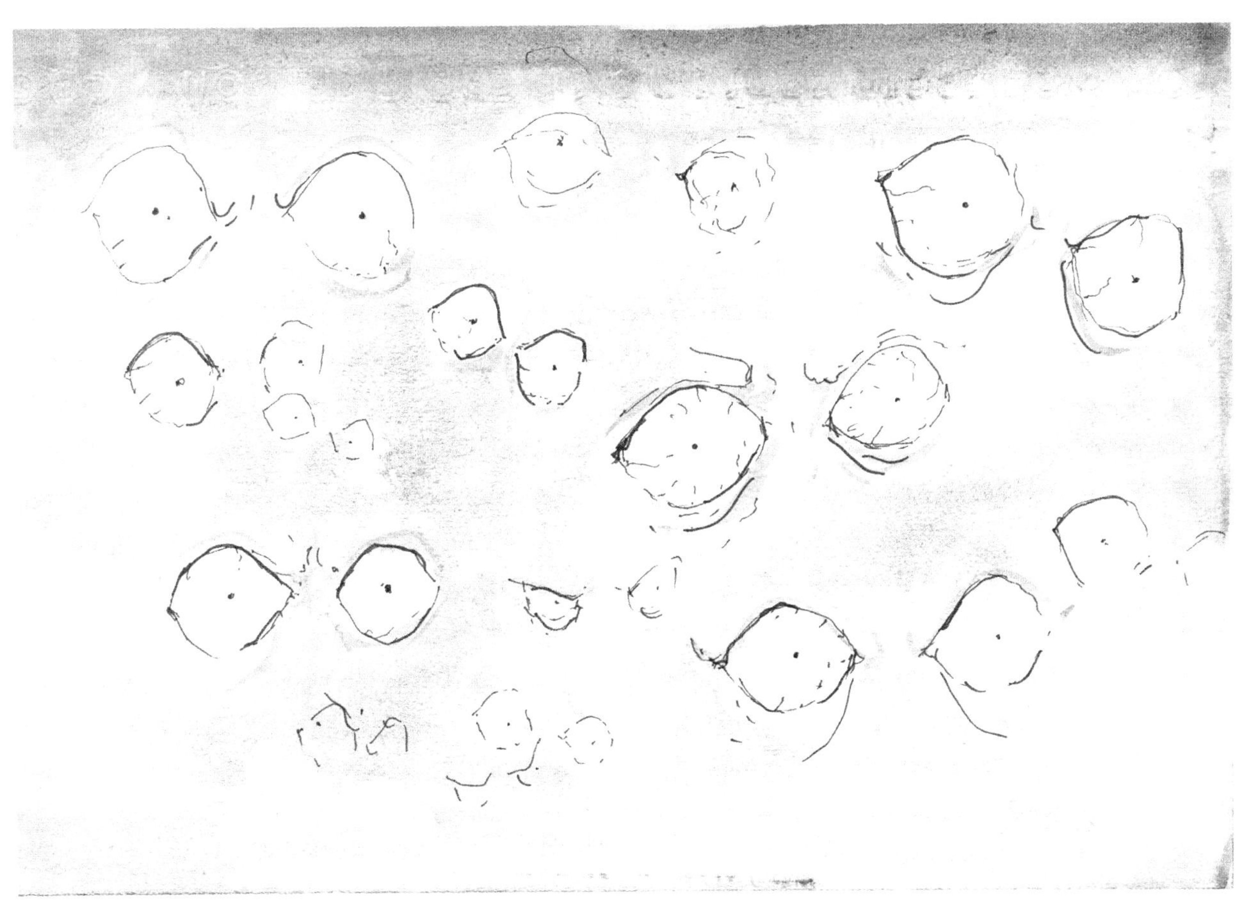

In a world of death where color was a moral sin,

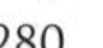

everyone, everywhere wore one shade of gray.

At all times.

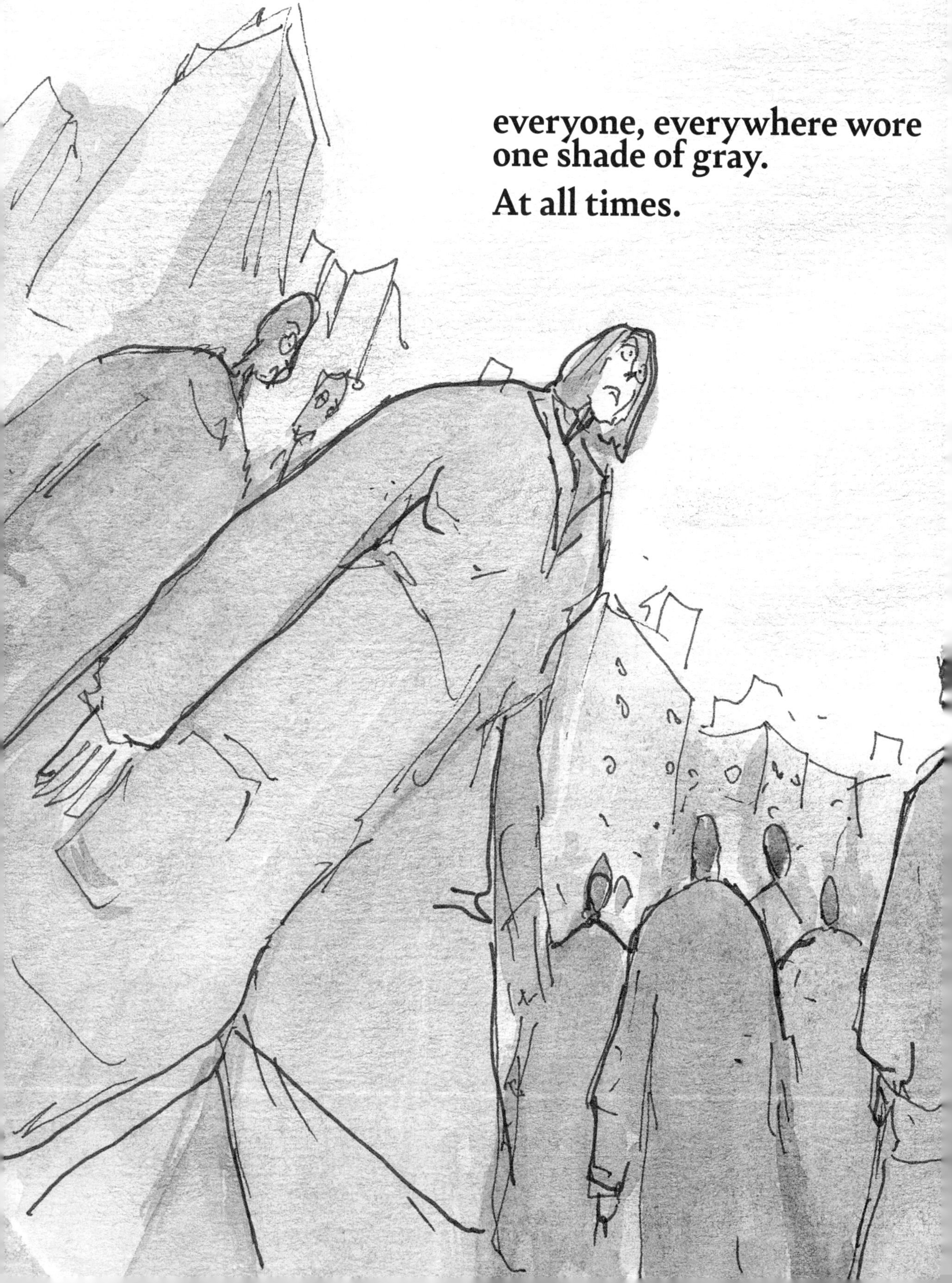

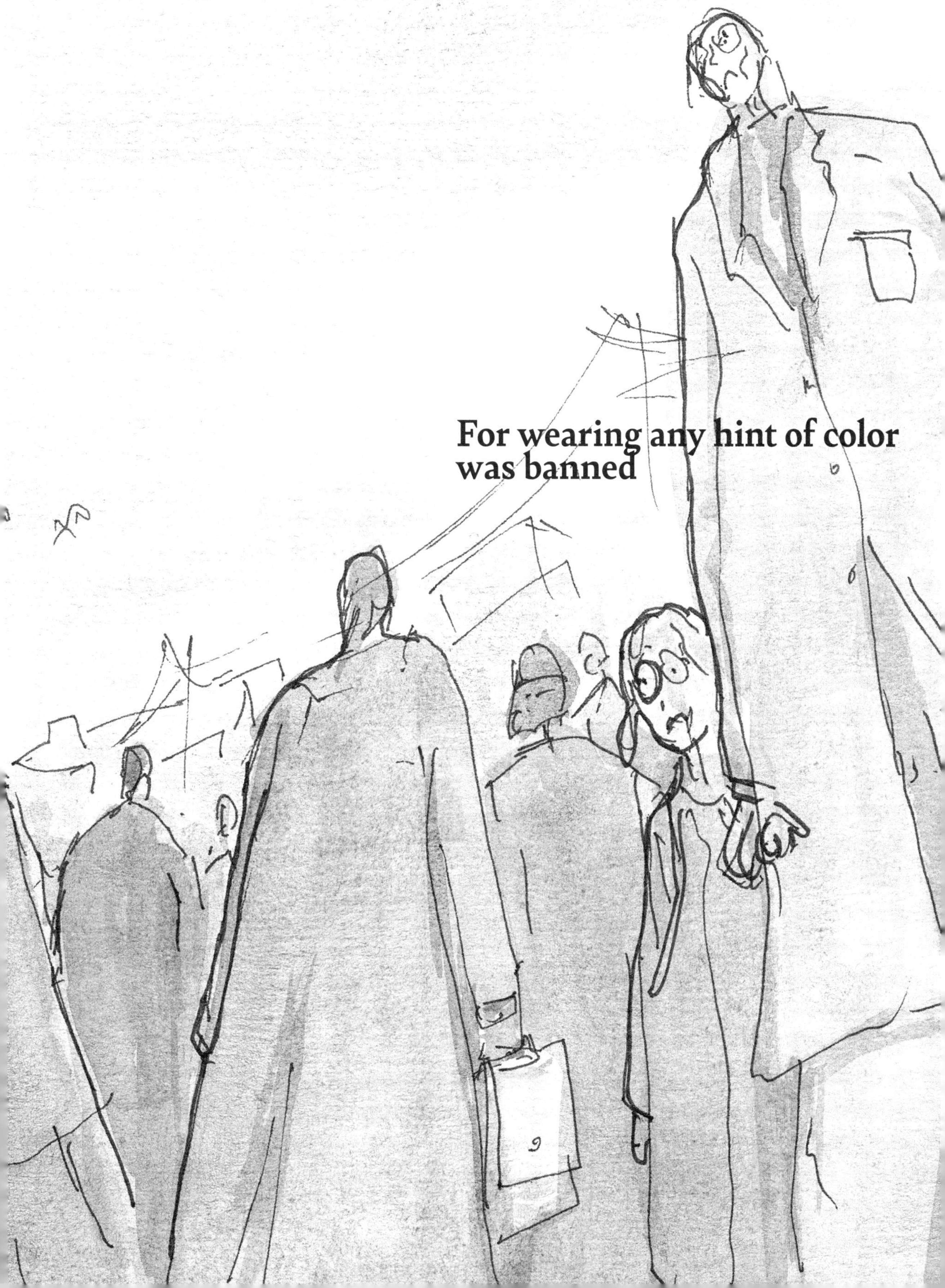

For wearing any hint of color was banned

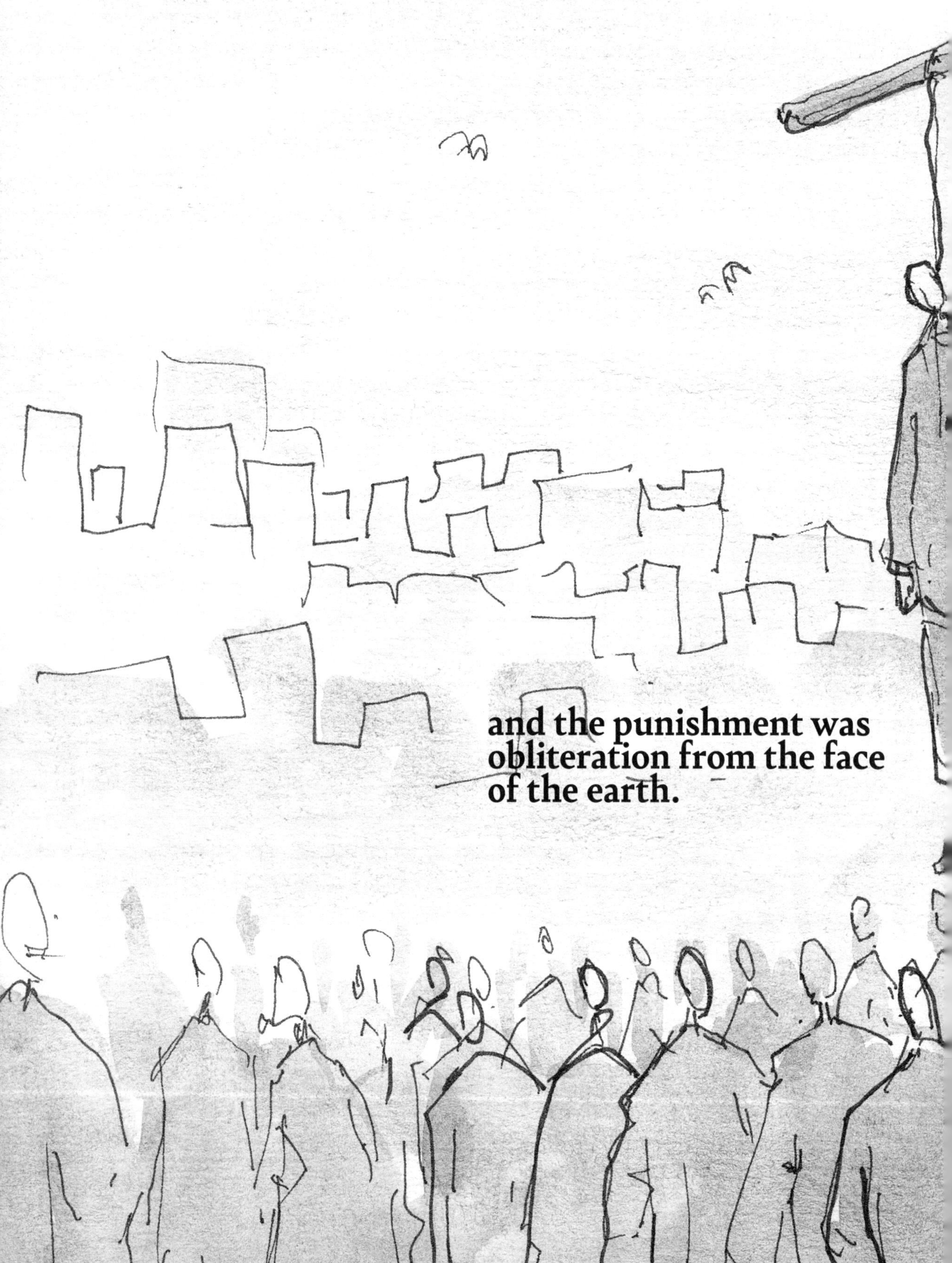
and the punishment was
obliteration from the face
of the earth.

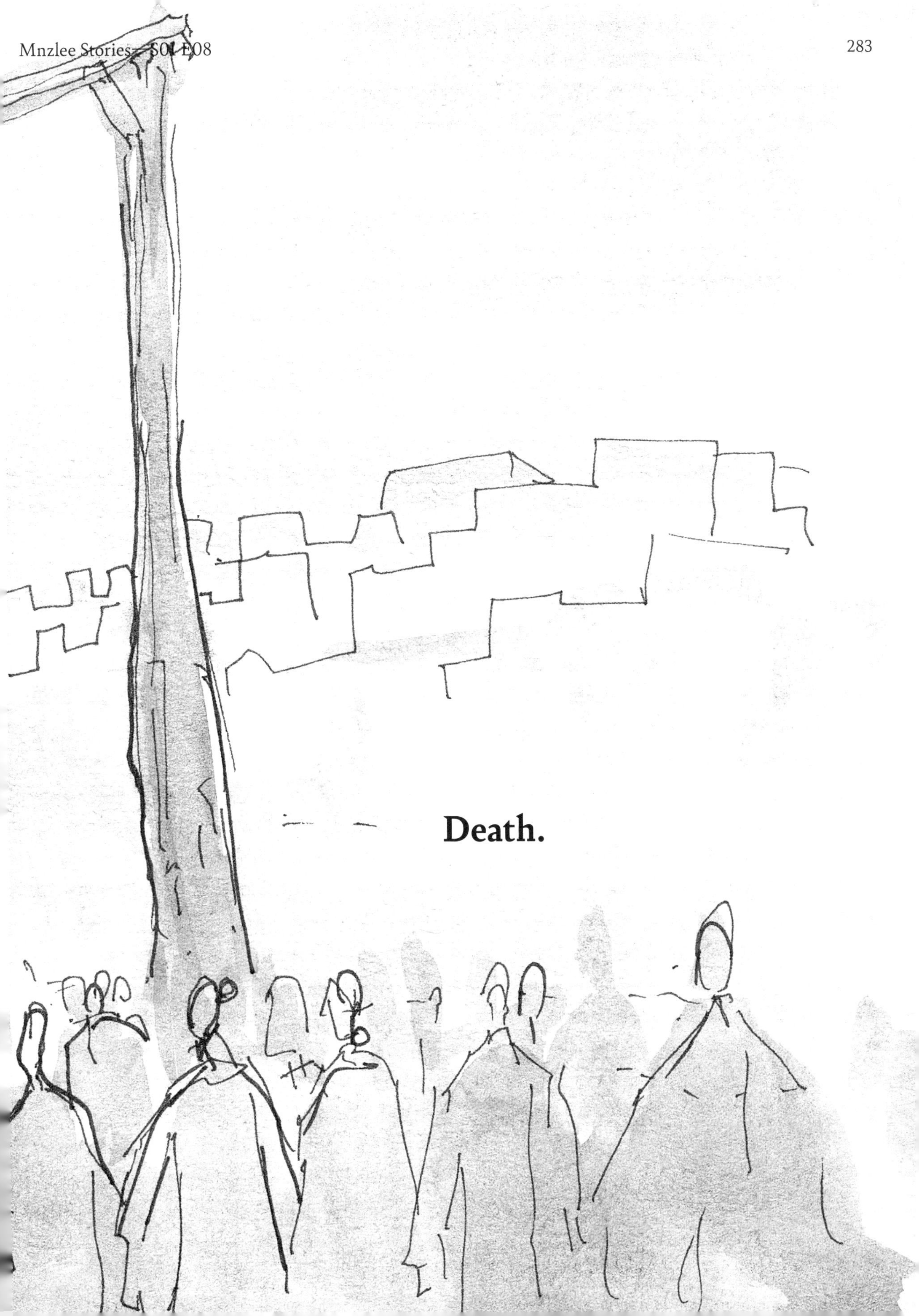

Death.

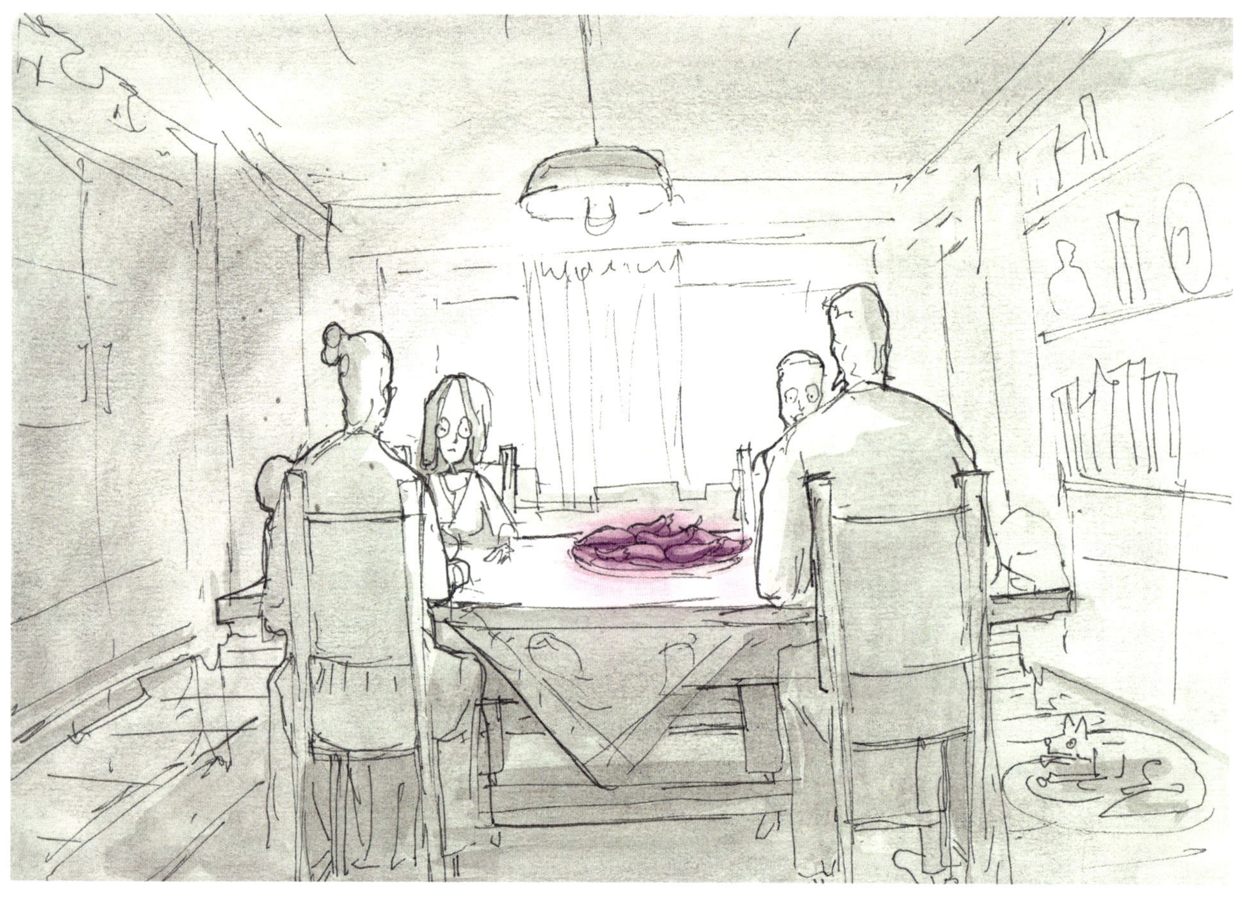

One day as a family was sharing eggplants over dinner at home,

all dressed in gray,

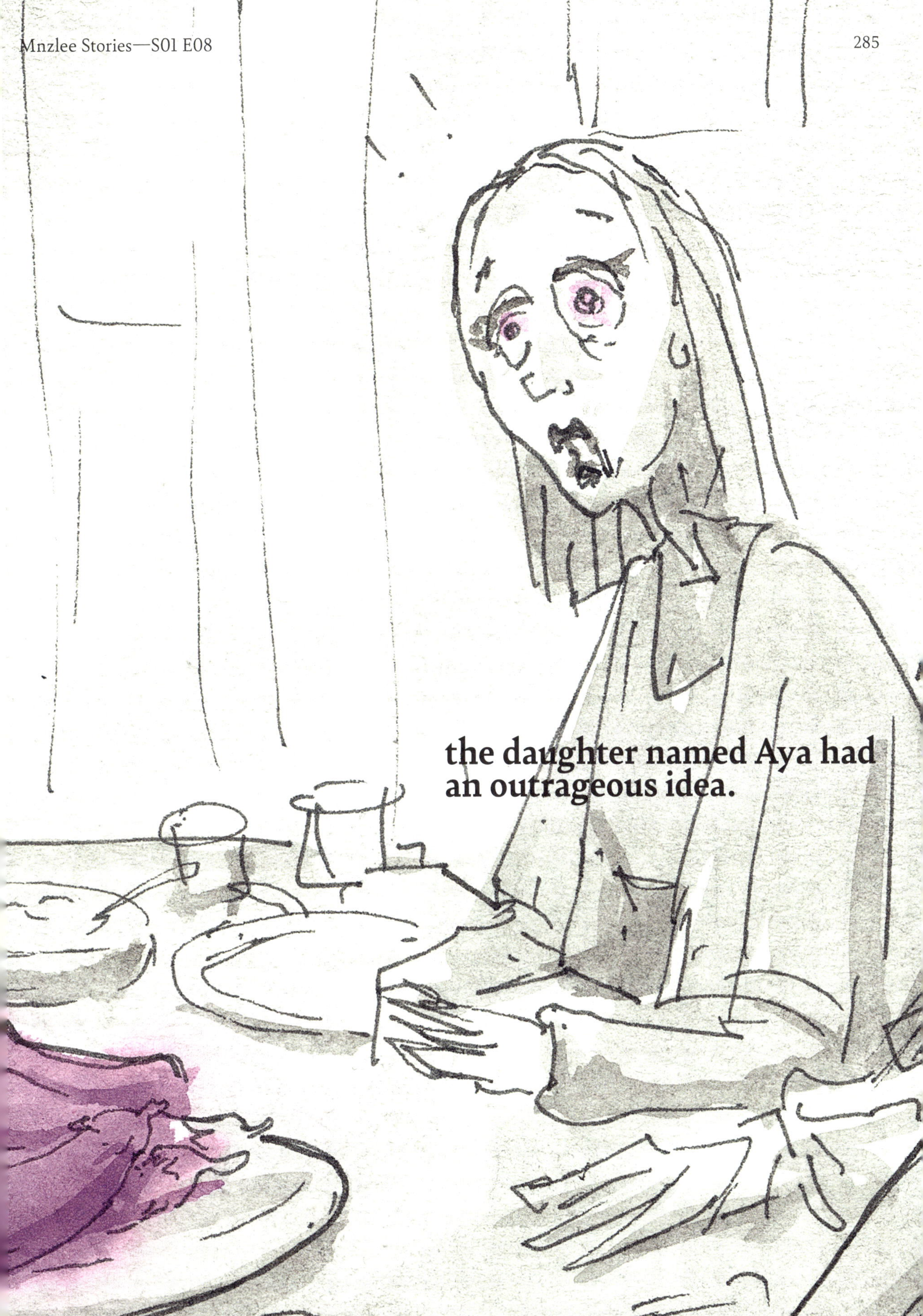

the daughter named Aya had
an outrageous idea.

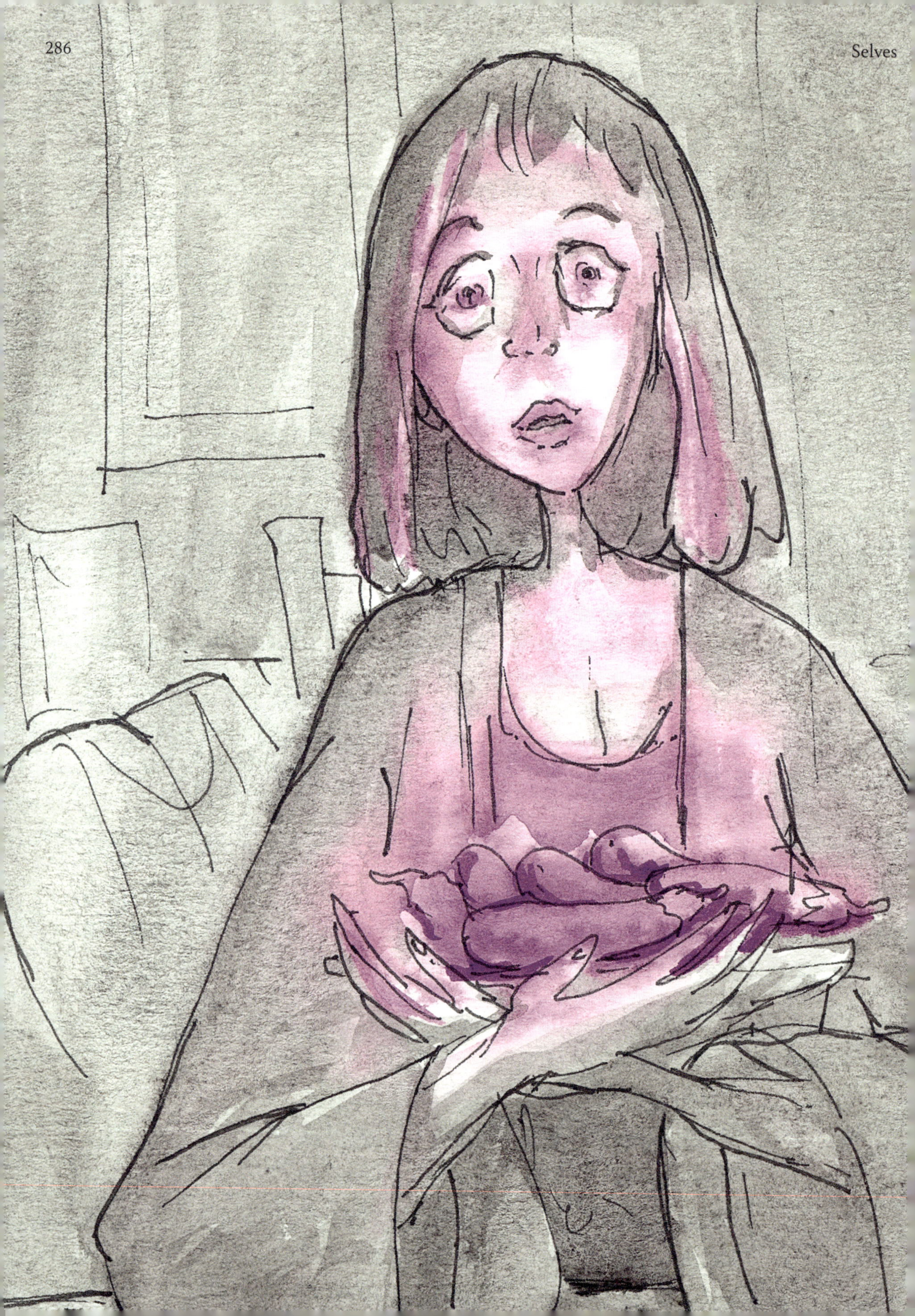

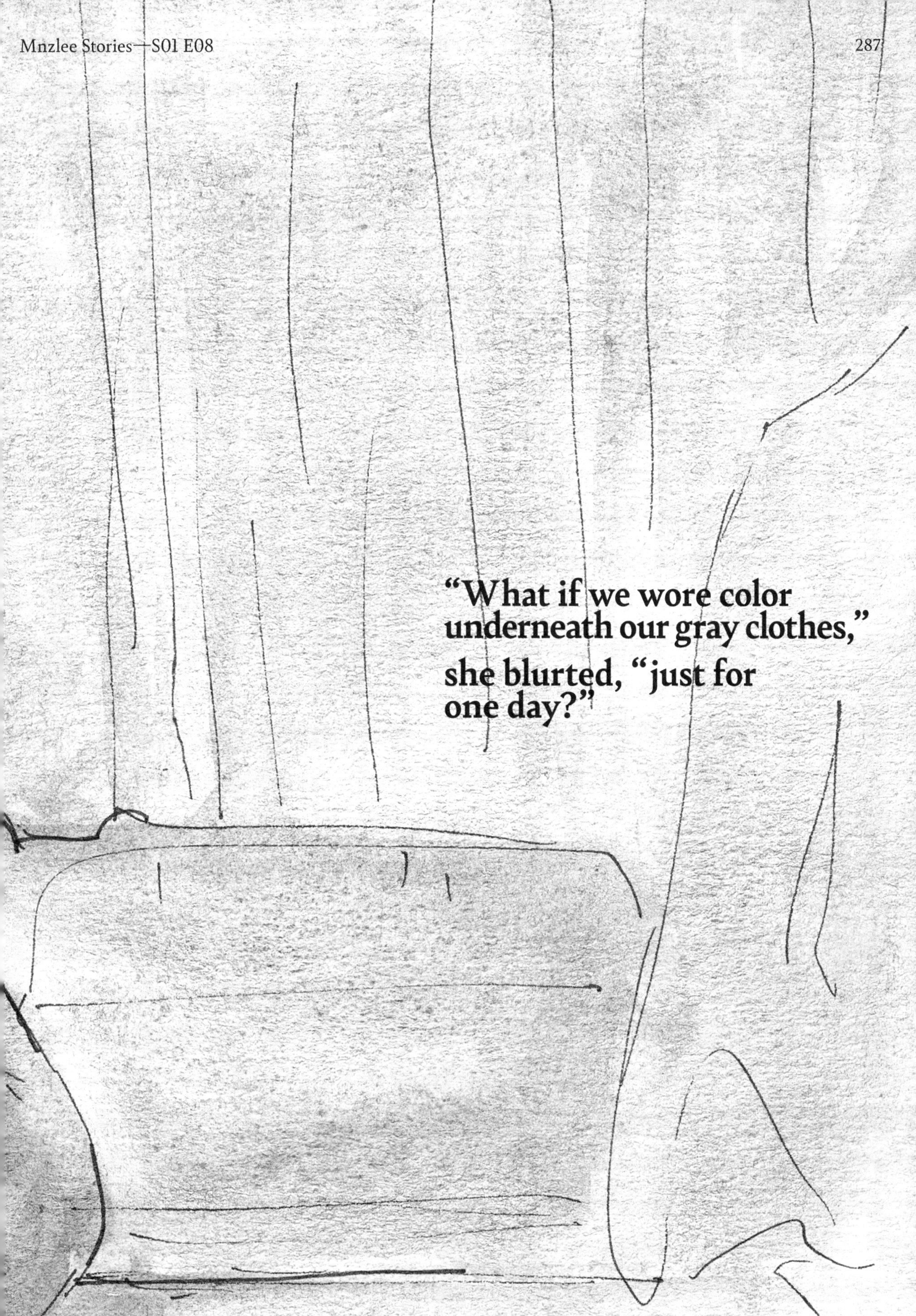

"What if we wore color underneath our gray clothes,"
she blurted, "just for one day?"

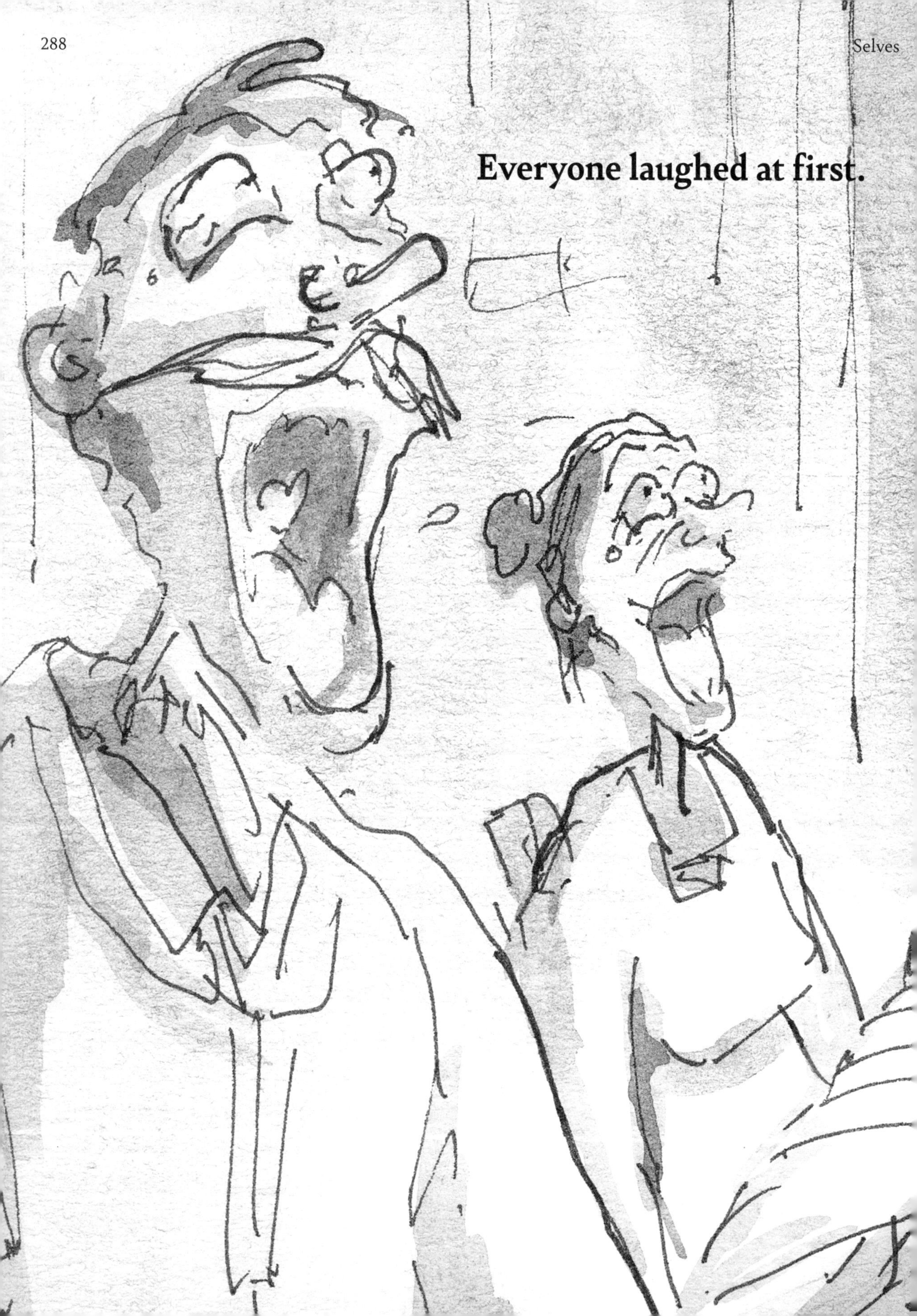
Everyone laughed at first.

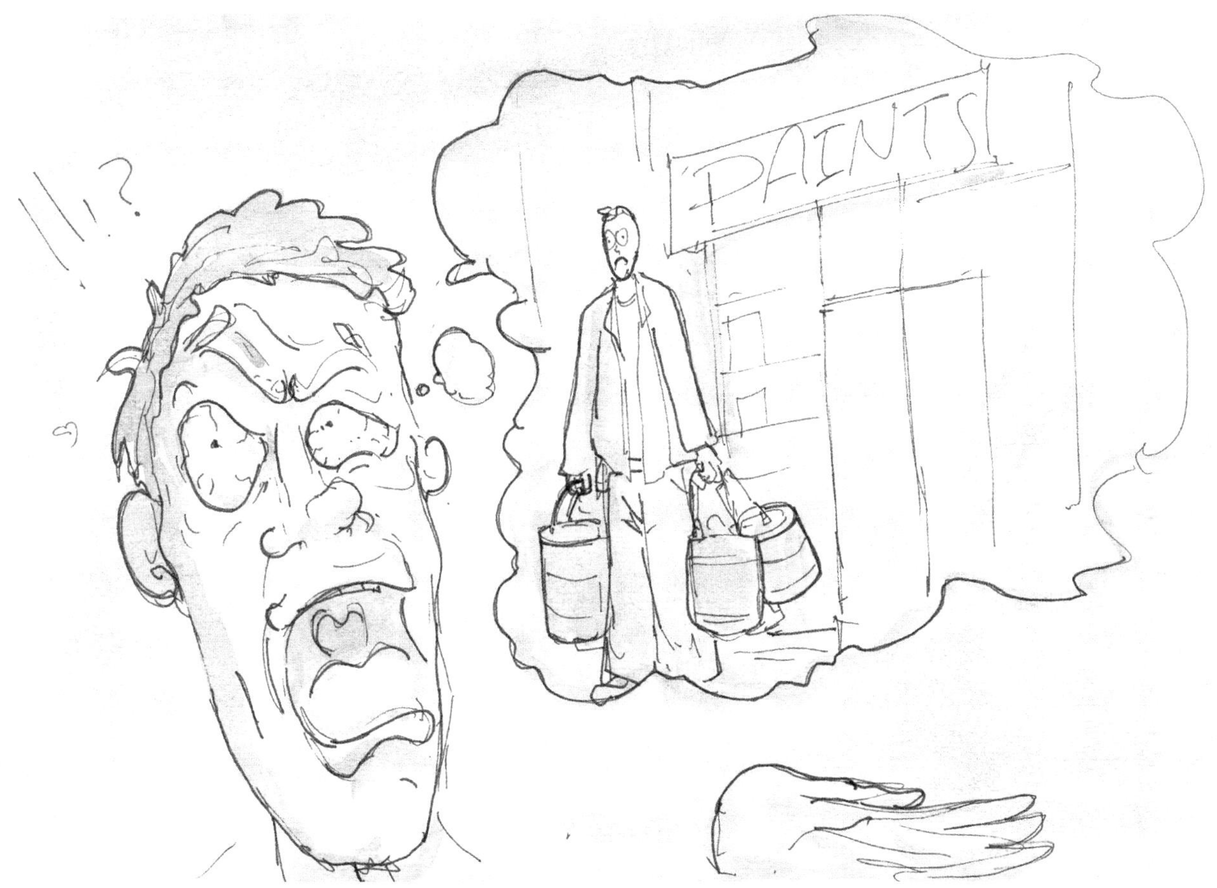

"Color underneath the gray clothes?"

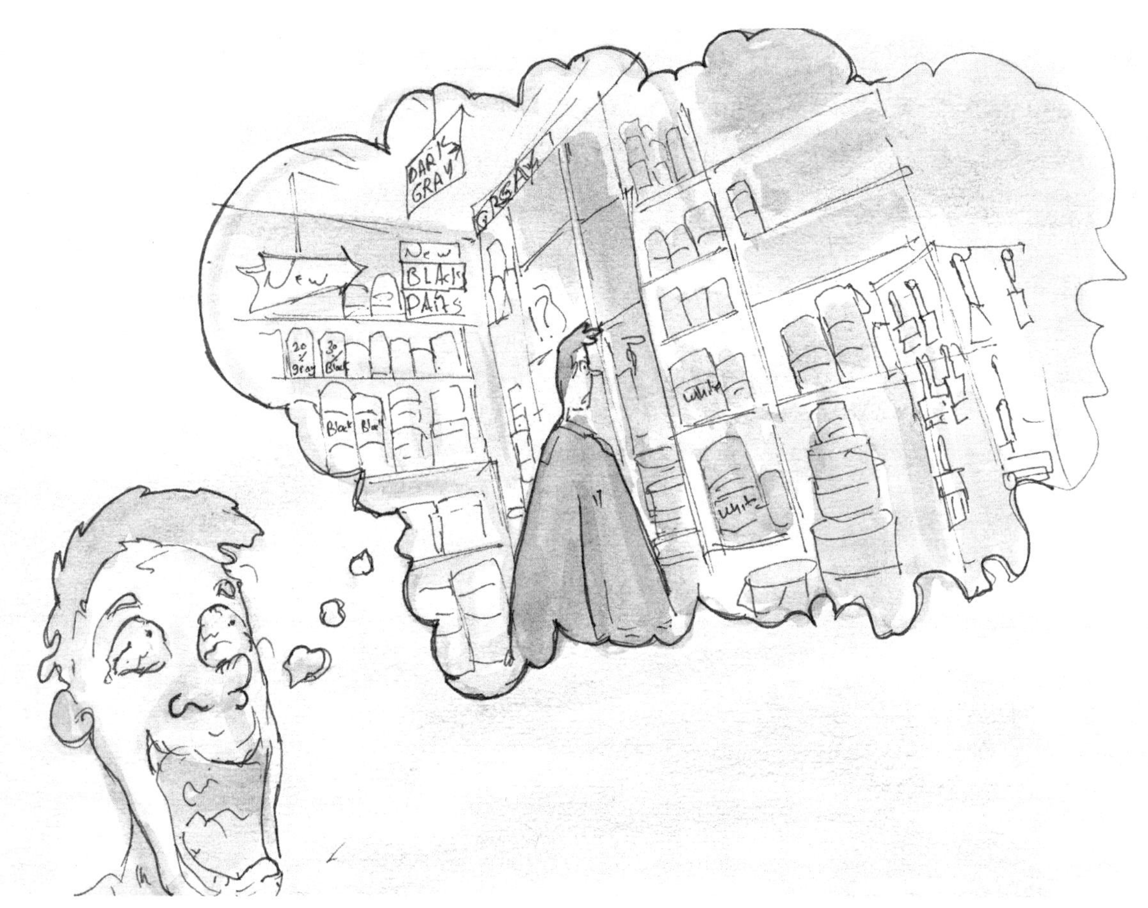

"How would we even make colored clothing?"
asked the brother.

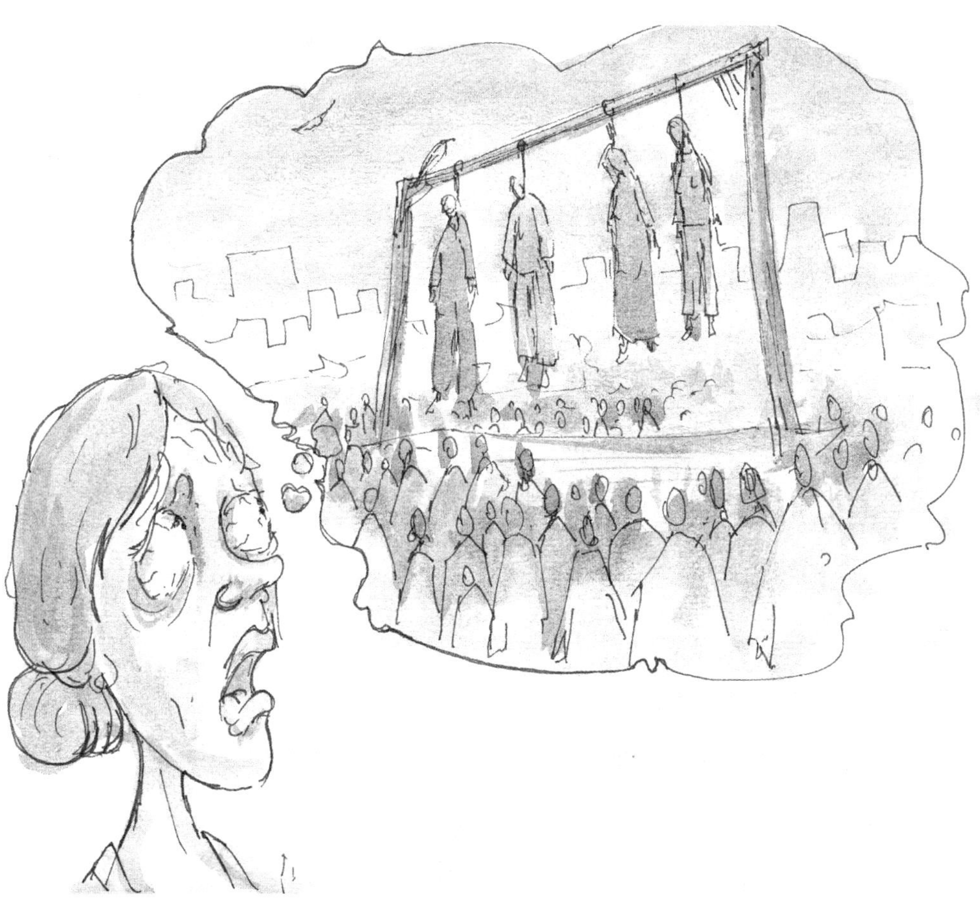

"And what if anyone sees us? What if we are caught?"
asked the mother.

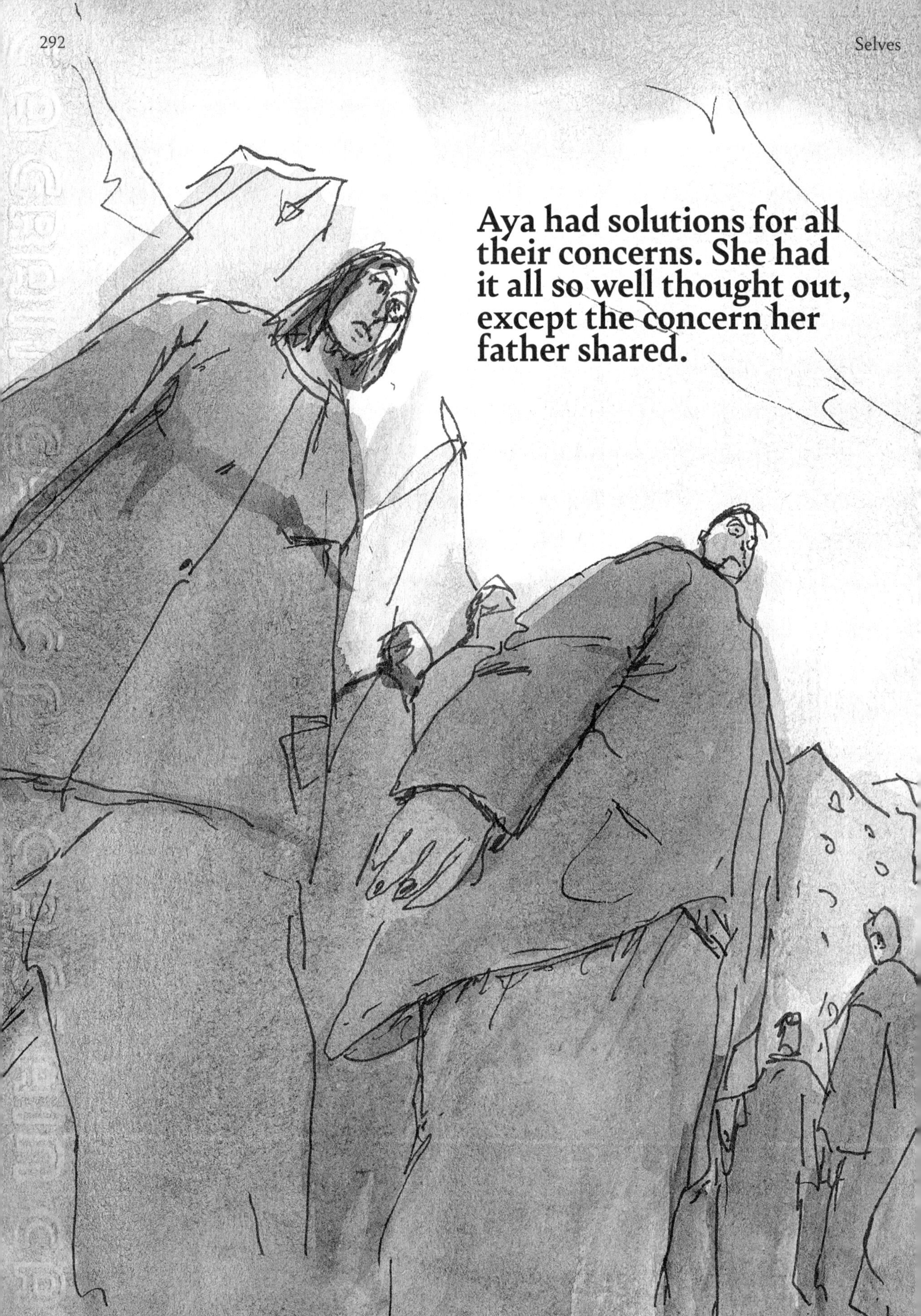

Aya had solutions for all
their concerns. She had
it all so well thought out,
except the concern her
father shared.

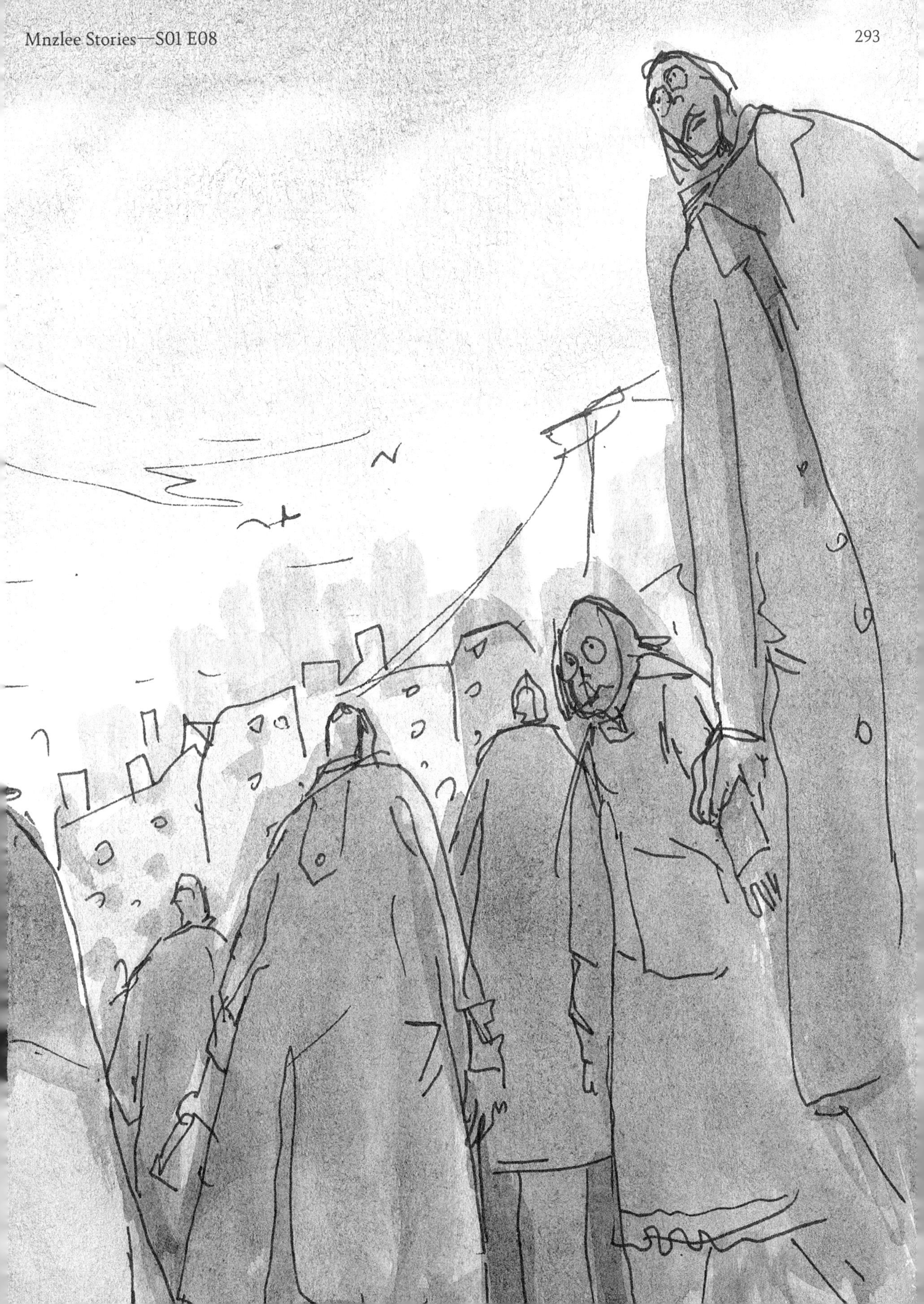

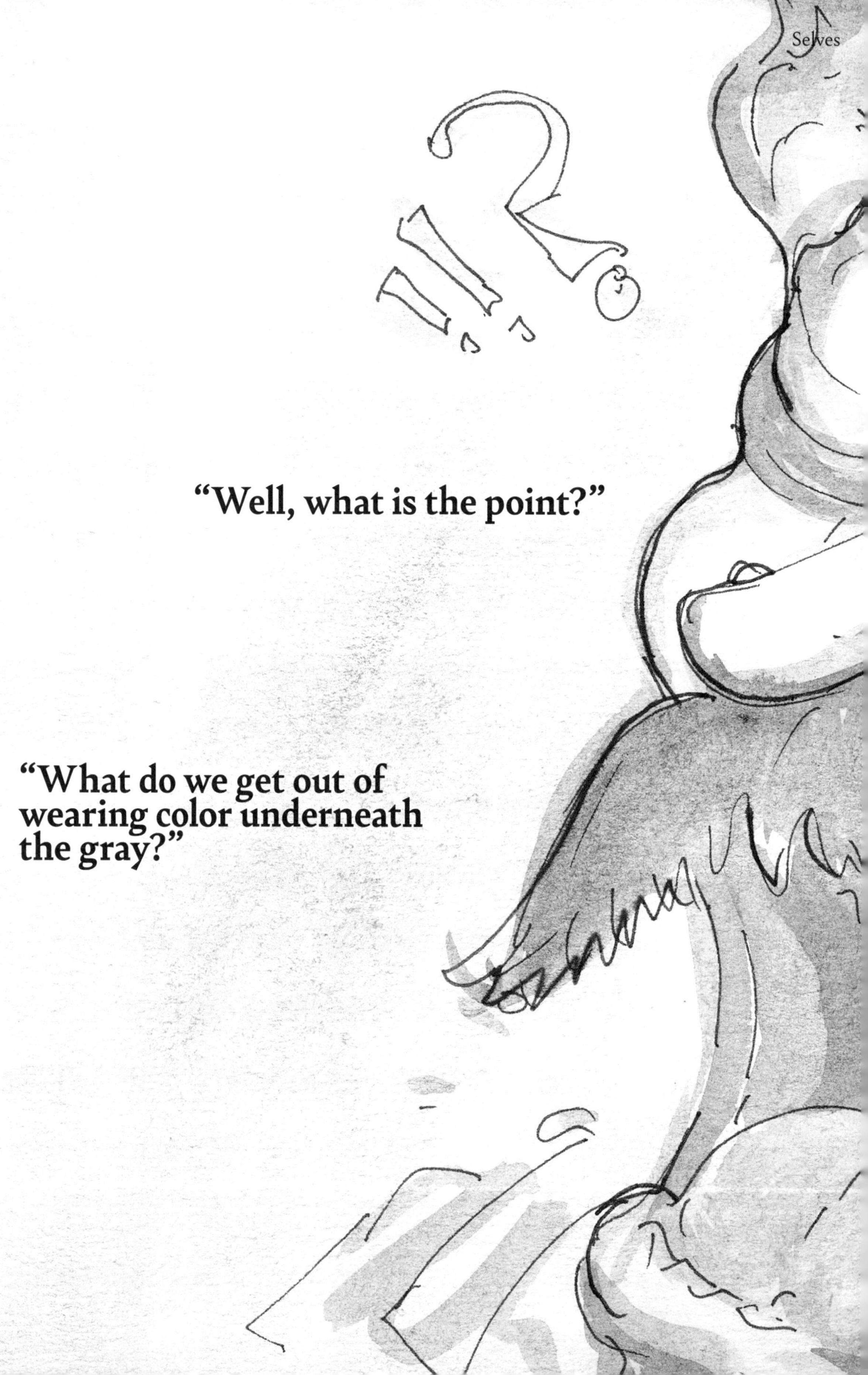

"Well, what is the point?"

"What do we get out of
wearing color underneath
the gray?"

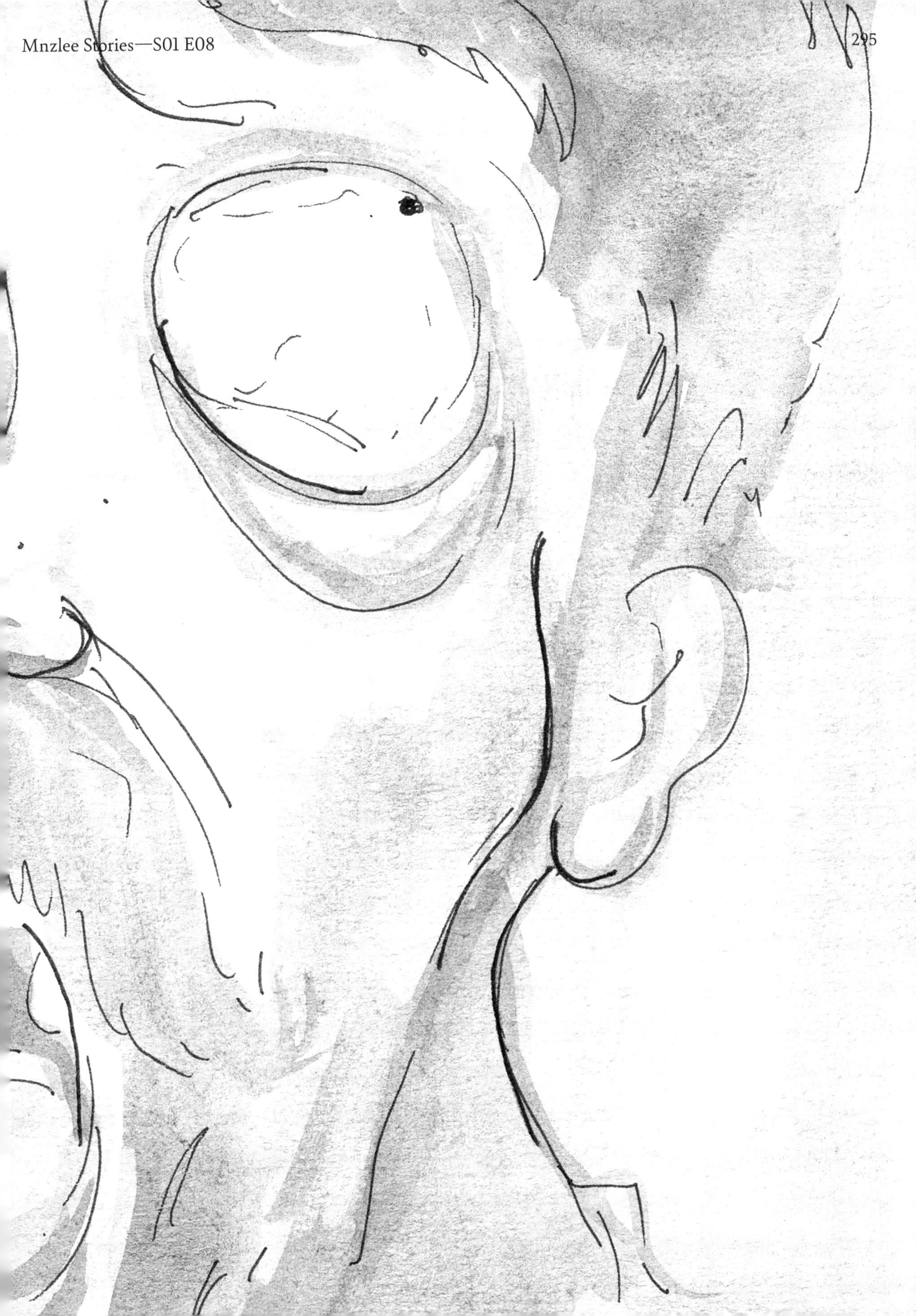

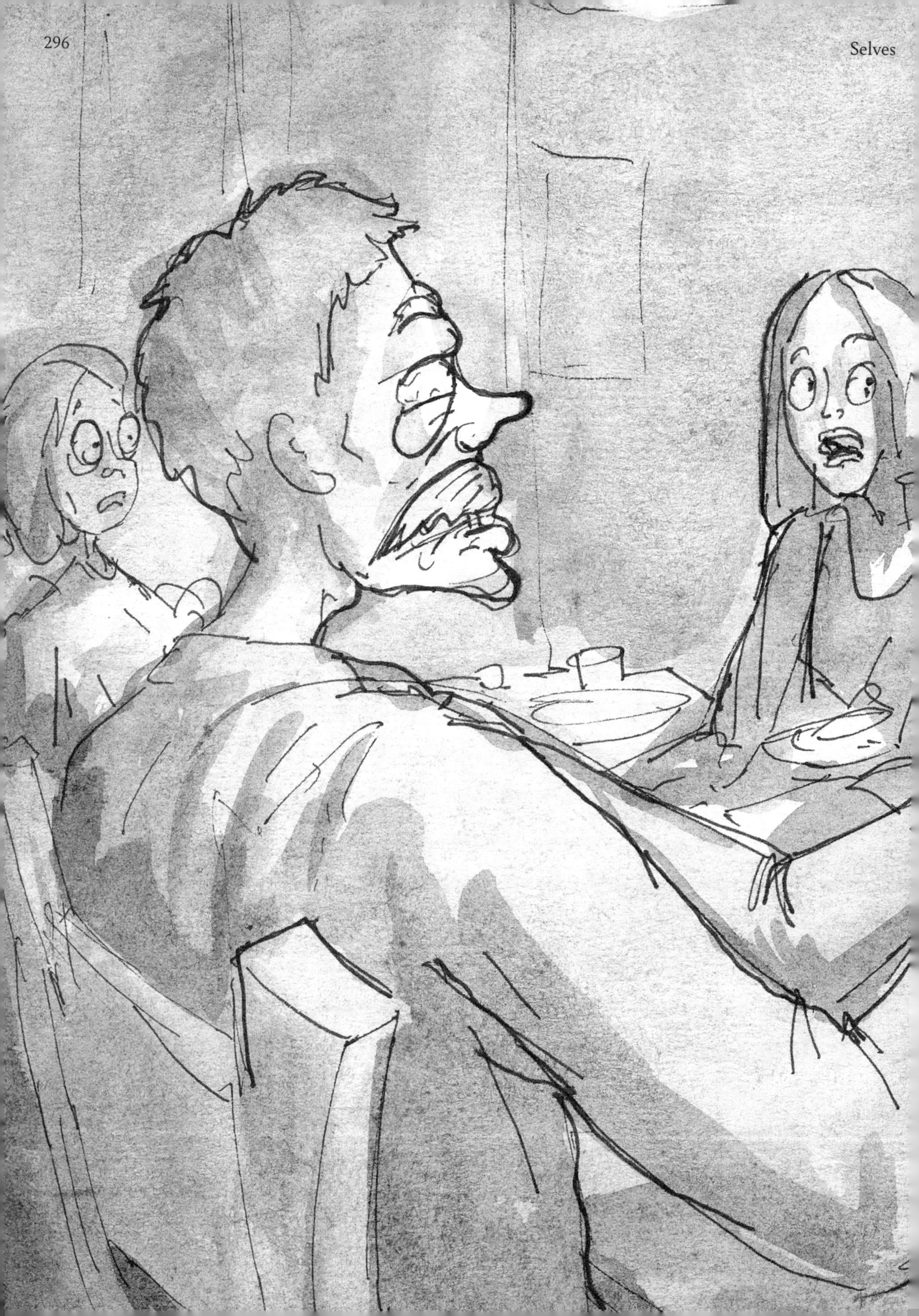

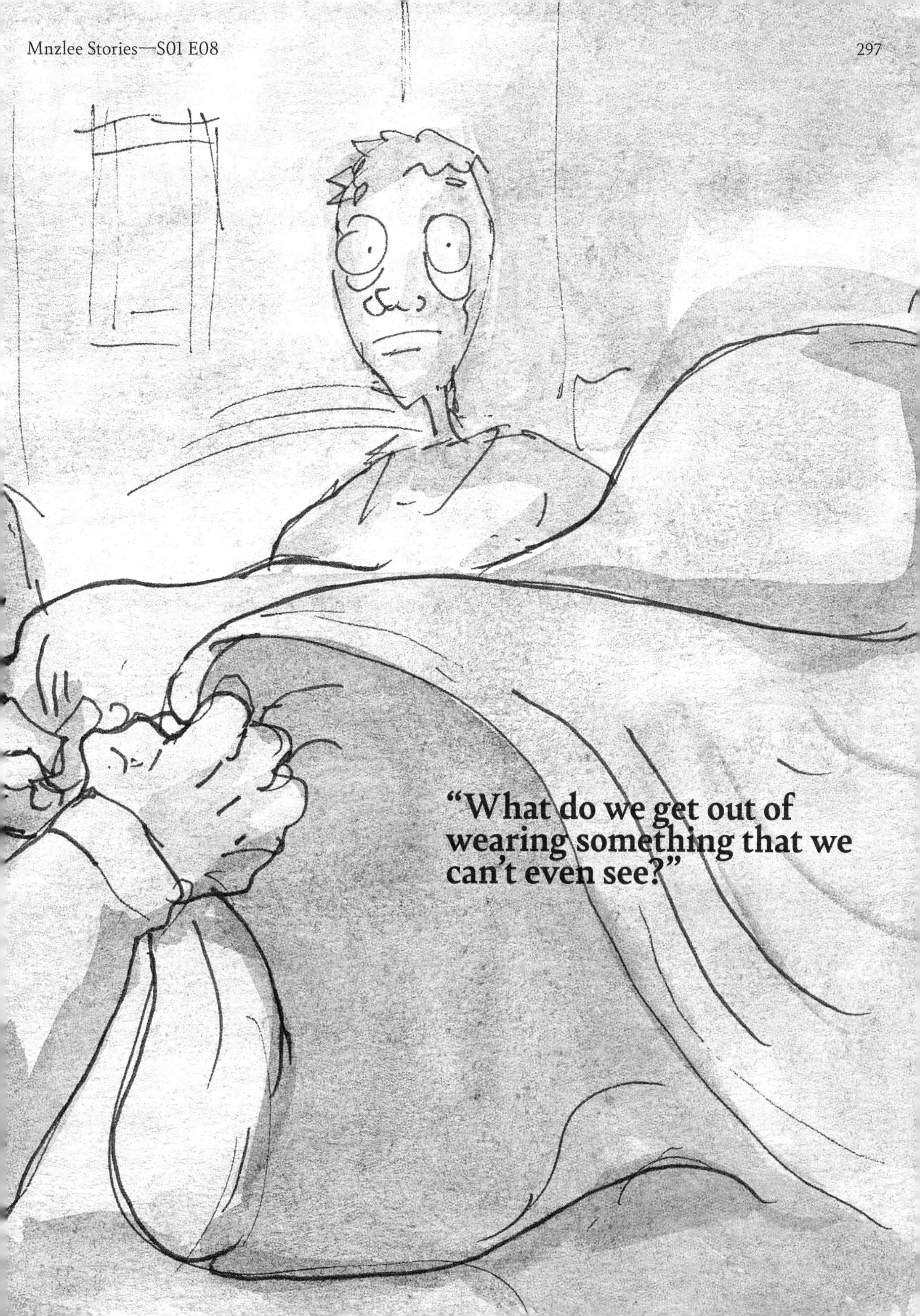
"What do we get out of wearing something that we can't even see?"

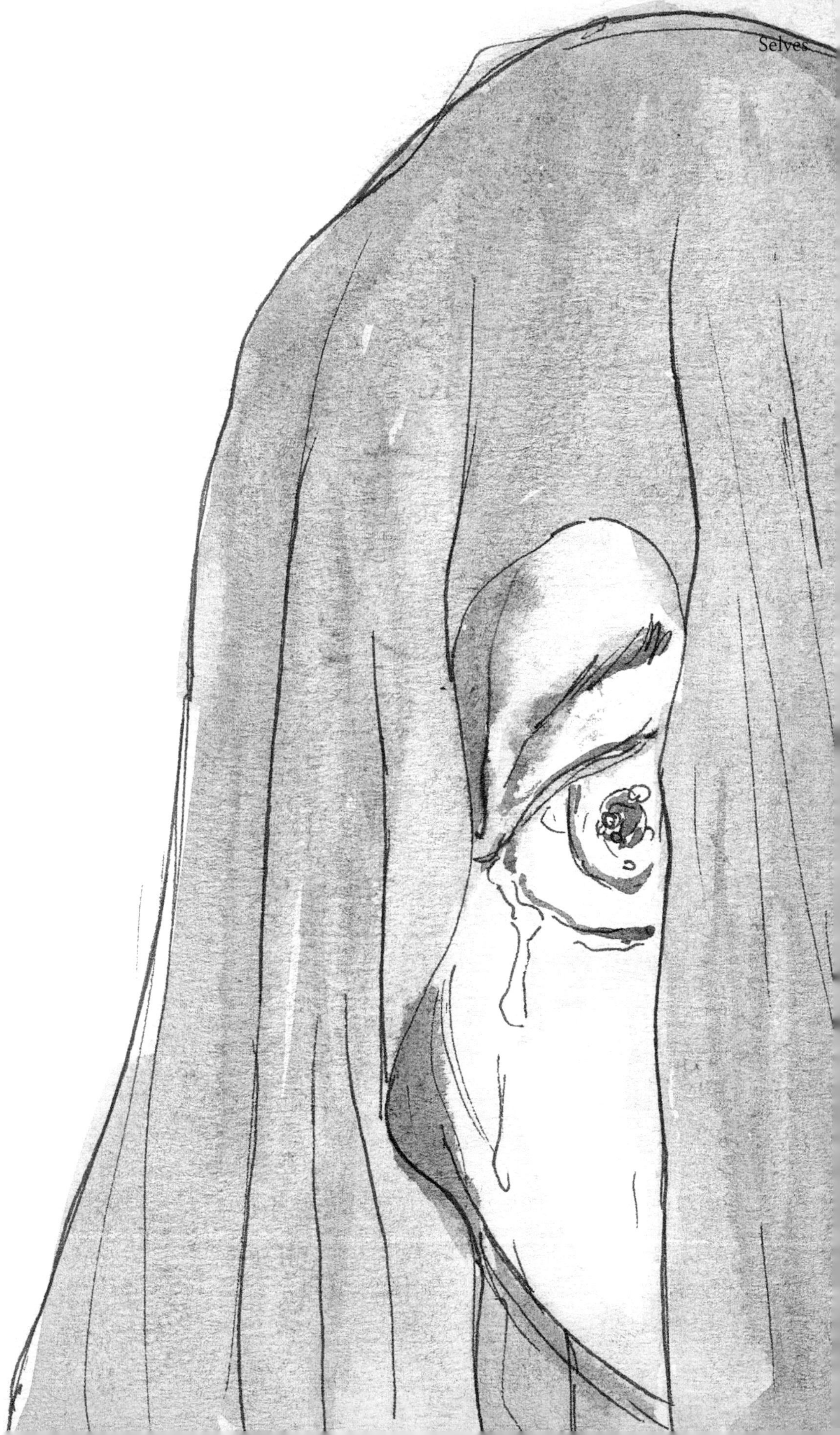

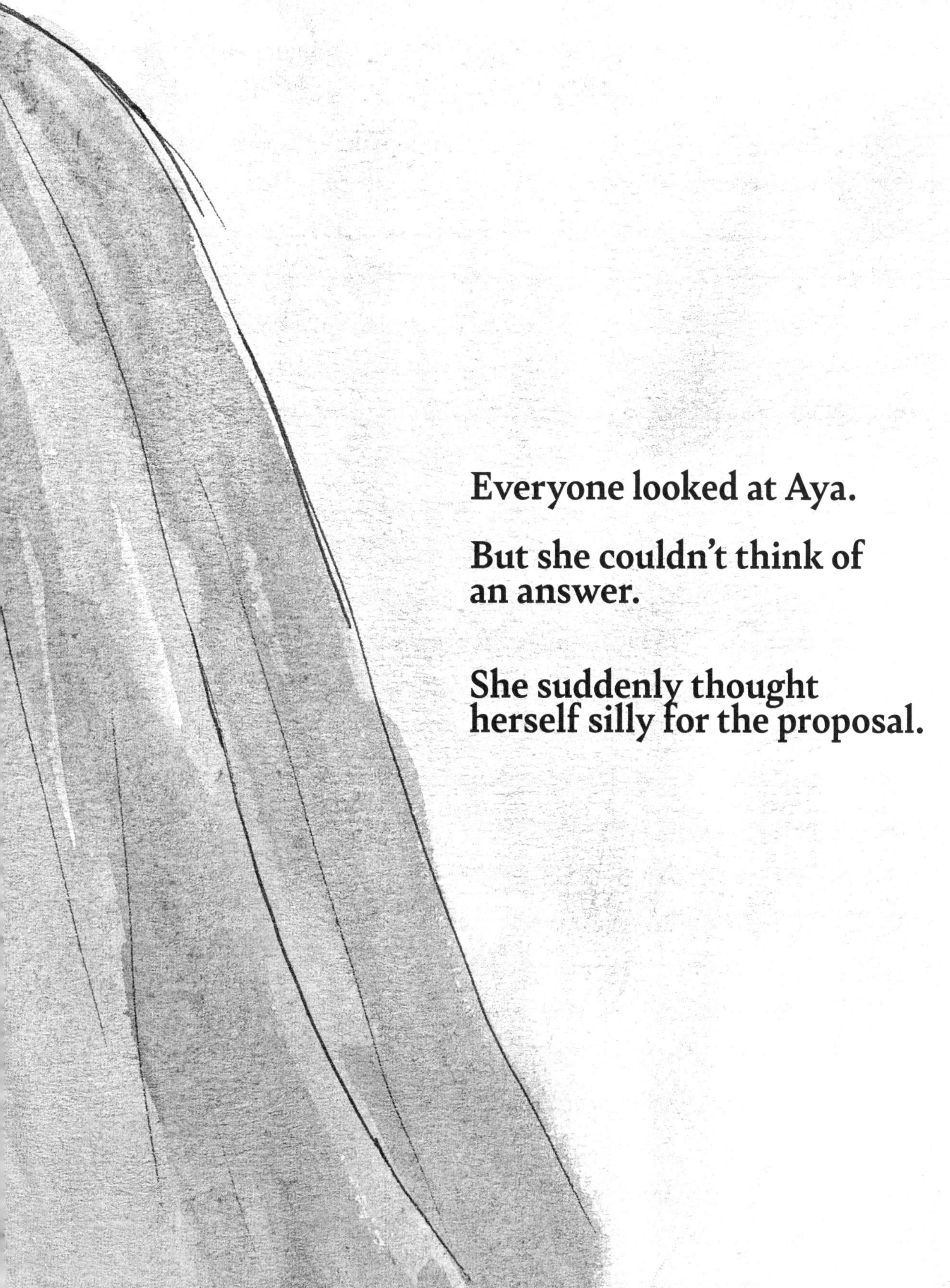

Everyone looked at Aya.

But she couldn't think of
an answer.

She suddenly thought
herself silly for the proposal.

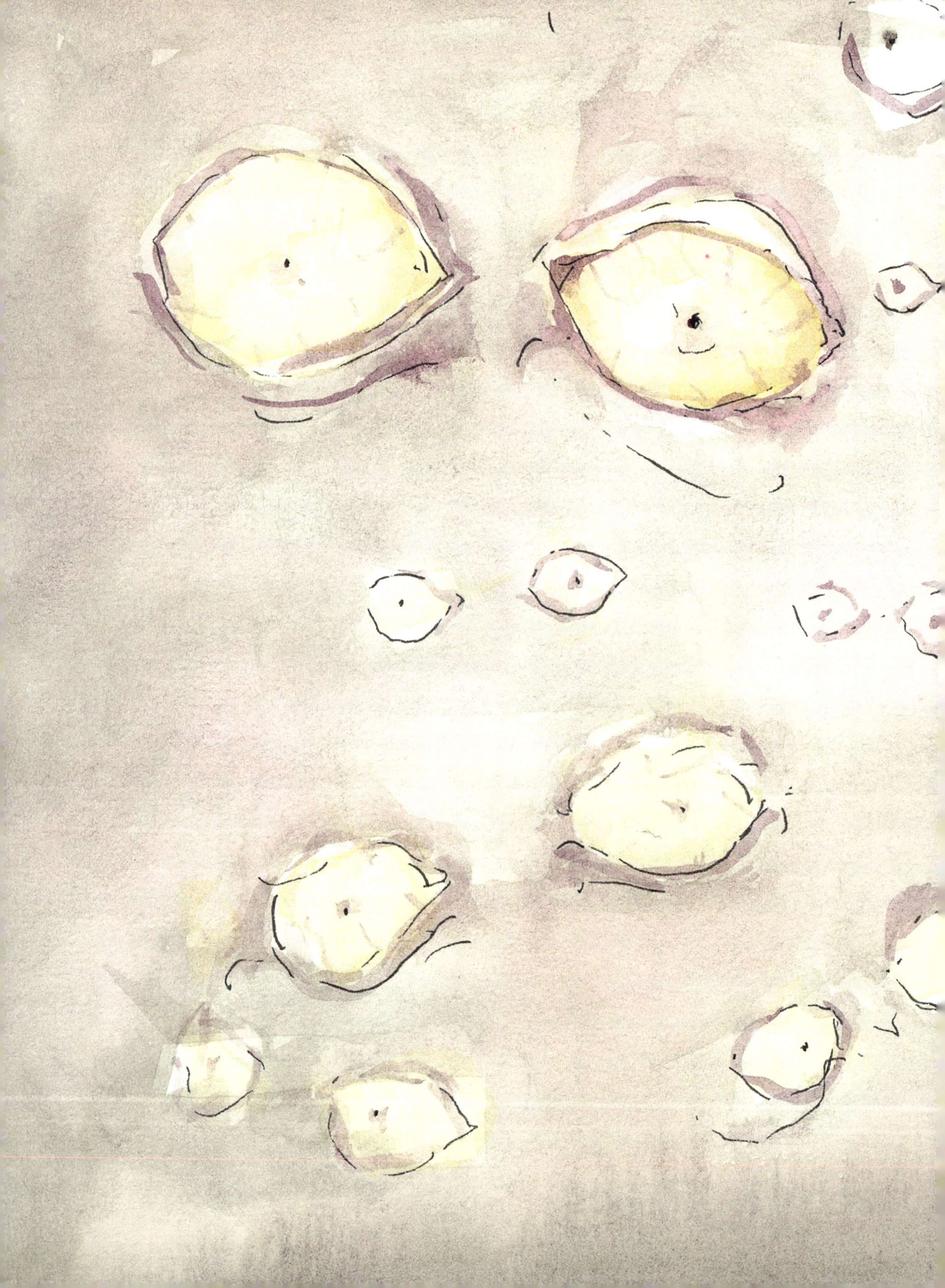

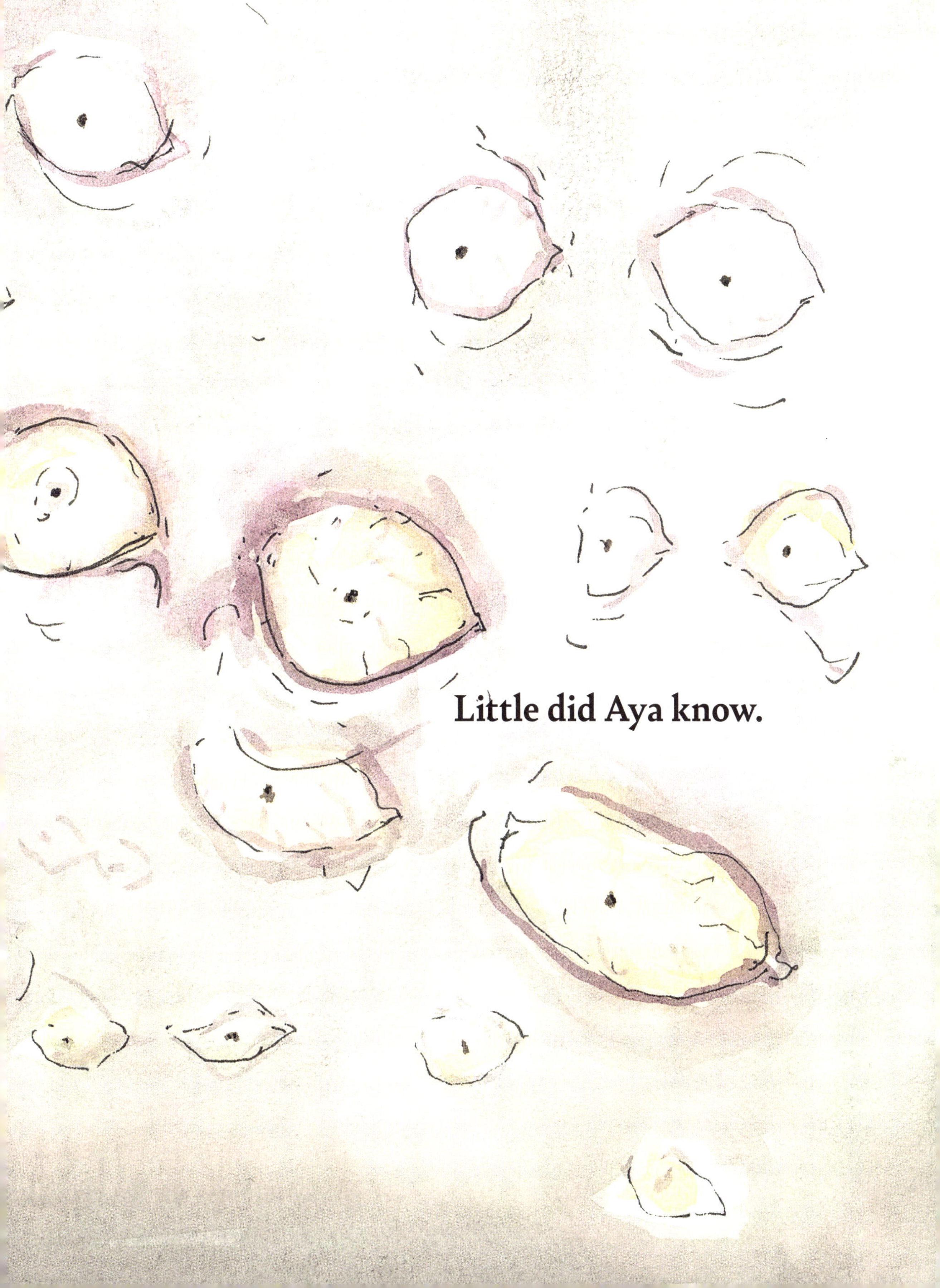

Little did Aya know.

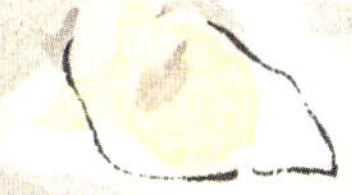

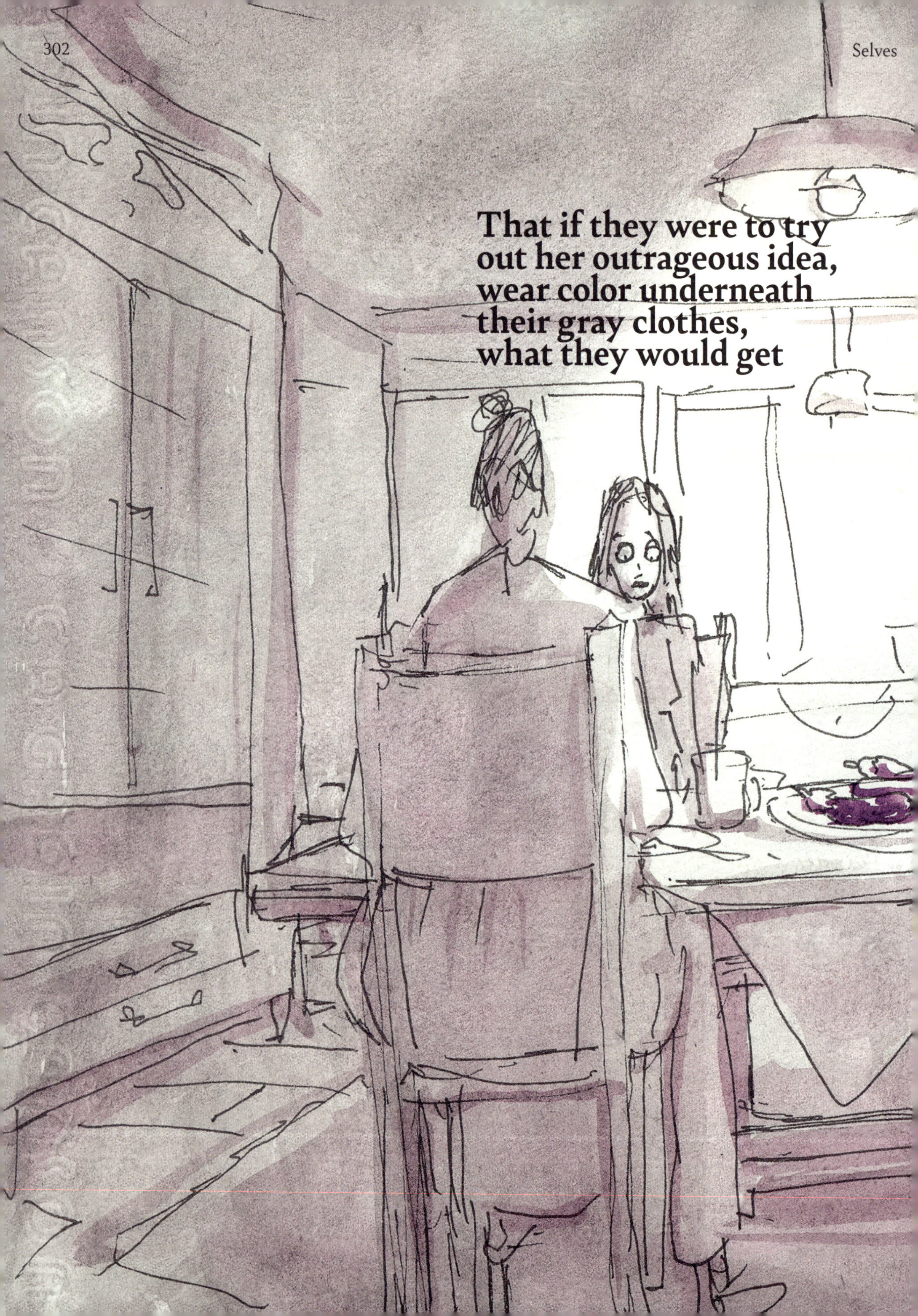
That if they were to try
out her outrageous idea,
wear color underneath
their gray clothes,
what they would get

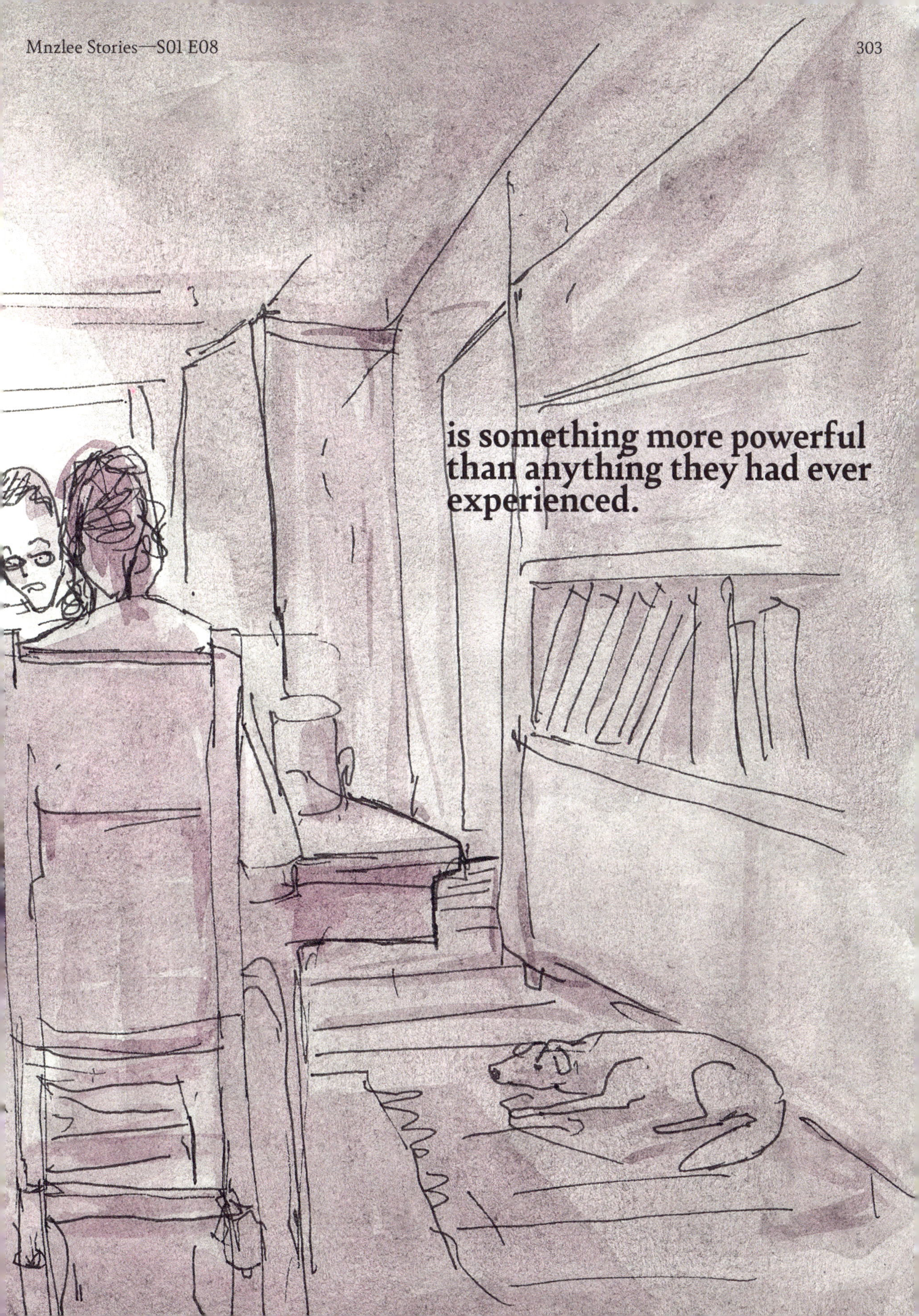
is something more powerful
than anything they had ever
experienced.

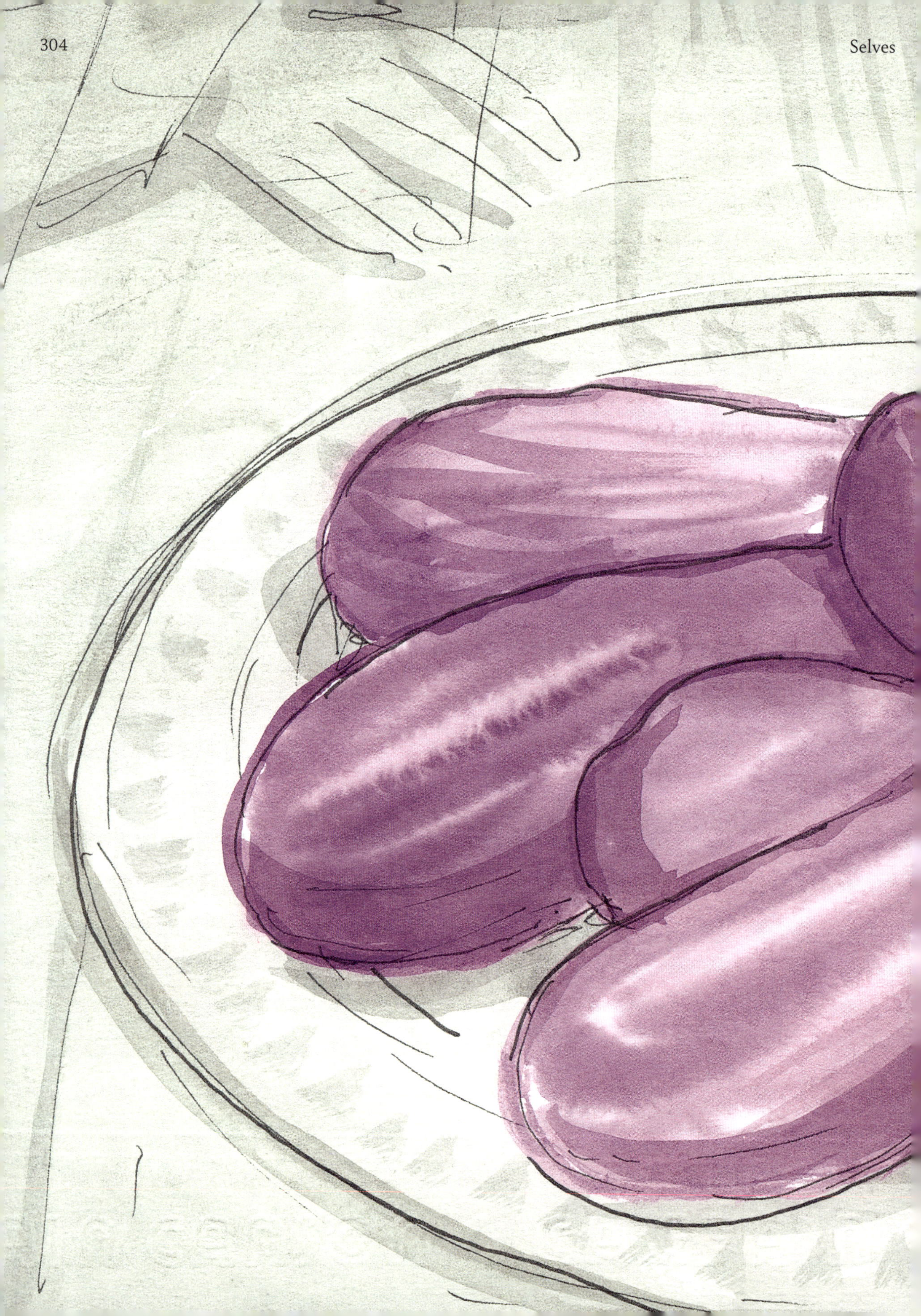

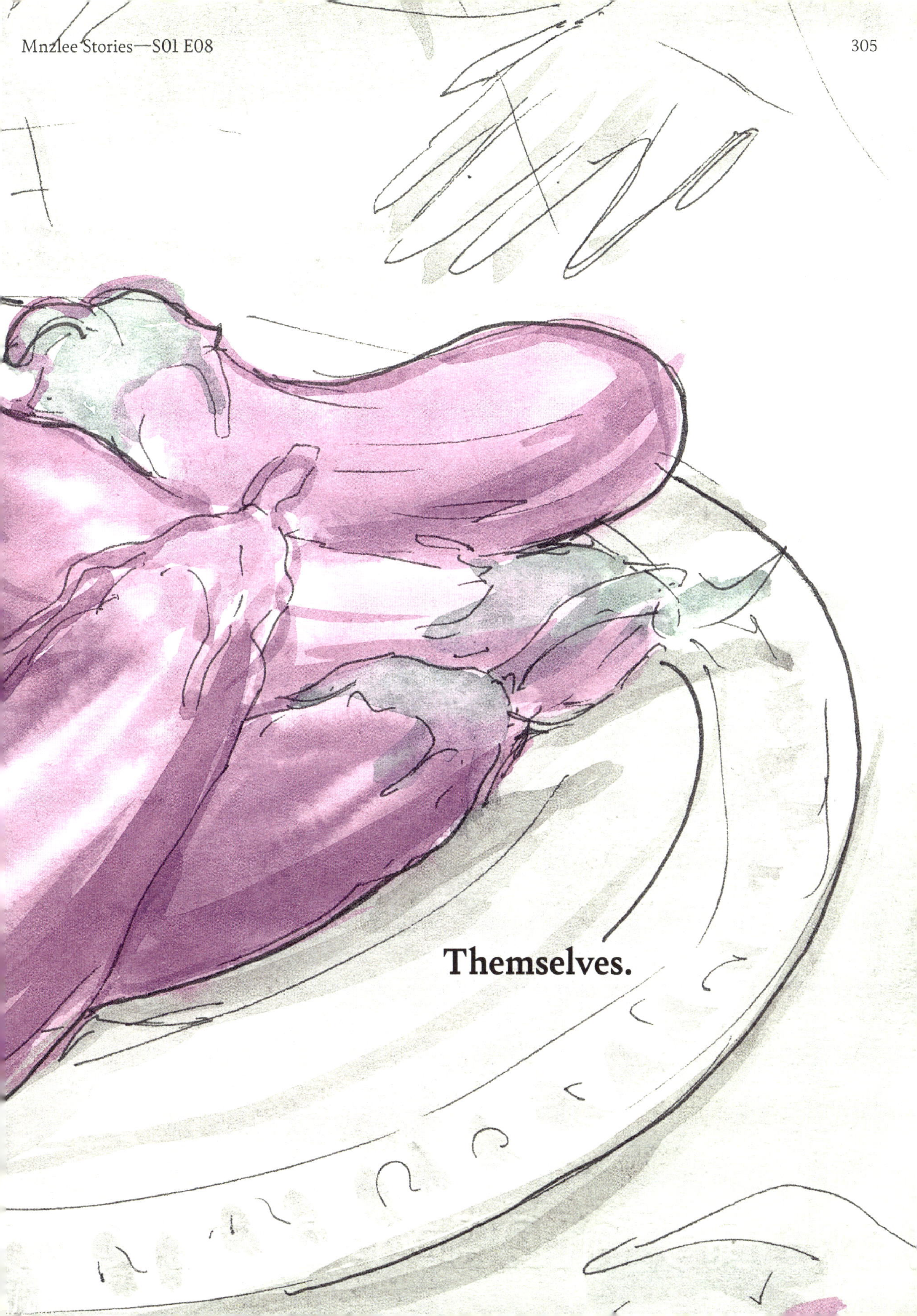
Themselves.

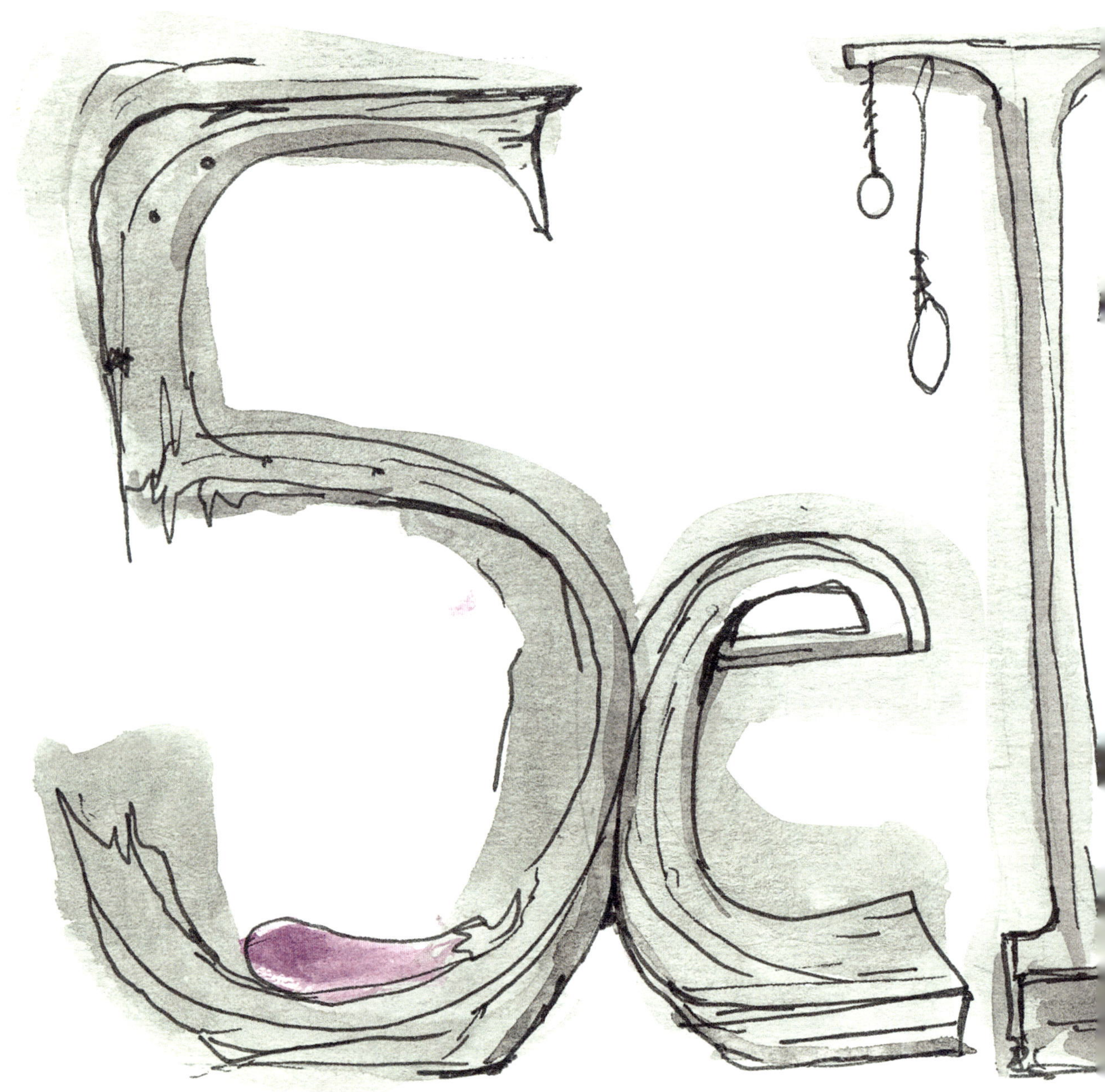

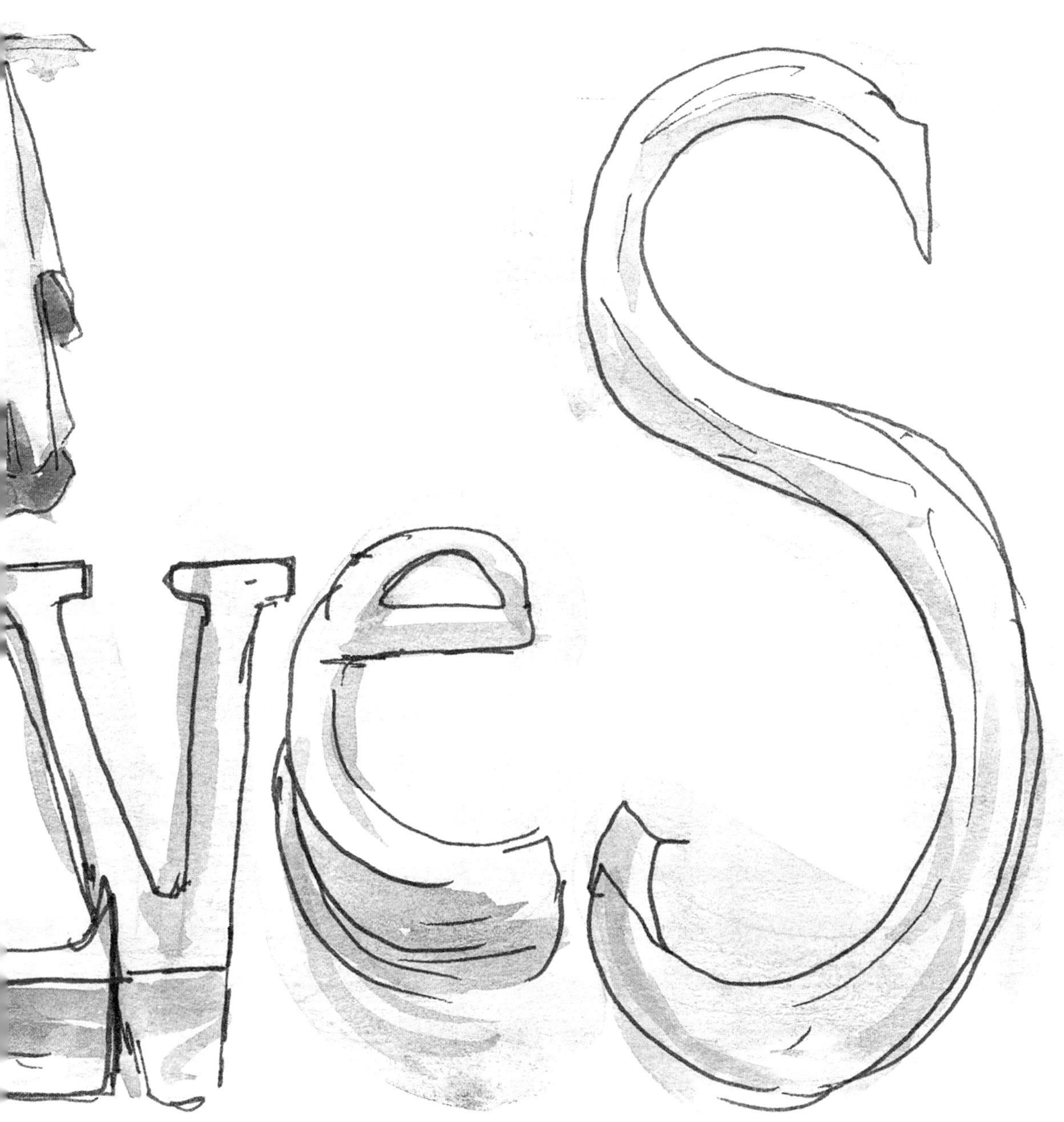

KALIMAT

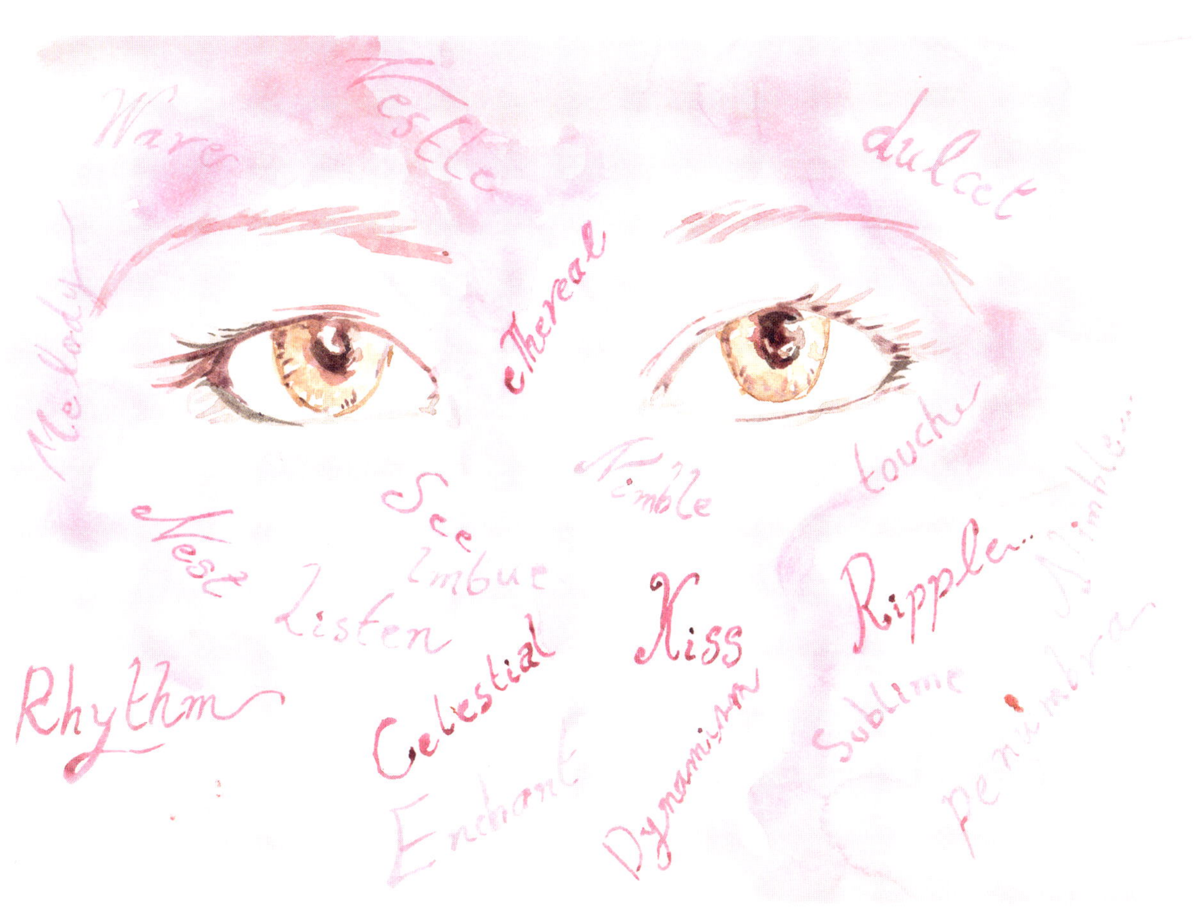

Kalimat was in love with words.

She wanted to savor them like you would savor hot chocolate on a cold day.

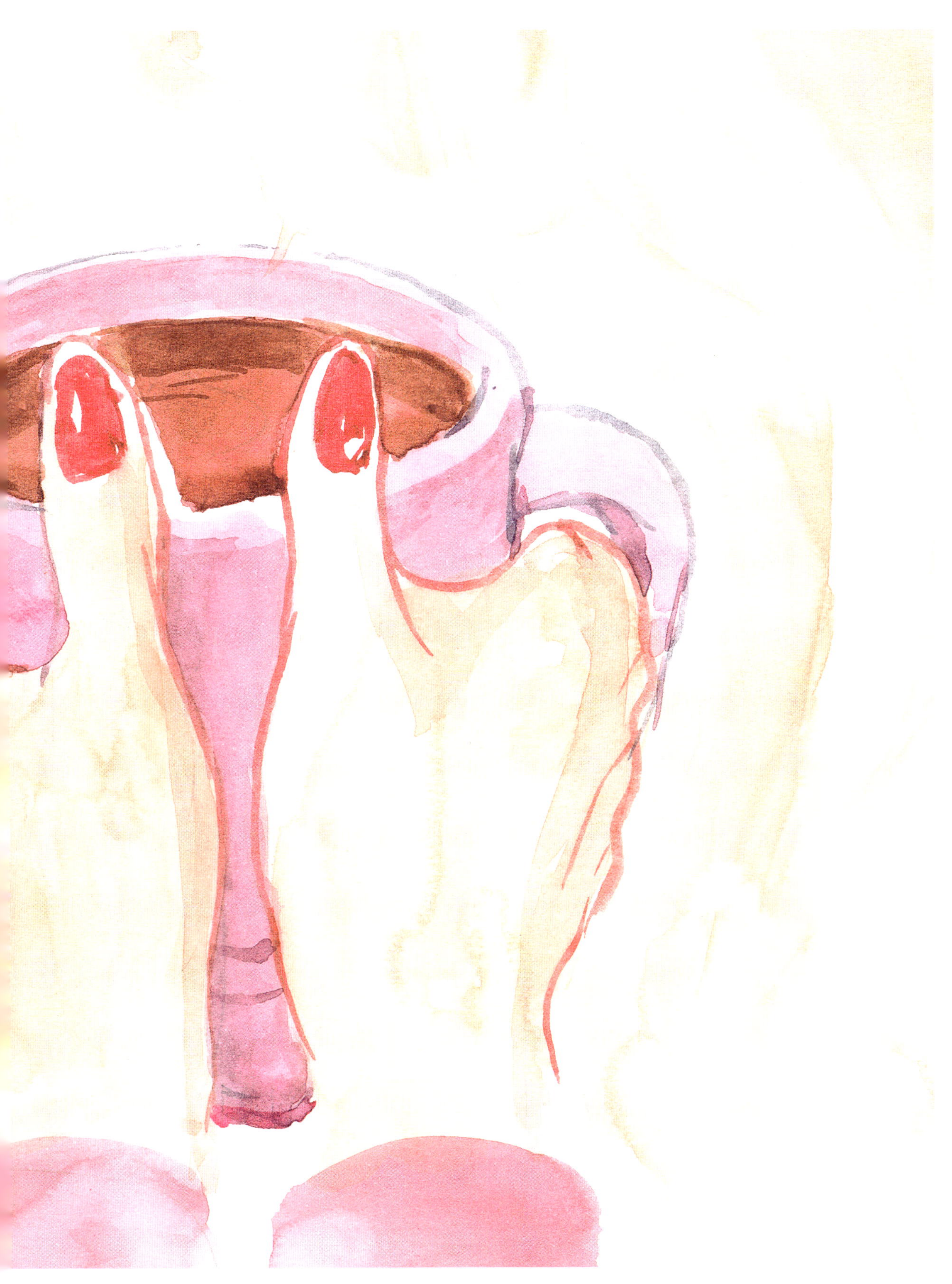

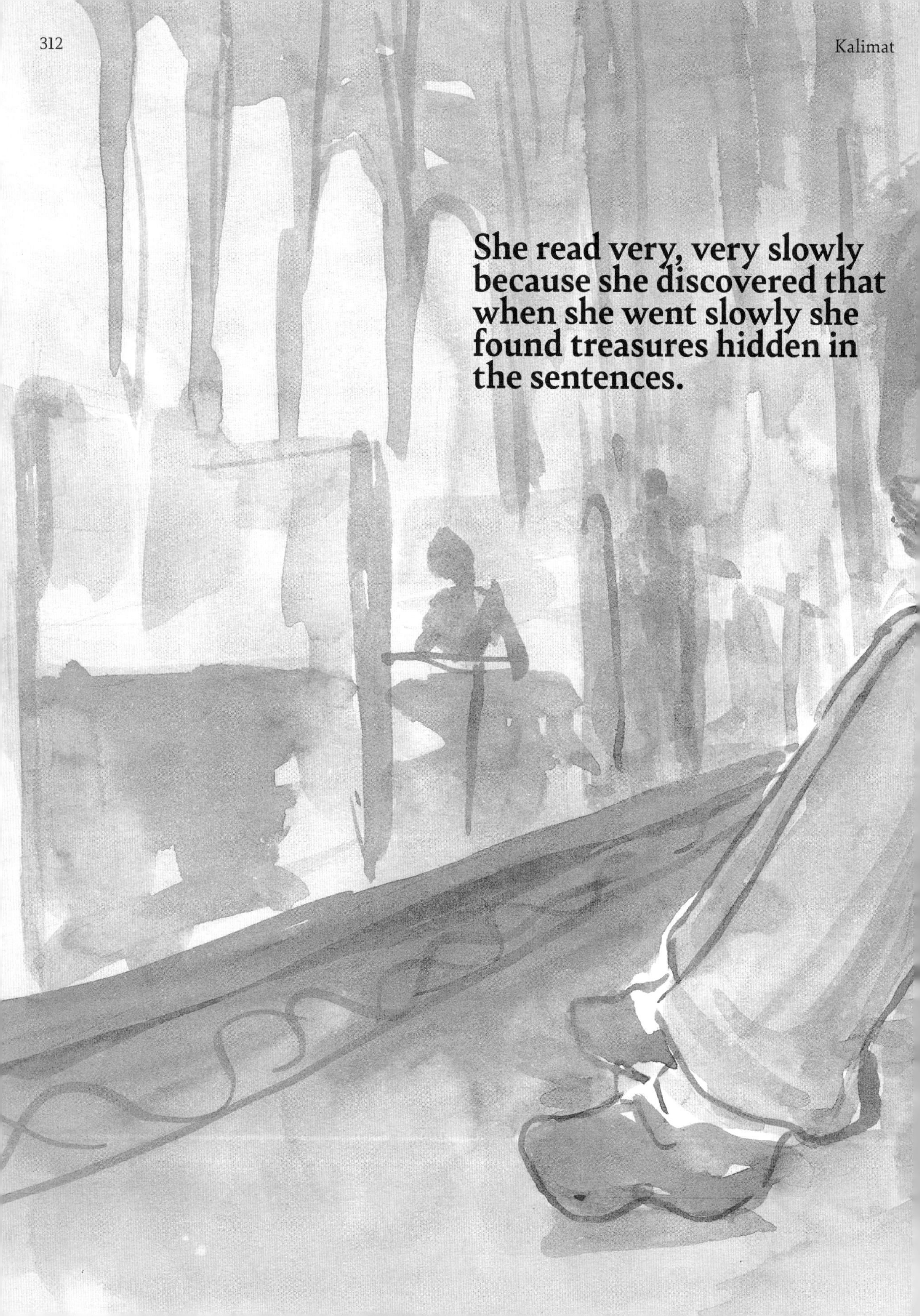

She read very, very slowly
because she discovered that
when she went slowly she
found treasures hidden in
the sentences.

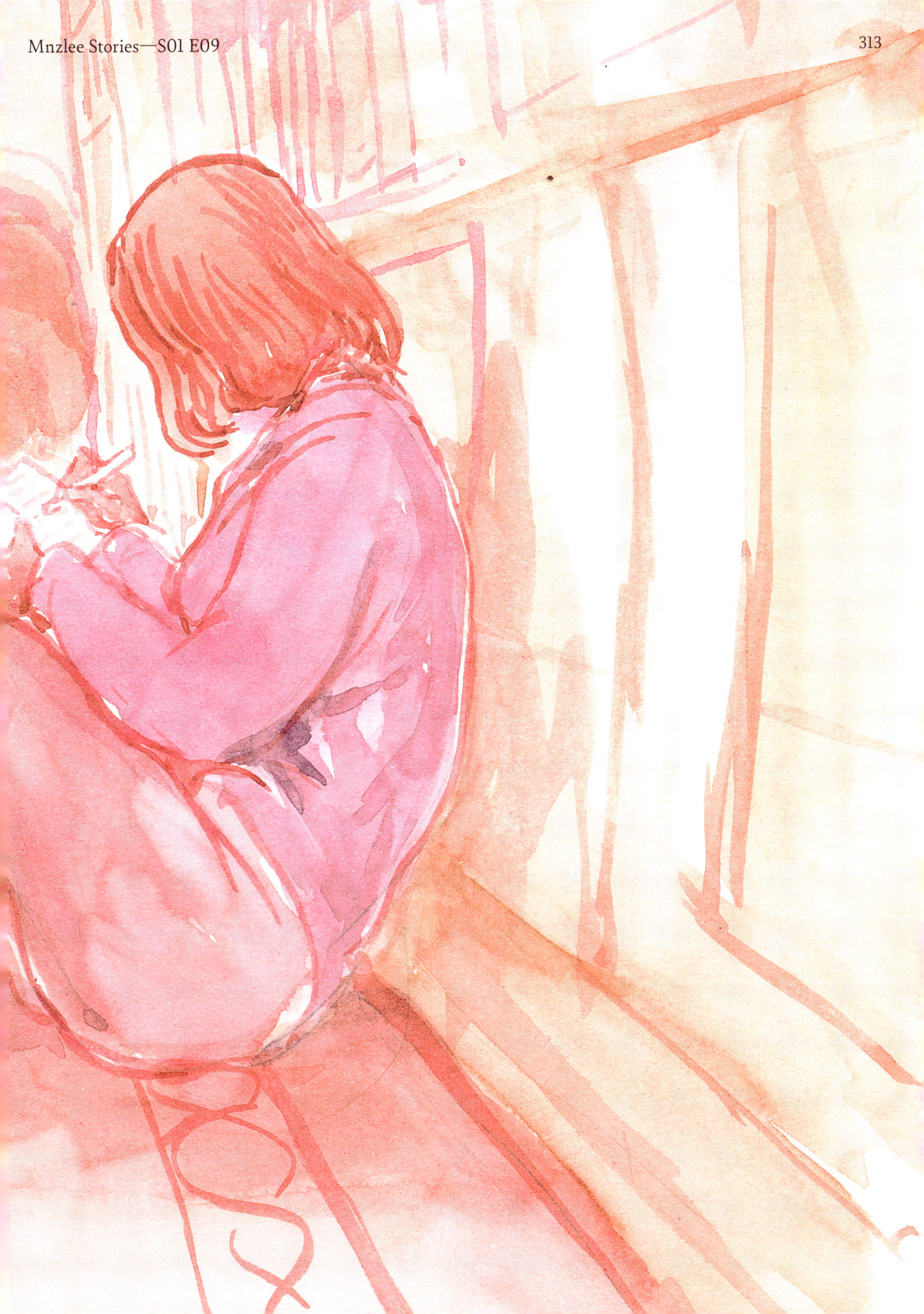

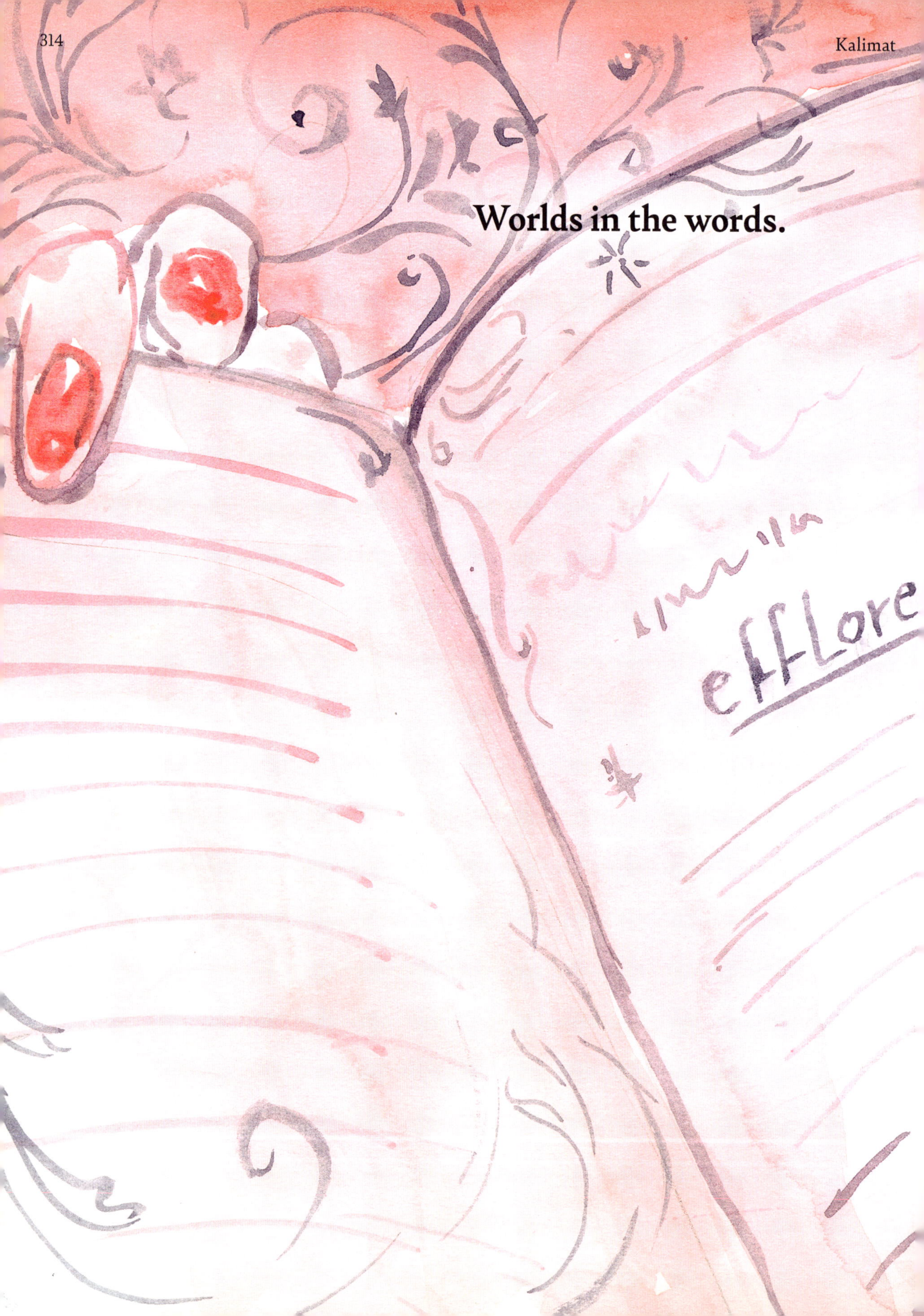
Worlds in the words.
efflore

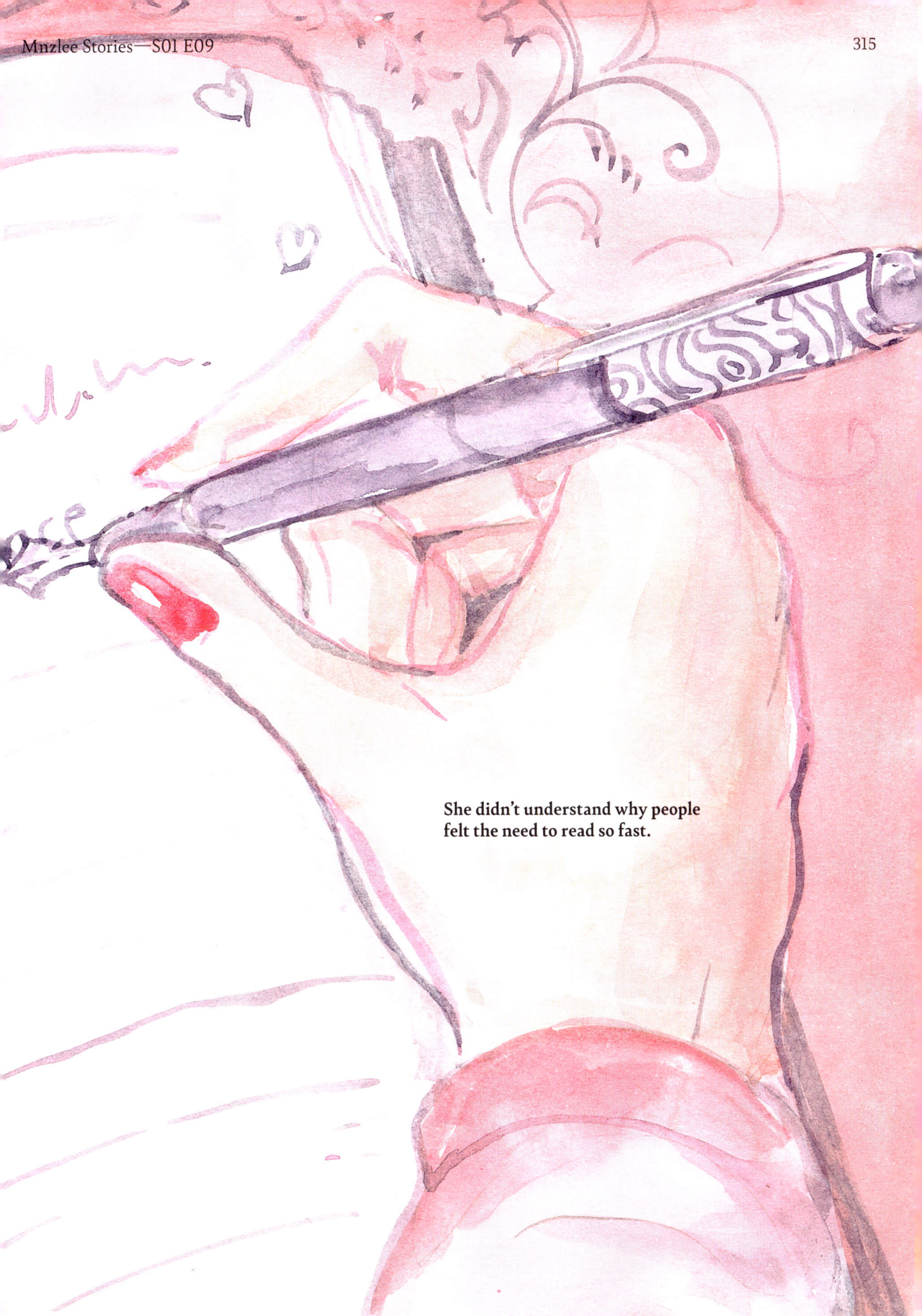
She didn't understand why people felt the need to read so fast.

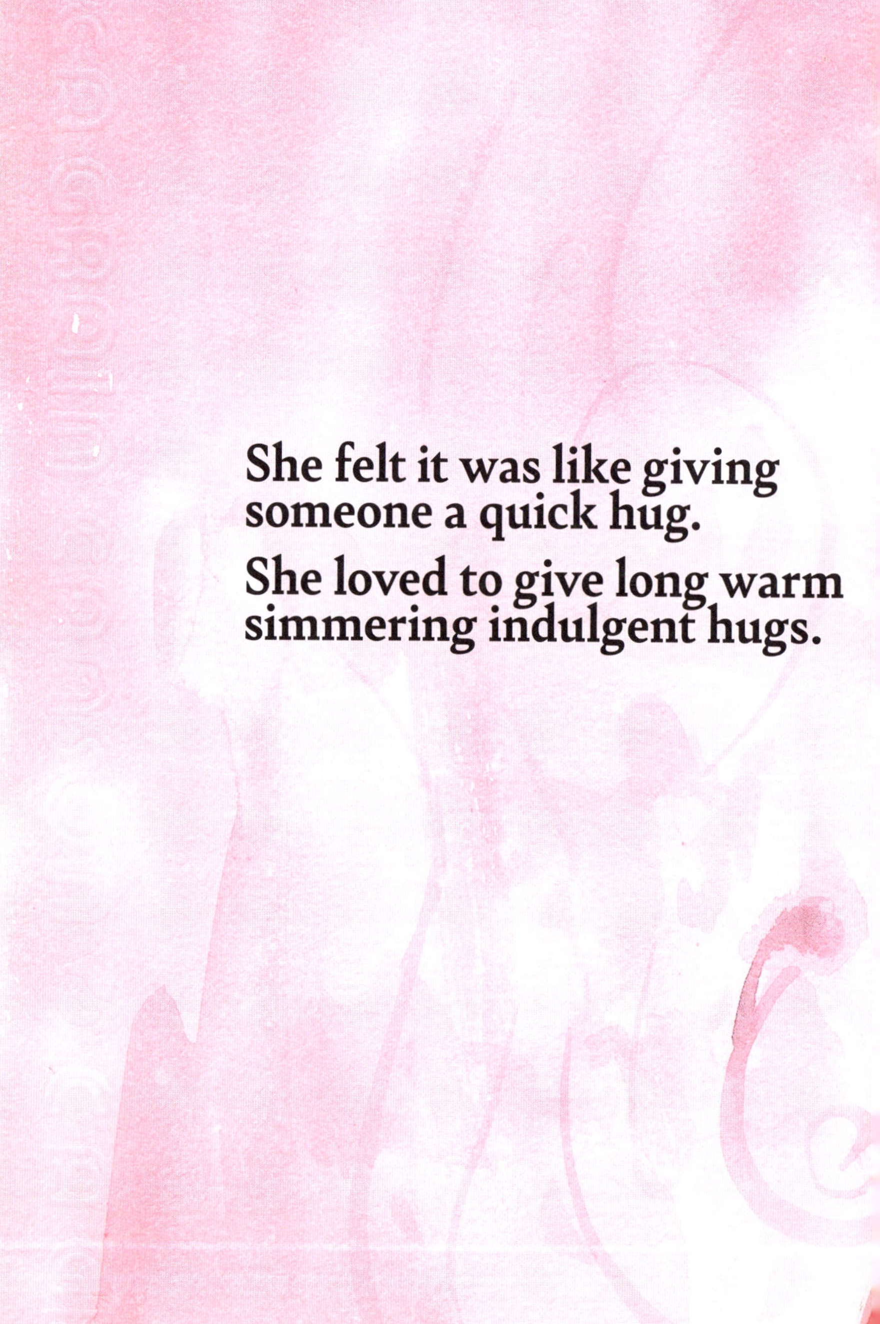

She felt it was like giving someone a quick hug.

She loved to give long warm simmering indulgent hugs.

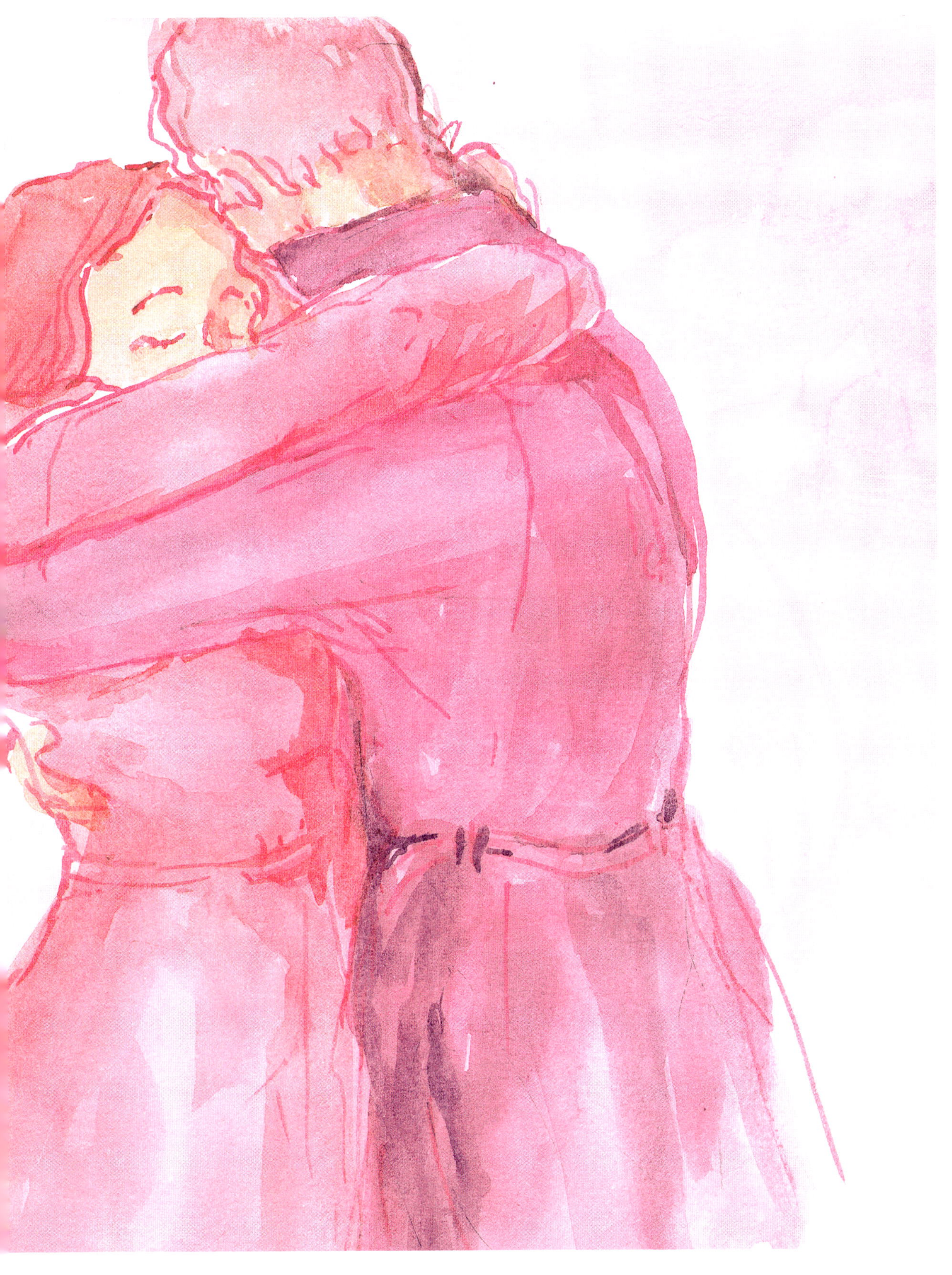

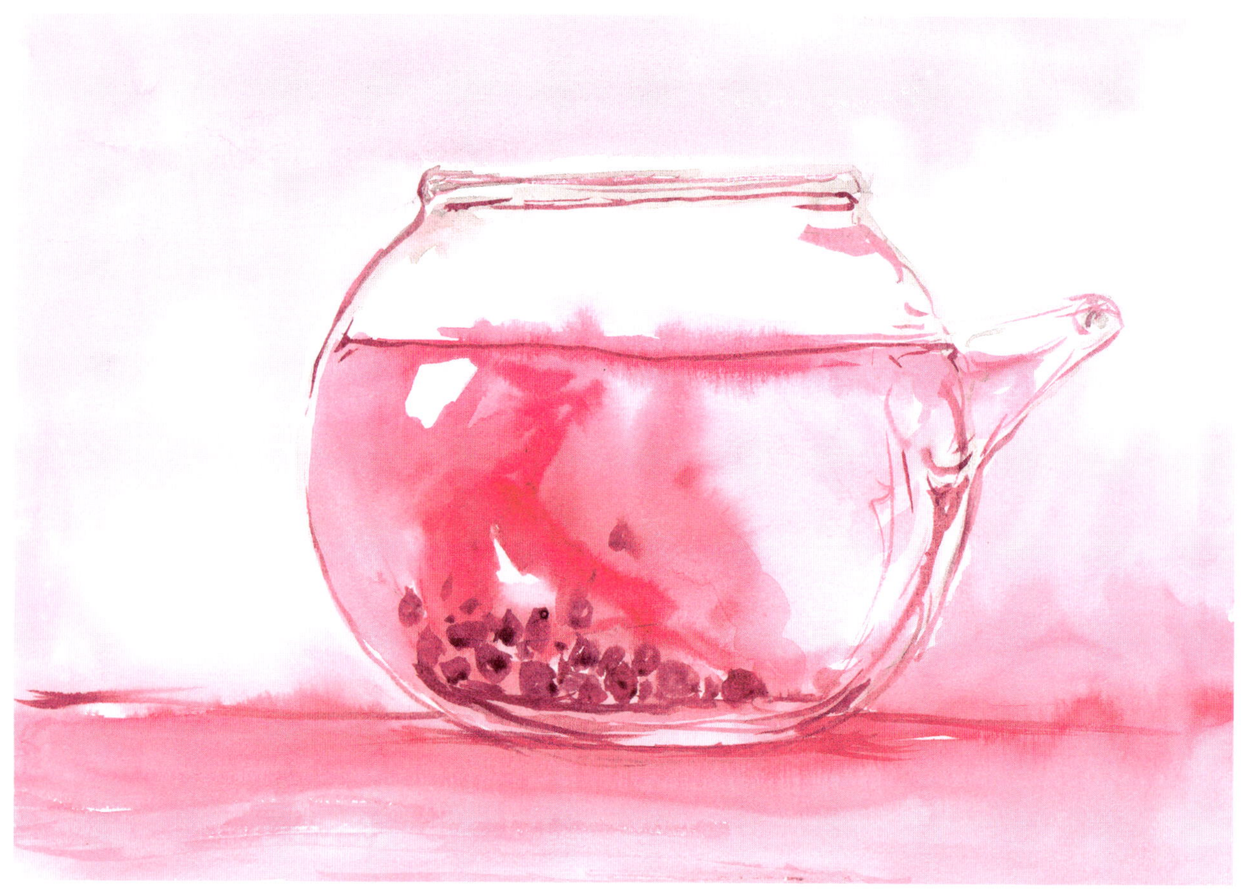

To steep the pomegranate in hot water and watch it turn maroon.

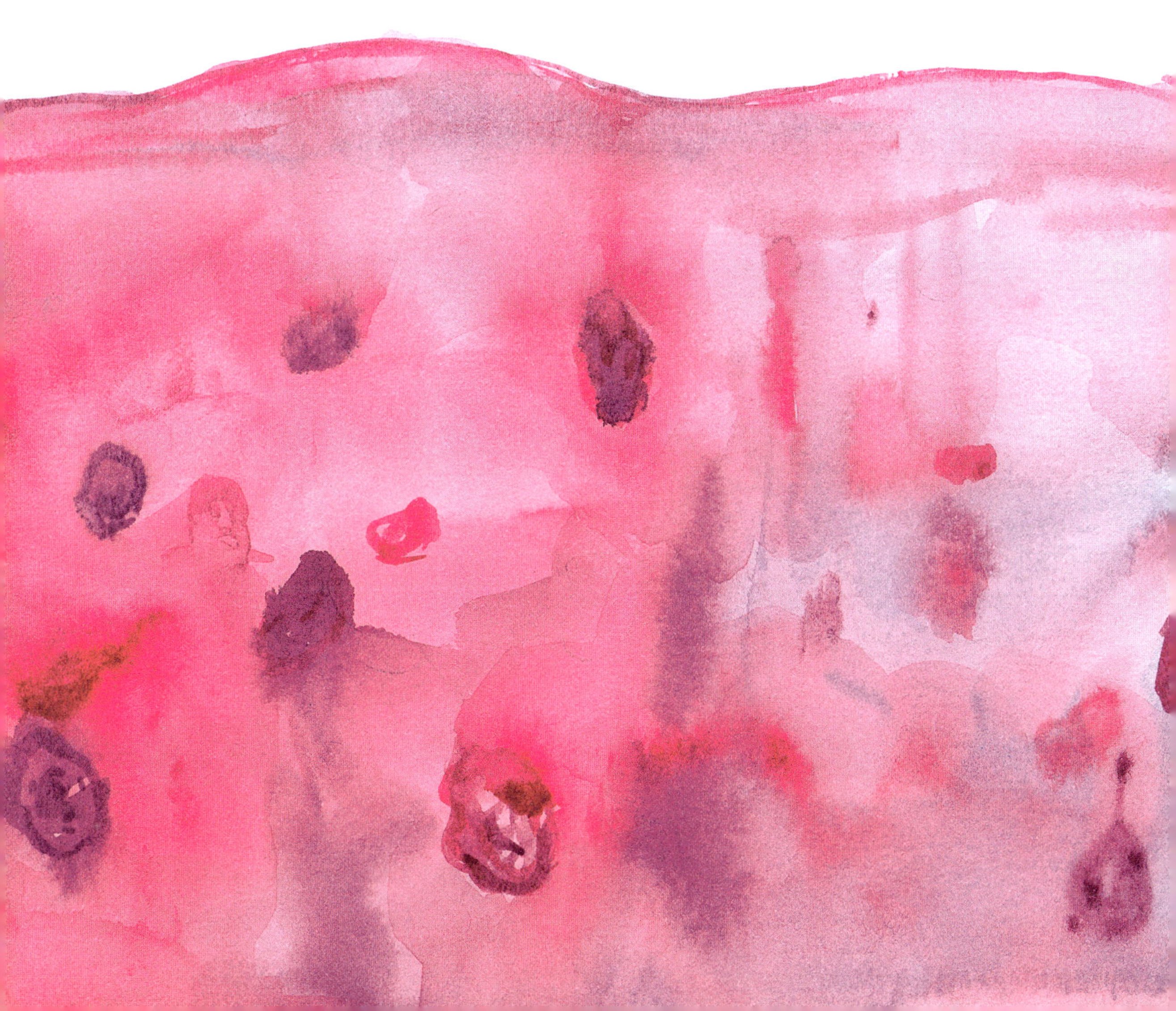

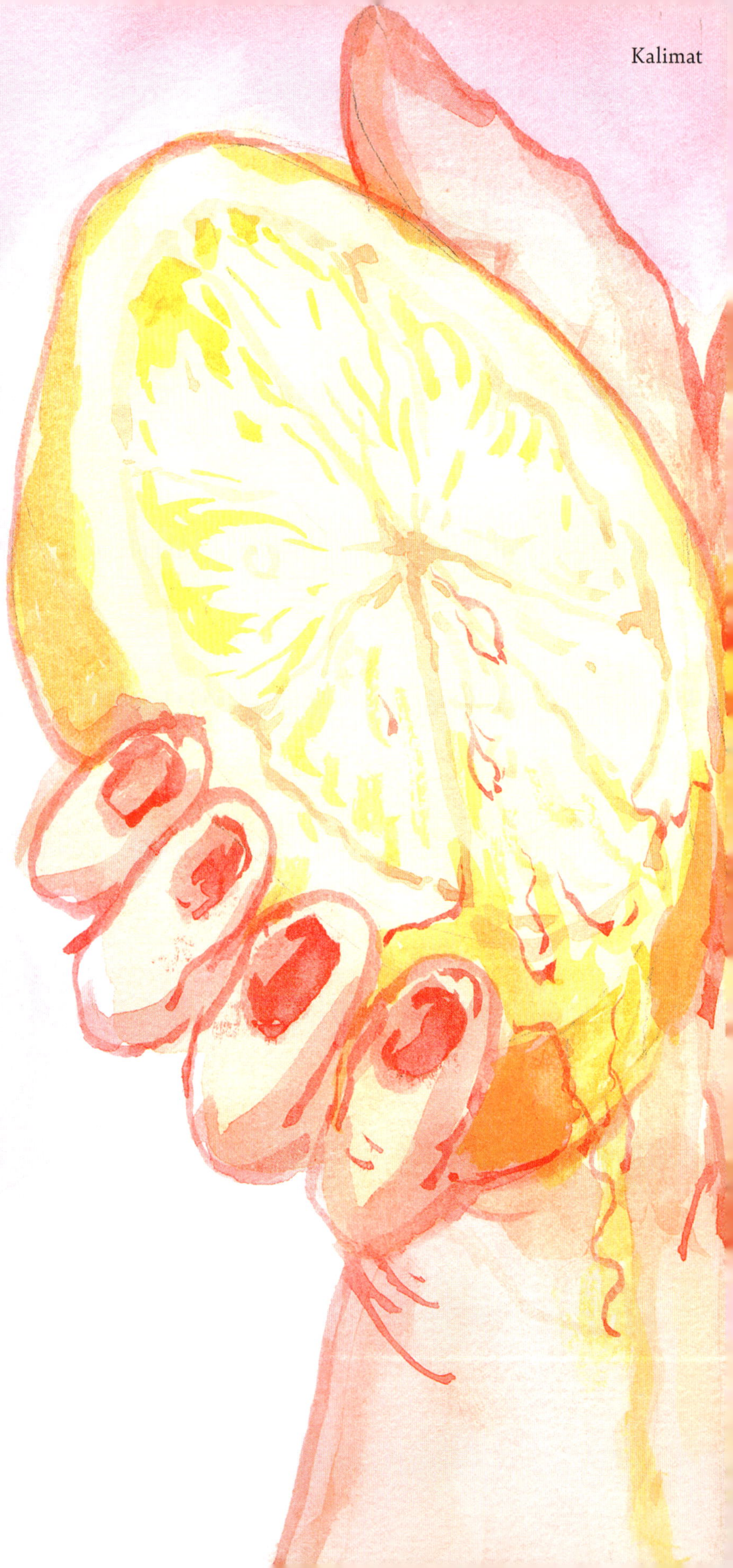

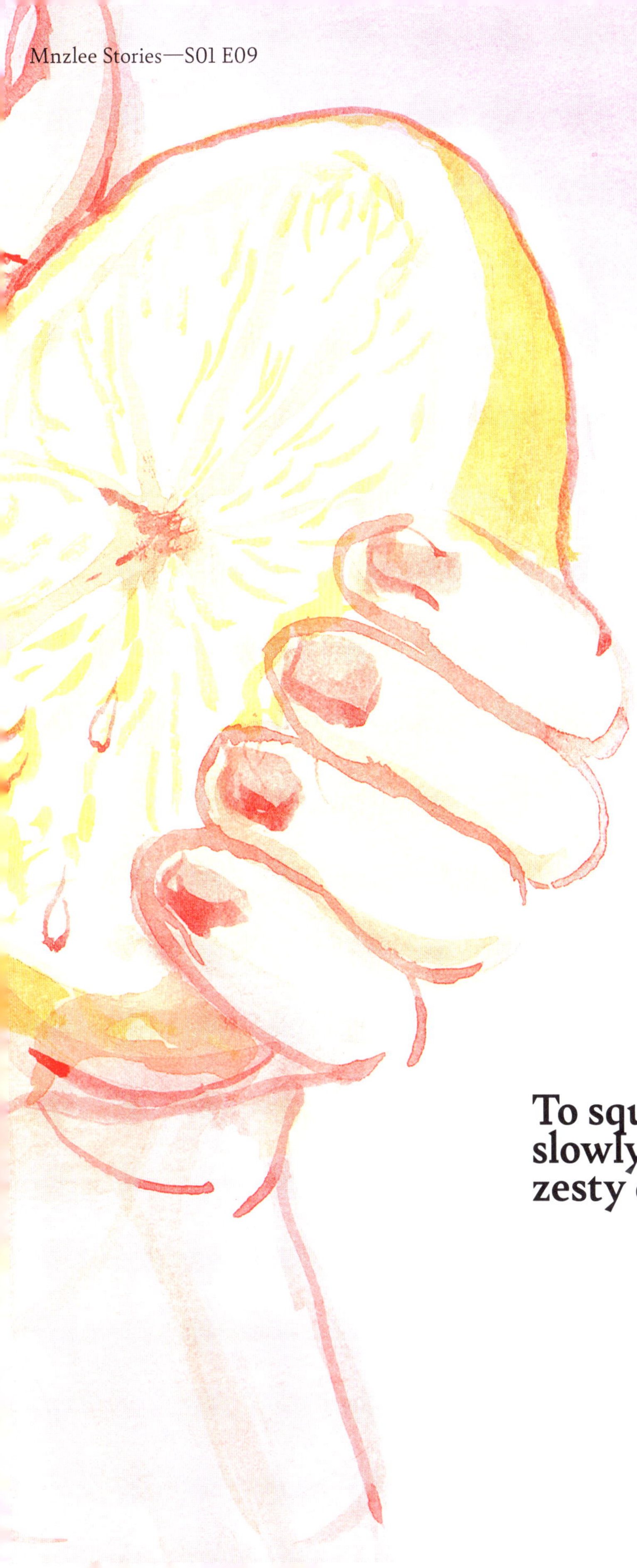

To squeeze a bright lemon slowly and get every last zesty drop.

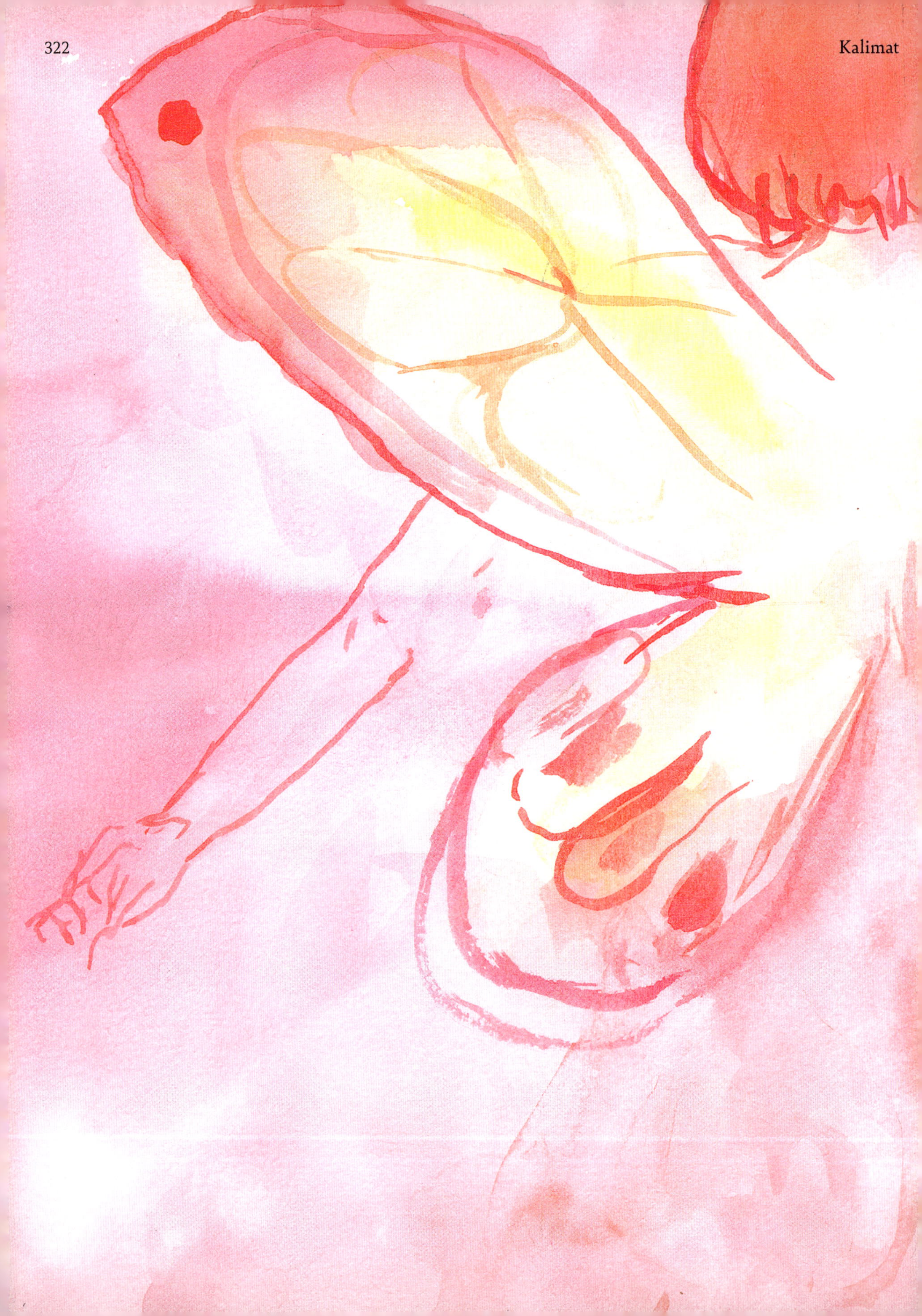

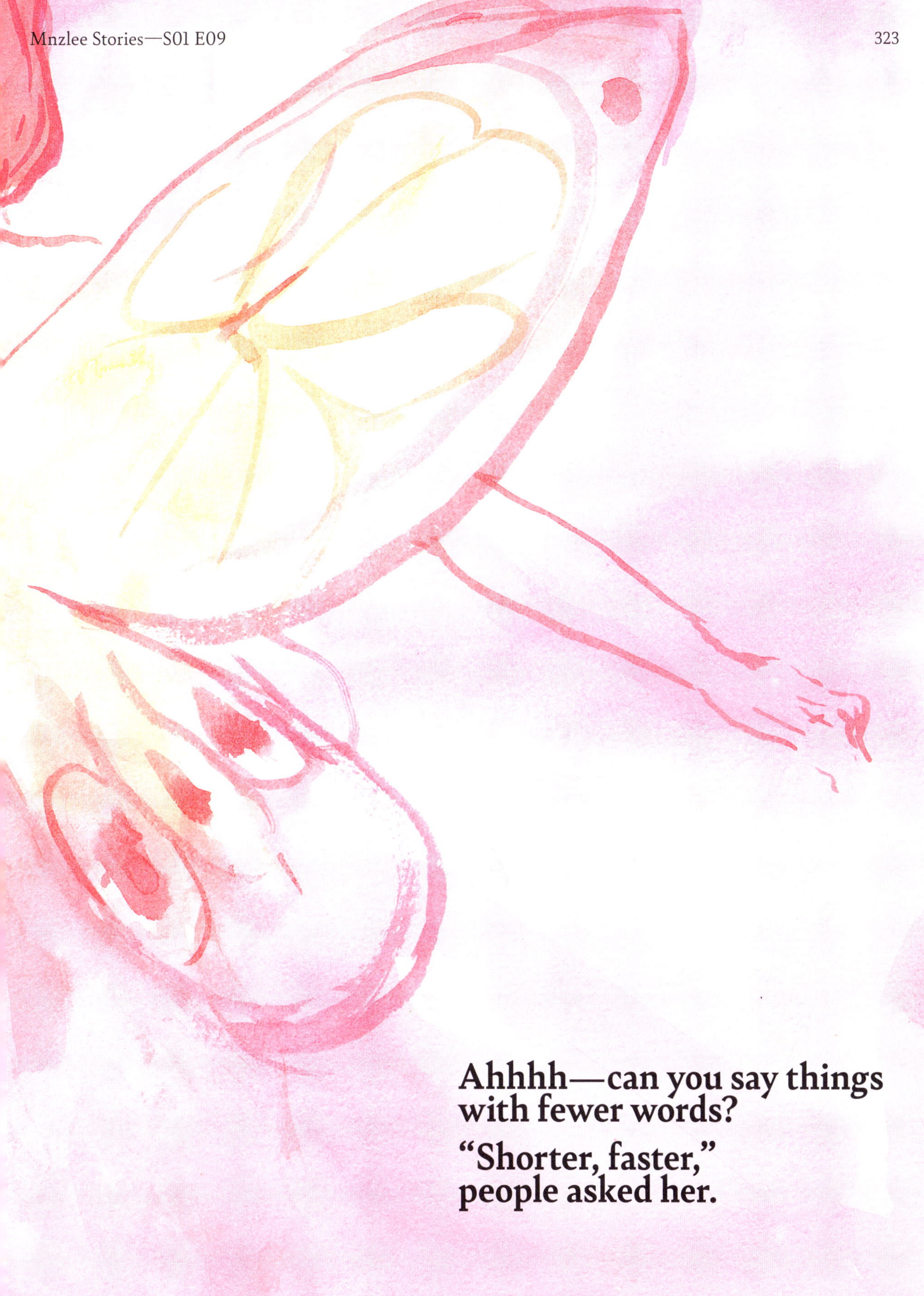

Ahhhh—can you say things with fewer words?

"Shorter, faster," people asked her.

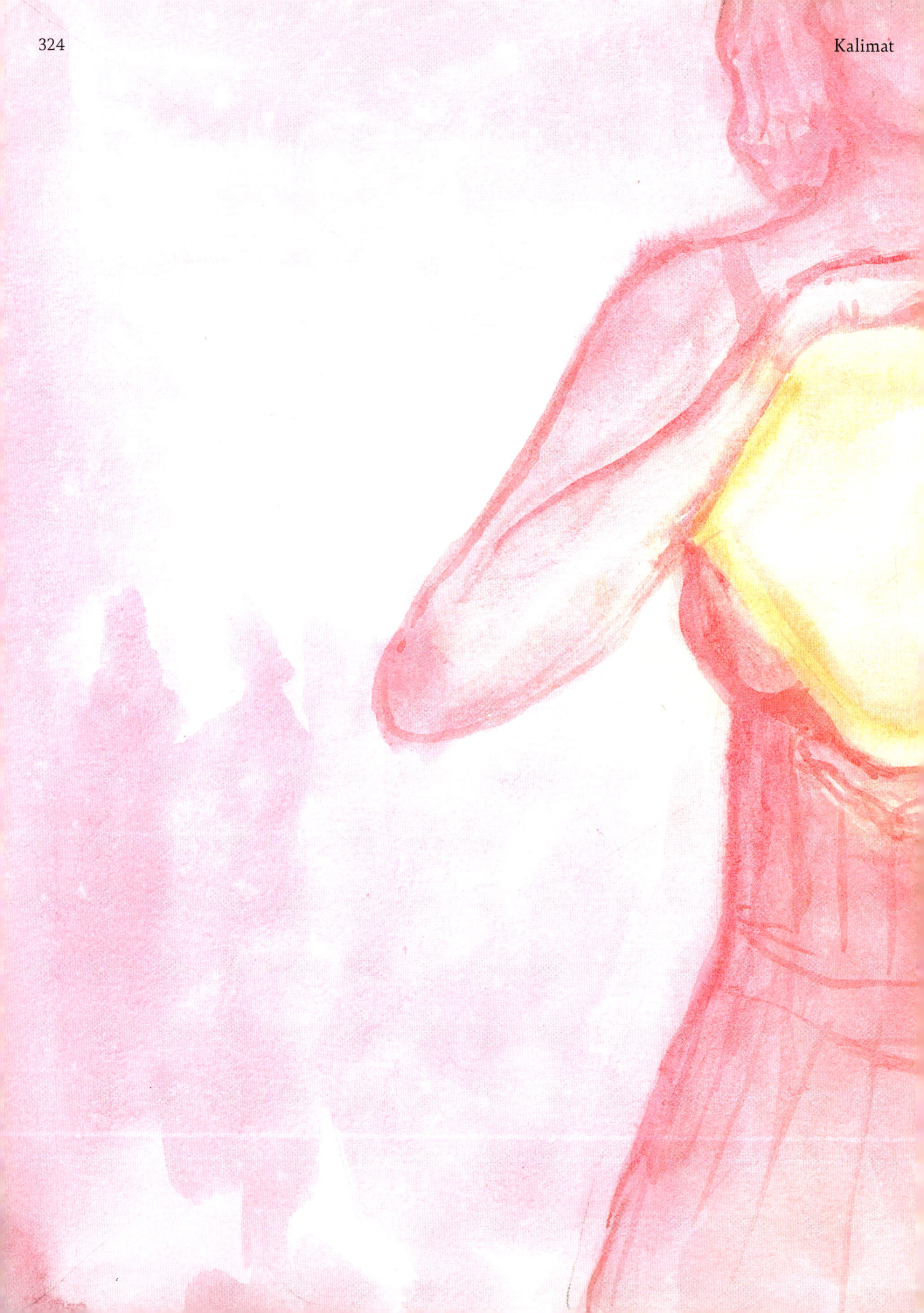

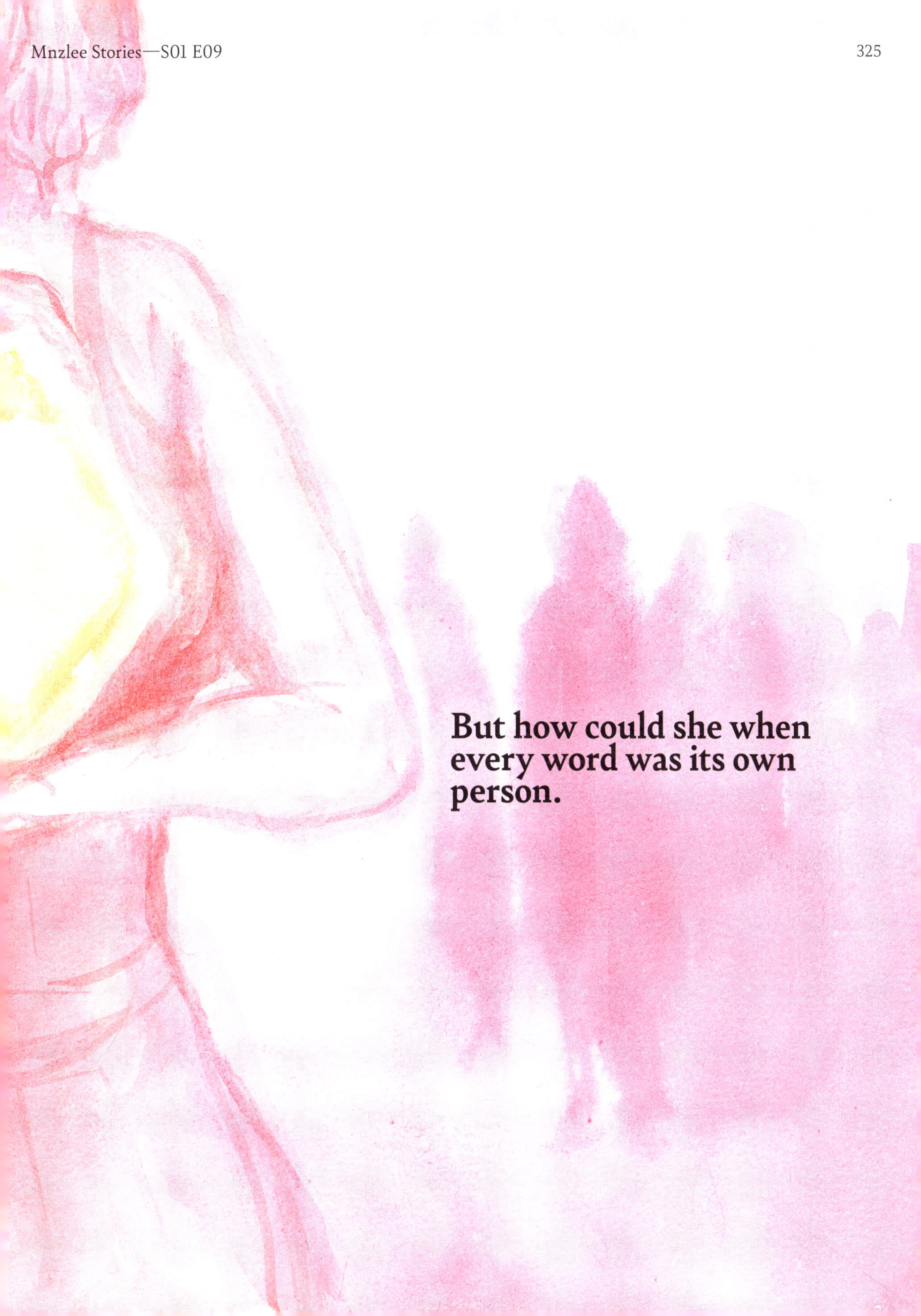

But how could she when every word was its own person.

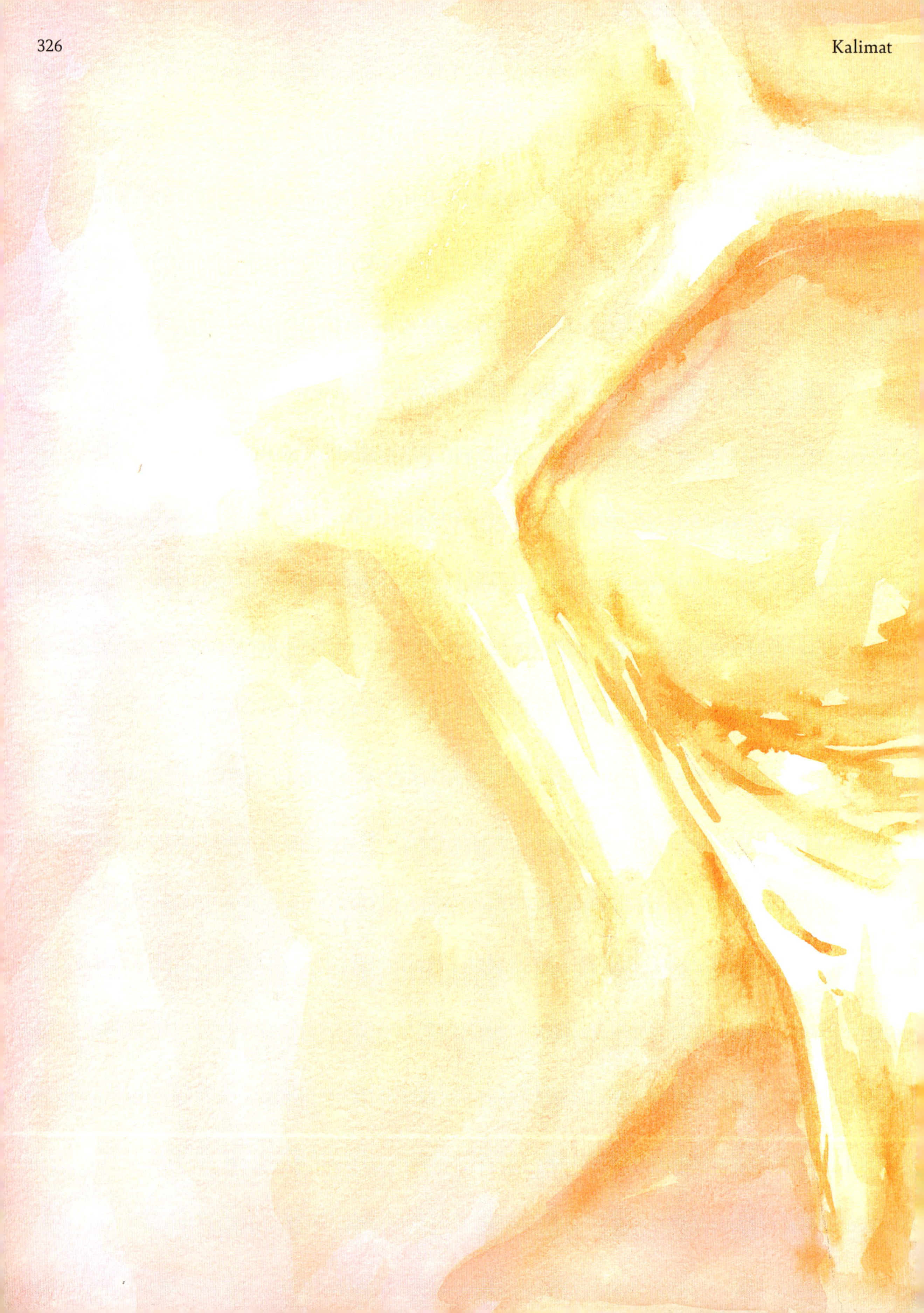

And every sentence, its own community.

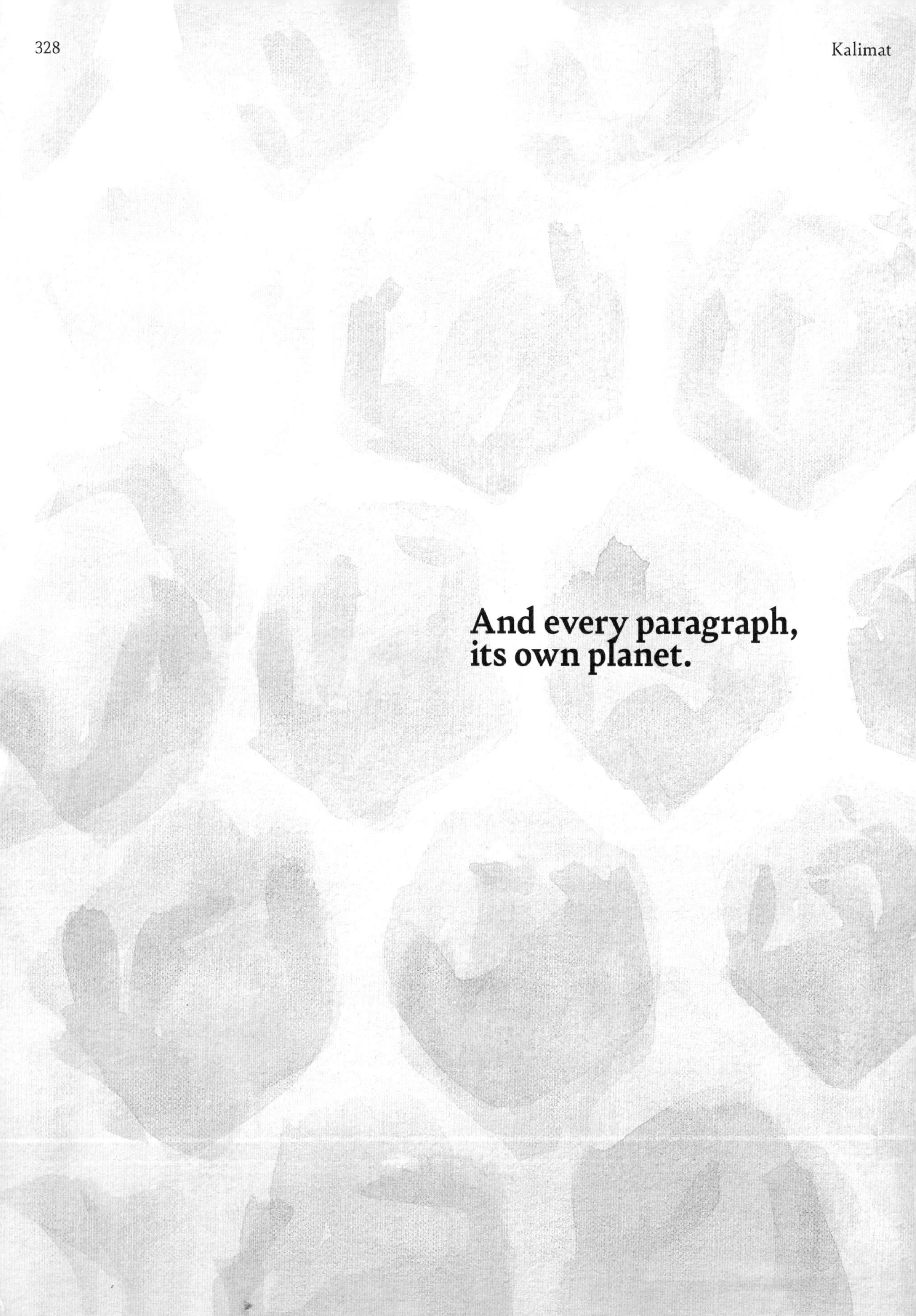

And every paragraph,
its own planet.

Person

Community

Planet.

Person

Community

Planet.

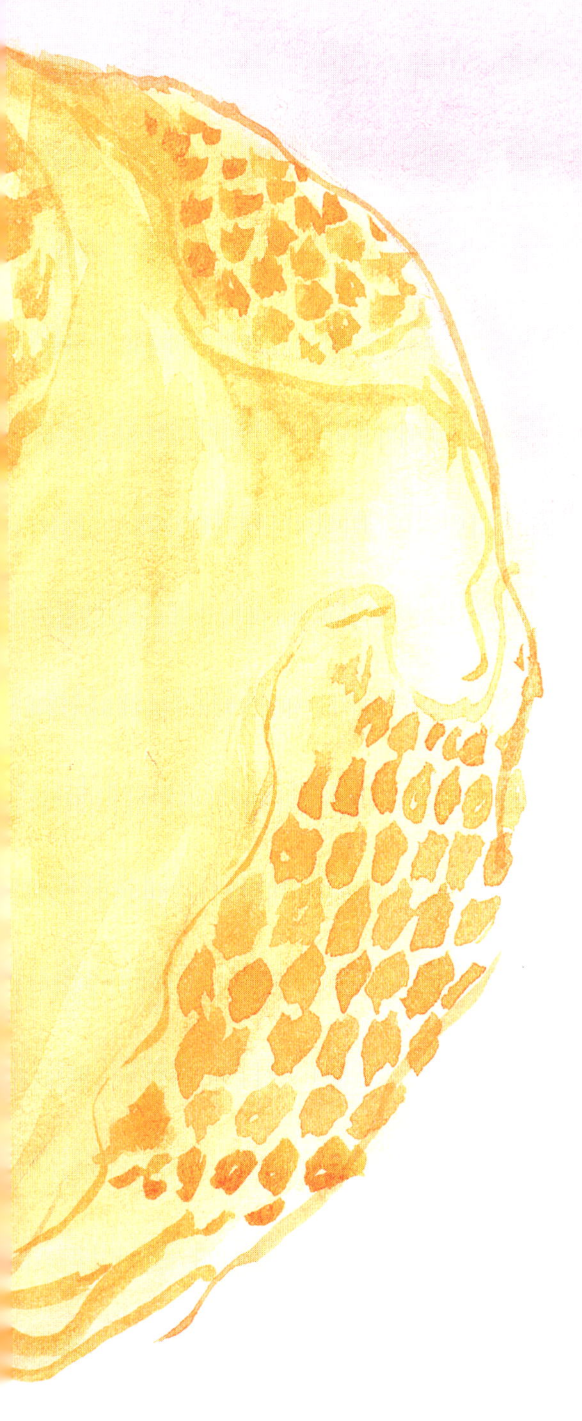

Person.

Community

Planet.

Person, community, planet, person, community, planet…

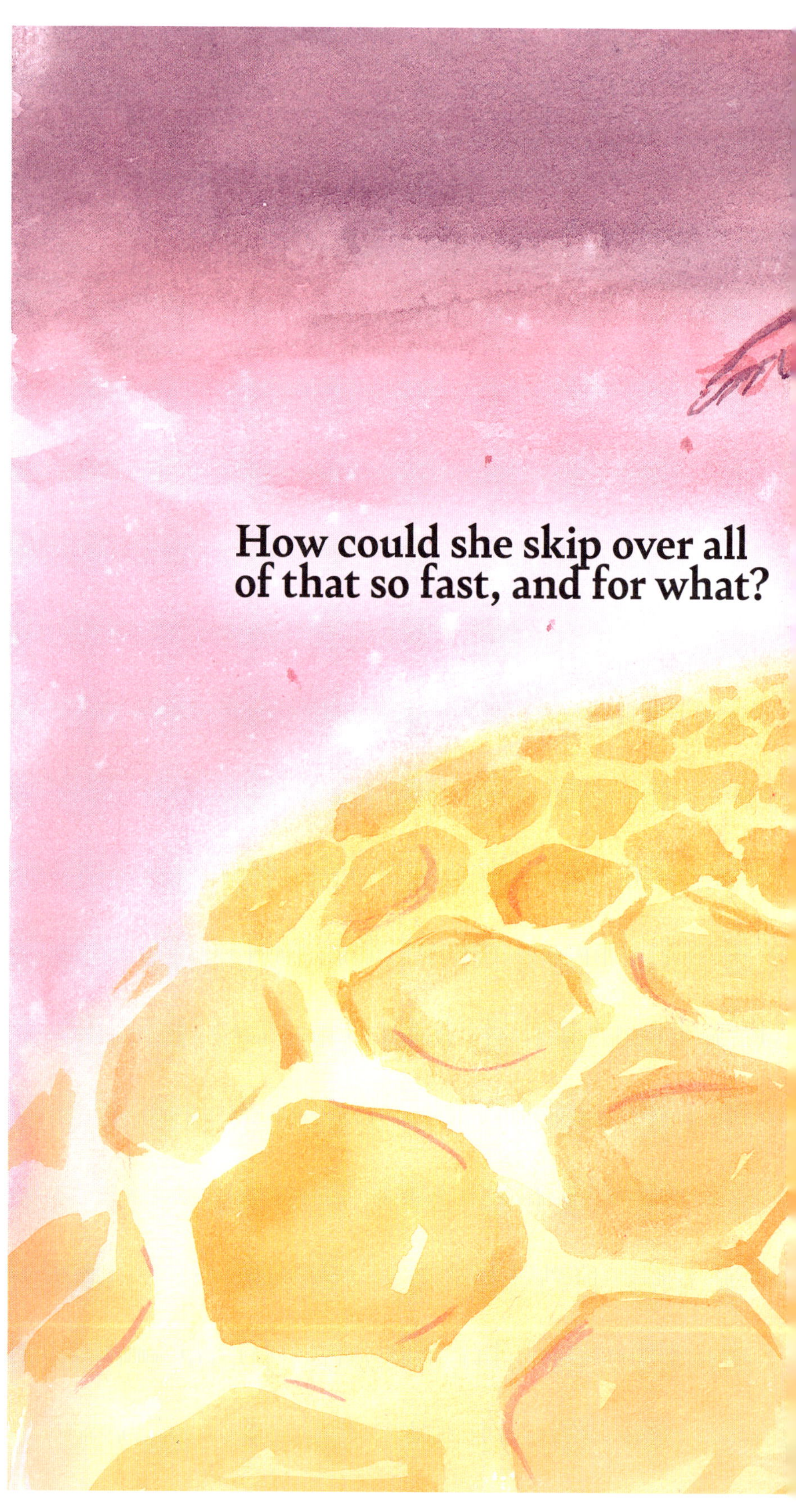
How could she skip over all
of that so fast, and for what?

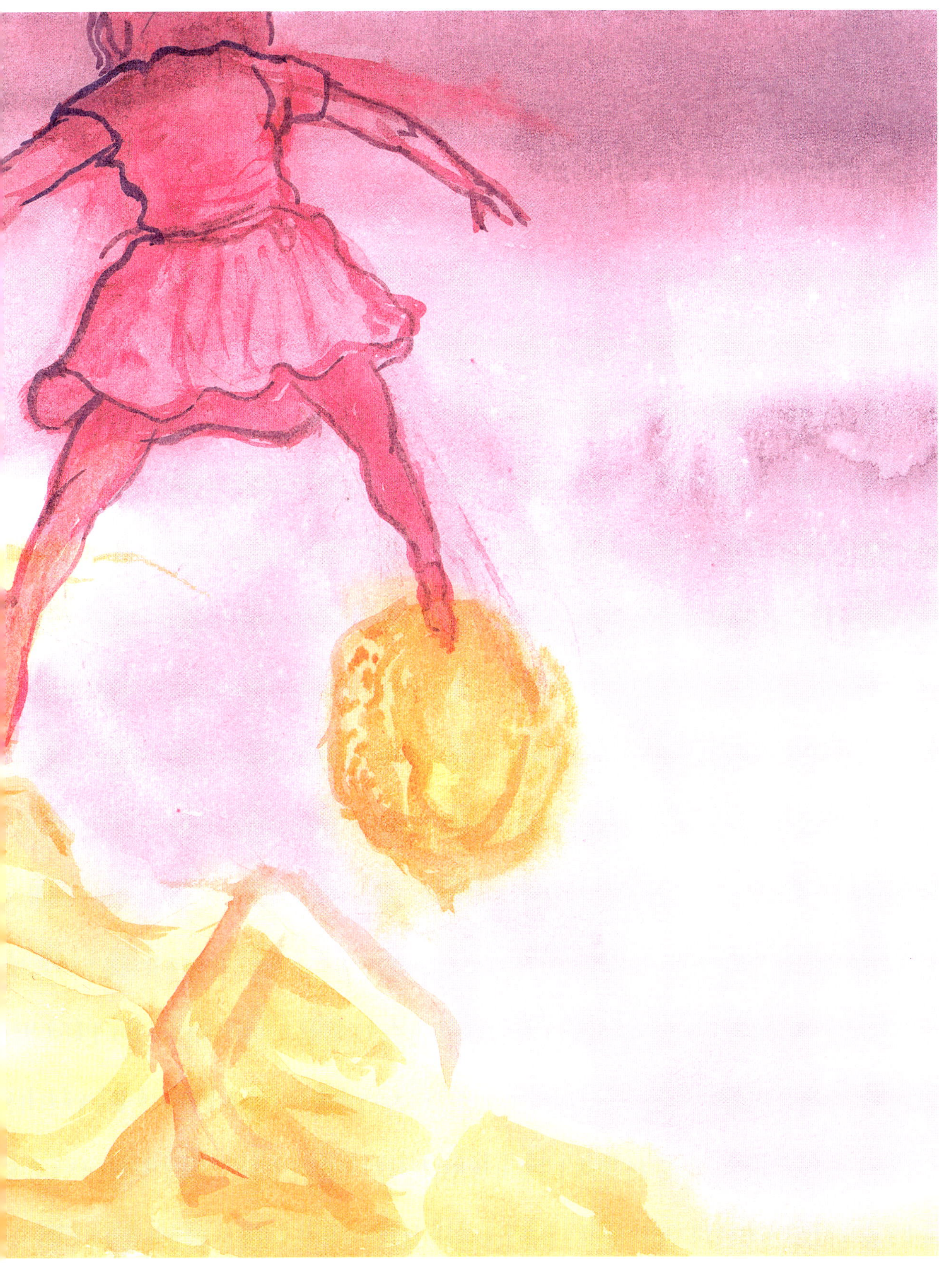

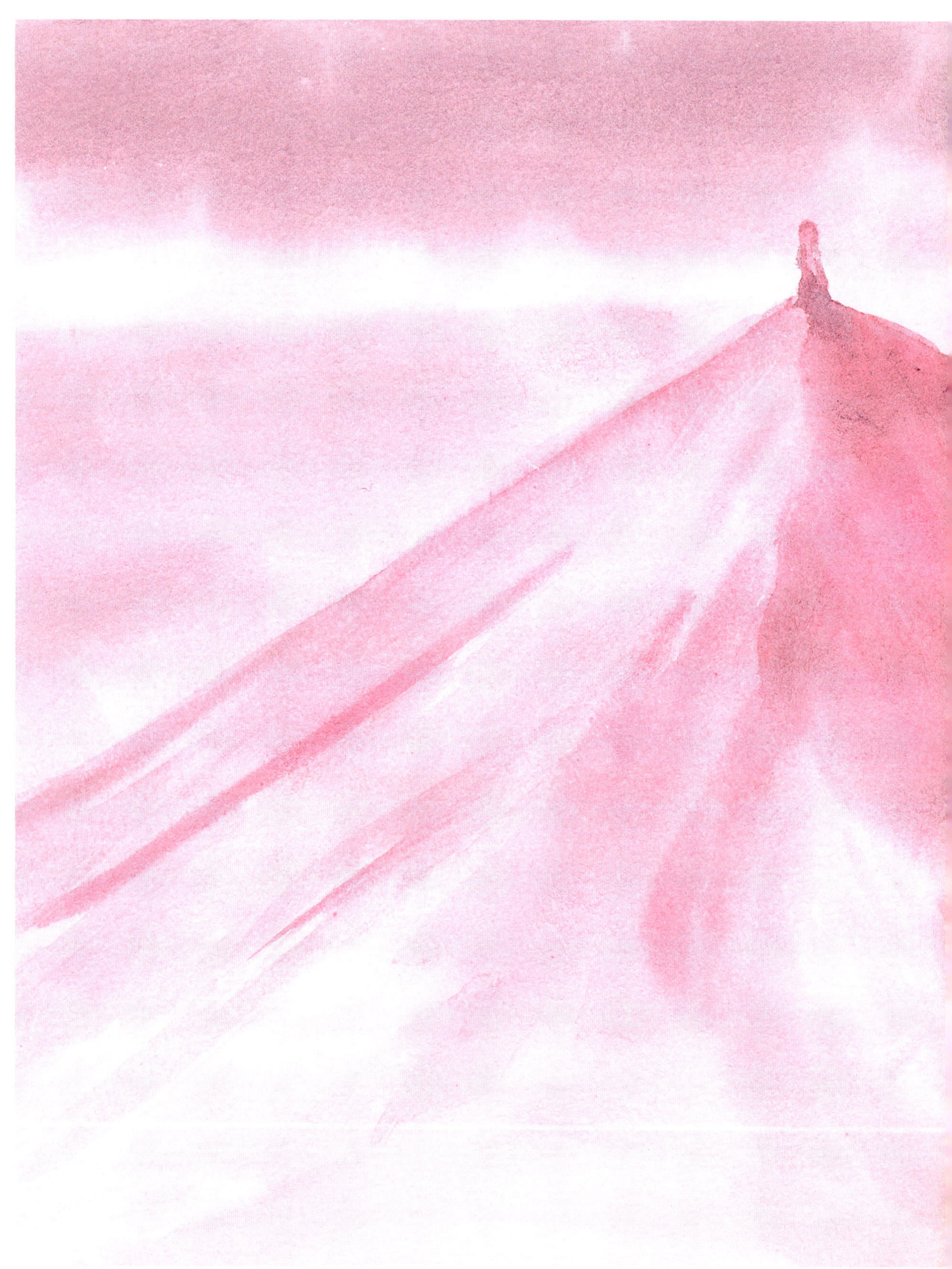

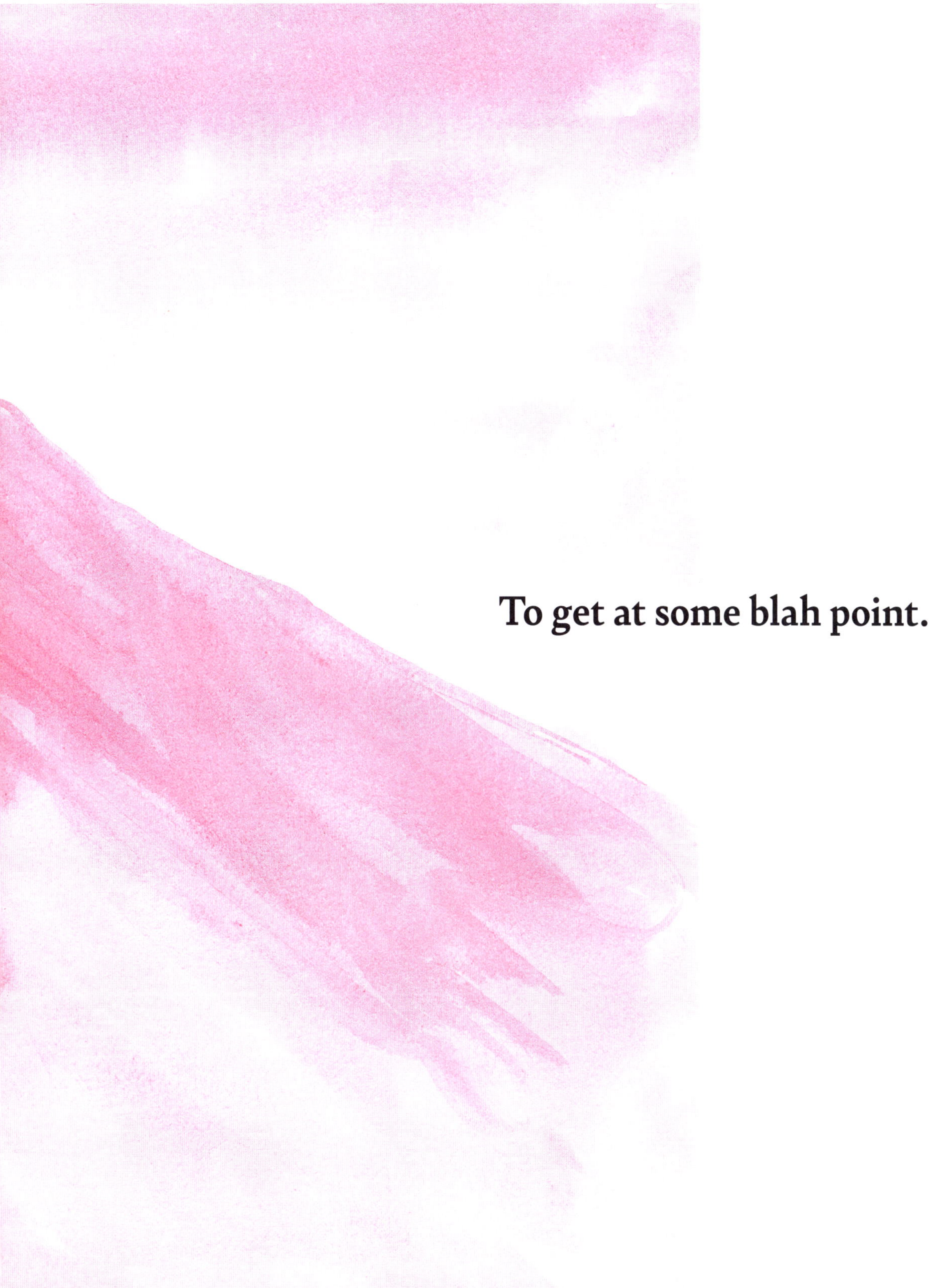

To get at some blah point.

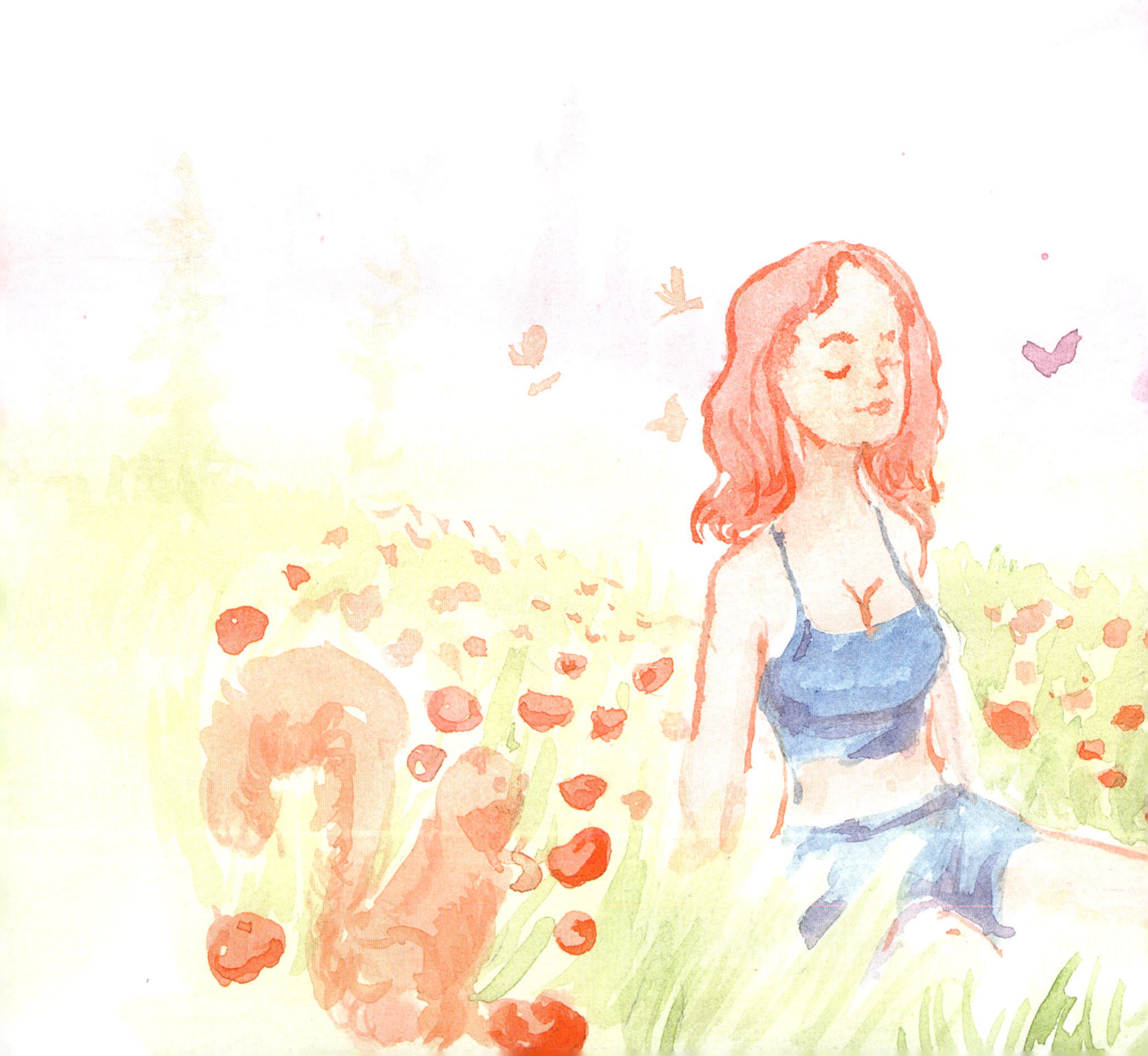

The green wild field was so much more interesting than the peak.

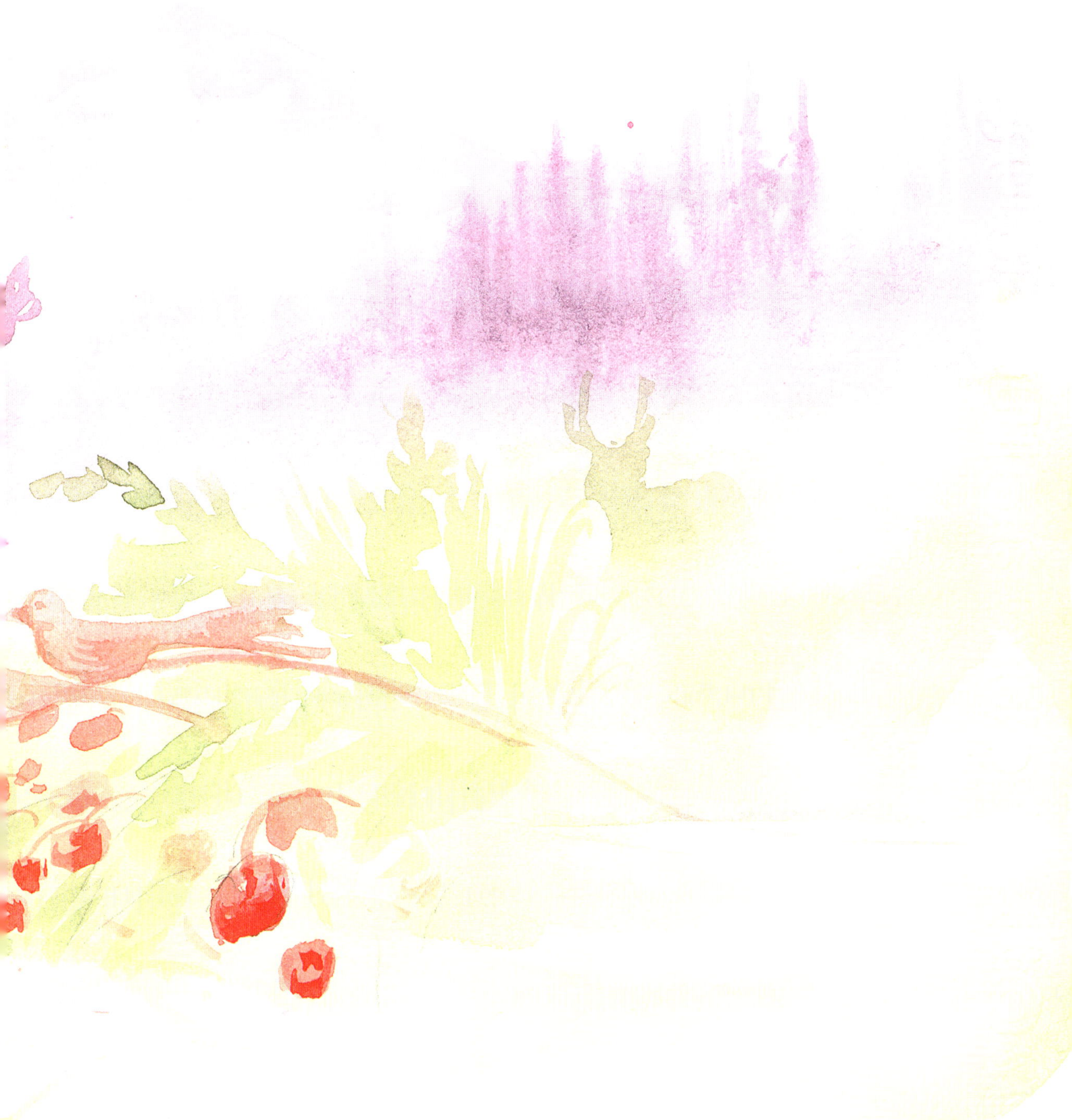

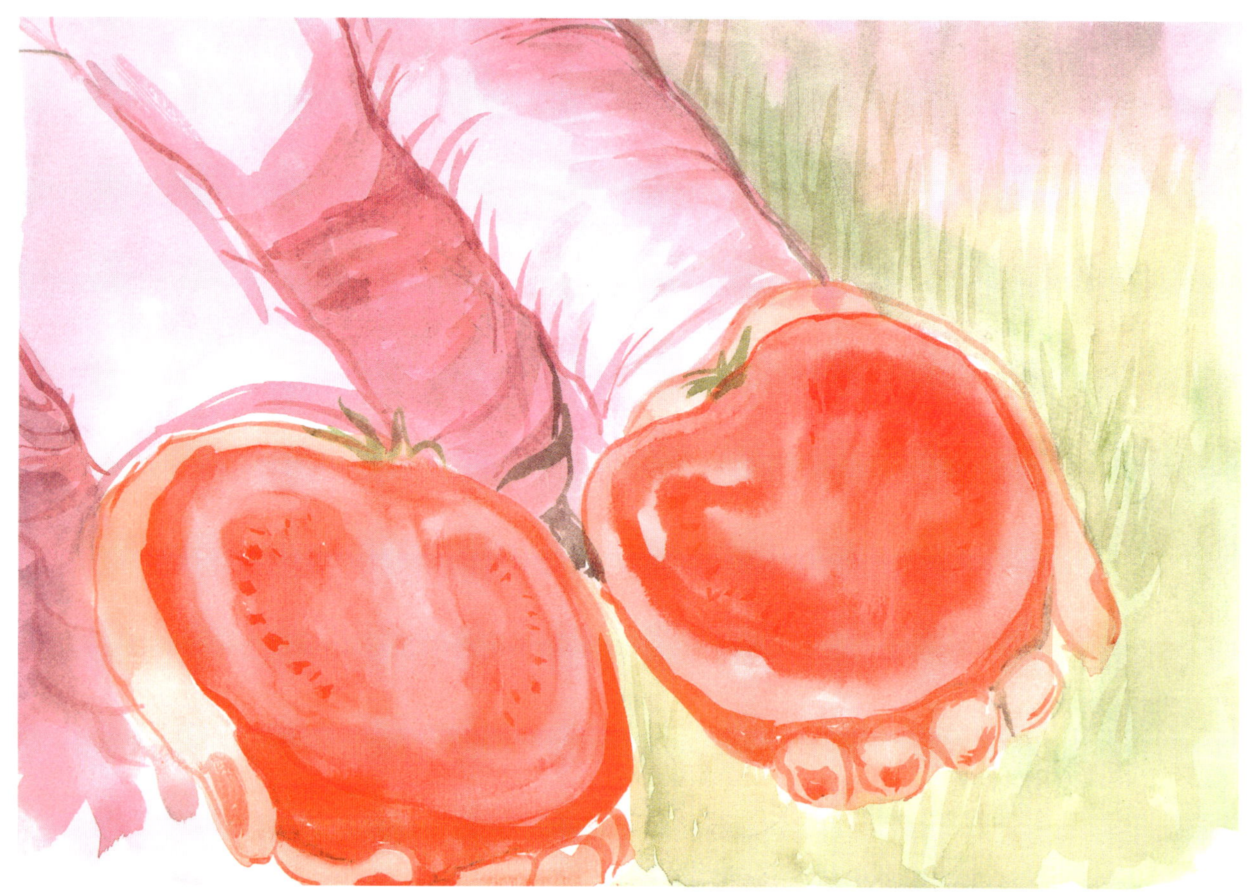

She didn't want to move along, she wanted to linger
right there.

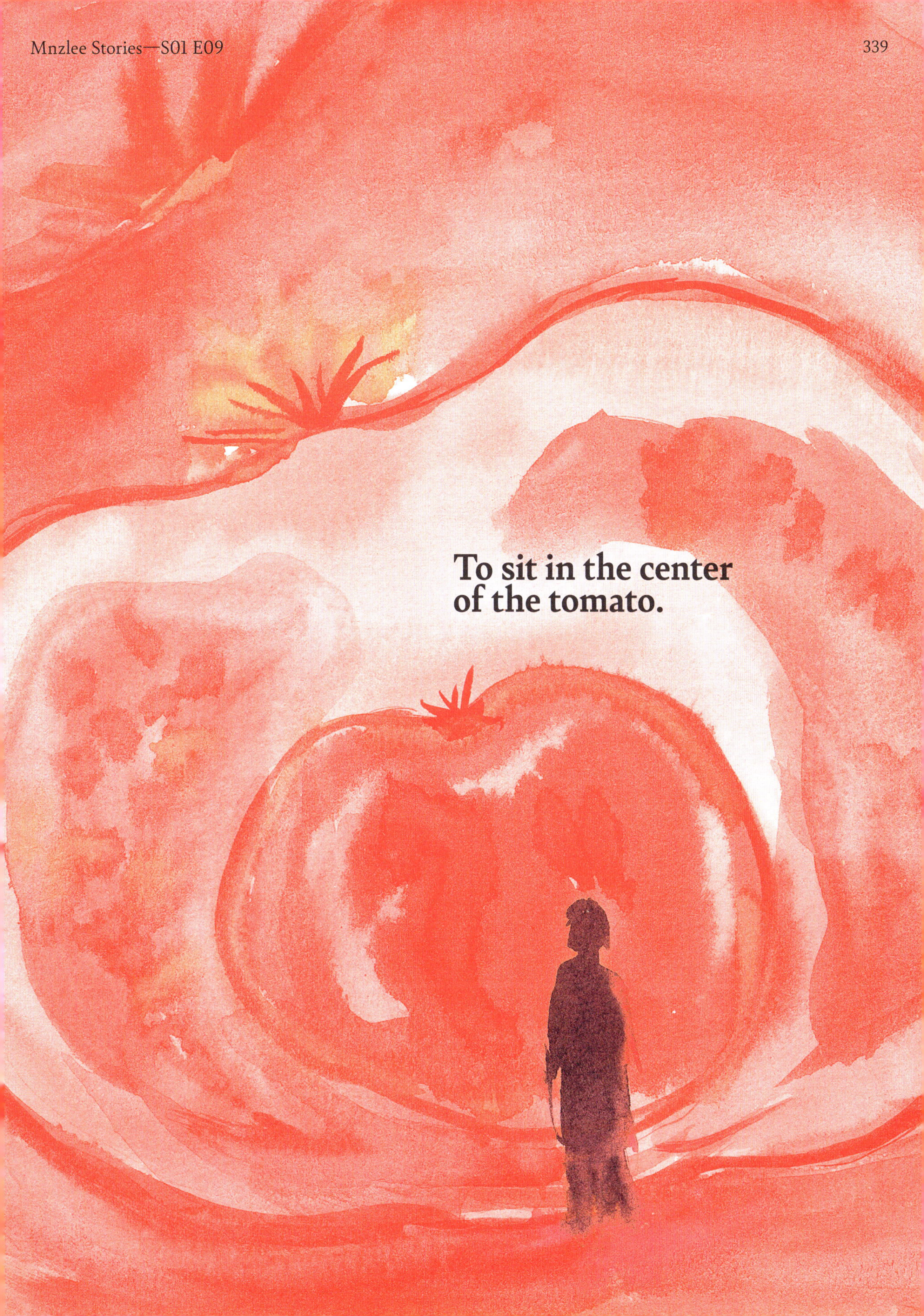

To sit in the center
of the tomato.

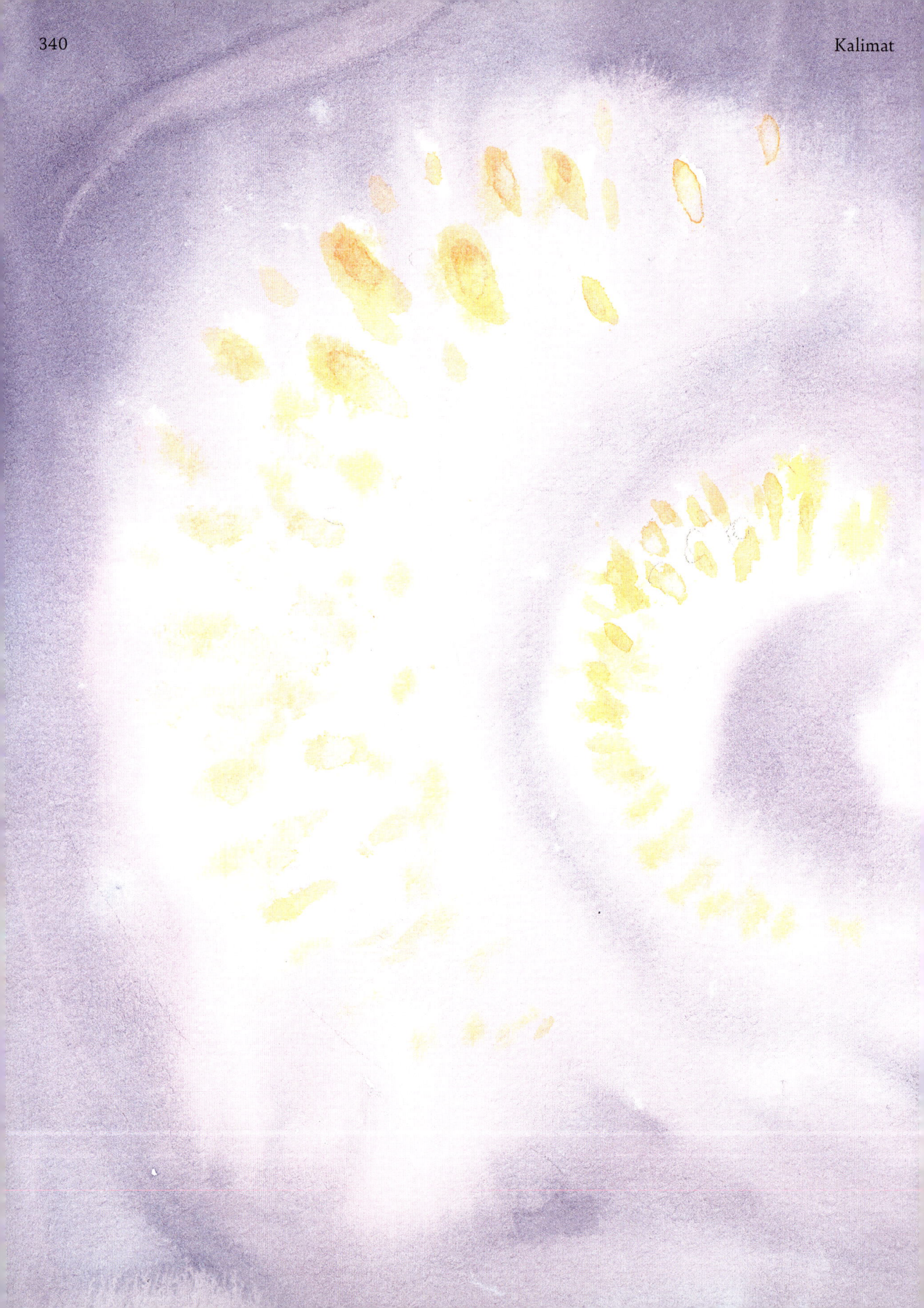

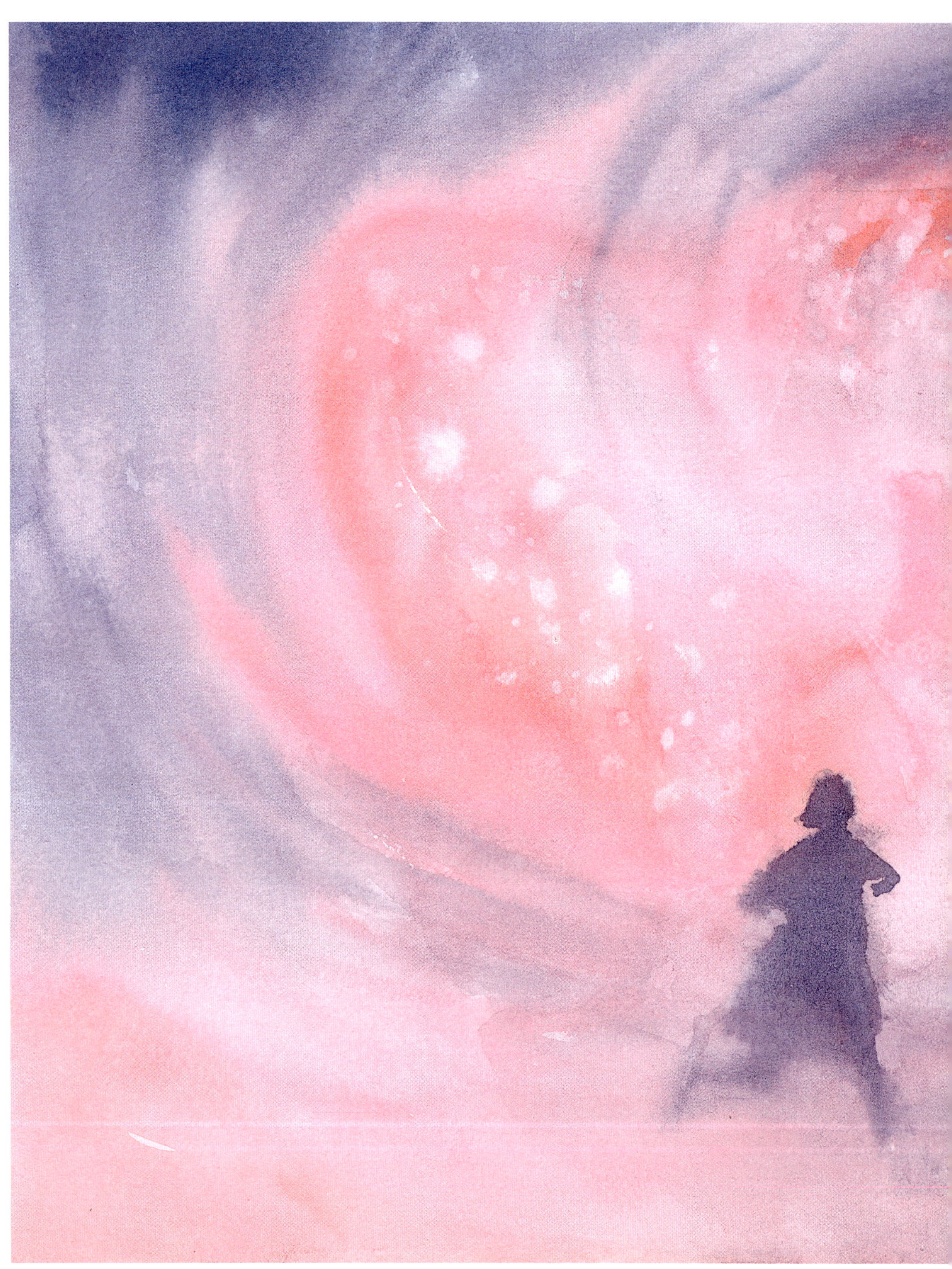

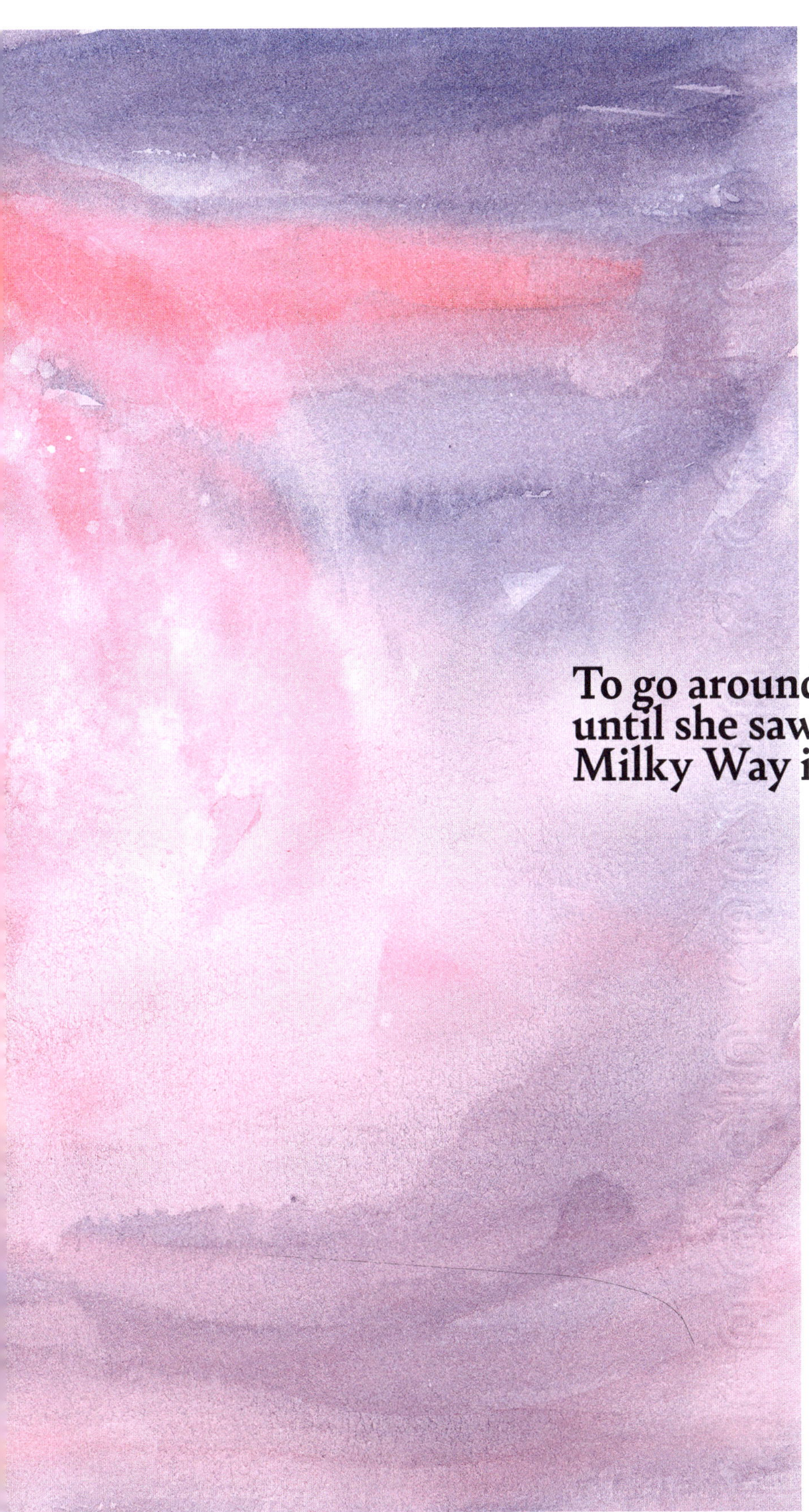

To go around in circles until she saw the entire Milky Way in it.

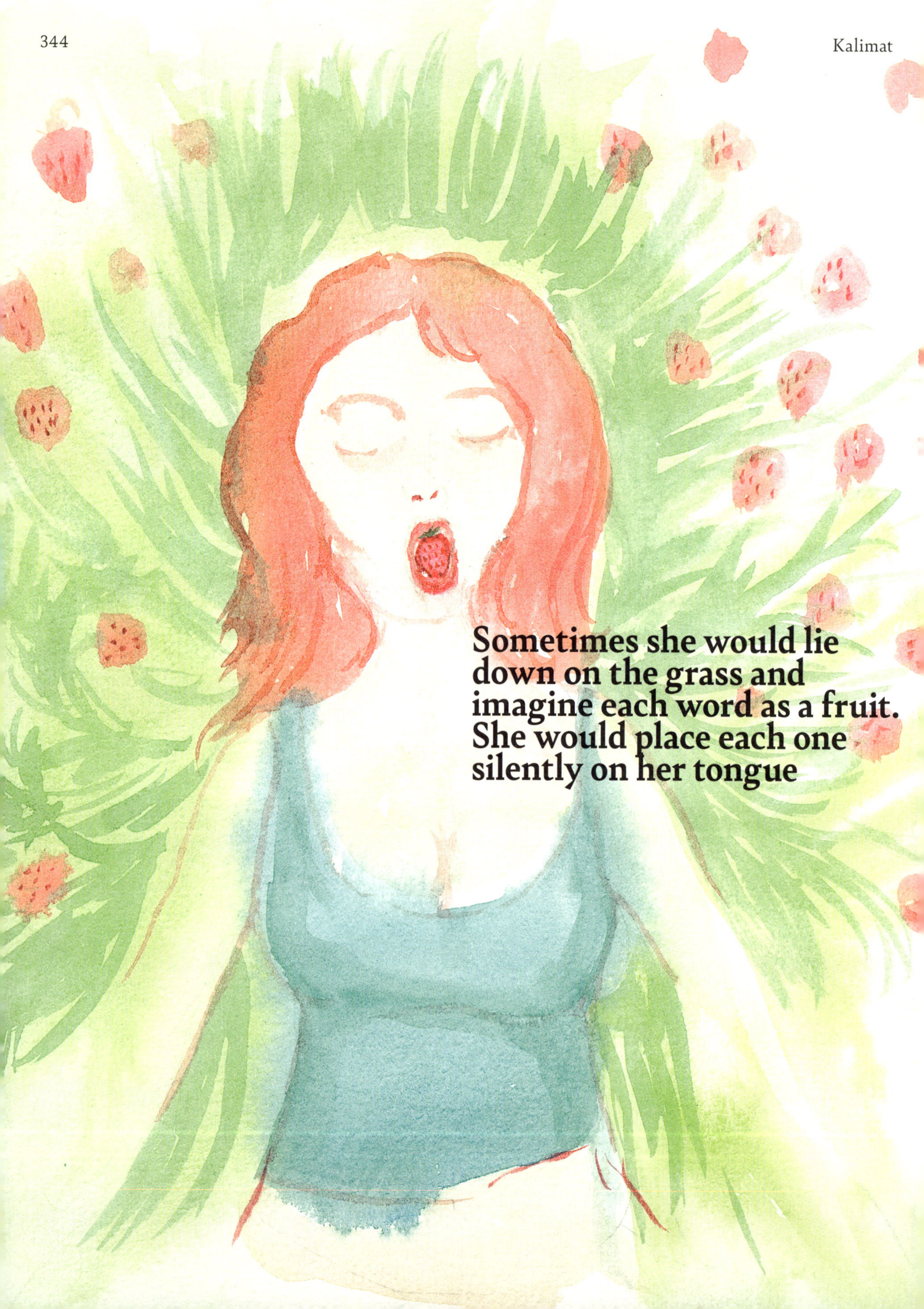
Sometimes she would lie
down on the grass and
imagine each word as a fruit.
She would place each one
silently on her tongue

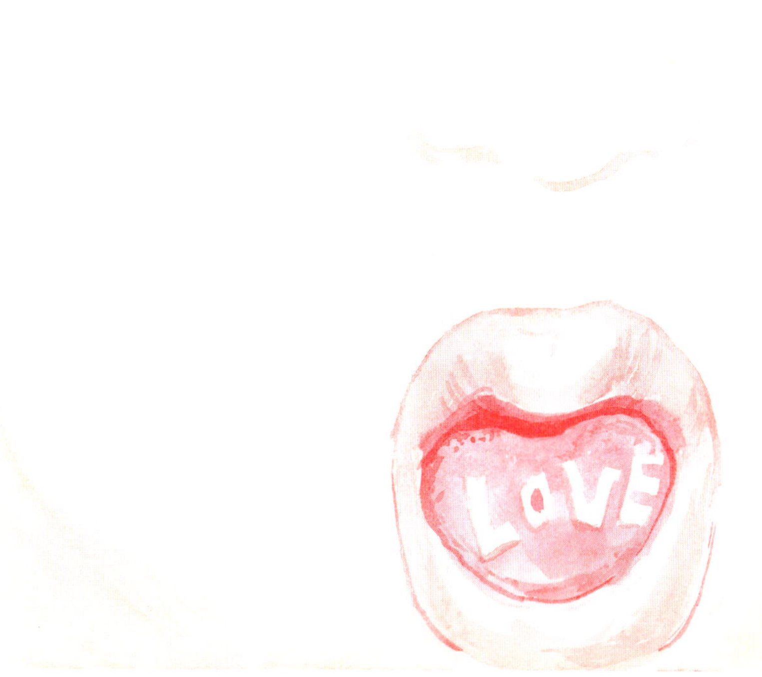

and let its flavor, color and feeling disperse in her body, like the word *love*.

She would hold it just enough to feel it fully,

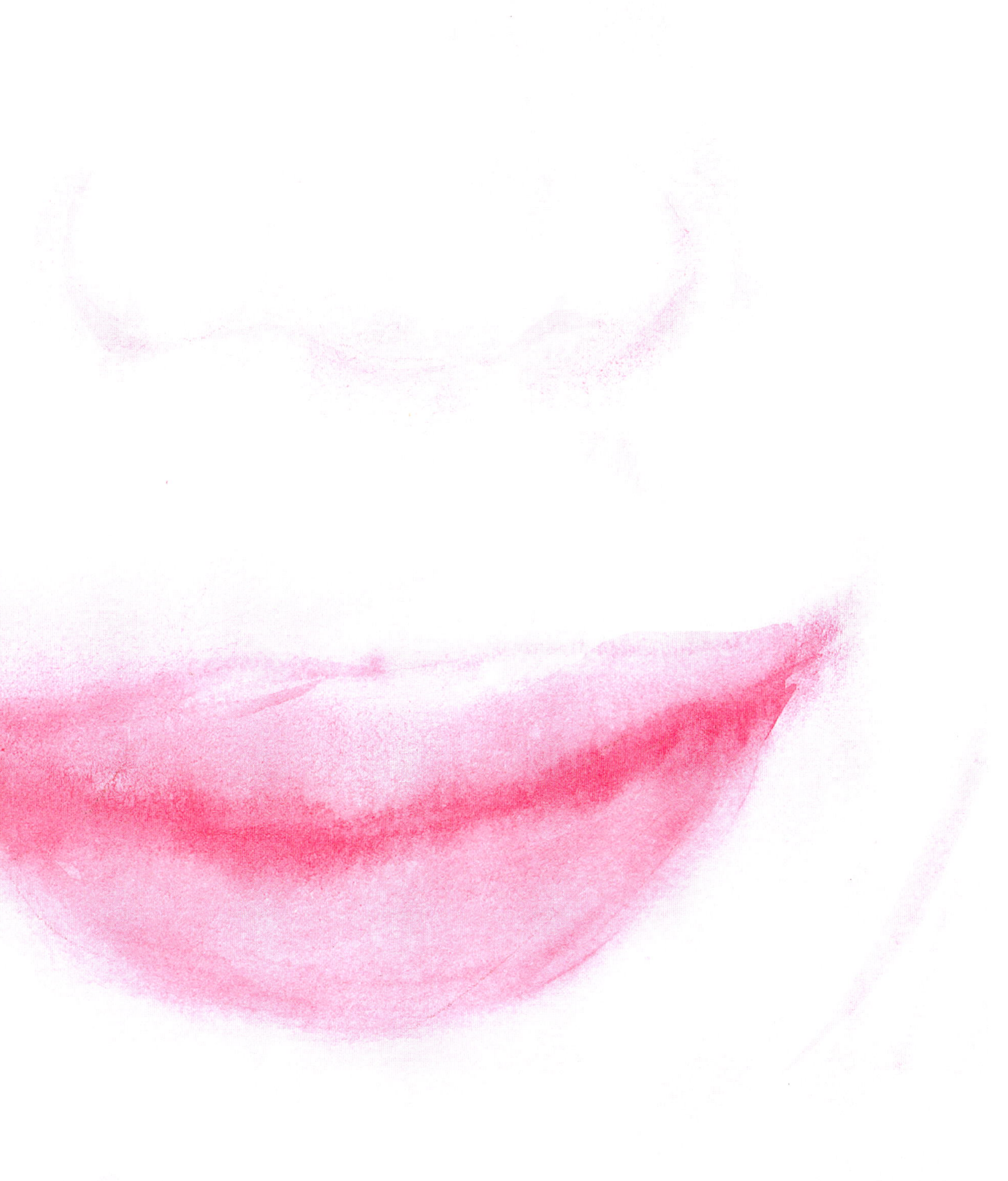

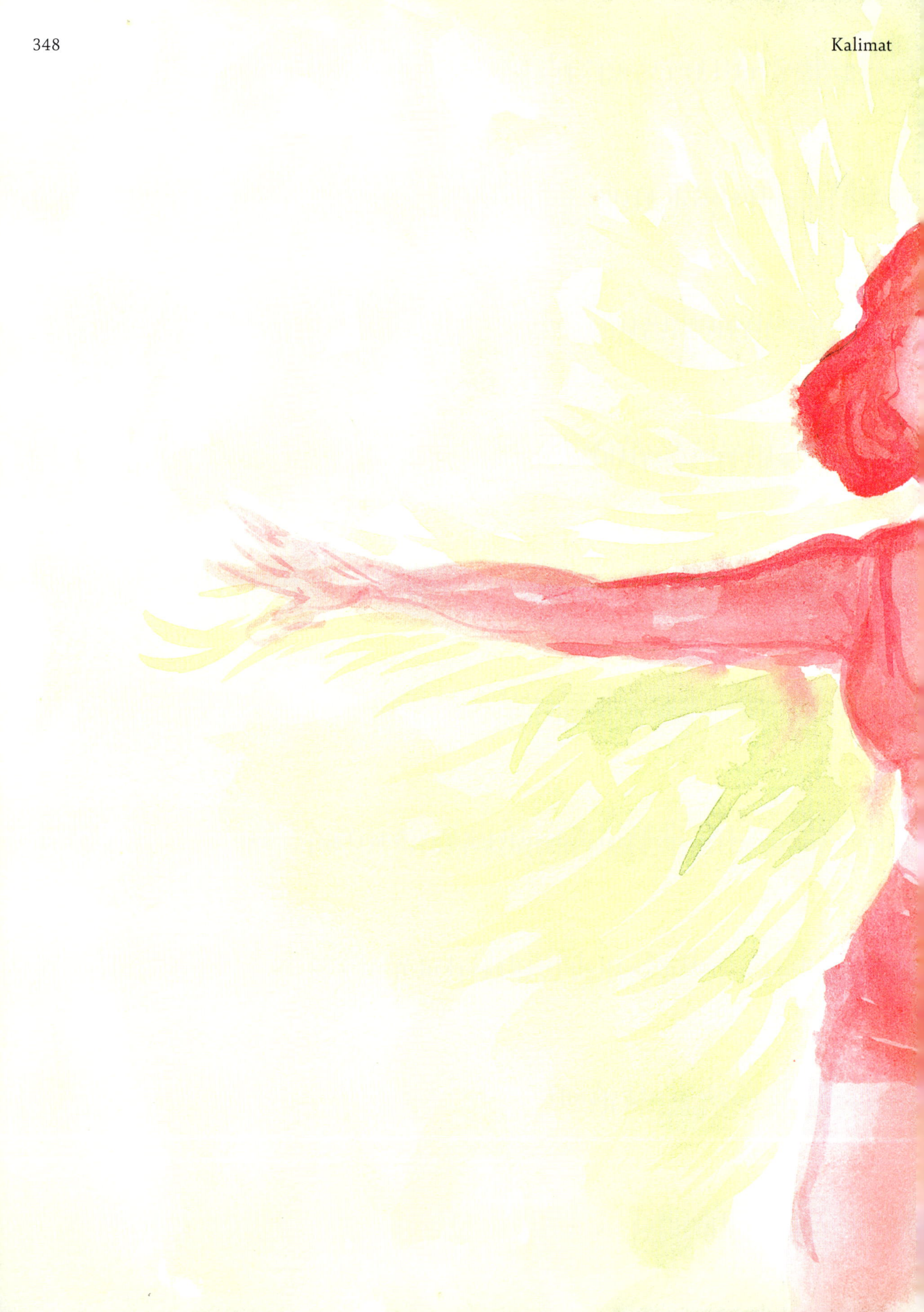

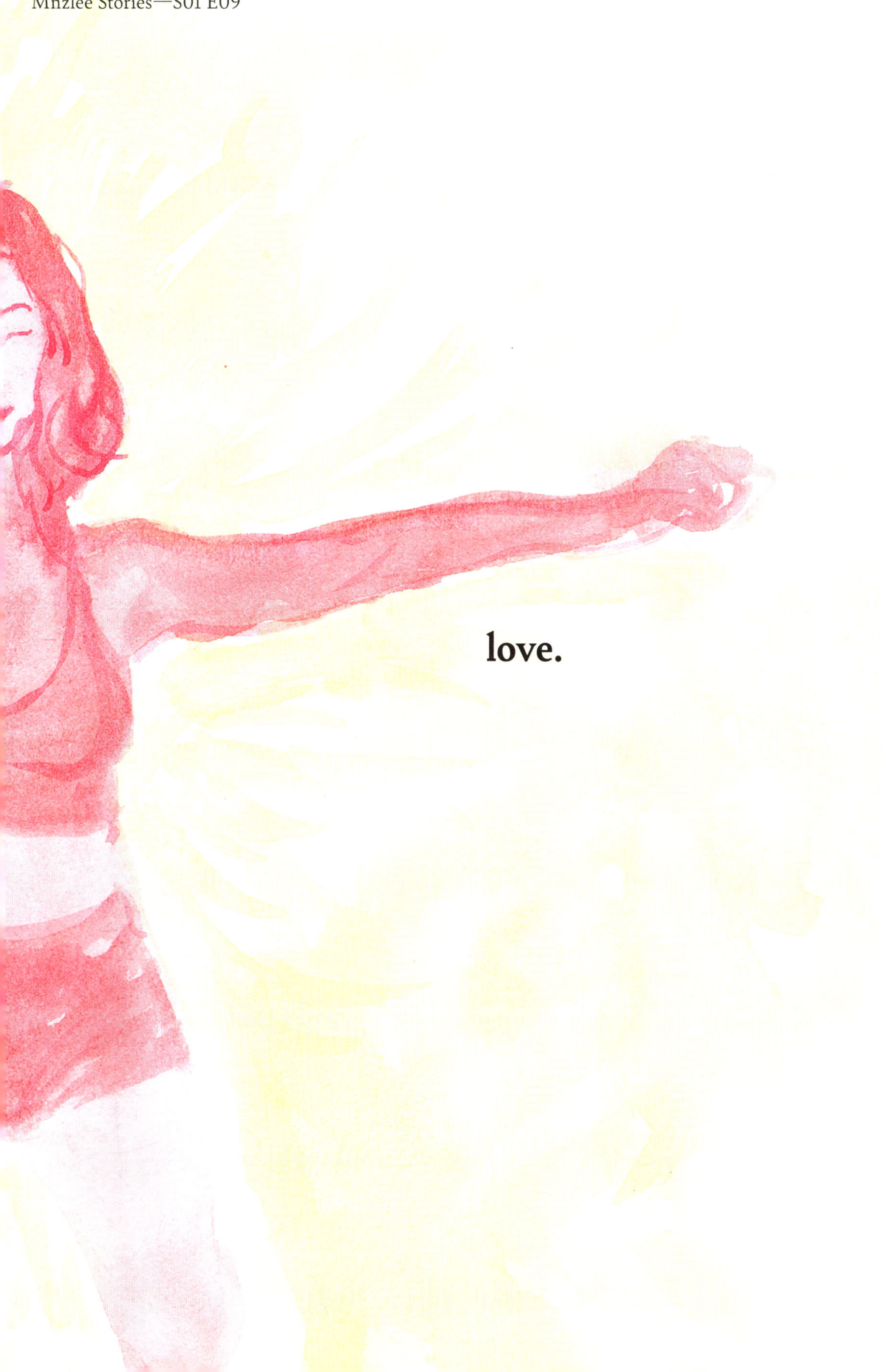

love.

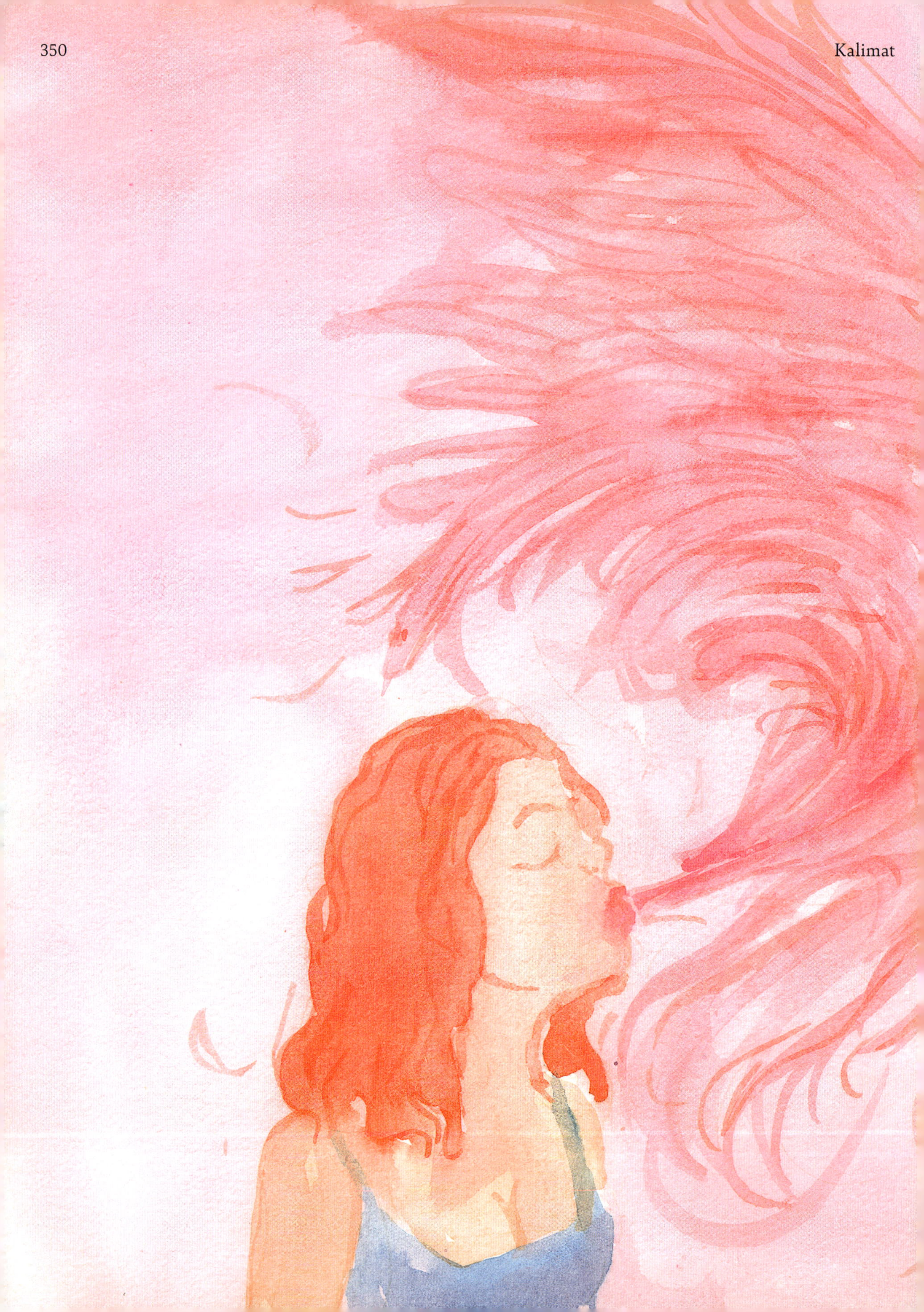

Then release it into the air like releasing a bird.

Kalimat dreamt of sharing her word treasures with others.

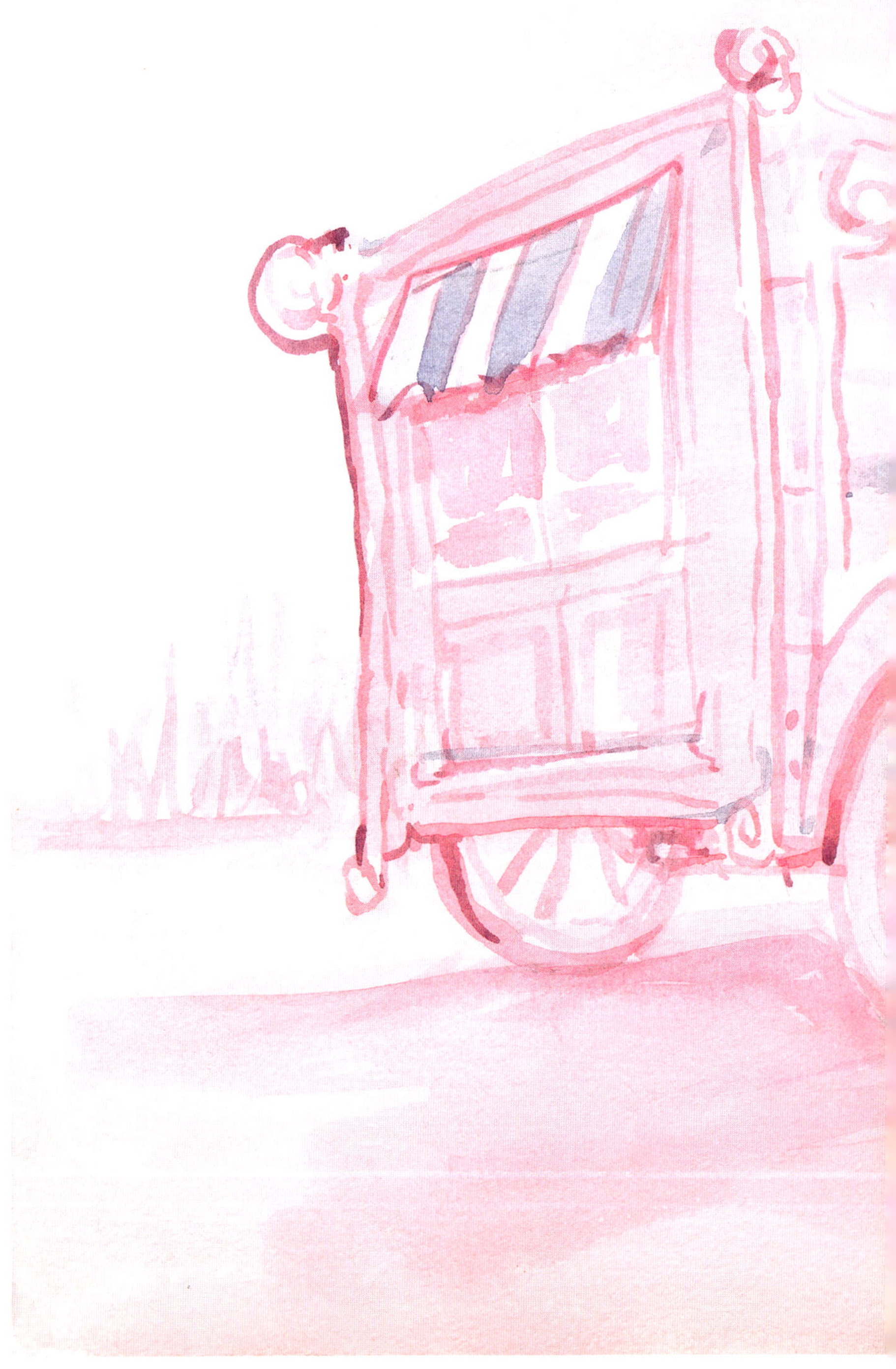

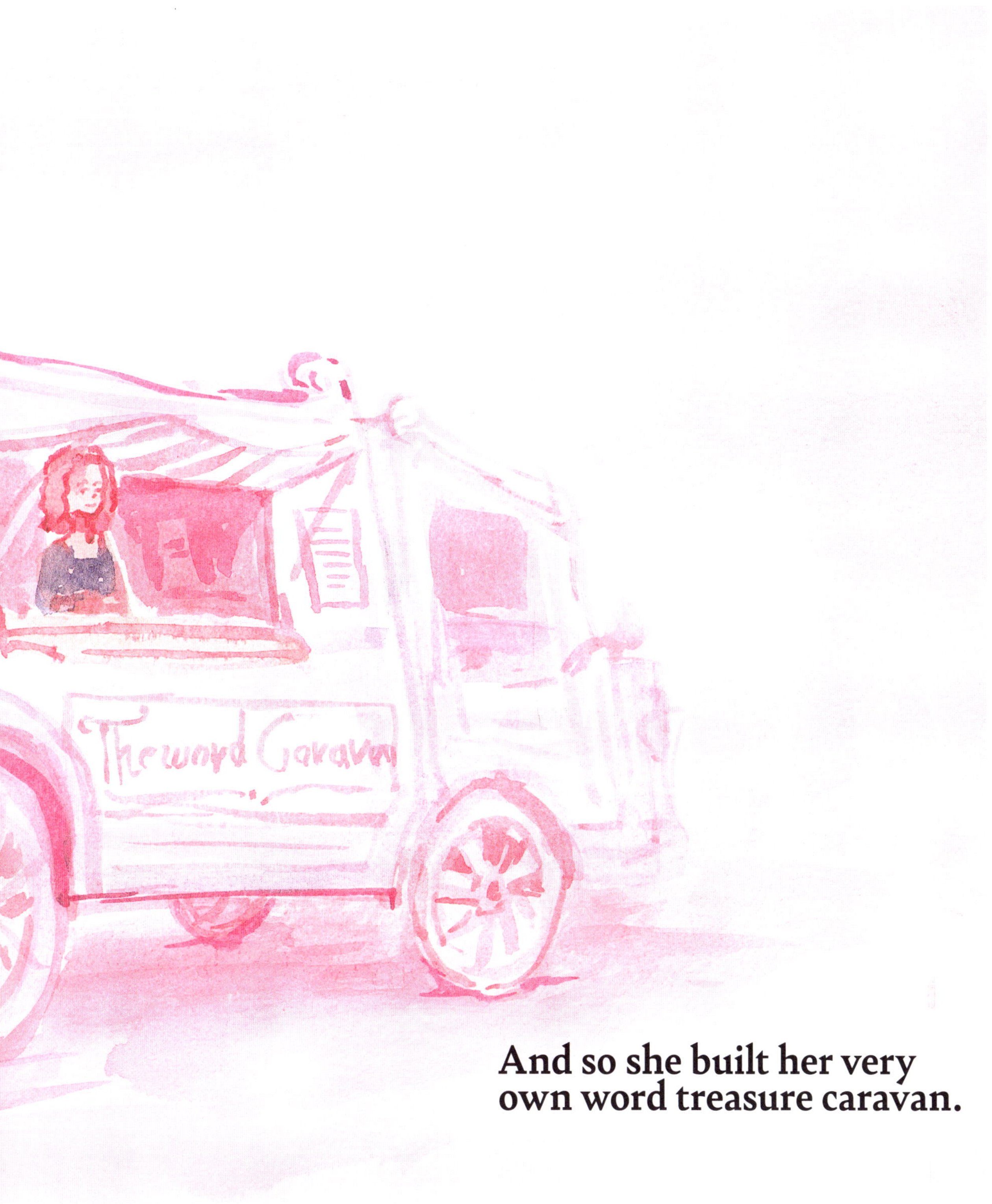

And so she built her very own word treasure caravan.

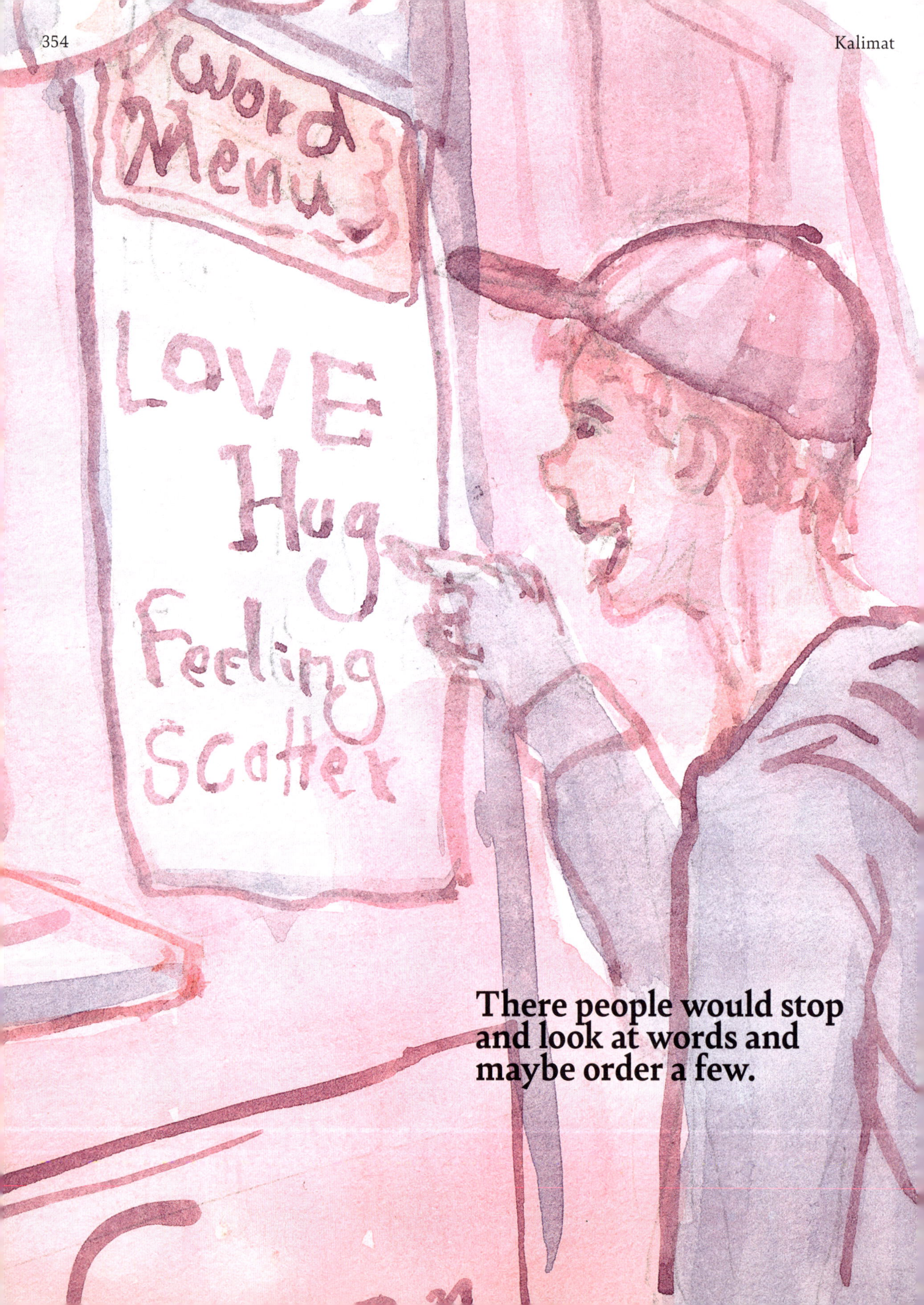

There people would stop
and look at words and
maybe order a few.

"One order of connection coming right up," she would say.

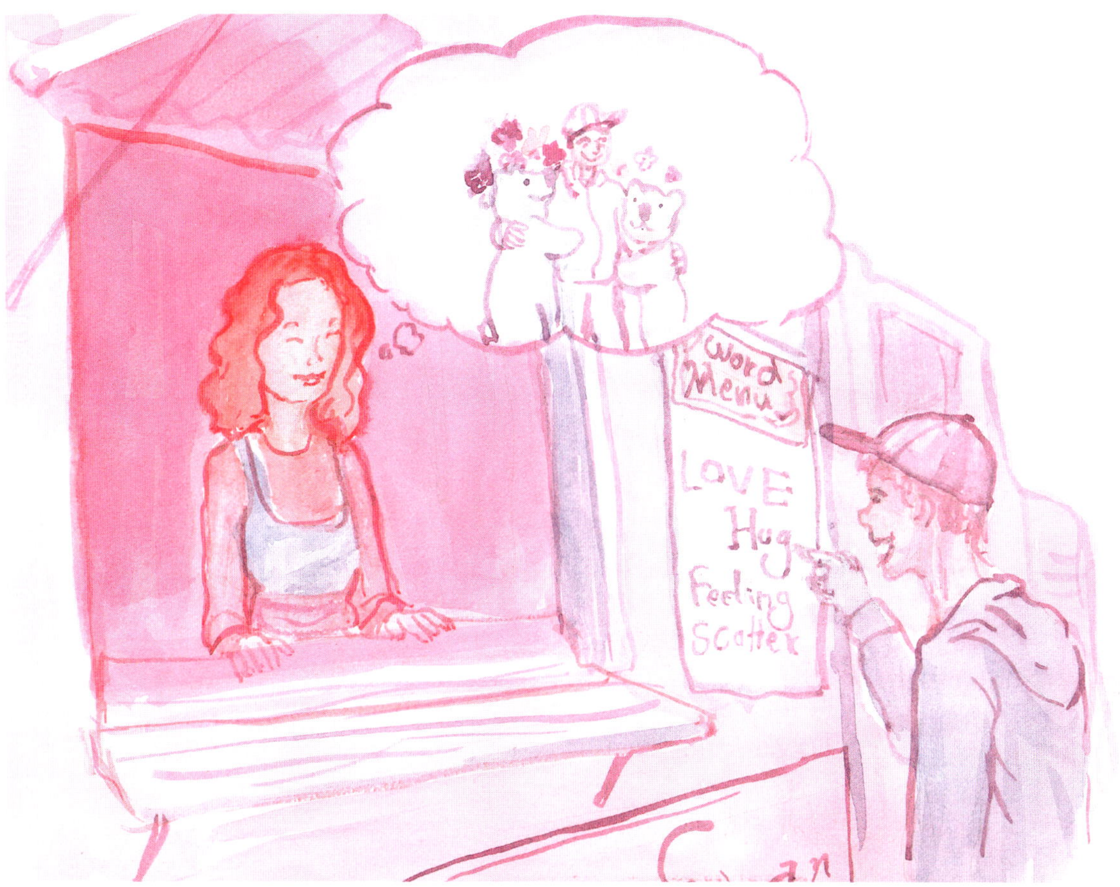

And a bunch of loving bears with flowers would come out
to hug the person, who paid them with a word.

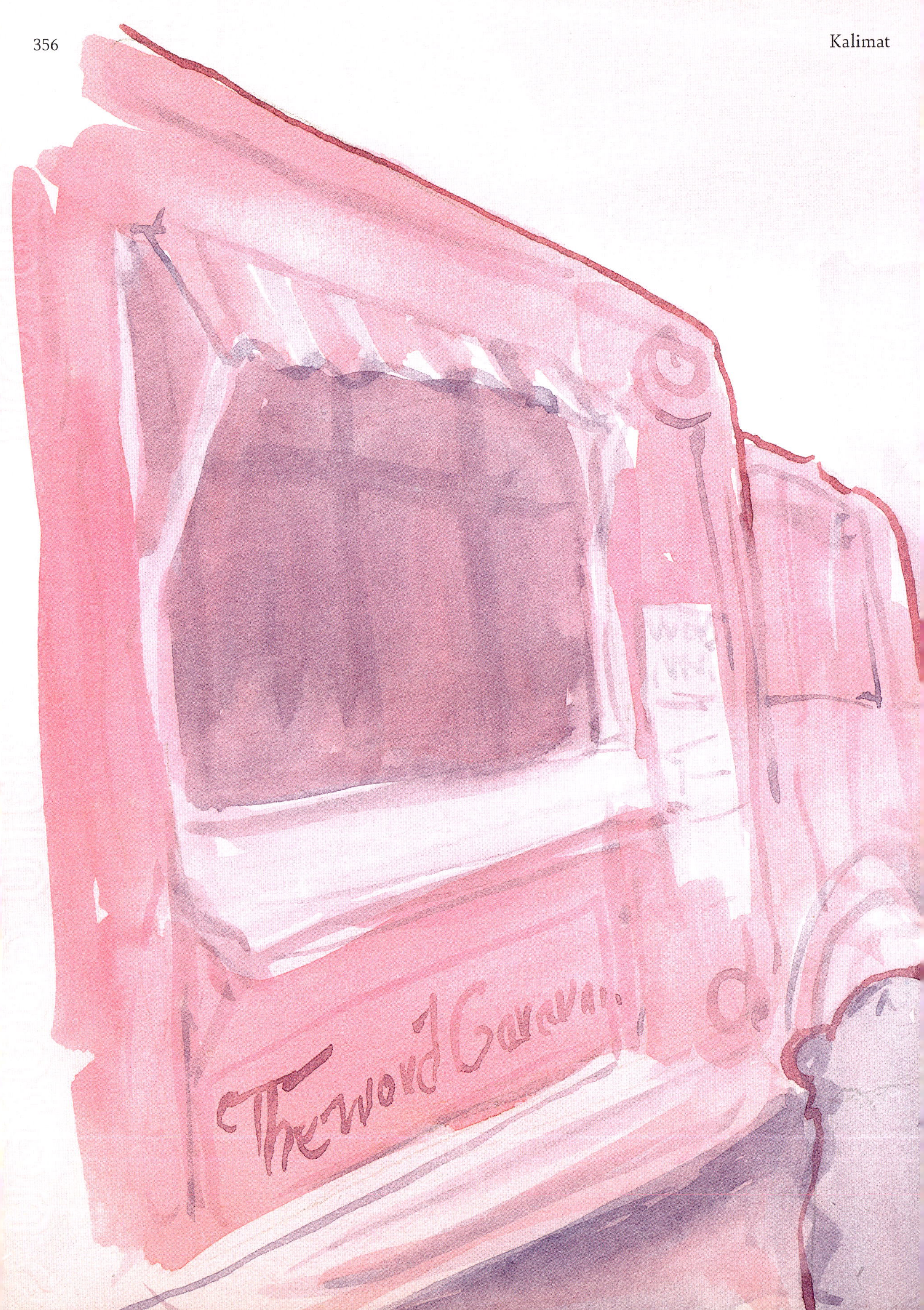
The word Caravan

There was one problem. No-one ever stayed long enough to receive the meaning of the words.

It was as if she was invisible.

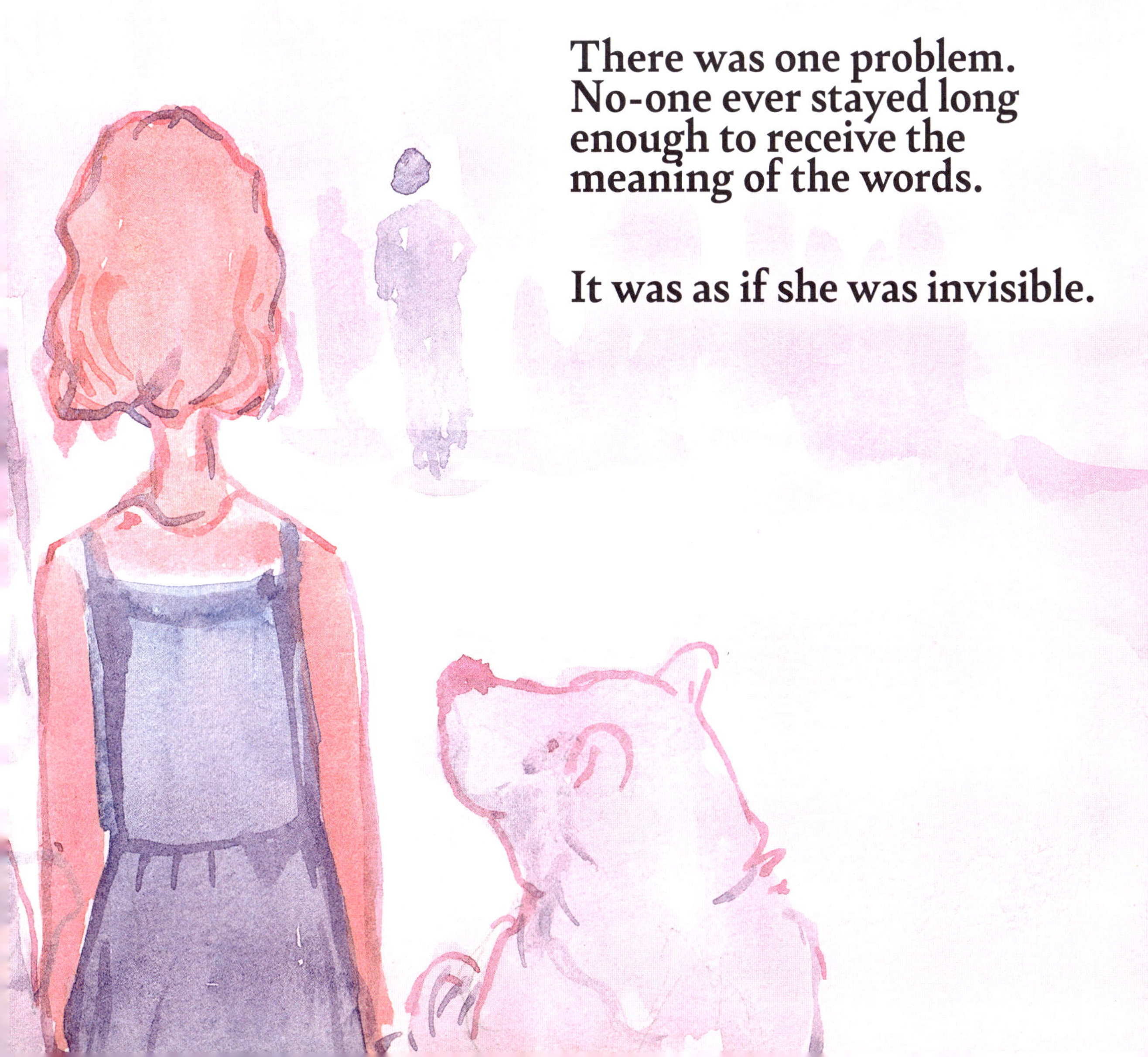

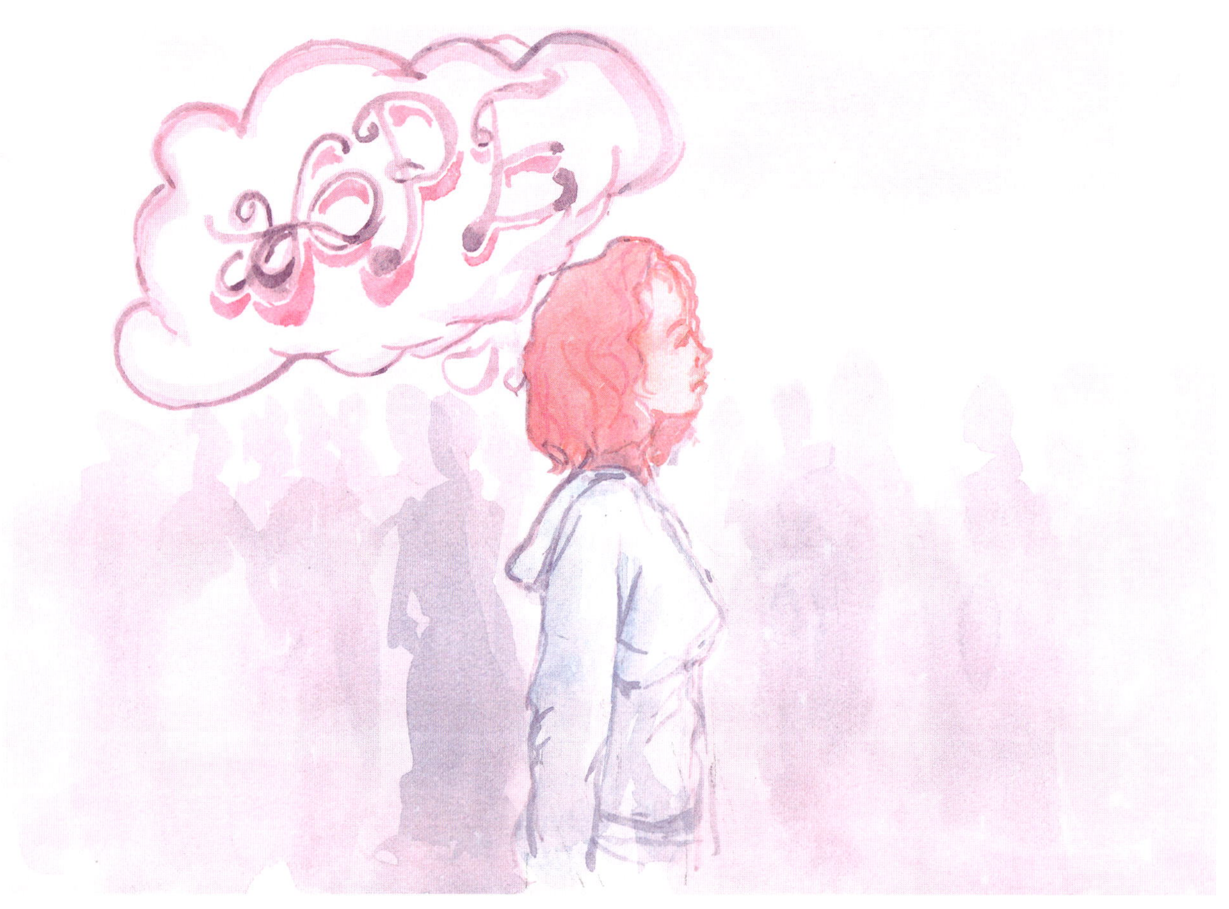

**And so one day as Kalimat was strolling down slowly
and exploring the word *hope*,**

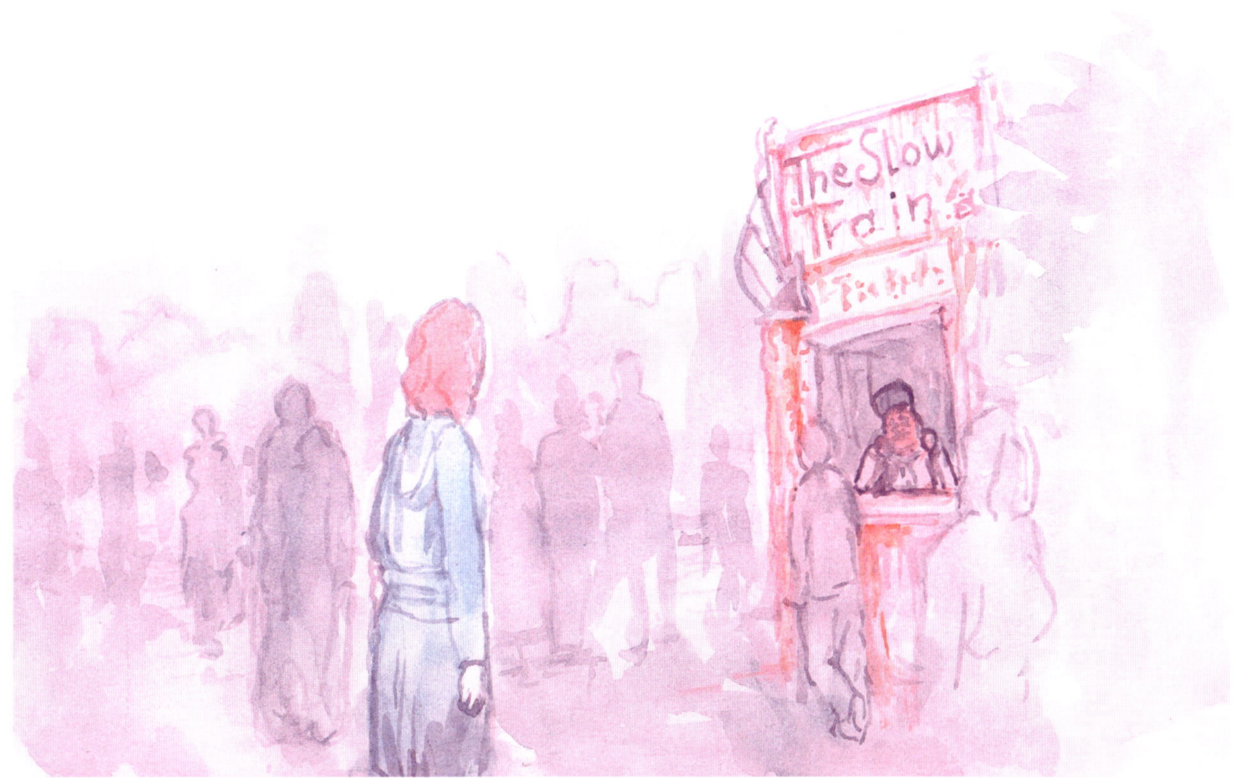

she saw a booth that read "The Slow Train." There was
no line and the ticket agent looked like she had not been
spoken to in years.

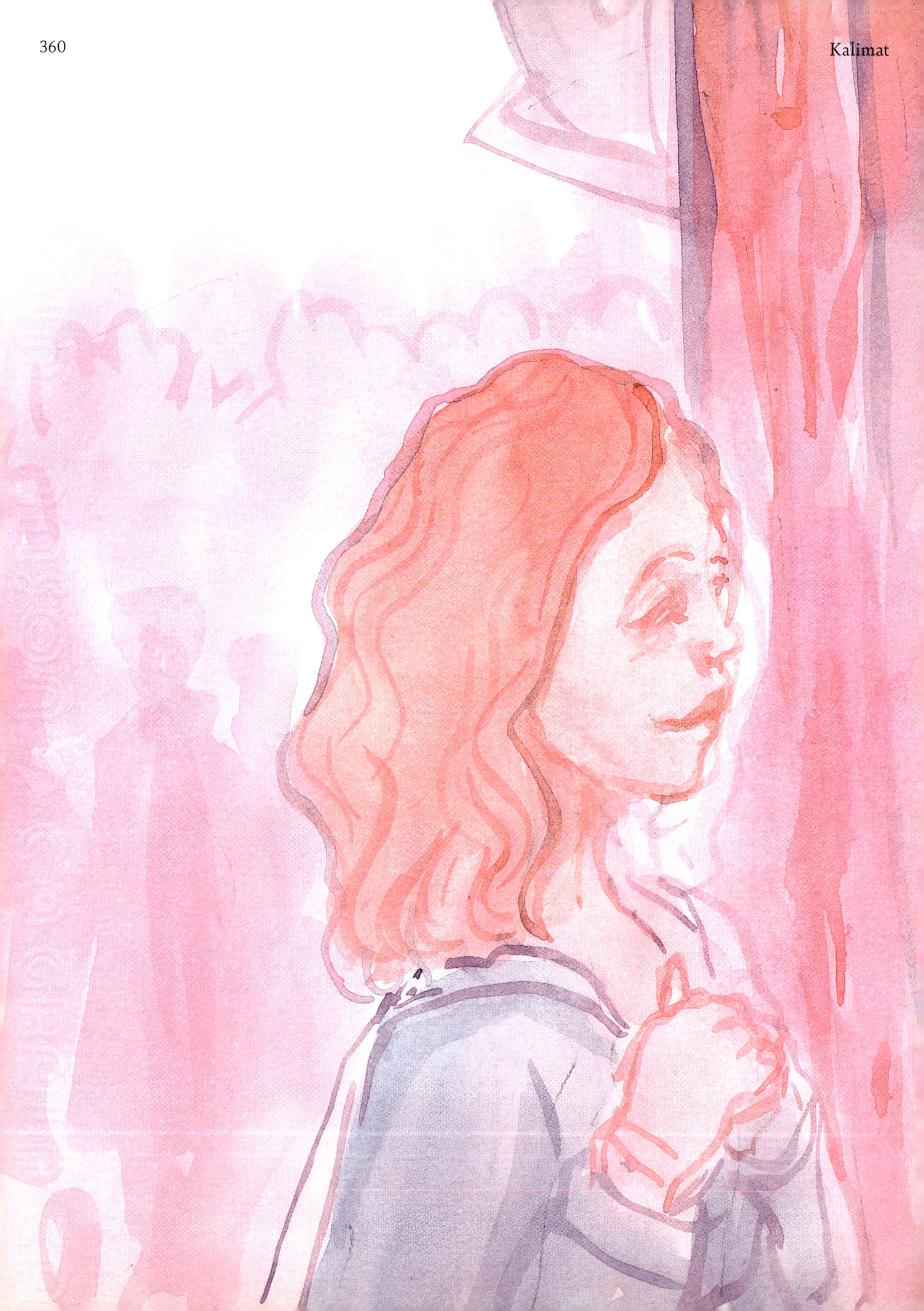

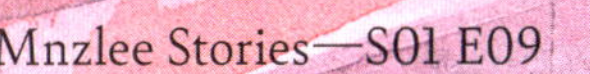

The ticket agent explained that the slow train was headed far, far, far into the future.

And it would take a very, very, very, very long time to get there.

A very, very, very long time
to get there sounded like
a very, very, very good idea.

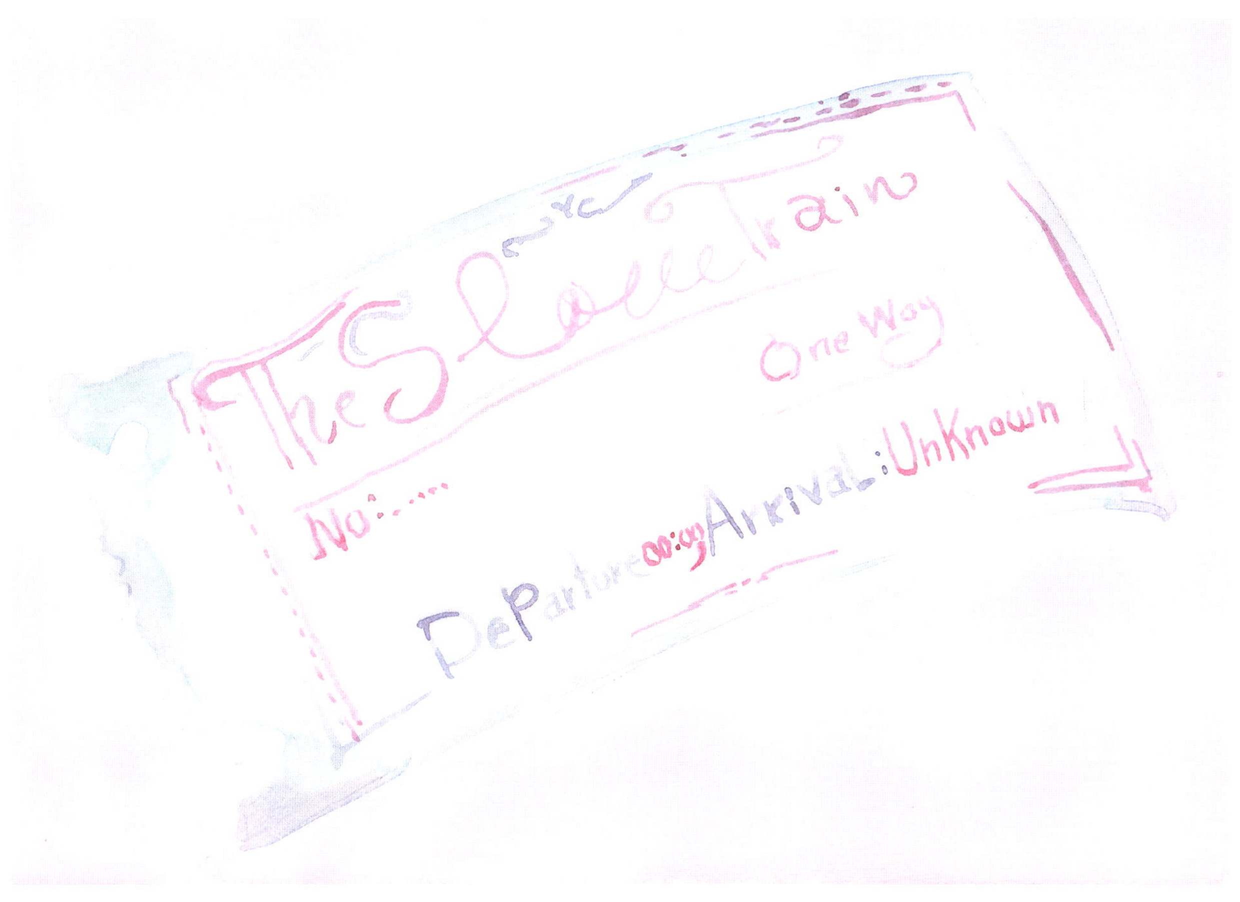

Excited, Kalimat bought a one-way ticket on the slow train, packed her word treasure caravan in a box and took off.

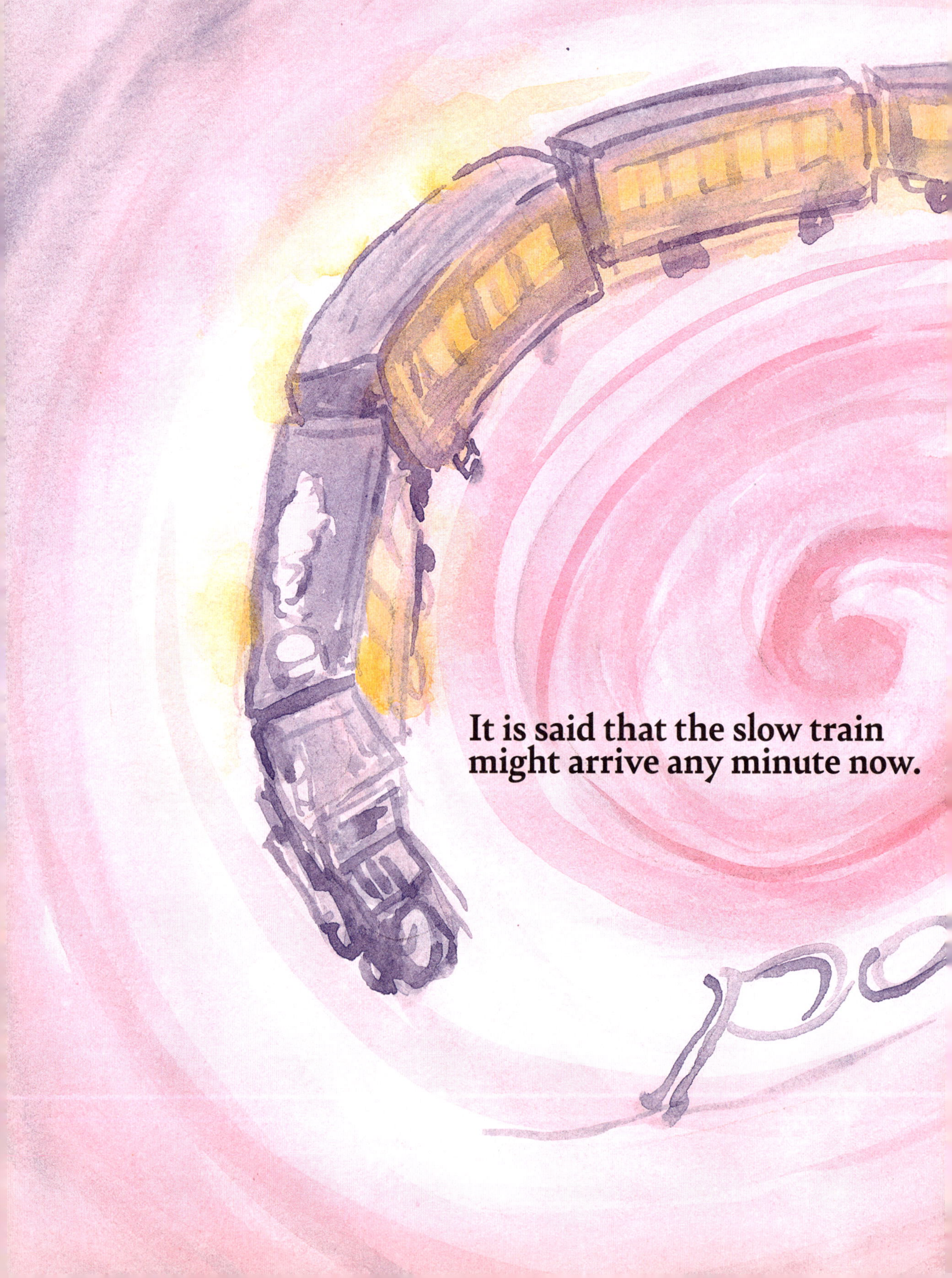

It is said that the slow train
might arrive any minute now.

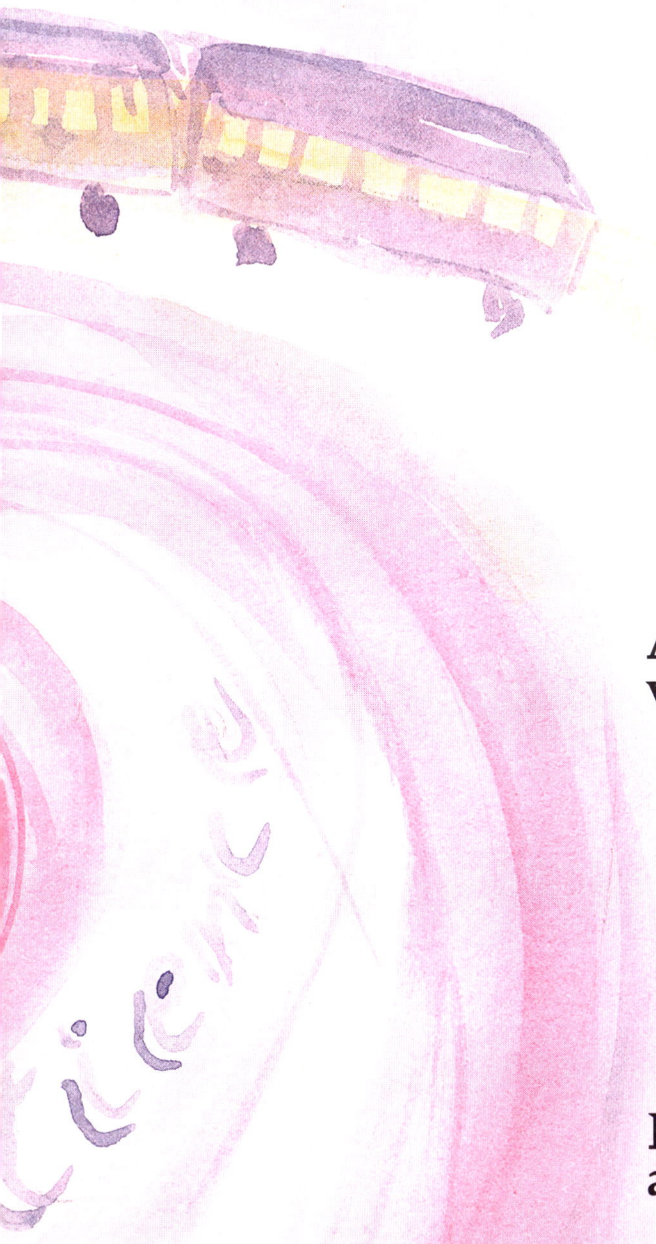

And that many people
wait for it.

It is said that it will arrive
at a future point called

Patience,

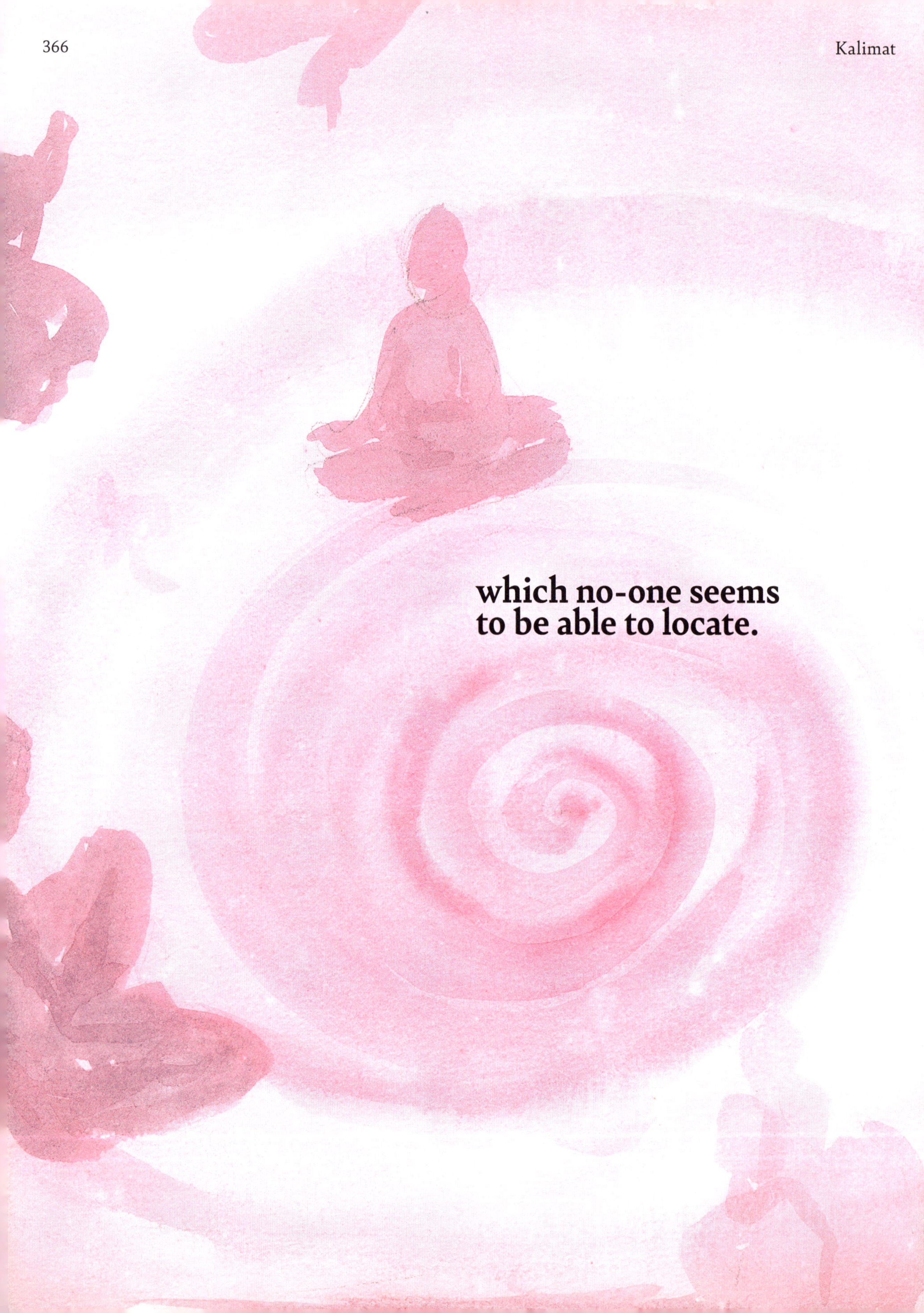
which no-one seems
to be able to locate.

Some people have been preparing for its arrival—well,

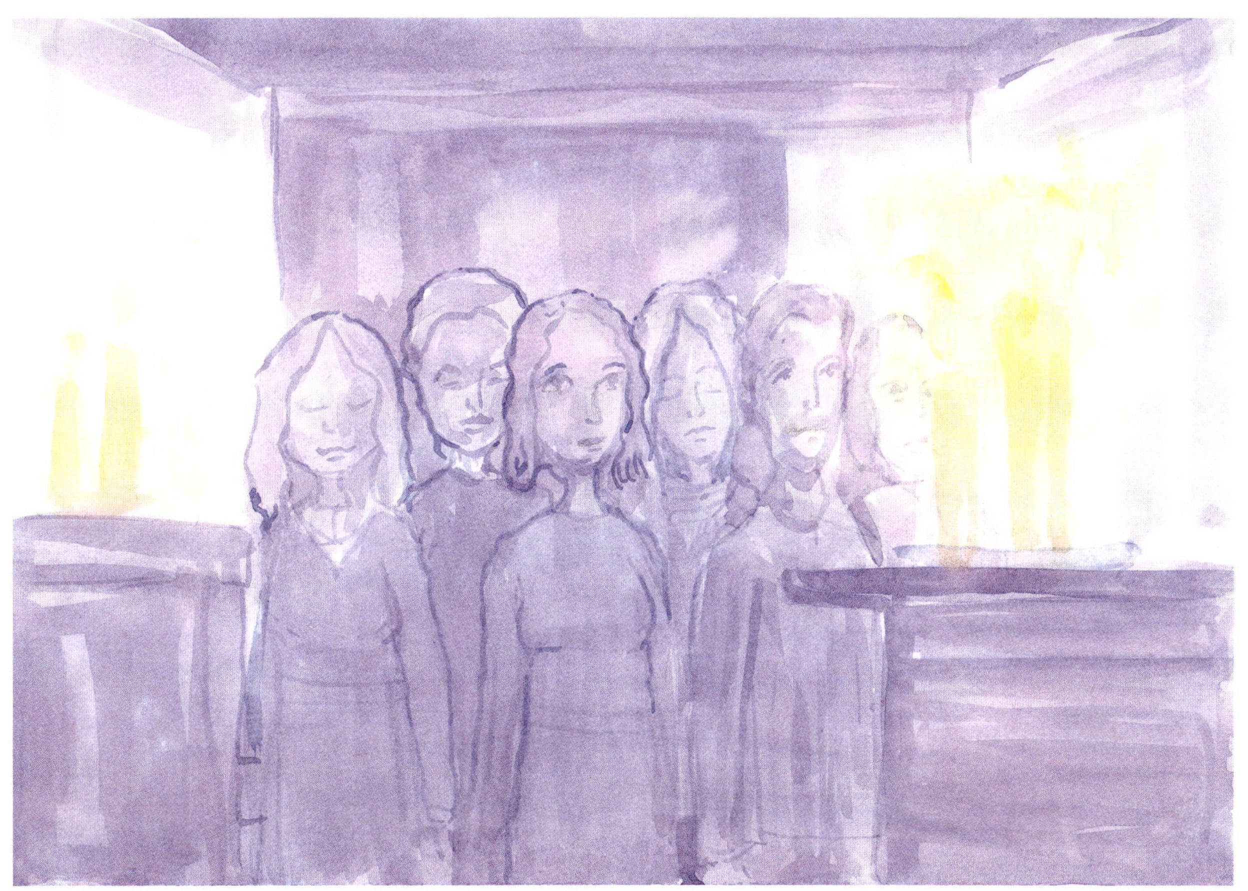

her arrival, in particular.

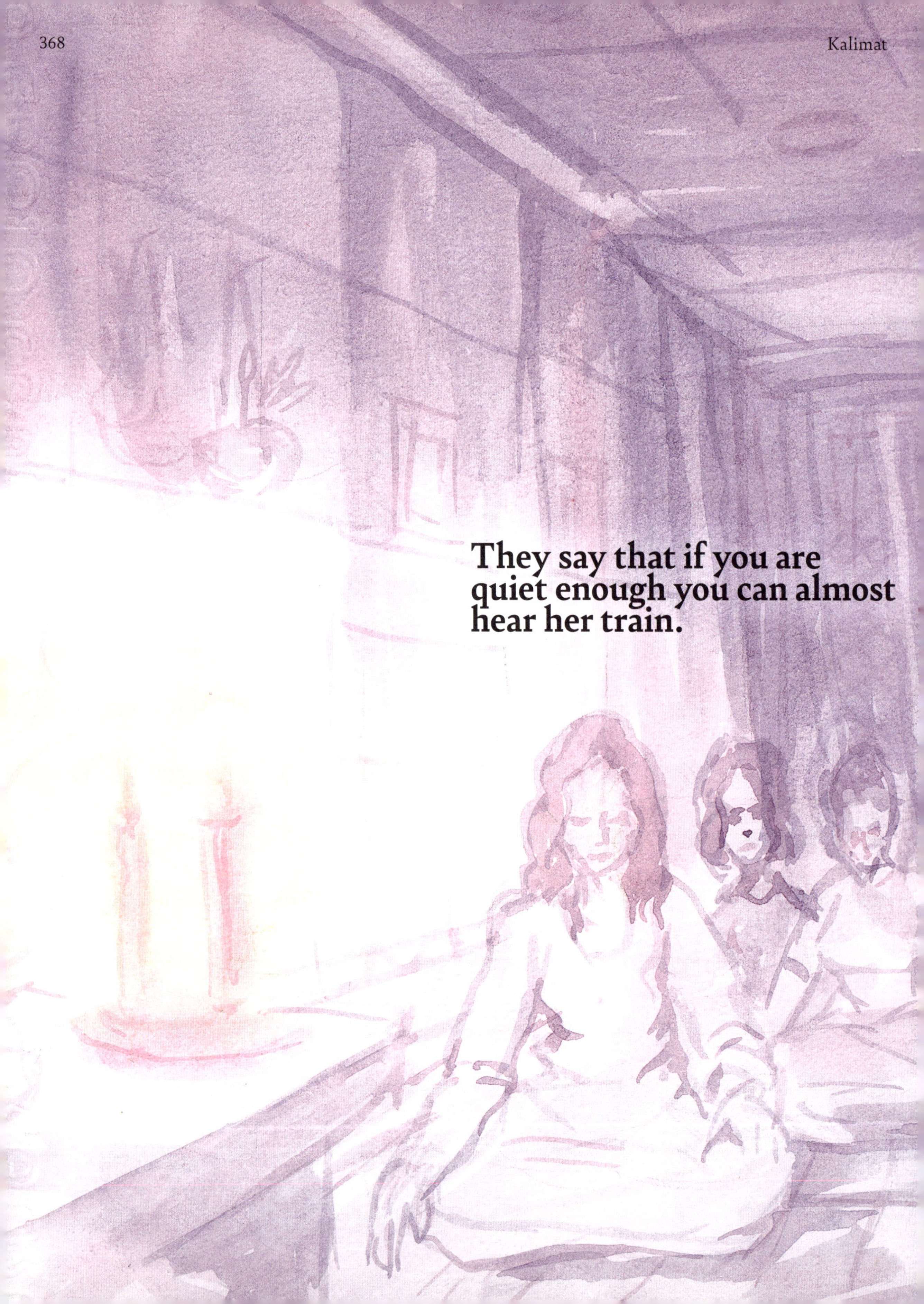
They say that if you are
quiet enough you can almost
hear her train.

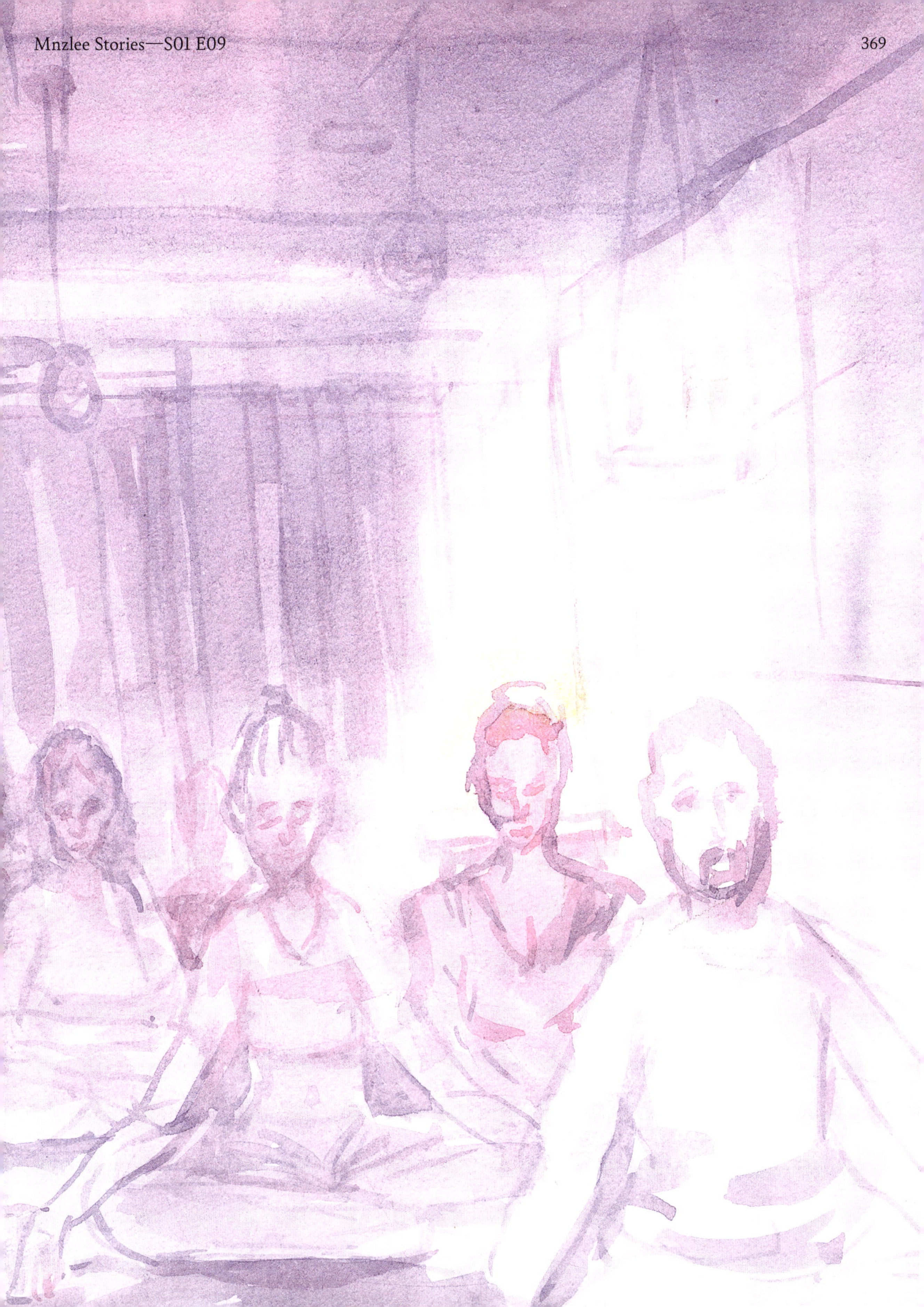

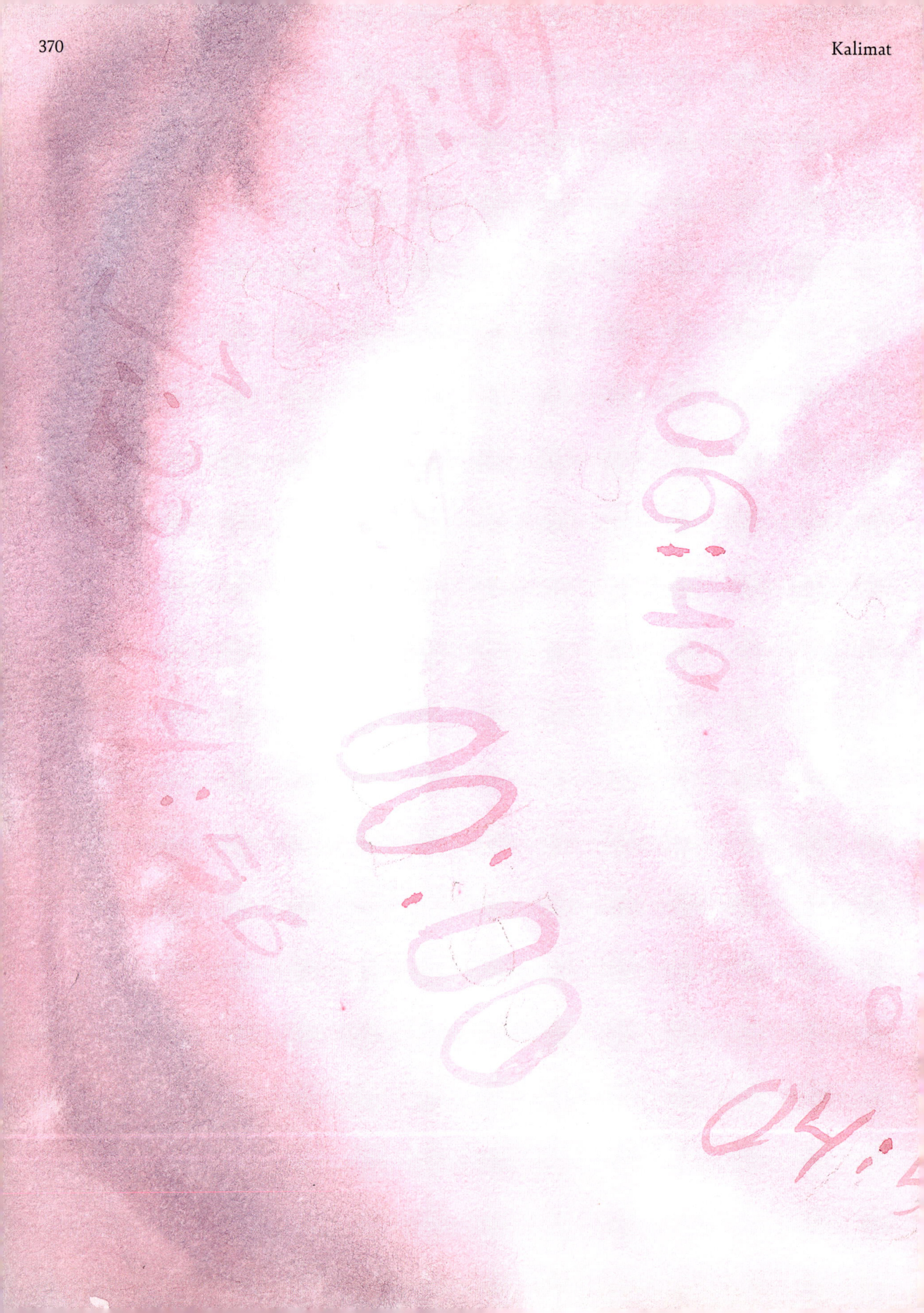

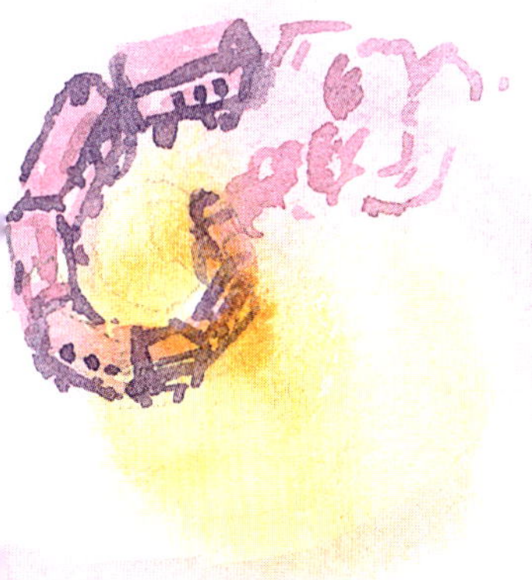

Toot, toot, toot.

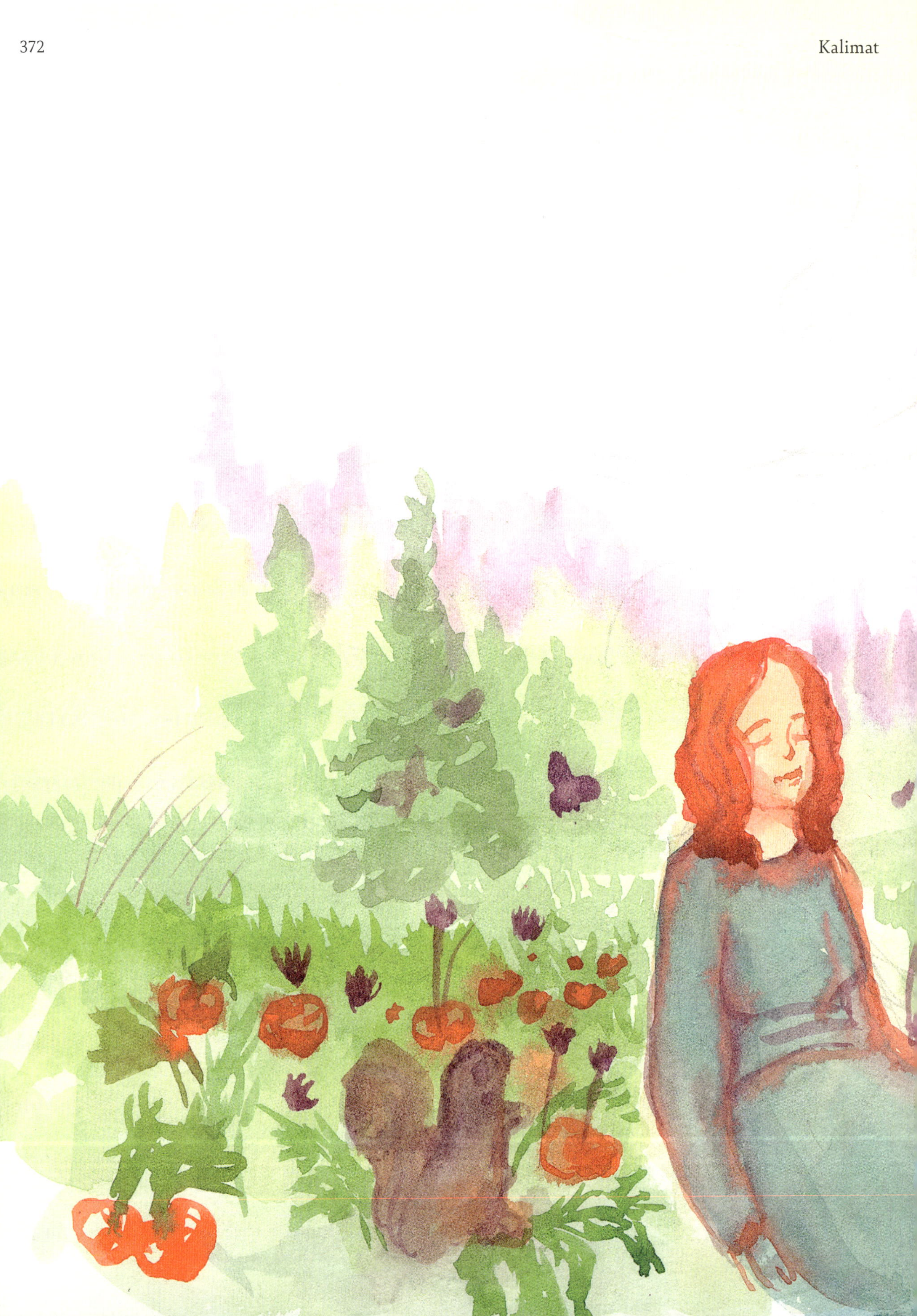

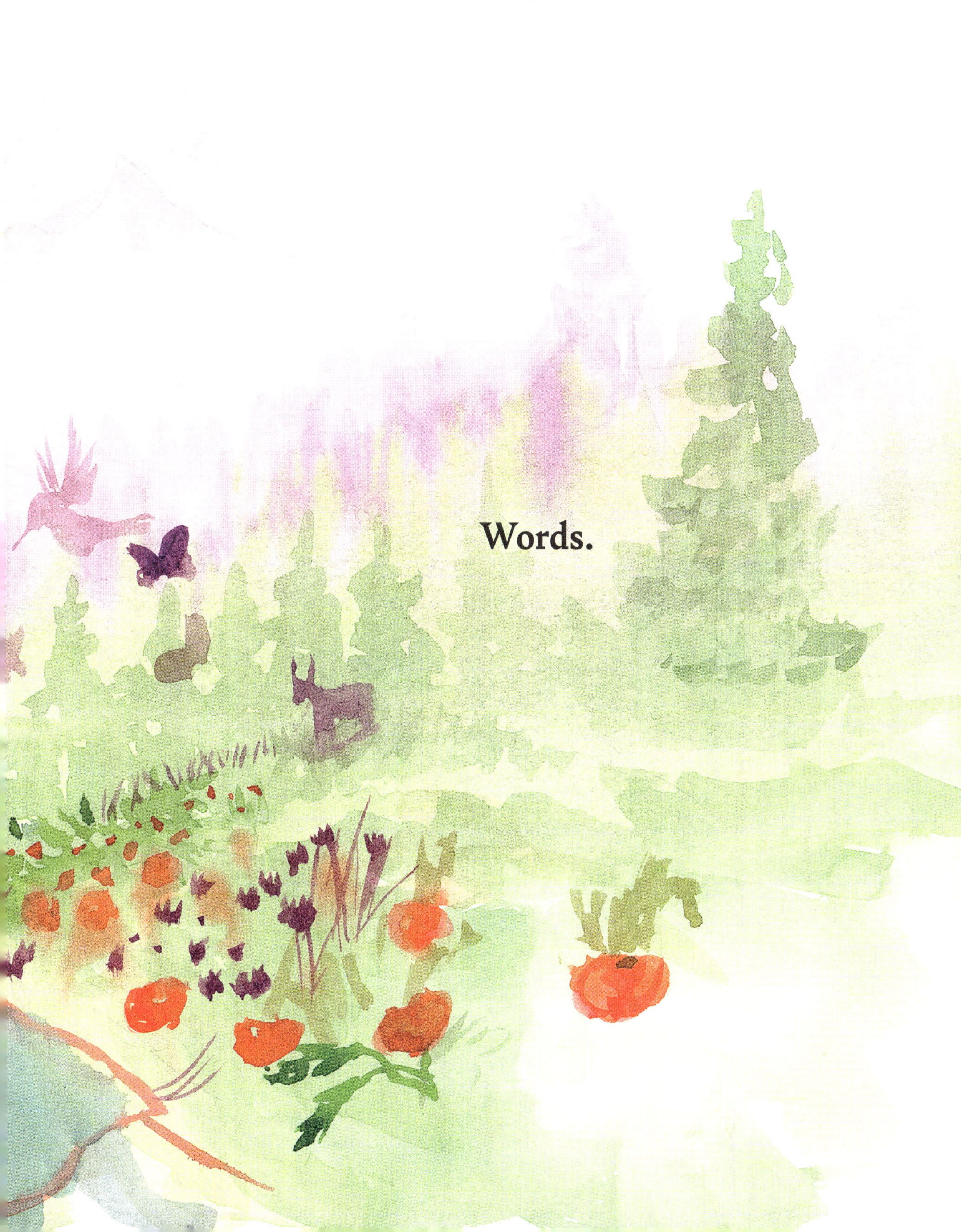
Words.

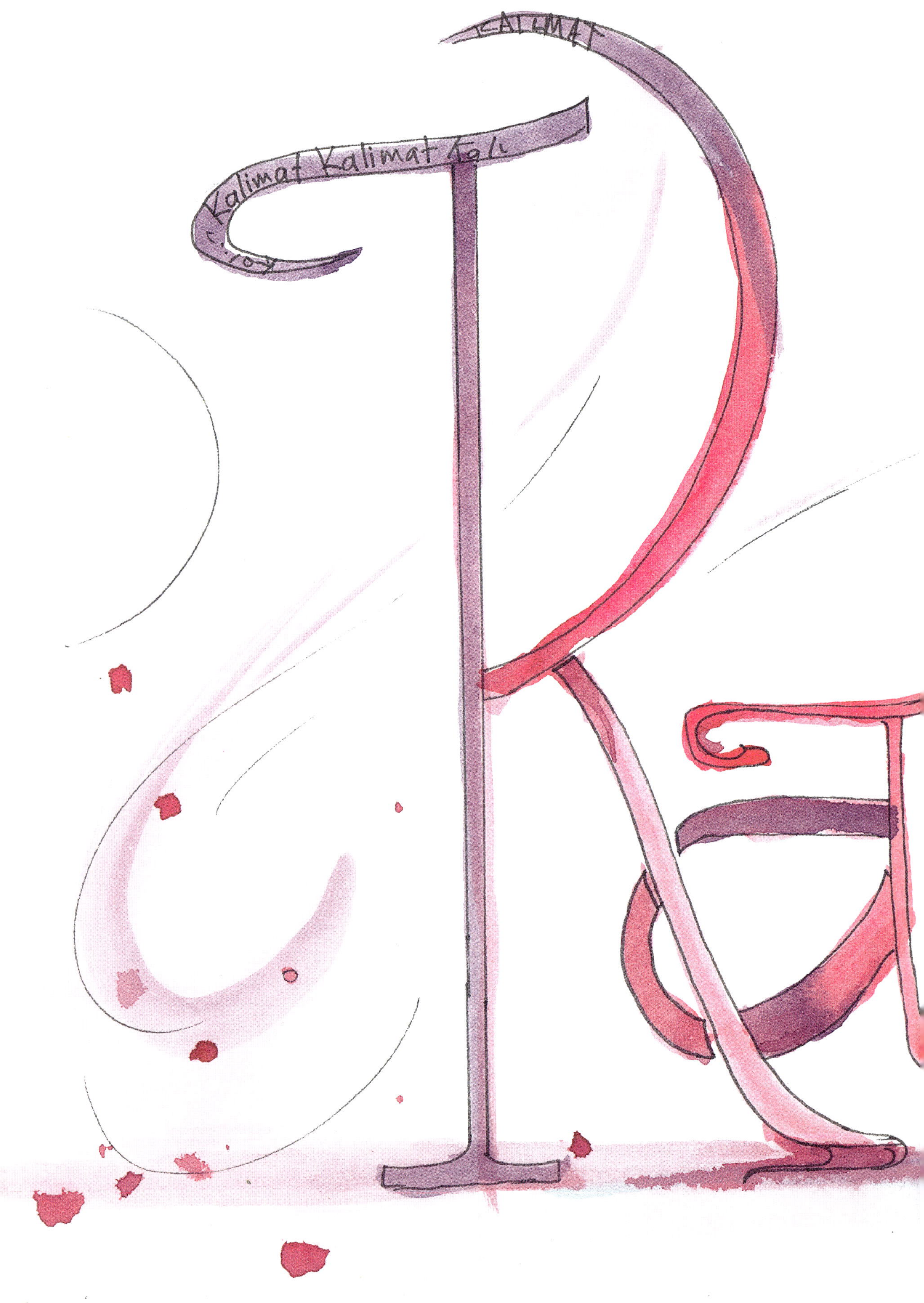

Kalimat Kalimat Kali
KALIMAT

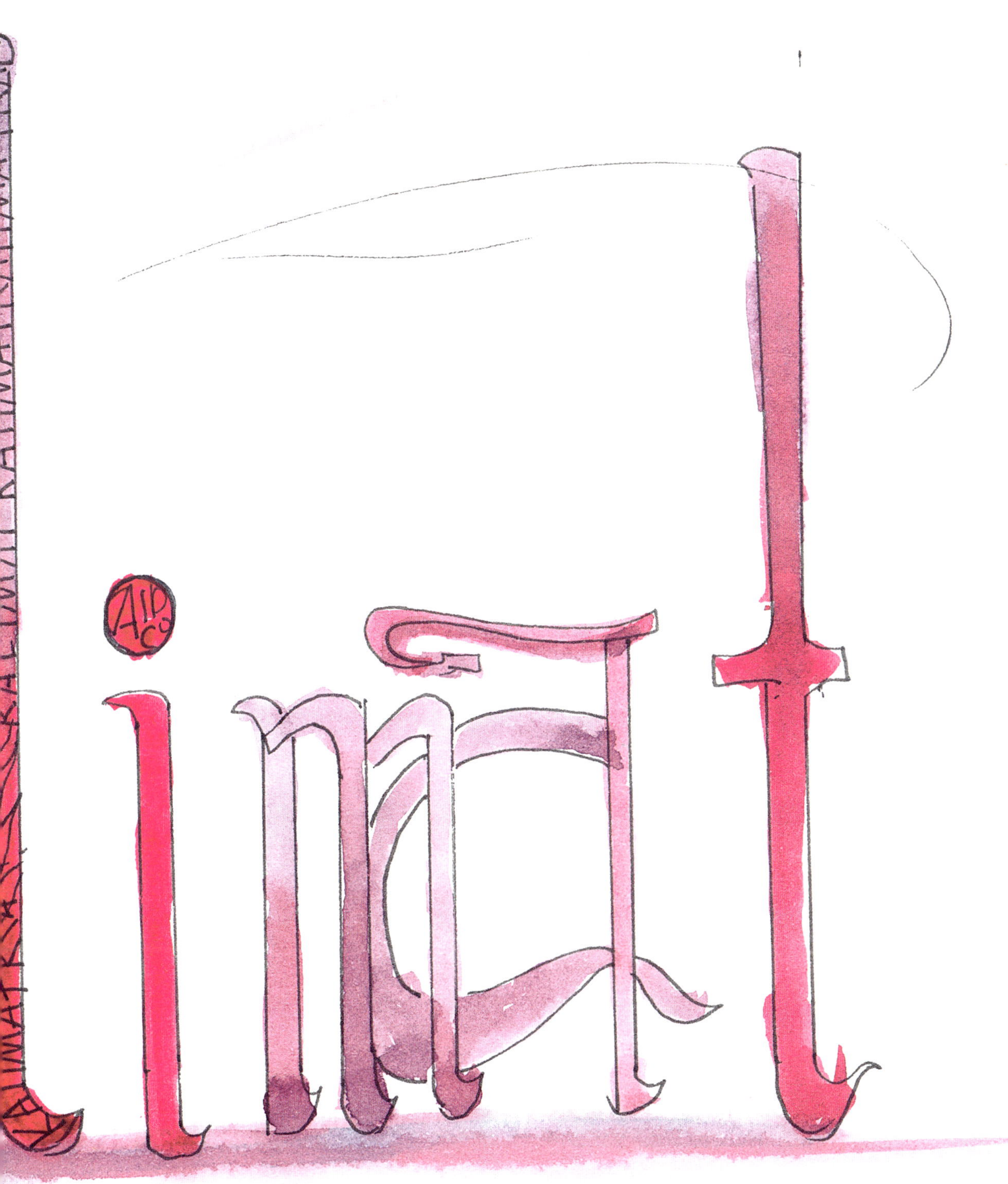

The Story of Mnzlee

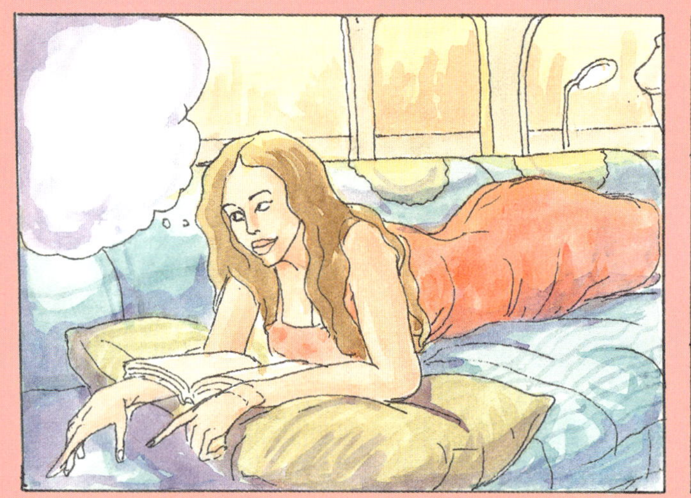

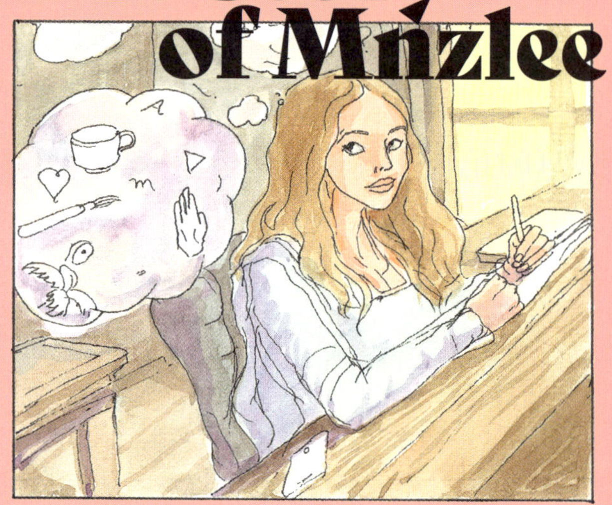

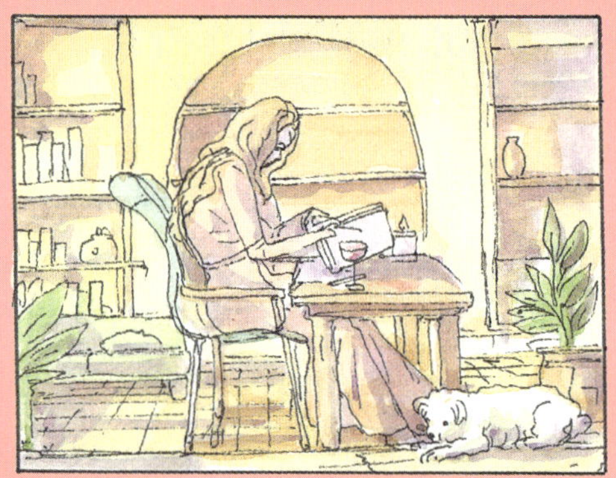

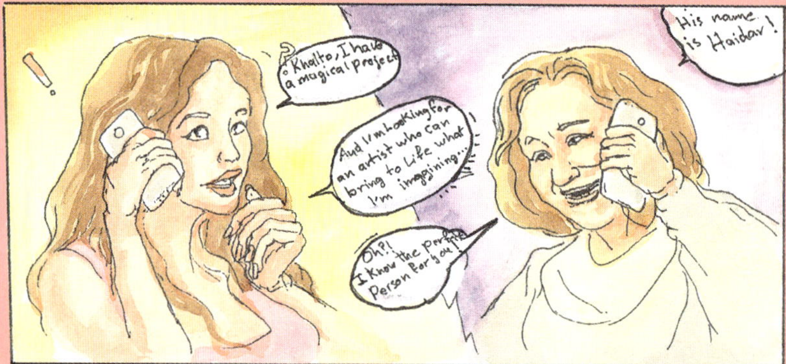

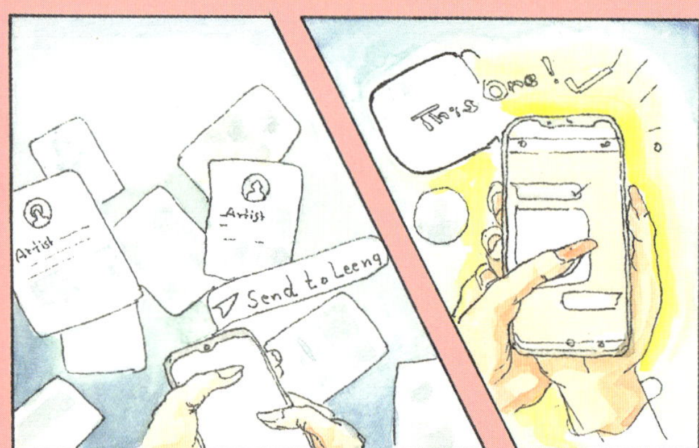

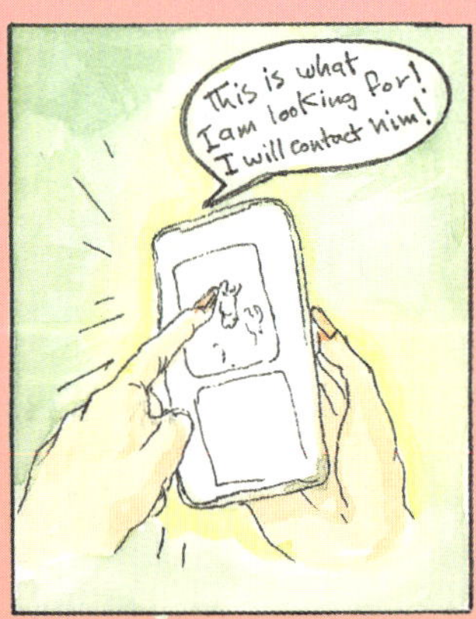

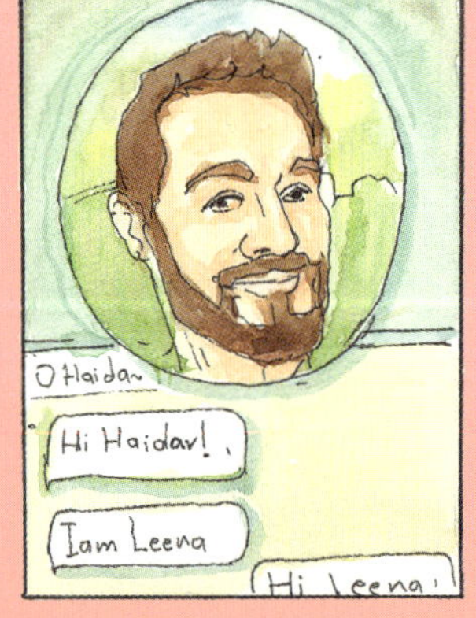

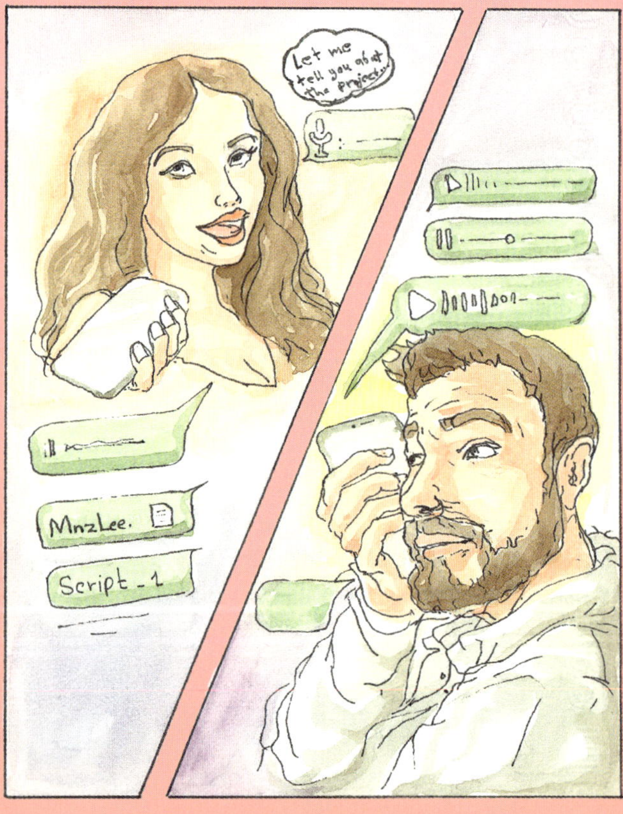

Mnzlee Stories — Epilogue

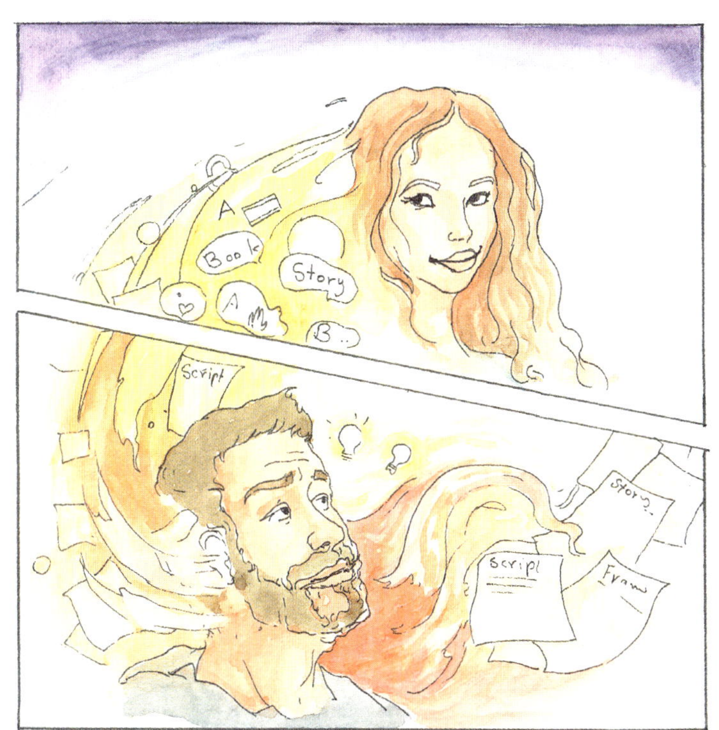

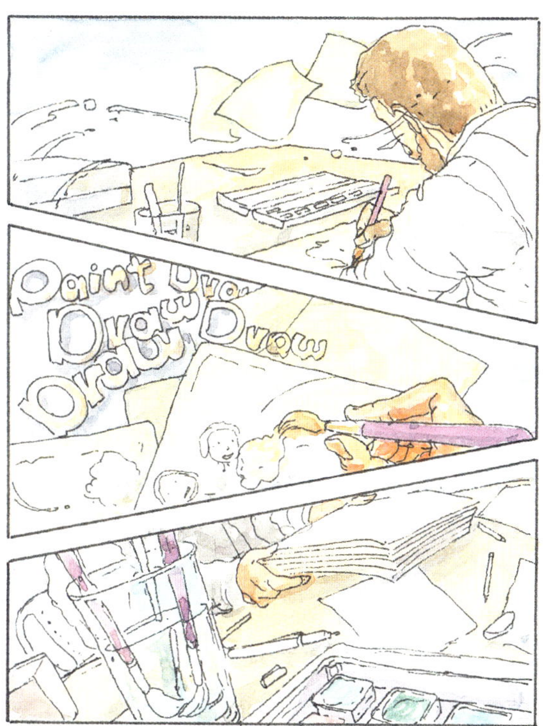

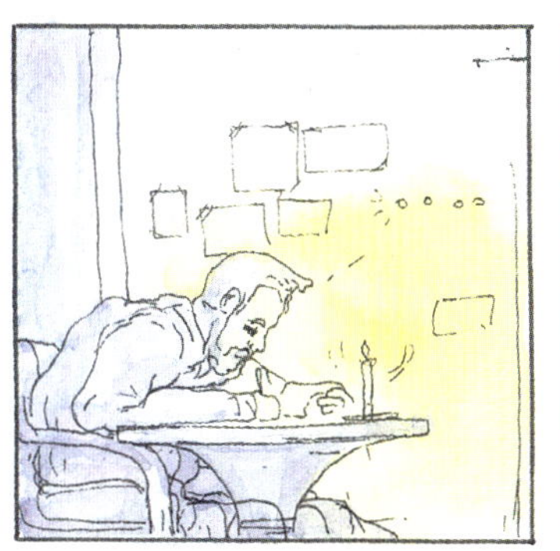

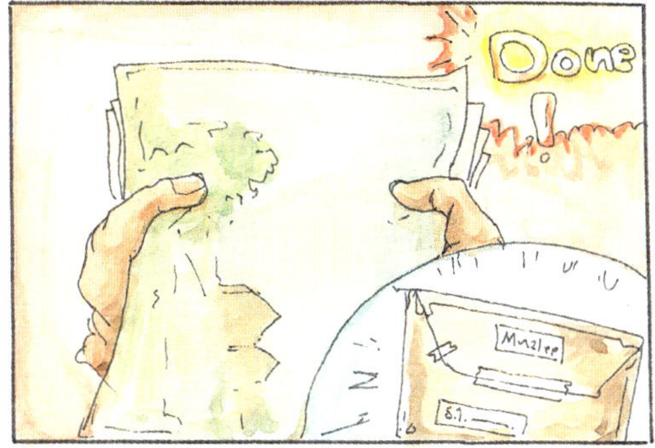

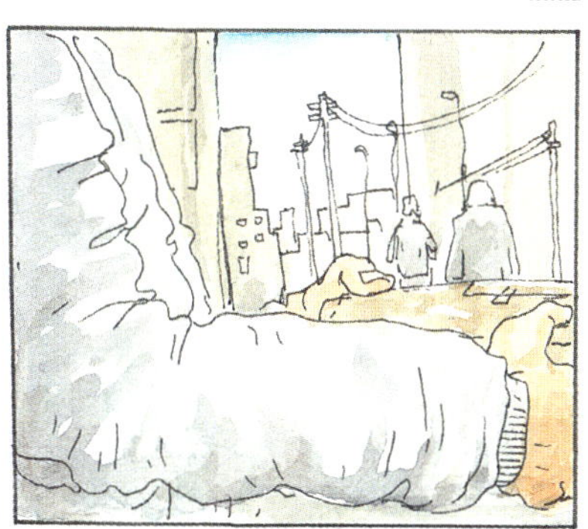

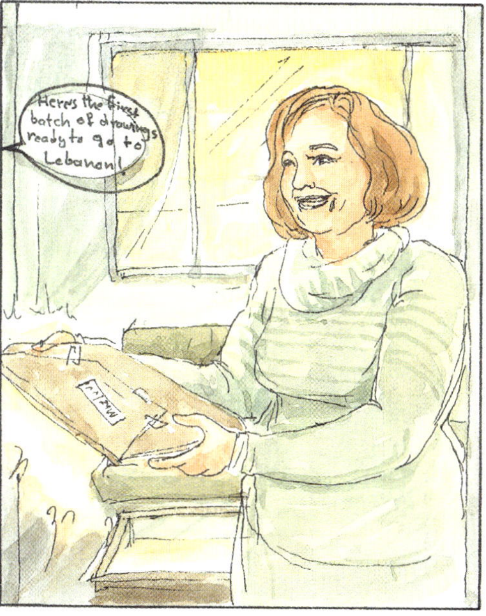

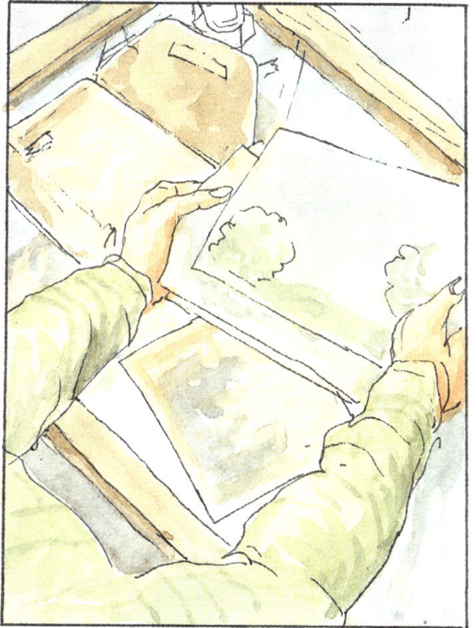

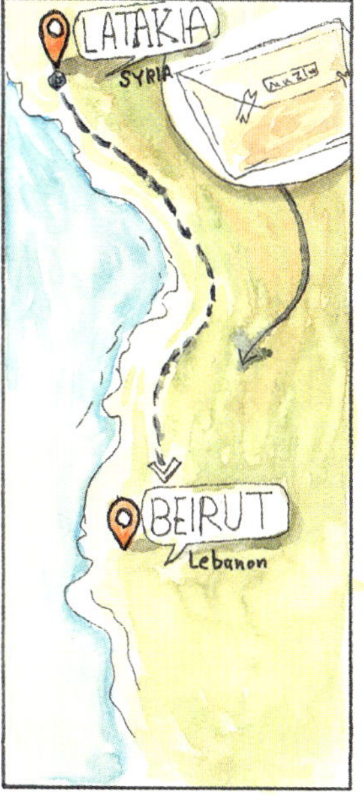

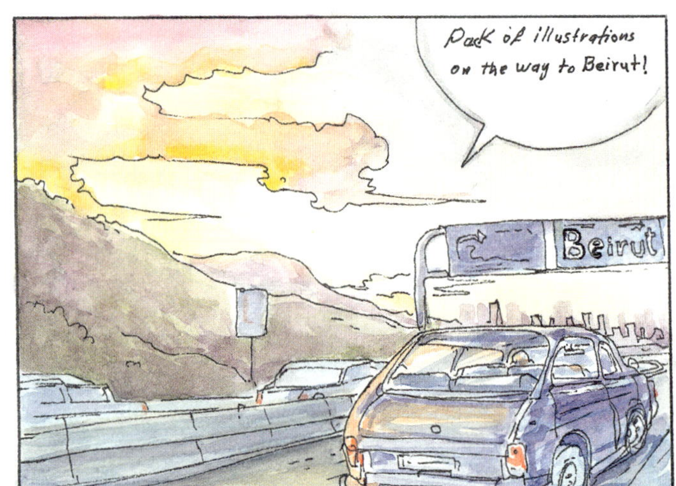
Pack of illustrations on the way to Beirut!
Beirut

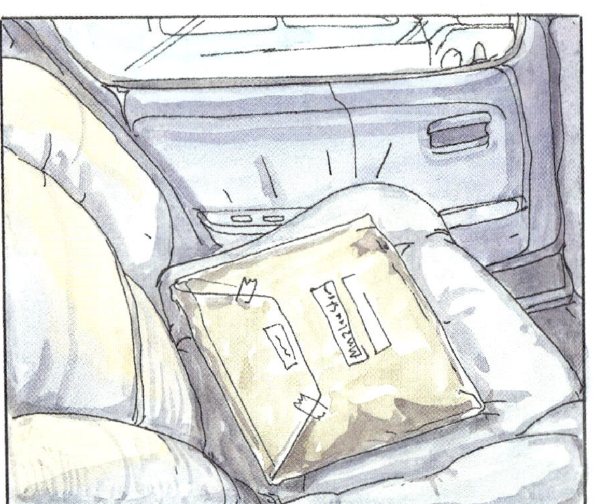

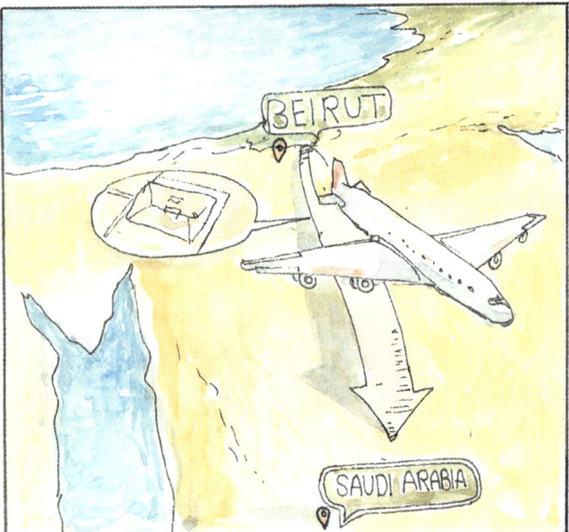
BEIRUT
SAUDI ARABIA

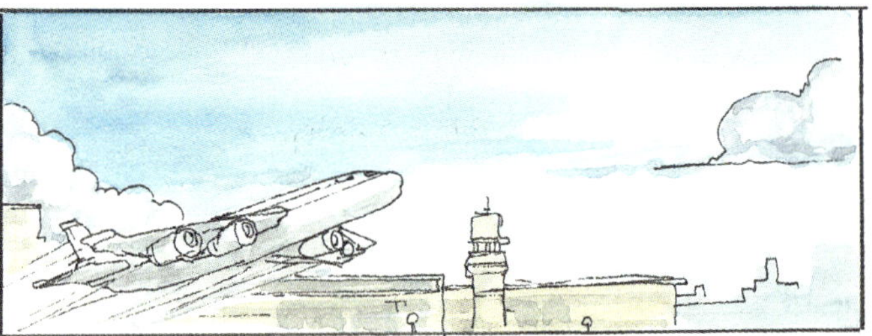

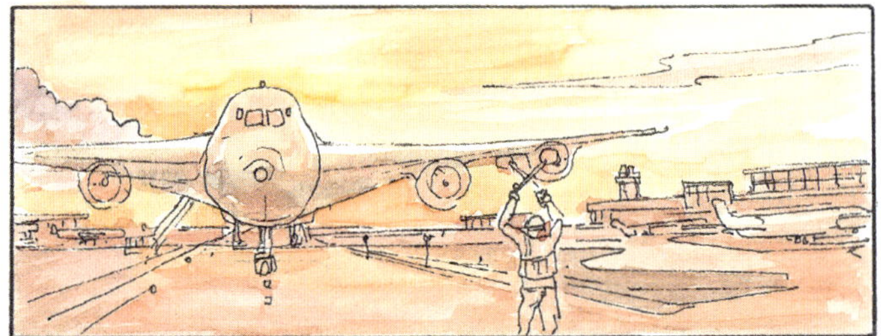

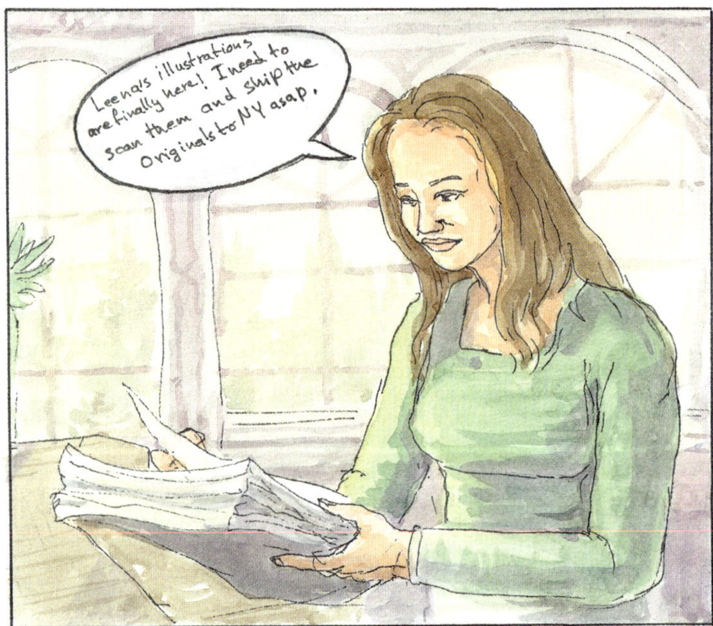
Leena's illustrations are finally here! I need to scan them and ship the originals to NY asap.

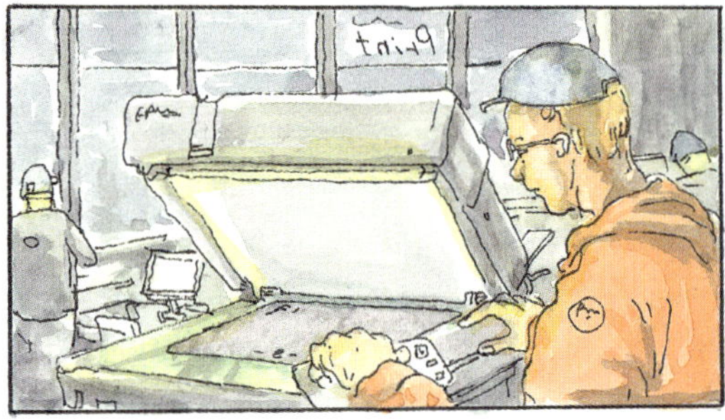

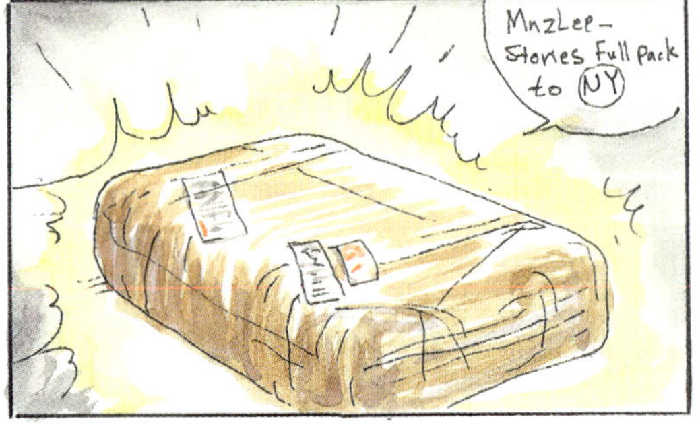
Mnzlee—
Stories full pack
to NY

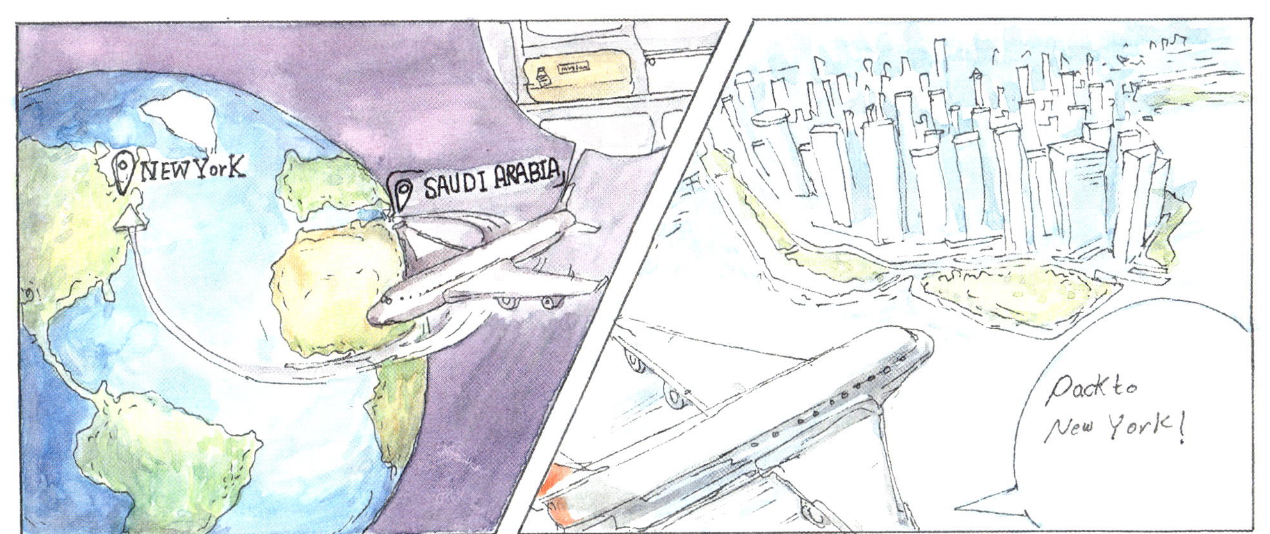
NEW YORK
SAUDI ARABIA
Back to
New York!

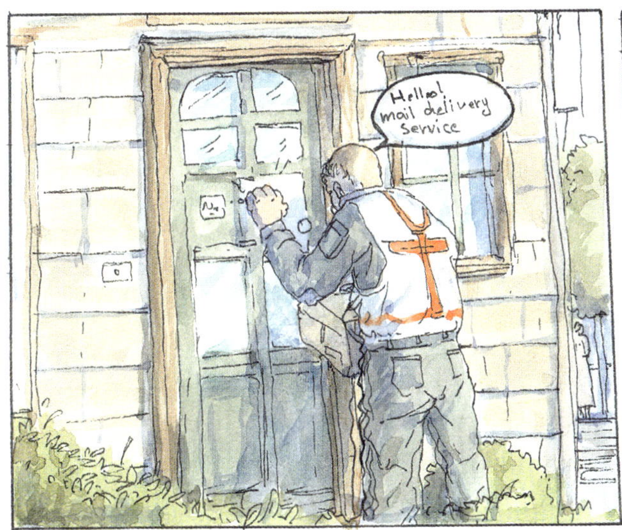
Hello!
mail delivery
service

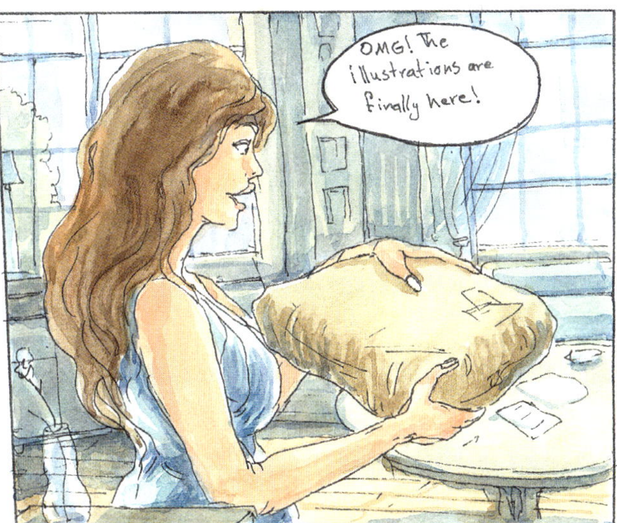
OMG! The
illustrations are
finally here!

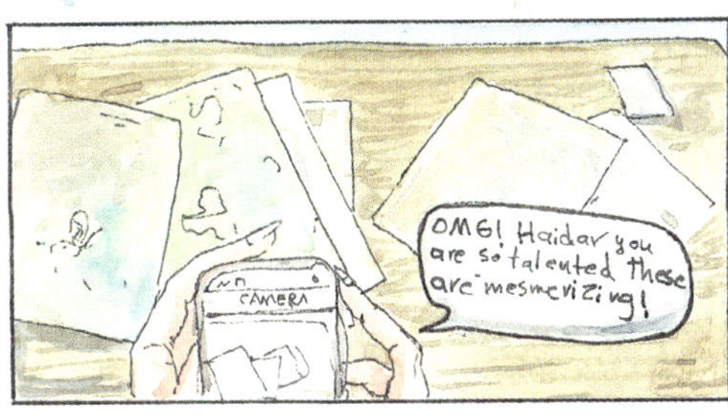
OMG! Haidar you
are so talented these
are mesmerizing!

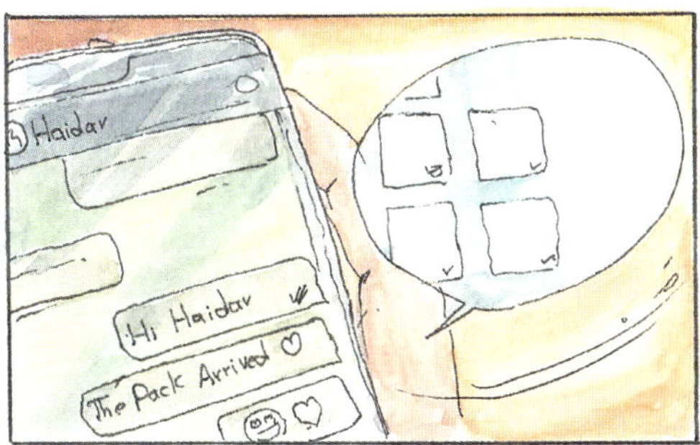
Haidar
Hi Haidar
The Pack Arrived

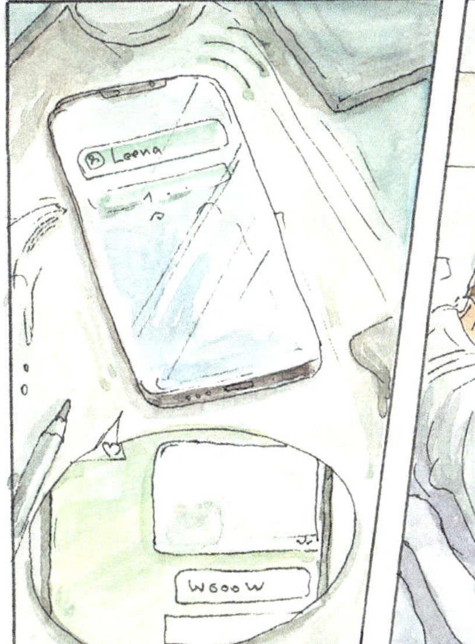
Leena
WOOOW

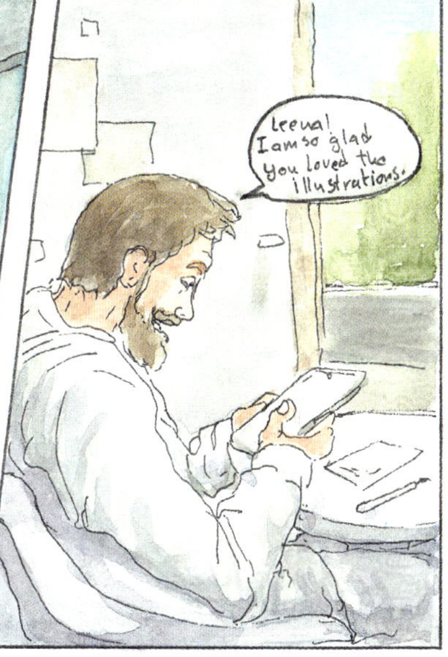
Leena!
I am so glad
You loved the
illustrations.

Biographies

Leena Al-Nasser

Leena Al-Nasser (b 1990, Dharan, Saudi Arabia) is a multimedia artist, writer and storyteller whose mission is to tell stories that offer a different way of understanding the world. Her work falls in the intersection between science and fiction, history and imagination. Central to all her creations is her process of discovery that drives whatever she makes. Al-Nasser received her master's degree in the Mind, Brain and Education program at the Harvard Graduate School of Education and has undertaken multiple creative projects, from writing and directing a short film exploring the female body in Arab culture to founding a space for artists of different disciplines to co-create. Al-Nasser is the founder of Mnzlee, a space created in service of imagining and reimagining what home means. She is a public speaker and a consultant on cultural and educational projects that aim to create social change and to cultivate a feeling of connection, creativity, and imagination. Leena lives between Buenos Aires, London, New York, and Saudi Arabia.

Haidar Al-Haibie

Haidar Al-Haibie (b 1996, Latakia, Syria) is a multidisciplinary artist, illustrator, graphic designer, and architect. Al-Haibie's works are inspired by nature, music, and personal experiences; his illustrations, paintings, and drawings come directly from concepts and imagery rooted in his own memories, bringing a unique perspective and intimacy to each piece. Al-Haibie's identity as a self-taught artist is central to his distinctive visual style, which is deeply informed by feeling and intuition. Al-Haibie's practice currently explores the boundaries of art and art production as a durational, co-determinate process. Al-Haibie holds a bachelor's degree in architecture from Tishreen University in Latakia. In 2022, he published hisfirst sketchbook collection and contributed work to university exhibitions and multiple group workshops. *An Imaginary Place Called Home* is Al-Haibie's first published book of illustrations. He lives in Latakia, Syria.

Loring M. Danforth

Loring M. Danforth (b 1949, Newton, Massachusetts, U.S.) is the Charles A. Dana Professor of Anthropology Emeritus at Bates College in Lewiston, Maine. He is the author of *The Death Rituals of Rural Greece (1982); Firewalking and Religious Healing (1989); The Macedonian Conflict (1995); Children of the Greek Civil War (2011)* with Riki van Boeschoten; *Crossing the Kingdom: Portraits of Saudi Arabia (2016);* and *Phantom Punch: Contemporary Art from Saudi Arabia in Lewiston (2016)* with Dan Mills. His teaching and writing uses symbolic and interpretive anthropology as lenses through which we can better understand and connect with others. For many years, Danforth has volunteered at the Adult Learning Center in Lewiston as a teacher of English for Speakers of Other Languages, where he has worked with refugees and asylum seekers from Somalia, Congo, Angola, and more recently Ukraine. He lives in Lewiston, Maine.

Acknowledgments

Family

Rania, mama, you make "mother" the most beautiful word on the planet. You are the biggest dreamer I know; my playmate, my yes-woman, my greatest gift in the world. Thank you for always supporting my imagination; you are the reason I never lost this part of me. Thank you for teaching me to dream big, and for being the Saudi port for the works that make up this book. This entire book is a love letter to the mother of all things—the imagination—who, to me, you reflect.

Amin, baba, my favorite tender eye, thank you for always supporting my passion! Without you nothing would be possible and this book would not exist. Your playfulness ever since my childhood, our deep conversations, and your interpretations of my art nourish my creativity so much. You provided a pillar that allows me to create. I love you.

Khalto Sawsan Al-Moualla, my artist aunt, my source of whimsy! Your artistic soul and tender spirit have lifted me up in ways I cannot describe. I am my truest, most vibrant self around you. Thank you for finding the talented Haidar for me, and for managing the transfer of the works in this book from him to Lebanon.

Amu Ziad Al-Abassi, the lover of art, music, imagination, and play; the DNA of our fustuq family! Thank you for showing us what it means to live every day like it's our last. Thank you for showing us the importance of lightness and play, and for always placing as much importance on the imagination as the "serious adult stuff". I know you would love this book, and are probably saying, "Where is the Arabic version?" It's coming, Amu. We miss you here.

Hala Al Abbassi, the worlds we created as children are most certainly still living today. Thank you for seeing me—the true me. You reflect this part of me back with so much strength, it amazes me.

Halool, Hatoom and Tarook Al-Abassi, thank you for receiving and shipping all the work for this book from Lebanon to Saudi, no matter the day or time. Hatoom, you live in my mind as the little child dreamer who dared to dream big. I hope you see yourself in this book. Tarook, we imagined a lot together as kids and we still do. Love you forever.

Halah Al-Nasser, my older sister and lifelong cheerleader. I don't think big sisters are thanked enough. You are the presence that allows us younger ones to take risks. You whisper sweet things in our ears that make us believe in ourselves. I love you.

Adam Al-Bahrana, my precious! It is a joy to be your khalto. I love how much you enjoy reading, learning, and exploring. Your curiosity amazes me! I can't wait to see what you'll uncover in this world, with this bright inner spirit of yours, and which story will be your favorite.

Maitham Al-Bahrana, my favorite, thoughtful brother-in-law! Thank you for always encouraging me to think bigger, it means a lot.

Faisal Nasser, my little brother who sometimes feels like my older brother. I adore you and all the ways we imagined together as kids. Thank you for always believing in my artistic side. Love you.

Teta Sukayna Al-Khayer, Teta ya sit il kul! If everyone saw me through your eyes, it would be a wonderful thing. You know my heart so well and you've always encouraged me to pursue my art. Our endless conversations always connect me to the idea of home.

Milou and Luna, my beloved dogs, you have been a team helping me with this book. Only the heavens know how many cuddles a writer and artist needs to make art! And our precious pets are never thanked enough. So how do I even begin? You have provided the unconditional love, comfort, and connection that has enabled me to do so much. You deserve loads of credit. And since you cannot read this, I will thank you with the gift of love and time.

Friends

Halah Al-Qahtani, my best friend, my family. Thank you so much for reminding me of the magic inside me and what I am capable of! Your endless love, and your faith in me—even when I don't have faith in myself—is always with me and is sprinkled throughout this book.

Nora Al-Dhuwaihi, habibti Norati, I love our endless listening sessions—so tender and kind. They have always left me filled with wonder. I won't forget how we started our own summer school at age 12! Through and through, seeing you always brings me back home.

Mert Karakus, we underestimate the impact it has on a person's whole life to be seen just for a moment through sacred eyes. And you have provided a sacredness for more than just moments. Your steady, unwavering presence has been a deep experience for me, and has shown me what the sacred masculine truly is.

Keti Vashakidze, you've shown me the definition of real friendship. Around you, I feel incredibly celebrated and unconditionally loved. I can't help but walk away a better version of myself. Thank you for always mirroring my strength, power, and abilities, and never failing to see my inner Beyoncé.

Lovelyn Souley, thank you for being the endless sunshine of my life. You remind me of the sacred power we have inside us. You remind me that I can create anything I envision. I love you so much.

Sarah Hamilton, I can't tell you how much our Inner Spaces Techniques work has transformed my life. But it's not just the IST—it's your generous, beautiful spirit that makes me feel so absolutely safe and curious about all of my parts.

Dani Severo, thank you for teaching me and showing me what it means to love unconditionally. I owe this to you. I can't wait to get this book translated into Spanish!

Tal Ofek, my friend, teacher, guide, angel! You have the innate ability to sense me no matter where you are, and it remains absolutely mysterious to me. I love you! May this book be the beginning of all that we've talked about.

Margaret Quinn, Mags, this book was developed across four different continents, and you and I both know that without you, that task would have been impossible! You are magical and I absolutely appreciate and adore you.

Molly Torres, many people design houses, very few create homes. As a designer and my friend, you have literally translated my insides into a home—my home. I don't think words can ever express how much your talent and friendship mean to me.

Nina Katchadourian, my favorite NYU professor of art. I can't find the words to thank you enough. All I will say is that you gave me the confidence to really start playing with my imagination, which this book is all about.

Emma Hitchcock, it's an incredible thing to know someone with whom you can truly be yourself! Thank you for being that friend who has always brought so much genuine curiosity—especially when I've needed it most.

Mohamad Nizam, you are the best and most brilliant advisor on all things miel and Mnzlee. Thank you!

Rose, Alma, Billy and Kathryn Atienza, you four did a lot behind the scenes while I was writing this book! Thank you from the bottom of my heart for creating a wonderfully supportive environment for me.

Blair Miller, I love your writing salons. They are so full of wonder; they spark such thought-provoking questions and always leave me thinking. Love you!

Casey Anderson, the magical woman whose sensitivity is the most beautiful part of her. Thank you for being in my life.

Samar Alauddin, I never felt strange dancing because it was something we did together. Love you and thank you for cheering me on, no matter the adventure.

Lulu Al-Mana, my inner child has never known a better friend! Life is too much fun with you and not nearly as beautiful without you. Love you so much.

Faheem Noori, I have one word for you: forwar! Love you and thank you for all the amazing guidance and support.

Conor Birney, you are such a thoughtful and talented human being! Thank you for creating my dream digital home, the Mnzlee website, to house all of my projects!

Eliza Cohen, your spirit is so beautiful. I adore you. Thank you for your genuine love, wisdom, and guidance—and all the pep talks that have helped me rise to my greatest potential.

Sultan Sooud Al-Qassemi, thank you for reminding the world of the many hidden treasures of Arab history and art! Thank you for dedicating your life to this. Your presence adds so much inspiration and strength to Arab artists and thinkers.

Contributors

Haidar Al-Haibie, the Mnzlee Stories artist; my friend, my brother. I could not have dreamed of finding a more magical artist to bring my vision of Mnzlee Stories into the world. I saw countless artist profiles when I was looking for you, but the moment I found your work I was captivated by your eye for magic, mysticism, delicateness, and the sacred feminine. To think that this book is being published without us ever having met... One thing I hope is that this book can somehow allow us to meet in person. I cannot wait for that moment.

Elisabeth Garaux, my PA, my manager, my advisor, my eye of magic, and my trusted friend! You have been there with me since the beginning, when this was all just an idea, to here, as it becomes fruit. You have been integral at every step of this journey and without you this book could not have come into the world. Your genuine love for this project, your creativity, your zest for dreams, your confidence, and your unwavering belief has made this experience an unforgettable one for me. I cannot thank you enough. I am so fortunate to have you in my life.

Loring M. Danforth, my teacher and my friend, I still will never forget how you believed in a 19-year-old enough to have her teach a class! Your faith in me is a gift that has never stopped giving. It is a huge honor that my first book starts with you.

Black Dog Press, thank you so much for publishing my first book! Your genuine love for art and books is so appreciated.

Other/Book Inspirations

Dr. Lewis Lapham, your magazine, *Lapham's Quarterly* was one of my biggest comforts during Covid. I particularly want to thank you for the Winter 2020 issue on memory, which has deeply influenced my work.

Maira Kalman, thank you for always mixing light, complex, silly, and serious things and sharing them with the world. You have been a huge inspiration to this process.

Manuel Lima, author of *Book of Circles* (2017). As a writer, I feel that if my work inspires just one person, then I am happy. And I want to tell you that your book really did that for me. "Memory", in this book, speaks to this. Thank you.

Steven Johnson, author of *Wonderland: How Play Made the Modern World* (2016). I have been a fan of your book since it came out. It is one of the books that connected me to my roots, and connected me to my faith in the imagination. It was a huge inspiration for the story "Imagine"! Thank you, thank you, thank you.

Ursula Leguin, my favorite writer who has inspired so much of my thought around the importance of the imagination. Thank you.

And finally, **Thumbelina**, my pearl, my imagination. Thank you for always making your voice heard, and for letting me inside your precious internal world. I love being there with you. You are the source of everything I make.

This book is published by Black Dog Press Limited, a company registered in England and Wales with company number 11182259. Artifice Press Limited is an imprint within the SJH Group. Copyright is owned by the SJH Group. All rights reserved.

Black Dog Press Limited
The Maple Building
39–51 Highgate Road
London NW5 1RT
United Kingdom
—
+44 (0)20 8371 4047
office@blackdogonline.com
www.blackdogonline.com

Creative direction by Mnzlee
Designed by Rachel Pfleger
Printed in Lithuania by Kopa

ISBN 978-1-912165-49-0

British Library in Cataloguing Data. A CIP record for this book is available from the British Library.

black dog press